"Si Dios Quiere"

(God Willing)

Cecilia Diaz Gruessing, MA

Photography: Ceil Gruessing, David Ashby, and Nimer Alvarado

INTRODUCTION – "Si Dios Quiere" – Cecilia Gruessing, MA – 2023

"Si Dios Quiere" is the story of an American woman who goes to La Ceiba, Honduras after 9/11 to teach dance in an International School. The book, which is intended as bi-lingual reading material, and also available for production, is written in theatrical manuscript form with many musical numbers. As historical fiction, the main points of the story are true as Ceci Diaz struggles for custody and visas for three little sisters she finds in a box on the street in 2003. Alone, for ten years, Ceci deals with the girls' disabilities, their health, education, their orphanages, and all the red tape involved with adoption in a third world country. "Si Dios Quiere" is a popular Latino expression meaning "God willing". It is used often in a culture where making things happen is totally dependent on God. In the beginning, there are several flashbacks which take the reader to a mystical place in the Honduran Mosquitia called "La Ciudad Blanca" (the White City). Here Mayan, Honduran, African, and Spanish ancestors convene to debate and resolve the ongoing problem of orphans in Honduras. Despite intense poverty, gang violence and political upheaval, Ceci carves out a family life in La Ceiba for Roxana, Angie, and Jazmin. Honduras is a beautiful tropical country with much untouched natural resources and land. The people are humble and compose the Trigueno population (Mayan, Indigenous, African Garifuna and Caribe, and original Spanish immigrant) that defines the Honduran culture. The story illustrates many of the cultural events (Carnaval, Christmas, etc) and customs that make Honduras a fascinating country.

After five visa attempts over 10 years, Ceci is granted the unprecedented request to get visas for the three girls. Finally, she is able to bring the girls home to her mother in Richmond, Va. who has been waiting for Ceci for 10 years to give the girls a life with her blessing in the USA. It is a bi-lingual story of love, tenacity, and dedication to motherhood.

In 2025 Angie and Jazmin are in college and Roxana is working with toddlers. This is an impossible story of a successful adoption that was "God willing".

This book is dedicated to my mother and father, Josephine and Joseph Gruessing, for their support of my commitment as an artist, and as a mother to my three adopted daughters, Roxana, Angie and Jazmin. Besides being wonderful parents, they have enabled my ability to rescue these precious sisters. My mother was very instrumental in the visa and adoption process, and my girls love her.

The following story is about the miracle they enabled.

Return to the Orphans June 24, 2004

Yesterday I returned to La Ceiba, Honduras after 2 weeks in the US, visiting my family and friends, and living in the American lap of luxury of food, clothing, and shelter. All I could think about on the plane were the orphans with whom I work in the Casa de Niños, and the SOS Aldeas, where there are also 3 little sisters I would like to adopt. I could not wait to bring my gifts to these kids, the dolls and doll clothing that my Mom so lovingly made for them, dresses for the girls, vitamins, and little ceramic angels for their bedsides. I want to describe my perspective on seeing these children again, as I would like to build an Art Clinic via an American University, to promote their artistic and psychological health through the development of an Expressive Arts Therapy program.

When I arrived at the SOS Aldeas, there was a huge celebration taking place for the Dia International del SOS. They were all sitting in a circle under the huge, open air social area where there is a stage. The director was organizing games, for which they were all enthusiastically attentive. As I approached, I could see Angie Nicole innocently hobbling across the floor in the midst of this action. Angie is 2 and a half, and had just started walking a week ago, despite her slow recovery from meningitis… she also does not see very well. This was so moving for me, as I know how intensely she has been trying to stand up since Christmas, 2003. At that time she and her sisters were removed from their negligent Mom's custody, and delivered in a box to the hospital around the corner from me, half naked, with fever and meningitis, full of parasites, and suffering from malnutrition. Her older sister Roxana, 3 and a half, does not talk, but was there too, in her kindergarten uniform, with the little shoes I had bought her before I left. She is smiling now, with her blackened upper teeth, and loves to throw herself into the laps of her orphanage brothers and sisters. Their 3 month old sister, Jazmin, is as adorable as she could possibly be, despite the anxiety she must feel being abandoned at this age.

At the SOS the children live in small ranch homes, in family groups, with a "tia" (aunt) and a mixture of teenagers who have grown up in the orphanage, and now help out. They all take care of each other in these homes, where there is a strong sense of family. They eat regularly and have clean clothing. There is a lot of love here, and I am thankful that "my girls" have arrived at this heaven-sent place, after all the trauma they have suffered in their lives. Three little boys ran up to me, with whom I had danced at the Casa de Niños, earlier in the year. They were now 5 and 6 years old, and wrapped themselves around my waist with the relief of familiarity... There are so few adults who can give their lives continuity.

I want to explain the feeling of looking into a crowd of over one hundred abandoned children, whose lives have been rescued from the Honduran streets where thousands of lost children still sleep every night. (There are over 150 thousand abandoned children in Honduras) They were so happy to be participating in something organized by civilized adults. The joy, the cooperation, and the love in the air were just overwhelming sentiments of happiness. I see hope, and a desire to become part of society.

Later that afternoon, at the Casa de Ninos, where I have worked on Sundays for a year, teaching dance, yoga, music and art, I delivered digital watches. What ecstasy was in the air as they all lined up to receive my humble donation from Richmond, Va. They could not believe that the watch also delivered the date. Since the hour was set for US time, they were all madly trying to figure out how to change the digital program. This was the first watch they had ever owned. Even the 2 boys with mental disorders, who had the watches upside down on their wrists, were glowing with pride. My heart was on fire.

It takes so little to make these children happy. They have not known what it means to have someone who cares exclusively for them in their lives... someone who wants to tend to their personal needs. Unfortunately, I only teach dance, and ask them to make wishes at the end of class. So many times they have told me that they want to belong to a real family in a real home. When we pray, I always say "someone in this room will be President of Honduras one day, because, if you can get through this, you will be able to address the problems of all the children after you, who are suffering from this poverty and abandonment."

I write this story of a day in my life with these 2 groups of children, because I want to help them in the only way I know how. I want to build three huge ART CLINICS in a summer camp outside of the three major cities in Honduras. Here these lost children can have an opportunity to make art with the teaching skills of employed Honduran artists. These artists would work with child psychologists trained in EXPRESSIVE ARTS THERAPY, to help process their emotions of abandonment and separation anxiety. Honduras has very little service in the field of Psychology. Art, is also an organized activity for the rich. I am trying to find an American university who will send Spanish speaking graduate students in the fields of psychology, performing and visual arts, and engineering to develop this program and finance the construction of these buildings. Within this model, the goal is to create a network to facilitate **easy international adoption** for children of all ages. Here prospective parents can come to see these children in their expressive modes, to know how tender, vulnerable, and precious they are as they try to figure out how they feel about their lives, being unconnected to parents. This is so evident once they begin to draw, sing, dance, and create art.

Thank you, Cecilia Diaz Gruessing, MA. Sanghita5@ yahoo.com

This letter was written in 2004 when I first arrived in La Ceiba to work before I even began the impossible journey of trying to get custody and visas for Roxana, Angie and Jazmin. If you are interested in "Helping Honduras Kids" you can go to their website. I encourage you to go to Helping Honduras kids with David Ashby and his work in La Ceiba, Honduras with the orphan population. https://www. helpinghonduraskids.org/

It has taken me 8 years to write the following story. Now these girls are young ladies. Roxana is working with toddlers and Angie has a seeing eye dog and is studying law at University of Mary Washington. Jazmin is also interested in law and advanced math at University of Lynchburg. They all want to give back. This is the story of our immigration.

Lovingly written, Ceil Gruessing   2023   Richmond, Va.

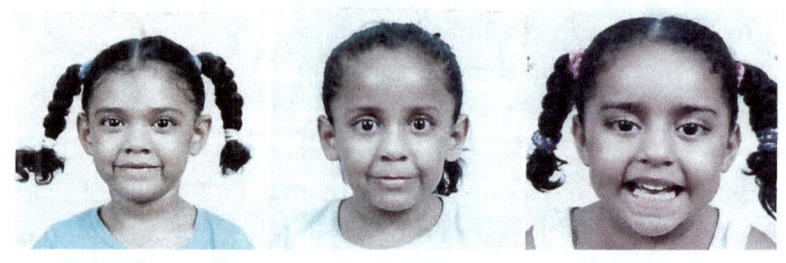

For Roxana, Angie, and Jazmin

I will love you eternally ….   Mom

"SI DIOS QUIERE" - A Honduran Story of a Gringa and Three Sisters

1. West Hollywood, Ca. – Dupree Dance Studio, Melrose Ave., 2002

We see a shot from above the Hollywood sign panning down along trendy Melrose Ave until we focus on the action and music inside Dupree Dance Studio. It is morning and nothing is happening on the street. A middle-aged woman locks her car and rushes to catch an early morning jazz dance class in the studio. She rushes through the green room where a few young dancers are stretching and gossiping.... She disrobes and hops into her jazz shoes.

This is Ceci Diaz, American choreographer, just returned to LA from earning a Masters Degree in Philosophy and Religion from California Institute of Integral Studies in San Francisco. She is 48, and perhaps in denial of her age as a dancer, yet devoted to her work as an artist and choreographer. Times are rough in Los Angeles, as all Americans are recovering from the shock of the recent attack on September 11th in New York 2001. There are few students in the studio, as people fear the onslaught of more attacks in LA.

Ceci arrives just in time to have a chat with the teacher, young, Puerto Rican, Domingo.

>   Domingo: Ceci! How are you doing?

>   Ceci: Bastante bien, buscando trabajo - glad to be here. Happy enough… looking for work.

>   Domingo: I'm glad you are here… not too many people are making it to class these days. Entonces, yo soy el maestro hoy… *He bows humbly.* So, I am the teacher today.

>   Ceci: I can't wait … vamos a bailar. We can get a coffee later. Let's dance.

Domingo puts on his hot, Latin music and the class begins in a huge studio which normally accommodates 40. Ceci is clearly the oldest of 10 other students, all young, aspiring and advanced dancers. She has all the style and technique of an experienced professional, despite a slight deficiency in strength. The scene becomes a montage of various Latin jazz/ballet exercises all danced to both romantic and sizzling Latin sound tracks. The final combination is a hot routine to a Mark Anthony salsa with loaded percussion and brass licks that would make anybody want to dance. The room transforms into a magical choreography of 10 male and female salseros... ripping across the floor with audacious joy, sensuality and power. Ceci's style stands out in this small group, and she is thrilled to be part of this experience... so sacred and exciting for serious dancers. She is fluid, full of Latina mobility, and spiritually transformed by the music and Domingo's choreography. At the end, all applaud Domingo's work and leave the studio, sweating, laughing, and satisfied. Ceci waits for Domingo, and they walk down the street towards the local diner on Melrose.

2. <u>**Melrose Ave – W Hollywood – trendy shops and restaurants**</u>

They exit the studio and enter the street. There is a strange mix of the trendy and the homeless as the afternoon approaches. Salesgirls stand in the doorways of boutiques waiting for business, calling out to passer bys to come shop. There are the wanna be trendy tourists, and teenagers..... some lost souls... a few skate boarders. Ceci and Domingo walk and talk.

Ceci: Hombre! Eso fue increible... Hay que terminar esta coreografia y presentarla. Man, that was incredible. You have to finish this choreography and present it.

Domingo: Gracias Ceci... coming from you that is a real boost. And I love dancing with you.

Ceci: A mi tambien Domingo. Vamos por aqui. Me too Domingo. Let's go here.

3. <u>**A Melrose Diner**</u>

They enter the diner and sit at the fountain bar. There are no other customers. Domingo addresses the Latino cook.

Domingo: Que pasa?... no hay negocios aqui tampoco. What's happening? No business here either?

Cook: Nueve/Once 9/11.... It's been like a ghost town this week.

Ceci counts her remaining dollars.

Ceci: Well we're going to eat. This is on me Domingo.... A reward for your brilliant choreography.

Domingo: Gracias hermana. *They hug.* AY... Why do we do this?

Ceci: Why do we dance? Because we get to go higher than most everybody else when we dance and especially when we know what we're doing. It's a big rush, and a super accomplishment to be able to put out so much energy in such a short amount of time. It's like magic. And I think it was Einstein who said that dancers are God's athletes.

Domingo: Well that sounds good. But it is still crazy... There's no money in it... no financial security... no longevity...

Ceci: You know... you need to finish that work and find a venue for it.

Domingo: Give me the dancers, tell me where and I'll do it for free. Choreography just can't compete with terrorism.

Ceci: I just don't understand why they hate us so much, and why they want to kill innocent people.'

Domingo: Oh I do... We poison the world with our cinematic violence and perverted exhibitionist sexuality, and continue to manufacture and sell guns to promote power and money for the NRA... Capitalism, in the name of democracy, is about excess, and lots of people don't like the global power behind it.

Ceci: So... are you an artist or an activist now?

Domingo: I don't know... I would go back to Puerto Rico if I didn't still have so many stars in my eyes.

Ceci: If I had work I would hire you... But I don't have any security in this business either... I never have.... with or without 9/11... It's hit or miss, and stay in shape if you can. My age and Masters degree isn't getting me anywhere either. I have to get a job.. somewhere soon, or go back to Mom in Virginia. *Waitress arrives.* I'll have a coffee and eggs benedict please. Order whatever you want Domingo…

Domingo: I'll have a burger well done and fries … and a coke… Thanks.

Ceci: Yes, so I applied on the internet for a job in Honduras teaching dance in an International school for $50 a week.

Domingo: $50 a week?

Ceci: Why not? It's on the equator… sunshine, mangos. You know my astro cartography says I have solar karma there. La Ceiba, Honduras lines up with the same longitude as NY where I was born, and Montreal, where I got a break working with Celine Dion. I wonder if that school job will come through?

Domingo: Ceci… where else are they going to find a bi-lingual choreographer, with all your experience *and* an MA, who will pay to go to Honduras and work for peanuts?

Ceci: I guess you're right… which doesn't say much for my self-esteem … But I am also thinking I could do more research on indigenous dancing…. I explored the roots of dance and theater in ceremony and ritual for my thesis…. So I could expand on that.

Domingo: Ceci, you are one of the few intellectual dance artists I know. Of course you should check out any kind of mystical history. You know, I just thought of something. I think the Ciudad Blanca is in Honduras.

Ceci: So what is that…. the white city?

Domingo: Ceci, It's right up your ally with all your mythological interests.

Ceci: Uh Huh… So where is it?

Domingo: I saw a documentary about it recently… It is somewhere in the mosquitia, deep in the Honduran jungles. But nobody can find it. It's like a Pre-Columbian, white walled city which Cortez found during the Conquista that is supposedly loaded with gold … Where the nobles of an ancient civilization lived… And it was also called the lost city of the Monkey King… with huge statues of apes. And the local Indians have legends about how people go there and don't come back. Even gold diggers have died looking for it… There are no roads nor land access. But now they have this super modern electronic lidar equipment which can fly over and photograph below the earth's surface, where they have seen outlines of plazas, and pyramids.

Ceci: Oooo .. I love all that, and you know I love the tropics.

Domingo: You go girl and get this job. You need an adventure.

Ceci: Tienes razon Domingo – Adventure brings out the gypsy in me. What will my mother say this time? I just got my MA and I want to go to the poorest nation in the western hemisphere?

Domingo: Well other than opening a Philosophy Shop on Silverlake Blvd, I don't know how soon any of us will be working again.

Ceci: Very funny. You know I want to make a difference with my work, with all the charity I've done over the years.

Domingo: Here's how I see it. Would you rather merengue in Honduras, or dry up in LA? The A list is waiting tables, and you are lucky if you can do fashion shows just for clothes… or maybe work for free teaching dance to inmates? Come on sister…. This is a shot at adventure. Jump on the wave.

Ceci: Hombre, not only are you a great dancer and choreographer, but you also are a brilliant influencer. Gracias…. Me empujaste bien! I will never forget you. Can I steal some of your steps?

Domingo: Gratuito… solo para ti senora! Free, only for you.

They clink coffee and coke cups.

4.CARNAVAL – Plaza in La Ceiba - May, 2003 – La Ceiba, Honduras

Fireworks explode over La Ceiba, Honduras. It is the madrugada (dawn) of the first day of Carnaval. The Ceiba Tree towers above the festivities in the park plaza where dawn begins to illuminate the action in the pueblo. Street cleaners are sweeping the street in front of the Plaza Central and City Hall as the bleachers are constructed for the VIP parade judges. Vendors begin to set up for carnaval. And the boys of the street start to wander out from the cozy corners of the park where they have spent the night. Honduran tourists begin to emerge, wearing the traditional carnaval beads to excess. The sound of merengue music fills the air, and the street kids begin to beg at the baleada wagon. Police begin to set up the orange street cones to make a pathway for the parade. The tourists mix with the marginal. Poor and disabled people come to beg in front of the church across from the plaza; the herb man has his wares displayed as usual; the crazy and the barefoot find their way into the preparations for the festival. Recovering alcoholics carry homemade tables and chairs for sale, like penance crosses at Easter. A juggler begins his routine in the intersection. The lottery ticket sellers are set up in their regular corner, and the vendors from out of town begin to unpack their cheap flashy merchandise onto the street. Add more tourists to this and the street is crowded.

In one corner of the park, the folk dancers are assembling and warming up. The ladies have long, colorful ruffled skirts with ruffled blouse bodices, sashes at the waist and special dancing shoes. They are fixing roses in their tied up hair. The men have white pants and shirts, with a straw hat, and red bandanas which are worn, but also used in their dances.

In another corner of the park the Honduran Garifuna (Afro-Latin) drummers and dancers are getting ready. The women wear identical dresses and head wraps in colorful fabric, and they warm up their bodies and voices to the beat of the male drummers. There are also young male dancers preparing their clown like costumes for the dance called Jean K'neau.

5. GRAND PARIS HOTEL - Lobby

The lobby of the Grand Paris Hotel, right off the park, begins to fill with the entourage of the Queen of Carnaval, the supporting princesses, various Indian Princess models, and of course, the sexy female plumage of the traditional carnaval bathing beauties partnered by muscular young men. They are all getting makeup and touches from famous fashion designer and Beauty Queen Contest Coordinator, Eduardo Zablah. The Queen of the Carnaval is having her makeup done, as workers flutter around her. In Latin America, beauty contests are like a return to Goddess worship.

6. Ceci's Small hotel room

There is a small hotel room with bed, table, telephone, and door. Asleep is the tourist, Gringa, Ceci Diaz. The phone is ringing and she sleeps through it. Finally, the bell hop bangs on the door.

Bell hop: Sra. Gringa, your mother is calling from the United States many times!! Can you take the call please??

Ceci: Oy… perdoneme Mom!! I am so sorry, I must have overslept. Yes it's me…yes me, mom, your daughter, Ceil,,,, really me…. I was just having the most amazing, surreal dream. Yes I am OK, I got in last night, and I am in La Ceiba at the Hotel Gran Paris. This place is miles from anywhere, and I cannot believe it is 2003. This is like National Geographic magazine. What? I can't hear you… I think the carnaval music is already blasting on the street. Today is carnaval Mom… Yes I will be careful. Yes I still have my credit card *(she checks)* and my camera. I've got to go Mom, the parade will start soon. I promise I'll call you later. Believe me, I am fine, I love you … Bye!

7. HOTEL LOBBY, STREET & PLAZA - Carnaval activity

The drums of a marching band are heard in the distance as the fantasy brigade of princesses hurries into the awaiting cars to join the parade. Eduardo Zablah runs around primping all of his models with their full length gowns at the last minute. Ceci, dressed tropically American, for her mission to photograph the event, with camera, hat, and backpack, descends the hotel staircase.

Mounting the stairs are a group of Doctors Without Borders arriving for a missionary trip. One good looking guy has a baseball hat that says "Virginia is for Lovers". Ceci approaches him:

Ceci: Are you from Virginia?

Gringo Doctor: My family is, and I have a house there… but I spend a lot of time in Italy.

Ceci: My family lives in Richmond, Va.

Doctor: Really? What are you doing here?

Ceci: I took a teaching job at the Mazapan school, and I'm doing research for a book on Latin American indigenous dance and cultural festivity.

Doctor: Well your timing is perfect. La Ceiba, Honduras is the best place for Carnaval in Central America.

Ceci: So I am told. And are you here for carnaval too?

Doctor: No I am here with a team of Doctors Without Borders, and we are going to the local hospital to see patients and do surgeries.

The drumming gets louder as the parade nears.

Ceci: A huh!.....Are you staying here at the hotel?

Doctor: Yes I am; maybe we'll see you later… Here's our mobile number. My name is Louis Harris. *He writes his number on her hand.*

Ceci: I'm Cecilia Diaz…. nice meeting you.

There is a connection in the mutual smiles and parting handshake. Ceci is a bit dazed at she watches him walk off into his medical van. She comes to… looks at her watch, and suddenly remembers that she needs to make a call, and runs back into the hotel to use the lobby phone.

8. <u>GRAND PARIS LOBBY PHONE BOOTH</u>

Ceci fumbles to find a number and dials. A voice answers:

Voice: Escuela Mazapan

Ceci: Buenos Dias. Yo soy Cecilia Diaz, la nueva profesora de danza. Yes Oh.. OK. I wanted Ms. Counsel to know that I have arrived and that I am at the Grand Paris Hotel...

Voice: Just a minute. She is expecting your call.

Ceci: Oh OK I will hold. Thank you.

Marta Counsel, Director of the Mazapan School, speaks.

Ms. Counsel: Hello Ms. Diaz, Welcome to La Ceiba. I am so glad you arrived safely and I understand you are at the Hotel Gran Paris?

Ceci: Yes, and I am looking forward to seeing Carnaval from this point of view. It's really interesting for me to see all this close up.

Ms. Counsel: Well I want you to come see your dance studio which is being converted from an old kitchen as we speak.

Ceci: I can't wait.

Ms. Counsel: And we should meet to discuss your contract and schedule. Of course, Ms. Diaz, you realize that having a dance teacher is a luxury over and beyond the best of schools in Honduras, and The Mazapan School is considered one of the better schools you know. But I am sure we can work something out. *Her tone changes to more familiar.* And I might add that you are welcome to run an after-school program as well as a badly needed summer camp.

Ceci: So when can we meet?

Ms. Counsel: We can start this Monday morning at 9am.

Ceci: Thank you so much for this opportunity.

Ms. Counsel: We look forward to getting some entertainment going for our parents. So this will give you plenty of time to acclimate to La Ceiba for the fall. If we hear of any available apartments, I will let you know. See you Monday.

Ceci: Thank you, Ms. Counsel. *Ceci hangs up, and puts on her sunglasses.* This is starting to look like a real job.

She plows through the busy lobby to get close to the parade to witness and record the carnaval festivities.

9. <u>CARNAVAL PARADE</u> – Main Street – La Ceiba

Ceci doesn't waste any time diving into the magical world of the carnaval. The majestic horses have just pranced down the street to open the parade. Next come the rhythm kicking marching bands from all over Honduras, which begin to strut their choreography for the judges and the VIP section in front of the City Hall. The drum sections mesmerize the public and everyone vibrates with this exciting Afro-Caribbean rhythm. The beat is contagious and the crowd rocks. The band steps in synch with their percussive Latino rhythmic sounds, as they fill the air with hip swinging tropical music. There is happiness in the air, and people are exchanging carnaval beads and wearing colorful masks and exotic feathered costumes.

After the marching band we can see and hear the young male Garifuna drummers, accompanied by dancers. The men are dressed in their raggy clown costumes with the screen mesh masks, (hopping rapidly with intense masculine energy in the "Jean K'neau" dance fashion). They are followed by the young women singing and dancing, question and answer libretto in Garifuna tongue, with the older women, who are dressed in colorful matching kitchen dresses, dancing up the rear.

The Garifuna tribes from the coastal villages of Corozal and Sambo Creek stop in front of the judge's seats and perform a traditional "punta" dance with each of the dancers executing short solos before the drummers in perfect accented synchronization. The singing and the dancing are feverish and powerful with tight, accented hip movements in synch with the drummers. This dance was originally part of funeral celebrations to call down the ancestor spirits, but is also performed for cultural and tourism performances.

Next in line, the drums are more subdued with the sound of flutes and conch shells, as a ceremonial parade of a Mayan Queen, her priests, and scribes, athletes and warriors, maidens and corn goddesses snake around in mystical formations. They carry out a short ritual at the judge's table which calls for rain and agricultural blessings from the Mayan Gods of Rain, of Corn, wind and fertility.

Next, the local indigenous tribes follow, wearing their traditional primitive dress using the woven bark of the coconut tree, the skins of animals…. Tunics are decorated with beans, rice, and corn seeds as symbolic decoration for the fertility of the land, and the agricultural pride of the native people. Mother Earth is honored with the young women dressed as princesses of nature and the men, as young farmers. Reed flutes, drums, and tambourines carry a humble beat to which the young natives dance.

Next come the Folklorico Dancers who represent the mix of the Spanish Flamenco influence with their broad skirts and fancy footwork. The men wear straw hats and carry bandanas which are used for partnering and dancing alone. They perform a medley at the grand stand, representing folklore with many songs and dances from Honduras.

At last, the Floats with the Carnival Queen begins. They call them Carosas... rose cars (floats covered with flowers) This is where "Car Naval" (floating car) gets its name from the Italian Carnavales in Venice, when huge boats filled with costumed party goers, would be dragged down the canals in Venice during Carnaval...(Car which floats on water)... Car Naval.

In these floats we will see all the princesses and beauty contestants, along with the CARNAVAL QUEEN, La Reina de la Feria, herself, accompanied by all her sexy feathered dancers. They all wave and throw necklaces and kisses as they float down the street. The Queen sits on her throne, decorated in huge orange colored feathers.

10. <u>**Discovering a box of girls – Hospital Atlantida, La Ceiba**</u> 2003
Ceci has been photographing all of these Carnaval parade events with great enthusiasm. There seems to be a mysterious swarm of

monarch butterflies surrounding the Carnaval Queen who looks at Ceci as she passes. She throws Ceci a green beaded necklace, and the butterflies swarm around Ceci. An army truck has pulled up in front of the hospital, interrupting the parade. Two masked soldiers with rifles guard a female police woman as she checks out a cardboard box holding three skinny little toddlers in worn clothing, who are crying. She accompanies the truck past the security guard. Ceci takes a final picture of the Queen who stands up at her throne, mystically pointing to the box of children, looking directly at Ceci.

Instinctively Ceci scurries through the closing metal doors of the hospital, showing her camera to the security guard as if it were a backstage pass at a rock concert. She runs after the army truck into the hospital courtyard as the truck pulls up to the emergency back door. The soldiers unload the box on the floor of the long line up to the emergency registration window. Butterflies continue to surround the box. The image of the children in the box is striking, riveting, and overwhelming for Ceci. She is awestruck and approaches the lady officer, who is filling out papers with the guard, while the girls begin to cry hysterically. Roxana is 2 ½, Angie 1 ½, and Jazmin is 3 months. Ceci addresses the policewoman:

Ceci: Disculpa Sra. Que pasa aqui? Donde esta la mama de estas ninas? Excuse me Mam, What is happening here and where is the mother of these children?

Policia: Disculpa Senora…. Permitame pasar… Let me pass.

A butterfly lands on Ceci's shoulder.

Ceci: Pero donde esta la mama? Quiero ayudar! But where is the mother, I want to help.

Policia: La "mama" casi les mato, y por eso, ha perdida sus ninas… The mother nearly killed them, and for that, she has lost her kids.

Ceci: Me parece que ellas están bastante enferma. Me voy con ellas Srita, por favor…. And they seem very sick. I am going with them inside, please.

The police woman looks at the kids and then looks at Ceci.

Là policia: Venga entonces. Ok come in.

Ceci picks up the box and follows the police lady as she cuts in front of the long line of humble sick people. The girls cry, and are taken through the emergency room door.

11. <u>Emergency Room Waiting area</u>

Ceci follows as the policewoman registers the girls with the clerk, reading their names from a scrap of paper. Ceci helps her juggle all three of them in and out of the cardboard box they came in, while they gaze hysterically into space. Neither Angie nor Roxana can walk because of visible weakness and malnutrition.

Police woman: Jazmin, Angie, and Roxana Rojas, sin papeles. No papers.

Ceci: They look very sick… y porque les sacaron de la casa? Why did you take them from the house?

Police woman: I can speak some English.

Ceci: Pleases tell me the story here.

Police woman: The vecino (neighbor) call from San Judas where there is epidemica de meningitis and mucho pobreza now. They have the gangs and drugs. The vecina sees the mother hit this one in the head because she crying so much. They are hungry with the fever…. So the vecina call and the militaria go to San Judas, because la policia no pueden. And I don't know if it's maybe too late lady. So here they are. Gringa… te digo -They are lucky, because somebody calls before they die.

A nurse, JOSIE, comes from behind the window and bends down to look at the girls in the box. Angie is beginning to shake like a seizure. Ceci picks her up and holds her tightly against her chest. It seems like twenty minutes of convulsive shaking takes over Angie's body, until Ceci finally calms her down.

Nurse Josie: Dios mio! Eres tu una enfermera?

Ceci: No… Pero quiero saber si podemos diagnosticar lo que pasa con estas ninas el mas pronto posible. Porque la epilepsia? No I am not a nurse, but I would like to know if we can diagnose what is happening to these girls as fast as possible. Why the epilepsy?

Nurse: Hello I am Nurse Josie… I speak English. I don't know why she is shaking. *She does a hasty examination and we see that their baby teeth are black.* I think they are drinking bad sugar water. Look at the black teeth and the big bellies… Maybe the little one has a chance…but she is sick too. I don't know….

Ceci: Oh my God, how can this be happening? Where are the doctors? Is there a laboratory?

Police woman: Sra, desfortunatamente no hay muchos doctores. Tienen suerte que pudieron entrar. Los jovenes siempre vienen en los últimos momentos… casi muerto. Lo veo siempre. Debes de ver los orphanatos. Sra, unfortunately there aren't many doctors. These girls are lucky they even got in. The young always come in at the last minute… almost dead. I see this all the time. Come see the orphanages. Goodbye Gringa. Goodluck. *She departs.*

Ceci: This is a child's worst nightmare.

Nurse Josie: You just have to wait. Thank you for staying with these girls. They remove from their family home. I take you to pediatrics right now. They have fever, and this one has the shakes again!!! Don't let her go gringa.

The nurse leads the way, carrying Jazmin…Angie begins to shake again violently in Ceci's arms, and her eyes roll back into her head. Ceci holds her close to her heart as they walk towards pediatrics. The nurse pushes Roxana in a Wheel chair with Jazmin on her lap.

Ceci: **Mira ninas… Tranquila… Todo bien. Tranquila…Ceci esta aqui…** Look girls, Calm down. Everything is OK. Ceci is here. *Addressing the nurse* Are't you going to call a Doctor? This child is really sick, can't you see?

Nurse Josie: The Doctor is busy. They must wait. I sorry.

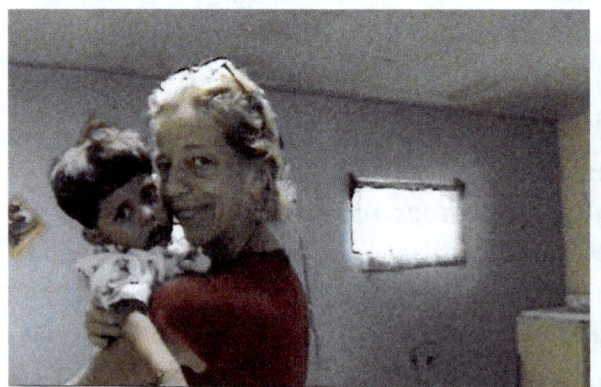
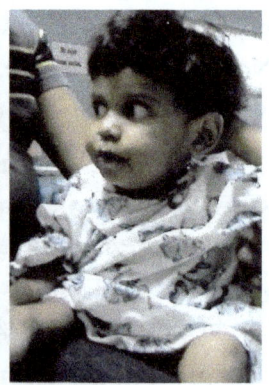

Angie   Roxana

12. <u>Pediatrics – Hospital Atlantida</u>

There is one vacant crib in Pediatrics, with no sheets and a broken plastic chair next to it. She assigns Ceci to the little crib.

Ceci: Are you kidding? One crib… One Doctor? For all these children? Can't you do something now? Where am I?

The nurse puts the other two girls in the same crib, and offers Ceci a seat next to a young mother with no shoes. She feels the fever on Roxana. Angie is still twitching in Ceci's arms.

Nurse Jose: **Las dos estan caliente. Aay! Creo que es meningitis. San Judas has epidemica now.** These two are hot. I believe it's meningitis. San Judas has an epidemic now.

Ceci: So what happens to them after this?

Nurse Jose: If they make it, they will go to IHNFA foster home and wait for a bed in un orphanato. I do not know which life is peor – the poor mother … or the bad orphanage. But, you will not be able to do much. They are property of Honduran government. I have to go now. I give you some advice. Don't attach too much… Visas are impossible. Good luck and thank you for to care about our children.

Nurse Jose leaves, and Angie continues to convulse. Ceci holds her tighter. Roxana can not stand up with her fever and malnutrition, and she screams…. She tries to give them water. Baby Jazmin just stares into space and kicks her left leg back and forth. The parade outside continues, and the music gets louder.

Ceci: **Donde estan los Doctores?** This child is slipping … I can feel it!! **Estoy preocupada por su corazon.** Oh Angie, let me make a call and then I will sing to you. If she keeps this up she will have a heart attack.

Ceci is almost hysterical talking to herself. She approaches a young mother who has a cell phone and offers her $5 to make a call. With Angie in her arms she dials the number written on her hand that the Doctor had given her this morning. The phone rings and is answered.

19

Ceci: Hello … This is an emergency. I am looking for Dr. Louis Harris. Is he anywhere near you? *She waits.* Oh, Thank God. *Ceci continues to hold Angie tenderly as she makes the call.* Hello, Dr. Harris? This is Ceci, the lady from Virginia. We met on the steps of the Gran Paris Hotel this morning? Yes, well I am in the Hospital Atlantida with a little girl who is having some kind of seizure and already has a high fever from what I believe is meningitis, and there are no doctors or nurses in Pediatrics and nobody seems to be doing anything!!

Dr. Harris: Well as luck would have it gringa, I am actually in Maternity at the Hospital Atlantida as we speak … Just hold on, I will find Pediatrics and be right there.

Ceci: Thank goodness… Please hurry!!! *She gets off the phone, and notices a bruise on Angie Nicolle's left eye.* And what's this bruise on your eye?

At this point all three kids are clutching Ceci and crying. She sings a "Mother Moon" lullaby as she swings Angie around and dances for Roxana and Jazmin until they are curiously captured by her act. The fan churns up the hot tropical air in the small hall of pediatrics. The music peaks again from the parade outside, banging around the cement acoustics of the barren hospital ward, and Ceci continues her Mother Moon song until Angie calms down.

Dr. Harris finally enters with a young Honduran student Doctor and Nurse, Josie. He examines Angie Nicolle and feels the fever… sees the wound on her left eye.

Dr. Harris: Looks like someone wacked her pretty good on her left eye from the size of this welt.

Ceci: The nurse said there was an epidemic of meningitis where they were living.

Dr.: Well that explains the fever. But this is definitely trauma to the head. And now she has a strabismus in her left eye which is why her pupil is not lined up properly.

Ceci: Oh no…

Nurse Jose rushes in drying her hands.

Nurse Josie: Hi, my name is Josie... The older one is with fever tambien. Many children come from San Judas with epidemica of meningitis, varicella, dengue. They bring them the last minute, and sometimes they don't live.

Dr.: Can we get a blood test?

Nurse Josie: Not today... the labs are closed with the carnaval.

Dr: OK, Can you find me the anti-biotic Rocephin?

Nurse Josie: We have very little medicine in the hospital Doctor.

Dr: What about Penicillin?

Nurse Josie: I'm sorry doctor, we don't even have bed sheets!

Long pause as the doctor intuitively diagnoses and prescribes medication for the condition, talking to himself in conclusion.

Dr.: OK ... These two have all the symptoms of meningitis. And this one is having neurological reactions from trauma. I am going to look in the Team's pharmacy wagon. I'll be right back.

Ceci: I'll pay for anything you need... anything!!

Dr.: If I don't find any, I will send you out to the local pharmacy. *The Doctor runs out of Pediatrics... Angie Nicolle continues to shake.*

Nurse Josie: Las pharmacias are closed during Carnaval.

Ceci: This is like a bad dream.

They both continue to juggle the confused girls.

Nurse Josie: Better here than San Judas. I think they did not get any milk or clean water

Ceci: *Voiceover of Ceci beginning to pray internally as she rocks Jazmin and puts Angie down.* Please dear God give these kids the strength to hang on and feel better... Please dear God,,, have mercy on these innocent little ninas.... They did not ask for this. (*This could be a lullaby song.*)

And the Doctor reappears with his syringes ready. They all hate needles and are hysterical while Ceci holds Angie and Roxana and the doctor injects each one. Jazmin continues to shake her leg in the wobbly crib.

Ceci: No se preocupen bellas, van a sentir mejor... les prometo.... And what about the baby, Jazmin? Don't worry beauties, you are going to feel better. I promise.

Dr.: Well I am pretty sure these two have meningitis. There doesn't seem to be fever with the baby, but we need to run blood tests on all three tomorrow.

Nurse Josie: I make sure for the blood test tomorrow.

Ceci: I hope that's the end of injections for today? They really hate those needles... So now what happens?

Nurse Josie: They will stay here tonight. Tomorrow IHNFA lady will come and put them in a home with a Madre Soltera. There is one around the corner, with lady named Adila, who I do not like much, but she is near the hospital.

Ceci: Where?

Nurse Josie: I not sure, but I can look.

Ceci: Then I will stay here and make sure they are OK.

Nurse Josie: There is no food in hospital. Only on the street.

Dr.: I must get back to delivering babies on the other side. They are all stable now, and I will check on them later in the day to make sure they have the right medicine.

Ceci: Thank you so much – Both of you. This has definitely been traumatic. *She embraces them both and breaks down.*

Dr. Harris... I believe you saved these girls' lives.

Dr: Just hang in there. They are definitely not out of the woods. I will see you later. *He answers his phone and rushes off.*

Ceci: OK... And thank you Nurse Jose... I will go for food. Esperenme ninas... me voy para comida... Yo vuelvo...OK? Besos. *Muttering to herself...*These girls are going to make it.

Nurse Jose: I hope so. *Hearing Ceci, she too mutters.* **Si Dios quiere.** God willing. **I must go, but will check on them later.**

The girls cry and reach out for Ceci as she backs out the door of pediatrics to find food. Nurse Jose moves on to the next crib. And again they are all alone in a crib staring into space, at the mercy of God, medicine, and public servants.

13. Back on the street – Carnaval continues

The parade still fills the street in front of the Hospital, and as Ceci fights her way through the crowd, another band of Garifuna drummers and dancers pass, decked out in their regalia, all singing and dancing to the punta beat. It is a fevered atmosphere, and provides the perfect transition to the Ciudad Blanca.

14. LA CIUDAD BLANCA – Flashback # 1

The Ceiba tree was significant in ancient Mayan history as it was believed to stand at the center of the earth. The 'Ceiba pentandra's' distinctive distinguishing hanging tendrils created an enclosure under it like a holy gathering place for the ancient Maya of Central America. These long, hanging vines were a sacred element of worship because they join together the terrestrial world to the heavens. The popular ritual incense, copal, comes from this tree. In the Popol Vuh (the Mayan creation story) the Mayan people were created under the Ceiba tree.

The history of La Ceiba starts under a huge Ceiba tree on the beach where the first settlers all congregated. This is an important symbol for the Mayan culture.

This is the first of several timeless flashbacks in the Ciudad Blanca, which will take place during this story. Legends also call it the Lost City of the Monkey King. The following monologue is a narration over images of the preparation for a spiritual meeting of famous Latin American ancestral tribal leaders who are meeting in the White City as the Carnaval punta drumming segues into the crackling sound of a fire and tropical night crickets.

A ritual is being performed in a beautiful stone plaza. There is a huge bonfire around which young women are dancing. Standing around the fire are several indigenous chiefs, kings, shamans, leaders and warriors from the past.

Cacique Lempira and his female assistant are constructing an altar with a collection of symbolic busts of Mayan, Garifuna, indigenous, Aztec and Spanish deities... the Catholic cross included. They all make their offerings and bows, then sit down on the semi circular stone bench in front of the altar to confront the problem of lost Latino youth.

Voiceover: Dawn breaks in the ruins of an overgrown ancient tropical city. The ancient, white stone walls are covered with the roots and vines of the Ceiba tree, towering over the plaza next to a crumbling pyramid, snaking its roots around a mystical white stone archway with the image of an upright monkey king. The two supporting arches portray a crocodile/lizard and a huge spider/ ant. In the blue light we can detect a smoking fire in the ruins of an old ceremonial plaza. Surrounding the fire, in earnest debate, is a congregation "in spirit" of tribal leaders from the last five centuries of native Mesoamerican royalty. They are meeting to address the demise of the Latin American family, and particularly the orphan children and gang population of Honduras. Leading the ceremony is the great Honduran Cacique, Lempira, who welcomes the sacred gathering of leaders from many centuries to the circle. He is serious, passionately sad, and violently angry at the plummeting status of abandoned children in Honduras. These ancestors and ancient tribal leaders are meeting in spirit to discuss the declining legacy of their descendants, as the fabric of their subaltern families crumbles under the invasion of modern culture, which constantly creates a divide between the classes. Lempira is crying out to the ancient leaders around him who were Mayan, Garifuna, Pre-Columbian, Toltec, Aztec, and Native Honduran Indigenous tribal kings, scribes, scientists, and shamans of the past.

Cacique Lempira: We thank the people of the Ciudad Blanca for letting us meet on these holy grounds. As we look at the present time, I am sad to watch the decline and constant struggle of our people. We come together to ask the powers of light and higher spirit to bring down their metal birds once again to boost the survival of our pueblos, to improve the educational and economic success of our humble people. Hondurans must reinvent their talents as indigenous natives to survive on our land, and also benefit from everything that modern society offers our children. We must find a balance. Help us… we need guidance!!

Cacique Benito: There was a time when the Maya were great and had the power of the heart of the sky. Now the technology out thinks our belief in nature.

Chief Copan Galel: And look where our people are centuries later? Prisoners in our own land. For this poverty we sacrificed our land, our women, children, and our lives to Europe? We weep for this land of the Latino population, who is confused by the suppression of their minority race. They struggle with their financial and class deprivation to participate in the next challenge of modernity, capitalism, white supremacy, electronics, speed, and the inevitable dissolution of the Latino family. The orphanages are full, and runaways are sleeping on the street.... Children are making more children and fathers are unable to support their families. The young men who form these gangs, are destroying their own culture, because they do not know what a loving family is. And the oligarchy who runs our country only think of themselves. This is like a tropical prison!

Garifuna Josephy Satuye: How could we defend ourselves against this electronic corruption, this false communication, this rapid transaction which excludes our native philosophy and our connection to nature?

Cacique Benito: We fight these wars and invasions against firearms, which bring us stress and death. Never mind the progress.... Have we lost all sense of brotherhood, family and friendship, and real human contact? What is this evolution which conquers and excludes the indigenous?!

Cacique Sicumba: We could not stop the conquistadores, and now we cannot stop modernity. The boys fall in love with these western gringas, they all want cars and cell phones, and they all want to look like television stars. I say we must reinforce their connection to mother earth and the benevolent ways of spirit. There is clearly a diminished connection to nature and family genetics while these electronic airwaves exist.

Cacique Lempira: Yes, I see that, but we cannot change the past. What I want to do is avoid more pain and disorder for the children. How can we bring them into a society where the schools are dysfunctional, where the police are powerless against the gangs and the drugs, and where there is so much poverty and disease?

Cacique Galel: I don't know where to begin? I did not fight for this... I did not lose my life and my people so that my great grandchildren would suffer like this at the hand of incompetent rulers from a distant land, who have evolved into the corrupt bourgeois oligarchy who cares not for us. Why must we fight to catch up and be equal in our own land?

Garifuna Satuye: I say that the only way is to operate directly from spirit to inject moral pride into these men to protect their families… enough pride to fight for their cultural survival and family and tribal dignity.

Cacique Benito: Quetzalcoatl, Great Feathered Serpent, what is your belief of this tragedy with our descendant children?

Quetzalcoatl: What I am about to say will baffle some of you. I will try to explain. There was an advanced civilization many moons before the Maya. They were the star people. We have reached the 13th heaven according to the Mayan Calendar, which finished its great cycle of evolution on December 22, 2013. Latinos have already suffered the lessons of bad education, discrimination, and domination. These children must be trained in humanitarian ideals, not eternal damnation and hunger. There must be a return to the heart of the heavens…. We are given life on a planet that takes care of us. So we must take care of it and its children. This must be done with the correct and noble intention of protecting and advancing the general welfare of the spectrum of all life on this planet.

Cacique Sicumba: When can we expect the feathered serpent to reincarnate? When does the new cycle begin? Why did the star people leave? What happened to the mighty Mayans? What happened to the intelligence?

Quetzalcoatl: The monkey scribes, whose legacy lies in this place where I last was alive know the history and the answer to these questions. This is the lost underworld of the 4th race of man, who lived as monkeys. The scribes can tell the whole story from the Popol Vuh of how the Gods came down from the stars to create life on earth.

Garifuna Satuye: And who are these Gods from the stars?

Quetzalcoatl: The star people are my people, who came to this planet to teach many things. What I know is that in the beginning there was nothing here but the water and the silence, and we called for land, and the ocean parted and land appeared. After that came the animals, the clay people, the wooden people and then the monkeys... But their bodies were imperfect and weak, and they had no hearts, nor could they respect their makers.... so the floods came to cleanse the population to start over and try again.

Francisco Morazon – This has to be mythology.... And yet more stories of the oppression of the humble by their so called "makers" and leaders. The Spanish did not do all of this.

Quetzalcoatl: We will overcome the mistakes of the past, and still be aware of our origins. Our people must promote the value of our culture despite the Spanish conquista. However, now is the emergency. We must look to the future ... for the destiny of Honduras and her children. May the Divine Spirit save our native souls and give our children a future on this planet to help support the wellbeing of all, with our intrinsic connection to nature.

Lempira: I thank you for this information, for which we must call the Divine spirits of alta luz (high light) for an immediate solution. Help us channel the energy of this young Latina generation into the production of healthy education and economic survival for days to come. We must offer copal to the God Supreme, not blood. I will start the ritual. We must call an army of angels.

Lempira begins to light the copal incense and sing to the heavens.... Dancing and shaking his rattle. The scene fades.

15. <u>AM – Hospital Atlantida – Doctor and IHNFA lady</u>

Ceci is waking up on the floor of Pediatrics, hugging her camera. The three girls are asleep in the crib. Children are crying everywhere. Dr. Harris returns to check on the girls.

Dr. Harris: Now why am I not surprised to see you here?

Ceci: There was nobody here last night and I could NOT leave them alone in this creepy hospital, OK?

Dr. H: OK... well meanwhile, your mother has been calling the hotel looking for you and leaving messages for you with every Gringo in the place.

Ceci: Well I am very sorry about that. I stayed with the kids last night to make sure the fevers went down, and then I fell asleep on the floor. There were no Doctors working last night. I couldn't leave them alone.

Dr. H: Welcome to third world medicine, where you are lucky if there even is a nurse. *He checks the girls for fever as they wake up.* They feel better, but these two need to continue the anti-biotic, and this one needs her vision checked. There is definite trauma to the head and eye here.

Enters the IHNFA (Instituto Hondureno de la Ninez y la Familia) *Lady, Melissa Calix, from Tegucigalpa with her assistants. She is looking at the file and reading names.*

IHNFA Lady, Ms. Calix: Angela Jazmin, Angie Nicolle, and Roxana Yadira Rojas. *She puts the file in her brief case and picks up baby Jazmin while her assistants take Angie and Roxana.*

Ceci: Where are they going?

INHFA Lady: Excuse me Gringa lady, but you cannot have these children. They are the property of Honduras now... and they are going to be placed in a foster home.

Dr. H: Disculpe Senora, pero dos de estas ninas tienen enfermedades graves y todas con malnutricion. Ellas necesitan mas tratamiento antes de salir del Hospital. Sus examines de sangre muestran meningitis bacterial, y son muy debiles. No deben de salir ahora! A trained nurse has to inject them regularly.

Excuse me Mrs., but two of these little girls have serious illness and all of them are malnourished and need more treatment before leaving the hospital. Their blood tests show bacterial meningitis and they are very weak. They should not leave now!

He injects them with the anti-biotic. Ceci holds Angie in one arm, Roxana in the other while she screams.

IHNFA Lady: I am sorry. They must be placed today, or there will be no room for them anywhere. I have an IHNFA lady who will take them today.

Ceci: And where is that?

IHNFA Lady: Excuse me Senora. But this is none of your business. Oye me bien! They are now the property of the Honduran government. Twenty years ago you could pick them up from the hospitals and take them home with you to your country, but not anymore. Please move, I am leaving with these children now.

The assistants each take a child, leaving Ceci with her mouth open. The children reach and cry as they are taken away.

Dr. H: Sra, these girls still need medical attention!

Ms. Calix ignores the doctor again. He is clearly frustrated. Ceci turns to the Doctor with this look of pain and horror on her face, not knowing whether to break down, or fight.

Dr. H: Don't give up now. There is a way to do this, and you will find it. Go back to the hotel and rest.

Ceci: Are you kidding? if I don't follow this IHNFA lady, I will lose them in this crazy system.

Dr. H: Then take this medicine and make sure they get it. They probably won't be given it otherwise. I will see you at the hotel later.

He hands her a plastic bag with needles and bottles of medicine.

Ceci rushes out of pediatrics to follow the IHNFA Lady, Melissa Calix. But she has already exited the hospital with the girls carrying Jazmin and Angie and hauling Roxana who can barely walk. As they are dumped into a taxi they look back frantically for Ceci. By the time Ceci catches up, the taxi has taken off. Ceci is in a frenzy.

16. <u>Street Scene – Aftermath of Carnaval – Madrugada (Dawn)</u> -

It's 8:30 in the morning. The carnaval street is hungover and strewn with garbage, the street cleaners are sweeping away. There are no garbage pails on the street in Honduras. Lost boys and drunks are asleep in the corners. The vendors have slept in their tents and begin again to set up, hoping to unload the last of their Carnaval bargains. We hear merengue music again kick in from a vendor's boom box.

17. <u>Hotel Grand Paris Lobby - Ceci, Nurse, Aguas Ocana Maduro</u>

Ceci wakes up in her hotel room to the sound of the phone.

Concierge: Excuse me Ms. Diaz, but there is a call for you from the USA. It's your mother again and again. She has been calling all morning.

Ceci: Thank you, I'm so sorry. Can you connect me? Thanks. *She takes the call, and her mom pops up in an aside or split screen.* Yes, mom I am OK. You're not going to believe what happened. Just listen ma. I have found and now lost three sisters who were dropped at the local hospital in a box.

Mom: Ceci, you sound like you are hallucinating. What about the job Ceci? Where have you been all night?

Ceci: I know you are going to think I am crazy, but I slept on the floor in the hospital to watch over these girls and their fevers. I had to Mom. It was a matter of life or death ... I swear.

Mom: Cecilia Diaz...Please get your priorities straight. Remember you are in the third world... children are dying of disease and starvation everywhere!!! And ... from what I understand. Honduras is the murder capital of the Western Hemisphere. *She has her glasses on and is reading a newspaper.* You have to watch your back. Ceil... these kids belong to somebody else.

Ceci: Mom I am OK, and I just have to do this.

Mom: You are alone, and I cannot help you if something happens. I AM worried!! So at least email me. PLEASE!!

Ceci: Yes Mom. Thank you for caring. And I swear to God, I promise to call more often. Bye ... besos. (kisses)

Ceci gets off phone, and Nurse Jose from the hospital, dressed in street clothes, approaches her in the lobby.

Nurse Josie: Hello Ms. Cecilia, I come with news of the ninas…. I know where they are.

Ceci: Oh Nurse Jose, you are an angel…Thank God… I was so worried that I would never see them again.

Nurse Josie: The IHNFA put them with Sra. Adila… not far. I will show you.

Ceci: You are so kind to come tell me this. They need their medicine.

Nurse Josie: And Ms. Cecilia, the Doctor tells me that you make dancing and are visiting Honduras.

Ceci: Yes, I am a choreographer, and I am here to teach dance at the Mazapan School and do research for a book.

Nurse Josie: You see I also work for orphanato se llama SOS, and they want for the children to dance there. Can you make some dancing for our kids? Because they do not go to Carnaval, we want to make special activity for them el Sabado.

Ceci: Of course, I would love to do that. Yes of course. But first I really want to see the girls.

Nurse Josie: Yes claro, this is why I come. I will take you to them.

Ceci: Oh thank you… I could barely sleep. And yes, I will gladly come to work with your children. And tell me about the girls?

Nurse Josie: The girls are around the corner from the hospital at the IHNFA casa de Sra. Adila. I will take you now?

Ceci: Thank you so much Josie… I must shower and change, and get my camera…. Can you wait? I want to see them as soon as possible…

Nurse Josie: Claro.

Nurse Josie sits in the lobby to wait for Ceci and watches the continuing hustle and bustle of Carnaval in the lobby and in the park across the street, where folk dancers are setting up. The first lady, Sra. Aguas Ocana Maduro, wife of President Ricardo Maduro, is being interviewed in the lobby. She is like an Evita, or even lady Di, blond, young, and beautiful.

Reporter: Sra. Maduro, we understand that you have put a high priority on your work with the homeless children in our country.

First Lady: Yes, and as a matter of fact, Ricardo and I are actually trying to adopt three children now from an orphanage in San Pedro, but it is very complicated with the IHNFA laws. We are trying to get children off the streets. That is our number one priority …. and to get them into the facilities that are available, so that further placement can be achieved. I am very sad about this destruction of the family, and I want to offer the children of these fractured families some hope. Statistics show that 50% of the Honduran population is under 15, and 80% of that group have no fathers named on the birth certificates. The tragedy is that many never ever find their way back into a family before the gangs find them.

Ceci arrives with her camera and finds her way through the reporters and onlookers.

Nurse Jose: This is the first lady, Agua Canas Maduro… She is from Espana. Please hear this.

Reporter: Sra., our resources say that the orphanages are overflowing with children who are sleeping two to a single bed in some cases, with insufficient food supply, and untrained staff trying to keep them disciplined and locked up in what seems like city jails. What do you think of that?

First Lady: The IHNFA is doing the best they can with the limited resources they have. Many of the children have escaped back into the streets in search of freedom, drugs, and food. They have no homes to return to after their fathers leave and new boyfriends enter the home, who will not accommodate the son's return. I go around with a fleet of vans every night collecting boys who are lost or stoned on resistol (glue) and sleeping in the parks and on the sidewalks. We give them a meal and put them in one of the residential facilities….. and believe me, I know that the El Carmen orphanage in San Pedro is not an adequate home for these children. So I am doing everything in my power to find the funds to create more civilized living conditions for them.

Reporter: We have also been told of significant corruption within the IHNFA (Instituto Hondureno de la Ninez y la Familia), which is supposed to be the agency assigned to the wellbeing of these children. We understand that administrators

First lady, Agua Canas Maduro

are embezzling funds, and using government money for unnecessary per diem costs….. That the women who are taking children into their homes for $100 each a month, are not able to take care of their complex medical needs. What is the story behind all this misuse of funds which are supposed to go towards the urgent care of these lost children?

First Lady: I understand that the government will be closing the IHNFA temporarily due to these allegations, with a serious goal to restructure their policies and facilities. At the moment all adoptions have been suspended. Fortunately, most of the orphanages run by North American Churches may be able to take up the slack in the meantime…. But I am doing everything I can, just to keep these kids off the street.

Reporter: Thank you, Sra. Maduro … for your kind heart and dedication. *The interview is wrapped up and the first lady is ushered away with her security guards.*

Ceci: Now that was interesting. *She comments to Nurse Josie.*

Nurse Josie: Come on, vamos.

Ceci: It's like these kids just have the luck of the draw or the toss of the dice.. as to where they will wind up. There's just no security. And none of these options can compete with a real mother.

Nurse Josie: Vamos Ceci. Piensas en las ninas. Think about the girls.

18. <u>**Nurse Jose takes Ceci to the IHNFA home**</u>

Folklore music begins in the park outside the hotel, and dancers perform for the crowds. Ceci and the Nurse cross through the festivities, and push through the street crowds to arrive at the IHNFA home where the girls are temporarily dumped.

Nurse Josie: Here is the house of Sra Adila, and I know she likes dollars and if you help her, she will let you see the girls. Please do not repeat that, OK? I must go to work.

Ceci: Thank you for doing this Josie.

Nurse Josie: I not supposed to get involved with patients, but I know that you saved their lives. Dios te bendice. But, Sra they need more care and vigilancia. The medicina and comida are very important now because they are so weak.

Ceci: The doctor gave me their anti-biotics. You have the heart of a sister.

Nurse Josie: I wish I could do more for these kids. I see them every day. They die in my arms, Senora.

Ceci: Not these girls. They are going to live. Porque Dios lo quiere y yo lo quiero. Because God wants it and I want it. *She pulls out the medicine. They hug.* **And when shall I come by to your SOS orphanage to do some dancing?**

Nurse Josie: Can you come this weekend? We will have some group activities, because they could not go to Carnaval.... They will love to dance.

Ceci: Tell me where, and I can come on Sunday afternoon.

A street boy comes by to try to hustle Ceci for cash.

Nurse Josie: *Writing on a paper...* Tell the taxista to take you to the SOS orphanage by the airport.....

Ceci: I will be there.

Nurse Josie: **Thank you so much... I must go back to work now. And do not give that boy any moneys, or he will go buy resistol with it.** *She takes off in a cab.*

Ceci: **What's that?**

Street observer: **It's glue. They smell it and go to sleep. It kills them. Better to give food.**

Ceci offers the boy a banana from her knapsack, and he scowls and grabs it....

Street observer: **Que lastima! Son como animales!!** What a pity. They are like animals.

Ceci turns to approach the house the nurse indicated, and there is a dark figure of a middle-aged, native Honduran woman, standing in the doorway. It is Adila. There are children running around playing in the small iron fenced-in porch in front of a tiny house. They are fascinated by the Gringa.

19. **Inside the IHNFA house of Adila - 2004**

Adila: **Como puedo servirle Senora?** How can I help you Mrs.?

Ceci: **Perdoname por favor. Vengo porque... hay tres hermanas que llegaron aqui del hospital con la IHNFA, y quiero darles la medicina para sus infeciones de meningitis y malnutricion. Me llamo Cecilia.** Excuse me please. I come because there are three sisters who arrived here from the Hospital with the IHNFA, and I want to give them medicine and vitamins for their meningitis and malnutrition. My name is Cecilia.

Adila: **Gringa verdad? Y que interes tiene ud. en estas ninas?** You are a gringa right? And what interest do you have in these little girls?

Ceci: **Puro corazon Senora. No me gusta ver sufrimiento a nadie si puedo ayudar.** Only heart Senora. I don't like to see anybody suffer if I can help.

Adila: **Pasa...**

She opens the door slowly, observing Ceci up and down. Ceci enters a small crowded room full of furniture and kids. It is dark,

and the electricity is off (which happens several times a week).
She follows Adila into a small bedroom. There lying on the bed
are Roxana, cleaned up, but hollow-eyed and skinny as death...
crying. Next is Angie, also long and skinny.... Both are lying
there, too weak to rise. Angie's head seems proportionally larger
than her body. They all have large distended bellies from bad
water. Angie still has that deep purple and red welt on the left side
of her head... her eyes bulging..... reaching out for Ceci when she
hears her voice. Angie remembers Ceci. And when she lifts her,
Roxana cries even harder. Little Jazmin is crying in a car seat,
shaking her left leg incessantly. Adila picks her up and shakes her
around, speaking in loud baby talk.... It is an uncomfortable
situation.... And Ceci is clearly moved and confused by all this
anxiety. She pulls out the medicine and prepares the needles to
inject Roxana and Angie. She juggles the girls back and forth until
the job is done, much to their dislike. The other kids play around
her. Jazmin looks up from her car seat leg shaking.

Adila: I can do that Gringa.

Ceci: Oh I didn't know you speak English. I wanted to make sure they got it. The medicine is difficult to come by and I will bring it on a regular basis, just to make sure. So what's the story with these girls?

Adila: The IHNFA lady brought them yesterday from the hospital. The father is furious, and I think he is part of some gang. The mother is in jail for abusing the kids. They haven't eaten in days. The little one at least got breast milk from the mom who probably does drugs. They say she is a little crazy. These two have fever still from the meningitis, and horrible diarrhea. They are pretty sick.

Ceci: I know they are, and I will pay for any more medicine they need. Here are the meds for the parasites and amoebas... and these are children's vitamins. They really should go back to the hospital for a checkup tomorrow.

Adila: You see how many kids I have here? I can't run to the Doctor every time a kid sneezes!

Ceci: But this one almost died with fever from meningitis yesterday! I can take them tomorrow. And there is a serious bruise on Angie's left eye.

Adila: I will take care of it Gringa... They are lucky to be here, believe me .... most of them just die in the hospital.

Ceci: Is there anything else you need? *She is reluctant to leave.*

Adila: Come back tomorrow, and I will tell you. I have work to do... VILMA! Hay que hacer compras! You must go shopping.

Ceci: Please take care of these little girls. They are very special. Please take this for any of their needs. Entiende Sra? *Ceci gives her 500 lempiras. Showing her out... Adila gives the cash to the trabajadora, Vilma, who will shop.*

Adila: We are all special Gringa.... Si Dios Quiere, viviremos.... Vilma!!! Comprame verduras, arroz, carne, y pampers chica.... Nos falta pampers! Ciao Gringa... God willing we will all live. Vilma, buy me vegetables, rice, meat, and pampers... We need pampers. Goodbye Gringa.

Ceci: Gracias Sra Adila... I will stop by tomorrow to check on the girls.

Roxana hobbles over to grab the bars on the porch fence to watch Ceci walk away. She begins to cry. Ceci kisses her through the prison like bars of Adila's porch. Vilma has waited for Ceci.

20. **On the Street with Vilma**

Vilma: Me dijieron que ud. salvo la vida de Angie ayer… que ella casi morio. They tell me that you saved Angie's life yesterday… that she almost died.

Ceci: Roxana y Angie tienen meningitis, pero van a sobrevivir. Si tu puedes darles buena comida y lo que necesitan le agradeceré. Yo no se como cualquier persona puede pasar una caja de ninas en la calle y seguir caminando. Roxana and Angie have meningitis, but they are going to make it. If you can make sure they eat and get what they need I would be so appreciative. I don't know how anybody could step over a box of three unconscious children, and keep walking.

Vilma: Eso pasa siempre. Yo trabajo… para poner comida en la mesa para mi familia. It happens all the time. I work… to feed my family.

Ceci: Vive con su familia? Are you living with your family?

Vilma: Vivo con mi madre y mis hermanas y sus hijos. Creo en familia. *Pause* **Sra Ceci… Puedo decirle que esta casa no es un buen lugar para estas ninas… especialmente como ellas estan enfermas. Adila no puede manejar bien todos esos muchachos. Ella toma el dinero para los niños del gobierno y lo gasta en viajes a Espana, y en su casa…. Y tambien ella pega los ninos.** I live with my mother and my sisters and their children. I believe in family. Pause… Sra… I can tell you that this is not a good place for these girls. Especially as they are sick. Adila cannot handle all those kids. She takes the money and spends it on herself, the house, and her trips to Spain. And she beats the kids.

Ceci: *(Mouth open in disbelief)* What? You know this? You see this? And you don't do anything about it? Oh My God, where am I? Porque no dice nada? Why don't you say something?

Vilma: Si digo algo, Adila me regana y amenaza mi trabajo. Es mi solo dinero Ceci. 300 Lempiras seminal ($15 a week) **Vivimos dia por dia.** If I say anything Adila scolds me and threatens my job. This is my work Sra…. 300 Lempiras a week, just to put food on the table for my mother. We live day to day.

Ceci: *Giving her money.* **Por favor cuide bien estas ninas. Ellas necesitan sus vitaminas y su medicina. Vengo manana. Tengo confianza en ti. Por favor. Quiero curarlas.** Please watch over these children for me. They need their vitamins and that medicine. I will come tomorrow. I am counting on you Vilma. I want to heal them.

Vilma: Con Angie yo no se. Ella no puede ver bien. Ceci… Serian muchos milagros para devolverle a la normalidad con todo el dano hecho. I can tell you Senora … I don't think she can see… You are going to have to make some miracles to bring these girls all the way back to normal with all this damage.

Ceci: Pues, ahora ellas necesitan amor sincero Vilma. Now they just need sincere love Vilma.

Vilma: Si, yo hare lo que puedo, pero la pobreza mata Ceci. Yes I will do what I can, but poverty kills.

Ceci: Yo se…. I wish I could help everybody.

Vilma pockets the money…and is about to enter a local bodega, when a Garifuna woman passes them, with a basket on her head. Vilma laughs and says goodbye to Ceci. Ceci is learning quickly that everybody expects payment in Honduras.

Vilma: Yo les cuidare bien Cecilia. I will watch over them for you. **Mira Ceci! Creo que se puede usar un pocito de esa magica Garifuna! Debes de aprovechar.** I believe you need a little of that Garifuna magic.

21. <u>Meeting Garifuna Eva – In Front of the Bodega</u>

Eva, a Garifuna woman, is coming out of a bodega where she sells her goods.

Eva: Hello Gringa lady!! Have you tried any of our Garifuna specialties?

Ceci: Like what kind of Garifuna magic are you selling?

Eva: Pan de Coco, tableta de coco, aceite de coco y casabe–the best in town, straight from Dona Eva's oven. I can also braid your hair right pretty.

Ceci: Well I definitely could use a little magic right now. How about that tableta de coco? Looks good. What is it?

Eva: Fresh ground coconut roasted with ginger and honey, and blessed by the spirit.

They sit under a tree and Eva unpacks her goods.

Ceci: Sounds delicious. *Handing her cash...* Tell me Eva... I am interested in seeing some authentic, Garifuna culture... music, dance, and any ceremonial events that I could possibly attend. I am writing about the indigenous culture and ceremonies in Honduras. Can you help me with that?

Eva: You know I belong to a dance group and we are having a ceremony on Sunday to celebrate the anniversary of my husband's death last year... right after carnival it was. Yes we are calling the ancestors. Do you want to come? It will be at my house in Corozal, near the beach.

Ceci: Yes I would love to come. I am honored that you invited me.... and I am so sorry about your husband.

Eva: He died in a storm in a fishing boat off the shore trying to save a young boy. It was a year ago today. I miss him... He made tambores *(drums)* and canoes for the community, out of the Ceiba tree. Sometimes when I sit on the beach at night, I swear I hear him playing the drum.

Ceci: I am so sorry for your loss Eva. *Pause* You know I would love to come. Where is your event?

Eva: It's up the coast in Corozal... a taxi can take you. You can have a great fried fish dinner at my friend Stella's Restaurant.... I live on the beach at the far end, in a bamboo house. That is where the ceremony is. Stella will show you. It will be late... like 9 or 10pm.

Ceci: I'll be there... Thank you for the tableta de coco. It is truly divino... *Ceci hails a cab which passes her by, and Eva shouts after her.*

Eva: And one more thing… that lady Adila is gonna take your money. Cuidado…..Watch out for her… She likes dollars. I will wait for you on Sunday… Adios gringa Cecilia!!

Ceci watches Eva walk away, while munching on her tableta de coco. She looks back at Adila's house confused, and turns around. Music accompanies her walk/dance home.

22. <u>Ceci arrives at the Mazapan School – Meeting with Director</u>

It is morning as Ceci leaves the hotel and crosses the tracks walking into the Dole Fruit Compound. She wears her jeans and a blue blazer with her sunglasses and camera round her neck. There are big, white, wooden, 1940s type beach homes lined up for the administrator's families. This scene provides a direct contrast to the mainstream lifestyle of the common people. In Honduras there are 3 distinct classes. The upper class, the lower middle class and the poor. The Mazapan School functions under the umbrella of Dole Fruit, called Standard Fruit of Honduras. The school was originally built to serve the children of the executives of Dole, but expanded with its great reputation and accreditation with American private schools, enabling possible college entrance to the United States for many upper class students in La Ceiba.

She comes to a guard house where she introduces herself.

Ceci: Hola Sr. Me llamo Cecilia Diaz y soy la nueva profesora de danza en la Escuela Mazapan, y Senora Marta Counsel me espera a las 9. Hoy es mi primero dia. Hello Senor. My name is Cecilia Diaz and I am the new dance teacher at the Mazapan school and Mrs. Marta Counsel is waiting for me at 9 am. Today is my first day.

Guard: Bueno, Bienvenida Sra. Permitame llamar a la escuela. Wonderful. Welcome Sra. Let me call the school.

The guard gets permission and allows her to pass. Ceci enters the palm tree shaded campus of the Mazapan School. On her way up to the main office stairs of one of the many white wooden buildings, Ceci sees students in uniforms changing classes, speaking Spanish *to one another and laughing with the spirit of students about to end the school year after Carnaval. They wear white shirts and blouses and navy blue pants and skirts. These children, K-12, are part of the Honduran, privileged upper class at $400 a month tuition. Ceci is greeted by the secretary, Diana, who is the hub of the wheel at Escuela Mazapan, and she escorts her to Ms. Counsel's office.*

Ms. Counsel: Buenos Dias, bienvenida, welcome Ms. Diaz.

Ceci: Thank you. It's very exciting being here.

Ms. Counsel: Yes Carnaval is exciting. La Ceiba is known as the party city and brings in many tourists at this time of year.

Ceci: Downtown is a gold mine for pictures and inspiration.

Ms. Counsel: Please be careful on the street Ms. Diaz. That camera is a flashy item for sure.

Ceci: I understand. Thank you for warning me. I hope to acclimate myself here poco a poco.

Ms. C: So let's talk about the job... and then Diana will take you over to the studio so you can advise in the set-up of the bars and the mirrors. They are working on the raised, wooden floor as we speak.

Ceci: I love it. How do you know about raised dance floors?

Ms. C: Well because you are replacing a Honduran ballerina named Mimi, who recently left us to marry an American Dole employee and return to the US with him... Anyway, we loved Mimi and she always insisted upon using the stage in the auditorium for classes because of the wooden floor. So we are moving the bars and the mirrors over to the old kitchen and building a new floor so you can have a real studio.

Ceci: Wow, I am speechless.

Ms. C: So what I would need from you is a curriculum for a bi-weekly elective dance class for the upper school kids... Grades 8-12.

Ceci: Do I have to stick to ballet?

Ms. C: Of course not. Any kind of dance that you can twist into academics, within reason and good taste now…is OK with me. *Pause as she thinks.* **What** also interests me is if you could coordinate our holiday productions for Mother's Day in the Spring and Christmas in December. Remembering that this is a very Catholic culture, perhaps you could coach our K-12 teachers to find thematic ideas for some kind of presentations in dance, theater, music, comedy, whatever… within theme and reason of course…. And help them polish it. Perhaps schedule them to come into the new dance studio to rehearse and see themselves in the mirrors. And just to get started, perhaps we can mount some kind of event for Dia Del Nino, which is a big celebration for Honduran families.

Ceci: Ms. Counsel, all of this is right up my alley. I can teach your staff a wonderful system for mounting shows so there is no waiting between numbers and everybody knows what's going on and at the same time I can learn about this culture and frame it.

Ms. C: Oh yes, all of that would be wonderful.

Ceci: And do you have a choral or instrumental teacher?

Ms. C: Yes, and she is wonderful, but she also needs technical theater support with her performances.

Ceci: Well, I was a stage manager before I got serious about choreography, so you have the right girl for coordinating and incorporating everybody efficiently into a dynamic sequence. I love to do that.

Ms. C: Magnifico Dona Cecilia. So we will send you Mimi's ballet students for the rest of the school year and I can offer you the use of the dance studio for a summer program if you are interested.

Ceci: Well that sounds good too. I will have to look at the logistics of advertising and charging tuition if you don't mind.

Ms. C: This free studio rent is what will compensate you for the salary we will pay you monthly to execute the plan we discussed… which is 3000 Lempiras a month… roughly $180.

Ceci: *Ceci smiles, pauses, and breathes and says:* Well that sounds OK too because you know what… if this studio is as beautiful as I imagine it, I can honestly say this is every artists' tropical dream.

Ms. C: I know you will be inspired when you see the studio. I have seen your resume and I know how much diversity you can bring to our students. And by the way, we speak only English in our classes. This is our policy. I don't know how much Spanish you speak, but this is why we like to have American teachers.

Ceci: Hablo bastante para comunicar… mi gramatica no es perfecto. pero mi madre es de Espana, que me dio muchos anos de oir la lengua en mi familia. I speak enough to communicate, even though my grammar isn't perfect. My mother is from Spain which gave me many years of hearing the language in my family.

Ms. C: Bueno.. Entonces.. vaya con Diana para firmar su contrato, y despues ella va a llevarse a ver el estudio en el otro lado. Ok then, go see Diana to sign your contract and afterwards she will bring you to see the studio on the other side of the campus.

She opens the door and shakes Ceci's hand.

Ceci: Ms. Counsel, thank you so much.

Ms. C: Llamame Marta por favor. Somos familia aqui… Call me Marta. We are family here. *Diana shows Ceci where to sign her contract and then escorts her to the studio.*

23. Inside Ceci's Mazapan Dance Studio

The charm and care of the Mazapan campus provide a direct contrast to the orphanage scene. The old bodega is being transformed into a dance studio for Ceci to teach and rehearse shows. It is small, with a charming outdoor covered patio. The studio will have everything a professional studio needs: a mirror, ballet bars, wood floor, sound system, music desk, waiting area, office, workshop, and changing room. It used to be a big social hall in the 40's. On the end is a tiled kitchen with huge ceilings where carpenters are finishing a raised wooden dance floor. It is small, with a charming garden outside. Diana introduces Ceci to the carpenter who is building the dance floor. He asks her for the correct height to hang the mirrors and the bars. Ceci takes off her jacket and her shoes to help them, and all of this progresses rapidly. Even the workers are stunned at how fast the room is ready to go. Ceci is stretching on the newly hung ballet bars.

Carpintero jefe Enrique: Senora, yo mismo estoy bien sorpresido saber que terminemos este trabajo en dos dias.. Ud tiene una fuerza inspirar y empujar al mismo tiempo! Senora, I am surprised to know that we finished this work in two days. You have the strength to inspire and push at the same time.

Ceci: Gracias Senor.. muy amable. Yo estoy muy alegre a ver un estudio de esta calidad, listo para los estudiantes. Thank you, very kind of you. I am very happy to see a studio of this quality ready to go for the students.

Ceci approaches him and extends her hand in thanks.

Carpintero Enrique: Su aire viene manana. Your AC comes tomorrow.

Ceci: Oh air conditioning.. Bueno.. Eso necesitamos. Good, we need that.

Carpintero: Entonces Dona Cecilia... Suerte con su nuevo suelo magico y original! Ok Dona Cecilia... Good luck dancing on this magical and original floor. *He makes a little dance step.*

Ceci: You know Enrique, I will remember that. Gracias por su trabajo.

<u>Dance Sequence</u> – Ceci baptizes the dance floor

Enrique and his men leave, and Ceci is left alone in the studio and begins to dance/baptize the studio on her new floor in front of her new mirror. She has a moment of dream space where she realizes she has found a home in Honduras.
Music accompanies this sentiment in a short solo dance sequence.

24. <u>Montage – Visiting the girls at the IHNFA House of Adila</u>

The following montage covers Ceci's visits to Adila's house mornings and evenings. She brings clothing, medicine, shoes, toys, diapers, food and whatever assistance she can offer to improve the lives of the girls and other kids around them.

Ceci introduces the girls to the songs she grew up with, attempting to translate them into Spanish. Sometimes she brings music for them to dance to. The following are some of the songs she would sing to the girls for play or lullaby.

<u>*This Little Piggy Went to Market - The toe wiggle baby song*</u>

Este cochinito fue al mercado, Este cochinito quedo en la casa, Este cochinito comio carne asada, Y este cochinito comio nada…. Y este cochino (pinky toe) llorro ."Wee wee wee" hasta la casa. This Little piggy went to market, this Little piggy stayed home, this Little piggy ate roast beef, this little piggy had none… and this little piggy cried wee wee wee all the way home.

Ring Around the Rosie, Pocket full of Posies, Ashes, Ashes, we all fall down!

Rock a-bye Baby, On the tree top, When the wind blows, the cradle will rock. When the bow breaks, the cradle will fall, and down will come baby, cradle and all.

Mother Moon, or Madre Luna

One day, Ceci arrives with a double stroller, which allows her to take Angie and Roxana out and about. Jazmin stays home always, seated in a car seat on the floor ... 3 months old ,,,, rocking herself with her left leg. She is too young to take out. The montage repeats this excursion routine for a few weeks, showing Ceci's regular arrival with gifts for everybody and the essentials for the girls... as alms to Ms. Adila. These donations allow her to take Angie and Roxana out of the house. They love climbing into the multi baby stroller to wander around La Ceiba.

When they go to the beach. Roxana is uncomfortable, always turning her back to the ocean, while Ceci walks the wobbling Angie, 18 months, to the shoreline. Then they walk up to the plaza, into the dance studio at the school, through the beautiful DOLE gardens... and perhaps to the Cafeteria in town. This whole time Jazmin stays home in a car seat on the floor. Usually, upon arrival, Ceci immediately goes to Jazmin and picks her up. Jazz is 4-5 months old and very observant... spending most of her time shaking her left leg to rock the car seat on the floor. Adila would not let Ceci take her out with the other two girls.., even after Ceci bought a special

stroller which would have accommodated all three of them. Whenever they return, Ceci would repeat the routine of picking up Jazmin and talking to her before she left. She always reaches out in panic when Ceci leaves. It was never enough, and Ceci always pulls herself away from the girls feeling guilty.

Clearly, they are happy to see Ceci, but their medical conditions are not good. Separating from the girls is always a difficult routine. The girls cry and Ceci does everything she can not to look back as she walks away. This particular time it started to thunder and rain… and the drums take over again in Ceci's mind…. transitioning again to the Ciudad Blanca.

25. CIUDAD BLANCA BAPTISM with Comizahual– Flashback 2

Another drumming transition takes us over the rainbow again to the Ciudad Blanca where there is another ceremonial congregation of the Gods and tribal leaders of the past. Jazmin, Angie, and Roxana are there in white tribal regalia riding a white tiger down a processional avenue lined with white pillars and images of animals… crocodiles, spiders, pumas, monkeys, jaguars.

They arrive at an altar area behind which is a long stairway, and a ceremonial platform above a cenote, or round body of water. Lempira begins to invoke spirit.

Lempira: There is a sorceress, a goddess named Comizahual who arrived from the stars two hundred years before the conquista. Her name means Flying Tiger, as she was white with hair colored like a tiger, riding on a huge triangular rock with the distorted faces of pumas on each side. She introduced civilization with her magic to the people of Cealcoquin *(also Cearquin),* which is now near Copan in the Dept. of Lempira. There she built a palace and although she was a virgin, she had three sons between whom she divided her kingdom. When she was old, she asked them to carry her bed to the highest part of the palace, whence she suddenly disappeared amid thunder and lightning. She had returned to the Gods… And a beautiful bird was seen to fly upwards and disappear.

Quetzacoatl: These three daughters are the reincarnated sibling sons of this ancient Mayan Goddess, Comizahual...The Flying Tigress. We are waiting for her return tonight, to baptize you in this life, because of your original miracle virgin birth with her as your spiritual mother. Comizahual is a great healer from the stars. We want to accelerate your evolution, in the name of all the Honduran orphans who suffer from illness, abandonment, neglect, and isolation. We pray that through the magnetic and supernatural strength of Comizahual, these girls will become examples.... by directing their souls to find the love and guidance of a family tribe whose culture allows them opportunity to be happy, to support themselves and their offspring. Hijas, this gringa, Cecilia, is the Flying Tigress reincarnated for you in this life to help you to fulfill your destinies....

And the music builds as the sky lights up with the zig zagging appearance of a triangular fiery rock, which slowly lands in front of them.... A beautiful tall, white woman with white and golden hair emerges from the flying, fiery rock... dressed in shamanic regalia like a tiger. She is Comizahual, and Ceci is playing the part. She performs a short ritualistic dance in front of the group... smiling and honoring the three girls individually... dancing with each one individually. Then she speaks:

Comizahual: Hello, I am Comizahual, and I am like your Madrina del Cielo, or Godmother in the sky. You are precious young beautiful children, with golden hearts that I don't wish to see broken, as so many without families, already are. You have been chosen to be rescued from a fate you could never control. And with the goodness of your hearts, you may transcend your disabilities by helping others one day. I have given wings to Cecilia, as my soul-spirit, so that you may fly over all mediocrity of character, that you may avoid all hate and pettiness, avoid tragedy, illness, and pain... and that you will always have your own strength of character to be safe and follow the right path. With the power of my magnetic force, I bless you with golden light, and the strength

50

of your souls to maintain goodness, generosity, and integrity towards others.

You may become instrumental in the reversal of the fate of so many Honduran orphans, who don't have the opportunity that this Gringa can offer you. Someday, perhaps you will help these people find homes and families. But surely…. You will not be sacrificial lambs again…

Lempira: Let it be known that we no longer believe in human sacrifice. Tearing out the heart of a living creature is a riveting shock to the spirit of any breathing witness… This fear reduced public power, and was clearly… bad leadership.

Comizahual: *addressing the girls* We Must Ask Quetzalcoatl to tell Hurakan and Guacametz to remove the blindness that the Creation Gods gave mankind and the MAYA to limit their powers. You my child (Angie) were challenged by meningitis and blinded by the limitations of your family situation. Roxana faced meningitis too along with possible trauma that took place in her mother's womb with physical abuse. And Jazmin has inherited anxiety and a hormonal growth deficiency, despite her brilliant intelligence. All of these children, however, are beautiful and have exceptional hearts. They must be legally united with this Gringa to facilitate their full potential. As we lift this blindness from your eyes, giving you the vision to see the future, you must help others with your intelligence and good fortune to see as well. This is the way you can survive, to lift others around you through the gift of inner vision.

Comizahual is smudging the girls with copal incense as she talks, and dancing around them like a tiger. Then, one by one they are baptized in the cenote pool. "The River Song" by Amy Grant, from the movie "Prince of Egypt" plays in the background. As they are dipped into the water they are brought up by Ceci/Comizahual and placed in a floating basket made of river reeds. In Mayan mythology, when a virgin is sacrificed by throwing her into a cenote… if she comes up and survives, she was meant to live and make an important contribution to society.

"RIVER LULLABY" From the movie Prince of Egypt - Amy Grant

Hush now, my baby Be still love, don't cry
Sleep like you're rocked by the stream
Sleep and remember My last lullaby
And I'll be with you when you dream

Drift on a river That flows through my arms
Drift as I'm singing to you
I see you smiling So peaceful and calm
And holding you, I'm smiling, too
Here in my arms, Safe from all harm
Holding you, I'm smiling, too

Hush now, my baby Be still, love, don't cry
Sleep like you're rocked by the stream
Sleep and remember this river lullaby
And I'll be with you when you dream

Comizahual: What other possible mission do we have in life but to pass on the wisdom of a resilient culture that sustains our families, our health and a future for our children? You must seek loving parents if you cannot find a community that can maintain this type of mutual order for the public. *She continues....*

We must not sacrifice our children to the spoils of civil disorder, crime, illness, and abandonment. Their increasing hunger for love and family security will deteriorate into darkness if they are surrounded by a culture of self-consuming destruction. In Honduras, the onslaught of modernity has touched enough hungry uneducated youth. An infatuation with technology, power and fashion has invaded all levels of society. Even humble farmers, living out in the hills without electricity, have cell phones in 2014, with great ambitions to advance and improve their lives with these devices. What they don't have is a political, judicial, educational, and medical infrastructure to facilitate the economic advancement of their civic and social rights. I want improvement, jobs, infrastructure! Not to hear that we are living in the murder capital of the world! Poverty and family disintegration continue to contaminate the future of our children. From the heart of the sky, I beg the Gods: Give us a miracle to save the souls of our unwanted children as they continue to be the sacrificed offspring of desperate sex. Help us to reverse the plight of orphaned children in these days. Give all youth a chance to grow and learn in a peaceful, healthy environment…. *Comizahual continues*

For the future of Honduras. I ask spirit to open the road for these three girls as an example for the survival of all orphans. That there may be a path to follow for family love.

Ceci/Comizahual carries them out of the water to a nearby palapa (palm leaf roofed hut) and gives them food in a coconut shell. The scene fades.

26. <u>**The Local Cafeteria – First words**</u>

Ceci has taken Angie and Roxana out on the town in their new double seated stroller. They have entered the local cafeteria. Ceci seats them in a booth, and goes on the cafeteria line to order. They sit there calmly, waiting. When Ceci arrives at the table, Angie is gone… looking for Ceci. She calls out to Angie, who she sees crawling with her limited vision. Angie bumps into some open plumbing on the floor and bangs her head hard. Ceci runs to pick her up… Angie is stunned. Ceci seats her back in the booth and examines her head. Suddenly she blurts out:

Angie: **Me golpi en la cabeza alla!!** I hit my head over there!

She points to an exposed pipe on the floor.

Ceci: **Did you hear that, Roxana? Did you hear her speak?** *Roxana also does not speak, but understands Spanish, as does Angie. Roxana nods with wide eyes and a big smile and joyfully grunts. Ceci grabs ice from the glass and puts it on Angie's head.*

Ceci: **Say it again Angie!! Te golpiaste en la cabeza alla?**

Angie: **Mi cabeza!**

Ceci: **Oh my God… She can talk… baby Angie can talk… Oh I am so proud of you Angie… Puedes hablar… bambina… Habla.. Habla … Habla!!! Cuando quieres… Verdad Roxana?**

Roxana: **Angie habla!!!** Angie speaks!

Ceci: **Y tu tambien Roxana. Oh my goodness!!! There is hope. My babies can talk!**

Big hugs as everybody processes these big emotions, and gets back in the stroller. Then it's back to Adila's humble and crowded IHNFA home to drop off the girls... She cuddles Jazmin for not long enough and then reluctantly leaves. They all cry upon Ceci's departure. This is never easy for Ceci... and with big besos, she runs out the door and doesn't look back. Here is testimony that when kids have attention they advance.

27. **Cab to the SOS Orphanage – Phone call with Louis**

It is Sunday. In the cab, Ceci asks for the SOS orphanage, and the driver tells her it will cost 300 Lempiras. Ceci asks to use his phone to make a local call... the driver agrees and takes her money. She dials the doctor.

Ceci: **Dr. Harris, is that you? ...... Yes it's me Ceci, how's it going? Well, they are OK... in the questionable home of Ms. Adila. ... Yes, I administered the medicine... they are better. It is not the best of situations. How's the Doctor business? .... I'm going to this orphanage called the SOS to teach a dance class. You've been there? Uh huh... Later? Well... I 'm going up the coast to Corozal for a Garifuna celebration tonight. Would you like to join me? I've been told about a little place called Stella's on the beach where we can get some delicious fish. Will you come? ...... OK I look forward to this. Bueno Doctor, Gracias! Hasta Luego!!**

28. **The SOS Orphanage Gate**

The scene changes as Ceci arrives at the SOS by taxi to a large gate with a guard. The taxi driver tries to speak for her, saying that she has been summoned by the nurse as a guest teacher.

Taxista: Tengo una gringa aqui que se mando la enfermera para bailar con los ninos. I have a gringa here that the nurse sent to dance with the kids.

Guard: Como te llamas gringa?

Ceci: Me llamo Cecilia Diaz! Me mando la enfermera Josie. My name is Cecilia Diaz. Nurse Josie sent me.

Guard: Momento!

He uses a cell phone to call the director, as kids gather by the gate talking about the gringa.

Ceci: Hola muchachos. Si, soy una gringa... Vengo a bailar con uds. Hello kids. Yes I am a gringa and I come to dance with you.

Ninos: Bailar? Si!!! Cuando? Vamos a bailar con la gringa! Baila, baila, baila con la gringa! Dance? Yes.. When? We are going to dance with the gringa!!! Dance, dance, dance with the gringa!

Clearly Ceci has immediately fallen in love with this adorable group of kids and interacts with them from the other side of the gate. Eventually the guard returns.

Guard: Entra....

Ceci: *She pays the taxista.* **Gracias senor.**

The guard points Ceci towards a small building near the gate. The ground walls surround a complex of 15 small homes, spread out, and connected by curved cement pathways, and a central plaza with a thatched roof (palapa). The SOS is designed after the Kibbutz system of common living in Austria, where the SOS headquarters operates. The La Ceiba SOS, home for orphans, is situated at the foot of a mountain, and it is hot and humid, with lots of insects. Boys are playing soccer in the fields... House mothers are washing clothes in the outdoor pilas (sinks). Small children are playing on the porch, as teenagers run about helping with the younger kids and the house chores. There is radio pop Latin music in the air... filtered by Evangelical church sermons. Everybody sings along in perfect lip synch, almost like they are in trance. Ceci walks into the office and is immediately greeted by the nurse Josie, who escorts her into Don Olman's office, the Director... where he is with his friend David Ashby, gringo volunteer, networker, and activist. David Ashby is a retired, American scientist who worked for Dole fruit and is now involved with the SOS.

29. SOS Director's office – volunteer job interview

Olman: Bienvenida Sra. Cecilia?

Ceci: Si... Cecilia Diaz... Thank you.

Olman: Welcome to the SOS. This is David Ashby, fellow citizen of your generous country.

Ceci: Ah... what part of the US?

David: Originally from California, but I have been here for decades. I am a retired DOLE scientist, turned activist, for the orphan population in La Ceiba. And we are looking for ways to offer culture and improvement to our kids here at the SOS.

Ceci: So, you are doing the real work!

David: No, Don Ollman is doing the real work and more... here at the SOS. And I do what I can. At the moment I am working on getting clean, filtered water for all the houses. So, we understand that you are a dance teacher and do shows? Is that right?

Ceci: That's right...My experience is in dance and theater. I will be teaching dance and mounting shows at the Mazapan School. And I am basically here to do research for a book about indigenous culture and dance. But I think I can help you here.

Josie: I told him you were famous because you work with big star Celine Dion! I think she is famous.

Ceci: OK. Well I am not famous, as hard work does not necessarily lead to fame in the US. But I was her first professional choreographer when she was 19. Anyway... tell me if these children have had any kind of dance training, any choreography, any yoga?

Olman: Let me tell you, these kids love to dance to cumbia and merengue, salsa and reggaeton... But it is mostly danza folklorico where they have had any kind of training. We have all age kids, from babies to 18 year olds, and they all love to dance.

Ceci: Magnifico! Vamos!

David: What about 2 groups, an hour each, boys and girls mixed? Ages 5 to 10, and 11 to 17

Ceci: OK,,, that sounds good....I know what to do... Take me to a boom box and a space to dance.

She pulls out her purse sized album of CDs that she uses for different dance classes, and unwraps a new one she has purchased on the street during carnaval.

Olman: Come with me. Josie, pide a Olvin traer la sistema de musica por fa. Josie, ask Olvin to bring the music system please.

Josie: Si Don Olman. A la orden.

30. **Central Plaza of the SOS**

Olman and David Ashby escort Ceci to the Central open air plaza which has a small stage and a sheltering roof for large gatherings. The kids are arriving, and gathering around Ceci with insatiable curiosity. With chalk, Ceci draws Xs on the pavement to indicate places for each child to sit. The kids are excited to participate and take their places.... The sound system arrives with the young boy named Olvin, and Ceci puts on her meditation music, as she takes her place on the makeshift stage in front of the kids. The house mothers encourage them to sit in the lotus position as Ceci is doing, with their hands on their knees.... Calmly breathing.....The older kids are watching on the sidelines. Ceci introduces herself.

Ceci: Buenas tardes damas y caballeros. Me llamo Cecilia y yo soy una bailarina. Vengo de los Estados Unidos, y quiero compartir mi amor por la danza con uds. Vamos hoy a empezar con una forma de ejercicio para estirar y meditar, se llama YOGA. Digalo... Good afternoon ladies and gentleman. My name is Cecilia and I am a dancer. I come from the USA and I want to share my love for the dance with you. Today we will begin a form of exercise to stretch and meditte called Yoga. Say it.... Yoga...

Todos: YOGA!

Ceci: Si... entonces, despues de conseguir su posicion en la lotus. Asi!, muy bien todos... vamos a cerrar nuestros ojos, relajar, escuchar la musica y vaciar la mente. Entienden? Pongan sus mentes en blanco, sin rezar, sin pensar de NADA... Pongan sus mentes en blanco, y bota lo que entra. Yes, then after finding your position in the lotus.. Like that.. very good everybody... we are going to close our eyes, relax, listen to the music, and empty our minds. Do you understand? Empty your minds, without praying, without thinking of anything. Put your mind in blank and throw out anything that enters. OK?

Todos: Si Tia!

Tia, which is Aunt, is what all these kids call anybody who shows them love. The housemothers are all called Tia, but Ceci has immediately earned the title.

Ceci: Vamos....

The meditation music takes over, and almost all of the 40 kids sitting on the cement floor become entranced with closed eyes. Ceci opens one eye now and then to check.

31. **First SOS Dance Class – yoga/merengue – Musical Number**

The music is hypnotizing. All the children have been tamed by the yoga lotus meditation with their eyes closed, as if magic is about to take place. Clearly a shift from the real... to a dream state has occurred while the kids become entranced by the music and follow Ceci's yoga moves. It is touching to watch them cooperate as Ceci takes them through a dozen classic yoga positions.

Ceci: Que buenos estudiantes son uds. Ahora quien sabe bailar merengue aqui? What great students you are! Now, who knows how to merengue here?

There is a unanimous positive vocal response

Ceci: Quien sabe jugar futbol? And who knows how to play soccer? *In Honduras, "futbol" is soccer. The boys respond picking up a few balls.* OK this is what we are going to do. Todos

van a aprender pasos de merengue. Everybody will learn merengue steps together.

And the merengue music begins. They all begin to follow Ceci with a hot little merengue step which faces the audience. Once they pick it up, Ceci instructs the girls to continue, while the boys dribble around them with their soccer balls. There is some serious athletic talent here. Then dancers partner off, as Ceci dances with Olvin, teaching the couples various partner moves which they repeat to the contagious beat of a hot, Honduran, tropical merengue.

Improvised solos, duets, and trios take place with Ceci's encouragement to enter the center of the circle, followed by a smashing company finish with all the kids dancing with each other. Josie, Don Olman and David Ashby are dancing on the sidelines. Although condensed in one musical number, the scene goes a great distance from shyness, through spiritual meditation, to the spirit of the merengue, and into a sizzling company celebration/ show stopper.

Ceci repeats the activity with the older group which is even more magical. There is a sudden shift when the music ends.... And we switch back to reality in the SOS Central Pavilion. The adults are stunned.

Ceci: I definitely see enough talent and material for a performance here.

Josie: Oh Ms. Ceci, when can you come back? They must dance again... We can make a real show.

Olman: Absolutely! A show!! Invite the investors!!

David: That's right... All the donating Padrinos and Madrinas!!! When shall we do this?

Olman: In two weeks, when that Good Samaritan Church Group comes down from Oklahoma... They would love to see this and donate money towards the water purification system.

David: Good idea Olman.

Ceci: Well I enjoyed working with your children very much. I can come maybe 2 times a week, and perhaps the dancers could join my students at the Mazapan school for the big shows. I am also doing research for a book... But more importantly, it occurs to me that I need to talk to both of you about some kids.

32. Meeting under the Central Plaza Palapa – Invitation to work at SOS

Don Olman invites Ceci to sit at a picnic bench on the stage under the Central Plaza thatched palapa.

Olman: OK what can we possibly do for you Dona Cecilia?

Ceci: I have become interested in three young sisters from San Judas, who are now the property of the IHNFA in the home of a woman named Adila, near the Hospital Atlantida.

David and Olman look at each other.

David: Yes I know that woman. I understand that her house is not the best place for any child to be.

Ceci: And I have heard the same thing from the trabajadora... I have been worried sick about their welfare with this woman. I found them entering the Hospital Atlantida in a box a week ago, and with Nurse Josie's help I have followed them every day since then. They are sick and although they have been treated for meningitis, there is other damage and they need to get better diagnostic care. Can you help me with this?

Olman: We can take them here at the SOS if you wish. It requires some paper work, but you are looking at all the people who need to register them right here.

Nurse Josie: I know about these ninas Don Olman, and definitivamente, they must have better care than the IHNFA can give. I was there when they come into the hospital. I know they will have disabilidades permanentes without better care.

Ceci: Oy Dios.

David: This is the best place in town... and we are beginning to purify the water, so they don't have to boil it anymore.

Ceci: Then, please help me get them transferred as soon as possible. Here are their names. *She pulls out a piece of paper and writes their three names with birthdays.*

Olman: We will do what we can right David? And we look forward to more of your dance work with the children here for our annual investors' gala. Sra. Cecilia…we will see that there is room for your little godchildren in casa # 9.

Ceci: Sounds like an offer too good to refuse. And, I believe that one day, I really will become their Godmother.

David: We can talk about baptizing them at Christmas in Por Venir if you're here so you can be their "madrina". That's one of my jobs here at the SOS. But now, I have to go to town, and will take you to your hotel if you want.

Ceci: Thank you for an exciting afternoon at the SOS… and for your hospitable invitation for the transfer of these girls. We must look into that immediately.

Nurse Josie: I help you to do this, with a report of their health. You must wait until you have contact from the IHNFA. I will check for this. Adila will not like this, because she makes money with more children in her house. I hope they can leave soon.

Ceci: Yes, because the care is substandard, and not good for their welfare? I mean it's a teeny house with fifteen kids in it. Way too crowded.

David: You have to let them do things their way… This is a very backwards country where history and habit preclude logic most of the time.

Ceci: Mr. Ashby, you must see these little girls. They are very weak, malnourished, and ill with meningitis. They need professional daily care.

David: OK… Let's do this tomorrow. What do we do Josie?

Nurse Josie: We meet there tomorrow at 9am, and bring that Doctor Ceci… David, you must come also to Ms. Adila's house where the Doctor can tell the IHNFA lady that they need more care and that the SOS is better.

Olman: I will deal with the IHNFA... Just get them out of there... I know about this Adila lady, and I think we should get them over here into Conchita's Casa 9 as soon as possible. I will talk to the IHNFA today.

David: In that case we will all meet at Adila's house at 9am... Let's go Ceci, we must run to town now. I have a meeting.

Ceci: Goodbye and thank you for this opportunity... Ciao Don Olman...

Olman: Thank you for your offer to train our children in dance and theater. This would be a great gift for us to raise funds with a performance.

Ceci: Hasta la proxima!! Until the next time.

The children all follow David and Ceci to the gate, as they leave in his pick up truck. This is the goodbye routine at the orphanage.

33. <u>**Driving back to town with David**</u>

On the way home Ceci and David chat. Then as they approach the bridge into town, traffic comes to a standstill. David asks a bicyclist coming from the opposite direction.

David: **Que pasa por alla?** What's happening over there?

Bicyclist: **Son los mareros con los impuestos de Guerra. Estan amenezando el autobus, y todos los pasejeros estan bajando ahora.** It's the gangs with their war tax. They are threatening the bus and all the passengers are dismounting now.

David: **Ah ha... ya mato el manejador?** Have they already killed the driver?

Bicyclista: **No, pero, el no quiso darles su dinero a los mareros.** No, but he doesn't want to give his money to the gang guys.

David: **Gracias.... Well that should be another 45 minutes at least.... And this is the only road back to town.**

Ceci: So what is going on?

David: Impuestos de Guerra. The local gang and their war tax on the bus drivers… they either pay up, or lose everything… sometimes, including their lives. They hit on restaurants, hotels and local businesses, and sometimes the buses.

Ceci: That's what's happening here?? Where are the police?

David: Mmm… we just wait it out. The police are no match for the gangs.

Then there is the sound of gun shots… Suddenly, people begin to run faster past their car in the opposite direction. Then we hear the forced sound of the bus accelerating forward, passing in the other direction.

Ceci: Oh my God what happened?

David: Looks like the marero killed the driver and took off in his bus …. Now, we can pass..

Ceci: You make it sound like it is all in a day's work.

David: Exactly… I just try not to make anybody mad, and keep looking forward. You have to be very careful here… especially as a Gringo… as they think we are all a bunch of humanitarian idiots. There are four police cars in La Ceiba, and basically no law. Please be careful, and don't make anybody mad. I have been here for 40 years, married a Honduran, and I try to stay low on the radar.

Ceci: OK , I'll try to remember that.

Ceci sits back and looks out the window. This is a musical/visual montage/ medley of the street with the local people making their way to and from home…. Old ladies carrying firewood on their heads, workers on bicycles, men carrying a newly made chair for sale, Garifunas carrying their bread and pan de cocoa in baskets balanced on their heads… Carts full of vegetables for sale…. Children playing barefoot with a soccer ball… a drunk or two…. Some lost, homeless kids begging. They arrive at the plaza in the center of La Ceiba.

David: Here we are… Thanks for making our kids so happy this afternoon… we hope you will come back.

Ceci: Sure thing Mr. Ashby… I will see you tomorrow at Adila's house, to get those girls over to the SOS..

David: There's no telling what the IHNFA will do with them first. I will do everything I can for you on that. See you in the morning.

34. <u>Grand Paris Hotel Lobby – Meeting Dr. Harris</u>

The scene shifts to Ceci's arrival at the Grand Paris Hotel, where the Doctor is waiting nervously on the steps.

Dr. Harris: Your mother has talked to every Gringo in the hotel, and wants you to call her immediately.

Ceci: I am so sorry about that… She thinks I am crazy and in constant danger.

Dr. Harris: I'm beginning to understand that.

Ceci: I've been busy. Just got back from the SOS.

Dr. Harris: So how did that go?

Ceci: Fabulous, those kids love to dance…

Dr. Harris: Please be careful when you walk around. This is not a safe place.

Ceci: I'm fine…So I am looking forward to our adventure in Corozal tonight.

Dr. Harris: Now I would not miss it for the world. Can we meet here in an hour?

Ceci: I am glad to see you. Thanks for waiting for me.

Dr. Harris: I am glad you are OK… You are walking some pretty tight ropes little Gringa.

Ceci: We can talk about it over Garifuna fried fish on the beach. I have been told to go to a place called "Stellas" in Corozal. Would that be OK?

Dr. Harris: Of course. And then?

Ceci: And then… some kind of ceremony to talk to spirit with a Garifuna lady named Dona Eva… which I do not want to miss.

Dr. Harris: How many guardian angels do you have?

Ceci: I beg your pardon, Doctor?

Dr. Harris: I'm joking. See you in an hour.

Ceci: I hope you are not on call Doctor, because we are going way out to the beach.

Dr. Harris: No problem. You better call your mother.

They go to separate rooms.

Ceci: Ok!

In the room at the Grand Paris, Ceci calls Mom in Virginia.

Ceci: Yes Mom I'm fine… how are you?

Mom: I've been worried sick Ceil… do you know how many times I have called Honduras?

Ceci: I have all your messages Mom, and I am OK. I went to teach dance at a local orphanage called the SOS, and I am trying to help these three precious little girls get in there.

Mom: Now don't get your heart broken over these little munecas honey. There are thousands of them everywhere… You can't save the world Ceil.

Ceci: Mom, I am doing research for my book too… So don't worry, not a moment lost. Te amo Mama.

Mom: Call me, please… collect… whenever… bye. Careful who you get involved with… Hello?

35. <u>Corozal – Stella's Garifuna Beach Restaurant and bar – Ceci & Dr. Harris</u>

Cut to Stella's beach restaurant/shack at sunset in Corozal, with a Garifuna band of drummers and women singing and dancing their repertoire. The place is hopping, and the fish platters can't come out fast enough. People are drinking beer and guiffityy, and into this come the gringos for dinner. Ceci is happy as they watch the band show off their punta music and dance. Finally, the band takes a break and we hear amplified, pre- recorded rancheros. Ceci sits with Dr. Harris up on the terrace overlooking the ocean. Stella comes upstairs to see them with a bottle of house guiffity, which is a rum drink with an odd number of medicinal herbs in it that is buried underground for a week. It is used for curative purposes, as well as getting you flying high.

Stella: Hola Gringa... Ud. es Ceci verdad? Yes because Dona Eva told me to look out for you, and make sure you got the total experience here before I take you over to her place...

Dr. H: Now that sounds like hospitality to me...

Ceci: Hola Stella, This is Louis Harris. He is a missionary doctor.

Stella: Welcome to the Garifuna zone Dr. Harris.

Dr. H: Thank you Stella. I am enchanted. Now, What do you recommend?

Stella: Our fried fish platter for sure.... And some beer and guiffity of course... to set you up for the right vibration... This is how we do the guiffity. *She demonstrates.* First you suck on some sweet grapefruit or orange, then you lick a little dab of salt from your elbow, and finally throw back the guiffity. Soon you will be dancing involuntarily!!

Dr. H: Uh huh? And what is guiffity? I don't dance much.

Stella: It is white rum with an odd number of herbs mixed in. There are 13 here. We bury it under the ground for three days, and then drink it as medicine. If you are willing to go with the high, it will cure anything.... It just goes right through ya and purifies everything!

Ceci: Ay gracias Stella! You are so kind. *Stella smiles and leaves.*

They look at the ocean, and drink the guiffity. There is a new moon. Some Garifuna boys are playing soccer on the beach... Men are bringing in their fishing boats, and some girls are braiding hair under a nearby palapa. Dr. Harris holds up his glass to make a toast.

Dr. Harris: I want to make a toast to you.... to your kindness and the way you are helping these kids survive.

Ceci: Well thank you Doctor. You are doing the same for so many more. *She throws back the rum and breathes the sea air in and out.* I am supposed to be on an academic sabbatical... but these sisters and their situation have me fixated. So I need to explain something to you...

Dr. Harris: Be careful... La Ceiba can be a Gringo black hole, easy to slip into, and difficult to get out of.

Ceci: Listen Dr. Harris, I need your help tomorrow.

Dr. Harris: Please call me Louis.

Ceci: OK Louis...OK...I need you to come with me to the IHNFA house where the girls are tomorrow at 9am to meet up with a brigade of people who will get the girls out of this dreadful holding tank and into the SOS orphanage. And I need you to speak up for their urgent medical needs, and emphasize that they must have clean water and be near a better equipped infirmary to monitor their recuperation from malnutrition and meningitis.... And that the SOS is the best possible situation under the circumstances, with their present bed availability, along with a trained nurse. Will you do that for these girls? Will you do that for me? Everybody will be there.

Dr. Harris: Of course I'll do it, yes of course, I will be there. I can do that. *He takes her hands across the table.* But, listen to me Ceci.... Then what? You get on the plane and go back to the USA with your photos and leave these kids to grow up in the orphanage with multiple broken heart episodes in their lives. I have seen these mission people come and go, in and out of the lives of these kids... like Santa Claus, year after year... I'm beginning to think it satisfies the egos of the missionaries more than helping the orphans.

Ceci: Louis..... I don't know what I am doing... All I know is that I responded to the suffering in front of me, as any woman would..... knowing that maybe I could do something to stop the pain of that moment for these dear precious innocent little girls.... *She begins to tear up, overwhelmed.* If I could throw them into my suitcase and bring them back home with me I would, but this is so way over my head. I just know I must do what I can today ... now... and taking them out of this disease and unhealthy danger they are in... is primary, and something you can help me do tomorrow... *She pulls it back together standing and walking towards the ocean....wipes* her eyes. Of course I have dreams of giving them a stable life. So...Thank you so much for helping me with this.

Dr. H: *He pours the remainder of the guiffity and makes a second toast.* Ok... Let's drink to this moment. I promise, I swear.... I will help you get these girls over the mountain, so they have a chance... OK?

Ceci: Thank You Dr. Louis... Jazmin thanks you, Angie thanks you, and Roxana thanks you. You are a kind soul, and you will be an important part of their history.

Dr. H: I tell you what Ceci... If you figure this out.... I mean... how to get custody of these kids one day.... I will send you money to support them. It will be almost impossible to take them out of the country, but you can stay here, and heal them..... if you are ready to give up a lot.

Ceci: I hope this is not the guiffity talking... Are you serious? I mean would you help me with that? I have been feeling guilty about not having a financial plan other than the money I make as a teacher and free lance choreographer. But somebody had to jump in and help them. You understand that right?

Dr. H: Hey... I believe in what you are doing... even if I know you don't know how you are going to do it. I believe in saving lives. I'm a doctor...and ... I don't lie. I will send you money for those girls, if you can get custody and take responsibility for them.

Ceci: Dr. Louis are you serious?

Dr. H: Yes I am serious. I'm a professional and I keep my word.

A joyful tear drops from Ceci's eye... and then she throws back more guiffity... looking at the ocean.... The fish arrives... Stella waltzes between them and whispers to Ceci....

Stella: Ahh... the spirit works in mysterious ways... You have much to learn from Dona Eva...Venga comer.

Dr. H: That looks absolutely delicious. *He ushers Ceci to her seat.*

Dona Stella: Claro Senor.... Just try my pescado frito... I make the best fried fish this side of the river... Just try it... You will feel like a million bucks... and my tajadas... and the beans and rice.... You will die and go to Garifuna heaven!

Ceci cuts into the fish immediately and takes a bite, and touches her heart with her left hand.

Ceci: Gracias Stella, absolutamente delicioso.. just what I need right now.

Stella: Buen Provecho!!

Dr. H: Please forgive me, I didn't want to insult you or upset you... I see what is happening to you, and your compassion for these kids.... But I have seen these hopes fall through with adoptions and the corruption of the IHNFA so many times. I don't want you to go through the same separation anxiety that the kids develop.

Ceci: I know all of that!!!! I also know that I am still... probably the only person able and willing to give these three girls any kind of shot at a real life. Nobody else can do this for them right now like I can, and they need a mama … This is the moment and I must seize it! And this fish is delicious Doctor… mmmm…. I forgot how hungry I am.

Dr. H: Please call me Louis.

Ceci: OK… Louis.

This is a picturesque moment as a voice coming from a solo Garifuna voice on the beach superimposes a romantic mist over Ceci and the doctor's dinner as the sun sets. There is a wonderful ambiance of happiness. Suddenly we can hear the faint sound of drums. Stella comes with a young boy who will take them to Dona Eva's house on the beach. The Doctor pays the bill, and they walk down the beach under the full moon. Ceci dances with the waves.

36. Corozal Beach Ceremony with Garifuna Eva

Ceci and Louis approach a thatched palapa on the beach where a drum circle is beginning to form. Young Garifuna girls are dancing "punta" in the sand. Families are arriving with food and flowers. A young woman greets them and they are introduced.

Garifuna boy: **Ella es Inez, la hija de Dona Eva.** This is Inez, daughter of Dona Eva.

Inez: **Bueno… Bienvenida. Mi madre me dijo esperarte.** My mother told me to expect you.

Ceci: **Si, yo soy Cecilia y mi amigo es Louis.**

Louis: **Mucho gusto.**

Ceci: **Y Eva?**

Inez: **Ella esta atras preparando para el ceremonio.** She is in the back preparing for the ceremony.

Ceci: **Ah ha! Por favor, se puede explicarnos lo que pasa en esta ceremonia? Que estan hacienda aqui… Yo quiero entender. Y por favor quiero regalarle mi ofrenda para gastos.** Can you please explain this ceremony to us? What you're doing here. I want to understand, and I want to give my offering for the expenses.

Ceci discreetly gives Inez 500 lempiras ($30) in an envelope.

Inez: Gracias Dona Cecilia... OK pues... Se llama un "velurio" para mi papa que murio hace un ano esta semana. Celebramos su vida con comida, alegria , musica y danza porque no nos gustan llorar con tristeza. Y rezamos que el espiritu de mi papa vuelve para hablar con nosotros.

Ceci translates for Louis: This is called a velurio which is like an annual memorial to her father who passed a year ago. And that they celebrate with food, music, dance and happiness to distract from the sadness. And they all pray that his spirit returns to speak to us. It's called ancestor worship.

Louis: Wow, that is beautiful... and definitely surreal.

Inez: I can speak English a little. OK, so my mother is a "buyei", like a shaman. And the Garifuna religious practice is called "dugu" which is an Afro-Indian mix of beliefs and rituals.

Ceci: You mean she is like a "curandero"?

Inez: The curandero is like a doctor and is a healer of physical problems. A "Buyei" is connected to the spirit world and can restore the balance of the soul and communicate with spirit. They can help guide the soul during life and after life by looking at the past, present, and future. A Buyei is the link between man and the supernatural for the Garifunas. My father had this talent and passed it on to my mother. Come with me to say hello to Eva before she begins.

37. <u>Eva's Altar to the Ancestors - and her late Husband's Spirit (Melvin)</u>

Inez takes them to the main altar in a cement home behind the palapa where Dona Eva sits smoking a cigar in front of her private altar which is laden with fresh fruits, flowers, sweet cakes, glasses of wine and guiffity, jewelry and cocos.... as well as a central photo of her late husband who was a fisherman and a drum maker. Eva is falling into trance, almost like sleep, and stands to greet them. She continues to fan her cigar and observe the ashes, constantly praying. Inez shows them where to sit in front of the altar. The musicians enter drumming with the dancers. The older women join the group, dancing in formation to the magnetic drum beats. They are dressed in matching gingham dresses. Inez joins Ceci and Louis to translate.

Inez: They will dance the "punta" to call the spirit of my father who actually made these drums. Even though this seems like a dance of joy, it was originally designed for funerals to generate the energy to call down the spirit to speak to us and help the soul cross over. My dad was a fisherman and would go to sea for long periods of time. Garifuna women spend a lot of time waiting for their men. And this song was a favorite song of my father when he was at sea.

The women sing in Garifuna question and answer format... dancing punta as they move around Eva, who prays at the center of the floor as the company sings.

I go to the Urupendula

I am a man without a home 2X

What is my destiny?   I would like to know.

When will my children greet me?

When will they come to me2X

So we can laugh together

Peace of mind does not come to me

Loneliness is what befalls me

Peace of mind does not come to me

It is only solitude that weighs heavy on my soul.

With the intensity of the drumming, dancing and singing, Eva falls into trance and begins to speak Garifuna in her husband's voice. Inez translates as she speaks.

Inez translates for her father, Melvin, through Eva:
Hello my family and loved ones. You know how much I miss my family, my beautiful wife and children and the community traditions. I have passed on the skill of *Buyei* to my wife, to help the community to determine the wishes of God and to pass them on to those in need. I watch you from my spirit body and with the grace of God I will help all of you in need tonight. First, I want to help this gringa with the big heart, and then I will get to my precious family and friends.
Louis stares at this in disbelief. Ceci is fascinated and whispers..

Ceci: I studied this trance business for three years in Venezuela with brujos, and I am working on a book about dance and shamanism. You know this is the roots of dance and theater when someone else is in your body...... and I love it. Trust me... it is riveting.

Eva continues to smoke her cigar and walks around Ceci with her eyes closed as she speaks.

Eva as Melvin: Good evening. I am Eva's husband Melvin. *Pause as his soul adjusts in Eva's body.* Gringa!... you have a good heart and a strong head...I see the three girls. How they need your love and attention... almost to the point of survival.... My God Gringa..... You *will* have these 3 sisters as daughters one day. It will be a long road of many papers and many words and much rejection. However, I can see it, but only with patience and determination, and most of all... the love of a pioneer for orphan rescue. Most orphan children will never see this love. Although, you must know that very few Garifuna children go to the orphanages. We take care of our children.

There is a long pause as she receives messages and images from spirit. There will be pauses. During this trance Eva's eyes are closed.

Eva as Melvin continues: Surely you know there is permanent damage with significant learning disabilities involved.... One is visual.... The other neurological... and the young one... there is something with her chemistry that is not right, although she is quite intelligent I believe. This all presents tests of determination and perseverance for you and these struggling little girls. They have come to you... for YOU to fulfill your own personal karma with motherhood, which coincides with their desperate needs at this time, for a real mother. As soon as possible, you must become their official Godmother to open the roads for future custody. Madrina.... Yes Madrina..... You have the blessing of spirit ... and the late father.... Who recently passed ..... and who gladly gives his grateful appreciation for your vigilance with his daughters. Their mother is unable to care for them, and the poverty and the sickness was just overwhelming the family. They are helpless in so many ways, and need your help gringa Ceci. Please take them as far away from this dreadful abandonment as soon as possible.

Ceci: I wish I knew more about their family.

Eva as Melvin: *Pause* The father is no longer alive... He was lost and unemployed in the cocaine. Yet he loved those girls.

Ceci: Help me... How do I do all this?

Eva as Melvin: You will have to find the mother...for only she can take them out of the orphanage by the law.... Even though it is she who almost killed them with neglect and abuse. *Pause*

I see that she gave them bad water and she is hitting the middle child in the head because she screams with fever and hunger... OHHH she is dying... this poor child!

There are still drums playing in the background.

Ceci: Yes that was Angie, but she is under care now... she had meningitis, with her sister, the oldest one, Roxana, who has also had the fever for some time. They are now both being treated with medicine by this doctor.

74

Eva as Melvin: Yes... there is an epidemic in the barrio where they were born. The water is contaminated, as are the chickens and pigs. They never would have survived there.

Ceci: And right now.... Do you think they are safe? I am so worried about them.

Eva as Melvin: You must remove them from this dark place they are in as soon as possible. Go tomorrow, and get them into a safe orphanage, with good house mothers... Then find the mother and get a lawyer... Until then, do everything you can to make sure they get the medical attention they need now... every day ... now... when the damage is being done as we speak.... Do you hear me doctor? Wipe out this bacteria now.... This one Angie, is already partially blind... I can see this....

Ceci: Oh please don't tell me this...

Doctor Lou: Yes... and I will make sure they are removed from their present situation tomorrow.

Eva as Melvin: You must take this responsibility to cure them. The orphanages will not have the perseverance to take care of this. *(Long pause and he switches from English to Spanish as there is a different Latino spirit speaking through him now)* There is another spirit here now.

Unidentified Latino Spirit: **Gringa ... las hermanitas tienen sus angeles al rededor, y definitivamente ellas te necessitan.... Que sigue con su fuerza... Y sabes que la sangre de estas ninas es especial... Que la madre tiene Maya mezclada con Afro Cubano..... Y el papa tiene sangre Hondureno Indio y guerrero mezclado con gitana de Hongaria. Son exoticas!!! Y los delphines del mar me dicen que tu eres bendecida por las estrellas a cuidar estas hermanitas hasta la luna,,,, si Dios quiere.... Se dice el papa que el pide perdon por sus pecados, las drogas, la pobreza.... Que las ama mucho a ellas, con su corazon... y el sabe que el futuro de estas ninas seria bien en sus manos.** Gringa... the sisters have angels around them and definitely they need you. Continue with strength, and know that the blood of these little girls is special. The mother has Mayan mixed with Afro Cuban. And the father has Honduran native warrior blood, mixed with Hungarian gypsy. They are exotic! And the dolphins in the sea tell me that you are blessed by the stars to take care of these sisters forever. God willing. The father also asks forgiveness for his sins… the drugs, the poverty. That he loves them very much with his heart and knows that their future is good in your hands.

Ceci: *Fanning herself rapidly with amazement.* Wow, that was too much…. Oh my God. Who was that?

Eva as Melvin returned: Some Indian from another land I believe.

Ceci: Could it be my Tamanaco?

Eva as Melvin: I do not know this spirt, but he wanted to come in with fuerza. *Her eyes are still closed.*

Ceci: Tamanaco es un cacique de Venezuela. El fue mi protector. Tamanaco is a chief from Venezuela. He was my spiritual protector.

Eva as Melvin: He is still protecting you Senora.

Ceci: I pray that he also protects the girls. He is a good man. Gracias Tamanaco!! Tambien quiero agradecerte Senor Melvin. Thank you so much for believing in me and these girls.

Eva as Melvin: Yes gringa…. Get them under your wing as soon as earthly possible… Think like an eagle…. Don't ever give up… you can do this…. I would like now to speak to my children.

Daughter Inez: *Speaking in Garifuna.* Father how are you? How wonderful to hear you speak, and to feel your spirit.

Eva as Papa Melvin: *Continuing in Garifuna*… Yes my daughter… how I love and miss you and your mother and sisters and brothers. Give me a hug. I am always with you, watching. Continue with the tambor business with everything I have taught you, to maintain the Garifuna culture. I have much to say, but first I must play my tambor.

Daughter Inez: Toma Papa. *She gives Melvin (Eva) a cigar, some guiffity, his drum, and splashes his back with alcohol.* Here is your favorite tambor.

Eva as Melvin: *in Garifuna.* I will play for my people... my sweet Dona Eva who lets me use her hands... yes I love you Eva. And then I will consult with whomever God gives me the fuerza to help.

And the drum begins with the spirit of his hands. All the drummers join in as the spirit of Eva's husband, Melvin, leads a dynamic healing drum circle. It is a magical full moon, smokey, tropical and mystical. Spirit begins to address the line of patients who have come for help as the drums continue. Ceci is mesmerized, and the doctor is stunned in disbelief.

38. <u>CIUDAD BLANCA – Healing Ceremony flashback #3</u>

Again, the energy of the drum circle will take us back to the ancestors with this drumming, as it blends with the drums in the courtyard. The audience hears a rhythm track that moves mountains, and we are lost in a flashback to the Ciudad Blanca, once again.

All of the ancestral chiefs, the scribes, and noble Mayans/ Aztecs/ Zapotecs/ and Olmecs, and Indigenous Lencas are dancing to this powerful rhythm around a fire. Standing in the corner alone is Francisco Morazan, Spanish conquistador.

QUETZALCOATL presides over the ceremony. It is a pivotal moment when the souls of motherless children begin to file down onto the ceremonial floor. Jazmin, Angie, and Roxana are there. They are not dancing... they are lost, as if their lives were taken from them suddenly, and now they are back in their bodies. Quetzalcoatl stops the music.

Quetzalcoatl: I am here to help you... I have finally come to make sense of this wandering journey. I am here to apologize for your sacrifice and pain. You have suffered because your parents have suffered in a society that doesn't provide for all, in an economy which could not care for you, and I weep for you along with all of your ancestors. And we ask your forgiveness, as you find a way to reincarnate into better circumstances, where you can make a difference helping other lost children. We must take this pain out of the network grid... It is turning innocent children into terrorists and gang members with no hope for solutions to this national problem. Know that we love you and don't want you to suffer any more. You are our descendants. We are offering our support to you now from spirit.... The knowledge to make a change in your next lifetime.... To fulfill your destiny and right to a good life in a society which supports you. We will give you guidance. There will be no more sacrifice.... No more war.

Quetzalcoatl takes a reed flute from his waistband and begins to play to the sky. The children surround him. The ancestors form a circle around the children. We see this from above, and then there is a sudden blackout. We continue to hear the sound of the reed flute until Ceci wakes up.

39. <u>RETURN TO EVA'S ALTAR</u>

We return to the Garifuna altar in Corozal where Ceci is now passed out on the ground. Dr. Louis is bending over her trying to revive her. Eva is now back in her own body and her crew have also gathered around.

Dona Eva: Do not worry.... She has gone into trance and she will come out of it. Spirit has chosen to give her a message.

Dr. Harris: I am a doctor and I have never seen these things.

Ceci begins to stir, as if waking up from a dream.

Dr. Harris: Ceci, are you OK? Try to open your eyes. It's me, Dr. Harris, from Virginia, remember?

Ceci: *(blinking)* Wow... what was that? I think I went to the White City with the big walls,

Garifunas: Ah La Ciudad Blanca! Dijo ella!!

Ceci: and I saw the three girls there.... And this shaman named Quetza something... It was so amazing.

The Garifunas start to speak to each other in their native tongue, with great interest.

Dona Eva: Quetzalcoatl!!?? What did you see Ceci?

Ceci: There were lots of lost children, and the girls were there, but they were like ghosts, and this shaman with feathers told them that they did not have to be sacrificed anymore, that the ancestors want to guide them into a better next life. It was so real....oooooof! And there were white walls, and white staircases, and statues of monkeys everywhere. I could see gold statues and animal designs on the white walls. I think it is the Ciudad Blanca that I have been reading about. Is it real Dona Eva?

Dona Eva: Cecilia – My spirits do not touch the Ciudad Blanca place. I have heard of it before. It precedes the Olmecs... Some say it was built by extra – terrestrials who were creating humans scientifically with primates. For this reason it was called the city of monkeys.... where hybrids were created. There are legends, that if you wandered too close to that city, you would never ever return. That it was a city of lights and flying serpents...

Ceci: I think I'm getting caught in a time warp... and they are trying to contact me!!!

Dr. Harris: Ceci, I think it's time to hit the road back to the hotel...

Dona Eva: One more thing, Dona Ceci.....You have been chosen to help these kids, but you must understand that you cannot save everybody. You must go now and do what you can for these sisters.... It will be a long road.... I wish I could help you more.... You know, we Garifunas take care of our young.... You do not see them in the orphanages...Go with the spirit Ceci, I must help the others.

Ceci: Thank you, Dona Eva, and know that I will always buy your tableta de coco.

Dr. Harris: Let's go Ceci, it is getting late, and we have to remove those girls tomorrow morning. Thank you, Dona Eva.

Dona Eva: Encantada hijo! *They leave walking down the beach in the moonlight.*

40. <u>Adila's House – To remove the girls</u>

NEXT DAY at Adila's house, where it is dark, and there is no electricity... You can hear somebody in the street yell "No hay luz en la calle!". The sisters are all sick with fever and "bitchos" (amoebas) from the bad water. They are crying. Adila cannot seem to get anything right. There is not enough food. It is dark in the little house, and the kids are fighting. Ceci and the doctor arrive at the door. Adila is slapping Roxana on the bottom, and scolding her for pooping in the bed...She is crying. She arrives at the door holding Roxana by the ear.

Ceci: What's going on here?

Adila: This is not a good time Gringa... there is no light, and everybody has diarrhea and lice.

Ceci: Did you give them the parasite medicine? And I also sent over lice shampoo.

Adila: I can't find it... Vilma, what did you do with the bitcho medicine?

Vilma: Senora, Ud. no me lo dio!! Yo no se!! You did not give it to me. I don't know!

Ceci: You should not punish them for being sick! How can you do that?

Adila: Gringa, I have my ways of running this house, and just because you come marching in here with your big gringa heart, doesn't mean you can tell me what to do. Go away gringa with your big morality. We have our ways of disciplining these half breeds. Eventually we all get used to the bad water

Ceci: They are children Adila, they don't want to be sick!! *The girls come to hug her.* Why don't you boil the water?

Dr. Harris: And the older two have meningitis... Did you give them the medicine for that? I can still feel the fever.

Adila: You gringos think you can solve everything with pills and shots. I have my ways of doing things, and your gringo medicine is not going to get these girls to the bathroom on time… They need to learn!!

Dr. Harris: Meningitis and constant diarrhea are serious problems Sra. They are not well. These girls need to go back to the hospital.

Suddenly there is a knock at the door, and the nurse Josie, David, and the local IHNFA lady, Mercedes Galinda, arrive.

Ceci: Oh Thank God you came Josie. These girls have not eaten, they are sick, and she is not giving them the parasite medicine.

Nurse Jose: Ceci … This is Mercedes, she is the Ihnfa Representative in Ceiba.

Mercedes: Miss Adila, these girls do not look well.

Adila: You know just because these gringos come in with their donations and charity does not mean they know how to deal with these kids.

David: Did you give them the medicine?

Adila: I was planning to do that today.

Ceci: Clearly, you are not taking care of these kids. They are miserable, hungry, and sick. This is no place for these girls.

Adila: You…Get out of my house!!!

Mercedes: Senora Adila, voy a traer estas ninas al hospital ahora, y les quito todos de su custodia. No es la primera vez que oigo de abuso en esta casa. Venga a mi oficina manana. Esta claro? No se puede tratar ninos asi, y la IHNFA no lo permitira. I am taking these girls to the hospital, and removing all these children from your care.. This is not the first time I hear of child abuse in this home. Come to my office tomorrow. Is that clear? This is not the way to treat children, and the IHNFA will not support this.

They each pick up one of the three sisters and leave. Adila is outraged. Ceci signals Vilma to come outside. The lights come back on. And they continue the conversation outside the house.

41. <u>OUTSIDE ADILA'S – On the Street – Ihnfa lady, Dr. Harris, David, Vilma and Ceci</u>

David: Sra. Mercedes... I have made arrangements for the girls to come to the SOS orphanage out by the airport, and we have an infirmary there. If you will sign these papers, we will take them to the hospital and then out to the orphanage now.

Mercedes: First of all, these kids are still the property of the state, and until I work up all the papers, the IHNFA will take them for further examination. And you, Senora... should not be giving money or medicine to this woman for these kids, just to have permission to take them off the premises on adventures!! Are you out of your mind? They call it buying orphans.

Ceci: Of course not!!! You are twisting this.

Mercedes: Look I am sorry. You will just have to get it out of your head that you can adopt them, because there is no way that will ever happen. Their mother is alive, and you cannot even consider this. I'm sorry.

Ceci: Clearly neither the mother nor the IHNFA can take proper care of them.

Mercedes: The law is the law.

Ceci: But can I still see them?

Mercedes: I can't tell you where I am taking them, but you can call me. *She writes a number on a small piece of paper.*

Ceci: Por favor Senora!!! Please.... I think I have a right to know what will happen to them now.

Mercedes: *Stopping and breathing* OK look...I have to do my job. I am going to close out this woman Adila now. This is not the first time I hear complaints about her. She is in it for the money clearly.

Ceci: This is unbelievable! If it's true... who loses? Innocent disabled kids.

Mercedes: I see it every day, Senora.

Ceci: Then help me adopt these girls.

Mercedes: Adopt? Nobody can adopt anymore. The adoption department is shut down because of IHNFA administrators who are pocketing funds and holding up cases for 4 to 5 years. Besides Senora, how old are you?

Ceci: I beg your pardon?

Mercedes: Forgive me but if you are over 50, forget it. Not possible to adopt.

Ceci: I am 52 with more than enough energy and heart for all three of these sisters.

Mercedes: Sorry... the best I can do is get them into the SOS orphanage down by the airport. You can visit them there eventually. But you will not be able to see them for a while. We must evaluate their mental and physical health before they are placed.

Ceci: What? That's crazy!! Nobody will take as much full responsibility for whatever they need as I will. They trust me, and they will be more traumatized if they can't see me. I am their only hope for safety.

Dr. Harris: What is your name Sra.? I am Dr. Louis Harris, and this is Cecilia Diaz.

Mercedes: I am Mercedes Galinda, Coordinadora de la IHNFA en La Ceiba. And I am truly sorry again... I understand these concerns, and I admire your intentions. But the truth is. I see dozens of you Americans come by with your big vacation hearts bleeding for these kids all the time. They come .. they go, and the kids are left hanging...

Ceci: I am not just everybody Senora. Look at me... I will do what it takes to facilitate the health and welfare of these three girls as long as they need it.

Mercedes: Ms. Cecilia,,,, the best thing is to donate and move on. You will never be able to get these kids past the IHNFA, nor adopt them. They have to be abandoned, first...

Ceci: Sounds like physical abuse, starvation and neglect are forms of abandonment, wouldn't you say?

Mercedes: The same parents, who abused them, are still the only legal parents. However, all rights to property, education, and wellbeing are now with the IHNFA and the republic of Honduras.

Ceci: It makes no sense. The girls are confused and really need love and attention now.

Mercedes: Believe me… the SOS is their best option. We cannot let any gringa come into the country and get back on a plane with our children. There are people who steal these kids to sell their organs as well.

Ceci: Senora please. I am not one of those people.

Dr. Harris: Ceci, they will be safe at the SOS. I know the place well.

David: Ceci, you may not think so, but I can guarantee you that the SOS is the Four Star Orphanage in Honduras, run by an organization in Austria… and it is structured like the Kibbutz, in Israel. You saw the place. This SOS has 15 houses, each with their own TIA, and a dozen other "brothers and sisters" with whom they will grow up until the age of 18. The Orphanage is very religiously run, and also has medical service for the kids.

Mercedes: It is the best and only option for them now. So you will have to forget these kids for a while and get back to your life. I will call you when the time is right to transfer these girls to the SOS.

Ceci: And what about the additional trauma they will go through now with more unfamiliar people and situations? This is wrong Sra Mercedes. Please let me take them back to the Hospital, and make sure they get the best possible care, which I will pay for… whatever they need. Do you understand? Here is my number at the Grand Paris Hotel. *She writes down her name and number.*

Mercedes: I will do what I can Senora Cecilia. Meanwhile… I also must shut down Adila's house and move all of those kids. This will not be pretty. I will be in touch with you.

Nurse Josie: Can I take them back to the hospital with Dr. Harris first?

Mercedes: Ok, but I will pick them up on my lunch hour. Is that clear?

Nurse Josie: Yes. Will you help me Doctor?

Doctor: By all means, they really need follow up care, and I am going there anyway to meet up with my team.

Ceci reluctantly hands over the crying and confused Angie to Dr. Harris, and the nurse takes Roxana and baby Jazmin. Adila is observing this with anger from the porch. The girls are all upset, and Ceci bursts into tears. Dr. Harris takes her aside. Mercedes leaves.

Dr. Harris: Ceci, calm down. I will meet you at the hotel this evening.

The IHNFA lady drives off with Dr. Harris and Josie as the girls look out the window crying.

David: I wouldn't give up if I were you. All of the kids at the SOS came through the IHNFA, and they do have space now.

Ceci: No I am not a quitter... I just don't understand the way things happen around here.

David: You can't trust anybody... That is the nature of the third world. Everybody is struggling just to get through the day themselves... promises are impossible to keep. The saying is .."Si Dios Quiere". So you see, it's all up to God, and not your fault if things don't go your way. I'll be in touch.

Ceci: Thanks David. I hope the transfer works.

David: You want a ride?

Ceci: No I think I'll walk this off.

David: Thanks for caring about these kids, Ceci... Hasta manana!

David takes off in his truck. As Ceci walks away, Vilma runs to catch up with her.

42. <u>Ceci and Vilma talk in the street</u>

Vilma: Dona Cecilia, gracias a Dios que veniste hoy, porque la Senora Adila tuvo una rabia gigante con las ninas esta mañana con su diarrhea. Sra. Cecilia. Thank God that you came today because Sra. Adila was in a rage with the girls this morning with their diarrhea.

Ceci: Hola Vilma. God works in mysterious ways. Vilma…Yo se que a causa de mi ud. ha perdido tu trabajo, y lo siento. Hello Vilma. I know that because of me you have lost your job, and I am sorry.

Vilma: Pues yo escuche todo lo que paso y fue un bendicion que ella perdio todos los ninos Adila es una bruja horrible. Ella solamente quiere ganar dinero de la IHNFA. Well, I heard all that happened and it was a blessing that she lost all the kids. Adila is a horrible witch! And she just wants to get money from the IHNFA.

Ceci: That's why I had to bust her… Me siento horrible. Hay tantos muchachos perdidos en la calle, Vilma. I feel horrible. There are so many lost kids living in the street, Vilma.

Vilma: Si Ceci. Por las condiciones economicas los padres no tienen dinero… que nadie tiene trabajo que paga bien… No hay derechos de ninos que funcionen bien para los pobres. Conoce ud. Los Derechos de la Ninez en Honduras? It's because of the economic conditions, that the parents don't have money, and no work pays well. There are no children's rights that actually are enforced for the poor. Do you know about the Rights of Children in Honduras?

Vilma pulls out a newspaper and opens it to a specific page, folds it over and gives it to Ceci.

Ceci: No, no sabía que había un documento de derechos. No, I didn't know there was a document of rights for children..

Vilma: Aqui esta un editorio sobre la realidad de los derechos de ninos en Honduras… en el periodico de La Tribuna hoy. Lealo cuando pueda. Here is an editorial about the reality of the rights of children in Honduras , in today's Tirbune. Read it when you can.

Ceci: OK, lo hare. OK I will

Vilma: Dona Ceci…Quiero trabajar contigo. Puedo ayudarle en la casa, en su negocios de danza, con las ninas. Cualquier cosa. Yo necesito poner comida en las bocas de mi familia. Dona Ceci.. I want to work with you. I can help you in the house, with the children, in your dance business. Whatever. I need to put food in the mouths of my family. *Ceci stops walking and looks at her and smiles and offers to shake her hand.*

Ceci: OK… wow… puede ser un bendicion para mi. Es la verdad que necessito alguien para ayudarme con mi escuela. This could be a blessing for me. It is true that I need someone to help me with my school

Vilma: Deberas? Really?

Ceci: Vilma….Manana venga a mi estudio en la Escuela Mazapan para trabajar conmigo y mis estudiantes. Yo necessito ayuda con muchas cosas, y me alegre tener esta oportunidad. Sabes como sacar medidas y costurar vestuarios? Vilma, tomorrow come to my studio in the Mazapan school to work with me and the students. I need your help for many things, and I am happy to have this opportunity. Do you know how to take measurements and sew costumes?

Vilma: Puede ser.. Maybe.

Ceci: OK , te enseno manana. Creo que tu eres una persona con quien puedo tener confianza. Dejare tu nombre con la guardia en el Porton de la Escuela, OK? OK we will see tomorrow. I believe that you are a person I can trust. I will leave your name with the guard at the school gate OK?

Vilma: Gracias, Ceci. Es un cambio bueno para mi vida. Una oportunidad creo yo. Thank you Ceci. I believe this is a good opportunity for me.

Ceci: Bueno Vilma… me alegre oirlo. Hasta manana. I am happy to hear that. See you tomorrow.

They stop in front of a small bodega and Vilma says good bye and enters.

43. <u>Downtown La Ceiba Streets – Declaration of Children's Rights</u>

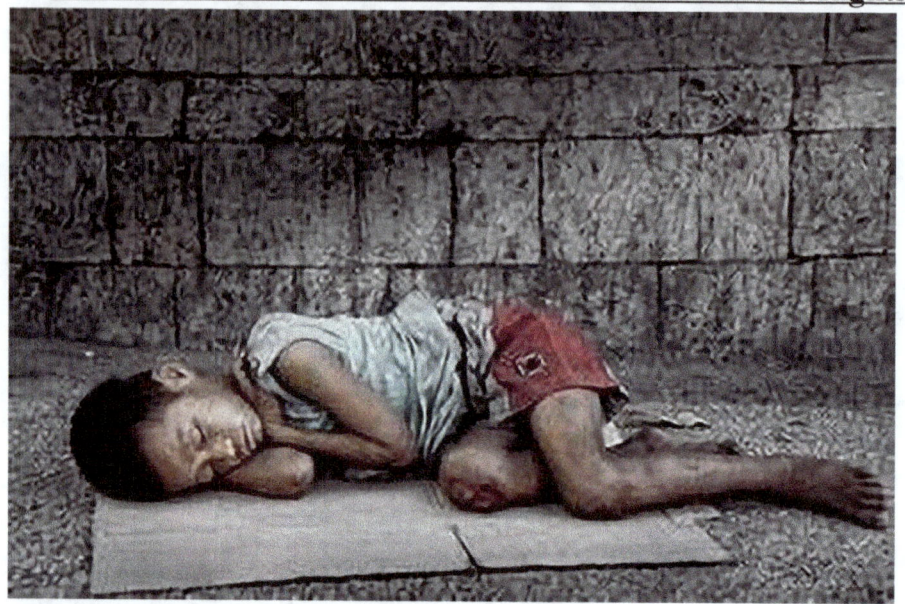

 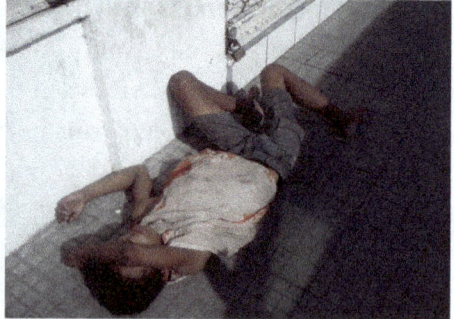

Ceci starts to walk, and finds herself walking around and over young boys lying on the street. She decides to stop for a café and read her paper as she watches the general drama on the street. This is accompanied by a voiceover of Ceci's translation of the Rights of Children which is taken directly from the United Nations Universal Declaration of Children's Rights. As she reads, the boys hustle her for money.

Ceci reads: *and her voiceover accompanies visuals of homeless street boys as she walks.*

http://hrlibrary.umn.edu/instree/k1drc.htm#:~:text=Every%20 child%2C%20without%20any%20exception,himself%20or%20of%20 his%20family.

Declaration of the Rights of the Child, G.A. res. 1386 (XIV), 14 U.N. GAOR Supp. (No. 16) at 19, U.N. Doc. A/4354 (1959).

PREAMBLE

Whereas the peoples of the United Nations have, in the Charter, reaffirmed their faith in fundamental human rights and in the dignity and worth of the human person, and have determined to promote social progress and better standards of life in larger freedom,

Whereas the United Nations has, in the Universal Declaration of Human Rights, proclaimed that everyone is entitled to all the rights and freedoms set forth therein, without distinction of any kind, such as race, color, sex, language, religion, political or other opinion, national or social origin, property, birth or other status, Whereas the child, by reason of his physical and mental immaturity, needs special safeguards and care, including appropriate legal protection, before as well as after birth,

Whereas the need for such special safeguards has been stated in the Geneva Declaration of the Rights of the Child of 1924, and recognized in the Universal Declaration of Human Rights and in the statutes of specialized agencies and international organizations concerned with the welfare of children,

Whereas mankind owes to the child the best it has to give, Now therefore, The General Assembly....

Proclaims this Declaration of the Rights of the Child to the end that he may have a happy childhood and enjoy for his own good and for the good of society the rights and freedoms herein set forth, and calls upon parents, upon men and women as individuals, and upon voluntary organizations, local authorities and national Governments to recognize these rights and strive for their observance by legislative and other measures progressively taken in accordance with the following principles:

Principle I -The child shall enjoy all the rights set forth in this Declaration. Every child, without any exception whatsoever, shall be entitled to these rights, without distinction or discrimination on account of race, color, sex, language, religion, political or other opinion, national or social origin, property, birth or other status, whether of himself or of his family.

Principle 2-The child shall enjoy special protection, and shall be given opportunities and facilities, by law and by other means, to enable him to develop physically, mentally, morally, spiritually and socially in a healthy and normal manner and in conditions of freedom and dignity. In the enactment of laws for this purpose, the best interests of the child shall be the paramount consideration.

Principle 3 -The child shall be entitled from his birth to a name and a nationality.

Principle 4 - The child shall enjoy the benefits of social security. He shall be entitled to grow and develop in health; to this end, special care and protection shall be provided both to him and to his mother, including adequate pre-natal and post-natal care. The child shall have the right to adequate nutrition, housing, recreation and medical services.

Principle 5 -The child who is physically, mentally or socially handicapped shall be given the special treatment, education and care required by his particular condition.

As Ceci walks, passing all these lost street children, her head begins to swirl with pain as she flinches over the irony and reality of children's rights. Tears come to her eyes. This intensity takes us back to the Ciudad Blanca.

44. <u>**Ciudad Blanca Ceremony – Quetzalcoatl -**</u> **Flashback # 4**

Offerings have been made to the altar... Shells, rocks, flowers, beaded necklaces, fruits and flowers. Kukulcan was the Mayan name of the Feathered Serpent. And Quetzalcoatl was the Aztec name. Quetzalcoatl will be used in this context because his name is part of the Popol Vuh, and is more recognized.

Lempira: Great Gods of the stars… please accept our offerings of nature, that shall no longer be the blood of innocent humans…. So many of our children have already been sacrificed as lost orphans. It's bad enough that human sacrifice was part of our history. This is almost as bad. We must change this mentality.

Garifuna Satuye: And what about this savage practice? Why did you allow this to happen? For all the intelligence of the Mayan scientists, the legacy is negated by this ruthless killing of innocent people as sacrifices to a God. Yes, we have this in Africa too… but mostly with animals.

Quetzalcoatl: I did not believe in the ceremonies of sacrifice. I fled many centers of Mayan power because of the loss of so many defenseless souls. This dramatic ritual, in the name of the gods, was a way of holding power for the great leaders. And if the truth shall be known…. This sacrificial blood was used by the great forefathers who came from the sky, whose civilization from another star was so advanced that they helped take humans from the monkey state to the human state through their experiments with human blood in scientific laboratories, where the Mayan tribe was created. This blood was the essential element which introduced genetically engineered life.

Francisco Morazan: Why would such advanced beings be so selfish as to witness pain as a sacrificial gift?? A holy God supports life in every way.

Lempira: Senor Morazan, even though you were the liberator of Honduras and enacted liberal reforms when you ruled the Republic of Central America….. Even with your reforms with the freedom of the press, speech and religion….. you came from Spain with the original conquistadores, who took over and imposed great pain and suffering on our people and culture.

Morazan: This is history now, and I did vow to protect all of your people from oppression.

Lempira: The oppression of the Spanish followed the oppression of the practice of sacrifice. They both crippled the Mayan culture.

Quetzalcoatl: I disagreed with the premise of ritual sacrifice. So I finally left Tulum to come here to the Ciudad Blanca, where the monkey scribes recorded the last remaining parts of the Popol Vuh, our great Mayan Creation Story. Let it be known that our ancestors came from the Pleiades star system, and they taught us how to build these beautiful pyramids throughout what is now Mexico, Belize, Guatemala, El Salvador, and Honduras. This Great White City where we stand now, has not yet been found and exploited, so it can still be visited by the star gods.

Lempira: Your historical account of creation is a shocking reminder of our present situation... as there has always been an upper class which controls the lower by manipulation and exploitation. Now, the government allows our children to sacrifice themselves unknowingly to poverty, hunger, crime, drugs, and negligence.

Morazan: This was not our intention. But the natives were unable to organize themselves. They were seeking order, a government, a way to move forward. This has happened all in the name of evolutionary progress.

Cacique Toreba: We had order and government. But the Spanish had fire arms.

Lempira: Our people were excluded from modern evolution, and considered savages and slaves since the conquista.... Dropped from the system.... Denied access to education and proper health care..... Immersed in an economy that has no jobs and refuses to explore improvement and progress for the masses. This is racism Morazan, and you were part of it... as a conquistador. You came from Spain looking for opportunity by invasion, at our expense!!!!

Morazan: Lempira... I had to pass over to witness this pain from the heavens. Forgive me.. if I ever come back I will be a champion for the indigenous. I weep at the suffering now.... I know not how to repair the damage.

Garifuna: No one could stop the white man. What's done is done.

Lempira: Have mercy... heart of the sky! Pray that our children are no longer sacrificed!

Quetzalcoatl: They shall evolve, with respect for nature, family, and progress. *They all reach skyward with both arms.*

45. <u>HOTEL Lobby – Dr. Harris waiting for Ceci</u>

Dr. Harris: I just came from the hospital. The girls will be OK under Nurse Josie's care. She has promised us that they will be recovered before delivering them to the IHNFA. So they will be in the hospital for further studies. But you cannot see them.

Ceci: But why?

Dr. Harris: Because they think you will run off with them.

Ceci: Oh God, I would never do that illegally. I just want to see them. Thank you so much for following up on their fever and infections. That really is the most important thing right now.

Dr. Harris: I have treated all of them and they are no longer infected or hungry. They plan to move them out as soon as possible to some secret location.

Ceci: I just don't get it.

Dr. Harris: Ceci, they aren't your kids. You just have to hang in there and play this out. Meanwhile, we will be leaving tomorrow for a flight to Tegucigalpa.

Ceci: Tomorrow? You can't leave now.

Dr. Harris: We have a whole itinerary in Central America. But I am going to a goodbye party tonight for the medical team. Do you want to come? I think you need a diversion.

Ceci: Not sure if I will fit in with the upper class of La Ceiba.

Dr Harris: Sure you will... They love Americans... and I would like to celebrate with you.

Ceci: Well, oh... OK... ummm... I only have one dress, and that will have to do.

Dr. Harris: That's fine, meet me here at 7pm

Ceci: OK . I'll do my best to clean up my act.

Dr. Harris: I'm sure you clean up real good.

46. Margie Dip's Coctail Party for Doctors Without Borders – Tom Weinberg

Cut to classy Honduran cocktail party in a private home, with the Doctors Without Borders group, mixed with the President Maduro and his blond wife, Aguas Ocanas, visiting Priests, and Doctors... as well as various upper class residents of La Ceiba. The event is being hosted by Governor of Atlantida, Margie Dip, and a local church with American affiliations to charity non profit groups. All are dressed in their Sunday best for this uppity affair. The party is elegant, with an open bar, a live band, and floating Afro Latino servants serving hors oeuvres. It is a far cry from the poverty of the streets.

Ceci arrives with the Doctor, and she is looking absolutely smashing in a simple jersey, salmon colored summer dress. There are fractions of dialogues revealing the characters at the banquet, as they drink their way into party mode. Guifffityy is being served in fancy glasses by the Garifuna servants. Clearly, there is an old world feeling to the scene with the black Garifuna servants, and the white upper class Ceibenos. They are seated at the table with President Maduro and his Spanish Diplomat Wife, Aguas Ocanas... and Mayor Margie Dip.

There is also an American at the party, journalist, Tom Weinberg, working in the Mosquitia on Aeronautical photography with a group of American scientists. It is called "lidar" recording and shows the subterraneous parts of swampy Mosquitia land, untouched by humans for centuries. They are in search of THE WHITE CITY... or Ciudad Blanca.

Ceci opens the conversation.

Ceci: Senora Aguas Ocana... de cual parte de Espana eres? *Long pause.* **Soy Americana, pero mis abuelos maternales son de Asturias.** Senora Augas Ocana... What part of Spain are you from? *Pause.* I am American but my maternal grandparents are from Asturias.

Aguas Ocana: Buenas Noches Senora? Good Evening Senora?

Ceci: Cecilia Diaz, de Virginia, USA. *Extending her hand.*

Aguas: Mucho gusto... Mi familia es de Barcelona. A pleasure to meet you. My family is from Barcelona.

Ceci: Sra... Quiero graciarle y hablar de mi admiracion por su courage en la lucha para los ninos de la calle en Honduras.... Este asunto toca mi corazon mucho.... Yo se que no hay soluciones rapidos... Conseguir famila es algo importante creo yo. Pero, como mantener la stabilidad economica de familias es el riego mas dificil en Honduras. Sra.... I want to thank you and speak of my admiration for your courage in the fight for the homeless children in Honduras. This issue touches my heart a lot. I know that there are no quick solutions. To find family is something very important I believe. But how to maintain the economic stability of the family seems to be the most difficult challenge in Honduras.

Aguas: Your Spanish is very good.

Ceci: Gracias...

Aguas: It's always about the money, and who has it to spend on building families. It's very complicated. All I know is that I must get these kids off the street. This is my immediate concern.

Ceci: Perhaps I might benefit from your advice and knowledge in these affairs. Because I also have my eye on three

little sisters here in La Ceiba, who were taken away from their family because of abuse and neglect. And I am dumbfounded about getting custody of them and don't know where to begin.

Aguas: Where are they now?

Ceci: They are between orphanages on their way to the SOS... which should be better than where they were with the Ihnfa lady....., but one is partially blind, the other has neurological issues, the youngest is only three months old... and I want to take them home... But.. tantas problemas, com ud. sabe ... First my age, second the living family members who can't take care of them, the grips of the orphanage business, the red tape with the IHNFA, papers of abandonment, investigations, visas, immigration, etc. etc.

Aguas: Yes I know Cecilia... I am going through this now with two children whom I love, and who are caught up in this Ihnfa red tape as you call it. Don't give up... Look at me Gringa... Don't give up. Even if you make a difference with only 3 girls, this will be three more girls who will make something great of their lives.

Ceci: You're right... But I will have to move to La Ceiba.

Aguas: Then move here. What's stopping you? You are still young.

Ceci: Oy! You say all the right things Senora!! You remind me of Evita!! Su estilo, su belleza, su corazon!

Aguas: Ay gracias! Vamos a bailar... Gringa!!

Margie Dip approaches them with a guiffity drink in her hand.

Margie Dip: Yes Cecilia, I am so happy that you will teach Dance in the Mazapan School at Standard Fruit. My Grandchildren go there. They will love you. You can make the shows... They need some professional spice over there... But.. come on let's dance.

Dr. Louis Harris: Just a minute Sra, I want Ceci to meet Mr. Weinberg.

Margie: Apurate! We need a professional on the dance floor.

Margie drags the first lady out onto the dance floor and starts the dancing. She is a charming and effervescent character as well as a beloved Mayor of La Ceiba.

Dr.: Ceci, Remember you told me that you were dreaming about the Ciudad Blanca, and how I told you I thought it was a legend…. And you disagreed with me?

Ceci: Yes…yes *Eyes wide open with curiosity…*

Dr. Well, this is Tom Weinberg, who says he knows you from TVTV, some video group you worked with in LA many years ago…

Ceci: Oh My God Tom!!!! I don't recognize you with a beard.

Tom: Ceil, it's been years, but you look the same. Still dancing?

Ceci: Yes of course. Teaching here in La Ceiba. Dios mio! Tell me what are you doing here.

Tom: I am working with a group which is doing scientific photography with lidar, a highly advanced technology that can map terrain under the densest rainforest canopy. We have found the images of a huge metropolis, which we believe is the lost civilization of the mythical CIUDAD BLANCA.

Ceci: *Having an inspired shock.* Holy wow Tom!… I am crazy for the Ciudad Blanca… I have actually had dreams about the place, And I've been doing some research about it too…. It's also called the City of the Monkey King, and this guy Theodore Moore, actually saw the place with its huge white staircases and plazas filled with gold and alligator, spider, and monkey statues.

Tom: I hate to rain on your parade, but that's been proven a myth and a lie… that Theodore Moore invented to compensate for used up research funds…. leaving a suicide note. There were several versions to the story, but we are already beyond that.

Ceci: That's no fun… and Tom, I just can't accept that. Every myth has a source. Maybe it's connected to a Honduran version of Big Foot. And…. Moore was probably murdered and accused of lying so somebody else could follow up and cash in.

Tom: Well…There are other theories which are being revealed around the origins of this White City… like Pre – Mayan, Pre-Olmec as another ancient, difficult access ruin for a lost civilization, way off the grid… yet integral to Central American indigenous development.

Ceci: Now that peaks my interest… I'd like to know more about that.

Tom: My pleasure… I am just getting the initial lidar images together to raise interest and funds for a formal expedition with anthropologists, archaeologists, biologists, scientists, Latin American geologists, Mayan scholars and video people. The geometric images are fabulous with plazas, pyramids, homes, deep under the jungle floor, miles from civilization.

Ceci: Tom, I love it.

Tom: I'm just a journalist stuck between the dreamers and the scientists. So I welcome all information…. Legend or fact. I'm working on a book about it.

Ceci: I'll buy it! Here's my email. *She writes on a napkin.* You know I gotta dance… We can talk about this a little later… Because I'm telling you… I have dreams about that place… It's calling me! Please stay in touch. Great meeting you Tom!!!

Dr. Harris: Now aren't you glad I found the only other American at the party?

Ceci: You're a prince. *She smiles.*

Dr. Harris: Go dance…

Ceci joins Margie and the first lady, Agua Canas on the dance floor. The live cocktail music increases in rhythm and then evolves from conservative rhumba, to salsa, merengue… and finally, the unbridled, Garifuna punta. This becomes a production number in which the guests and the Garifuna servants perform in tropical Broadway Latino style. Ceci joins them. As the drinks circulate. the dynamic begins to swirl. The evolution of dance, costume, and the increase in energy becomes a surreal dance number in every way, as this is not typical upper class party entertainment. The spirit starts to take control of Ceci. Louis intervenes as she begins to fall into trance. He carries her outside to the patio for air near a bonfire as she passes out. The frenzied drumming continues.

47. CIUDAD BLANCA # 5 – Strategy for the Three sisters – Lempira calls Comizahual

This intense performance leads to another magical transition to the Ciudad Blanca….. into a dusky, and fiery setting in a jungle wilderness, surrounded by Mayan ruins … where indigenous women are dancing ceremoniously to primitive flutes and drums. The three sisters, Jazmin, Angie and Roxana, are at the center of a ritual platform with a fire pit, and a pyramid shaped throne with an altar behind it. They will be ritually cleansed. There, once again, in spirit are the elders in their ceremonial garb. Chief Lempira speaks to all the ancestors and leaders – Mayan, Aztec, Garifuna and indigenous as he begs spirit for help.

Ceci is dreaming all of this within the trance that the dancing took her at the party. The famous Lenca warrior, Lempira presents his case.

Lempira: Here we dance a war dance to banish the evil around us… more profoundly the neglect of our family culture and children… Again, our legacy as the first settlers on this land has been hijacked, as those who are close to the earth and mother nature, are penalized by their inability to succeed in the current world of electronic modernity. So our children are not considered equal… and there is not enough work for our men. So what of our royal Mayan history, built of blood, sweat and tears in working the earth and taking care of our family and tribal ways... living off of nature. It has been taken over by Western Coffee and Fruit companies who exploit OUR land, and pay us barely enough to work it for their profit. How can our people maintain their families without causing suffering to their own children? *Walking round the circle, looking at the ancient leaders,* **Lempira** *continues talking from the heart.*

These three children represent thousands in our country, who are lost with no futures. The children must become our priority, through family. I hereby wish to end their struggle for survival, health and love, and open their roads to the possibility of a real family and future. Please take away their pain, and as much of the damage that your mercy can empower, as they suffer from blindness, anxiety, abandonment, mental confusion, and growth issues all caused by the abuse, neglect, and inability of their misdirected parents. I ask this with all my heart.

This is OUR land. Here Great Spirit, we must initiate more of our trigueno philosophy - to overcome the struggle of all of our lost children in the twenty first century. We must believe in the blended family.... The world tribe. That mothers and fathers of any color, can take on lost children anywhere in Honduras now... especially if their blood parents cannot and will not care for them. And since the government cannot help the Honduran family, nor rescue these children properly... we must inspire and facilitate compassion from the realm of spirit.

I call the Great Spirit.... There is a white woman willing to be a mother. We endorse this woman, who I believe is a reincarnation of the Goddess Comizahual, for her interest in these three precious young sisters, Jazmin, Angie, and Roxana... as they face the most important opportunity of their lives in these coming years.... The chance to advance their karmas and become healed. The ordeals and trials this American will endure to cross the border to the USA with these girls will be almost impossible, with all the odds against her. It will take years. BUT.....We stand behind her and these young girls in spirit, as they make this journey... and hope that this woman sets an example to our supposed Honduran Democracy to step up to the job of caring and legislating. People should not be walking over their bodies as they sleep on the streets. Bless those who can help our Honduran children to survive.

We ask that all available parents take the initiative in Honduras and around the world to take on the courage to rescue and adopt a child. An orphanage cannot develop their hearts and minds as can the true love of a family. Bring in the Goddess Comizahual again. She must help us in this blessing with her invaluable feminine presence.

Ceci, suddenly appears as the spirit of Comizahual, descending from the sky like a flying jaguar in her golden robes. She lights incense and blesses the girls muttering a strange language. Then she envelops the girls in her long sleeves and begins a ring around the rosy circle as the drums intensify. The company of elders dance around them in the opposite direction swishing them with branches of rue. Concentric circles take the Ciudad Blanca in a swirling time tunnel of energy. There are flashes of moments between Ceci and these girls through the past, present, and future. When the rotation and speed slow down, Comizahual literally floats up and away into the sky with the girls reaching upward for her.

48. Return to Party – Ceci and the Doctor dance

And we return to the party which is almost over. The servants are cleaning up. Ceci is seated with the Doctor on the patio on a lounge chair, her head on his shoulder. It is a very "Casablanca" moment. A guitarist plays a dreamy ranchero in the corner, and Ceci awakens.

Doctor: Como esta mujer?

Ceci: Wow…. *She looks around and tries to pull herself together…***You won't believe what I just dreamt… or where I just went?**

Doctor: You were definitely out there again. How often does this happen Ceci?

Ceci: I swear it was the Ciudad Blanca.. like an ancient ceremony, but the girls were there. Yes they were, Louis.

Doctor: Are you OK?

Ceci: I think so... forgive me for passing out again... I swear I normally don't do this... must be that guiffity... Wow.

Doctor: No problem Ceci... I am fascinated by this Garifuna medicine....and you are a great dancer... But I want you to come down to earth now. How about some coffee? *One of the waiters brings her a cup.*

Ceci: Looks like the party's over. *She sits up.*

Doctor: Our party isn't over. I was hoping you would save the last dance for me, if you are up for it. Although I can't compete with your technique. *He offers her his hand.* May I have this dance Dona Cecilia?

Ceci: I didn't know you could dance.

Louis: Are you sure you are up for more dancing?

Ceci: Hmmm... Maybe you can ground me.

Ceci smiles, throws back some coffee, stands up, and rearranges her dress. This becomes a romantic bachata duet choreography. The dance segues into a taxi arriving at Ceci's hotel. Dr. Louis accompanies Ceci to her room.

49. <u>Return to Ceci's Hotel Room – Night</u>

Ceci: Thank you for an exciting evening, and again.... forgive me for passing out. I must have a psychedelic connection with that guiffity. Did I make a fool out of myself?

Doctor: I can say that you were the best dancer at the party.

Ceci: Well I can honestly tell you that I left my body.

Doctor: Ok Ceci... now we don't want you leaving your body anymore.

Ceci: Yes Doctor...I can take care of myself, and I know I can take care of those girls.

Doctor: I told you I would help with the girls, and I mean it.

Ceci: I wish you weren't leaving. Just my luck, when I find someone who can dance, he's gotta go.

Doctor: I know it's not going to be easy getting custody of these girls, but if anybody can do it you can. Please call me with your bank routing number when you get settled. **OK?** *He hands her a card.*

Ceci: Thanks for all of this support....I will miss you. *She takes a pen from her purse and writes her email address on his arm.* Write to me OK?

Doctor: I Promise. Their welfare is now my fatherly instinct.

There is a clumsy moment of silence, followed by a kiss. He leaves.

Ceci: And what kind of instinct was that? *Talking to herself.*

50. <u>AM Hangover – Summons from Adila</u>

Ceci wakes up with hangover the next day. But pulls it together to get ready for her first day of classes at the Mazapan School. She puts on her dance clothes, packs her music and shoes, and leaves for the school. On the way out she finds a letter on the door. She opens an official looking envelope from the City Municipal Building, which is a summons for her appearance at court for allegedly threatening Adila with a dagger. She talks to herself as she walks to work.

Ceci: Oh my God, what is this? A summons? *Reading...* For threatening Sra. Adila with a dagger?!?! So she has taken revenge for losing those poor kids, and I have to respond to this lie and squeeze this into my already crowded agenda? Yes, that Latino revenge factor did not enter my mind. Taking care of these kids was a business for her.... Way beyond her heart .... and now she has no money source. Ay yuy yuy! What am I in for now? OK breathe Ceci. You are in the third world. Shit happens, with very creative misinformation. But right now you have to go to class. Pick it up Ceci. This is the price you pay for protecting these kids.

51. <u>Mazapan Dance Studio – Deni May - First dance class with adolescent students - 2004</u>

Ceci meets Vilma outside the studio and unlocks the door and bathes for a moment in the joy of having a place to dance again.

Ceci: Look Vilma… a real dance studio… mio…y aqui esta la oficina, con espacio costurar, organizer vestuario… Telefono, escritorio… todo. And here is the office, with space to sew and organize costumes, telephone, desk… everything.

Vilma: OK Ceci – como puedo ayudarte? So how can I help you?

Ceci: Well primero necessito decirte que no se donde estan las ninas. Hable con la gente en el SOS si ellos pueden acceptarlas alla, y me dijieron que si, pero la IHNFA no quiere que yo sepa donde estan ellas ahora. Y eso mata mi corazon. Well, first I have to tell you that I don't know where the girls are. I spoke with the SOS people if they could accept them there, and they told me yes, but the IHNFA doesn't want me to know where they are right now… which breaks my heart.

Vilma: No entiendo Ceci. Ellas te necesitan. I don't get it Ceci. They need you..

Ceci: Y la senora Adila me cargo con el crimen de amenezarle a ella con un cuchillo en la calle, que es una mentira, y ahora necesito buscar un abogado, etc. etc. And Senora Adila has accused me of the crime of threatening her with a knife in the street, which is a lie, and now I need to look for a lawyer.

Vilma: Si, ella esta enojada por perder su trabajo. En Honduras uno se tiene la culpa hasta que se puede probar su inocencia. Y esta mujer sabe hacer venganza. Ademas me dijieron que ella salio por Espana para cuidar un viejito alla. Yes, she is mad because she lost her job. In Honduras you are guilty until proven innocent. And this woman knows how to make revenge. And I was told that she left for Spain to take care of an old man there.

Ceci: Ella invento esa mentira y ella lo sabe. She invented that lie and she knows it. **Basta de este problema!** Enough of this mess!

Vilma: Pues, buena suerte con eso. Entonces que quiere que yo hago hoy para los estudiantes? Well, good luck with that. And what would you like me to do today for the students?

Ceci: Bueno hoy se puede organizer la oficina, y cuando vengan los estudiantes quiero que tu marques la assistencia, y empieces a tomar sus medidas. Te enseno. *Ceci shows her the different body measurements she needs to make costumes.* **Cuando empieza la clase yo voy hablar sobre mis planes para la clase, y despues les ensenare una coreografia de salsa... mi musica Latina favorita... Especialmente salsa vieja big band. Y durante eso, se puede medirlas, y empezar a conocerles una por una?? OK?** OK today you can organize the office, and when the students come you can take attendance, and begin to measure them. I'll show you how. When class starts I will speak about my plans for the class, and after I will begin to teach a salsa choreography, and during that you can get to know them and measure them one by one. OK?

Ceci shows her how to measure the students: bust, waist, hips, shoulders width, waist to ankles waist to knees, neck to waist, shoulder to wrist, etc.

Vilma: Esta bien. Deme la lista de asistencia con los nombres. That's good. Give me the attendance list with the names.

Ceci: Toma... Gracias Vilma. Hay que trabajar. Thank you Vilma. I need to work now.

As they are working, in walks Deni May, a gringa first grade teacher from the Mazapan school. She introduces herself.

Ceci: Hello, can I help you?

Deni: Are you Ceci Diaz?

Ceci: Yes Mam.

Deni: I am Deni May, the first grade teacher and I heard about your arrival and I wanted to meet and welcome you to the Mazapan school.

Ceci: Thank you so much, I am just starting today. This is Vilma, my assistant.

Deni: I also came by to tell you that I have two left feet as a dancer and I would be really happy if you can help me out with my first graders for the Dia del Nino show. They love to dance.

Ceci: That's what I'm here for, and I have lots of ideas for the Dia del Nino that would be great options for first graders. So we can decide on a song you like and then schedule them in during the school day for rehearsals.

Deni: That is exactly what I wanted to hear.

Ceci: If you can come by after school tomorrow, I can give you a few ideas before I go to the SOS... say about 2:30?

Deni: I can be here at 2:30 tomorrow. And I understand that you have taken interest in some Ceiba orphan girls.

Ceci: Yes, I have fallen in love with three sisters whose fate seems to be in God's hands... you know what they say... "Si Dios Quiere".

Deni: I hear that every day. And I know what you are in for.

Ceci: What do you mean?

Deni: I have a three year old boy who was "given" to me, and I keep running into visa problems with the American Embassy. It's a nightmare. The paper work will drive you crazier than the waiting. Now they want DNA samples.

Ceci: Evidently many American women and couples have gone through this for many years in Honduras. And many were successful.

Deni: That was back in the day. Then the IHNFA tightened up because of the talk about selling the kids for their organs. Can you believe it?

Ceci: So you never get to discuss what a better life you can offer them?

Deni: No... that never comes up. And the IHNFA has been so corrupt with financial pilfering and improper care, that it had to be shut down for any kind of custody or adoption proceedings until accusations were settled by the courts. That's why Ale's mother just gave him to me, rather than going through all the red tape, knowing Ale would be in a limbo orphanage indefinitely.

Ceci: Ah what we do for love, other than dance. And what's your son's name?

Deni: Ale... Alejandro

Ceci: I hope we can all meet up someday soon if I can coordinate something with the girls. And of course, we will find a great number to mount with your students. I already have an idea.

Deni: And I would be happy to help you in anyway with the custody of your girls. I know how confusing this road is. I would love to meet the girls... And I will see you tomorrow. Thank you... Great meeting you.

Ceci: Likewise, Adios.

As Deni leaves, we hear a 3pm school bell for last period and the students come in. They are all girls who had originally been studying ballet with the previous dance teacher who left.

Ceci greets them as they come in while setting up her music and playing around with some salsa steps. She dances as they change into dance attire. They slowly come back into the studio, and sit themselves hesitantly on the floor. They do not know Ceci. And they are all ages 15 – 18.

Ceci: Welcome to my first dance class at the Mazapan school. My name is Ceci Diaz, and I am a choreographer from the United States, where I have worked in theater, rock n roll, videos, film, TV, and just about any kind of venue where people want dance and entertainment. And I am here to learn about Honduras and Latin music. This is Vilma, my assistant, who will be helping with classes, with our shows, and today she will be taking your measurements for costumes while we work, if you are all OK with that. So as I was saying. I am not a ballerina like Mimi, but I do use ballet at the bar in my classes and in occasional choreographies. I am hoping that you are all willing to embrace different kinds of dance which may be a shift from the style of Ms. Mimi. I will be preparing you and the students from Escuela Mazapan, along with my after school dancers, and dancers from the SOS .... for a Dia del Nino show, for a Christmas concert, and Mother's Day and Carnaval next year... And we will start one of those dances today. Any questions?

Marbella: Like what kind of dance?

Ceci: I have studied and worked with jazz, tap, ballet, modern, folk, hip hop, merengue, flamenco, lyrical jazz, rock n roll, modern dance, African, Latino, so I do it and use it all in my work .... Mainly because for so many years I worked as a commercial choreographer, and when they called me up and said can you make me a Quebecois clog dance, I would always say yes, and find out everything there was to know about Quebecois clogging as fast as possible. So no warm up today. Just want to start you off on some simple salsa steps. Let's see how you do, and then you can decide if you are up for a Dia del Nino salsa performance that can also work for Christmas. OK?

Dancers: OK?

Ceci: Great. *She puts on some background salsa music.* I would like you all to line up in front of the mirror. Let's just warm up with some little steps ... like this ... yes... very good.... *They all follow Ceci with basic salsa steps as she continues talking.* You guys are naturals. You know this salsa ritmo originates in Cuba and Puerto Rico and has a sophisticated African origin. I hope you are going to show me some Latina personality. So, we will go one by one now, in the mirror, and introduce ourselves through dance with 8 counts that show me how you like to move? I will start and then Marbella .. you pick it up.

They agree and Ceci throws out 8 beats of "My name is Ceci... Watch my feet and you'll see". Marbella continues with surprising swagger, and the introductions flow from each girl to the next, saying her name with a little dance to match. Ceci stops the music applauding.

Ceci: Great... I love dancers who dive right in.. I am very impressed with your intrinsic "estilo". Gracias. So this salsa is a modified version of a choreography that a Puerto Rican friend of mine in Los Angeles, showed me before I came to Honduras. So this is dedicated to Domingo... with music by Marc Anthony. Let's break it down.

Ceci then begins to break down salsa steps with lots of little jazz touches facing the mirror. She takes it very slowly, over and over again to join the first 8 counts with the music, which she puts on a slow speed. Then she breaks down the next 8 counts and adds it on... and by the time the class is over the girls are swinging their hips in their ballet attire, repeating the phrase over and over with more and more flair. Vilma has managed to measure all the girls in and out of their enthusiastic practice. The bell finally rings and the girls are laughing and wiping the sweat off their necks. Ceci's first class was a success. As they leave, she slaps a high five with Vilma.

Ceci: Gracias Vilma... You are fabulous. Vamos a trabajar juntas con todos sus talentos... Cuando no estas aqui en el estudio me puedes ayudar en la casa y tambien en el SOS con mi trabajo alla. Definitivamente te necesito. Thank you, Vilma, you are fabulous. We are going to work together with all of your talents. When you aren't here in the studio you can help me in the house and also in the SOS with my work there. I definitely need your services.

Vilma: Yo quiero el trabajo. Gracias Ceci. I want the work... Thank you Ceci.

Ceci: Espero que pasas un buen fin de semana. Saludos a tu familia. I hope you have a good weekend... regards to your family.

Ceci hands Vilma some cash for the day and she leaves. Left alone, Ceci walks around her newly christened studio with hope and pride before she locks up.

52. <u>Encounter with a Homeless boy – Adan</u>

It is Saturday, and a song takes Ceci into the central park in front of the Hotel Gran Paris, where she sits alone, until a homeless boy asks her for money. After giving the boy a banana, Ceci is surprised that he scowls. A passing pedestrian comments.

Pedestrian: **Como un perro!** Just like a dog!

Ceci: **Y porque dice eso senor?** And why do you say that?

Pedestrian: **Porque son animales todos – malcriados, desgraciados, y quieren su dinero para comprar resistol...** Because they are all animals… badly raised, ungrateful, and they want your money to buy resistol. **(*A glue which is inhaled as a drug*)**

Ceci is alarmed by the disgust this woman has for street children. She pursues the boy.

Ceci: **Disculpa chico. Puedo preguntarle donde vive ud.?** Escuse me chico. Can I ask you where you live?

Boy: **Vivo en la calle gringa...** *Big smile* .. I live in the street gringa.

Ceci: **Y donde estan sus padres?** And where are your parents?

Boy: **Mi madre vive lejos en las montanas cerca Tocoa con un senor diablo.** My mother lives far away in the mountains near Tocoa with a devil man.

Ceci: **Y su papa?**

Boy: **No conozco mi papa.. Y el senor diablo es el novio numero cuatro de mi mama.** I don't know my father. And the devil

man is the number four boyfriend of my mother.

Pause

Ceci: **Y como se llama ud?**

Boy: **Adan Maldonado**

Ceci: **Y cuantos anos tiene?**

Adan: Creo que tengo casi 12. I think I am almost 12 years old.

Ceci: Y porque vive en la calle? And why do you live in the street?

Adan: Porque no quiero vivir con el novio de mi mama ni en la Casa de Ninos tampoco. Because I don't want to live with my mother's boyfriend nor in the Casa de Ninos either.

Ceci: Que es la Casa de Ninos? What is the house of boys?

Adan: Es un orfenato en Barrio Inglais donde estaba yo por un ano. It's a boys orphanage in Barrio Englais where I was for a year.

Ceci: Y porque prefieres estar en la calle? Au menos hay comida y camas en los orfanatos, no? And why do you prefer to be in the street? At least there are food and beds in the orphanages, no?

Adan: Porque no quiero compartir la cama con otro muchacho. Somos encarcerados, como presos.... Y en la calle estoy libre. Because I don't want to share the bed with another boy. We are locked up like prisones. And in the street I am free.

Ceci: Oh my God!!

Adan: Deme dinero senora. Tengo hambre... No comprare drogas hoy. No he comido por dos dias. Give me money Senora. I am hungry. I won't buy drugs today. I haven't eaten for two days.

Ceci: OK, vamos. Voy a comprarle una hamburguesa en Wendy's. OK let's go. I am going to buy you a hamburger at Wendy's. *He follows, willingly, smiling.*

53. <u>Wendy's Hamburguesas – with Adan</u>

Adan is caught off guard with Ceci's generosity. They arrive walking and talking on the way to the local Wendy's across the street from the park. As they leave the park, they pass other "muchachos de la calle" who know Adan, who heckle him with lines like "Adan consiguio una gringa madre". As they enter the Wendy's to wait in line, the manager approaches Ceci y Adan.

Mgr: Disculpa muchacho pero ud. sabe que no tiene permiso entrar aqui. Excuse me boy, but you know that you don't have permission to enter here.

Ceci: Que pasa senor? Yo tengo dinero y quiero comprarle almuerzo. What's happening Senor? I have money and I want to buy him lunch.

Mgr: Please senora... We have many problems with this boy and he is not welcome here.

Ceci looks at Adan who smiles at her with his strange smile, and Ceci realizes that this young boy is capable of more trouble than she thought.

Ceci: Espere afuera Adan, y te traigo su hamburguesa. Y lavete sus manos. Wait outside Adan and I will bring your hamburger. First wash your hands.

Mgr: Aqui no! Afuera! *Pointing towards the door and raising his voice.* Here no! Outside!

Adan: Ok! Me voy! *He leaves* OK I am going!

Mgr: Sra, You do not know what you are doing. Be careful. *Ceci remains in line, humiliated.*

Ceci: Disculpa Senor... El tiene hambre. I am sorry Senor. He is hungry.

54. **Picnic with Adan in the Plaza park**

She gets a 'to go' meal for Adan and marches out of the store. Adan is seated in the park across the street. He calls her and waves.

Adan: Gringa!

Ceci joins him on the grass and watches him inhale the Wendy meal

Ceci: Ok Adan... So this is what we are going to do.

Adan: *Smiling with food in his bad teeth,* **No speaka engleesh missus!**

Ceci: Bueno... Ud y yo vamos ahora a la casa de tu mama en Tocoa... por autobus... y yo lo pagare. OK, so you and I are going to go to your mom's house in Tocoa by bus, and I will pay.

Adan: Estas loca gringa.... no.... no vale Are you crazy gringa? No, it's not worth it.

Ceci: *In his face*... **Si... porque yo quiero saber como tu madre puede permitirte salir de su hogar para vivir asi en la calle.** Yes, because I want to know how your mother can permit you to leave home to live in the street like this.

Adan: *Back at her*... **Yo te dije... Porque yo quiero estar libre en la calle .** I told you.. because I want to be free in the street.

Ceci: Y nunca falta su familia... comida...seguridad... cama... ni techo? Mires tu vida – no tienes bano ni ropa limpia... Necesitas tu Mama chico...Despiertate muchacho o vas a morir asi en la calle. Ven conmigo... Vamos al estacion de buses ahora.

And you never miss your family, food, security, a bed, a roof? Look at your life. You don't have a bathroom or clean clothes. You need your mother chico. Wake up boy or you will die like this in the street. Come with me. We are going to the bus station now.

Long pause as Adan saves half his hamburger by carefully wrapping it up. Still a child, he knows he has found the friend of the moment.

Adan: Visitar...nada mas... Y el autobus dura tres horas. To visit… nothing more. And the bus takes three hours.

Ceci: No importa... tu debes de estar con tu familia... y un angel me dijo que necesito entregarte alla... y bueno...caso cerrado... vamos. It doesn't matter. You should be with your family. An angel told me to deliver you there. And so,case closed-we are going.

Adan: Yo nunca veo angeles. I never see angels.

55. **Bus Ride to Tocoa with Adan**

It is a long bus ride to Tocoa – away from any metropolitan infrastructure. The bus passes fields of bananas, pineapples, palm trees, and cacao. Adan points to the fields.

Adan: Mira gringa. El dueno de estas cosechas es DOLE – Estandard Fruta... Los Estados Unidos explotando nuestra gente en nuestra propria tierra. Look gringa. The owner of these crops is DOLE/ Standard Fruit. The USA exploiting our people on our own land.

Ceci: Yo trabajo por Estandard en la Escuela Mazapan, pero yo no quiero explotar a nadie. Estoy aqui para ayudar, y aprender su cultura. Yo no soy DOLE, ni Estandard. Soy una professora. Y quiero entender porque las familias no cuidan sus hijos... Y debes de saber que yo estoy ayudando tres hermanas ahora que estan en la IHNFA. I work for Standard Fruit in the Mazapan school, but I don't want to exploit anybody. I am here to help and learn about this culture. I am not Dole, nor Standard Fruit. I am a teacher. And I want to understand why families don't take care of their children. And you should know that I am helping three sisters now who are in the Ihnfa.

Adan: Si... yo conozco la familia de estas ninas. He visto uds. en la calle. La problema que tienen las familias es pobreza senora... pobreza que causa hambre, enfermidad, problemas entra esposos... la infidelidad... Yes I know the family of these girls. The problem that these families have is poverty Senora. Poverty causes hunger, illness, problems between couples, infidelity, etc.

Ceci: Como conoce esta familia? How do you know this family?

Adan: Ellas vivian en San Judas donde hay muchos mareros en crimen y drogas. They were living in San Judas where there are many gang members in crime and drugs.

Ceci: Que son marerros? And what are mareros?

Adan: Son tribus de criminales, drogas, pandillas, hombres perdidos... como el papa de las ninas. El conocio todos los mareros, y siempre fue al Barrio Englais buscando drogas. Y yo mismo le ensene donde comprarlas cerca de La Casa de Ninos. Yo le vi cuando el fue assasenido – piedra en el cuello...boom! Un solo golpe! They are tribes of criminals, drugs, gangs... lost men... like the girls' father. He knew all the gang leaders, and always went to Barrio Englais looking for drugs. I showed him where to buy

them near the Casa de Ninos. I saw him when he was murdered...
rock on the neck. Boom... one hit!

Ceci: Oh my God again...

**Adan: Y yo conozco las hijas... Hay cuatro en San Judas... y
yo le he visto a ud. con dos pequenas en la calle.** And I know the
girls. There are four in San Judas. And I have seen you with two of
them in the street in Ceiba.

Ceci: Cuando y como? When and how!?

**Adan: En el parque. Porque vivo en la calle con ojos en todos
los partes. Compartimos informacion para comida y drogas
entra todos los muchachos de la calle.** In the park....Because I
live in the street with eyes everywhere. We share information for food
and drugs between the boys in the street.

Ceci: Adan, que mas sabes? Adan, what more do you know?

**Adan: Que la mayor, Cynthia, estuvo en escuela cuando
vinieron los soldados para sacar las otras de la casa, y por eso
Cynthia no fue con sus hermanas.** That the oldest, Cynthia, was in
school when the soldiers came to take the other girls away, and for
that Cynthia didn't go to the hospital with the other three.

Ceci: Y que mas? And what else?

**Adan: Yo se que el papa, Carlos y la mama siempre peleaban
como gallos... y que el casi morio con tristeza cuando las ninas
fueron sacadas con fuerza... y por eso fue a buscar drogas sin
dinero.** I know that the father, Carlos, and the mother always fought
like roosters... and that he almost died of sadness when the girls were
taken away by force. And for that he went to look for drugs without
any money.

Ceci: Y por eso le mataron? And for that he was killed?

**Adan: Si, yo lo vi... el debia demasiado dinero. No fue un mal
hombre... Fue perdido, sin trabajo...** Yes, and I saw it. He owed
too much money. He wasn't a bad guy... just lost, without work.

Ceci: Como ud? Like you?

Adan: Ademas, ella fue con otro hombre, bien rapido... Ella es una puta te digo. And she went right away with another guy. She is a whore I tell you.

Ceci: Oy Adan...... Yo se que pobreza es el problema. Oy Adan. *pause* I know that poverty is the problem.

Adan: Gringa... Mujeres Latinas no pueden vivir sin un hombre. Gringa… Latina women can't live without a man.

Ceci: Adan, llama me Cecilia por favor. Sabes que estoy buscando la madre ahora para hablar de custodia. Adan, call me Cecilia please. Do you know that I am now looking for the girls' mother to talk about custody?

Adan: Tu pierdes su tiempo buscando ella... Mi madre ya no mas tiene nada legal conmigo. You waste your time looking for her. My mother no longer has any legal connection to me.

Ceci: No entiendo. I don't understand.

Adan: Soy abandonado.... como las ninas. Cuando sus ninas fueron inscritas en la IHNFA a causa de abuso y malnutrition, la familia ya no mas tiene custodia, y el gobierno de Honduras se convierte en el dueno oficial. Entiende? Yo no se cual es peor. I am abandoned, like the girls. When kids are registered in the IHNFA because of abuse and malnutrition, they are no longer the legal property of the family, and the Honduran government takes over officially. Get it? I don't know which is worse.

Ceci: Si. *Ceci gets it and is visibly frustrated.*

Adan: Entonces... Piensas tu Cecilia, que yo, Adan Maldonado, quiero ser la propriedad de este gobierno corrupto? No senora! Nadie es mi dueno! Therefore, Cecilia… do you think that I, Adan Maldonado, want to be the property of this corrupt government? No senora! Nobody owns me!

Ceci: Ok, Adan....

The bus comes to a stop in Tocoa... another run down, third world bus station. They change buses. The place buzzes with independent merchants. Local girls come on board selling baleadas, fruit, candy, etc. ... Ceci buys two baleadas (tortillas folded in half around beans, cheese, chicken, whatever), a bag of mangos, and a drink for Adan. Adan smiles and eats vigorously.

Ceci: Vamos estar claro Adan… Esta comida es mejor que resistol, verdad? Let's be clear about this Adan. Good food is better than resistol, right?

Adan: Si Senora….

Ceci: Cuanto mas tiempo? Estamos lejos? How much more time? Are we far?

Adan: Una hora… y despues caminando otra hora para subir la montana y yo no dormi a noche. *He yawns.* Another hour And after, we walk another hour up the mountain and no sleep last night.

Ceci: Ven descansar. Come rest.

Adan puts his head on Ceci's shoulder… A lady next to them on the bus nudges Ceci when he falls asleep.

Woman: Yo vivo cerca la familia de este chico. Conozco la mama, se llama Gloria. I live near the family of this boy. I know his mother, Gloria.

Ceci: Y que paso? El vive en la calle en Ceiba ahora. What happened? He is living in the Ceiba streets now.

Woman: Su papa fue un taxista. El tuvo hijos con novias en todas las partes de Tocoa. His father was a taxi man. He had children with girlfriends all over Tocoa.

Ceci: What?

Woman: Por fin la madre le boto de la casa. Pero ella no pudo vivir sola. Adan peleaba con todos los novios hasta que el salio por fin el ano passado. El ultimo novio le ataro en su cama para que el no pudiera salir… como un perro…. Y por fin el se escapo para Ceiba. Finally, the mother threw him out of the house. But she couldn't live alone. Adan fought with all her boyfriends, until he finally left last year. The last boyfriend tied him to the bed so he wouldn't leave….. Like a prisoner, and finally, he left for Ceiba.

Ceci: Dios mio… y la mama?

Woman: **Gloria?... Ella todavia llora por Adan.** She still cries for Adan.

Ceci: **Y todavia ella se queda con el mismo hombre?** And she is still with the same guy?

Woman: **Si, porque el trabaja. El compra la comida.** Yes, because he works. He buys the food.

Ceci: **Pues, es interesante como la pobreza y la desesperacion de supervivencia mata la dignidad. ...** Wow, It is interesting how poverty and the desperation of survival kills dignity.

Woman: **Mira senora ... Yo viajo una hora cada dia para trabajar en Tocoa. Vivimos sin luz, con solamente la comida diario en mi mano para mis hijos. Es una lucha gringa... Dia por dia... Si Dios quiere, comemos.** Look Lady. I travel one hour every day to work in Tocoa. We live without electricity, with only the daily food in my hands for my kids. It's a struggle gringa. Day by day. God willing, we eat.

Ceci: **Todavia... todos los ninos son inocentes en el principio.** Still, all children are innocent in the beginning.

Woman: **Pero Senora, te digo... Este muchacho es malcriado.. sin Dios... sin reglas...sin morales... con hambre siempre.** But, also I tell you. This boy is badly raised, without God, without rules, without morals, with constant hunger.

Ceci: **Sin amor sincero...** Without sincere love

Woman: **Oh... Senora Gringa... si supieras!** Oh Mrs. Gringa, if you only knew!

56. Hike up the mountain in Tocoa to Adan's family home

Ceci looks out the window and sighs. We pass more and more rural surroundings until the bus comes to a stop and the woman signals Adan to wake up and tells Ceci this is their stop. She grabs her chicken and points Ceci in the direction they must hike towards Adan's home on a dirt road, past jungle, along the river to the thatched palapa hut of Adan's mom, Gloria.

57. Adan's home – Mother and boyfriend

Ceci follows Adan and says goodbye to the woman from the bus. After a long uphill climb on a dirt road lined by adobe houses… we come to Gloria's house. Out front sits a young man wearing suspenders over a white under shirt, with a bandana around his head…. drinking a Salva Vida beer. As Ceci and Adan approach, a woman comes to the door with a pot and a rag in her hand.

She sees Adan and drops the pot screaming as she runs to embrace Adan. They look alike… Clearly Mom misses Adan. He is smiling and she is crying. The man on the porch continues to sit and finish his beer, tilted back on his chair. Ceci introduces herself.

Ceci: Hola Sra… Yo soy Cecilia Diaz, una amiga de Adan. Hello Mam, I am Cecilia Diaz, Adan's friend.

The mom holds Adan close to her heart.

Adan: Mi madre se llama Gloria… My mother's name is Gloria.

Hombre: Y yo soy Enrique – hombre de la casa. And I am Enrique, man of the house.

Gloria: Si Sra Cecilia, gracias.. Dios te bendiga por traerme mi hijo… Chico …donde has estado por tanto tiempo? Yes Senora Cecilia, thank you. God bless you for bringing me my child… Boy where have you been for so long?

Enrique: En la calle como un perro. In the street like a dog.

Gloria: Basta Enrique!! Enough Enrique!

Ceci: Gloria… Yo le traje aqui porque creo que este muchacho debe de vivir con su familia. Gloria, I brought him here because I think this boy should be living with his family.

Gloria: Es porque la casa es demasiado pequena para tres. It's because the house is too small for three people.

Adan: Demasiado pequena para ud Enrique!. Too small for you Enrique!

Ceci: Gloria, Adan es su hijo verdad? Gloria, Adan is your son right?

Gloria: Claro!

Adan: Digale a ella ... entonces Mama? Diga la senora que hizo el con mis manos y mis pies!! Tell her ... come on Mama. Tell her what he did with my hands and feet!

Enrique: Fuiste como un tigre! You were like a tiger!

Adan: Un tigre atarado en captividad! A tiger tied up in captivity!

Enrique: Sin disciplina... Without discipline!

Adan: Abusador!

Gloria: Basta!...por favor!!

Ceci: Sra... Ud. es la mama de este muchacho. El tiene solamente once anos. Senora, you are the mother of this boy. He is only eleven years old.

Adan: Me perdiste mama... You lost me mom.

Gloria: *crying* **Y todavia te amo mi hijo!** And I still love you my son!

Enrique: Y yo pago la renta. *He grabs Gloria by the waist.* And I pay the rent.

Ceci: Pues... yo creo que Adan tiene el derecho de vivir aqui con su mama como el todavia es menor de edad. I believe that Adan has the right to live here with his mother especially since he is still a minor.

Enrique: Este muchacho prefiere vivir libre en la calle con las drogas y los otros joven mareros. This boy prefers to live freely in the street with drugs and the other young gang boys.

Gloria: Adan, ven a banar en el rio... Comeremos pescado frito esta noche, como te gusta. Adan, come bath in the river. We will eat fried fish tonight the way you like it.

Adan: Y invitamos a mi amiga? Can we invite my friend?

Gloria: Si ...claro.

Enrique: *Showing Ceci a beat up plastic chair...* **Si sientete... Te invito a tomar una cerveza.** Yes sit down. I invite you for a beer.

Ceci: No gracias… Necesito volver a Ceiba esta noche… Debo de salir ahora… Deme un abrazo Adan…Espero que todos pueden resolver sus diferencias para vivir en paz como una familia. No quiero verte en la calle mas Adan. No thank you. I need to return to Ceiba tonight. I should leave now. Give me a hug Adan. I hope that you can resolve your differences to live in peace like a family. I don't want to see you in the street anymore Adan.

Adan: Gracias Sra. Cecilia. Ella cree en milagros. Thank you Cecilia. She believes in miracles.

Ceci: Si creo en lo que debe y podria de ser posible… Buena suerte Adan… Yes, I believe in what should and could be possible. Good luck Adan.

58. Ceci leaves Adan's home in Tocoa

Ceci hands 100 lempiras to Gloria, hugs Adan, and turns around to make her way back down the mountain to the bus stop. Adan goes to the river to bathe while Gloria cleans the fish and sings.

Enrique throws wood on the fire… Ceci turns around to see Enrique drinking his beer, staring at her as she walks down the hill.

59. Bus ride back to La Ceiba – Musical Montage of landscape

The return to Ceiba is a montage of the agricultural landscape that the bus passes. In and out of flat lands of pineapple, bananas, palm oil, and coffee beans… spotted with small, humble towns teaming with market life on the bus route. Young children rush on to the bus during their brief bus stops trying to sell goods to passengers.

60. Hotel Bar – Ceci arrives in La Ceiba

It's late when Ceci returns to the hotel in the dark, exhausted from the day's journey. She stops in the hotel bar for a drink before she goes to her room. The bartender greets Ceci as she climbs up on the bar stool.

Bartender: Hola Gringa Cecilia… como le fue su dia? Que quiere tomar? Hello gringa, how ws your day? What do you want to drink?

Ceci: Hello Jorge. Deme una bebida dulce y tropical por favor. Give me a sweet tropical drink please.

Bartender: Mi "Ceiba libre", es la bebida de la casa… con ron, guiffity, pina, y coco OK? My Ceiba libre is the drink of the house with rum, guiffity, pineapple and coconut juice,

Ceci: Perfecto…

Bartender: Entonces, gringa, cuenteme todo? So gringa, Tell me everything. *He is fixing a beautiful drink.*

Ceci: OK.. Entonces… yo vuelvo ahora de Tocoa donde fui con un muchacho de la calle para reunirle con su familia… Well, I am arriving now from Tocoa where I went with a street boy to unite him with his family.

Bartender: Como se llama el? What's his name?

Ceci: Adan… 11 anos… flaco. Adan, ll years old, skinny.

Bartender: Tiene un sicatriz de un tiro en su pierna? Does he have a scar from a bullet on his leg?

Ceci: Fue un tiro? That was from a bullet? *She sips the drink.* **You mean he was shot? I may need two of these.**

Bartender: Si le conozco. Y le digo…manana… este mismo muchacho, Adan, va estar en la plaza pidiendo en frente del hotel, y dormiendo en el parque de nuevo. Yes I know him. I am telling you that tomorrow, this same boy, Adan, will be in the plaza begging in front of the hotel and sleeping in the park again.

Ceci: No le creo eso senor. I don't believe that Senor. **Ooooh! That guiffity is psychedelic! His mother loves him.**

Bartender: Si guiffity es real… Y tambien son mis consejos. Y voy hablar Englais contigo gringa. Yes guiffity is real, and so is my advice. And I will speak English with you gringa Cecilia. **And those girls that you want to adopt… They are the property of the IHNFA, our most corrupt government agency. Forget it. You**

are breaking your own heart and theirs for nothing. For what? The drama? A few heroic moments with them, with this Adan? Gringa…. Us Hondurans… we are used to suffering… Don't make it harder than it has to be. Eventually you will give up and go back to your golden American streets.

Ceci: Well thank you for that realistic and sobering advice. I will file it with all the other pessimistic advice I get… as I continue to monitor the health and welfare of three innocent little girls BEFORE they are cast into the Ceiba streets.

Bartender: Buena suerte Senora… you will become tired of being the good Samaritan.

Ceci pays the bartender, finishes her Ceiba libre, and gives him a huge tip as she throws him a final comment and smile, and retires from a long, but educational day.

Ceci: May I quote your jaded comments about orphans in my book? Thanks for the Ceiba libre Jorge. See you in church?

61. <u>The SOS Orphanage- 2004 -05 – Casa 9 – Tia Conchita</u>

Left – L to R -Angie, Jazmin, Conchita, Roxana

R to L bottom – Angie, Roxana, Jazmin

We move to the SOS where the girls have taken residence in Casa 9 with Tia Conchita, their house mother. Ceci has come to visit the girls and set up a dance class. David is there photographing them and watching the other kids get to know them. There is Angela, Luz, Norma, Olvin, Blanca, and Juny. The girls are feeling confused as they have recently arrived. Ceci bursts in the door calling their names. She is so happy to see them after waiting for

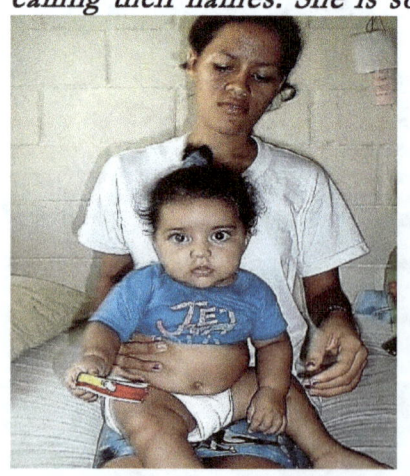

the IHNFA to place them. The girls are overjoyed to see Ceci again. She has gifts for everybody in her suitcase, and drops everything to hug the three little girls. Jazmin is still in a car seat. Angie barely stands, Norma has Jazmin in her arms.

And Roxana wobbles around on skinny legs. The other kids watch in awe as the scene unfolds. Ceci takes each sister on her lap, one at a time, while all the other kids watch vicariously, silently absorbing, reliving the faint memory of motherly love that they recall as Ceci gives attention to these girls.

Conchita: Hola Senora Ceci… Soy Conchita, La Tia de la Casa # 9… Y esta panchita, Angie, estaba llena de bitchos antes que le di la medicina…. y chica, le juro cuando te digo que salieron como 20 gusanos asi en sus panales. Mira!! Hi Ceci.. I am Conchita, the Tia from House #9… and this little pancha (stomach), Angie was full of parasites before I gave her the medicine. And I swear when I tell you that 20 huge white worms came out in her diapers… Look I will show you!!

Out back she takes Ceci to see all the white six inch worms crawling in the dirt outside.

Ceci: Dios Mio!!! Como pudo ella vivir con gusanos en su cuerpo? Entonces, creo que la senora Adila nunca les dio la medicina para los parasitos. Oh my God! How could she live with those things in her body? Then I believe that Adila never gave them the parasite medicine.

Conchita: Claro… Pero ahora, ella esta limpia, y creo que va a caminar en poco. Obviously, but now she is clean, and she will walk soon.

Ceci: *Taking Angie in her arms and standing her up.* **Really?? Do you think you can walk today baby? Angie, vas a caminar hoy? Poco a poco mi amor**

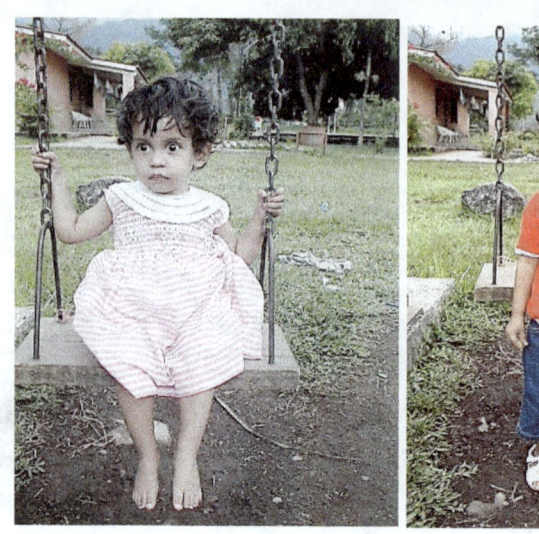
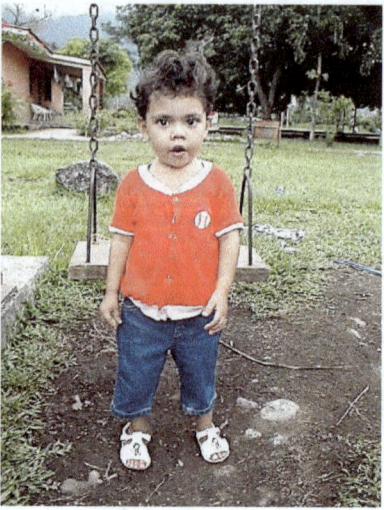

Angie   Roxana

Ceci cuddles Angie while the others watch.

Conchita: Y tu sabes… que…hay algo malo con sus ojos. Creo que ella es completamente ciego en la derecha, y la izquirda es torcido. And you know that there is something wrong with her eyes. I believe she is completely blind in right eye and the left is also off center.

Ceci: Si … yo se… aqui con el golpe…. Oh my God, gracias Conchita. I will take her to the eye doctor. Yo le traere al doctor de ojos para ver que es el problema. Pobrecita…. Yes I know, here with the wound, I will bring her to the doctor… poor thing.

Roxana is pulling at Ceci and trying to talk, as she just grunts.

Ceci: Roxana como estas mi amor… Oigame.. Un dia hablaras y yo te ensenare Englais. I have a doll for you. Roxana how are you my love? Listen, one day you will speak and I will teach you English. I have a doll for you.

Ceci gives the girls their own dolls, and little presents for the other kids…. Make up for the older girls, socks for Olvin…and she has an interesting pacifier for Jazmin who is reaching out for her anxiously.

Ceci: Oh mi bambina Jazmin, Como te amo bella. Oh my baby Jazmin... how I love you bella. *Jazmin has a smile that can melt snow, and she lights up on Ceci's lap with her new doll.*

David enters the house after taking pictures of the kids outside.

David: Hello Miss Ceci. Como estas?

Ceci: Oh I am happy to see the girls in such good hands. Thank you for helping engineer this David. I love these guys so much. I just want to squeeze them forever. Y me alegre conocer sus hermanos aqui en casa 9 con Mami Conchita. And I am happy to know your brothers and sisters in House #9 with Tia Conchita.

Conchita: Aqui tenemos Olvin... con todas sus "hermanas" Norma, y Luz, y Angeles, y Blanca y tambien Juny. Here we have Olvin, with all his sisters. Olvin and Norma are teenage syblings; Luz and Angeles are young twins, sisters of Blanca; and adolescent Juny.

Ceci: Mucho gusto, ... Diganme... Hay bailarinas aqui? Quiero saber! Busco bailarinas del SOS. Vamos a practicar con pasos hoy. Necesito sus ideas. Nice to meet you. Tell me, are there dancers here. I want to know. I am looking for SOS dancers. We will practice today and make a dance. I need your ideas.

They shyly laugh in their self conscious adolescent way.

Conchita: Ellos van a participar... Deles tiempo.... Son timidos al principio. They will participate. Give them time. They are timid at first.

David: I know Ceci! What about the baptism day when we have the festival after the church services? You could do a little dance number there maybe. We can invite investors to that perfect, authentic, fundraising event. And you could baptize the girls and be their madrina.

Ceci: OK... We'll see how it goes.... I don't know much about raising money. I guess I will be extending my stay in La Ceiba. And yes I love the idea of adopting the girls formally.

David: Money is what sustains the orphanages.

They walk towards an open field with trees.

Ceci: I also have to tell you about a summons a got this morning from Sra. Adila, saying that I threatened her with a deadly weapon, and I have no idea where she got that idea. So I have to go to court for the first time in my life.

David: You caught her red handed and she lost her job... this is the hidden Latina revenge lie for exposing her sins. You will have to ride this one out. The lawyers do it all. She will probably not even show up, and you will not be allowed to face a judge. It is all done behind closed doors with a lawyer, a district attorney, and a judge.

Ceci: Oh my God, where am I?... in the middle ages? I'm supposed to overlook the abuse of innocent children?

David: In Honduras .. you re guilty until proven innocent. And the law is not designed for anybody but the accusers. I suggest you get in there early with your case. If there is any chance at all at getting custody of those girls, you will need to clear this.

Ceci: Well, just one more reason to stay in Honduras. I can see that this rope is full of knots. I hope you know that I would never threaten anybody with a knife... much less touch a weapon of any kind.

David: Like I said... Adila is inventing this for revenge. You have formally exposed her history of abusing orphans for years. It takes a sacrificial lamb to make things right some times. I am sorry. Just know that you cannot trust anybody, no matter how generous you are.

Ceci: OK... moving on... What about the baptisms? I really think that is important. Will you be their Godfather?

David: You know how many kids I have baptized? I will do it gladly, but don't expect a vigilant Godfather? I am overloaded as it is. And you can't even trust me with that role. But I will do it.

Ceci: Just get them to the church on time, and I will get the dresses and the props together. This I know is important for some reason. And I will put together a dance performance for the event, as promised.

David: Yes, I think Godmother status will help you. But, you really need a lawyer who can help you with this Adila problem, and maybe the custody of the girls. It will not be fast and easy, but you should begin with that, and then the IHNFA lady is the one to see where you can go with custody.

Ceci: Thanks David... It all makes me cross eyed... So ... I want to start the dancing. Do you have a big room with a door, which would cut down on escape and diversion?

David: Right now you can work under the pavilion, but there is an old Kinder room which is full of boxes we could empty.

Ceci: Open spaces are not the best for dance class, because the kids get distracted... I would like to clean that room out eventually... if you are up for that. And I can help rip through, consolidate, and throw away like a pro when I see unused space.

David: Let me see what I can do about that.

Conchita: *Entering on phone with boyfriend/arguing in Spanish.* Te llamo mas tarde, Antonio. Tengo que trabajar. Voy a decidir hoy, te juro , mi amor. Mas tarde OK? I will call you later, Antonio. I have to work. I will decide today I swear my love. Later, Ok? *She hangs up cell phone.* Hola Ceci, David, como estan?

David: Hola Conchita... como esta el novio? Hello Conchita.. How is the boyfriend?

Conchita: Aay David... Es complicada. Oy David, It is complicated. *Wiping tears from her eyes.*

129

David: **Pues, me voy a arreglar un estudio de danza.** I will begin to clean out the room next to the nursery for you. That's where you can dance. Give me an hour.

Ceci: Perfect. I'll meet you there, with the girls.

David leaves, Ceci sees that Conchita is not feeling right/

Ceci: **Que pasa contigo Conchita? Venga, sientate!! Estan tomando una siesta, las ninas?** What's wrong Conchita? Come sit. Are the girls sleeping?

Conchita: **Si, estan dormiendo....y estan muy bien... despues de acostumbrarse con los otros hermanos ... estan feliz...** Yes they are napping, and they are well... after getting accustomed to the other kids... they are happy.

Ceci: **Me alegre oir eso, para saber que estan en buenas manos.... Y que mas Conchita?** I am happy to hear that, to know that they are in good hands. And what else Conchita?

Conchita: *She sits across from Ceci on the sofa...* **Pues, tengo que hacer decisiones importantes hoy.** Well, I have to make important decisions today.

Ceci: **Como que?** Like what?

Conchita: **Tengo un novio por muchos anos, que vive cerca mis padres en mi pueblo en el sur de Honduras. El esta esperandome salir de aqui para casarnos.** I have had a boyfriend for many years who lives near my parents in my village in the south. He is waiting for me to leave here and get married.

Ceci: **Y que quieres tu?** And what do you want?

Conchita: **Mira, tengo nueve anos aqui en el SOS, como madre para bastante ninos. Es mi familia, mi trabajo... Las Tias son mis hermanas. Vivo aqui.. Pero amo a mi novio tambien. No se que hacer.** Look, I have been in the SOS for 9 years, like a mother for many kids. It is my family, my work. The Tias are my sisters. I live here. But I love my boyfriend too. I don't know what to do.

Ceci: **This is a turning point in your life, Conchita. Entonces, que piensa de su futuro como mujer, madre, esposa, etc?** Don't

do what I did …. You can ignore this issue for only so long…..
**No quiere su proprio familia? No vas a conseguir amor en el
SOS, ni en el mercado en Ceiba!! Cuantos anos tienes ahorita?**
So what are you thinking about your future as a woman, a mother, a
wife? Don't you want your own family. You are not going to find love
at the SOS nor en the Ceiba Market. How old are you now?

**Conchita: Tengo 33, y vivo dia por dia con corazon para estos
muchachos.** I am 33 and I live day to day with my heart for these
children.

Ceci: Oy chica! Vamos hacer sus cartas. Let's read your cards.

62. **Behind Casa # 9 – Under a coconut tree with Conchita – Musical
    Tarot Divination number**

*Ceci pulls out a tarot deck from her purse, and indicates that they
should go to an area more private under a palm tree behind the
house, sets up a table and two chairs, lights a candle, smudges,
starts to shuffle the cards… and prays to her Venezuelan spirits.*

**Ceci: En el nombre de Dios poderoso. Con el permiso del padre,
hijo y espirito santo, y la Santa Madre Maria… yo pido permiso de
mis protectors…de Venezuela… La Reina Maria Lionza, El
Libertador de los esclavos, el Negro Felipe, el Gran Cacique
Guacaipuro, y mi protector personal, el Gran Cacique Tamanaco…
Quiero abrir la puerta de consejos en este momento por su aviso y
sabiduria… para esta mujer, Conchita Alvarez, con su situacion en
el servicio de Dios con estes ninos del SOS, y su destino como
esposa y madre. Con su corazon pido el consejo de Espiritu con sus
mensages en estas cartas. Gracias…** In the name of God all powerful.
With the permission of the father, the son and the holy ghost and the
holy mother Mary, I ask permission from my Venezuelan protectors, the
queen Maria Lionza, the liberator of the slaves, el Negro Felipe, and the
great chief, Guacaipuro, and my personal protector, the great chief
Tamanaco. I want to open the door of consultancy in this moment for
the advice and knowledge for this woman Conchita Alvarez, with her
situation in service of God with these children from the SOS, and her
personal destiny as a wife and mother. With her heart I ask for your advice
with the messages in these cards. Thank you.

63. **DREAM DANCE SEQUENCE** – Conchita/ future husband/ other woman - Ballet Trio

This interaction with the tarot session as Ceci reads the cards, becomes a silent ballet-drama, fantasy sequence, which Ceci describes verbally to Conchita as it plays out in a blue light ballet. We see Conchita dancing with all her children, as a man watches on a nearby hill. There are intermittent rendezvous, but she must always return to the kids, whom she dearly loves like a Mom. Finaly, the man makes an ultimatum. There lingers another woman in the background, ready to replace Conchita, if she does not comply. The man, loves Conchita dearly, but wants to make a family. He has waited 9 years. At the end of the reading/dance-drama, Conchita gets up and dances with the man,,, leaving the orphanage children. It is poetically romantic and tragic as the children say goodbye.

64. **Return to the Coconut Tree – Casa 9**

Conchita opens her eyes and takes Ceci's hands.

Conchita: Thank you, Gracias, Ceci por ayudarme con este problema. Lo veo ahora. Es doloroso decider. Sin embargo, quiero mi propria familia feliz. Antonio me ama y voy a casar con el. Hay que salir del SOS y sera dificil porque me siento como estos muchachos son mios. Pero necesito pensar de mi futuro y mi familia que estara en el otro lado del pais. Gracias por ayudarme a verlo. Espero que puedo hacerlo. Thank you for helping me with this problem. I see it now. It is painful to choose. I want to make an example of a good family. Antonio loves me, and I must marry him. I must leave the SOS difficult as this will be, as I feel like these are my children… But I have to think of my family. Thank you for helping me see this. I just hope I can do it.

Ceci: A veces, lo que se ofrece el universo es un pedazo de oro, que no puedes ver. Conchita, tu siempre seras la Madre de estos muchchos. Tu les criaste… eso no cambia, y siempre ellos van a buscarte como mama, no importa donde vives. Sometimes the universe offers you a piece of gold that you cannot see. Conchita,

you will always be the mother of these children. You raised them… that doesn't change, and they will always look at you like a mother, no matter where you live.

Conchita: Tiene razon hermana…. Hablare con Don Olman hoy. You are right sister. I will speak with Olman today.

The girls have awakened and are approaching Ceci and Conchita, so excited to see Ceci again. They return to Casa 9.

65. **RETURN TO INTERIOR – Casa 9**

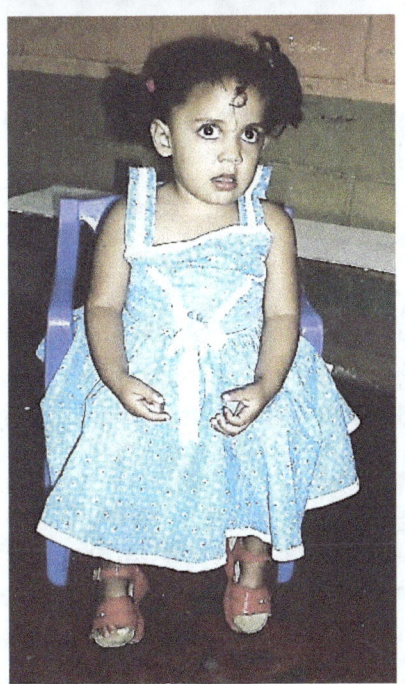

Angie

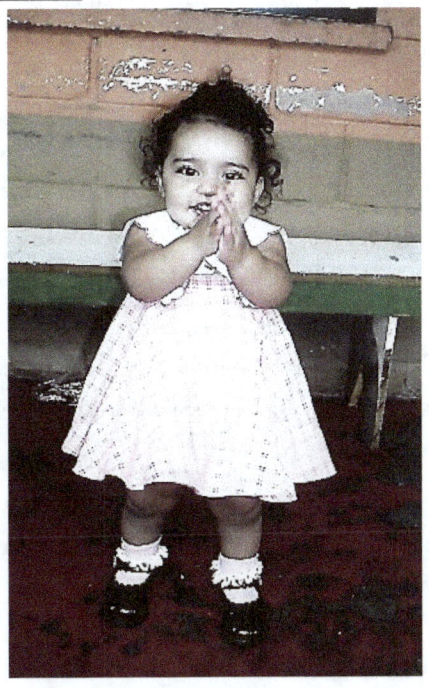

Jazmin

The light shifts, and we are back to reality as Vilma arrives by taxi to help and calls Ceci from Casa 9. Conchita and Ceci greet Vilma and walk back into the house.

Vilma: Ceci, mira lo que consegui para el baptismo de las ninas!! Ceci, look what I found for the girls' baptism!

She pulls out three frilly white children's dresses from a used shopping bag for the upcoming baptism.

Ceci: Vilma, they are beautiful, and I bet they will fit perfectamente. The kids just woke up from their naps, maybe we can try them on before class. Roxana Pueden probarlos? Can they try them on?

Conchita: Vayan ayudarles chicas. Go help them chicas.

The other kids, Norma , Juny, and Blanca take the dresses to put on the 3 sisters.

Vilma: Ceci ... tengo noticias que el papa de las ninas morio la semana pasada. Ceci, I have news that the girls' father died last week. *She has a newspaper.*

Ceci: Que dijiste?

Vilma: Carlos Iraheta Alvarez...Aqui esta en el periodico. En Barrio Inglais. Que alguien le golpio la semana pasada con una piedra en la cabeza... por una problema con drogas. Carlos Iraheta Alvarez... Here in the newspaper. In Barrio Inglais...That someone hit him with a rock on the head last week.

Ceci: Dios mio!!! Como dijo el muchacho. Adan was right. Como supiste que es el papa de las ninas? Oh my God, just like the boy said. Adan was right. How did you know that it was their father?

Vilma: Porque yo vi la mama de las ninas en la calle de San Judas. Se llama Karla, y ella vive con la familia de Carlos. Ayer yo realize la conexion con las ninas... como mi barrio, Las Mercedes queda al lado de San Judas. Yo recuerdo el papa del autobus... Siempre el estaba sentado atras sin destinacion. perdido. Y ahora muerto...O Ceci... No hay trabajo para los hombres... ni para nadie!! Because I saw their mother in the street in San Judas. Her name is Karla, and she lives with Carlos's family. Yesterday I realized the connectin with the girls, because my neighborhood, Las Mercedes, is right next to San Judas. I remember the father from the bus. He was always seated in the back lost, without a destination. And now he is dead. There's no work for these men… nor for anybody!!!

Jazmin, Angie and Roxana are silently listening, although they don't understand.

Ceci: Increible!!! Era joven yo imagino. Incredible! He was really young I imagine.

Vilma: Si Ceci…. La Ceiba es un pueblo pequeno. Yo se donde vivian las ninas, y donde esta la mama. Quiere que te enseno? Yes Ceci. Ceiba is a small town. I know where the girls were living and where the mother is. Do you want me to show you?

Ceci: No lo creo!!! Wow!!! OK… Hay que visitarle. David esta areglando un taller de danza, y voy a ensenar una clase de danza para preparar danzas para el Baptismo. Hay que visitar manana si puedes. Hoy no puedo. Pero… Gracias Vilma, por comprar tan bellas vestidas!!! I just don't believe it. Wow! OK I must visit her. So Vilma, David is arranging a dance studio and I am going to teach a dance class and prepare dances for the Baptism. We must visit tomorrow if you can. Today I can't. But Thank you Vilma, for buying such beautiful baptism dresses.

Vilma: OK… Vamos manana. Let's go tomorrow.
Norma and Juny enter holding hands with Roxana and Jazmin who wobble over to Ceci in their beautiful white dresses.
Mira, que bonita son las ninas Sra. Ceci. Look how beautiful the girls are Sra. Ceci.

Angie suddenly comes through the door walking for the first time… wearing her new white dress with a big smile on her face. All the other girls from casa #9 are excited for her, following her out of the room. She is giggling as she walks, and suddenly falls. Ceci runs to pick her up.

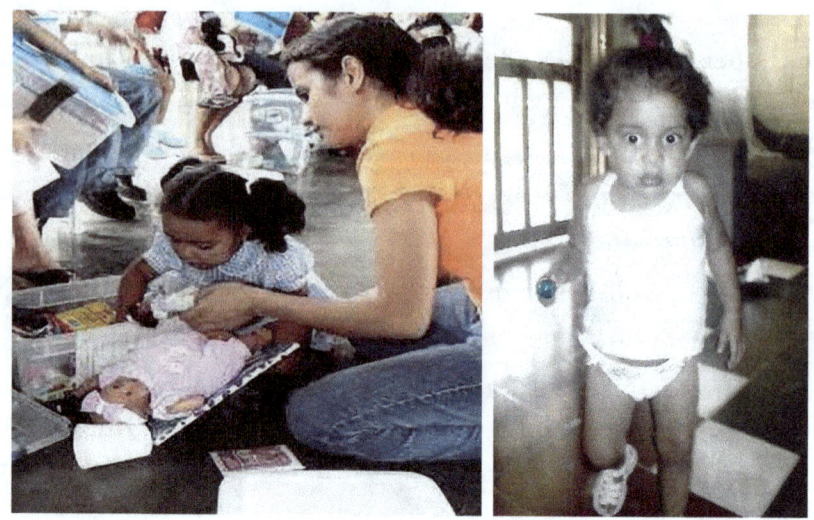

Jazmin, Blanca,   Angie's first steps

Ceci: Oh my God… Like little angels!!! Donde esta Angie? This is a miracle, look at this… Baby Angie can walk finally. *She picks her up and squeezes her when she to cry.* **I just can't believe it. I'm so happy. Puedes caminar!**

Angie, Roxana, Jazmin

Angie: No llores Ceci. Don't cry Ceci.

She wipes Ceci's automatic tears away and makes a little wobbly dance step.

Ceci: It was those horrible little worms that were holding you back. I am so happy that you can walk now.

136

Roxana struts over to Ceci to show off her dress. She grunts a little, asking for attention. Conchita is bouncing Jazmin on her lap in her pretty white baptism dress.

Ceci: Y Roxana y Jazmin tambien… que bonitas estan en blanco. You guys are so beautiful!!

Vilma: Y uds. van a poner estos bonitos vestidos para su Baptismo. And you will wear these pretty dresses for your Baptism.

Ceci: Son bien juapas las muchachas!! Ahora, vamos a cambiarnos, y prepararnos para la danza!! Venga conmigo mis ninas bellas!! Quisas Angie va a bailar por la primera vez!!! They are really pretty. Now we are going to change and prepare for the dance class. Come with me my beautiful babies.

Norma, Juny, and Blanca take them back to the little bedroom to change them into dance clothes and shoes. Maybe Angie will dance for the first time.

Jazmin, Roxana, Angie

66. <u>Makeshift Dance Studio – SOS – "Where is Love" from Oliver</u>

The following dance class takes place in the make shift dance studio which is a storage room and has boxes piled up all around the perimeter. Ceci sets up her boom box and sits in her meditational lotus yoga pose and asks everybody to join her. Angie sits in her lap. Roxana sits next to some older girls. Little by little they all sit down and pretend to close their eyes in meditation. Vilma scrambles after Jazmin, who, like Angie, is also just learning to walk... Conchita comes in and joins them. Soon they begin to stretch and go through different yoga moves... the music is calming. Then it shifts into a simple choreography that starts on the floor to "Where is Love" from the musical Oliv music from Oliver

Almost like an emotional release, they follow Ceci's moves in a lament of longing, desire, confusion, and indecision following Ceci. Near the end Ceci runs to embrace the girls for their beautiful dance. Angie, Jazmin, and Roxana are also trying to imitate the dance. Angie and Jazmin keep falling down, but Ceci and Vilma keep picking them up. They stay by Ceci. When it is time to leave, Ceci returns the girls to Casa 9. They still want to dance their Ring Around the Rosie, but Ceci and Vilma have to leave. This is always really difficult. The other kids try to distract them while they run out the back, but the girls see her and run to catch up with her. They walk her to her car, asking if they can come with her. Ceci bends down to their height and hugs each one of them telling them that she will return tomorrow. They cry, and don't understand why she is always leaving them. Finally, Ceci and Vilma driveaway, and as she pulls out of the gate, she looks into the rear-view mirror, and sees the girls crying and reaching out. She burst into tears and drives away. This image becomes a recurring struggle for Ceci.

Ceci & Angie

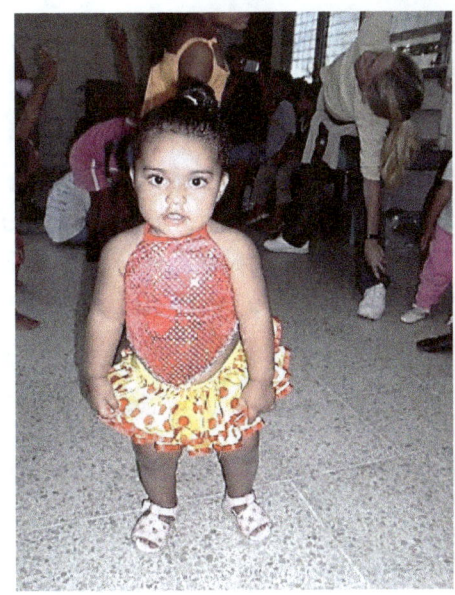

Jazmin

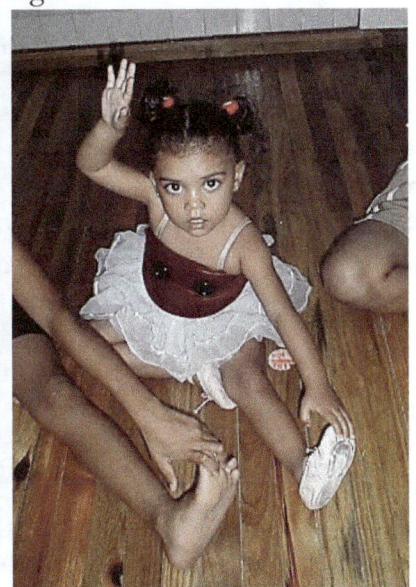

Roxana

67. <u>Next Day – Courthouse, La Ceiba – with Lucia Urbizo – lawyer</u>

Ceci enters with female lawyer, Lucia Urbizo, to respond to Adila's false accusation that she assaulted her with a dagger. The accused is not allowed in the closed courtroom, where Ceci's lawyer goes with a District Attorney and a local Judge in a back room to determine Ceci's fate as a criminal offender. She gives her oath of honesty over the bible, and waits while the verdict is hashed out behind closed doors between lawyers and judges. In Honduras you are guilty until proven innocent and have no part in the trial. Adila isn't even there. She has left the country. Ceci bows her head closing her eyes.... The lawyer returns after almost an hour.

Lawyer Lucia Urbizo: I have good news. You have been admonished of all criminal intent as Adila has left the country, and has obviously invented lies to take vengeance upon you for losing her job as an orphanage house mother. There have been numerous complaints about her abuse, and she has rightfully been terminated. Our concern at this time, was to cleanse your name of any wrong doing in the matter of the children. The children will continue to stay in the SOS, where they are protected by Honduran law. Let's talk in the cab.

Ceci is relieved and confused at the same time.

68. Ceci and Lawyer return to town in a taxi together

As they talk in the taxi, we are aware of the mix between the first and the third world, as we pass mule drawn fruit wagons, alongside modern SUVs; people on bicycles; vendors by the road; drunks; mothers with kids, old ladies carrying fire wood on their heads.

Lawyer Urbizo: Tuviste suerte esta vez Cecilia. You were lucky this time Cecilia.

Ceci: Thank you, Lucia, for fixing this. I am not used to revenge politics.

Lawyer: Welcome to Honduras and the lies of desperation.

Ceci: Por favor escuchame, Lucia.... I know I am too old to adopt... but I am not too old to take care of them, and give them a much better life than the orphanage can offer. There has to be a pathway here somewhere.

Lawyer Urbizo: Well... Good luck, and keep moving forward with this. I will support you in whatever way I can. The IHNFA is going through so many changes with these corruption allegations, along with the growing number of street children, the drugs, the crime… It is a cancer in our society that needs a miracle cure. Adoption is impossible now.

Ceci: You know I wish there was a way to harness the potential of all these kids. There has to be an overall solution for their welfare. But at the moment God has put these three girls in my path and I have to focus on them.

Lawyer: The SOS is the best possible place for them.

Ceci: I know. But now I'm going to go to the Casa de Ninos to see about helping there.

Lawyer: Just to prepare you… If the SOS is a 4 star orphanage, the Casa de Ninos has no stars at all. I don't know why you engage in these hopeless affairs.

Ceci: I just have to do something about suffering if I can. I can't ignore it.

Lawyer: You need to understand the tragic role that poverty has played in the lives of Honduran children. With a better economy, parenting, and education these street kids could have a life, instead of being unwanted.

Ceci: Seems like the only future women have in Honduras is to make babies.

Lawyer: Ceci, Hondurans love their children. They want only the best for them. I want you to realize that the intention to care for the youth of this country has always been there. But the economic and political failures have put family survival at the low end of priority in these days.

Ceci: It is the lower class who suffers because of mismanagement and corruption around the selfish greed of those in power. I can only help whom I can see.

Lawyer: Good luck with the girls Ceci

Ceci: Thanks again… I appreciate your help for taking one more obstacle out of my path. *Ceci writes her a check.*

69. <u>Montage of Street Kids</u> –
As Ceci walks home through the streets of La Ceiba that evening, she begins to realize the extent of the homeless, misdirected youth barely surviving in the streets. They are mostly boys. This collage of images is accompanied again by Ceci's voice reading the 2nd half <u>of the Declaration of Honduran Children's rights.</u>

Principle 6 - The child, for the full and harmonious development of his personality, needs love and understanding.

He shall, wherever possible, grow up in the care and under the responsibility of his parents, and, in any case in an atmosphere of affection and of moral and material security; a child of tender years shall not, save in exceptional circumstances, be separated from his mother. Society and the public authorities shall have the duty to extend particular care to children without a family and to those without adequate means of support. Payment of State and other assistance towards the maintenance of children of large families is desirable.

Principle 7 - The child is entitled to receive education, which shall be free and compulsory, at least in the elementary stages. He shall be given an education which will promote his general culture and enable him, on a basis of equal opportunity, to develop his abilities, his individual judgement, and his sense of moral and social responsibility, and to become a useful member of society. The best interests of the child shall be the guiding principle of those responsible for his education and guidance; that responsibility lies in the first place with his parents.

The child shall have full opportunity for play and recreation, which should be directed to the same purposes as education; society and the public authorities shall endeavor to promote the enjoyment of this right.

Principle 8 - The child shall in all circumstances be among the first to receive protection and relief.

Principle 9 - The child shall be protected against all forms of neglect, cruelty and exploitation. He shall not be the subject of traffic, in any form.

The child shall not be admitted to employment before an appropriate minimum age; he shall in no case be caused or permitted to engage in any occupation or employment which would prejudice his health or education, or interfere with his physical, mental or moral development.

Principle 10 - The child shall be protected from practices which may foster racial, religious and any other form of discrimination. He shall be brought up in a spirit of understanding, tolerance, friendship among peoples, peace and universal brotherhood, and in full consciousness that his energy and talents should be devoted to the service of his fellow men.

http://hrlibrary.umn.edu/instree/k1drc.htm#:~:text=Every%20 child%2C%20without%20any%20exception,himself%20or%20 of%20his%20family.

70. The Casa de Ninos – Barrio Inglais

This voiceover segues into the next day as Ceci arrives in a taxi at the Casa de Ninos in Barrio Inglais down by the ocean. She has her boom box, a roll of paper and a big box of markers. She walks in unannounced to a rundown cinder block building exploding with the echoing noise of boy's voices. She is greeted by the cook and asks if she can speak to the Director. He greets her with a big smile, and the boys surround her like flies on honey. The Director appears.

Director: Hola Senora. Como puedo servirle? Hello Senora. How can I help you?

Ceci: Pues actualmente yo quiero servirles a uds. Me llamo Cecilia Diaz.. Soy una coreografa y estoy en La Ceiba por algun tiempo para ensenar en la Escuela Mazapan y para averiguar y escribir sobre la cultura y danza Hondurena… Cuando yo vi la situacion de huerfanos aquí, mi punto de vista cambio. Quiero ayudar. Entonces estoy disponible ofrecerles clases de yoga, danza, y arte si quieres. Y estoy libre hoy y soy una profesora… y pues… I just wanna help you. Well actually I want to help you. My name is Cecilia Diaz. I am a choreographer and I am in La Ceiba for some time to teach at the Mazapan School and to research and write about Honduran culture and dance. When I saw the orphan situation here my point of view changed. I want to help. So I am available to offer you yoga, dance, and art classes if you want. And I am free today and I am a teacher. And well… I just want to help.

Director: Dios mio… Ud. es un regalo de los cielos… Seguramente quieremos su ayuda. Los ninos necesitan mucho mas atencion que podemos darles. My God, you are a gift from heaven. Surely we want your help. The kids need a lot of attention, much more than we can give.

Suddenly all the boys start to enter the room, crowding around Ceci and the Director. With typical orphan curiosity, they are all hugs.

Boys in the Casa de Ninos orphanage -2005

Director: Pues se puede ver la necesidad. So you can see the need.

Ceci: OK and I haven't even done anything yet! *Addressing the boys.* **Hola muchachos como estan?** Hello boys how are you?

Boys: Bien Tia… que vas hacer con el radio? We are good Tia. What will you do with the music machine?

Orphans in institutions tend to call the women workers "Aunt"- "Tia", as if they are family and really care.

Director: Esta senora es una profesora de danza y quiere darles lecciones de yoga y danza. Y me parece que ella esta lista empezar ahora, verdad? This lady is a dance teacher and she wants to give you lessons. And it appears that she is ready to begin now, right?

Ceci: Solamente si quieren… Only if you want.

Boys: Si Queremos!!!! Yes we want!

Director: Bueno, muchachos… muevan las mesas en el comedor por favor, y podemos bailar alla. Ok boys, move the tables in the cafeteria please, and we can dance there.

Ceci: Bueno, vamos chicos. *They all go to work moving tables and sweeping the floor.*

71. <u>Musical Yoga sequence of Casa de Ninos boys</u> –

The following scene begins with everybody seated in the lotus position with their eyes closed and meditation music. This is new for these boys, but they think it is magic... so they follow.

Ceci: OK . Sientense en el piso por favor, y vamos a empezar con yoga. Ok please sit on the floor and we are going to begin with Yoga.

After they settle down, Ceci puts them through lots of simple yoga moves... Then she changes the mood and puts on merengue music and does a few merengue steps with them... They absolutely love it, and the smiles are everywhere.

For a moment Ceci takes her mind off the lost three sisters... and the boys take their minds off of their lost lives and immerse themselves in joyous movement. After that they draw self portraits, or pictures of their mothers. There are many touching moments in this session between Ceci and the obvious need for love in the hearts of these young boys. Conversations about their mothers are dramatic. She becomes more aware of the magnitude of the orphan problem.

72. <u>Plaza in front of Hotel – Vilma sells truck to Ceci</u>

Around 5 pm Ceci arrives at the hotel in a taxi, and as the Taxi pulls away, Vilma and her brother pulls up behind in his funky black pick up truck loaded with run down furniture.

Vilma: Ceci, Mi hermano quiere vender su camioneta barato. Ceci, my brother wants to sell his truck cheap.

Hermano: Si Sra.... Lo vendo ahora mismo para 16,000 Lempiras ($500), si tu puedes entregar estes muebles a nuestra casa de mi Mama en Las Mercedes con Vilma primero. Despues es suyo. Tengo que irme, trabajar... ahora, Funcione bien, y es barato Sra..!! Porfa?

Yes mam, I will sell it now for 16,000 lempiras, if you can deliver this furniture to our mother's house in Las Mercedes with Vilma first. Then it is yours. I have to go to work now. Really cheap Sra. Please?

Ceci: That's about $500 dollars …. I don't know.

Vilma: Ceci… Necesitamos el dinero ahora. Y tu necessitas un caro. Cuanto tienes..? Ceci, we need the money now. And you need a car. How much do you have?

Ceci: *Counting money in her wallet.* **Tengo solamente mils lempiras ahora.** I only have 1000 lempiras ($60) now.

Vilma: Perfecto… Mas tarde vamos al banco para el balance… Firme aqui… el camion es tuyo. Felicidades Ceci… tiene su proprio burro Hondureno… Perfect. Later we can go to the bank for the balance. Sign here and the truck is yours. Congratulations Ceci. You have your own Honduran donkey!! *He gives her the keys.*

Ceci: OK… I hope I'm doing the right thing here.

Hermano: *Taking the L 1000 and giving her the signed form…* **Entonces.. mas tarde nos vemos para el balance de L 15,000, y mas informacion… Pero ahora hay que llevar Vilma arriba con los muelbles, antes que esta oscuro en la calle.** So, later we will see you for the balance of 15,000 lempiras and more info. You must bring Vilma up the mountain now with this furniture, before the street is dark.

Ceci gets in the driver's seat, ready to drive this beat up old black manual drive pick up truck. Vilma's brother takes the money and leaves.

Ceci: OK… Vamos a ver si puedo manejar este burro. Y Vilma, ahora seria posible ensenarme donde vivieron las ninas en San Judas. Quiero hablar con la madre. Ok let's see if I can drive this donkey. So now I can drive and you can show me where the girls lived in San Judas. I want to speak with their mother.

Vilma: Si Ceci – Primero hay que entregar estas cosas a mi casa en Las Mercedes, y quisas manana buscamos Karla en San Judas…. Si Dios quiere. Yes Ceci, first I must deliver these things to my Mom… and maybe tomorrow we can look for Karla in San Judas. God willing.

Ceci: OK vamos. Pero, digame porque están mudando? OK let's go. But tell me why you are moving.

Vilma: Ahora tu sabes que es peligroso allá en las Mercedes. Vamos a mudarnos a causa del ocupacion de los marerros. Son mas y mas agresivos. Y por eso necesitamos vender el camión por el dinero mudar. Si Dios quiere todo pasara bien y conseguimos otra casa. Now you know that it is dangerous en las Mercedes. We are going to move because of the infiltration of the gang members. They are more and more aggressive. This is why we needed to sell the car for the money to move. God willing, everything will be OK if we can find another house.

Ceci: Uds. dejaran la casa de su mama? You will leave your mother's home?

Vilma: Estamos colectando muebles y dinero para mudar toda la familia el mas pronto posible. We are collecting furniture and money so the whole family can move together as quickly as possible.

Ceci: Yo te ayudo Vilma. Vamos. I will help you Vilma. Let's go. *Vilma crosses herself.*

73. <u>Vilma's Barrio - Las Mercedes</u>

After going to the bank, Vilma directs Ceci to her barrio, Las Mercedes, high atop a mountain on the outskirts of La Ceiba. As they enter the long winding road that climbs straight up, Vilma tells Ceci to put on the high light beams, which is a signal to the gang member guards in Las Mercedes that only residents can pass. They pass young gang members with cell phones and rifles. They all know Vilma by the truck… but report by cell phone the vehicle's entrance into the barrio to the next guard up the mountain…. That a gringa is driving.

Vilma: No se preocupas Ceci… Estas conmigo. Don't worry Ceci. You are with me.

Ceci: Que pasa aqui Vilma? So what's happening here?

**Vilma: Hay que apurarnos para entregar las cosas rapido…
Los mareros son los duenos de la calle en estos dias… y no le
gustan mucho a los gringos. Es peligroso para ud. Vamos con
sonrisas Ceci… Y no mires nadie con sus ojos.** We have to hurry
and deliver these things fast. The gang guys own the streets these days,
and they don't like Gringos very much. It's dangerous for you Ceci.
Let's go with a smile and don't look at anybody with your eyes.

*They wave and smile and soon arrive at the top of the hill where
Vilma's mother and sister are waiting. They embrace and unload
the used furniture fast. She whispers to Vilma's mother as she
passes her the remaining cash for the truck in a greasy lunch
bag, so as not to call attention to the mareros who are lurking
around.*

**Ceci: Por el
camion y su
nueva casa. Lo
siento lo que pasa
aqui.** This is for
the car and your
new house. I am
sorry that this is
happening here.

**Vilma's mom:
Gracias Dona Cecilia.**

Vilma climbs back into the truck.

Vilma: Hay que bajarnos ahora… We have to go down the hill
now.

Ceci: Vilma, me gustaria conocer tu mama. But Vilma, I would
like to get to know your Mom.

**Vilma: Es peligroso aqui para ud. Entiende Ceci? Yo te veo
manana OK? Hay que bajar conmigo ahora antes que caiga el
sol.. Vamos Ceci, ahora.** It's dangerous here for you. Do you
understand Ceci? I will see you tomorrow. You have to leave now
before the sun sets. Let's go now, Ceci.

Vilma's mother gives her a hug and thanks her for her help. Mareros are beginning to gather around the house.

Vilma: **Con sonrisas vamos.** Don't forget to smile Ceci, Let's go.

They take off down the hill so Ceci can get out of Las Mercedes. They talk on the way.

Ceci: **OK listen Vilma... Escucha. Tu tienes la seguridad de tra bajar conmigo. Siempre te ayudare... Su familia siempre tendra accesso al camion para mudar cuando lo necesitas...** Listen Vilma. You have the security of work with me. I will always help you. Your family will always have access to the truck to move when you need it.

Vilma: **Ceci...Gracias por su ayuda. Entonces... Puedo ir contigo a San Judas manana...Yo se donde vive la familia del papa de las ninas. Creo que su mama se llama Karla Rojas, y vive alla todavia. Ud va a esperarme cerca un kiosko de frescos en la calle principal mientras yo busco ella. OK?** Ceci, thank you for your help. So... I can go with you to San Judas tomorrow. I know where the girls' father's family lives. I believe that their mother, Karla Rojas, still lives there. You can wait near a kiosk on the main street while I look for her. OK?

Ceci: **Y quien esta buscando un hogar?** And who is looking for a home?

Vilma: **Mi hemana tiene algunas ideas y esta averiguando ahora.** My sister has some ideas and is researching it now.

They have passed mareros again along the way down the hill, with telephones and rifles. They all recognize Vilma. When they arrive at the foot of the hill in Las Mercedes where the curling mountain road leads into a main road with kiosks and a taxi stand, Vilma gets out of the car. She will walk back up the hill alone.

Ceci: **OK Vilma, . Suerte con la casa. Cuidate chica. Te busco aquí mismo en la manana** OK Vilma, Good luck with the house. Take care chica. I will look for you here in the morning.

Vilma: **Gracias por el dinero.** Thanks for the money.

Ceci: Gracias por el camion. Thanks for the truck.

74. <u>Walking through San Judas- Vilma seeks Karla</u>

Next day, Ceci and Vilma drive into San Judas, the barrio next to Las Mercedes, in the rolling hills outside the main pueblo of La Ceiba. This barrio also has a gang population. They pull up next to a rickety kiosk selling vegetables... and park under a tree.

Vilma: Espereme aqui... Tambien hay mareros en San Judas... Yo vuelvo con Karla, si Dios quiere. Wait for me here. San Judas also has gangs. I will return with Karla, God willing.

Ceci: OK... Si Dios quiere. I need to write a song about that.

Ceci waits under a huge ceiba tree, while Vilma goes looking for Karla. We follow Vilma as she walks through the barrio. As she arrives at the foot of a mountain where Karla is supposed to live up on the cliff with her in laws... Vilma meets a woman whose child of 7 years is completely afflicted with meningitis and cannot do anything but be carried around. After getting directions, Vilma climbs up the ravine, covered in trash and dripping water, to where the mud house is seated, on a chiseled out ledge of the mountain. Karla comes out of a doorway with a bowl full of yucca she is peeling.

75. <u>The Iraheta Home on the mountain in San Judas</u>

Karla: Hola? Que buscas? Hello. What are you looking for?

Vilma: Karla Rojas?

Karla: Si, Quien quiere saber? Yes, who wants to know?

Vilma: Yo soy Vilma.. Yo trabaje por la Senora Adila donde estaban sus hijas con la IHNFA. I am Vilma. I worked for Senora Adila where your daughters were with the Ihnfa.

Karla: Y donde están ellas ahora? And where are they now?

Vilma: Estan bien ahora en el SOS... They are OK in the SOS now.

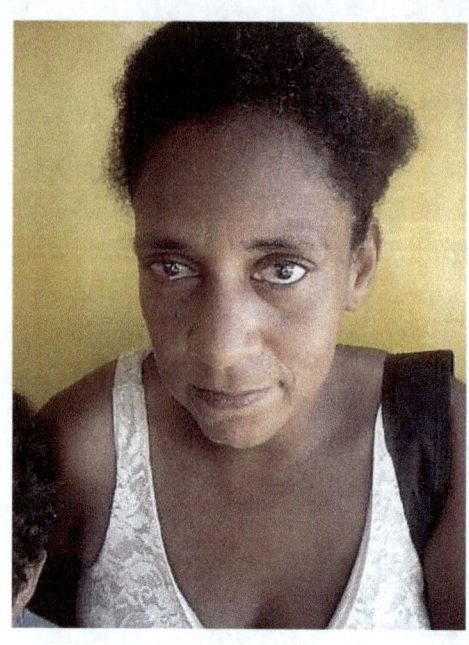

Karla: Bueno… el papa estaba bien enojado…. Well, their father was really mad.

Vilma: Y que paso con el? What happened to him?

Karla: Alguien le mato en Barrio Inglais. Someone killed him in Barrio English.

Vilma: Lo siento. Karla… Estoy aquí porque conozco una gringa que quiere cuidar estas ninas… Ella esta abajo esperando hablar contigo sobre este asunto. I am sorry about that. Karla, I am here because I know a gringa who wants to take care of the girls. She is below waiting to speak with you about this.

Karla: Tiene pistos ella? Does she have any money?

Vilma: No se Karla… Yo se que las ninas tuvieron meningitis y que ella salvo las vidas de ellas en el Hospital Atlantida. Creo que ella quiere darles una buena vida… Debes de hablar con ella…… para ellas Karla!! I don't know Karla. I do know that the girls had meningitis and she saved their lives in the Hospital Atlantida. I believe that she wants to give them a good life. You should speak with her… for the girls Karla! *Long pause*

Karla: Solamente si ella tiene dinero…. OK. Espereme. Only if she has money. OK, wait for me.

Karla turns around to go clean up her act. Vilma looks around and sees the pila (a cement water hole loaded with bacteria) with the animals walking around. There are lots of barely dressed kids running around the carved out moutain shelf of a small family settlement on the ridge. Karla emerges, pregnant, and cleaned up in tight jeans and a T shirt. They descend the slippery ravine, and make the hike through San Judas to the main highway below where Ceci waits.

76. <u>Return to Ceci Waiting in the Truck – San Judas Border – Ceci/ Karla/Vilma</u>

Ceci is hanging out at the nearby kiosk where a few Garifuna men are playing drums, when Vilma and Karla show up. Karla is visibly pregnant. Ceci approaches them as they walk towards the truck.

Vilma: Ceci... Te presento Karla. Ceci. This is Karla.

Ceci: Wow... Angie looks just like you!! Hola ... como esta? Yo soy Cecilia Diaz.

Karla: Hola Gringa... Entonces... se puede sacar mis ninas del SOS? So can you get those kids out of the SOS or what?

Ceci: Es lo que quiero hacer. That's what I want to do.

Karla: Vilma me dice que tu puedes cuidarlas. Yo firmare lo que quieras pero hay que darme pistos... ayudame gringa. Estoy embarasada con el ultimo hijo del padre de las nina, mi quierido Carlos. Dios le bendice ... el morio hace poco. Vilma tells me that you can take care of them. I will sign whatever you want, but you have to help me. I am pregnant with another baby.... This is the last child of the girls' father, Carlos... God bless his soul, he just died.

Vilma: Que paso? Yo recuerdo Carlos. El siempre estaba en el autobus atras. What happened. I remember Carlos. He always was in the back of the bus.

Karla: El debia dinero supuestamente. Yo no se que paso. Pero nosotros le enteremos sin una tomba en el cemetario publico la semana pasada. He owed the guy money. I don't know what it was about. But now he's gone and we had to bury him without a stone in the public cemetery last week.

Ceci: Quisas podemos visitarle alla un dia con las ninas. Maybe we can go there sometime with the kids.

Karla: Ellas casi no le conocian. Solamente Roxana un pocito. Puedo firmar culaquier cosa, pero hay que ayudarme. Soy pobre. Y hay otra hermana, Cynthia, mayor que Roxana, que estuvo en escuela el dia que vinieron los soldados. *Holding* *her belly.* **Y tengo otro aqui.** They hardly knew him…Only Roxana maybe a little. So what do you want me to sign? I can sign anything, but you gotta help me. I am really poor. And there's another sister, Cynthia, older than Roxana, who was in school the day the police came, so they didn't get her. And I have another one on the way.

Ceci: Y que pasa con el meningitis aqui? What is going on with the meningitis here?

Karla: Hay una epidemica en el barrio con la agua mala. Mi vecino tiene una nina con 7 anos abajo, que no puede hacer nada… como un vegetal. There is an epidemic in the barrio with the bad water. My neighbor has a 7 year old down the hill. She can't do anything, almost like a vegetable.

Ceci: Hay que buscar la medicina imediatamente!

Vilma: Fortunatamente Angie y Roxana tuvieron tratmiento temprano. Y que paso con el ojo de Angie? Fortunately Angie and Roxana were treated early on.. And what happened to Angie's eye?

Karla: Un ladrillo cayo en su cabeza. Estuvimos construyendo una pared y un ladrillo cayo en la cama. Ella lloro para horas.. no habia comida, y con meningitis, fiebre … Roxana lo tuvo tambien por mucho tiempo, y mi suegra, Celestina, intentaba curarlas con hierbas. Ella es una enfermera y partera, y es la sola que gana dinero y trae comida para la casa. Fue mal la semana pasada. Necesito ayuda Gringa. Se puede ser mi co madre. Como tu quieras. Ayudame. A brick came down on her head. We were building a wall… and a brick fell on the bed. She would not stop crying… and there was no food, and meningitis with all the kids… fever everywhere. Roxana had it for a long time, and my mother in law, Celestina, tried to cure it with herbs. She is a nurse and midwife, and is the only one bringing in any money. We had a bad week last week. I need help… You can be my co-madre. I just need some money.

Ceci: Me contaron que ud. le golpio a Angie para silenciar sus gritos de dolor…. Y por eso vinieron los soldados y las sacaron. The soldiers said the neighbor told them that you struck her, and that is why they were removed.

Karla: Puedas creer lo que quieras! Un ladrillo le pego en la cabeza.. disculpa!. El facto queda que no puedo cuidarlas sin pistos. Entonces, se puede guardarlas como co-madre. Si o no? You can believe what you want. A brick hit her in the head.... And the fact remains I can't take care of them... no money! So you can keep them like a co-madre. Yes or no?

Ceci: Pues. I'm not sure I believe that brick story. Deme su numero telefonico y yo averiguare lo que tenemos que cumplir para darme la custodia. Estoy seguro que no es facil. Pero.. Gracias por hablar conmigo. Permitame ver lo que puedo hacer para conseguir un hogar y una vida estable en la Ceiba. OK? But give me your phone number and I will find out what we have to do to give me custody. I am sure it is not as simple as it seems. But thank you for talking to me. Let me see what I can do to make a proper life here. I have to find a place to live.

Karla: Y deme tu numero tambien. Se puede venir visitarme, donde vivimos arriba, aunque de creo que me mudare en poco. No cabo bien con mi suegra desde la muerte de Carlos. And give me your number too... You can come visit where we live. Although I may be moving soon. I don't get along too well with my mother-in-law since Carlos died.

Ceci: Mantengas contacto conmigo Karla. Me voy al doctor de ojos con Angie mañana. Tambien la semana que viene baptizare las ninas para ser su madrina oficial. Quiero hacer todo legal. Entiende? Stay in touch Karla. I am going to the eye doctor tomorrow with Angie. Also, next week I will baptize the girls and become their Madrina. I want to do everything legally. Do you understand?

Karla: Y tiene pistos ahorita? *Ceci reluctantly gives her money.* **Bueno, gracias co-madre. Hablaremos.** *She walks away. And Vilma looks at Ceci annoyed, as Ceci stares after Karla in stoned disbelief. The drummers continue to play on in the street kiosk.*

Vilma: Ceci, tengas cuidado con esta mujer. Ceci, be careful with this woman.

Ceci: Su cara parece exactamente como Angie. Her face looks just like Angie's.

Vilma: Si Ceci, pero escuchame... Ella va a buscarte por dinero para siempre nada mas.. sin interes en las ninas ni su bienestar. Te digo Ceci.. cuidado. Ella es una manipuladora. Ceci listen to me. She is going to hunt you down for money always... nothing more. Without any interest in the girls nor their wellbeing. I'm telling you to be careful. She is a manipulator.

Ceci gets into the truck and leans her head on the wheel. The street drum volume increases.

Ceci: **Vilma estoy seguro que tengas razon... Most desperados are manipulators. No se como escaparle.** Vilma... I know you are right. Most desperados are manipulators. I don't know how to escape her. **But now I just have a headache from trying to do the right thing, when I knew it was the wrong thing.**

Vilma: **Ella tiene su numero!.** She has your number!

77. CIUDAD BLANCO- Orphans and Conquistadores flashback 6

Once again we return to the Ciudad Blanca with the drumming at the street fruit stand which segues into the ancient ceremony. These caciques are dressed in primitive ritual regalia yet will speak sophisticated English, which becomes a device of these spiritual interludes to express the historical injustice of the Spanish conquista.

Cacique Toreba: Where now are the leaders who can address the needs of this lost generation of children and their families?

Quetzalcoatl: The Hero Twins, Hunahpu and Xbalanque are my monkey scribes, patrons of the arts and music. They had a mysterious plan that was written up in the Popol Vuh. It is hidden here in these ruins of the White City. They are here today to help us understand this evolution of the Native Latino, and may be able to rewrite this course of history. I believe this Ciudad Blanca, land of the lost Monkey Kings, holds the answer to the positive destiny of the youth of Honduras. We must re think the culture of the Maya.

Hunahpu: Perhaps these gangs are only recycling history, avenging the violence of the conquistadores with rebellion and retaliation towards the present day upper class and their white man's ever present doctrine of slavery and law and order.

Garifuna: But why should these gang members be destroying their own in the process? It makes no sense.

Xbalanque: They have nothing to live for, when everything has been taken away, starting with their parents, and continuing with the discrimination against their race and class. The future seems hopeless.

Lempira: What other possible mission do we have in the spirit world but to pass on the wisdom of our ancestral heritage, and a sustainable lifestyle for our descendants. If the community cannot maintain this order, then we must rethink the survival of the blood family. We must not sacrifice our children to the spoils of civil disorder and corrupt abandonment. Their increasing hunger for love and family security within a gang, can only emphasize the decay of a culture already on a self consuming spiral of destruction.

Cacique Entepica: In Honduras, the onslaught of modernity has touched enough hungry, uneducated youth. The infatuation and desire for technology, money and power has invaded all levels of society. Even humble farmers, living out in the hills without electricity, can't live without a cell phone and instant communication.

Cacique Cicumba: What they don't have is a political, judicial, and educational infrastructure to reform the social injustices that keep them without a real economy, clean water, electricity, and education for the young. This produces exclusion and outrageous crime, poverty and family disintegration which continue to contaminate the future of our children.

Hunahpu: From the heart of the sky, I beg for a miracle to save the souls of our unwanted offspring. I REPEAT: These orphans are the modern sacrificial victims of this Mayan century. Their hearts have been cut out, and this is how they become gang members…

Morazan: We have already witnessed the fall of the agricultural and political Mayan civilization causing the decline of the indigenous masses, even with the ongoing adoration and respect for the Gods who created them.

Cacique Benito: We were told, that without sacrifice to these higher powers of the sun, and the moon, the stars, the wind and the rain, there would be no life, no vegetation, no animals….. We lived in subordination to these great fears of celestial punishment, making bloodletting and sacrifice a ritual sport, designed by the nobility to control the masses.

Hunahpu: This is not holy sacrifice in the enlightened mind.

Xbalanque: Fear will tear your heart out… Athletes who lost in the Mayan game of football were beheaded for the Gods. Virgin women, warriors, and children were also sacrificed. These brutal dramas were unfairly, illogically, and painfully damaging to the souls of families of thousands of Mayan spirits. Tearing out the heart of a living creature was a riveting shock to the daily life of any breathing witness. This subjugating pressure of destroying humans out of respect for the Gods can only breed fear, hypertension and apocalypse.

Quetzalcoatl: There was rebellion and escape. Then the floods came to wipe out the humble defenseless masses. The nobles fled to the pyramids, until the rivers subsided. Those who survived, continued to worship and subdue the anger of the Gods with more sacrifice and war …. leaving more and more children homeless with the graphic memory of their sacrificed parents.

Morazon: At least you can thank the white man for eliminating this barbaric ritual of sacrifice, and introducing Christianity.

Cacique Toreba: Senor Morazon, may I again remind you that your Spanish brothers invaded and murdered our people. They also brought us small pox.

Cacique Benito: So which is worse, being invaded or being sacrificed, or infected with lethal disease? Our people were doomed on both ends of history.

Cacique Copan Galel: And still, the modern day Saturday night Evangelical screaming sermons and testimonials go on... "Please God, help me from drowning in this river of pain and poverty. Rescue me from this horror... I have passed through this underworld one too many times." Where is this Christian God now???

Hunahpu: Others, who survived the floods of rain, poverty, gang war, disease, and family heart break, fled to the hills hanging high in the Ceiba trees.... Like monkeys, living on God's fruit ... until the floods subsided. We became the scribes who recorded our Mayan creation story in the Popol Vuh.

Xbalanque: They were all waiting for your return, Quetzalcoatl, the feathered serpent.... the great white feathered God who once ruled the Mayan empire... You did not believe in sacrifice... Your intention was that all creatures on the earth had the right to life, and should coexist in nature peacefully. With the cultivation of corn, beans, and squash, people can survive.

Quetzalcoatl: But the noble class was too ambitious and greedy to support a culture of blissful paradise for the working class. There were great stone pyramids to be built, wars to be waged, land to be conquered.

Morazon: Yes... these imperialistic principals have lasted for posterity on all continents... Might makes right.

Quetzalcoatl: But I fled this tyranny to the kingdom of the white city,,, Place of the lost Monkey Kingdom... birthplace of the aurora borealis. ... to get away from this manipulation.

Lempira: The star gods were powerful. They held the Mayan kings in the palm of their hands. How could our ancestors compete with those who could engineer the construction of our miraculous pyramids?

Xbalanque: It is still a mystery to Western Civilization why this White City is lost. Clearly it holds the source of the mystery of the Mayan cycle of creation and time.

Quetzalcoatl: This is where we are now. Gentlemen … we must re-write this final chapter of the Popol Vuh, so that the cycle can begin again, just as the Aurora borealis exploded over the skies of the Ciudad Blanca before…. They will shine their brilliant lights again with the return of the compassionate star gods to regenerate a spirit of hope and regeneration amongst our precious children…. To grow in their own time and manner. Let us send these wishes to the star gods.
A circle dance ensues around the fire to the mystical beat of ceremonial drums.

78. <u>Next Day – SOS and First trip to Eye Doctor with Angie & Olvin</u>

Ceci arrives at the SOS in the funky black truck to pick up Angie and Olvin to go to El Progresso where there is an ophthalmologist. When she arrives at Casa 9, she sees that Angie and Roxana's black teeth have been removed, and that all three girls have their ears pierced. Ceci is examining the teeth and ears of all three of the girls.

Ceci: Hola mis amores. Conchita, que paso con los dientes de Roxana y Angie? Hello my loves. Conchita, what happend to Roxana and Angie's teeth?

Conchita: Una dentista missionista los hallaron ayer. A missionary dentist pulled them yesterday.

Ceci: Pero porque? Tu sabes que ahora van a comer con sus encillas, y eso va a darles dientes adultos irregulars. But why? You know that now they will eat with their gums and that will give them crooked adult teeth.

Conchita: Pero fueron negro , feo y infectados Ceci. But they were black, ugly and infected Ceci

Ceci: Entonces ellas van a necesitar frenos seguramente cuando vienen los dientes adultos. Oy y tambien veo huecos en sus orejas. Dios mio! Muchas lagrimas cayeron con todo esta surgeria yo imagino. Well, now they will need braces for sure when their adult teeth come in. And I also see holes in their ears. My God! Many tears must have fallen with all this surgery I imagine. **OK,,, never mind… today we go to the eye doctor with Angie. One doctor at a time.**

Conchita: Vas al Progresso con Angie verdad? Are you going to the doctor in el Progresso with Angie?

Ceci: **Si, y con Olvin tambien. Porfa?** Yes, and with Olvin too if that's ok.

Conchita: **Bueno... ellos estan listos.** Sure, they are ready.

Norma brings Angie out of the bedroom with her hair in little pony tails. Olvin takes her hand and they say goodbye. It is a two hour ride down a single lane road, along the ocean with pineapples, bananas, and palm oil plantations on both sides. Olvin is 12. He and his sister, Norma, lost their parents in a car crash and were sent to the SOS. They live in the same house in the SOS as the girls, and consider the girls like sisters.

79. <u>EYE DOCTOR – EL Progresso</u>

They arrive at a very crowded public medical center and get in line to see the doctor. Hours go by as Angie waddles around the waiting room. She sees a woman who looks like Conchita, and goes to climb in her lap. Ceci quickly gathers her.

Ceci: **Disculpa... la nina piensa que ud es su Tia del SOS en La Ceiba. No puede ver bien ella.** I'm sorry. The little girl thinks that you are her Aunt at the SOS in La Ceiba. She can't see very well. *Ceci takes Angie on her lap.*

Olvin: **Interesante como esa senora se parece mucho como Conchita.** Interesting how much that lady looks like Conchita.

Ceci: **Pobrecita... Ella esta buscando alguien familiar... Es dificil perder una madre...** Poor thing. She is looking for someone familiar. It's difficult to lose a mother.

Olvin: **Es mas dificil cuando la madre no le quiere, como su madre de sangre.** It's even more difficult when the mother doesn't want her, like her blood mother.

Ceci: **Gracias a Dios que ellas tienen uds. en el SOS.** Thank God that they have love in the SOS.

Olvin: **Ud. va a tener custodia un dia Ceci... Sigue con la lucha... Ellas te necesitan.** You will have custody one day Ceci. Keep up the fight. They need you.

Ceci: Gracias Olvin. Everybody needs a real mother.

The nurse comes out to call Angie. They go into the office to meet the doctor.

Doctor: Buenos Dias senora… Esta nina no es tuya verdad? Hello Senora. This little girl isn't your child right?

Ceci: No soy su mama, pero, soy su angel… y quiero saber que pasa con la vista de ella, y si ud. puede curarle. La madre de sangre le golpio hace 6 meses, y sabemos que ella no puede ver bien. Es posible diagnosticarla? I am not her mother, but I am her angel. And I want to know what is happening with her vision, and if it can be cured. Her blood mother hit her in the head 6 months ago, and we know that she can't see very well. Is it possible to make a diagnosis?

Doctor: Bueno, vamos a ver. *He looks inside her eye, and she cannot bear the light.* **Mira… I speak a little English. I need to put her to sleep to take a better look. Will you allow that?**

Ceci: How long will she be unconscious? *She is uncomfortable with this.*

Doctor: Maybe 30 minutes….It is the only way I can determine exactly what is going on.

Ceci: OK… I hope you know what you are doing… This is totally unfamiliar to me.

Doctor: If you want a proper diagnosis we must do this.

Ceci: OK but can I hold her?

Angie is all of two years old, and does not know what is happening. Ceci holds her close while the doctor injects the anesthesia and administers the eyedrops. Olvin consoles Ceci as she begins to cry when Angie passes out.

Olvin: Todo va estar bien Ceci… No llores. Everything will be all right… Don't cry Ceci.

Ceci: I can't help it. I hate all this suffering.

As Angie falls asleep the doctor examines her eyes with a bright light, and after what seems like forever, he is ready to make the diagnosis.

Doctor: She has something called Optic Nerve Atrophy, which is about her sensitivity to light. The trauma to her head has ruptured her optic nerve almost completely in her left eye, and partially in her right eye. And with the simultaneous meningitis, the fever did not help. Unfortunately, God does not replace the optic nerve, and she will be unable to recover from this.

Ceci can't hold back the tears, and holds Angie close.

Ceci: Oh my God… what does that mean? Will it get worse? Will she become totally blind?

Doctor: With the right care she can maintain the vision she has…. But people with this problem have been known to get worse with the demands of eye strain. She must get a proper diet, and be well cared for. Clearly, she will be legally blind for the rest of her life. There is nothing I can do for her.

Ceci is rocking Angie and holding her close. Olvin holds Ceci who can't stop crying with the realization that there is no cure for Angie's blindness.

Ceci: OK… It's time to go. Thank you Doctor. Hay que ir. Olvin… el no puede areglar la vista de Angie.

Doctor: I'm sorry Senora.

Angie begins to wake up. Ceci carries Angie back to the car, and lays her down. There is a man selling ice cream.

Ceci: Esta bien Angie… Vamos a comer una crema helado OK? Olvin… Vaya comprar dos conos para uds… It's OK Angie. We are going to have an ice cream OK? Olvin go buy two cones for you both.

She gives Olvin money and strokes Angie's head as she slowly wakes up. Olvin returns with the cones and they get ready to leave. A popular song comes on the radio.

Ceci: **Vamos a cantar juntos.** Let's sing together.

Ceci dries her eyes, dismisses her fears and turns up the scratchy radio... They pull out onto the open road home to La Ceiba singing with the music at top volume to hide Ceci's tears.

80. Meeting for MISS HONDURAS CONTEST -Eduardo Zablah

Ceci arrives at the Gallo de Oro store in the middle of La Ceiba, which sells everything from bicycles to beautiful imported fabrics. She is greeted by Eduardo Zablah, fashion designer and coordinator of the Miss Honduras Contest.

Eduardo: Miss Cecilia, thank you so much for coming. I understand that you are American and have come here to teach dance at the Escuela Mazapan, and we would be so honored if you could help us with the opening number of my next Miss Honduras Contest.

Ceci: Yes I am a choreographer and I would love to work on your show. I came here to research your national culture and dance, so this is a great opportunity for me. I actually saw you getting ready with your girls in the plaza during carnaval.

Eduardo: Excellent!!! So you know how much I love feathers and glitter.

Ceci: Yes, this is very exciting. So... When is it? How many girls? What about the music? And how big is the stage?

Eduardo: I love Gringas... they get right to the point. Yes...the show is in two weeks... thirty girls... I have the music and some ideas... and I will show you the maquette of the stage. Come to my office.

In a small workroom in the back of the store, filled with glamorous dresses and beautiful, young, naïve Honduran girls trying them on, Eduardo shows Ceci a model of the stage.

Eduardo: So you see I am creating a tropical/cabaret theme this year with a medley of Honduran music. We will present all the contestants and then bring in last years' Ms. Honduras for a special solo. They will be at rehearsal next Monday and Tuesday at the Quinta Hotel on the beach. Can you dream up a fabulous opening number for me?

Ceci: Give me a copy of the music, and I will work on it. Do your girls have any dance training? That will affect my choreography.

Eduardo: Probably not, because they do not have the same cultural dance training as young girls from the states. But they all know how to merengue, salsa, and punta. Make it basic, and simple, and use our native dances, and it will be fabulous.

Ceci: Mr. Zablah, I am honored to work with you. Your dresses are so glamorous. This is such a world of fantasy.

Eduardo: Cecilia, you will see that there is a great cultural divide between the rich and the poor here, but we all love our Latin music.

Ceci: I can see that the poor are really poor, and the rich are really rich... I am now trying to help three orphans I found in front of the Hospital Atlantida a few weeks ago.

Eduardo: Are you trying to get custody of them?

Ceci: I am, difficult as it seems to be.

Eduardo: Good luck with that my dear... because the IHNFA is so corrupt, and there are so many abandoned children here. They sleep in the park down the street. Be careful, as everybody will charge you for their legal services, and you may never get them out of the orphanage.

Ceci: I will stay until I can find a way to improve their lives... whatever it takes. Meanwhile, I will need to work with your music as soon as possible.

Eduardo: Here is the CD, fresh off the computer from my technology expert Bryan. Call me as soon as you have you are ready to talk, and I can set up dance rehearsal time for next week.

Ceci: Hello Bryan. Ud. sabe cortar musica verdad? Me gustaría tu numero por favor para ayudarme con montajes

musicales. You know how to cut music? I would like your number to help me with musical montages.

Bryan: Si, claro…. Toma… *He writes it on a papelito. Ceci's cell phone rings, and she ignores it to shake Bryan's hand and make clear that she will be in touch regarding the sound track.*

Eduardo: *continues:* **AND, think about this… Your whole life will change if you take on these kids…. You will not be able to help as many other orphans, nor will you have the freedom to continue your work teaching and choreographing. And don't think that once you get them under your roof that it will be easy, as they will surely have physical and mental disabilities.**

Ceci: Yes of course I have considered all of this, my age, my instability, the children's potential futures as Americans, and their disabilities. But I am not the gringa who flies down for two weeks with the church, pours my heart into these darling children, and THEN waves goodbye, and gets back on the plane forever….. Thank you for your advice Mr. Zablah… I am a woman, and I cannot shut down my heart in this case. *Ceci's phone rings again.* **Hence….I will listen carefully to your music and get back to you with some fantastic ideas.**

Eduardo: Wonderful… I can see you are a woman with guts. Call me Eduardo, Ceci. See you soon.

Ceci: Ciao then… Eduardo

<u>Street</u>

Ceci leaves Eduardo's store and answers the phone on the street. It is Karla calling from the hospital with news about the birth of her new baby boy, Carlitos.

Ceci: Hola Karla como esta? En el hospital, Porque? Hembra o baron?....You're kidding. No puedo ahora Karla. Tengo clase … tengo que trabajar en dos horas….. OK por un rato. Hello Karla how are you? In the hospital why? Oh… girl or boy? I can't come now Karla. I have class, and I have to work in two hours. Ok, just for a moment.

81. <u>Hospital Atlantida – Karla's next baby, Carlitos</u>

Cut to Ceci walking into the Hospital Atlantida and heading for the maternity ward right next to pediatrics - the same exact place she was with the three girls. There are many young girls in beds without sheets, holding their newborn babies. Ceci finds Karla who has baby Carlitos on her tit.

Ceci: Hola…. Como se fue? Hello… so how did it go?

Karla: Rapido…no hubo problema. Fast… I didn't have any problems.

Ceci: Y como se llama? And what's his name?

Karla: Carlitos, como su papa … en el cielo. Carlitos, like his dad, in heaven.

Ceci: Parece exactamente como Jazmin. He looks just like Jazmin.

Karla: Si… hay un ano entre ellos. Yes, there's only a year between them.

Ceci: Y quien son todas estas jovencitas… And who are all these young girls?

There are many young girls in the ward with babies.

Karla: Son las mujeres de los mareros … las jovenes. Para marcar su territorio… ellos les ponen embarazadas. They are the women of the gang guys… the young ones. They mark their territory by getting the girls pregnant.

Ceci: What? *Ceci exhales and closes her eyes.* And what about birth control?

Karla: Ceci… nadie puede pagar por eso. Ceci, nobody can pay for that.

Ceci: Tu lo necesitas… Espero que se puede cuidar Cynthia y Carlos ahora. Well you really need it. I hope you can take care of Cynthia and Carlos now.

Karla: Pues… Ahora tengo un novio. I have a boyfriend now.

Ceci: So fast? Carlos morio hace poco, no? Y que piensa su novio de un bebe que no es de el? But Carlos just died a little while ago. And what does your new boyfriend think of a baby that isn't his?

Karla: El me quiere Ceci…. Y no puedo quedarme mas con Celestina. He loves me Ceci… And I can't stay with Celestina anymore.

Ceci: Puedo entender eso. Karla…Celestina es su suegra, madre del padre de sus hijos. Ella no quiere ver otro hombre en la cama de su hijo! I can understand that. Karla, Celestina is your mother in law… mother of the father of your kids. She doesn't want another man in the bed of her dead son!

Karla: Y no tengo pistos Ceci!!! Y tengo Yarel ahora. El trabaja… y puedo vivir alla con su familia. I don't have money Ceci. And I have Yarel now. He works, and I can live there with his family.

Ceci: Y Carlitos y Cynthia van a vivir donde? And where will Carlos and Cynthia live?

Karla: Con su abuela, Celestina en San Judas. With their grandmother, Celestina in San Judas.

Ceci: What? Vas abandonar ellos? Are you going to abandon them?

Karla: Necesito dinero Ceci, por favor. Yo no quise este nino… I need money Ceci, please. I didn't want this child.

Ceci: Ni Roxana, Angie, o Jazmin tampoco. You need birth control… control de nacimiento. Nor Roxana, Angie, or Jazmin either.

At this point all the girls in the maternity ward are looking at them as Ceci is angry and upset.

Karla: Hay que comprar comida Ceci. I need to buy food Ceci.

Ceci: OK… toma… *Ceci gives her more money* **Tengo que trabajar Karla. Suerte con Carlitos… El es bello. Ciao.** Ok here… I have to work Karla. Good luck with Carlitos, He is beautiful… Goodbye.

Ceci looks around at all the young teenage girls holding their babies… and leaves.

82. <u>AFTER SCHOOL DANCE in Mazapan Studio – Dia Del Nino preparation – Vilma emergency</u>

Ceci is working on various dance pieces with her different classes of young students at the school in preparation for her first performance. One is a ballad to "Where is Love" from Oliver. There is a ballet about seeds becoming flowers with the help of worms and butterflies; A Honduran pot pourri merengue with folklorico costumes; and a salsa with long skirts. As students come in, she realizes that Vilma has not arrived to help her. She calls, but nobody answers the phone. We watch a montage of four different group rehearsals and the numbers they are preparing.

1. Where is Love? From "Oliver" – Lament

2. Seeds to Flowers - Bambinas

3. Pot Pourri Merengue folklorico

4. Salsa – Candelito– Santana

Ceci is pleased and dismisses all the dancers. As the students are leaving, Vilma runs into class with her brother Hernando, asking for the truck.

Vilma: Ceci, Necesito su ayuda. Podemos prestar el camion? Ceci, I need your help. Can we borrow the truck?

Ceci: Claro, chica,, que pasa? Me preocupaste cuando no veniste esta tarde. Of course girl.. What's happening? You had me worried when you didn't show up this afternoon.

She takes them into her office.

Vilma: Disculpa Ceci, me robaron el telefono. I'm sorry Ceci… my telephone was robbed.

Ceci: What? Quien te lo robaste? Who robbed you?

Vilma: Hay que mudarnos pronto… Por fin los mareros llegaron a nuestra casa para amenezarnos con machetes…. Hay que mudarnos ahora!. Mi madre esta alla sola… We have to move fast. Finally the gang guys came into to our house threatening us with machetes. We have to move now! My mother is there alone.

Ceci: Oh my God!!… la policia? No los has llamado? And the police? Did you call them?

Vilma: Ellos no suben por Las Mercedes nunca, Ceci… hay que ir… They don't go up to Las Mercedes ever. Ceci, we have to go.

Ceci: Vamos… Vilma… pero donde se van a mudar? OK let's go. But where are you going to move?

Vilma: Conseguimos una casita en las lomas para aquilar. We found a little house in Las Lomas to rent.

Ceci: Pero su mama es la duena de la casa en Las Mercedes no? But the house is in your mother's name no?

Vilma: Si Ceci… pero no vale a perder nuestras vidas. Tenemos que irnos… Yes Ceci, but it is not worth losing our lives. We have to go!

Ceci: Bueno…. Vengo contigo manejar donde quieres. No entiendo como pueden robar la casa de tu madre? OK I am coming with you and I will drive you where you want. I just don't understand how can they just take your mother's house??!!

Vilma: No se Ceci, es barbaro…. I don't know Ceci… It's barbaric….. *She starts to cry.*

Ceci: Vilma, te ayudare. Vamos…Vilma, I will help you. Let's go. *She embraces her.*

Hermano: Ceci no… es demasiado peligroso. Te robaran…. Ud. es una gringa… simbolo de todo lo que ellos odian…. Demasiado peligroso. Yo manejare. Ceci No! It's too dangerous. They will rob you … you are a gringa, symbol of everything they hate. It's too dangerous! I Will drive.

Ceci: *(getting into car)* **Entonces… yo les esperare en el kiosko de frutas al pie de la montana. Me voy contigo. Yo voy ayudarlas mudar, en cualquier manera.** Allright then… I will wait for you by the fruit kiosk at the foot of the mountain. I am coming with you and I will help you move in whatever way I can.

Vilma: Bueno Ceci… Gracias…

83. LAS MERCEDES – Fruit Stand and Vilma's House- Moving

The following scene takes us in the black truck to the foot of the mountain in Las Mercedes where there is an intersection with the same small fruit stand near San Judas, a bus stop, a taxi stand, a bicycle repair, and a funky food stand. They drop Ceci there and continue straight up the hill to Las Mercedes, where once again they pass gang members with rifles, talking on their cell phones. Vilma and her brother wave as they pass. They arrive at Vilma's mother's small wooden home on a cliff, where her family is stacking boxes of things on the road for pickup. Two gang guys stand there with machetes, smoking cigarettes.

Hermano: Mama… solamente las cosas mas importantes. Mama, only the most important things.

They load up as much as possible in the truck, and there is still more to move. Vilma's mother timidly addresses the gang guy.

La madre: Podemos volver para los muebles? Can we return for the furniture?

Gang guy: Si… rapido… necesitamos esta casa hoy. Yes, move it. We need this house today.

La madre: *(to Vilma)* **Vayan rapido, y su hermana y yo vamos a sacar los muebles para la calle.** Go now fast, and your sister and I will remove all the furniture from the house and have it ready on the street.

Hermano: Mami no… ven ahora… Y me voy a quedar para sacar todo de la casa. Mom, no come now. I will stay to move the furniture.

Vilma: Pero quien va a manejar? But who will drive?

Hermano: Ceci puede manejar….. Venga ahora! Ceci can drive. Come on now!

The mother starts to cry… she is leaving the house where she was born and gave birth to all her kids.

Madre: Mi casa... Dios mio... porque? Soy humilde... no hice nada.. My house – My God why? I am humble – Haven't done anything.

Gang guy: Vaya senora... Get out of here Senora.

Madre: Y yo conoci tu madre muchacho... Que paso contigo? Yo me quedo aqui hasta que estoy lista. And I knew your mother boy. What happened to you? I will wait here until I am ready to leave.

Vilma and her brother into the truck... it is painful for all of them.

Hermano: Yo vuelvo en quince minutos... entiende? I will be back in fifteen minutes, OK?

The mareros have already gone in to check out the house, as the loaded truck pulls away. Ceci is waiting at the kiosk drinking from a coconut, sitting on a broken plastic chair, talking to a woman with a baby on her tit who is waiting for a bus. Vilma's brother arrives and gets out of the truck.

Hermano: Ceci, traiga las cosas para Las Lomas por favor... Nuestra hermana esta alla. Y vuelva despues de descargar... Yo me quedo con la casa hasta que tu vengas... Ceci, take my family to Las Lomas please. Our sister is there. And return after dropping them off.

Ceci: Esta bien... *getting into car...* **Vilma, sabes donde vamos?** OK Vilma, do you know where we are going?

Vilma: Si Ceci

Ceci: *directed at the brother...* **Vamos a reunirnos aqui en una hora o menos... estas claro?** We will meet again right here in about an hour. Is that clear?

Hermano: Esta bien... a las 4pm...Ciao That's good... at 4pm, Ciao!

The following is a montage of images showing us Vilma's teeny new house in a barrio on the other side of the mountain. This is a beautiful, mountanous barrio with small, cement houses and lots of vegetation. No sooner have they unloaded, we cut back to the bus stop to meet Vilma's brother to repeat the routine. In no time they return with a truck load of furniture, and they all take off for the new home. The whole family, is there to help unload, and as soon as the truck is empty... Vilma approaches Ceci and hands her back the keys to the truck.

84. <u>Vilma's new house in Las Lomas</u>

Vilma: Gracias Ceci. *Trying not to cry... Ceci hugs her.* **Mira... OK... Hay otra problema... Mis sobrinos no pueden salir de la escuela sin pagar los mareros impuestos de guerra. Mi hermana no puede pagar hoy. Me presta 100 lempiras mas Ceci? Necesito recogerles ahora. Disculpa Ceci.... Seria nuestro ultimo dia en esa escuela allá.** Thank you Ceci. Look.... OK .. there is another problem. My nieces and nephews are unable to leave school without paying war tax to the mareros every day. My sister doesn't have the money to pick them up today. Can you lend me 100 lempiras? I have to pick them up now. I am sorry Ceci. This is our last day in that school.

Ceci: Yes....yes...Oh my God! What is going on with these gang guys? OK ... Vamos...

Ceci, Vilma, and Sayda – (Vilma's sister), get into the truck.

Sayda: Tienes Lempiras Vilma?

Ceci: Cuanto cuesta para hacerlo? How much does it cost to do this?

Sayda: Fue 100 lempias esta manana para entrar.... Y probablemente otro cien para sacarles. It was 100 lempiras this morning, to enter. And probably another hundred to get them out.

Ceci: I can't believe this is actually happening. Vamos a ver... Y donde esta la policia con todo este crimen? Let's see what happens. And where are the police with all this crime?

Vilma: La policia tiene miedo entrar Las Mercedes. The police are afraid to enter Mercedes.

Ceci: Tambien en las escuelas publicas? Con ninos? Even in th e public schools? With kids?

Sayda: Los mareros no tienen miedo de la policia… Quieren sus impuestos de guerra… y matan por nada. The gang guys are not afraid of the police. They want their war tax and will kill for no reason.

85. <u>**The public school in Las Mercedes**</u>

They pull up to the school where an old beat up car is blocking the entrance. Ceci gives Vilma more money. Four gang members with pistols get out of the car.

Vilma: Quedese aqui Ceci. Stay here Ceci.

Ceci: OK… *Reluctantly she stays in the truck. Vilma and Sayda talk to the leader, who asks her for money.*

Sayda: Pero yo te pague esta manana. But I paid you this morning.

Gang guy: No importa… Quiere ver sus hijos? I don't care. You want to see your kids?

Vilma: *angry* **Que paso contigo? … Yo conozco su hermana… sin verguenza hombre… No crees en Dios?** *Flaring her nostrils* **Cuanto quiere?** What is wrong with you man? I know your sister… you have no shame?? Don't believe in God?

She reaches into her pocket for the money Ceci gave her earlier.

Gang guy: Dos cientos lempiras, y tengas cuidado como hablas conmigo chica. Two hundred lempiras, and careful how you talk to me chica.

Ceci: *Getting out of the truck and addressing the marero...* **Yo lo pago... y voy con ellas para recoger los ninos.** I will pay for it, and I will go with them to get the kids.

Gang guy: Quien es ella? Who is she?

Vilma: Una maestra Americana... Yo trabajo con ella. An American teacher. I work with her.

Gang guy: Otro cien. Another one hundred...

Sayda: Porque? Why?

Gang guy: Porque ella puede... Because she can.

He gets in her face, and then wanders over to Ceci for the extra money. There is a stare down.

Ceci: This is insane... they all think I am a bottomless dollar pit. *She willingly pulls out another 100 lempiras.*

Vilma: Venga Ceci...

Ceci: Sayda, como les pagan los padres a ellos todos los dias? How do the parents pay them every day?

She walks towards the school, maintaining her gaze at the marero who took her money.

Sayda: Los niños no van a estudiar mas aqui. Gracias a Dios hoy es nuestro ultimo dia. Vivimos dia por dia Ceci... Eso es la vida. The kids won't study here again. Thank God today is our last day here. We live day by day Ceci... That's life here.

They walk into the school. It has been raining and there are pails and puddles all over catching drips with one student desk for the teacher and lots of broken chairs. The kids are writing on their laps in their journals. The teacher is walking around. When she looks up, you can see that she has barely been able to keep her composure to teach with the gang action outside the school.

Teacher: *Approaching Sayda* **Desculpa Sayda... La Policia no vinieron.** I'm sorry Sayda, I called the police but they didn't come.

Sayda: Yo se... Puedo salir con mis hijos ahora? I know. Can I leave with my kids now?

Teacher: Si claro... Yes, of course.

Sayda: No vengamos manana. Hemos mudado a causa de los mareros en Las Mercedes. Buscaremos una nueva escuela en las Lomas. Ciao...y Gracias... We will not come tomorrow. We have moved because of the mareros in Las Mercedes. So we will look for a new school in Las Lomas. Goodbye and Thank you.

The teacher tries to hide her anxiety, and hugs Sayda's kids knowing it is the last time she will see them. It is a silent brigade that passes from the school to Ceci's black truck. They all get in and drive away.

86. <u>**Driving to Vilma's House with Sayda's children**</u>

Sayda: Como se fue escuela hoy muchachos? How was it in school today you guys?

Muchacho: Los mareros entraron en la clase hoy. The mareros came inside the class today.

Ceci: Porque? Why?

Hijo: Para escapar la lluvia.... To get out of the rain.

La hermanita: Si, contando su dinero atras ... con sus pistolas en el piso. Yes, while they counted their money in the back, with their guns on the floor.

Vilma: Dios Mio!!

Ceci: Sin duda es una bendicion que mudaron hoy. Uds. van estudiar en otra escuela alla en las Lomas. Without a doubt it is a blessing that you moved today. You will study in another school in Las Lomas.

Vilma: Te veo manana en el estudio Ceci. Gracias..... So I hope to see you tomorrow in the studio Ceci.. Thanks.

Ceci: Es un principio nuevo… hay que estar positivo… Que sean fuertes chicas. It's a new beginning. You have to stay positive… Stay strong Senoritas..!!!

Ceci drives away and is clearly troubled by Vilma's situation

Ceci: *She mutters…*And I thought I was living on the edge!

87. Mazapan School Performance – Dia Del Nino – 9/10/05

Deni May enters the dance studio with her first grade students to dress them up for the DIA DEL NINO… Ceci and Vilma simultaneously greet the bus from the SOS with the girls and the other orphans who will also participate in a Dia del Nino parade and performance. Both groups have learned the same choreographies separately. Ceci brings the girls to meet Deni May who is dressing her students.

Ceci: Girls this is Deni May. She is the first grade teacher.

Deni: Hello girls. It's a pleasure to meet you. Sus nombres?

Angie – I'm Angie.

Jazmin: Jazmin

Roxana: Y Roxana y somos gusanos !! We are worms!

Deni: They are pretty girls.

Ceci: They are all beautiful! And they will be little worms in the flower dance.

Meanwhile, both groups (the Mazapan students and the SOS kids) gather and silently stare at each other as Vilma checks costumes.

Deni: And these are some of my students.

Ceci: You all look so beautiful dressed in your costumes. And you will be dancing the same dance together which we will practice. Now let's take a photo… both groups.

Ceci organizes both groups together in the studio against the ballet bars for a photo. The younger children, ages 4,5,6 and 7 have costumes that are made of burlap, dried corn kernels, coffee and frijole beans all glued to the dresses. The theme is about seeds with emphasis on nature and the innocent, humble beauty of these kids.

 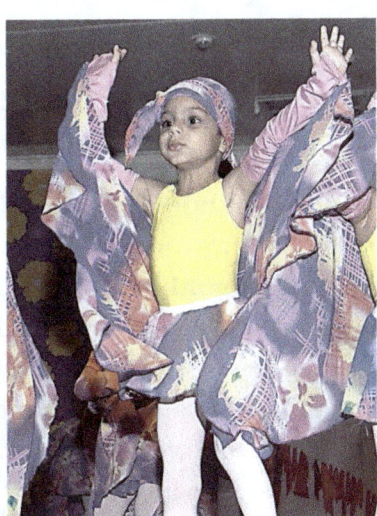

Ceci organizes both groups together in the studio against the ballet bars for a photo. The younger children, ages 4,5,6 and 7 have costumes that are basically made of burlap with dried corn kernels and coffee and frijole beans glued to the dresses. The dance theme is about seeds - very Indio, with an emphasis on nature and the innocent, humble beauty of these kids.

The older groups, ages 8-16, are dressed in traditional Honduran folkdance attire… the girls in wide skirts with flowers in their hair… The boys in white pants and shirts with cowboy hats and red bandanas. Again, both groups will dance together for the first time.

The salsa dancers are flapping their skirts. The 3 sisters follow Ceci around as she organizes.

Ceci: Todo el mundo… Hablo Espanol porque es la idioma todos aqui. Oyeron? OK…Hoy estamos bailando con dos grupos que conocen las mismas coreografias. Pero nunca han bailado juntos en el mismo escenario. Entonces… hay tres danzas. Ahora vamos a practicar las posiciones de entrar y sus lugares en el escenario juntos para cada danza. OK? Tias y profesoras, yo pido tu ayuda con Vilma para ensenarles sus "places". Everybody… I will speak Spanish because it's everybody's language here. Do you hear me? OK. Today we are dancing with two groups that know the same choreographies. But you have never danced together on the same stage. So, there are three dances. Now we are going to practice the positions for entering and your places on the stage for each dance. OK? Aunts and professors, I ask your help with Vilma to show them their places on stage.

Ceci continues: Nosotros bailaremos tres numeros. Mirame y oigame bien, y cuando yo les llamo, preparense para sus entradas. Primero las bambinas con EL BALLET de LAS SEMILLAS… Con el viento uds van a entrar de dos lados y mezclanse en el escenario, corriendo en circulos de direcciones oposito. Entonces empezaran a pasar los obstaculos. Vamos! We will dance three numbers. Watch and listen to me well, and when I call you, get ready for your entrances. First the babies with the Ballet of the Seeds. With the sound of the wind you will enter from both sides and mix on the stage, running in opposite directions. Then you will dance the obstacle course. Let's go!

The music of wind starts and the kids run out into circles from both sides of the stage and then take the path over and under all the obstacles on the stage, just like in class.

Ceci: Esta bien…de nuevo por favor. Very good.   Again!!

They do it correctly next time and then begin to roll on the ground as if they were burying the seed. A thin grey fog (blanket) comes over them with the sound of rain, and under the blanket the kids remove their seed costumes to reveal green legs and arms in leotards. The worms begin to crawl around. Ceci stops the music and tells everybody to find a hole and stick their arms through it like plant stems. They practice without music.

Ceci: **OK... ahora hay que sacar la cascara de su semilla encima de su cabeza, sin ayuda. Y despues buscar su hueco en la tela. Y poco a poco van a seguir con la danza. Que pasa despues de esto?** Ok now you must take the shell of your seed over your head. Without help from Mom. And afterwords, look for your hole in the fabric covering the stage. And little by little you will continue with the dance... So what happens after this?

Student: **We stick our hands out of the holes like the stem of a flower.**

Ceci: **Then what? Y despues?**

Other student: **We grow out of the ground and wave our green scarves like leaves.**

Another student: **Then we make flowers like this.**

Ceci: **And where do the flowers come from again? Ensenenme!**

Everybody: **Like this!** *They whip out a folded round fan which has been attached to their belts. Vilma is under the tent distributing props.*

Ceci: **Yes and you all know what to do after that right?**

Todos: **Si.. La manzana!** Yes... the apple!

Ceci: **OK, let's run it once.**

<u>Seed to Fruit – Bambinas</u>

The youngest group of dancers (ages 4-6) filter onto the stage running as if blown by the sounds of wind and rain. Some are dressed like worms and others are dressed like seeds in brown burlap and traverse an obstacle course track which requires hopping through hoola hoops on the floor, jumping over blocks, crawling under limbo sticks, summer saulting across gym mats, and tight rope walking on balance beams until the rain intensifies and the seeds "take root" in the earth. The worms crawl around. Soon the sun breaks on the horizon and a stem (arm) shoots out of the rooted seed, and they rise up from the ground discarding their burlap coverings. The worms become butterflies. With scarves the little dancers start to grow leaves that wave in the afternoon breeze. As the music reaches higher crescendos, a beautiful flower emerges from a small bud on the branch, which grows into a flower (fan) in their hands. After that an apple emerges from the flower, coming from a pocket. They throw it up and catch it over and over. The fruit dance becomes a short finale to the piece, and a larger child comes in to pick the flowers and they eat the fruit. The girl exits and the dance ends with the repeated sound of wind, as new seeds (thrown by the kids) scatter. The circle of life continues on the Dia del Nino. Jazmin is in this group.

Ceci: OK – This will be fabulous.... Excelente, Bellas mariposas, gusanos, and semillas! Next... Merengue folk dancers!! Listos? Los dos grupos?

They assemble on stage with their partners and Vilma and Ceci place them, mixing the 2 groups yet leaving them with their original partners. Partner shifting is part of the choreography. Right away you can see all the students checking each other out. Initially there is hesitation and reluctance between the two groups. But Ceci cracks it.

She places them on stage equally, then practices a weaving step. Without music they mark the different positions of the dance as Ceci counts them through it and defines the changing spaces. There is shyness and giggling, but a mutual respect when they see that they both know the same steps.

Ceci: OK now the Salsa... Alguien va a introducir la salsa, y cuando empieza la musica sus primeros posiciones estan aqui: Someone will introduce the salsa, and when the music starts your first positions are here.

Ceci arranges everybody in their offstage positions carefully mixing students from the two groups. Then she counts them into dancing onto the stage and clarifies all the positions on stage, and how they change for the different formations. They are all wearing colorful clothes and by the time they realize how much fun they will have on stage, there is very little edge between these two different social classes of students.

   Ceci: **OK… Muy bueno trabajo todos… Ahora arreglamos la formacion para el desfile hasta el escenario en la cancha. OK Tias y Professoras? Vamos afuera.** Great work you guys. Now we will fix the formation for the parade that goes to the stage on the sports court. OK aunts and teachers? Let's go outside.

88. <u>Outside studio - Preparing the Parade</u>

Ceci and Vilma, once again arrange and mix both groups for their places in the parade formation. There is a distinct contrast between the two classes of children, but Ceci makes it work, and they all unite around the tradition of the Dia Del Nino, with traditional music. Both groups will march in the same parade around the campus at the distinguished Mazapan school. The Mazapan students begin to arrive to line up for the parade. Ceci organizes the drummers from the SOS into formation outside the studio, and they start to warm up. There are two boys in the drum line from the SOS who team up with the Mazapan drummers.

Ceci: **Bueno… todos saben como marcar el ritmo con sus pies. A ver?** OK, everybody knows how to mark the rhythm with their feet? Can I see?

The drummers start a primitive, native rhythm which is subtle and suggests a stomping step that the younger kids have rehearsed before…

Ceci: **OK, cuando llegamos en la cancha, vamos a formar un gran circulo. Despues de rezar, you guys open the show. Las bambinas son las primeras con el ballet de las semillas OK? Y sus madres van estar alla… con su familia, y sus sonrisas, y sus cameras… y yo siempre estare en frente. Son tan bellos todos. Entonces, hay alguien que quiere usar el bano antes de ir?** Allright… when we arrive in the court, lets form a big circle. After praying, you guys open the show. The babies are the first with the Ballet of the Seeds. And your mothers will be there, with your families and your smiles and the cameras. And I will always be in front of you at all times. You all look so beautiful. So, is there anybody who needs to use the bathroom before we go? *Three children raise their hands, and are taken away while we wait. Ceci hugs Vilma.*

Ceci: **Vilma… Gracias por su ayuda y su trabajo… los trajes son bellos…** Vilma, thank you for your help. The costumes are beautiful.

Vilma: **Gracias Ceci… como tu dijiste… cuando estamos preparadas, todo va bien.** Thank you Ceci. Like you said…. When we are prepared, everything goes smoothly.

Ceci: **Exactamente…** Exactly. *As she fans herself vigorously in the morning heat.*

Vilma: **Tu necesitas un vacacion Ceci.** You need a vacation Ceci

Ceci: **Interesante, sabes que? Quiero irme a Copan para el fin de semana… para sacarme de todo por un minuto… y averiguar**

las ruinas, y posiblemente conseguir un curandero alla... como shaman... sabes? Interesting that you should say that. I want to go to Copan for the weekend to get me out of all this for a minute... to see the ruins and possibly find a healer there... like a shaman... you know?

Vilma: Si Ceci, hay curanderos alla en las montanas. Hay que pedir en el Hotel Thelma. Yes Ceci.. there are healers there in the mountains. You must ask at the Hotel Thelma.

Ceci: Gracias Vilma... exactamente lo que queria hacer, además visitar las ruinas. Copan es un mundo que me encanta. Thanks Vilma, exactly what I wanted, along with visiting the ruins. Copan is a world that enchants me.

Vilma: Estan listos Ceci, vamos. They are all ready. Let's go.

Ceci: OK ... a marchar... vamos tamboristas! OK... Let's march... Come on drummers!!

The combined drum section heats up the moment with some great beats and the parade officially begins. Both the SOS orphans and the Mazapan school students march together into the school grounds of the Mazapan school... in parade formation... They hold the banner... Dia Del Nino. Parents, teachers, and staff are waiting to cheer the kids on.

89. Dia del Nino Performance in the Cancha of Escuela Mazapan

They arrive at the cancha and form a large circle, and the student body gathers around. A pastor from a local church makes an invocation for EL DIA DEL NINO... and the future success of youth generations. The music begins, the drummers join in, and the kids get ready for their presentation for the student body and parents. It is ethnic and contemporary ... simultaneously.

This becomes a musical montage of pieces of several different performances from the different grades of the Mazapan school.

Included in the show are the 4 numbers that Ceci has composed with her after school program integrated with the choreographies of the SOS dancers.

The Ballet of the Seeds, The Folklore Merengue; Salsa, and the "Where is Love Ballet"

All of these numbers are great successes in Ceci's eyes, as are all the numbers presented on this cherished holiday for children. The audience and staff are delighted, as there are no glitches in continuity. The afternoon ends with pictures of both groups together...... with Ceil and the girls. Jazmin, Angie and Roxana don't want to separate from Ceci. The older SOS girls, Norma, Juny, Blanca... try to get them on the bus.

David Ashby: Great show Ceci. Thank you. They had a ball.

Ceci: And they were great.

David: Es la hora de salir todos! - It's time to leave everybody.

The girls run to grab Ceci's legs.

Ceci: Uds. saben que les amo muchisimo... pero todavia... viven en el SOS con sus hermanos y Tia Conchita. You guys know that I love you very much... but you still live in the SOS with your brothers and sisters and Tia Conchita. *More tears.*

Ceci: Ademas... me voy a Copan esta fin de semana... y no vengo para la misa Domingo. And I am going to Copan this weekend. And will not be at the mass on Sunday.

Angie: Quiero venir contigo Ceci... por favor. I want to go with you Ceci, Please

Roxana: Yo tambien. Me too.

Ceci: No se permite mis amores...*(whispering in a huddle with the three girls)* **Pero un dia te prometo que van a venir conmigo en cualquier direcion, en cualquier momento... y por cualquier razon, sin permiso de nadie... Les prometo, OK?** It's not permitted my loves. But one day I promise that you will come with me wherever I go and whatever moment and for whatever reason without permission from anybody. I promise OK?

David: Vamos Todos! Let's go everybody.

Angie: Dios quiere que vamos contigo Ceci.

Jazmin: Adios Ceci!

Kids on the bus: Ciao Tia Ceci!!

Ceci: Yo se que Dios quiere. I love all of you... y vuelvo el Lunes... Todos bailaron buenisimos.

Ceci gives out hugs and kisses and manages to tear herself away from the girls as they pile into the back of David Ashby's pickup truck to return to the SOS. Ceci can NOT stand the separation anxiety. Once again it is the rearview mirror blues.

90. **COPAN – Ceci travels alone**

Ceci takes the bus to Santa Rosa de Copan, where the breathtaking views of Honduras on the bus, give a wide panorama of landscapes and pueblos to remind us that we are not in the twenty first century much of the time. Five hours later she gets off the bus in Copan... to hike along the narrow, cobblestone streets in search of Casa Thelma, where she has made a reservation... Suddenly a young boy yells out from a balcony.

91. <u>Thelma's Hotel - COPAN</u>

Boy: Hey Gringa...Bienvenida a Casa Thelma... te gusta pancakees?

Ceci: Oooy! Si echa miel Hondurena, absolutamente! Yes, if you have Honduran honey, absolutely!

Boy: At your service gringa! You come to Casa Thelma!

Ceci: Excelente, y donde esta Thelma? And where is Thelma?

Thelma: Aqui estoy Sra Cecilia? Here I am Sra. Cecilia. *She appears on the balcony wiping her hands.*

Ceci: Si... Mucho gusto. Mi secretaria, Vilma Reyes, me mando. Yes pleased to meet you. My secretary, Vilma Reyes, sent me.

Thelma: Sube senora. Venga a ver.. el mejor cuarto en la casa... para ti. Y te presento Luis... mi hijo.... Come on up... Come to see the best room in the house for you. This is my my son Luis.

Ceci climbs the stairs of a four floored building built into the mountain. Thelma and Luis greet her on the second floor.

Ceci: Si.. muy amable.. Yes, you are so kind.

Thelma: Luis… traiga comida para la gringa… Ella esta cansada de viajar. Luis, bring food for the gringa. She is tired from traveling.

Ceci: Gracias Thelma….

Thelma: Aqui esta su cuarto…

And it is a beautiful room with a terrace overlooking a garden with a huge mango tree and a view of the valley. There is a small kitchen, with a table… a big bed, closet and wonderful bathroom… all well lit by huge windows. It is better than ever. Thelma puts away the towels and asks.

Thelma: So I speak English and want to know what does a single gringa do alone in Copan I ask?

Ceci: Oh … well… that's a good question. You see I am living in La Ceiba, teaching at the Mazapan school, and doing research on indigenous culture and dance. I was a choreographer in the United States, but I am definitely here now.

Thelma: And you will go to the Copan Ruins?

Ceci: Yes of course… tomorrow..

Thelma: Y que mas?

Ceci: What else?

Thelma: Yes I know there is something special with you.

Ceci: Well, as a matter of fact… I am hoping you can help me with a spiritual matter.

Thelma: Que pasa mama? *Thelma sets up two chairs on the porch.*

Ceci: OK… long story as short as possible….

Thelma: I have all day.

Ceci: I am trying to get custody and visas for three Honduran orphan sisters who are in the SOS in La Ceiba, who are very young, and have disabilities. I am too old to adopt., and I am up against big walls with the IHNFA and the American embassy as a result. But more pressing, for me, are their disabilities, which I want to help with if possible and then bring them home to my mother's house in the states someday.

Thelma: Yes. That is a very big wish. It is difficult to understand why the IHNFA is so corrupt, but these are the times we are living in, at the expense of the children, unfortunately.

Ceci: And that's why I live here and I am totally committed to work this out.

Thelma: And what can I do for you?

Ceci: Frankly Thelma…. Verdaderamente…. Yo quiero hablar con espiritu… Entiende? What I really want is to speak to spirit. Do you understand?

Thelma starts laughing.

Thelma: Si Gringa… Yo entiendo… Y tambien ud. quiere abrir sus caminos – open your roads. I have a few ideas. Come with me right now. *Thelma changes into a white robe.*

92. Thelma's Rooftop Altar

Thelma leads Ceci all the way upstairs to a roof top world with a place to hang laundry… a fogata (a fireplace on a table for cooking)… and a sheltered altar with several Mayan statues … candles… and flowers. She motions to Ceci to sit down, and she lights up some candles and cigars as she mumbles a prayer in Mayan. She smudges Ceci and the altar with copal and hands Ceci a tobacco.

Ceci: Wow…. Ask and you shall receive! This is exactly what I wanted to do. Are you a real bruja?

Thelma: Since the gringos do not like the word "bruja", I prefer to use "curandera". I am puro Maya and my mother was blessed with the spirit. I participate and hold sessions here in Copan. So ... I am bruja enough to feel the hair on my arms stand up in your presence... and to know that you are a spirit of high light.

Ceci: Well thank you... I am glad that all my somewhat crazy pursuits of ritual and magic have not gone to waste in obscurity...

Thelma: OK, so hermana... Vamos hablar con espiritu...Dios mio! I can tell you that I feel the fuerza on my arms again... and that spirit is in the room. You can talk.

Ceci: OK good...so... I would like to find out if there is any medical hope for three orphan sisters in La Ceiba. Two of them had meningitis... Roxana has some delay and memory issues that seem impossible to repair... along with Angie, who is partially blind because of trauma to her optic nerve... and Jazmin, who suffers from asthma and anxiety, along with other infant vitamin deficiencies. I wish I could correct all of them now, and I don't know if modern science can.

Thelma: Bueno... first dear Gringa... Spirit is listening. *She is smoking her cigar and looking at the altar.* And they tell me that you have saved these girls' lives. These girls do not know love other than yours. *She closes her eyes and chooses her words carefully.* I believe that their disabilities are permanent.

Ceci: Oh please don't tell me that. *Tears surface.*

Thelma: Now listen. *She opens her eyes and examines her cigar ashes.* You must be strong. We want to open the roads for you and the girls. You will go to the ruins tomorrow, and there you will find my older brother, Leonel Blanco who also has my mother's blood like me. She descends from pure Mayan sacerdotal (priestess), so you see whatever Mayan souls that are here with us now, will reach out if they can help you. And they have told me to send you to my brother, Leonel. Entiende?

Ceci: Yes! Donde y cuando? Estoy lista. Where and when... I am ready.

Thelma: I will tell him to meet you by the Macaw birds at the entrance, and he will introduce you to the Mayan ruins. I can see that your children have *our* native blood, but mixed with many others from different parts of the world. They are special children. After you go to the ruins, and spirit sees you there, my brother and I will do a trabajo for you.

Ceci: Yes... their maternal grandmother was Mayan from Belize. How did you know this?

Thelma: *She laughs and whispers with a smile.* Because they tell me. *She points to the sky....* I will tell Leonel that you are coming, and then we will talk later. Some day you must bring these girls to Copan.

Ceci: Thank you Thelma. I will go to the Ruins in the morning and look for Leonel. And I will gladly pay you for these services...

Thelma: No .. this comes with the rent. You are helping our children.

93. The COPAN RUINS – meeting Leonel Blanco

It is early morning when Ceci enters the gate to the Copan ruins. As soon as she walks past the gate she feels chills up and down her spine. There aren't many tourists there yet. As she walks down the path, she feels almost weightless, and she comes to a leafless tree with several colorful macaws. There under the tree is an old man feeding the birds. One is on his shoulder. At the base of the tree is a small altar with: a three stoned hearth, a candle, a small cement bust of Quetzalcoatl, and burning copal incense. It is almost like a dream, and Ceci is excited. She approaches the old man, who also resembles Quetzalcoatl from her dreams.

Ceci: **Perdoname Sr. Leonel? Me llamo Cecilia, y su hermana, Thelma, me dijo buscarle aqui por los pajaros.** Excuse me Sr. Leonel? I am Cecilia, and your sister, Thelma, told me to look for you today by the birds.

Old Man, Leonel: Hola Sra. Estoy esperandote. Yo soy Leonel Blanco. Mucho gusto. Hello, I have been waiting for you. I am Leonel Blanco. Pleased to meet you.

Ceci: Mucho gusto tambien… *shaking his hand.* **Yo soy Cecilia Diaz.** *Pause* **Te conozco senor? You look familiar. Digame… Que esta haciendo?** Me too. I am Cecilia Diaz. Do I know you sir? You look familiar. Tell me… what are you doing?

Leonel: Estoy pidiendo los pajaros para permiso usar sus plumas para trabajar. I am asking the birds for permission to use their feathers to call spirit.

Ceci: Son bellos estos pajaros. These Mckaw birds are beautiful.

Leonel: Son magicos Sra. Este pajaro se llama Quetzalcoatl. They are magical Sra. This one's name is Quetzacoatl.

Ceci: El serpiente con plumas…. Quetzacoatl por los Aztecas, Kulculcan por las Mayas. The snake with feathers. Quetzalcoatl for the Aztecs and Kulkulcan for the Mayas.

Leonel: Si, pero nosotros preferemos el nombre "Quetzalcoatl"… Como sabia estas cosas Gringa? But we prefer the name Quetzacoatl. How do you know these things gringa?

Ceci: Porque he estudiado mucho de las Mayas. Because I have studied the Mayans a lot.

The bird jumps from his shoulder onto Ceci's shoulder.

Ceci: Oh my goodness!!

Leonel: No tengas miedo! Quetzacoatl sabe porque estas aqui. Do you feel the chill in your bones? Don't be afraid! Quetzalcoatl knows why you are here. Do you feel the chill in your bones?

Ceci: Yes I do… ever since I entered. This gets better and better every minute.

Leonel: You are Cecilia, and my sister told me about you. I can speak English, because I am also a guide for the turistas. I will give you a special tour of this magic place, so that spirit will

see you, and so you will know the Maya philosophy a little more. You want history, you go to the books.

Ceci: Are you also a curandero?

Leonel: I am more shaman... I speak with spirit.

Ceci: Well then... show me the spirit of Copan. I am ready.

Ceci continues holding the bird, while Leonel packs up his altar in a small knapsack. He leaves his three stoned fire place intact... and extinguishes the flame with a prayer of thanks.

Leonel: Let us go then.

Leonel takes his colorful pet macaw bird on his shoulder and they walk towards the ruins. It is quiet, and Leonel walks with a cane, carrying his sacred items in his beautiful Mayan sac on his back. This man has a twinkle in his eye, and a lift in his step that invokes respect and fascination. They walk in silence until they get to the Grand Plaza, where there is an open field of stepped pyramids and inscribed sculptures (stelae). It is breathtaking. Ceci is wide eyed and grabs her heart.

Ceci: Oh, this is just magnificent... so mystical.... So ancient and impressive... What happened here?

Leonel: OK... let us sit for a moment. *He takes Ceci and the bird to a small pyramid called Mound #4 right in the middle of the Grand Plaza, and sits her and the bird on a bench to watch. He takes out a branch of ruda... brushes and snaps it around Ceci... and begins his lecture. Ceci records with her camera.*

Leonel: First I will give you some important background. Even though Copan is smaller in size than many of the other Mayan ruins, it was the center of great achievements in science and mathematics... Their advanced studies in astrology created specific signs to compute time. They invented the most exact calendar in the world by plotting the rotation of Venus...They were the first to use the concept of "0" in math... Scribes who invented an independent written language with the use of ornate hieroglyphs on buildings and sculptures having exceptional artistic finishes, were of the finest quality…. As well as the design and engineering of water irrigation and drainage flow based on the principles of gravity. Scholars say that all this sophisticated culture began in Copan around 1500 BC… and ended for reasons of decadence that seemed to have been caused by the depletion of the land, starvation and illness around 900 AC… We don't really know.

Leonel has moved closer to the pyramid without his cane and has begun to preach/ perform/ invoke.

Ceci: Leonel, is it possible that these pyramids are much older than 1500BC?

Leonel: In my heart I know how sophisticated this culture was, and it did not happen overnight. There is so much mystery connected to the origins and history of the Mayan people

Ceci: I want to know more about that.

Leonel: There were many complex agricultural accomplishments during the Pre-classic period. They were the first to cultivate turkey, sweet potatoes, squash, tomatoes, and beans. Peanuts and chocolate came from Mayan culture. They also grew chili peppers, sunflower seeds, papaya and vanilla. They were the first to cultivate cotton and tobacco.

Ceci: Basic things that we take for granted. Where did they learn all this? Please continue.

Leonel: Ahora....

Leonel Steps up on the pyramid. A crowd is gathering. Leonel becomes more profound. Ceci continues to record Leonel's lecture.

Leonel: Hablo de las cosas basicas.... There were three Mayan classes: The elite were the governors, the priests, and the nobles. The middle class was made of the commerciantes, the warriors, the artistas, and the arquitectas of these grand palaces.... And finally, the lower class was composed of the farmers, the servants and other types of workers. And above all of this were the kings who were the political and religious leaders who in turn were dominated by the Gods. The shamanic priests were responsible for the prosperity, security, and health of their people. The king and his noble class communicated with the Gods and presided over all the ceremonies. It was a theocracy built around a priestly class.

Ceci: Sigue Leonel, por favor!! *She continues to shoot the performance, which becomes more and more dramatic and the tourists become more engaged. Leonel is inspired and is visibly on the verge of falling into trance.*

Leonel: The life of the Maya was ruled by their supernatural beliefs, their gods, spirits and invisible powers that were in the world of nature around them... animism... with the spirits of animals, streams, mountains, trees. They considered caves to be like entrances into the underworld, a world of the dead. They believed that their lives and souls were in a constant fight between the powers of good and bad. The good souls were said to rest in the shade of a Ceiba Tree, or YAXCHE in Maya, where peace and tranquility, along with an abundance of food and drink, were always found. The bad souls were condemned to a hell of hunger, cold, fatigue and sadness. You can see how the Catholics took hold of this.... Like heaven and hell.

Suddenly a guard comes and very kindly asks Leonel to get off the pyramid, as it is forbidden to stand on this monument. He knows Leonel, and speaks to him in Spanish... then turns to the audience that has gathered.

Guard: Muchas gracias todos... Este Senor Blanco conoce mas que nadie de Copan sobre Las Mayas, y para oir sus cuentas hay que inscribir en la entrada por favor..... Gracias. Thank you everybody. This Mr. Blanco knows more about the Mayans than anybody in Copan, and if you want to hear his stories you must register at the entrance please. Thank you.

The crowd dispenses, and the guard approaches Leonel.

Guard: Cuidado Leonel... No se puede caer en trancia aqui.... OK hermano? Senor Leonel, You can not fall into trance here. Ok brother?

Leonel: No hay problema... Nos seguimos en nuestra tour privada con la Sra. Cecilia. No problem. We will continue our private tour with Ms. Cecilia.

Guard: Pero no mas brujeria aqui OK? But no more brujeria OK?

Ceci: Hay un problema senor? Yo he empleado este Sr. Leonel como Guia. Is there a problem senor? I have employed Sr. Leonel as a guide.

Guard: No, no hay problema.

Leonel: Esta bien Jorge... Saludos a sus padres. It's OK Jorge. My regards to your parents.

They enter the Gran Plaza... Ceci stops recording.

Ceci: Seguimos?

Leonel: Seguimos. Let's continue.

They walk to the center of the plaza, past many Stellae of rulers... and mostly the king, 18 Rabbit.

Leonel: Entonces... This Grand Plaza was the place of public announcements, religious ceremonies, festivals, and sports. All of this was built by the 13th ruler, 18 Rabbit, who is the major king figure in most of these stellae. These hieroglyphs talk about the past and the future. The nobles and the priestly class spent time in the Grand Plaza, and only on special occasions would the working class participate in ceremonies.

Ceci: **What do you think about the theory that all this complicated apparatus strapped around them in sculptures and stellae are like space suits, with helmets along with the mechanical dashboard of space ships?**

King Rabbit – Copan   King Pacal - Palenque

Leonel: *He digs into his backpack for a book about the Maya and turns to a photo of King Pacal's sarcophagus lid in Palenque.* **I can tell you that I do believe that there was contact with extraterrestrial life in our beginnings because of the unusually quick evolution of sophisticated culture and social structure that developed...** *He shows the picture to the camera.* **But we do not talk about this with the tourists, despite the popular theories of the tombstone in Palenque of King Pacal... which I am sure is not a Ceiba tree, but a spaceship for sure. Many people see the mechanical handles and breathing devices of space ships in the stellae. The Ceiba tree is symbolic to the Maya for it's connection between the lower and upper worlds. But, this appears to be a fire beneath his seat, and that he is going towards the upper world.**

Ceci: **Yes, I have studied that picture. It definitely looks like a spaceship and astronaut.**

Leonel: **There are many elders who will not discuss any of this, so as not to anger the established archaeologists. Which reminds me of another example of our alien origins in the** <u>Rosalila Temple</u> **which has many interesting images. It was** built on top of another temple. And Temple 16 was built over that. Here we are.

Ceci: This is a big wow!

Leonel: This temple was recently discovered around 1988. It had been ceremoniously buried for some reason to keep the red stucco intact. But now we can go in. They believed they were entering the underworld.

Ceci: Oh this is so exciting. I've got the chills.

Leonel: The images on the outside are of the sun god K'inich Ahua. Do you see the wings? But what I want to show you is inside. Come. Look at these images on the wall. What do you see?

Ceci: They look like astronauts, dressed with helmets, space suits, and technical gear all around them.

Leonel: I do not discuss this with the tourists.

Ceci: The flight gear makes it so obvious. And what is so fascinating, is how the culture became so advanced. It had to be from extra-terrestrial contact with a very sophisticated culture.

Leonel: Someday this will be included in our history. We better move on as it looks like rain is coming. Now on to the famous Ball Court, which is also part of the public activity in the Grand Plaza. Come Cecilia.... This place was thought to be another entrance to the underworld, and if you look at these round stones they depict the king of Copan playing the ballgame against an underworld god... a struggle between day and night deities. The ball symbolized the sun and the rings signified sunrise and sunset, or equinoxes. The idea of the game was to use only your hips and your legs to keep the ball in the air. The goal was to send it through those tiny rings adorned with the macaw bird, an almost impossible task. Points were awarded, but the ball could not touch the ground. Sometimes, as in times of the gladiators, athletes were like warriors, in that losing the game could cost them their lives as sacrificial victims.

Ceci: I just don't get all this cruelty and sacrifice from such an evolved society. I mean this sounds like a complete scam that the rulers were running. *Ceci pretends to bark.* "Big event this Saturday night... we will cut out the heart of some innocent ball player, and throw it down the stairway".... So that everybody can stand there with their mouths open, wondering if it could ever be them next time... or their family ... All for the Gods? Honor them or else?? Talk about riveting theater, Dios! They lived in fear Leonel!!! Religious fear and control by distant gods. How could it be an honor to give up your life, and abandon your family for a god you did not know?

Leonel: The Kings were like the Gods, and they wanted blood for performing miracles. However, it wasn't always this violent you know. The sacrifices came during the decline of the civilization when people were desperate.

Ceci: That makes sense. And... Quetzalcoatl was against it.... He supported these people... Why would he want to celebrate murder? I think the kings did it to cultivate power and population control with fear.

Ball Court

Leonel: And our fear has not changed, mi hija! Calmate! We accepted our fate. And the calendar predicted it.

Ceci: *Ceci mutters to herself.* I just don't see the future for children in Honduras.

Leonel: I am only a humble tour guide and cannot change history or the future unfortunately. So we will move on to the Hieroglyphic Staircase over here, for which Copan is very famous. Which again is a testimony to the dates, lifetimes and achievements of the rulers. There are 63 steps and two thousand glyphs which tell the story of the royal lineage of Copan. This is the sight of the longest known text in Mayan Civilization, and it is all connected to the calendar and astronomical calculations. And now you see that they have covered the stairway with a tent so the rain doesn't continue to destroy it as they reconstruct it. We must preserve these artistic sculptures and hieroglyphs for posterity.

Ceci: And who was the genius that translated these glyphs?

Leonel: Oh there have been many... starting with the Spanish Bishop Diego De Landa who translated an alphabet, then the Spanish Friar, Francisco Ximenes in 1701... and his Spanish translation of the Popol Vuh. There was a Soviet linguist named Yuriy Valentinovich Knorozov who was very successful at translation in the 60s employing the phonetics of the language as well as the visual meanings of the glyphs. And also a J Eric Thompson followed up with the symbols as ideograms. I don't know how they did it.

The Hieroglyphic Staircase

Ceci: They had to be geniuses... This calendar is too complex for me to understand. So...ahora donde vamos Leon el?

Leonel: Well right here you see Altar Q, which is famous for it's 16 rulers of the Copan Dynasty passing the baton of power from one to the other... built in 763 AC... during the fall of Copan. It is not a conference of astrologers constructing the Mayan Calendar. It is the succession of the kings.

Ceci: Yes.. I want to talk more of your theories on the fall of the Mayan Empire, Leonel...

Suddenly the sky gets dark and we hear thunder.

Leonel: I will tell you that when we finish. Right now we will climb up Temple 22, which was called the "Montana Sagrada" and the Temple of Meditation with many symbols of the Mayan cosmos. *Pause as they walk.* And into the Acropolis, which is the domain of the king and his court. Each king was buried in the temple he built, and then the next king built on top of that... so that the Acropolis grew higher and higher.... We will enter the Acropolis through Temple 11, which has an entrance into the other world... and there you can see the Copan river, which had to be rerouted because it was eroding the Acropolis. *Pause as they walk.* Then we pass over here by the Eastern Court on your right which is the Plaza of the Jaguars where great ceremonies and musical performances took place for the king. Here you can see across all of Copan.

Ceci: I love all this....

The Passage of power from king to king

Plaza of the Jaguars

Rain starts to fall as the thunder continues. Ceci shouts over the thunder. She is inspired and Leonel is also excited.

Ceci: Yes… and right here, in the court of the jaguar, I would like to make a dance with 50 dancers and lots of feathers, and fur, and the flutes and the drums, and the rattles.

Ceci goes down to the center of the plaza to feel the ancient vibe of the dance floor.

Leonel: Y porque no?

Leonel pulls out his drum and mallet and begins to play. Ceci starts to dance in an interpretive form of a jaguar. Leonel joins her in the plaza in front of a jaguar altar. He gives her the Macaw feathers he had gathered in the morning, which Ceci places in her hair. The rain continues to fall. The beat of Leonel's drum formalizes the magic of her dance. Her performance smile turns to a serious, priestess like gaze as she defines the sacred space and begins her testimonial to the Court of the Jaguars. She appears to be dancing around jumping flames. The drum sound increases in volume. Once again we go to the Ciudad Blanca.

94. CIUDAD BLANCA – Popol Vuh parallel – flashback # 7

There is a transition to a ritual dance around a fire in the ruins of the Ciudad Blanca… There again are the leaders from all different races and tribes. We see the two scribes, Hunahpu and Xbalanque, Lempira and all the Honduran Caciques, along with the Garifuna leaders… all in spirit, convening once again to resolve the problem of the present decay of the Latino family, as manifested by unemployment, adultery, and lost children. Ceci is there, as a Priestess Comizahual (Flying Tiger). She arrives in her golden robes and silently watches the ceremony until she is moved to start dancing around the fire.. Leonel is Quetzalcoatl. (In all these flashback situations, the crossover use of performers from the reality scenes is encouraged).

There is the spirit of Francisco Morozan, a Spanish conquistador in Honduras who has repented for the Spanish torture and degradation that invaded and destroyed the Mayan culture. He is speaking to the circle of caciques, kings, and ancestral leaders in ritual conference at the Ciudad Blanca… around the fire.

Morozan – These are the original lessons of history repeating itself – white supremacy rule, based on claims of superior DNA and the manipulation and intimidation of false information which uses fear and violence to invade and dominate. From spirit, we watch the corruption of Democracies get crushed by the selfish consolidation of wealth that lobbies power by Oligarchies manipulating the masses psychologically and economically. This breeds a society of autocratic rule and class division. I tried to unite Central America but this racial and class division seems endless.

Leonel, as Quetzalcoatl, begins to speak around the fire as they talk.

Quetzacoatl: Conquerors all through history have demonstrated this obsessive control of populations all the way back to creation stories… as does our very own POPOL VUH…. Which is why we are here today…. To reconcile the decisions made in the Popul Vuh to give life to man, and then to reduce his intelligence and vision, so as not to conflict with or surpass the Gods. This has constricted our people. We must tell the story and resolve to take a position with respect to the welfare of our families and our people first. This divine dominance cannot be sustained at the expense of the people… and these children must not suffer any more. We will tell the story… and with all respect to the Gods, change the ending. I call my scribes so they can revisit the history of the Mayan people in the Popol Vuh.

The monkey scribe story tellers, Hunahpu and Xbalanque rise to tell the story of the Popol Vuh. Hunahpu starts with a very short form of the story.

Hunahpu: After the clay people melted in the rain, and the wooden people floated away in the flood, they mixed maize with the pulverized bones, mud, and the blood of monkeys and our star people. They had discovered genetics and something called

DNA. And... a race of man with exceptional intelligence was created ... one who could record time, respect the seasons and worship their creator Gods. They made four men and four women to populate the earth. And in the middle was the great Ceiba Tree to connect the heavens with the underworld. And this is how our Mayan world was formed.

Lempira: But you must start at the beginning of this story.

Morazon: Yes, please review this for me again in detail, as I don't understand the Popol Vuh.

Quetzalcoatl: With pleasure... It is an epic drama... Hunahpu and Xbalanque please review our origins - from the beginning please.

Hunahpu: First there was nothing but dark water. Then, the gods caused the winds to blow, and the waters to part to reveal a beautiful land, where life could grow. First, they made plants, then animals... but the animals could not talk. So they created the first model of man in the form of clay. But these people could not think or feel or talk very well, or even hold themselves together, and they dissolved in the great flood waters.

Xbalanque: Then there were the people fashioned of wood. But they were not smart enough to function, or more importantly, to worship or appreciate the life they were given by the Gods... so they too were washed away in the great flood waters.

Hunahpu: Next came another race that the gods made of clay and powdered bones. These people were smarter, but did not have respect for the Gods... So they were turned into monkeys and survived the flood waters by living in the trees on the highest mountains.

Xbalanque: Finally, the Gods mastered a race of man, making a hybrid model in their own image by combining their own DNA with corn and previous upright mammals on earth. In the Popol Vuh, the goddess Xmucane took her flour milling tools, the metate and the mano, and ground the corn nine times. These beings, although unable to reproduce, were brilliant, could walk and talk, could learn complicated sciences, were able to see far and wide, to understand the past, present, and future, could read and write... they were super human!

Hunahpu: This genetic engineering finally produced four brothers of supreme intelligence, with great vision and sensitivity of heart.

Xbalanque: The brothers were created to live on the land by their four Bacab tree posts at the corners of the world, surrounding the great tree of life – The Ceiba Tree. They were given four wives with which to procreate, and so the Mayan Creation began, around the Ceiba tree.

Lempira: But these people advanced rapidly and became more and more sophisticated in their progress. The Gods realized that this intelligence was pre-empting the worship and respect they demanded in return for giving them life. They could be overthrown by the intelligence of their very own invented humans... who were meant to be slaves, not to jeopardize their ultimate power. And now we get to the tragedy of the creation story.

Quetzalcoatl: Yes, there is another part of this creation story that I believe is very significant with regards to what is happening to our children now. After those four men and four women were created to live on the earth, grow food, and make children, the Gods decided that their human experiments were designed to be too smart. They had a supreme vision to see way beyond their immediate surroundings, they were innately gifted with math and scientific procedures, and they had great communication abilities which did not require language. This worried the Gods, as they wanted a population which would be subservient and respectful of their makers.... So they blinded and dumbfounded the newly created humans... they took away their powers of memory... and installed training and strength... so they would have to make slow progress in their way in life, inch by inch, in constant awe and debt to the Gods and their sacrificial requests... to live a life of religious service.

There is much discontented reaction to this explanation.

Hunahpu: So, a blindness was cast over these first families, a veil of forgetfulness... that limited their powers and intelligence.... that disabled memory of past lives and the journey of the soul, ... A blindness that came from the sky Gods... some of the original settlers of earth... They were called the Annunaki and they came from the star system, the Pleiades.

Xbalanque: The Mayan Gods demanded sacrificial blood, not only to instill fear and respect for the gods among the people... But also to collect their blood and pursue more genetic engineering to produce humans that could serve their purposes.

Morazon: Are you crazy? Where do you get these notions?

Hunahpu: From the memory of all the Mayan books that the Spaniards burned Senor. The books that held thousands of years of knowledge of the stars, of medicine, of science, of numbers, of the calendar, of the pyramid construction... infinite knowledge, which could have been passed on to our children.

Comizahual dances with more speed around the fire.

Lempira: And what do we have now in the third world? These precious, lost children are being born, as fast as they are cast out into the street. They live under the economic class system of global power I call White Supremacy, which renders the poor and humble powerless, through lack of education, proper housing or nutrition, opportunity, medicinal care, and family support..... unable to advance... eternal slaves to the rich for insulting wages, paying rent on their own land, where they are mere political afterthoughts.

Morazan: All of this has increased even further with modernity, fast food, television, electronic devices, computers and phones... into the daily struggle for survival.

Quetzalcoatl: Yes, to keep them subservient, and unable to participate unless they work for small wages, on their own land. (*The Green Prison….PRISON VERDE by Ramon Amaya Amador)*

Morazon: I apologize for my people, as this imperialistic domination seems to be the ongoing refrain of history and power.

Xbalanque: And so the great divide between the haves and have nots has kindled the production of more lost, innocent kids, who grow up thinking that adults and the people in charge are not to be trusted. And we have: poverty, hunger, rebellion, drugs, terrorism, gangs, and the suffering of the humble.

Lempira: How do we heal this crushing manipulative decay? Is this suppression now being bred into the DNA of our children as the new normal of mediocrity? So they cannot begin to compete educationally with the children of the elite and upper classes?

Hunahpu: Hopeless humility is the product of overwhelming fear and confusion until the pain of that isolation turns into the anger and power of the criminal gangs of today.

Xbalanque: And that is terrorism… lost innocence… that brought on the great flood waters… the nuclear bomb… all because of the great Gods who by example, taught the ruling class to oppress the lower classes to maintain power.

Quetzalcoatl: We must break the pattern of this abuse… for these poor Latin orphan children who come from nowhere and who see all their bridges to safety burning…They feel betrayed by adults. It breaks my heart…

He begins to sing a wailing lament, pleading to the beneficial spirits to unite the races with sensitivity. A cold wind sweeps through the ceremony as Comizahual intensifies her silent dance around the fire, conjuring feminine, warrior energy.

95. Return to Thelma's Rooftop

Ceci suddenly wakes up from this dream in front of Thelma's altar at the Hotel, with Leonel on one side smudging her with copal and Thelma on the other dowsing her with holy water. Clearly, Ceci has no idea how she got from the ruins to Thelma's roof. She sits up abruptly.

Ceci: Oh my wow! So what happened?

Leonel: The spirit took you into a trance, gringa!... And fortunately, not me... I could feel the fuerza in the courtyard.

Ceci: Yes... I went to the Ciudad Blanca again, and without the guiffity this time.

Leonel and Thelma: Oh... *looking at each other in disbelief.*

Leonel: How do you know about the Ciudad Blanca?

Ceci: Well ... I've been researching about it a lot recently, and I have actually been there in my dream trances now twice. So how did I get here?

Thelma: In one of those Copan buggy taxis... Leonel knows everybody.

Ceci: Oh thank you. I'm sorry.

Leonel: So what else happened?

Ceci: Well they told me about the Popol Vuh... and there was Francisco Morozan, and Chief Lempira, and Quetzalcoatl and two scribes... and at the end there was like a flying white lady tiger.

Thelma: Hombre... sabes quien es ella? La Sacerdota de las Lencas.. Comizahual.. the flying tiger goddess. You know who she is? The Lenca priestess, Comizahual... the flying tiger goddess.

Leonel: Y que mas, Ceci? And what else Ceci?

Ceci: And Leonel,,,I swear you were Quetzalcoatl!!! And he kept saying that Los Hondurenos need a big change of mind. That there has to be leadership that shows the people how to use the land and the resources to turn the work into paying jobs and turn the profit into education and infrastructure... to boost the self esteem of the people. Not to lose their land to invaders.

Leonel: And you saw me as Quetzalcoatl?

Ceci: I am pretty sure it was you.

Leonel: Gringa... this may not have been what you were looking for, but I believe this is the message spirit wanted to give you... right there in the ruins of Copan in the Court of the Jaguar, where you have arrived to celebrate your reincarnation as the Flying Tiger. the great, legendary Sacerdota Comizahual. She was blond... and a warrior who had three sons. These are your three warrior daughters who will survive only because they must learn your brave talents as a female warrior and goddess. For this lesson, you have come to Copan... to understand that your mission is to fight for these children, and to teach them to fight for their survival.

Ceci stands up. She is speechless. This spiritual message has taken her by surprise. In shock she looks up at Thelma and Leonel.

Ceci: Oh dear... I have to get back to the girls... I have to go. You have been so kind... Thank you so much, Thelma. Let me get my things and I will pay you on my way out. Thank you Leonel... You have taught me more in one day than I could have learned in a four year degree.

Leonel: Spirit told us to work with you. There are three Mayan children who have the chance of a lifetime under your care. They chose you and you chose them. You must remember, the children are the future. Your children are my children. In Mayan we say: In lak' ech, Hala ken - I am another you. You are another me. Go with God Cecilia.

On the way to the bus station, Ceci stops by the phone company and calls Conchita in Casa 9 at the SOS. Angie gets on the phone.

Angie: **Ceci donde estas?** Ceci, where are you?

Ceci: **Estoy en Copan y vuelvo hoy... y te veo manana ok?** I am in Copan and I will return today and will see you tomorrow OK?

Angie: Ok Ceci... big besos... moi!! Kisses

Ceci: Besos para ti tambien... Explique a sus hermanas que les amo OK? Kisses for you too. Explain to your sisters that I love you all, OK?

Angie: Si Ceci.. Te amo.

96. CECI'S HOTEL ROOM – return to reality – Rental home

Ceci returns to her hotel room in La Ceiba, exhausted from the bus ride. She drops her suitcase near the door of her hotel room and collapses on the bed. Night turns to early morning and the phone rings. Diana, the school secretary calls with a lead on a house for rent in Naranjal. Ceci jumps out of bed, dresses, and runs.

Ceci: Dios Mio – Una casa? Si seguro ... Quiero verla.... Vengo ahorra. Gracias Diana! Oh my God.. a house? I want to see it. I am coming now. Thanks Diana!

97. CASA in Naranjal – Avenida Roatan

Cut immediately to Ceci arriving at the house rental appointment in Naranjal, which is considered an "upscale" part of town... and originally had been an orange orchard. The house is a modern duplex in disrepair, situated, unbeknownst to Ceci, in the low point of a former river on Avenida Roatan. This causes flooding, and is owned by a young woman who cannot repair anything and will continually raise the rent. But it is a pretty house with big mango trees in the yard, and big cement walls and a gate. There are three upstairs bedrooms, 2 bathrooms, with a balcony and ensuite off the master. Downstairs there is a great room salon with an area to dance, a kitchen, an outdoor maid's quarters, laundry room, a garage porch, and a yard full of fruit trees. It is perfect for the girls, if they ever become part of her life.

This is a gift from the Goddess. She takes it, pays, and starts to move in... to a musical sound track... Vilma helps and finally, Ceci is settled.... She also sets up an altar with Mayan statues, the Venezuelan Cacique Tamanaco, the queen Maria Lionza, the Virgin Mary, candles, pix of the girls and her parents. When she is comfortable, she puts on music and she begins to work on choreography for the Ms. Honduras theme song.

** Just for the record... Ceci lived in three different places in La Ceiba. First she was in a 3rd floor apartment next to a gas station and down the street from the soccer stadium. This was down the street from the hospital where she originally found the girls. In reality, Ceci went back to the USA for a year to make money teaching dance in a charter school for the Arts in Henrico County, Va. Unable in her heart to abandon the girls, she returns after a year, making enough money to set up a house in El Sauce, upon initial custody. This was a rented house behind a golf course, in a middle class suburban development near the mall outside the city of La Ceiba. This was the property of the brother of the President of Honduras, and Ceci had to relocate when the house was needed. Hence, the housing episodes have been condensed to further the story. Needless to say there were many hoops to jump through to maintain a comfortable life style in La Ceiba for 10 years.

98. The Quinta Convention Hall – Rehearsal – Miss Honduras

Ms. Honduras Rehearsal – This is Ceci's first rehearsal with the beautiful female candidates for the Ms. Honduras Contest. The repetition of the Miss Honduras theme song takes us through lots

of dance sequences for 31 young girls, who also learn an opening number choreography to a tropical medley of salsa, merengue, and punta. Ceci takes them in groups and we see the initial lack of confidence in the young girls until they get into the music. This tropical cabaret theme, with a rhythm for a Latina feminine strut, repeats until they all eventually pick up the routine... There is confidence with repetition. Ceci must leave to keep her promise for a dance rehearsal at the SOS. The young, beautiful, but mostly untrained Ms. Honduras candidates practice their steps. He director, Eduardo Zablah then takes over with his flamboyant demeanor to direct modeling sequences. It is a huge enterprise.

99. <u>SOS – Casa 9 – Tia Dunia arrives -2005</u>

Ceci and Vilma climb out of the black truck, to a waiting group of kids at the SOS gate. Ceci has brought a tricycle and the double stroller for the girls. The girls are waiting patiently outside the crowd. Angie and Roxana have just returned from public kindergarten. She goes to hug them each with tender love and care. They go back to Casa 9 to change into their dance leotard and tights (donated to all the girls by Ceci). Tia Dunia is there. She has replaced Conchita as the new Tia.

Ceci: Bienvenida Tia Dunia. Como esta con su nueva familia en Casa 9? Welcome Tia Dunia. How are you with your new family?

Dunia: Poco a poco Dona Ceci. Hay que acostombrarnos. Aqui esta Jazmin. Little by little Dona Ceci. We have to get used to each other. Here is Jazmin.

Ceci: How are you bambina Jazz?

Takes Jazmin on her left knee... Roxana is driving her new tricycle around in circles, and the older kids are pushing Angie around in the double stroller.

Jazmin: Te amo. *She gives Ceci a big hug.*

Jazmin, Ceci, Angie, Dunia, Roxana

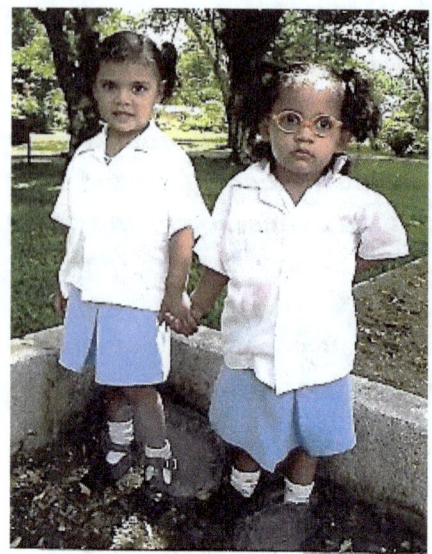

Roxana and Angie

Roxana & Jazmin

Angie: Te amo mucho Ceci. *She screams from the twirling stroller.*

Roxana: *mumbling as best she can.* Y yo tambien.

Ceci: And I love all of you… and I wish I could spend more time with you, but at least we know you are healthy. Let's do the Ring Around the Rosey dance… OK?

"Ring aound the Rosey" is the classic circle nursery rhyme, which has been a popular tool for teaching English to the girls. They love it…. Especially the falling down part. The other kids in Casa 9 are watching Ceci, Vilma and the girls, But eventually Olvin, Luz, Angeles, Blanca, Norma, Juny join in as they all lie on the floor laughing. Jazmin is laughing and wheezing.

"Ring around the Rosey, Pockets full of Posies, Ashes, Ashes, we all fall down!!!"

Norma: Ceci, Jazmin respire mal en la noche. Ceci.. Jazmin breathes badly at night.

Roxana: Asi... *Roxana grunts, imitating Jazmin's breathing. Ceci listens to Jazmin's chest.*

Ceci: Maybe you have some asthma from sleeping near those mosquito ridden pools of water in the back of the house. Now what can I do about that? Hay que ver un doctor.

Olvin: Ceci, nosotros faltamos mucho a Conchita. Ceci, we really miss Conchita a lot. *And the tears begin to flow from all.*

Angeles: Ella fue nuestra Madre. She was our mother.

Blanca: Y ella nos dejo... con esta Senora que no nos conocemos. And she left us with this Senora who we don't know.

Ceci: OK.. Yo entiendo. Vamos a hablar todos ahora mismo.. Vengan... Hay que discutir sobre esta situacion con Tia Dunia y todos los hermanos en casa 9. OK I understand. We are going to talk now Come. We have to discuss this situation with Tia Dunia with everybody in Casa 9.

Ceci and Vilma sit with the girls, while the other kids from Casa 9 gather, and Tia Dunia enters. Ceci makes room for Dunia next to her and addresses the kids.

Ceci: Sientese a mi lado Dunia. Muchachos...Nosotros sabemos como suffren uds. sin parientes. Es dificil, mas que yo puedo imaginar. Hay que tener mas fuerza que la mayoridad de ninos en el mundo. *Pause* Y ahora, se fue Conchita para casar, y aqui esta su nueva Tia... Dunia... Ella será alguien muy importante en sus vidas. Yo se que es bien dificil cambiar tias, despues tanto tiempo con Conchita. Pero... Conchita queria una vida, con un senor que le esperaba por mucho tiempo. Puede ser un ejemplo por uds. Que un dia consiguiran sus familias. Ella hizo su decision con mucho dolor a dejar uds... y fue por el amor de un buen senor. Pero ella les dijo a uds. que siempre seria en contacto como familia, como su madre, con visitas durante Navidad y por siempre. Sit down by me Dunia. Kids... We know how you have suffered without parents. It is difficult, more than I can imagine. You must be strong. Stronger than most children in this world. And now here is your new Aunt Dunia.

She is going to be someone very important in your lives. And I know how difficult it is to change Tias, especially after so much time with Conchita. But Conchita wanted a life with her boyfriend who has been waiting for her for a long time. This could be an example for you.. that some day you find your own family. Conchita made a decision with much pain to leave you all, and left for the love of a good man. But she told you that she would always be in contact with you like family, like your mother, with visits, and forever after leaving the SOS.

Olvin: Pero.. como podemos cambiar tan rapido… tener confianza con una senora que no conocemos? But how can we switch over so fast… to have confidence in a woman we don't know?

Ceci: Ella esta aquí porque tiene experiencia. Y porque yo se que Dios les mando una buena mujer con un grand corazon. She is here because she is a professional And because I know that God sent you a good woman with a big heart.

Dunia: Saben que?… Yo siento su dolor… Yo se que todos quieren vivir con padres suyos…. Y espero que un dia uds van a tener sus proprias familias buenas. Por el momento, para el futuro indefinitivo, yo soy su tia y voy a cuidarles y ensenarles lo que yo conozco… en el nombre del Padre, hijo, y Espiritu Santo. Con todo el amor que tengo en mi corazon. You know, I understand your pain. I know that all of you want to live with your own parents. And I hope that one day you will have your own families. But for the moment, for the future indefinitely, I am your aunt and I am going to take care of you and teach you what I know… in the name of the father, the son and the holy ghost. With all of the love that I have in my heart.

Ceci: Oyen? Dunia es una madre professional. Y Conchita siempre va estar en sus vidas. Are you listening? Dunia is a professional mother, and Conchita will always be part of your life..

Angeles: En el otro lado de Honduras!!! On the other side of Honduras!! *The tears continue.*

Ceci: Fue dificil tambien para Conchita. It was difficult also for Conchita.

Olvin: Si,, me dijo eso. Yes, she told me that.

Norma: A mi tambien. Me too.

Dunia: Yo entiendo su tristeza chicos..es dificil cambiar Tias. Que me den un chance para cuidarles… ayudarles con sus vidas… I understand your sadness, and the difficulty to adjust to someone else. Give me a chance to take care of you and help you with your lives.

Ceci: Haremos un circulo para rezar… antes de bailar… Dunia…a rezar por favor. Let's make a circle to pray…. Before we dance… Dunia… please pray for us.

Roxana, Blanca, Angie, Dunia, Jazmin, Luz

Taking hands, they all rise and make a circle. Dunia begs in her Evangelical way… for the Lord to give her the strength and the knowledge to heal and love these children, and that they will love her in return… They open their eyes and hug. Mami Dunia will be at the SOS for many years.

Ceci: Bueno… Ahora… Vamos al estudio para bailar. Ok now, let's go to the studio to dance.

100. Dance studio –SOS - Angel Dance

Everybody goes skipping out of casa 9, over to the old Kindergarten where all the SOS dancers are gathering. Once situated in the make shift studio, the music begins and they do their yoga and rehearsal of a Christmas angel pot-pourri ballet they are preparing. Jazmin, Roxana and Angie are mini angels with the older girls accompanying them. They are all celebrating the birth of Jesus as a Mary figure holds the baby in an upstage manger to the music of "River Song", by Amy Grant, which repeats throughout the story.

101. On the Swings outside Casa 9 - SOS – Another exit drama

Then then all the children go out to the swing and push Jazmin and Angie while others spin hoola hoops or chase soccer balls…. Roxana is fervently riding her new tricycle.

Soon it gets dark and Ceci and Vilma must go, and as usual she must escape the goodbyes in casa 9, as nobody will let go of her. Ceci tries to leave, and really dislikes having to slip out unnoticed, as the girls never want to let go of her. Ceci always regrets leaving them like this… more abandonment. How often can this happen before they learn committed security. Ceci and Vilma sneak away….

Angie, Ceci, Roxana

102. <u>In the Truck –View in the RV mirror (My deepest memory of all)</u>

Ceci wipes away a tear, as she looks in the rearview mirror image of the girls running towards her as she leaves. This has become a re-occurring nightmare for Ceci, as she too goes through separation anxiety for the bond that is forming between her and the three sisters. This is the abandonment that so many orphans live over and over, from their parents, to housemothers and missionaries coming and going, or with anybody who plays temporary mom. Still in 2022 with the current custody in the USA of the girls, this abandonment issue raises its ugly head as permanent psychological damage.

103. <u>Returning Vilma to her new home</u>

Ceci takes Vilma home to her new house where her family has begun to get settled. Her mother, is upset about leaving the family home in Las Mercedes, but remains strong despite the grief of being pushed out by gang members. Police do not go into Las Mercedes because gang members will shoot them. Their new home is a small house in the hills, with a little land and pretty views. Clearly it is a humble barrio, but it is safe and neighborly. Ceci gets out to greet Vilmas's sisters and her mother who is the same age as Ceci, and has issues walking. She is a matriarch and tells Ceci that she raised two neighbor's children with unofficial custody whose lives she saved from the orphanage. Ceci knows that their financial situation is not good, and asks Sayda, Vilma's sister if she will join Vilma and work for her on the Xmas show this week. Any work is hard to come by in La Ceiba. Ceci climbs back in the truck and they wave as she descends the hill.

104. Christmas Show at the Mazapan School – "Angeles de Ballet"

Authors note *** - Over the course of 9 years in La Ceiba Ceci produced EIGHT Xmas productions. Many hours of choosing music, choreographing, making costumes, and rehearsing took place to create these productions. In this book we talk about only three, but extra playbill programs from different productions are presented for the memories. These are three out of eight productions.

This will be a montage of the first Christmas production which includes the Mazapan students and the SOS orphans. Vilma and Sayda help Ceci mount the backdrop on the stage. It is an image of a nativity with the light of a star beaming down on the manger. Honduras is a Catholic country and there is no hesitation to portray the Nativity Story and the birth of Jesus in schools. Dancers and parents start to arrive and there is excitement backstage in the 4th grade class dressing room as they get ready. Moms do makeup and hair. Soon the house lights dim, and the show begins with the following numbers from:

La Escuela de Danza Axis Mundi – La Ceiba, Honduras Numeros "Angeles de Ballet" - Diciembre 2003

1. **Happy Holidays Tap – Intermedios**

2. **Waka Waka - Avancados** (Student choreography)

3. **Angelitas – Bambinas**

4. **Tiki Tiki Ballet – Principios**

5. **Pata Pata Ballet – Intermedios**

6. **I Could Have Danced All Night – Avancados**

7. **Merengue Navideno Folklorico – Principios**

8. **Santa Claus is Comin to Town – Avancados – Student work**

9. **The Give Love Ballet - Intermedios**

10. **Birth of the Baby River song - Bambinas**

11. **Angelina Raton – Principios**

12. **Adestes Fideles – Avancadas**

13. **Finale – Angels We Have Heard on High – Todos**

(FOLLOWING YEAR)

<u>**EL ARBOL DE AMOR** – Diciembre 2004</u>

1. **The Simple Things – Avancadas (Student choreography)**
2. **The Lost Dolls – Las Bambinas**

3. **Prayer – Intermedios**

4. **Deck the Halls/Jingle Bells – Principios**

5. **DUET – Irena & Sarahi Martorell (Student choreography)**

6. **I Want a Hippopotamus for Christmas**

7. **Home for the Holidays – Intermedios**

8. **Santa's Elves – Bambinas & Santa**

9. **Let's Get it Started – Principios**

10. **Transformations – Avancados**

11. **FINALE – Santa Claus is Comin to Town – Todos**

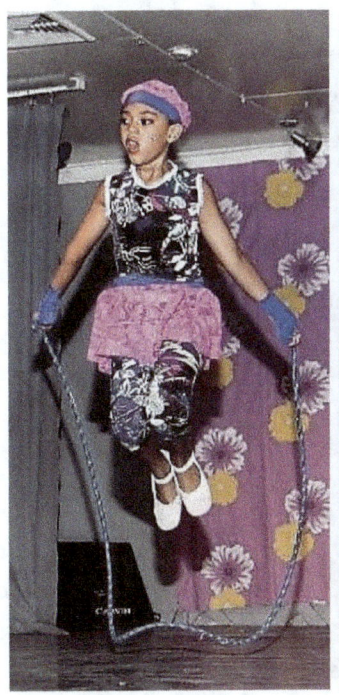

Roxana **Roxana and Angie on stage**

(FOLLOWING YEAR)

Cuentos de Hadas Navidenas – Diciembre 2005

1. **The Cha Cha Slide – The company**

2. River Song – Avancadas *(Nativity Ballet)*

3. Hoola -Twist & Shout / Penguinas – Bambinas

4. Evergirl- Principios

5. Pray – Intermedios

6. Twinkle Twinkle – Bambinas

7. Ano Nuevo – Avancadas

8. Opera of the Bells- Principios y Intermedios

9. Bon Bon – Bambinas

10. FINALE – We wish you a Merry Christmas

105. BAPTISM – La Union

There is a small, humble Catholic chapel in La Union, outside La Ceiba. It is a small beach community. Lots of parents and children congregate outside the church dressed in long, well used, white, fluffy dresses. There will be a mass communion and baptism ceremony. David, Ceci, Vilma, all the kids from Casa 9, and Tia Dunia, attend.

The three sisters are dressed in the pretty white dresses Vilma got for them. They look beautiful. David and Ceci will fill out an important document with the Padre that declares their status as Madrina (Godmother) and Padrino (Godfather). This will later be the key to Ceci's custody.

Inside the church, Ceci and David are monitoring several children who will be baptized and confirmed during this festive Winter holy day at the humble, coastal Catholic Church in La Union. The following factory line baptismal ceremony would be effective in slow motion, and/or black and white. There are many poor people there. The second hand white dresses are pretty, even if they don't fit perfectly. A Catholic Priest/Padre, prepares the altar while several dozen children, wait their turn in the front rows of the small, village church, ready to be baptized. After everybody is settled, the Padre starts the long process of the mass, and then one by one, each child is blessed with holy water. Ceci holds baby Jazmin, Vilma is with Angie, and Mami Dunia is with Roxana. There are other SOS kids from Casa 9 present…along with other young SOS children who are also being baptized. The ceremony continues in dream like musical fashion, where each child is individually baptized with a pitcher of water. Then the chorus sings and they all go outside the church to take photos.

Angie, Ceci, Jazmin, Roxana

Roxana, David, Luz, Dunia, Ceci, Angie, Blanca, Olvin, Norma

106. Back inside the CHURCH – Ceci and the Father/ Priest

Ceci goes back into the church to pray at the altar.

Ceci: Dear Mother Mary, thank you for bringing these children into my life. Thank you for my father and mother, Joseph and Josephine, who showed me the love that has given me the ability to do what I can. Please help me do everything possible to do the right thing in this impossible situation. I now must move on to the beginning of my next struggle, which is to get legal custody of the girls. Can you show me the way? Stay with me Mary, please stay with me. I know how important this baptism is for the girls.

There is a spiritual moment when we see a tear in the eye of the Mary statue.

The padre watches from the chapel door. The three girls run into the chapel looking for their madrina ...calling Ceci's name. The padre goes to speak to Ceci.

Padre: Querida Sra Cecilia... venga aqui.... El espiritu de Dios esta contigo. Dejame bendecirte. Estas haciendo todo posible para estas ninas. Yo lo veo, y me lo siento. Dios te bendiga con suerte. Vas a ver exito un dia…. Porque? Porque nadie les quiere como ud. Cualquier persona puede ver eso… y con tiempo, ellas van a salir contigo. Tengas paciencia con nuestra sistema de custodia… Es lento. Pero… tiene Dios en su lado. Vaya con Dios hermana…. Dear Sra. Cecilia come here. The spirit of God is with you. Let me bless you. You are doing everything possible for these girls. I see it, and I feel it. God blesses you with luck. You will have success one day. Why? Because nobody wants them like you do. Anybody can see this and with time they will leave with you. Have patience with our custody system. It is slow. But you have God on your side… Go with God sister.

Ceci: Gracias Padre… Hay dias cuando yo pienso que nadie lo vea asi. Sus palabras me inspiran…. Gracias… En el nombre de Maria, su hijo, y Dios Poderoso. Thank you Father. There are days when I think that nobody sees it like that. Your words inspire me. Thank you in the name of Maria, her son, and the all powerful God.

Angie comes up behind Ceci and grabs her leg.

Angie: Venga Ceci!!! A prender una luz para la virgin!!! Para pedir mi vista!!! *Angie sees the Padre.* **Hola Dios!!….Ella es mi Madrina…** Come Ceci! To light a candle for the virgin. To ask for my sight… Hello God. She is my Godmother.

Padre: *laughing*…**No soy Dios… Soy solamente un ayudante de Dios. Bendiciones bellas. Y su madrina… un dia va a ser su Mama …. Recuerden mis palabras.** I am not God.. I am only a helper of God. Blessings beautiful girls. And your godmother, will be your mother one day. Remember my words.

Angie: Si Padre… Donde esta Dios entonces? Yes Father… Then where is God?

Padre: Esta en el Cielo, con Jesus, y Maria… pero cuando les llama, ellos pueden oir… Hay que aprender a rezar ninas… He is in heaven with Jesus and Maria… but when you call them they can hear and see you. You must learn to pray girls.

Angie: El Padre Nuestro? Si yo puedo. I can pray the Our Father.

Padre: Hazlo entonces… Let me hear it. *He takes Angie on his knee. Angie recites El Padre Nuestro, the Our Father in Spanish with her eyes closed in deepest earnest.*

Padre nuestro, que

estás en el cielo.

Santificado sea tu nombre.

Venga tu reino.

Hágase tu voluntad en la tierra como en el cielo.

Danos hoy nuestro pan de cada día.

Perdona nuestras ofensas,

como también nosotros perdonamos a los que nos ofenden.

No nos dejes caer en tentación y líbranos del mal.

Amén.

Padre: Bien hecho. Y que es su deseo mas grande? Well done. And what is your biggest wish?

Angie: Quiero mi vista, quiero estar con mis hermanas y con mi Madrina, Ceci. I want my vision, I want to be with my sisters and my Godmother, Ceci.

Padre: Yo rezare para uds…. Pero uds. tambien necesitan rezar. I will pray for you. But you also need to pray.

Angie: Ceci nos quiere tanto con un grand corazon. Nos sentimos triste cuando ella va. Ella nos ama mucho. Verdad Ceci? Ceci loves us a lot with a big heart. We feel sad when she leaves us. She really loves us. Right Ceci? *Angie hugs Ceci*

Ceci: You know I love you baby… You and your sisters… I'm gonna take care of you.

Padre: Bendiciones para uds.

David comes along.

David: So are the kids going to do their Christmas Ballet? Are they ready to go?

Ceci: **Of course, forgive me. I got lost in the rhapsody of my little Goddesses. Gracias Padre.** (*To David*) **I will organize the kids for the performance now.**

107. <u>Plaza – Outside the Church – Photos and Performance</u>

Ceci goes to the outdoor plaza where the SOS Tias are decorating the Virgin with flowers and offerings. It is tropical Christmas time with the outdoor pavilion decorated like the Nacimiento with villages around a cresh stable with Baby Jesus. The SOS chidlren are gathering nervously. Ceci plugs in her boom box, and all the kids who were baptized from the SOS get ready to dance in their beautiful white baptism and holy communion dresses as angels. The three little sisters perform as the three queens bringing gifts ceremoniously to baby Jesus, played by a very young orphan baby boy from the SOS. Once again, we hear the beautiful, haunting melody of Amy Grant's "River Song". Everybody is there: Dunia, Vilma, All the brothers and sisters from casa #9... Norma, Juny, Olvin, Blanca, Angela, y Luz.

108. <u>After the Baptism – Celebrating at Porvenir Beach</u>

Not far from the church one can see the ocean. The entire entourage from the SOS walks down to the beach in their white dresses to have a barbecue and swim in Porvenir after the mass. They all change into swim wear in the bamboo hut behind the restaurant. It is a joyous occasion. Ceci sits with David as the Tias barbecue chicken, and they toast to their new status as OFFICIAL MADRINA y PADRINO of the girls (Godmother and Godfather).

Ceci: Well David, I am hoping this is the first step towards any possibility of custody.

Roxana & Angie

David: You can't take them out of the orphanage you know. It's impossible. They were taken away from the Mom because of abuse, yet she is the only one who can remove them from the SOS. Go figure that logic.

Ceci: I will go to the IHNFA tomorrow to explore all these possibilities.

David: And even if they were eligible for adoption, which they are not because the Mom is alive.... You are too old to adopt.

Ceci: I don't take no for an answer David. I am the only one who will upgrade their lives and give them a chance, and they deserve it. I know it and God knows it. Angie is legally blind according to the eye doctor in El Progresso, Roxana has developmental issues, and God knows how being abandoned at three months will affect Jazmin. How will they survive? Somebody has to see them through this.

David: All from general abuse and a whack on the head from a bad mother. I hear about this everyday Ceci.

Ceci: I just can't go on just teaching dance for the rest of my life when now I know how all these children suffer emotionally. It's just putting artistic bandaids on moments for underprivileged kids. I want to make a real difference.

David: Adoption is really rough in Honduras. The IHNFA is closed for corruption, all the adoption cases are on hold. The US embassy insists that you set up a two year residency with the children in Honduras before they will even consider a visa. You will have to establish residency.

Ceci: Ok well, I have a job teaching dance and theater and mounting all the school shows over at the Mazapan School now, and that will get me a work visa.

David: I admire your tenacity Ceci...But... Nothing will be harder than getting custody of these girls and getting them into the USA. I have seen Americans come and go with great big aspirations and plans....

Ceci: They need medical help, therapy, and special education David. We're not going to get that here. I want to take them on a medical visa at least to start.

David: Ceci, you fit the profile of a gringa who won't come back. I have seen it a dozen times. Twenty five years ago, I went to the Hospital Atlantida where you found the girls, and picked up a kid in pediatrics.... Took him home as my son. Now he is a lawyer in LA. But those days are over with all the sex trafficking and organ rip off. It's not going to be easy.

Ceci: I know David, but nothing I do has ever been easy.

The 3 girls come running over to Ceci with wild beach flowers and throw themselves into her lap.

Angie: Te amo Ceci.

Roxana: *Mumbles something- She cannot talk.*

Ceci: Uds. son tan bellas!!! Les quiero mucho. Saben verdad? You guys are so beautiful! I love you very much. You know that right?

Angie: Ahora tenemos otra madre Ceci…. Tenemos Conchita y Dunia y Ceci. Now we have another mother, Ceci.. We have Conchita and Dunia and Ceci.

Ceci: Para siempre mi amor… Soy tu madrina… y David es tu Padrino. Dele un beso. For ever my love. I am your Madrina, and David is your Padrino. Give him a kiss.

David: *David gives the three girls a big squeeze.* **Vamos a comer todos!!!** Time to eat!

The Tias have prepared a barbecue. Kids are swinging in hammocks, singing along to the music, eating, or enjoying the cool river in the hot northern Honduran sun. Olvin begins to play the drums and Angie, Jazmin, and Roxana join some of the other girls who enter the water dancing. The whole gang cheers them on, as they dance, laugh and splash. David is standing at the rivers' edge.

David: I may not be much of a godfather for the next few years, but I am beginning to think that this baptism could very well be the key to your future custody. Love can make miracles.

Ceci: Thanks David… Part of the dream is that I am now official.

David: Even though I am a pretty straight arrow, I wish all the Padrinos had the guts to fight for these kids like you. They definitely need and deserve you Ceci… Good luck… Let's pack up… the rain is coming.

They all scramble for shelter as the tropical thunder and rain begin.

109. <u>With Lawyer Segovia with Karla – First Custody Paper.</u>

Ceci is sitting on the porch of her new house. She calls Karla.

Ceci: **Karla, Como estas? Todavia puedes venir ahora hablar con el abogado sobre la custodia?** Karla how are you? Can you still come to speak to the lawyer now to talk about custody?

Karla: **Si Ceci… Pero estoy en el mercado sin pistos.** Yes, but I am at the market without money.

Ceci: **Busques un taxi para llevarte a la oficina de Abogado Segovia en la calle 15 de Septiembre cerca La Escuela Maria Regina. Yo voy a cobrarlo. Diez minutos OK?** Take a taxi and come to the office of Lawyer Segovia on the 15th of September street near the Maria Regina school. I will pay for it… 10 minutes?

Ceci enters an office, where she meets Licenciado Roberto Segovia, abogado/lawyer.

Segovia: **Buenas Tardes Sra. Cecilia… Me dicen que un senor David Ashby te mando para mi servicio.** Good afternoon Sra. Cecilia. David Ashby sent you for my services.

Ceci: **Si senor, gracias por su audiencia. Esperamos ahora la madre de tres ninas en el SOS que quiero cuidar y conseguir custodia oficial. La madre les perdio a ellas porque no pudo mantenerles, y por fin ella tiene confianza que yo puedo cuidarles bien.** Yes, thank you for seeing me. We are now waiting for the mother of the three little girls in the SOS whom I want to care for and find custody for. Their mother lost custody because she couldn't maintain care for them, and she has confidence that I will take good care of them.

Segovia: Excelente senora. *Taking notes.* **Vamos a ver lo que dice la madre.** Excellent. Let's see what the mother says.

Karla enters in her flip flops and tight jean shorts with another baby in her belly and Carlitos on her hip. He is the last child of the father Carlos conceived with Karla.

Segovia: Sientete Sra. Bienvenida. Welcome, please be seated.

Ceci: Hola Karla, como estan ud y Carlitos? Hello Karla, how are you and baby Carlitos?

Karla: *In a whisper.* **Bien tengo prisa. Hay que pagar la cuenta de luz antes de que ellos la corten.** I'm OK.. I am in a hurry because I have to pay the electricity bill before they turn off the lights.

Segovia: Bueno, Sra. Rojas... Hello Ms. Rojas.

Karla: Iraheta Rojas, Sr. El papa de mis ninas se llama Carlos Alvarez Iraheta. Mi esposo. Aqui esta su ultimo hijo, Carlitos. Karla Iraheta Rojas, Senor. The father of the girls was named Carlos Alvarez Iraheta... my husband. Here I have his last child, Carlitos.

Segovia: Y donde esta Carlos? And where is he?

Karla: El ya morio el invierno pasado. He died last winter.

Segovia: Mis sentimientos, Sra. Iraheta, tiene el acto defuncto? I am sorry to hear that Sra. Iraheta. Do you have the death certificate?

Karla: No, todavia, no he reportado la muerte de Carlos. Esta en el cementario publico. No, I haven't yet reported his death. He is in the public cemetary.

Ceci: Yo voy averiguar el processo de obtener el acto defuncto. And I am researching the process to obtain the death certificate now.

Segovia: Pues, vamos a continuar. Entonces sra, ud. esta lista dar custodia a esta Sra Americana para sus tres hijas Jazmin, Angie, y Roxana. Y porque? OK, so let's continue. So Sra, I understand that you are ready to give custody to this American woman for your three children, Jazmin, Angie and Roxana? And why?

Karla: Si, Porque yo se que seria mejor para ellas estar con ella en vez de estar trancadas en el SOS. Yes because I know it is better for them to be with her than to be locked up in the SOS.

Segovia: Y porque Sra?

Karla: Porque yo se que Ceci puede darles una mejor vida… Una vida que yo no puedo darles en 100 anos. Me naci en esta clase baja, y es donde ellas se quedarian conmigo, o en el SOS. Cual es peor, no se. Pero… con Ceci, ellas tienen un chance. Y ella seria mi co-madre. Because I know that Ceci can give them a better life. A life that I can't give them in 100 years. I was born in this lower class, and that's where they would remain with me or in the SOS. Which is worse I don't know. But with Ceci, they have a chance. And she will be my co-madre.

Segovia: Ademas, ud. entiende que ellas tienen enfermidades, que afectaran sus futuros. Besides, you know that they have illnesses which will affect their futures.

Karla: Si, Roxana y Angie eran enferma con fievre y infection por mucho tiempo… y un ladrillo cayo en la cabeza de Angie Nicolle cuando ella tuvo un ano. Yes, Roxana and Angie had meningitis with fever and infection for quite some time… and a brick fell on Angie's head when she was one year old, and she is blind from that.

Segovia: Y eso fue cuando vinieron los soldados para sacarles de la casa verdad? And that's when the soldiers came to take them away, right?

Karla: Si, porque mi vecina les llamaron. *Rolling her eyes.* Yes because my nosey neighbor called.

Segovia: Se dice aqui… que tambien ellas tuvieron mucho hambre con agua mala, y que había meningitis y mucho violencia en la casa. And it says here in the report that they also were very hungry and that there was meningitis and much violence in the house.

Karla: No hablamos de estas cosas Sr. Les regalo a la gringa. Escriba el papel y vamos por favor. Let's not talk about those things Sr. I will give them to the gringa. Please write the paper and let's go.

Segovia: Bueno.... Con permiso, voy a preparar el documento. Ok... with permission I am going to prepare the document. *He leaves the room.*

Ceci: Tu sabes, Karla, que voy hacer todo en mi poder para mejorar las vidas de ellas.... Y que es bien valiente que ud. esta arreglando este camino para ellas. Te prometo que voy a darles toda mi vida. You know Karla, that I am going to do everything in my power to improve their lives. And it is really valiant of you to arrange this path for them. I promise that I will give them my life.

Karla: Lo que necesito ahora Ceci son pistos para mudarme de la familia en San Judas. Desde el muerte del papa, toda la familia me odia, y quiere que me vaya. What I need now Ceci is money to move me out of the house in San Judas. Since Carlos died, the family hates me and wants me to move.

Ceci: Entonces, toma. *She slides Karla 500 lempiras.* **Y con discrecion, porque tu sabes que no debo de darle dinero.** All right, take it... and with discretion, because you know that I should not give you money.

Karla: Porque?.... Porque tu lo tienes, y yo no tengo nada. Why? Because you have it and I don't.

Ceci: La ley dice que es como comprar ninos. The law says it is like buying kids.

Karla: Chica, tu quieres custodia de las ninas?... hay que ayudarme... me entiendes? Girl, you want custody of the girls? You have to help me. Do you understand?

Ceci: Si Karla.... Spoken like a true swindler. You don't care about these girls at all.....clearly.

Karla: Hay que comer, co-madre... Tengo mas ninos! Con hambre!! We must eat co mother. I have more kids... who are hungry!!

As she smiles maliciously, the lawyer Segovia returns. He places papers in front of both the ladies and proceeds to read in Spanish....

After which they both sign. There is music over this. When all is said and done, under the music, Ceci writes a check to the lawyer, hands are shaken, words are spoken, they leave and Ceci goes her way/ precious document in hand. She puts Karla in a taxi.

110. <u>Return to IHNFA – La Ceiba – Mercedes y Melissa</u>

Ceci gets out of her black pick up truck in front of a dilapidated old public school turned into the Government Children's Services or La IHNFA (Instituto Hondureno de la Ninez y la Familia) de La Ceiba. She waits in a humble cement brick office in Barrio Alvarado for La Directora, Mercedes, who is a middle aged, motherly lawyer constantly limited by backwards law, and insufficient funds. She is the one who originally removed the girls from Adila's house. Despite the struggle of her work with the IHNFA, Mercedes has helped many orphaned children. She has a warm heart.

There is a woman named Melissa Calix from the Tegucigalpa IHNFA who Ceci also remembers from the hospital. She has come especially to talk to Ceci about her interest in the sisters. There is also a young, male assistant in the office.

Mercedes (Ceiba Ihnfa Lady): La Senora Cecilia…. Como esta? Con mucho gusto te saludo.

Ceci: Buenas Dias Senora.

Mercedes: Cecilia, le presento Sra. Melissa Calix de la administracion de la IHNFA en Tegucigalpa…que quiere oir su cuenta sobre las ninas Iraheta Rojas. Cecilia, this is Sra. Melissa Calix from the IHNFA administration in Tegucigalpa, who wants to hear your story about the Iraheta Rojas girls.

Ceci: Bueno Senoras… Gracias por su audiencia. Vengo hoy para decirle que tengo un papel con la mama de las ninas que me da permiso para cuidarles. Aqui esta. Y quiero saber si piensan uds. si puedo segurar la custodia de ellas? Hace poco yo me converti en la madrina de ellas con un padre de la Iglesia Catolica. Alright ladies. Thank you for seeing me. I come today to tell you that I have a paper with the girls' mother that gives me permission to take care of them. Here it is. And I want to know if you think I can get custody. Recently I became their Godmother with a priest in the Catholic church.

Mercedes: Te aseguro, Sra Cecilia, que las ninas estan en buenas manos... y que estan bien en el SOS... Yo, personalmente, visito alla seminal para chequearles en Casa #9 y o tros. I assure you Sra. Cecilia that the girls are in good hands and that they are OK at the SOS. I have personally visited them weekly to check on them in Casa 9 and others.

Ceci: Yo se Sra. Mercedes... pero quiero darles una vida mejor que eso... Aunque de yo le agradezco a Dios todos los dias que ellas tienen techo y comida en el SOS.... Pero.... I know Sra. Mercedes, but I want to give them a better life than that. Even though I thank God every day that they have a roof and food in the SOS, but...

Mercedes: *Interupting...* **Yo entiendo lo que quiere ud. Y por mi cuenta, yo preferiria ver todos estes ninos en hogares familiares... con madres, padres, hermanos, primos, abuelos..... Pero, para validar la seguridad de estos ninos con familias extranjeras...es un trabajo increible para mi gente... y por eso, adopcion es bien dificil.** I understand what you want. And from my side, I would prefer to see all these kids in family homes, with mothers, fathers, brothers, cousins, grandparents... but to validate the security of these kids with foreign families is incredible work for my people, and for that reason, adoption is really difficult.

The Male assistant: Ms. Diaz, permitame hablar Englais. The Adoption circuit is frozen anyway because of the IHNFA shutdown. Abandoned children remain in the orphanages meanwhile. The law dictates that to leave the orphanage they can only go back to their blood and extended family as first priority. You say that you are the Madrina. That is good. But, if a parent is alive, even if the child is legally taken away from her, that parent is the only person, other than secondary family members, who can repent and legally remove children from an orphanage. Maybe later you can arrange some kind of foster care. But it will be difficult to leave the country. You will also need the Acto Defuncto (Death Certificate) of the father. And it is

often difficult to find the police report to begin the process. What you are trying to do is next to impossible. I am sorry Senora Cecilia.

Ceci: **OK bien... pero hoy... No veo la familia visitando el SOS. Mira...aqui, tengo un papel oficial de la madre Karla Rojas....diciendo que podria yo tener custodia. ... dice aqui...** Understood, but today I don't see the family visiting the SOS. Look here... I have an official paper from the mother, Karla Rojas, saying that I could have custody... It says here.

Mercedes reads with her glasses... and then looks up... and shows it to Ms. Calix, who has been maintaining silence with pursed lips.

Ms. Calix: **Sra Diaz.... Estas ninas ahora son la propriedad del gobierno de Honduras – de la IHNFA, desde que les quitaron de la mama, por su negligencia y abuso. Entonces, esta misma mujer no puede hacer nada con estas ninas hasta que su situacion se ha resuelto. Ella no tiene poder con este papel... es una broma.... Burla!! Disculpa...** Sra. Diaz These girls are now the property of the Honduran Government... of the IHNFA, since they were taken from the mother, because of negligence and abuse. Therefore, this same woman, cannot have anything to do with these girls until the situation is resolved. She has no power with this paper, it is a joke... I am sorry.

Ceci: **Entonces, Un nino entra el SOS, y no se puede salir para nada.** So.. a child enters the SOS and cannot ever leave for any reason.

Ms. Calix: **Hasta que tengan 18 anos, y francamente, es la mejor vida que podrian tener.** *Approaching her....* **Ademas, Sra. You should not have been entering, touching, paying for, or removing these sisters from their home with Ms. Adila. Clearly this woman took advantage of your generosity. And you had no business taking them out of the house. They are under the care of the IHNFA ... the Honduran government. Do you understand?** Until they are 18 years old, and frankly it is the best life they could possibly have.

Ceci: *Indignantly* I gave them care they never would have received with Ms. Adila. Her hands were full. And these girls were really sick!! *She pauses to collect herself...* Y que pasara con ellas cuando tengan 18 anos? How will the street give them a healthy future? And what happens to them when they are 18?

Ms. Calix: No... Les ayudaremos buscar careras y educacion.... *Looking out the window.* Si no hacen sus proprios bebes antes.... *Sigh, and she mutters in bad English.* Babies making babies.... Mira Dona Cecilia... Necesitamos los orphanatos en Honduras. Las calles serian mas llenas de ninos perdidos. No.. We help them look for careers and education. If they don't make their own babies before. Babies making babies... Look Dona Cecilia ... we need the orphanages in Honduras. The streets would be more filled with lost kids.

Ceci: Sra Calix, ... Estas ninas, tienen disabilidades medicales, y necesitan mas atencion que se puede darles en un orphanato... Y no poderian sobrevivir por mucho tiempo en la calle.... Son bellas... y llegaran embarasadas rapido. Yo se que conmigo hay una mejor vida... que pueden evitar estas huecos, con una madre real. Sra. Calix. These girls have disabilities and need more attention than they can get in an orphanage. They would not survive for much time on the street, even at 18. They are pretty, and they will get pregnant fast. I know that with me there is a better life, that can avoid these pitfalls, with a real mother.

Ms. Calix: Mira, Sra. Cecilia... Yo repito,,, Cuando se entran un orphanato, como el SOS, ellos estan alla hasta que tengan 18 anos... Solamente la madre o padre, o familiares pueden sacarles, con prueba de responsibilidad para las ninas. Y sabemos que la madre, Karla, vive, pero no sirve, que quiere decir que ellas NO estan abandonadas. Hay que estar abandonada para adoptar. Ademas el circuito de adopcion en la IHNFA esta gelado, y casi cerrado. End of story. Tengo que irme, para hablar con otra madre ahora. Disculpa... Le dejo con Sra. Mercedes. Look Cecilia... I repeat. When one enters an orphanage like the SOS, they will be there until they are 18. Only the mother or father or family members can take them out, with proof of responsibility for the children. And we know that the mother, Karla, is alive, but is not a good mother… which means that they are not abandoned. And they must be abandoned to adopt. Besides, the adoption circuit in the IHNFA is frozen and almost closed. End of story. I have to go, to speak to another mother now. I am sorry. I leave you with Sra. Mercedes. *She puts on her glasses and leaves the room with her stack of papers.*

Ceci: Yo soy la Madrina, oficial, con papeles… Mercedes!! Yo estoy buscando el acto defuncto del papa, yo aquile una casa para acomodar las ninas, tengo ropa, juguetes, escuela privada lista para ellas, doctores listos, y mucho mas. Yo se que estoy mirando un camino largo para lograr custodia. Y ud. sabe que nadie va a cuidar estas ninas como yo. Y este compromiso es lo que me maneja en los ojos de Dios. I am the official godmother, with papers Mercedes! I am looking for the death certificate of the father, I have rented a house to accommodate them, I have clothing, toys, private school, the right doctors, and so much more. I know that am looking at a long journey to get custody. But you know that nobody is going to take care of them like me. And this commitment is what drives me in the eyes of God.

Mercedes: Con respecto de su amor y fuerza…. Desfortunatamente, hay que entender que la misma IHNFA que les sacaron las ninas a causa del abuso, puede reponerles en los manos de la misma mama mala de nuevo….a causa de este ley incomprehensible. Porque, segun la ley, SOLAMENTE un familiar puede sacar un nino del custodia del gobierno… y la IHNFA. Esta mujer Karla, es triste y peligrosa…. te digo. La situacion es muy dificil. With respect for your love and strength… Unfortunately, you must understand that the same IHNFA that removed the girls because of abuse, can put them back in the hands of the same mother again… because this law is incomprehensible. Because according to the law, only a family member can take the girls back from the government, and the IHNFA. This woman Karla is sad and dangerous, I am telling you. The situation is very difficult.

Ceci: Whose side are you on anyway? Por favor!!

Holding her head in her hands.

Mercedes: Sra. Cecilia.... Yo se que sus intenciones son admirables. Cada dia yo rezo que adopcion en este pais desarrollaria mas rapido... No piensa ud. que yo quiero que todos estes ninos consiguen un padre y una madre algun dia??? Yo quiero ayudarte... yo quiero ayudar Roxana, Angie, y Jazmin, con todo mi corazon... pero por el momento, mis manos estan attaradas. Sigue con su exploracion. Tu tienes amor, y poder en su espiritu... Vaya con Dios , y si Dios quiere, un dia, tu vas a lograr esta custodia con estas preciosas angelitas. Personalmente, yo no puedo hacer mas. Sra. Cecilia. I know that your intentions are good. Every day I pray that adoption in this country would be faster. You don't think that I want all these kids to find a mother and father some day? I want to help you, I want to help Roxana, Angie, and Jazmin with all my heart.... But for the moment my hands are tied. Continue with your exploration. You have love and power in your spirit. Go with God and God willing, one day you will have custody with these precious little angels. Personally, I can't do more for you.

Ceci: Gracias Mercedes....me siento como la oveja negra aquí with the backbends, the suspicion of organ selling and child abuse, the wrong lawyers, the cash, the endless tenacity... Es incomprehensible!! Thank you Mercedes, ... I feel like the black sheep here. ...... It is incomprehensible!!!

Mercedes: Yo se!!! Pero Karla es la mama Cecilia.... Ella vive.... con o sin el abuso.... Y segun la ley, solamente ninos abandanados son candidatos para adopcion.... Tambien, recuerde que, con 51 anos, ud pasa el limite para aplicar para adopcion. No veo ningun puerta abierta hoy... Disculpa Dona Cecilia. Si Dios Quiere ... las cosas cambiaran. I know. But Karla is the mother Cecilia. She is alive, with or without the abuse. And according to the law, only abandoned children are candidates for adoption. Also remember that with 51 years you pass the limit to apply for adoption. I don't see one open door today. I am sorry Cecilia... God willing things will change.

Ceci: Bueno, au menos, haga me el favor de estar pendiente de ellas siempre. Y sabe que .... vamos a vernos mucho... Tambien... no olvide que soy la Madrina legal con papeles. Esa

es la llave que voy usar un dia. OK… at least do me the favor of being very aware of them. And know that …. we are going to see each other a lot. Also don't forget that I am their Godmother with legal papers. This is the key that I will use one day.

Mercedes: Claro Cecilia!!!!, que Dios te bendigas. I understand Cecilia… may God bless you.

As she leaves, the male assistant follows her into the street.

Male assistant: Sra Cecilia. Tenga este numero de un abogado, Merlyn Vazquez, que yo recomiendo. Take this number of a lawyer, Merlyn Vazquez who I recommend. *He whispers.* **His mother is the Children's Judge of La Ceiba. Don't tell anybody we talked about that. OK?**

He turns without a word more, and Ceci stands there with her mouth open…. Until she realizes…That she must learn about the inside connections in La Ceiba.

111. <u>**Dance class at SOS – Preparing for Mother's Day**</u>

Ceci jumps out of her funky black pickup truck, to be greeted by a group of kids at the SOS. Waiting patiently outside the crowd are Jazmin, Angie, and Roxana. She goes to hug them each with tender hugs. Ceci often feels guilty that she cannot provide the same love for all the other kids that look on while she gives the 3 sisters her a+ttention.
They are all ready for dance class in their leotard and tights. Once situated in the make shift studio, the music begins and they warm up… shifting directly into the rehearsal of the dance number they are preparing for MOTHER'S DAY. After, Ceci takes Jazmin on her knee.

Ceci: How are you bambina Jazz?

Jazmin: Te amo Ceci… *Hug*

Ceci: **And I love you too sweetness. I wish I could spend more time with you, but I have to work too. We have to look into your asthma… And I think you all could also be lactose intolerant. I will have to get you tested.**

Roxana & Angie

SOS Dancers, Ceci

Ceci and Angie

Angie crawls up onto Ceci's other knee.

Angie: Ceci, manana es mi cumpleanos. Tomorrow is my birthday.

Ceci: **Of course I remembered Angie. How could I forget? Because tomorrow... we will have a special birthday at the dance studio in Mazapan oK?**

Angie: **Con pastel Ceci?**

Ceci: **Claro chica - con pastel... Les amo mucho,,, Adios!** Of course chica - with cake. I love you very much... Goodbye.

Soon it gets dark and Ceci must go, and as usual she must escape the goodbyes in casa 9, as nobody will let go of her. This is always a difficult move, having to slip out unnoticed, as the girls never want to let go of her.

112. Angie's Third Birthday Party – Dance Studio – 4/28/2006

Outside the old plantation type bakery, turned dance studio at the Standard Fruit company International School... is a modest little picnic area covered from the rain where Vilma and Sayda are decorating the outdoor patio for a Saturday birthday for Angie and her SOS family and friends. After Ceci's dance, class, David Ashby shows up with a pick up truck of SOS kids, ready to party. Angie and her sisters jump from the truck into Ceci's arms. Vilma takes Angie to change into party dress, and the festivities begin.

Angie is 3, and as cute as cute can be with a smile that can only be described as "la boca mas grande del mundo". From running the labyrinth in the field, to three legged races, and sack leaping, carrying eggs in spoons in the mouth, to the piñata and cake... Everybody is having a wonderful time. Then they all start dancing to local merengue, salsa, punta, and holiday beats. Everybody shows up, including Karla, Deni May, a friend of Ceci's, the IHNFA lady, the Tias from the SOS, David Ashby, Tia Dunia, and Vilma and her sister, Sayda. There is food and a great moment of silence, when Angie makes her wish....

Ceci: **Angie make a wish... Piensa en su deseo?... antes de sofflar las velas.** Think of your wish before blowing out the candles.

Angie: *Angie is confused, and the other girls explain this to her.* **Tengo dos deseos.** I have two wishes.

Angie's Birthday

Ceci: **You can have as many wishes as you want … Lo que quieres Angie Nicolle.**

Angie: **Por favor Dios… Quiero ver con dos ojos…. Y quiero estar con Mami Ceci.** Dear God.. I want to see with two eyes, and I want to be with Mami Ceci.

Ceci hugs her with tears in her eyes. Karla is there and it is an interesting moment.

Ceci: **I do have the strength and tenacity…..I will make sure that you and your sisters have a good life…. And I promise that I will do everything I can for your vision. Souffle Angie…** Blow!

Angie blows out her 3 candles in one shot and everybody laughs as they push her nose into some icing on the cake… (A Honduran custom which is disturbing, but is popular). Hence Angie has icing on her nose as they sing to her… and pass the cake around.

113. Karla's Lament – What happened to me?

There in the background is Karla... who looks so much like Angie, and who has so little connection to these children since they were removed from her custody. She stands back from the party packing up food she has taken. She will leave early with her sack full of food. Ceci sees this and realizes she cannot help everybody. Karla will sing her lament at being an unqualified mother.... She cannot get them back... but realizes from this moment... that they should not be caged up in an orphanage when they have the opportunity to go to a private pre-school, and have their medical issues addressed in a more secure living situation. Karla admits privately to this, and submits to it.... But not without expecting something in return... least of which is a relationship with her kids. She sees Ceci as a link to financial survival... almost like a mother. But she sees herself as the victim, not her children... a real identity crisis for many poor mothers in Honduras... who can only be defined through a man.

This is a tender moment which merits this song of desperation from an undeserving birth mother, whose only self worth comes from making babies..... There are many women like this in Honduras. Ceci runs to give her a piece of cake and say goodbye. Karla then sings... walking alone away from the party.

Once again, she says goodbye to the girls as David drives them back to the SOS. The Birthday good byes are difficult as usual.

114. Montage of Paper Trail for Father's Death Certficate

The next day at the REGISTRO (Hall of Records)– Ceci is waiting in line to get Birth Certificates of the girls and their father. One can see a true cross section of humanity on this line. Ceci learns that there is a birth, but no death certificate for the father. She gets birth certificate copies of the girls, and is directed upstairs to another lawyer to file for the father's death certificate. That discussion takes her on a journey. The lawyer requests police report of fatality due to assault, hospital report, and burial confirmation. This takes place in Spanish, when Ceci really begins to understand the complexity of the paper trail which is a serious test of her patience....

The following montage is cut musically in dramatic edits of paper trails that Ceci follows through the police station, hospital, and graveyard. Whatever dialogue takes place is fostered through improvisations set up to reveal the devoted perseverance needed to follow all the paths towards getting a formal death certificate (acto defuncto) of Carlos Iraheta Alvarez. The musical montage begins....

1. *Police Station – Ceci climbs on ladders, looking through shelves of files (for days) looking for the hand written police incident report of finding Carlos Iraheta Alvarez dead at the scene of the crime in Barrio Inglais and why.. February, 2004.*

2. *Hospital Atlantida – Records dept. – Ceci is looking for info about DOA (Dead on Arrival) at the emergency room where Carlos was brought and then delivered to the morgue. This is the same hospital where Ceci originally found the girls. Walks down these halls will show the condition of the public hospital.... Nurses smoking, rats, no sheets, families hanging out, lack of doctors, AC, light, medical supplies, and hope.*

3. *Public Graveyard – Ceci visits the graveyard and speaks to the proprietor who actually knew Carlos. He signs a hand written note authenticating the burial of Carlos Alvarez Iraheta at the Municipal cemetery in La Ceiba, Honduras... Feb, 2004.*

Here the music stops, and real time, improvised dialogue and montage take place:

Ceci returns to the Registro to see the same lawyer she saw over a month ago. With a smile and more directions to go to the Court to file for the printing of the actual Acto Defuncto, and to come back after that, the lawyer dismisses Ceci. She exits elated for another hard earned accomplishment towards getting custody of the girls.

The final part of the music includes the last stop back at the Court house to file for the Acto Defuncto paper. She gets into the car and collapses....Starts the car and says, knowing that she must now just wait for the death certificate to be printed some time in the not too distant Honduran future, return a copy to the Registro and breathe... She drives towards the river Cangrejal. Despite the achievement, she needs to discharge the stress of getting this far.

115. Flash of Carlos – Cangrejal River

Ceci: It's out of my hands.... Pero los caminos estan abiertos!... Gracias a Dios

Music begins as Ceci has stopped by the side of the river road, and has descended to the banks of the river where she dances to the re-occurring melody of Amy Grant's song, RIVER LULLABY, after which she jumps into the river with her clothes

on. This will be a repeating melody throughout the story.

Mystical Moment with Carlos

Ceci jumps into the stream. As she comes up for air, on the other side of the river, in the glare of the sunlight, she sees a man standing on a rock about to dive in. She is not sure if it is real, and the shimmering sunlight on his body suddenly turns to twilight, and Ceci recognizes this as the spirit of the recently deceased father of the girls, Carlos Alvarez Iraheta. He shouts to her across the river:

Carlos: Les cuidese bien a mis ninas por favor! Son inocente ellas.... Gracias Gringa!! Take good care of my girls. They are innocent. Thank you Gringa.

Flash into a spiritual dimension with Carlo's departing soul as he rises to the heavens. He was a misdirected, sacrificial warrior, lost to drugs, without work opportunities to provide for his family. In this dream sequence... tinted in blue light... Carlos is dressed as a

Honduran warrior who comes home from battle defeated.... He was actually raised in Guerero, Honduras, which was a battlefield during the conquista. Ceci witnesses this in a dream state while floating in the river. She looks over to the other river bank with the afternoon sun glaring and wipes her eyes. She returns to reality to drive back to town realizing she is barely on time for a Miss Honduras Rehearsal.

116. <u>Ms. Honduras Pageant - 2nd Rehearsal</u>

The rehearsal takes place in the ballroom of the Quinta Hotel on the beach. She will review the opening number and stage the bathing suit and gown modeling numbers. The girls are oooing and aaahing over Eduardo's collection of stunning gowns back stage. He is running around talking to everybody...

Ceci sees the former Miss Honduras whom she remembers as the Feria Queen from the Parade during Carnaval. She had signaled Ceci to notice the girls in the box on the street. She approaches Ceci and reminds her of the encounter. This is an emotional moment for Ceci. As the Former Miss Honduras, she will also be participating in the pageant.

Former Ms. H: Ms. Cecilia, I remember you from the Carnaval parade!

Ceci: Yes I remember you too... I had just arrived in town that day.

Former Ms. H: Please tell me what happened with those little girls in the box in that army truck in front of the hospital? I was so glad that you helped them. I was so ready to jump off the float and rescue them myself.

Ceci: That was a powerful moment for me too. Thank you for connecting with me, because it was truly a shock for me, and I think your zap is what kicked me into action. Believe it or not, I am now trying to get custody of them. They have been placed in the SOS orphanage, and are doing much better, although there are some medical issues.

Former Ms. H: Dios Mio... that is incredible news. What a story. When I think of how many don't get rescued, it breaks my heart. You know I dreamt of them that evening, and I was so relieved that you saw my concern... You are an angel.

Ceci: And so are you to care so much.

Former Ms. H: You know we have such a big problem with these orphans in Honduras... I have made this my major platform since my reign as Miss Honduras, and I feel so helpless that the problem just gets worse and worse.

Ceci: I have decided to take on this challenge by trying to care for and get custody of just these three little girls. And I am also teaching dance classes at the SOS to help the other kids. Meanwhile... you know that the girls will be carrying your train when you enter at the end of the show.

Former Ms. H: This is such magic! I can't believe it... You have made my day. I am so honored.

Ceci: Believe me... THEY are honored.

Eduardo approaches, kisses Ms. H.

Eduardo: Cecilia can you work with her for a little while so that I can organize the rest of the fittings?

Ceci: Of course Eduardo... I am ready for her.

Former Ms. H: Aqui estoy! Lista. *She puts on her dancing shoes.*

Ceci takes Ms. H to the stage and begins to review her choreography. She is a good dancer compared to most of the other girls. Ceci goes through the choreography for the departing queen. Then Ceci begins to work on the opening number. The smiles on these beautiful women are scintillating. Ceci starts and stops the music a few times to polish various spots in the number. It is stunning, exciting and glamorous. The former Miss Honduras enters at the end of the number with her dancing cameo.

Eduardo: Fabulous darlings... We still need to work on this more. But...Ceci I want to run the bathing suit routine now so these girls can get used to parading around in bikinis.

We see various clips of the bathing suit number. Then the staging for the final gown routine. And then a review of the opening number. The girls all complain about their feet after hours of dancing in high heels. Ceci is confident it will come together, and packs up and leaves while the girls try on their gowns.

117. <u>Garifuna Bar – Zona Viva</u>

After the rehearsal, Ceci goes down the beach to the Zona Viva to a very funky palapa Garifuna bar right on the beach.... to "descargar" (to discharge or unwind) and drink guiffity. She is curious yet comfortable in the bar, despite being the only white person there. It is Friday night and there are live drummers interspersed with canned music. Men and women are dancing. The bartender approaches her.

Bartender: What can I get for you mam?

Ceci: Thank you for speaking English. I would like some guiffity?

Bartender: A tu orden Senora. I speak three languages... mostly Garifuna.

Ceci: Tell me about guiffity.

Bartender: OK, this is very old for the Garifunas and was invented mostly for medicinal purposes. So they take white rum and put an odd number of herbs in the bottle, they bury the bottle for at least a week, and then give it to a sick person to burn out the disease.

Ceci: And the disease can be physical or mental?

Bartender: Yes mam...

Ceci: Please tell me more. *As she throws back the guiffity, she begins to take notes.*

Bartender: Garifunas come from the black Caribe culture which is a a mixed population of black Africans from Nigeria and the Arawak Indians (Caribs) of the Lesser Antilles. The Africans migrated to Guyana and Venezuela from the island of St. Vincent in the Caribbean, many centuries ago. Evidently an English ship capsized, and the black prisoners swam to freedom on the island of St. Vincent all around the 1600s. So these Africans never actually experienced the slavery of American blacks. And with the interbreeding between them and the conquered South American Indians during the next forty years, a new race and culture was created known as the black Carib or the Garifuna.

Ceci: Wow,,, I will quote you in my book. Thank you. That finally explains it. Two oppressed cultures coming together for survival.

Bartender: Yes, and our Garifuna language, the music, the dance, the food and the rituals have all survived to this day.

Ceci: This is a fabulous, spiritual, inspiring culture. I love it!

One of the young girls approaches her dancing punta, and non-verbally invites her to dance. Despite her fatigue, she gets on the dance floor to Punta. We see the dancers one by one dancing directly in front of the master drummer, synchronizing their movements with his attacks on the drum. Ceci struggles with the intensity of the punta beat, but manages to keep it as she performs her short solo for the drummers with a full gringa smile. She lacks the tenacity, but is applauded graciously for her correct rhythm and energy. Ceci is happy with this totally inspiring experience of guiffity and punta.

118. Court House – next morning – Karla and Ceci

Ceci is leaving the court house triumphantly waving Carlos Alvarez Iraheta's death certificate document in her hand. Karla is waiting in the truck with her new boyfriend, Yarel. Ceci gives her a copy of the paper. Karla will go see the Judge about removing the girls from the SOS, with the Acto Defuncto.

Ceci: OK Karla, aqui tenemos el acto defuncto de Carlos... por fin... Y con este papel yo puedo pedir por la custodia. Karla, here we have the death certificate for Carlos. And with this document I can ask for custody.

Karla: Gracias Ceci, porque mis manos estaban demasiado llenos para hacerlo. Te presento Yarel, mi novio. Thank you Ceci, because I have been too busy to do that. This is my boyfriend Yarel.

Ceci: Hola Yarel. *Ceci mutters to herself.* Well that was fast... Carlos just died. Donde esta viviendo ahora? Where are you living now?

Yarel: Con su guapo esposo Yarel... y mi nuevo bambino adentro.... With her handsome husband, Yarel, and my new baby inside her. *He grabs Karla's belly.*

Karla: Por favor Yarel. Si, ahora vivo cerca aqui con la familia de Yarel. Please Yarel... Yes, now I live near with Yarel's famiy.

Ceci: But you just had a baby!!! Donde estan Carlitos y Cynthia?

Karla: Estan todavia con su abuela, Celestina, en San Judas. Mira.. Ceci... Yo le voy a explicar al juez. Deme pistos por favor... Hay que comer. They are still with their grandmother, Celestina in San Judas. Look Ceci. I will explain it to the judge. Give me some money please.. we must eat.

Ceci: Si Karla... cuando salgas con el orden para las ninas... Yo se que tienes hambre. Pero necesito pensar primero en el hambre de las ninas... entiende? And why are you making more babies? This is crazy!! Yes, Karla, when you come out with the order for the girls to leave the SOS. I know you are hungry. But I must think primarily for the girls' hunger and needs.. Understand?

Karla: Estan comiendo mejor en el SOS que yo. They are eating better in the SOS than I am.

Ceci: Y conmigo ellas van a comer bien para siempre. And with me they will eat well forever.

Karla: Ah co-madre, deme pistos... Come on co-madre... give me money.

Ceci: **No Karla. Tu sabes que cambiando dinero entra nosotros es illegal… como comprar las ninas. I feel like a broken record. Lo hago para ayudarte, pero tambien para accelerar este proceso imposible.** No Karla. You know that exchanging money between us is illegal. It's like I am buying the girls. I feel like a broken record. I do it to help you, but also to accelerate this impossible process.

Karla: **Tenemos hambre Ceci.** We are hungry Ceci.

Ceci: **Por favor Karla, vaya buscar el orden… Estas claro en lo que va a decir? Que vas a trabajar en una casa donde las ninas pueden vivir contigo.** Karla, please go get the order. Are you clear in what you will say? That you are going to work in a house where the kids can live with you.

Karla: **Si Ceci… Lo tengo.**

Karla gets out of the car angrily, takes the death certificate,, and walks into the court house for an appointment with the judge. Ceci and Yarel wait in the truck.

119. Judge's Chambers - Karla

Karla enters the chambers of Judge Irasema Guillien.

Judge: **Bueno Karla, como estas?** Hello Karla, how are you?

Karla: **Bien Sra… Gracias por la cita.** I am fine Sra. Thank you for the appointment.

Judge: **Y como puedo servirle?** And how can I help you?

Karla: **Pues… morio en Febrero, el papa de las ninas… y ahora estoy trabajando. Quiero sacar las ninas del SOS por favor.** So the girls' father died in February, and now I am working. I want to take the girls out of the SOS please.

Judge: **OK… Que paso con el papa?** What happened to their father?

Karla: **Alguien le mato.** Someone killed him.

Judge: **Drogas?** Drugs?

Karla: **Yo no se.** I don't know.

Judge: Fue drogas entonces. Lo siento Karla. Then it was drugs. I'm sorry Karla.

Karla: Aqui tengo el acto defuncto. Here is the death certificate.

The judge examines the document.

Judge: Bueno, y que tienes en la bariga... Hay otro nino? O demasiado baleadas? OK so what do you have in your belly? Another child? Or too many baleadas? *(Honduran bean quesadillas)*

Karla: *She lifts her shirt and beats on her stomach.* **No Sra... tengo Cynthia y Carlitos y no mas a cuidar ahora.** No Sra I have Cynthia and Carlitos and no more to take care of now. *She is lying about a new pregnancy (Lilliana) who belongs to Yarel.*

Judge: Y las extrana a las ninas? And do you miss the girls? *Pause* **De la verdad, Karla... No me mientes!** Truthfully Karla... don't lie to me.

Karla: Claro las extrano. Yo les di a la luz no? Of course I miss them. I gave birth to them didn't I?

Judge: Y como vas a cuidarles esta vez? Cuando hay enfermidades, y no hay comida?? Ya casi les mataste con neglegencia y abuso Karla... Como y porque le debo yo darte custodia de nuevo a estas ninas indefencibles!! And how will you care for them this time... when they are sick or hungry? You already almost killed the girls with negligence and abuse Karla. How and why should I give you custody again with these indefensible children? *Clearly, she is angry.*

Karla: Porque tengo una nueva vida ahora con un novio bueno que me quiere y trabaja. Carlos me pegaba... y no pude vivir con su problema de drogas... Fue una mala situacion.... Pero ahora estoy mejor...y lista para cuidar las ninas. Tengo un trabajo con una Sra. En Naranjal. Because I have a new life now with a good man who wants me and works. Carlos would beat me and I couldn't live with his drug problem. It was a bad situation. But now I am better and ready to take care of the girls.

Judge: Como puedo creerte Karla? How am I supposed to believe you Karla?

Karla: Porque yo soy la mama y tengo trabajo y apoyo ahora. Because I am their mother, and now I have work and support.

Judge: Apoyo de su nuevo novio… o de esta gringa bailarina que esta en el pueblo? Support from your new boyfriend, or from this gringa dancer who is in town?

Karla: De que esta hablando Sra.? What are you talking about Senora? *Now Karla is nervous, annoyed, and angry.*

Judge: El pueblo es pequeno… y conozco todo lo que paso en su caso, su negligencia, las enfermidades de las ninas, y su tiempo en la IHNFA, y por fin en el SOS. Yo se que morio el papa, y que conseguiste otro hombre, y que una gringa quiere custodia de estas ninas. This is a small town, and I know everything that's happening in your case, your negligence, the illnesses of the girls, and their time in the IHNFA and finally in the SOS. I know how the father died and that you found another man, and that the gringa wants custody.

Karla: Sra… No quieria dejarles en un orfanato donde no hay un futuro. Estas ninas merecen mas…. Y yo voy hacer lo que puedo para ellas. Deme el orden para sacarles del SOS… por favor. Sra. I don't want to leave them in an orphanage where there is no future. These girls deserve more, and I am going to do what I can for them. Please give me the order to get them out of the SOS. *The judge takes a long moment as she files her nails and thinks.*

Judge: Quiero saber todo de lo que pasa con estas ninas …Oye? Quiero verles aqui cada mes, limpia y sana con sus notas de escuela. Estamos claro? Ok Karla… I want to know everything that happens with these girls. Do you hear me? I want to see them every month, clean and healthy with their school grades. Are we clear?

Karla: Si Senora.

Judge: Esta vez, es su ultimo chance…. Oye? *She signs a release paper that she gives to Karla.* **Con este papel se puede sacar las ninas del SOS…. Suerte Karla….** This time is your last chance. Do you hear me? With this paper you can remove them from the SOS.. Good luck.

Karla... Si Sra... Gracias...

Judge: Karla, Yo repito. Quiero reportage regular... A ver estas ninas con mis ojos regularmente. Entiende??? Karla, I repeat. I want a regular report... and to see these girls with my own eyes regularly. Undestood?

Karla: Si Entiendo Senora. Gracias. Yes, I understand Sra, Thank you.

Karla leaves the office and gets into the truck, waving her paper of gold. The judge peeks out of the window to see this.

120. **Ceci waiting for Karla in Truck with Yarel**

Ceci: No lo creo... por fin! Entonces, cuando vamos por las ninas? I don't believe it! Finally! So when can we go pick up the girls?

Karla: Cuando quieres Ceci... por favor deme los pistos. Whenever you want Ceci... Please give me money now. *Ceci gives Karla 500 Lempiras*

Ceci: La pregunta es Karla... lo haces para las ninas o para el dinero? The question is Karla.. are you doing this for the girls or for the money?

Karla: Los dos Ceci. Both Ceci.

Ceci: *Ceci shakes her head in disbelief and sighs.* Entonces, no podemos ir al SOS manana porque tengo que montar un espectaculo para Dia de la Madre. Pero el sabado si, te busco temprano en la manana y vamos. OK? Se puedes venir al espectaculo manana si quieres. Ok then... we can't go tomorrow because I have to mount a show for Mother's Day. But Saturday, yes.. I will look for you early in the morning and we will go.. OK? You can come to the show tomorrow if you want.

Karla: No se Ceci.

Ceci: Por favor Karla, guarde este papel de la Juez con tu vida. Tengo que ir ahora para el ensayo. Hasta el sabado Karla... Y gracias... Dios te bendiga por esta ayuda. Please Karla. Guard this release document from the judge with your life. You will need it. I have to go now for rehearsal... I will see you Saturday, and thank you... God bless you for this help.

Ceci drives off leaving Karla in front of the courthouse counting her lempiras.

121. <u>**Mother's Day Show – SOS & Mazapan Students**</u>

Dancers are arriving with their families and costumes to go backstage and prepare. **There is music in the house. Sayda is collecting tickets, Ceci is running around coordinating everybody and waiting for David Ashby to arrive with the SOS dancers and the three sisters. Finaly the bus arrives and the three girls rush in to find Ceci. They all have special hair dos.**

Angie: Hola Ceci. Mire mis cabellos. Look at my hair.

Ceci: Que bonita!

Jazmin: Y yo tambien soy bonita.

Ceci: Y Roxana tambien. Quien lo hizo? Who did it?

Angie: Norma y Juni.

Ceci: Me alegra verles. Estan listas bailar? I am so happy to see you. Are you ready to dance?

Angie: Ceci, Roxana esta nerviosa. Donde vamos? Ceci, Roxana is nervous. Where do we go?

Ceci takes the three girls onto the empty stage with the closed curtain to whisper to them privately.

Ceci: Ninas, ven aquí... cerca mis amores. Quiero hablar con uds. Vilma esta backstage lista para vestirse. Pero necesito explicarlas algo importante que va a cambiar sus vidas. Estan escuchando? Manana vendra Karla para recogerles del SOS y llevarles vivir conmigo. Pero Karla es la unica persona que puede sacarles del SOS. Porque ella es su madre. Entienden? Espero que esten listas para este cambio. OK? Es un secreto, pero yo queria que uds. lo sepan. Girls, come close my loves. I want to talk to you guys. Vilma is backstage ready to get you dressed. But I need to explain something very important to you that will change your lives. Listen carefully? Tomorrow Karla will come to collect you to bring you to live with me. But Karla is the only person who can get you out of the SOS. Because she is your mother. Do you understand? I hope you are ready for this change. It is a secret, but I wanted you to know.

Angie: Vamos las tres a vivir contigo Ceci? The three of us will live with you Ceci?

Ceci: Si mi amor. Roxana entiende? Espero que quieren hacerlo. Yes my love. Roxana do you understand? I hope you want to do this.

Jazmin/Angie: Si Ceci....

Angie: Roxana va a llorar. Pero yo soy feliz y Jazmin tambien. She is going to cry ... But I am happy and Jazmin also.

Jazmin: Y yo quiero mi propria cama. And I want my own bed.

Ceci: Es importante que entienden lo que va a pasar. Y es un secreto. Que van a dormir en mi casa manana. Diga si, si me entienden. It's very important that you understand what is going to happen. And it is a secret. That you are going to sleep in my house tomorrow. Tell me Yes I understand. *The three girls look at each other and nod their heads up and down, not exactly sure what emotion to feel.* **I know it's crazy, but you will thank me some day.**

Angie: Si Ceci.. Es bueno.

Ceci: OK...Come here Roxana... Te amo mucho... Y vas a bailar bien ...Mira, ahora nos preperamos para el espectaculo OK? Estoy tan argullosa de uds. Empezamos en poco. Vaya con Vilma para vestirse. OK Come here Roxana... I love you very much... and you are going to dance well tonight. So look.. now we are getting ready for the show. I am so proud of all of you. We will start soon. Go with Vilma to get dressed in your costumes.

Directors note ** - Once again, there were 8 Mother's Day shows at the Mazapan School. Mother's Day is a very big holiday in Honduras. Every May for several years, Ceci presented shows that included the SOS orphans, the Mazapan school students, and *dancers from other schools in La Ceiba. The following programs are the private dance concerts originating from her after school program. Listed below are three of the eight programs.*

When the house lights go down, Ceci enters to introduce the show and welcome the families. These shows will become a tradition in La Ceiba for the years that Ceci lives there. The Bambinas group 4-6 years old; Principios 7-9; Intermedios 10-16; Avancadas 12-18

"TOMANDO MANOS" Taking Hands– 24 Mayo 2007

1. **Spanish Numba Rumba y Arroz Con Leche- Bambinas Tradicional con Guillermo Anderson**

2. **Boy From NY City- Principios – Manhattan Transfer**

3. **Jungle Punta – Intermedios – Les Baxter & Punta Garifuna**

4. **Lavender Blue & I Love you – Bambinas – Barney's Great Adventure**

5. **"Ka Ching" – Avancadas – Shania Twain**

6. **Ninos de la Calle- Principios – "Jeux d'eau" from "0" Cirque de Soleil "Somewhere Out There" – Linda Rondstadt/ James Ingram**

7. **"Ch-Check it Out" – Intermedios – The Beastie Boys**

8. **Cinicienta- Duet, Nicole y Elizabeth – "Sonar es Desear"** Disney

9. **Belly Dance– "Caravan" Suzanne Sterling**

10. **"Oooshalallla" – Principios – Disco Hippie –**

11. **Shop Window ballet – – Intermedios**

12. **"Jeux de enfants" & "Valsapena" – Alegria – Cirque de Soleil**

In this ballet, the dancers are ballerinas in a shop window. When the store turns out the lights to close up, a little fairy prances through the window throwing fairy dust. The manikins come alive and dance their way to the toy dept. where they find ballerina dolls dressed just like them. The scene turns into a full on ballet of duets between the dolls and the living manikins. In the morning the store manager finds the manikins in the window holding the dolls.

13. **" Los Conejos Panaderos – Cri Cri**

14. **FINALE – Todos "Ciclo Sin Fin"** Circle of Life – **Rey Leon** Lion King

"SUENOS" – Mayo, 2008

1. Payasos – Bambinas – Nino Rota (Fellini Soundtracks) Jack Constanzo – "Inchworm"

2. "Llueve" – Principios - Cri Cri

3. "Step up" – Intermedios - Cheetah Girls

4. Nightclub Fantasy – Avancadas – "Deep Night Softly" Terry Snyder

5. Lasso – Intermedios II – "It's My Turn Now" – Keke Palmer

6. Munecas – Bambinas – "Waltz of the Doll" Coppelia – Leo Delibes "The Enchantment" – Fairy Doll – J Baker

7. Suenos Rosados – Principios – "Dream" – Peabo Bryson

8. "A Dream is a Wish your Heart Makes" – Intermedios – L Rondstadt

9. "When You Wish Upon A Star" – Intermedios II – NSYNC

10. "Wind up" Rainbow Ballet – Avancadas – Marbella Rubio y Darell Garcia – student choreographers This ballet is designed for 7 groups, in which each piece of music inspires a different style of dance within the 7 colors of the rainbow. At the end they all dance together.

11. "You've Got the Moves" y "Penguinas" – Bambinas – Sesame St.

12. Chiquita Banana – Principios – "Chiquito" – Ruben Calzado "Frere Jaques Conga" – Los Albinos

13. "Let's Dance" (tap) – Intermedios – Hannah Montana

14. "Ain't No Man" – Avancadas – Christina Aguiliera

15. Ballet de Tela/Honey Rag – Intermedios II All That Jazz/Chicago

16. FINALE – "What Time is it?" – High School Musical

<u>CARNAVAL DE DANZAS – 22 Mayo, 2009</u>

1. Diamond Cabaret – Avancadas

2. El Banquito (the bench) – Bambinas

Ceci starts the music and the girls come skipping out and begin to circle their little benches on stage. Ceci stands in the pit and dances the choreography in reverse with them. While they sit, stand, lift, and dance with their benches to Cri Cri's Spanish song… un Banquito, the girls scream and yell in their glee to be on the stage.

3.Four Minutes – Intermedios II

4. Chair Dance - Adv

5. **Ballet de La Madre Naturaleza – Intermedios**   This ballet begins with each dancer standing on a pedestal in Goddess robes. The music reflects ancient ceremonial sounds with brass, flutes, and dramatic percussion. There is a central altar. The goddesses come to life and perform a slow ceremonial dance that is an offering. They honor the four directions; then present flowers, water, incense, burning candles and great passion as they build the altar and honor Mother Nature. The music escalates in rhythm and intensity until the dancers huddle around the altar. At the crescendo in the music, the dancers reveal a small child (Jazmin) materializing from their huddle. The goddesses lift her onto the altar and they return to their pedestals. The child performs a solo on the central altar. They all do the same movements choreography together on their pedestals.... And then freeze, returning to their original positions.

6. **Fashion Show – Avancadas**
7. **Let's Sing – Bambinas**
8. **Beatles Ballet – Intermedios II**
9. **The Boys Are Back – Intermedios**

10. **Counting Ballet – Principios**

Angie, Cecilia Dip, Jazmin

11. **Make A Change – Avancadas**
12. **Shake a Tail Feather – Bambinas**
13. **Sofrito Salsa – Intermedios II**

14. Java Jive Tap – Intermedios

15. Gypsy Dance – Principios

16. FINALE – Todos

At the end of the show, Ceci is taking pictures on the stage with students. The three girls come up to hug Ceci. She takes Jazmin on her lap.

Ceci: You guys were great tonight!! *Squeezing Angie and Roxana.* I was so proud of you! Bailaron bellas. Verdad Tia Dunia?

Dunia: Si, bien bonita... Todo Ceci... Gracias por esta noche divina. Yes really beautiful... everything Ceci... Thank you for this divine evening.

Angie: *Angie whispers.* Queremos ir a su casa contigo. We want to go to your house with you.

Ceci: Yo se y eso es exactamente lo que quiero yo. I know and that is exactly what I want. *She whispers back to Angie.* Vamos a ver lo que pasa manana cuando viene Karla OK? Recuerdas que es un secreto Angie. Si Dios Quiere, tu vas a dormir en mi casa manana. Let's see what happens tomorrow when Karla comes. Remember that it is a secret Angie. Godwilling you will sleep in my house tomorrow. *She puts her finger to her lips* Secreto... shshshsh!

David Ashby: Great show Ceci... Thanks so much. They needed this ego boost.

Ceci: They have a copy of the music, so please let them keep dancing in the studio.

David Ashby: Of course. Come on kids... the bus is leaving.

Ceci: OK babies... give me a kiss... I love you.

As Ceci walks them to David's pick up truck and they all pile in the back and pull away waving... Ceci mutters to herself.

Ceci: Si Dios Quiere I will soon be saying good night instead of good bye. Hasta manana mis angeles.

122. In the truck and at the Bustop – the girls exit from the SOS

Saturday mid morning, Karla, Yarel, Vilma and Ceci are driving to the SOS, Ceci is excited talking to Vilma about preparations of the girls' bedrooms…. Tooth brushes, clothing, toys, little beds, uniforms for school, etc. This will be a long day and a milestone in the lives of the girls and Ceci.

Ceci: **I can't believe this is really happening!!! No creo que este milagro esta pasando Karla! Tu no sabes como has cambiado el futuro de estas ninas.** You don't know how you are changing the future of these girls.

Karla: **Yo quiereria saber el futuro mio tambien?** I would also like to know my future?

Yarel: **Y un nueva bicicleta para mi?** And a new bicycle for me?

The new boyfriend, Yarel wants everybody to know that he is part of the new act. Vilma rolls her eyes, and buttons her mouth. Ceci drops them at the SOS bus stop.

Ceci: **Bueno, llegamos. Volveremos a la casa para esperar su llamada.** We are here. We will return to the house to wait for your call.

Karla: **Si Ceci…**

Ceci: **Suerte… Te esperaremos.** We will wait for you.

123. The SOS Gate

Karla and Yarel walk the long driveway to the SOS gate with the Judge's release paper. The guard greets her.

Karla: **Estoy aqui para recoger mis ninas por orden de la Juez de la Ninez. Me llamo Karla Rojas.** I am here to collect my children with the order from the Children's Judge. My name is Karla Rojas.

Guardia: **Esperen aqui por favor.** Wait here please.

The guard takes the paper and goes to the main office and Karla and Yarel wait outside the gate. It is hot. Inside the main office is Ollman, the director of the SOS.

124. Olman's Office – SOS Director – September 6, 2006

The guard gives Olman the paper.

Olman: Que pasa? What's happening?

Guard: Hay una mujer en el porton que dice que es la madre de las hermanas Irahetas/Rojas. There's a woman at the gate that says she is the mother of the Iraheta/Rojas sisters.

Olman: La madre que casi las mato?!! En el nombre de Cristo, quiero saber que pasa aqui. Con quien esta ella? The mother that almost killed them? In the name of Christ, I want to know what's happening here. Who is she with?

Guard: Un hombre joven... novio, yo imagino. A young man... boyfriend I imagine.

Olman: Pero morio el papa de las ninas... *(pensando)* **.... Y la gringa?** But the girls' father died. And the gringa?

Guard: La gringa no esta Sr. Ollman... Es la madre... con la misma cara de Angie.... Con ese papel de la Juez de la Familia. The gringa isn't here Sr. Olman. It's the mother, with the same face as Angie. And with that document from the Judge of the Family.

Olman: Dejales esperar.... Let them wait.

125. Return to the SOS Gate

Guardia: Hay que esperar senora. Don Olman esta ocupado. You must wait. Don Olman is busy.

Karla: Esperar para que?... son mis ninas. Le di el orden de la Juez Irasema Guillien. Wait for what? They are my children. I gave you the order from the Judge Irasema Guillien.

Guardia: El director dice que esperen. The director says to wait.

Hours go by. We flash between Karla and Yarel waiting in the sun by the gate; Ceci and Vilma are waiting at the house and the girls are on the swings at Casa 9 with David Ashby. There is clearly a standoff taking place.

126. The House in Naranjal – waiting for the call

We switch to the house in Naranjal where Ceci and Vilma are waiting for the call.

Vilma: Son las cuatro, Ceci.

Ceci: I am so excited Vilma I can't stand it.

Vilma: Y el dormitorio es bello. Ellas les gustara mucho. And their bedroom is beautiful. They will love this.

Ceci: Quiero saber que sucede con Karla. Ya ha pasado cinco horas desde les dejemos en el SOS. Maybe this was too good to be true. I wonder what is happening with Karla. Five hours have already passed since we left them in the SOS. *She calls Karla.*

Ceci: Hola Karla… que pasa?

Karla: No quieren darmeles… estoy esperando afuera. They don't want to give them to me. I am waiting outside.

Ceci: Pero porque? Tienes el papel del Juez! But why? You have the paper from the Judge.

Karla: No se Ceci…El director me dijo esperar afuera. No me voy hasta que les tengo… Nos tratan como animales en este sol caliente. Estoy enojada ahora …. te llamo. I don't know Ceci. The director told me to wait outside. I am not leaving until I have them. They are treating us like animals in this hot sun. I am mad now. I will call you.

Yarel and Karla

Ceci gets off the phone discouraged.

Vilma: Ceci, oye bien. Tu sabes que es complicada cuando los ninos estan la propriedad del gobierno. Las leyes cambian todo el dinamico con la familia... pero tambien protégén los ninos de madres como Karla. Ceci.. listen . You know that it is complicated when children are the property of the government. The laws change the whole dynamic of the family... but also protect kids from mothers like Karla.

Ceci: Pero la ley dice que solamente la madre puede recogerles,,, es la unica manera. And now when Karla is finally trying to do the right thing. Oh my God. And the girls are caught in the middle. But the law says that only the mother can take them out... it's the only way.

Vilma: Mi madre crio dos ninos... ninos abandonados de vecinos pobres. No habian papeles... Estuvimos seis en la casa. Para cada nino perdido en el SOS hay tres mas viviendo con abuelos, tios, vecinos.. o en la calle. My mother raised two boys who were abandoned by poor neighbors. There were no papers. We were six in the house. For each lost child in the SOS there are 3 living with grandparents, aunts, neighbors, or on the street.

Ceci: *Walking around in a frenzy.* **Y aunque de la abuela de las ninas supuestamente es una partera y curandera de hierbas... todavia ella y Karla les dejaban a ellas sin leche y medicina, con fiebre y hambre, y con una epidemica de meningitis alla en el barrio. San Judas no es un lugar para sobrevivir enfermidades, ni hambre, ni picadillos!!!** And even though their grandmother supposedly is a midwife and an herbal healer, they both still left the girls without milk and medicine... with fever and hunger ,,, with an epidemic of meningitis there in the barrio. San Judas is not a place to survive sickness, nor hunger, nor molesters.

Vilma: San Judas es el segundo barrio mas pobre y peligroso en Ceiba... Actualmente, los soldados salvieron sus vidas cuando les sacaron de alla... El barrio mio, Las Mercedes, es el mas peligroso... San Judas is the second poorest and most dangerous in Ceiba. Actually the military saved their lives by taking them away from there. My neighborhood, Las Mercedes is the most dangerous.

Ceci: OK… entonces… es bien tarde. Voy a llamar a David Ashby… El esta alla trabajando con los ninos adentro el SOS ahora. Well now it's really late. I am calling David Ashby. He is there inside the SOS working with the kids now.

127. **David at SOS with ninas – Casa 9 – Phone conversation**

Ceci: *dialing cell phone –* **David,… How are you? ……….. It's me Ceci. Where are you?............... Are you with the girls?............Are they OK?...............Karla is outside ready to take them, but Olman won't release them…. She has a court order.**

David is on the swings in front of Casa 9 with the three girls.

David: Now Ceci… I can't get involved in this. I'm already walking on egg shells in this place. Everybody knows you are behind this.

Ceci: David, are you with the girls?

David: Yes Ceci, and I can't do anything.

Ceci: OK, Just tell Dunia to get them dressed.

David: Dunia is crying. She doesn't want to let them go. Listen Ceci… Don Olman doesn't want to make this a precedent. You realize, they lose money every time a bed is emptied…. Those are the rules from Austria… and he needs every penny.

Ceci: Oh God… David, whose side are you on? There is a legit court order from the judge. Karla has been waiting at the gate for hours. It is getting dark. Let's look at the larger picture here….. even if I never leave Honduras… I can take much better care of them than the SOS… Or do you want them to stay in the orphanages? Please go talk to Don Olman … David please! You know I am right.

David: Ok Ceci – you know I go by the book. This is crazy, but yes… I will go talk to Olman.

Ceci: Now?

David: Yes, now.

Ceci: Thanks David. ... Vamonos Vilma... Hay que ir ahora. **David hablara con Don Olman.** Let's go Vilma.. We have to go now. David is going to talk to Olman .

128. **Karla and Yarel in Olman's office**

Karla and Yarel enter Olman's office and sit down.

Olman: **Hola senora... Yo soy Don Olman, el director del SOS. Quien es el senor?** Hello Sra. I am Don Ollman, director of the SOS. Who is this gentleman?

Karla: **Mi novio, Yarel. El trabaja.** My boyfriend Yarel. He works.

Olman: **Y que son sus planes para las ninas? Y donde van a vivir con ellas? No debe de presentarles con un nuevo novio cuando su padre morio hace poco.** What are your plans for the girls? And where are you going to live with them? You shouldn't present them with a new boyfriend when their father just died.

Karla: **Soy la trabajadora para una Senora en Naranjal, y las ninas van estar alla conmigo.** I am a worker for a lady in Naranjal, and the girls will be there with me.

Ollman: **Es la gringa Cecilia?** Is it the gringa Cecilia?

Karla: **Aqui es la direcion Senor.** Here is the address Senor. *She hands him a paper.*

Olman: *Standing up,* **Escuchame bien.... Yo se como Angie Nicolle perdio su vista. Yo se que tienes un nuevo bebe cada ano. Yo se que morio el papa de las ninas hace poco por drogas.... y que tu no puedes cuidar las ninas, ni la mayor muchacha, Cynthia ni el nuevo pequeno, Carlitos en la casa.... y mas que todo, por casualidad, yo se que Cecilia la gringa bailarina.... esta enamorada con estas mismas tres ninas Iraheta Rojas.** Listen to me clearly. I know how Angie Nicolle lost her sight. I know that you have a new baby every year. I know that their father just died because of a drug deal, and I know that you can't take care

273

of these girls, nor the older daughter Cynthia, nor the new baby Carlitos. And I also know by chance, that Cecilia, the gringa dancer, is crazy about these same three girls Iraheta Rojas.

Karla stares ahead while Olman circles her with his speech.

Karla: Pero tengo el orden del Juez…. Seis horas hemos esperados afuera de su porton. Y aqui estoy. Porque esperamos mas? Soy la madre… mire mi cara… mire mi cedula, y mire el orden de la Juez Senor. But I have the Judge's order to release them. Six hours we have waited outside your door. Why are we waiting? I am the mother. Look at my face, look at my Cedula (ID), look at the order from the judge.

BIG PAUSE – Turning point of the entire story

Olman: Sra. Rojas, puedes, quieres, sabes cuidar estas ninas? Tienes amor por ellas? Porque yo no lo veo senora. Are you able, do you want them, do you know how to take care of these girls. Do you love them? Because I don't see it Senora.

Karla: Su padre, Carlos fue loco cuando ellas salieron de la casa, y el tuvo mucho amor por sus hijas y no quisiera que esten en el SOS. Son mis ninas Senor!! Y tengo el papel y el derecho! Their father went crazy when they were taken, and he really loved them, and did not want them in the SOS. They are my children Senor. And I have the paper and the right.!!!

Olman: Esperen afuera mientras yo hago algunas llamadas por favor. Necesito hacer lo que creo seria la mejor cosa para las ninas. Wait outside while I make some calls please. I have to do what I believe would be the best thing for the girls.

Karla: La Juez ya hizo la decision Senor. The judge already made the decision Sr.

Olman: Por favor esperar afuera. *They leave. He calls in the guard.* **Jorge…. Mantenga un ojo en esta gente mientras yo decido lo que vamos hacer.** Please wait outside. Jorge, keep an eye on these people while I decide what we are going to do.

Jorge: Si Don Olman… pero no me gusta. Yes sir Don Olman… but I don't like it.

Olman: Por favor Jorge! Please Jorge!!

Don Olman is clearly in conflict about the situation and goes back into his office as the Guard seats Karla and Yarel on a bench outside the office.

David

129. <u>David Ashby talks to Olman in SOS Director's office</u>

David arrives at the front office and goes in to see Olman. They have a long relationship.

David: Entonces…….. que pasa con las ninas Irahetas? So what's happening with the Iraheta girls?

Olman: La palabra viaja rapido aqui no? The word travels fast.

David: Puedo ver el papel? Can I see the paper?

Olman shows David the release order from the Judge.

Olman: Yo se que es la Gringa….. Y tambien yo se que con ella sus vidas pueden estar mil veces mejor. Pero, si empezamos con esta Gringa, van a seguir otras….. y la gerencia en Tegucigalpa me retirara... Ya quieren sacar todos los voluntarios de aqui... los grupos de missionarios... y ud. tambien David... Es serio.... I know it's the Gringa. And I also know that with her the girls' lives would be much better. But, if I begin this with this gringa. others will follow... and the management in Tegucigalpa will fire me. They already want to get rid of all the volunteers that come in here... the missionaries and you too David. It's serious.

David: The difference here Olman is… that she is their legal Godmother, and they will have a real home with her. You want them back on the hill in San Judas,,, really? With the gangs? Or do you want them to graduate from here in 10 years and get pregnant 3 months after being released? Give them a chance Olman. I know this woman. I have seen how she gets kids to dance, how she puts a show together…., and I know she will give those Iraheta girls everything she has got. I am their Godfather and I believe it's the best option for the girls.

Olman: *A long moment of silence, and Olman calls the guard…* OK.. Busca la senora por favor. OK Jorge, bring the lady back in here please.

Guard: No me digas que vas a sueltar estas ninas?! Es la gringa jefe…. Es ella seguro que si. Y ella piensa que puede dar estas ninas una mejor vida que nosotros? Hmph!!! Gringos…. Todos egoistas!! Don't tell me that you are going to let these girls go. It's the gringa boss. It's her for sure. And she thinks she can give these girls a better life than we can? Gringos… ego maniacs!

Olman: Basta Jorge!!! Busca la senora Karla. Enough Jorge!! Go get the lady Karla.

The guard is dumbfounded. Olman turns to David.

Olman: I could lose my job for this.

David: I don't think so…. They are going with Karla by court order…. Not your problem.

David leaves the office as Jorge confronts Olman again.

Olman: Y Jorge, después de llamar Sra. Rojas busque las hermanas Rojas en Casa 9. And Jorge, after calling Ms. Rojas. go get the three girls in Casa 9.

Jorge: Jefe, por favor… porque hombre? Boss why are you doing this?

Olman takes Jorge aside and corners him, whispering with anger.

Olman: Porque yo he decido que es la mejor opcion para las ninas, y que ud. no tiene que pensar en este asunto, ni hablar de las ninas Irahetas Rojas de nuevo. Estamos claro Jorge? Because

I have decided that it is the best option for the girls, and that you don't have to think about this situation, nor speak about the Iraheta Rojas sisters any more. Are we clear Jorge?

Jorge: A su orden Jefe. At your service boss.

He stomps off to call Karla and then find the girls, and Olman, with his head in his hands, goes into his office and closes the door.

130. **Leaving Casa 9**

The three sisters are on the swing when David approaches Casa 9 to tell everybody what is happening. Norma & Juny are pushing them on the swings. They follow him into the house as he is looking for Tia Dunia.

David: Dunia, la madre de las ninas esta aqui para llevarles. Norma, Juny, pueden vestirles? Dunia, the girls' mother is here to take them. Norma and Juny... Can you dress them?

They all rush into the back bedroom with the girls, while David talks to Dunia.

Dunia: Pero porque? No puede ser. But why? This can't be.
She starts to cry

David: La madre tiene papeles del Juez de la Ninez para recogerles. The mother has a paper from the Judge to take them.

Dunia: Pero ella casi les mato. But she nearly killed them.

David: No podemos pelear con el Juez Dunia. We can't argue with the Judge Dunia.

Dunia is clearly overwhelmed with separation anxiety, despite the short time she has had this job. In the bedroom, Norma and Juny are cleaning up the girls and whispering to them in direct, fast informative whispers. Jazmin is speechless, but remains silent as they dress her. Roxana is in shock. Angie remembers Ceci's promise.

Angie: A donde vamos Norma?

Norma: Ah Panchita … Algo bueno va a pasar. Oh Panchita, something wonderful is going to happen. *Norma calls Angie Pancha because of her extended belly.*

Juny: No tengas miedo porque creo yo que uds. van a vivir con Tia Ceci… Pero shshshs! Don't be afraid because I believe that you are going to live with Aunt Ceci…

Norma: Es un secreto, y una adventura, OK? No llores! But shshshs… It's a secret, and an adventure, OK… Don't cry!

Jazmin: Yeah! *Jumping up and down.*

Roxana starts to cry. She has great difficulty understanding and adjusting to change.

Angie: Roxana esta confundida. Roxana is confused.

Roxana: *Grunting with big eyes. Juny takes her in her arms and sit them all on the floor. She whispers.*

Juny: Ninas me escuchen bien. Van a tener una familia… una casa, con su proprio cuarto, comer en restaurantes…escuela privada… hablar Englais… posiblemente ir a los Estados. Girls, listen to me. You are going to have a family, a house, with your own room, eat in restaurants, private school, speak English… poissibly go to the United States! This is good!

Olvin: Van a tener mucho amor con Ceci. You will have a lot of love with Ceci.

Norma: Pero no digan nada, porque solamente tienen permiso salir con Karla. Oyen?

Angie: Vamos con Ceci verdad? We are really going with Ceci, right?

Juny: Shshshsh! Creo que si. I believe so. *Whispering…*

Angeles: Pero ellas son nuestras hermanas. No pueden salir asi. But they are our sisters. They can't leave like this.

Luz – Angeles… es un sueno para ellas… Yo se que es Cecilia. Aqui tienes tu muneca Roxana. Angeles… it's a dream for them. I know it's Cecilia. Here, take your doll Roxana. *She hugs Roxana who clutches the raggedy ann doll that Ceci gave her.*

Blanca: Y si no es Ceci?, y se van con la madre bruja que golpio Angie? Huh? And if it isn't Ceci, and they go with the with the mother who hit Angie? Huh?

Norma: Vamos a creer que Dios las mando un ANGEL para que Cecilia tendria custodia legal para darles un futuro magnifico. We are going to believe that God sent an Angel so that Ceci would have legal custody to give them a magnificent future.

Olvin: Yo se que es Dona Cecilia… y es una cosa buena. Vaya con Dios chicas. I know it's Ceci. It's good.. Go with God chicas.

He hugs and kisses them, as everybody gets in a hug for each girl. In comes Dunia crying hysterically. She embraces the girls as she washes their faces. They are having their shoes tied and hair combed. Roxana cries when she sees Tia Dunia.

131. Ceci calls David

David steps outside to take a call from Ceci, as a group of young children swarm around him.

David: Dunia is combing the girls' hair. She is hysterical. This will be traumatic for a lot of the kids. Ceci… I can see that you are playing with fire… Better be careful.

Ceci: OK I'm already on my way. David… you know I am doing the right thing.

David: Si Dios Quiere Ceci…

He hangs up and proceeds to organize the parade to the gate.

Roxana: Mami Dunia!

Dunia: Oh mi bella Roxana! Angie, Jazmin…

They all embrace, and Roxana starts crying. Jazmin and Angie are stunned. David enters the room to tell them that the guard has arrived to collect the girls.

David: OK Todos… Vamos.. besos… Adios…etcetera. Hay que irnos. Ok girls, Let's go… kisses, adios, etc… We have to go.

Dunia carries Jazmin, Norma takes Angie by the hand and Juny and Olvin take Roxana by the hand. She can't stop crying.

Karla and Yarel are waiting by the gate. All the other SOS kids start to gather around the porton with their Tias to say goodbye to the girls. The girls are transferred to Karla. The gate closes and Karla and Yarel walk the sisters down the long driveway to the street. Behind them the locked gate and fence are covered by dozens of kids yelling out goodbyes to the girls.

Olvin: Suerte ninas!... No nos olviden! Good luck girls. Don't forget us!

Norma and Juny whisper together through their tears, as everybody yells Adios.

Juny: Es un oportunidad para ellas... una bendicion de Dios! It's the opportunity of a lifetime for them.. a blessing from God.

Everybody watches as they leave. Karla struggles with Roxana who is crying as they walk towards the street down the long driveway.

Karla: Callate Roxana! Shush Roxana!

Yarel: Pues Karla. Este trabajo vale mas de 2000 lempiras, esperando todo el dia en el sol para caminar cinco minutos con las chicas. Wow Karla... This job is worth more than 2000 lempiras, waiting all day in the hot sun to walk 5 minutes down the road.

Angie: Donde vamos Karla? Where are we going Karla?

They arrive at the bus stop bench on the main highway. These moments are difficult, as the girls are once again in limbo, with a blood mother who just doesn't know how to care.

Karla: Sientense aqui. Viene la gringa. Sit down here. La gringa is coming.

Jazmin: Ceci?

Karla: Si Ceci... para llevarles a su casa en Naranjal donde van a vivir como princessas. Yes, Ceci, to bring you to her house in Naranjal so you can live like princesses.

Roxana continues to whimper.

Angie: Roxana no llores ... Viene Ceci para cuidarnos como ella nos prometio. Roxana don't cry. Ceci is coming to take care of us like she promised.

Jazmin: Ceci, Ceci, Ceci... *Shaking her left leg.*

Karla calls Ceci. Ceci answers her cell phone in the car.

Karla: Ceci... Estamos en la parada... Listos.. Te espero. Ceci, we are waiting at the bus stop.

Ceci: Whoppeee! Estamos cerca. Voy! We are not far... I'm coming!

Angie: Roxana calmate! Viene Ceci... Es como Cinicientas. Roxana, calm down... Ceci is coming.   It's just like Cinderella.

132. In the car – Ceci and Vilma

Ceci: Vilma I can't stand this... They are waiting at the bus stop. Estan en la parada. I must be out of my mind. I don't know whether to laugh or cry.

Vilma: Ceci, Dios mio... Hay que relajarse un pocito... Ceci, my God... relax a little.

Ceci: No puedo relajarme. Sabe cuantos anos yo he esperado por este momento? I can't relax, You know how many years I have waited for this moment?

Vilma: Mira Ceci... Alla estan ellas en la parada! Estan libre! Look, there they are! Liberated!

133. Ceci and Vilma arrive at the SOS bus stop

They pull up to the bus stop on the main highway in front of the SOS and there are the three girls in their Sunday best dresses, sitting on the bus stop bench waiting with Karla and Yarel. Ceci parks and jumps out of the car and hugs them.

Angie: Mira mi vestido Ceci... my dress.

Ceci: *Trying to hold back the tears behind her joy.*   **Si mi amor... que bonita tu eres... y todas sus hermanas en sus**

vestidos. **With the clothes on their backs that I gave them. Good lord.** Roxana… no llores… *She wipes away Roxana's tears and hugs her.* **Vamos a su casa nueva. I am going to give you a better life.** Yes my love. How beautiful you are as well as your sisters in their beautiful dresses. With the clothes on their backs good Lord. Roxana please don't cry. We are going to your new house. I am going to give you a better life.

Everybody piles into the black truck with Karla and the three girls in the front seat. Vilma and Yarel sit in the pila. Roxana is crying. Angie sits next to Ceci… Ceci thanks Karla for hanging in for the long wait at the SOS.

Ceci: Karla, Gracias… Yo se que fue dificil. Tu sabes que este dia va a marcar un cambio de vida grande para ellas. Thank you Karla. I know that was difficult. You know that this day will change their lives.

Karla: Estoy acustombrada estar rechazada…. He aprendido quedarme como una piedra, hasta que tengo lo que necesito. Soy pobre, pero tengo tenacidad. I'm used to being rejected. I have learned to stay put like a rock until I have what I need. I am poor but I have tenacity.

Ceci: Que paso con el papel de la Juez?… no entiendo porque habia una problema. What happened with the paper from the judge? I d on't understand why there was a problem.

Karla: Ellos conocen a ud… y saben que las ninas quieren estar contigo… Y no me creyeron que tengo trabajo en Naranjal.

They know you and know that the girls want to be with you. And they don't believe that I will work as a trabajadora in Naranjal.

Ceci: Entonces….no he terminado con la Juez seguramente. Well I guess I haven't finished with the judge yet.

Karla: No importa… Lo que es claro… es que las ninas estan libre, y van a vivir bien… hablar Englais… comer bien etcetera … verdad ninas? *The girls are somewhat confused.* It doesn't matter. What is clear is that the girls are free and that they will live well.. speak English, eat well, etcetera… right girls?

Jazmin: Yo me gusta chocolate. I like chocolate.

Karla: *Whispering to Ceci..* **Nunca me dejes Ceci… Son mis ninas… y yo vengo con el paquete, tu sabes…no lo olvides.** *Karla catches Ceci off guard with this comment… and then points to a corner.* **Se puede dejar nosotros por el Restaurante Hamacas por favor.** Never leave me Ceci. They are my girls, and I come with the package, you know. Don't forget it. You can leave us by the Hamacas Restaurant please.

Ceci: OK Karla…. Gracias… *She gives Karla 2000 Lempiras. The girls start crying, thinking that they are returning with Karla. Karla turns to them, tucking the money in her bra…she leans into the faces of the crying kids and says:*

Karla: Se portan bien ninas!!! Oyen?? Somos co-madres… Ceci… Behave yourselves girls… Hear me? We are co-madres, Ceci.

Vilma shakes her head disapprovingly as she knows Karla will always beg for money.

134. **Yarel's family shack along the old railroad line -Karla's home**

Karla and Yarel exit behind a new housing development where we see an old row of shacks that used to border the old railroad tracks running to the shore where pineapples, bananas, and coconuts were harvested and shipped out to the La Ceiba seaport. Many native Hondurans worked on these farms, and lived minimally alongside the tracks to guarantee their work and fruit trade. Karla's new man, Yarel, 20 years old, lives with his family who has two shacks side by side near a creek. *Yarel's Mom and Dad and older sister and her children watch as Karla and Yarel are dropped off. Karla at 30, is an odd match for Yarel, but she has found herself a home with this family. There is no plumbing, and when it rains, the muddy trail in front of the shacks becomes a river. They cook outside on fogotas (fire tables) and share out houses. They wash clothes in the creek. There is a cement block Pentacostal church at the corner. This is Karla's new neighborhood in a small 2 room shack with a young boy and his family, whom she met while selling chicken at a street kiosk. Ceci climbs out of the car with them as they depart. Vilma gets in the front with the girls and starts singing songs with them.*

Ceci: Gracias Karla y Yarel. Me siento mal que duro tanto tiempo, pero nosotros todos lo hicemos para ellas. Thank you Karla and Yarel. I feel badly that it took so long, but we all did it for them.

Karla: Si Ceci, yo se ... lo que quiero saber...es mi futuro.. lo que tu puedes hacer para mi. Yes Ceci, I know. What I want to know .. is my future... what you can do for me.

Ceci: Karla... buenos parientes trabajan para sus familias. Ninos no pueden trabajar. Yo necesito gastar mis pistos para ellas. Me ayudaste para el bienestar de ellas,,, Gracias... pero YA!!! Tengo limitos. No soy su banco. Digan adios a Karla ninas... Karla... good parents work for their families. Kids can't work. I need to spend my money on them. You helped me for their welfare. Thank you... but that's it. I have limits. I am not your bank. Tell Karla goodbye girls.

Ninas: Adios Karla.

Karla: *She and Yarel get out of the car, and Karla turns back to Ceci...* **Les cuiden bien Ceci. Yo se donde esta su casa. Buenas noches.** Take good care of them Ceci. I know where you live. Good night.

Ceci sees the poverty in her rearview mirror, and swears that the girls will never return to that. And although she pities Karla's situation, she knows that she cannot allow herself to be manipulated by Karla, who clearly makes babies she can't support.

135. <u>Under Ceci's roof – The house in Naranjal – Jazmin's Birthday</u>

**There were actually two suburban rented homes where we lived in La Ceiba over a period of seven years. For purposes of efficiency, I have condensed the time dramatically to combine the events we shared together in El Sauce and Naranjal, La Ceiba (where oranges used to grow). The house in Naranjal has huge, cement walls around it, with barbed wire layers above that, and a big iron gate to let the car in and out. The first house was in El Sauce, where many Ceibenos have created a humble, middle class settlement just outside the city. We had to move when the owner's family needed the home. Needless to say, both homes were a huge upgrade for the girls, despite regular problems of leaky rooves and theft.

The following scene introduces the girls to their new suburban home in Naranjal... straight from the SOS orphanage. It has been a long day and the sun has set. Vilma and Ceci usher the girls in with great suspense. It is a modern home in disrepair, with high ceilings, a dated kitchen, and a nice backyard with fruit trees, a swing set, and an inflatable pool. Bedrooms are upstairs.

Roxana: Wow! Mira el tele! Grande! Wow, look at that big television.

Jazmin: Y columpios! Y una piscina atras! And swings and a pool in the backyard!

Angie: Y un espejo para bailar. Y Ceci. Donde esta nuestro cuarto? And a mirror to dance. And Ceci, where is our room?

Ceci: Upstairs honey... **Vamos... todas!**

Upstairs there are three bedrooms... For the moment the three will share the same room, where there are three little red metal beds with little bed tables and stuffed animals and dolls waiting for all of them. Ceci instructs Vilma to prepare Jazmin's birthday cake with three candles.

Jazmin: Mi cama... sola!!! Como las ninas!!!! With my own big girl bed like the girls!!!

Ceci: Si - no more crib... you're a big girl *Ceci takes Jazmin in her arms and squeezes her tight.* **You know it was just your birthday yesterday, September 5**th**, 2006, and we must celebrate tonight that you are THREE YEARS OLD.... Tres anos mi amor... Cumpleanos... Birthday cake... ahora!!!**

Angie: Mi cama.. My bed... Ceci gracias... y una biblioteca con libros. And a bookcase with books.

Jazmin: Y Peluches!! And stuffed animals!

Angie: y Barbies y un escritorio... And Barbies and a desk.

Ceci: It's your room. Your own beds. No more sharing beds.

Roxana: Wow...*She wanders into the closet and sees all the dresses hanging neatly, shoes lined up.......* **Y Ropa .... ninas!!**

Angie: Es Como Navidad!!! It's like Christmas!

Jazmin: Y es mi cumpleanos!!! AND it's my birthday.

Ceci: That's right... Hay que festejar. *She presents a gift wrapped box.* **Su abuela, Josephina, mando este regalo de los Estados para todos. Ella costuro los vestidos para uds... y las munecas.** *Inside the box are three dolls with homemade dresses with matching dresses for the girls They are thrilled.* That's right and we have to celebrate. Your grandmother, Josephine, sent this present from the States for everybody. She made these dresses for you and the dolls.

After considerable excitement and over stimulation from the doll clothes Jazmin speaks...

Jazmin: Y mi pastel? And my birthday cake?

Vilma: Esta listo aqui! Vengan cantar! It's ready. Come and sing!

Vilma puts a cake with three candles ablaze on the kitchen table, cantando en Espanol. They all sing happy birthday Honduran Style to Jazmin – "Cumpleanos a ti, etc."

Jazmin: Suplo ahora? Do I blow now?

Ceci: Primero, hay que pensar de un deseo, y despues puedes suplar las velas. First you have to think of a wish, and then you can blow out the candles.

Jazmin: Deseo a ti... Ceci, que tu sea mi mama. I want you, Ceci... that you are my mother.

Angie: That was my wish too.

Ceci: You're not supposed to tell everybody your wish... But it's OK. You all have me ... Soy tu madre!! Now blow!!

Jazmin blows the candles and Vilma cuts the cake which they gobble up with big smiles. They have found a real home... This is a moment to remember, and the moon rises in the night sky.

Vilma: Felicidades Jazmin... *(big hug and a kiss)* **Tres anos y que guapa!!!** Happy Birthday Jazmin. Three years old and how pretty!

Ceci: OK.. now I hate to spoil the party, but we are not laying our heads on any pillows in this house until we kill those little bugs in your hair. Vilma... quiero sacar los piojos de las ninas antes que ellas tocan las camas. Tengo el shampoo y te pago mas... mas el taxi.. Hay que hacerlo ahora. Vilma I want to get rid of the lice in the girls' hair before they touch the beds. I have the shampoo and I will pay you more... plus your taxi. We have to do it now.

Vilma: Te entiendo…OK ninas… vamos a banar…. nuevos pajamas… nuevas camas.. y no mas piojos!!! Whoppee! I understand. Ok girls.. let's bathe… new pajamas, new beds and no more head lice.

The next hour is devoted to hair washing and nit picking. A nightmare that will continue until they leave Honduras. The girls climb into their pajamas and brush their teeth. It has been a very long day, and Vilma has been there through it all.

Vilma: Tengo que irme Ceci, es tarde. I have to go Ceci. It's late.

Ceci: Gracias por su ayuda con este milagro Vilma… Thank you so much for your help with this miracle Vilma.

Vilma: Es un milagro Ceci…. Saludos ninas… hasta manana… It is a miracle Ceci. Good night girls… see you tomorrow.

Angie, Jazmin, and Roxana: Ciao Tia… te amo. Ciao Aunt… I love you.

The girls give hugs to Vilma as she leaves. Ceci gives her money. When they are all in the bed, she sings MOTHER MOON… a lullaby that will stay with the girls forever.

136. CIUDAD BLANCA - Song to Quetzalcoatl & Comizahual

The Mother Moon melody is echoed by the same haunting flute melody line, floating over another mystical ceremony in the Ciudad Blanca. The members are sitting around the fire with no action, as they all stare into the fire unable to speak. With a distant roar of a spinning wind, Comizahual lands on the altar.

Ceci as Priestess Comizahual: Greetings comrades. Forgive my tardiness, I appreciate the invitation, I have been following the release of my god children from the orphanage. Thank you for the invitation… I have been listening…. And I hear that you have defined the problem as if all is doomed evolution… What shall we do about it?

There is silence.

Comizahual walks around with her majestic cape looking close up at all the leaders of the many indigenous tribes of Central America.

Comizahual: Well? What are you thinking gentlemen? Have you no solutions for this matter of great spiritual and political importance to our people? Come on!! If spirit cannot help, nothing will help. I know you have feelings about this.

Suddenly the inspiration takes the form of independent lines spoken from individuals all around the group in succession... like declarations of independence.....

Satuye: We must change the self identity of those who are governed as much as those who govern.

Cacique Copan Galel: The priority of the ruler must be to create a safe space for his people... then he can create the work that sustains that living society.

Cacique Entepica: And within that work, the people must feel that they are contributors to that survival ... not slaves to a higher power.

Morazan: That every citizen is part of the whole...

Cacique Benito: And so we must infiltrate the spirits of all Mayans to believe in their individuality, their health, their families, and not to participate in sacrifice.

Cacique Cicumba: We must not leave our children behind, as the Sun will still rise, without having to sacrifice the lives of our children.

Cacique Toreba: Because we have a beautiful country, full of resources and good people who have the energy to work for a better economy... a fair economy... a better life, right here in Honduras.

Cacique Mota: Yes, we must do this….We must create faith in Honduras and our people… Or go down with the orphans in history? No…

Cacique Lempira: We must take this to the scribes to write us a song, which we will then inject into the Honduran culture. It must be a beautiful song. Scribes where are you?

Scribe Hunuhpu: Yes we will work on this immediately.

Scribe Xbalanque: I have many poems with these exact themes.

Quetzalcoatl: No violence   This is not a revolutionary war. This should be an anthem to the spirit of our land, to the self-esteem of our people, and to the future of our children… We must have more intelligent leadership for our economy, our educational system, and our political system… with leaders who care and know how to construct community infrastructure. This is the tribal spirit which got lost in western modernity.

Priestess Comizahual: Then so be it…we will infiltrate spiritually with the wings of this song.. Yes, The FLYING TIGER and the FEATHERED SERPENT shall return from the heart of the sky to bring back the rightful destiny of these Latino orphans. And spirit will answer the call.

This song begins as an instrumental and as a dance of lifting energy and becomes a lyrical anthem that is performed in tribute to Comizahual and Quetzalcoatl. It is a tribute to the ancestors and their bravery for giving the Maya life

Clearly there is a need for compassionate, leadership amongst the current Hondurans population. Someone who can lead them out of economic decay.

FLYING TIGER AND FEATHERED SERPENT – Ceil Gruessing

Someone had to part the waters, root the trees, create the spark,
so many tries to start up life had left the planet in the dark

But then you came with birds and trees, mangos, fish and jaguars
We learned to farm and count the days, and understand the stars.

We call you back Quetzalcoatl, to bring some truth to life
To teach us how to live in peace with wisdom to survive.

Make   us   fearless   Comizahual
your   rules   of   Justice   make   the   call
Inspire our kids to stand up right

all as equals, see the light

CHORUS

Flying   Tiger,   Feathered   Snake,   Spirits   from   the   sky
We   call   on   evolution,   to   spread   our   wings   and   fly
Comizahual   and   Quetzalcoatl   teach   us   all   you   know
Come back to sow future seeds, to let our children grow

You gave us nature's treasures, a home, a family name.
From dawn to dusk we work to live, on this our home terrain
This land belonged to Ancestors who taught us how to pray
But we must open up our eyes, see the light and seize the day.

We all have vows we made for free, To pass down love as legacy
Our children need clean air to breathe without the fear of tyranny
Science is the magic trick we ask you to explain
The mystery of the sacred linked to science must remain

CHORUS

Thank you for your knowledge from the heart of the sky

You are angelic messengers who bring us tools of light

We ask you for the vision to live for common dreams
to give our kids a guarantee - a chance to be free.

137. <u>**Pre-School – Nursery, Pre-K, and Kinder**</u>

Next day, Ceci wakes up humming the tune from her dream to see three faces staring at her.

Ceci: School!!! I almost forgot! You have to go to school. Escuela muchachas. Banos, dientes, uniformes, lunches, smoothies, vitaminas!!!

We hear Honduran radio music, as Ceci gets the kids ready for their first day at pre-school right down the street. They put on uniforms, she does their hair, makes the lunches, gives them vitamins, breakfast, back packs just like any other Mom in the world times three, and out the door.

When they arrive up the street to the school, there is a moment of abandonaphobia, which Ceci gets to know in each of their faces when they are "dropped off a new cliff", alone again. Ceci stays and watches. Angie is hesitant and Ceci holds her. Roxana makes friends, somehow, without talking, on the jungle gym. Jazmin stays close to Ceci. We see the timidity of the girls, who have known too many mother figures in the past 2 years: Karla, Adila, Conchita and Dunia. Ceci's girls have again, another change, in a very short period of time. Ceci stays and watches and leaves when they are somewhat adjusted. <u>September 6, 2006.</u>

Ceci: Mami has to go to work... Hay que trabajar.... Te veo mas tarde,,,, and I love you. Big embrazo!!!   *Lots of hugs.*

138. <u>**Foster Home Charade – Deni May**</u>

Ceci is on her way to work when she gets a phone call from David Ashby.

David: Ceci... How's it going with the girls?

Ceci: Actually, they are in their first day of school today even though it started two weeks ago. Better late than never I guess.

David: Well I have some bad news.

Ceci: OK... *She pulls over and puts the phone on speaker*

David: The assistant Director of the SOS, Estefan Rodriguez, doesn't believe that the girls are with Karla...so he is on the way over to your house to bust you.

Ceci: Oh my God... I thought this was too good to be true.

David: I told him that Karla was a trabajadora in a foster home living there with the kids. But he is sure it is your house.

Ceci: What am I going to do now? They can't go back to the orphanage.

David: You know I hate to lie as I am a strict Catholic. So I told him I didn't know anything about the situation other than they went off with Karla yesterday. They think it's you Ceci.

Ceci: Ok... I have to do something quick. I won't let him take them back to the SOS

David: Good luck Ceci. I don't know what to tell you.

Ceci gets off the phone and calls Deni May.

Ceci: Deni.. are you awake? I need you to do me an outrageous favor.

Deni: I am half asleep. What's going on?

Ceci: That big guy, assistant director at the SOS is on his way over to my house because they don't believe that Karla has the girls. So I need you and Ale to go to my house and pretend that you are a foster parent and that Karla is the trabajadora. That's what Karla told the SOS Director when she got them out yesterday.

Deni: WHAT?

Ceci: That's it Deni. I can't be there. I need you to cover for me, and I also have to teach in 15 minutes.

Deni: Why do they care so much with 150 other SOS kids to worry about?

Ceci: Because they never ever let kids out of there unless the judge clears it for them to return to their original parents. And we both know how impossible it is to adopt orphans in this country. Ademas... they get money from the government for every bed they fill. And they don't want to set a precedent by letting gringas adopt and reduce their population.

Deni: Is this the guy that makes them stand on their head when they break the rules?

Ceci: Yes.. the fat assistant Director, Estefan. Deni I need you to go there now and pretend it's your house. The girls are in school. Take Ale with you, like he lives there too. I can't think of anything else and I have class in 5 minutes.

Deni: But what about Karla? She's a good liar.

Ceci: I don't know where she is and it's too late to look for her. Please come Deni….You can tell him she's at the Mercado and that the girls are in school up the street..... Deni, you are the only one who can do this. I will forever owe you.

Deni: OK … I'm on my way.

Ceci: Thank you Deni. Call me when he leaves. I will be at the studio.

She hangs up and lays her head on the steering wheel for 10 seconds and then realizes she is late and gets back on the road.

Ceci: Please God help me. I know I am breaking the law. This is the only way.

139. <u>SOS Inspection Visit – Naranjal home</u>

Deni is waiting on the porch when Estefan arrives at the porton.

Deni: **Hola Senor... Como puedo ayudarle?** How can I help you?

Estefan: Yo soy un Director con el SOS. Quiero ver las ninas Iraheta Rojas. I am the assistant director with the SOS. I want to see the girls, Iraheta Rojas.

Deni: Ellas estan en escuela ahora. They are in school now.

Estefan: Y la madre Karla? And the mother Karla?

Deni: Ella esta en el mercado haciendo compras. Que quiere senor? She is at the market shopping now. What do you want Senor?

Estefan: Necesito ver la casa para verficar la residencia de las ninas aqui. I need to see the house to verify their residence here.

Deni opens the gate and he enters strutting around the yard. He goes in the back yard and sees the swings. Deni follows him.

Estefan: *(referring to Ale)* **Y quien es el?** And who is he?

Deni: Mi hijo senor. Que es el problema? My son. What is the problem?

Estefan: Otra gringa con un hijo Hondureno? Another gringa, with a Honduran child?

Deni: Que quiere senor? Ud. llega sin noticia... Estoy perdiendo mi patiencia. What do you want Senor? You arrived without notice. I am losing my patience.

Estefan: Quiero ver la casa. I want to see the house.

Deni takes him inside the house and shows him the girls' bedroom with the 3 little beds and the clothes neatly organized in the closet.

Estefan: Y donde esta la escuela? And where is the school?

Deni: Al fin de la calle. Ellas vuelven a las 2pm. At the end of the street. They return at 2pm.

Estefan: Y donde duerme la madre? And where does the mother sleep?

Deni shows him the trabajadora's room which is clearly unoccupied.

Estefan: Pero nadie vive aqui senora!! But nobody is living here Senora!

Deni: Las ninas llegaron ayer y Karla empezo ayer tambien... Todavia no tuvo tiempo recoger sus cosas... Fue al mercado a comprar comida para la cena. Eso es todo. The girls arrived yesterday and Karla just started to work yesterday. She still hasn't had time to collect her things. She went to the market to buy food for dinner. That is all.

Estefan: Yo creo que la gringa Cecilia es responsable por la salida de las ninas. Conoce ella? I believe that the gringa Cecilia is responsible for the exit of the girls. Do you know her?

Deni: Si la conosco. Ella va a seguir apoyandoles sin duda. Yes I know her. She will continue supporting them without a doubt.

Estefan: Y ud cree que se puede darles una mejor vida aqui que en el SOS? And you believe that you can give them a better life here than in the SOS?

Deni: Claro que si Senor!! Estan en una escuela bi-lingual y privada con acceso a doctores y atencion mucho mas personal aqui. Senor, preferia ud. que sus hijos esten en el SOS o en su casa? Absolutely Senor! They are in a bi-lingual, private school with access to doctors and much more personal attention here. Would you prefer to have your children in the SOS or in your home?

Estefan: *Ignoring her.* **Ahora Senora, no creo nada de su cuento. Puedo tomar su nombre?** *He opens his notebook and pen.* Now I don't believe anything of your story. Can I have your name?

Deni: Lo siento Senor. Pero ellas estan mas seguro aqui que en el orfanato. Que mas quiere saber? Tengo una cita en 15 minutos. *Grabbing her purse and keys* I am sorry Senor. But they are much safer here than in an orphanage. What more do you want to kn ow? I have an appointment in 15 minutes.

Estefan: Esta inscrito con la IHNFA esta casa? Como se llama Senora? Is this home registered with the IHNFA? What is your name?

Deni: Es una casa privada Senor. Jane Doe, OK? *She spells it.* This is a private home Senor. Jane Doe OK?

Estefan: **Yo fui esta manana a la casa de la familia en San Judas donde vive Karla supuestamente con sus otros hijos, Cynthia y Carlos. Es claro que las condiciones alla son horibles. Quiero saber porque ud. no puede cuidar a los otros hermanos aqui tambien.** I went this morning to the family's house in San Judas where Karla supposedly lives with her other children, Cynthia and Carlos. It's clear that the conditions there are horrible. I want to know why you didn't take the other siblings as well.

Deni: **No hay espacio aqui para mas ninos Senor. Eso es bien evidente... Entonces que mas? Tengo que irme.** There is no space for more children here Senor. That is obvious. So what else? I have to go.

Estefan: **No se preocupe senora...hay mas. Yo voy a contactar la Juez y hablaremos de nuevo en poco tiempo.** Don't worry Senora... there is more. I am going to contact the Judge and we will speak again shortly.

Deni: **Buenos Dias senor. Aqui esta la puerta.**

Estefan: **Buenos Dias Senora..**

Deni: *Watching him drive away.* Pig! At least they won't be standing on their heads as punishment here. *She calls Ceci.*

Deni: Ceci...he just left. I showed him the house, but he doesn't believe Karla is living here, so I told him that she just started working today. I don't know... He really pissed me off with his attitude.... but I got through it. But I can tell you.... it's not over.

Ceci: Thank you, Deni... I would do this for you.

Deni: Nobody knows how hard it is to rescue a kid in this country. They think you are a criminal, when the real parents are the problem.

Ceci: Poverty is the problem... but that's for another argument.

Deni: Hang in there strong lady.

Ceci: Deni... Thank you so much for this landmark favor. I mean it was like a Hollywood block buster moment from Oscar nominee Deni May... It was Carpe Diem, and I thank you for stepping up to a shaky plate at the last minute. You are a sister and I will never forget it.

140. <u>High School Dance Class – Prepping Presidential Tribute and Christmas</u>

Ceci is distraught when she arrives at the studio, but pulls it together and continues working.

Female students enter and take their places at the bar. Ceci puts on the music... they do the jazz bar routine which has been memorized as part of the class warm up. Ceci walks around checking each of the ten girls for technique and energy. The Mazapan Students have been working on a medley of Honduran songs for a performance on the La Ceiba Beach in tribute to President Maduro and his wife Agua Ocanas. It is a Caribbean mix of indigenous, ceremonial sounds, followed by Moises Canelo and a tribute to the struggle of Honduras after Hurricane Mitch, including Garifuna music and dance with Aurelio Marinez classic punta, ending with a colorful Caribbean Carnaval finale with poet/musician, Guilliermo Anderson. The scene opens with a rehearsal of this epic medley of famous Honduran music. We watch them work.

Ceci: OK.. girls, that is really looking good... fun to watch, and exciting to be around. We will be doing that for President Maduro in a few weeks on the beach here in La Ceiba... so keep it alive in your bodies and spirits. I am very proud of you. .... Please have a seat por favor.

Ceci changes the music. The girls gather in a circle on the floor.

Ceci: Now what I would like to do today girls....make the circle tighter ... OK...What I want to talk about today and hopefully begin, is a study with authentic expressive sections of your own choreographies....that can call your emotions up when you move: like love, or hunger......desire, pain.......valor....curiosity... discovering any movement that you can attach to a feeling, and then expressing it.

Ceci continues **And in this case, for this song, I have chosen a theme of love and longing for Xmas with Mary's longing for her son Jesus .... For which I will choreograph the chorus, and function as the quilt master, as you all do 8 bars of 8 count choreographies for the verses...one of which will repeat in the beginning and the end.**

There is mixed reaction to the assignment. Ceci continues...

Entienden? Easy formula... One that will always work, if you can learn to diagnose a song .... And then to have an intention with an idea how to express it, and repeat it, and bring it to life over and over in different ways. Then you are a choreographer. And I will not judge your style of movement if you can dig deep to find it and set it to music.

Student: Ms. Ceci, I have never made a dance before. I don't know how.

Ceci: I am going to help you and teach you all of this... how to break down a song mathematically, to see the verses, the repeats, the modulations, the crescendos, the intro, the drama, the instrumentals, the end... and bang bang... OK? It becomes a formula, that you use in your own way, to make your own story. Trust me... the person who taught me this was my artistic mentor when I was at Antioch college *(Michael Fajans, painter)* **He gave me the mathematical secret for keeping track of music and choreography.** *She continues*

This is an exercise more than a work of art, at this beginning point.... To stimulate your creativity and collaboration in response to this music. So I will teach you the chorus today, and give you the mathematical break down of the song afterwards so you understand the structure of the song with verses, choruses, musical breaks, etc. Are there any questions?

Marbella: Do we know the song?

Ceci: Yes I am sure you do... es una cancion Latino...

Andrea: But I didn't sign up for this class to choreograph. I can't do that.

Ceci: Andrea, you are an A math student...

Andrea: What does math have to do with dancing?

Ceci: Choreography is math... Music is math.... When you understand the structure of a song you like, you count the measures, then you plug your personal moves into the given mood, time and music.... You see the structure of the song, its repetitions, and instrumental breaks, its symmetry and shapes. It's definitely math. You put the pieces together and "voila".. arte!

Andrea: How do I make my feelings into movements?

Ceci: Do you feel pain, hunger, love, and desire?

Andrea: Of Course...

Ceci: Then you can learn to let your body respond to those feelings, when the music and lyrics connect with your heart. There is no right or wrong. I chose this song because it reminded me of the longing I had for my little girls, when I knew how lost they were in the orphanage after having survived absolute hell in their first few years, ... and how much I wanted to give them a life, and yet how impossible the whole custody thing seemed to be..... That journey was and still is so difficult and intense within me, as a mother, as a woman, as an American, and as an artist. I long for the safety and happiness of these three little girls as any mother does. Can you imagine how that feels? It's just a universal motherly instinct... which we will plug into xmas and Mother Mary.

Andrea... I will help you. I will help everyone who needs help. You all have it in you.

All the girls agree in their own shy way. They are inspired.

Student: Oooh ... I just got the chills..!!

Ceci: Ok so let's learn the chorus to this Mark Anthony salsa and see how it goes. Just concentrate on the footwork for now.

Ceci begins to teach the choreography for the chorus which will repeat. It is basic salsa with fast foot work in various patterns. The girls are slow to pick up the footwork at first, but with the music, it all starts to kick in.

Ceci: That's the spirit!! For real… Very nice work for the first rehearsal. You are becoming very good salseras. Now rub your hands together like this and then hold them an inch apart. Can you feel that vibration between your hands? The heat? The buzz? With the right intention, that is what you want to feel when you dance, and of course what you want to express… Chills, spirit, maya, fuerza, mana…magic… I learned that from a modern dance choreographer named Jose Limon.

Student: I have the chills too…

Ceci: Then you too can choreograph. Use your muscle memory… You have to be able to create this in your dances. 8 eights….64 counts .. got it? And you may collaborate in partnerships. Yes work that out.   Entonces, that is homework for next week. Right now we will get ready for your part in the "Breath of Heaven Ballet" with the rest of the company. Listas?

Other students enter for the rehearsal for a different ballet, all together, including the three sisters. The dancers take their place in front of the mirror, and Ceci begins to teach the choreography of Angels and Mary to the music of "Breath of Heaven" (Amy Grant)

The dancers are miming the washing of clothes with other young girls. The music shifts and the wind blows. Angie will appear as the angel Gabriel and offers a lily to Mary. She blesses Mary and circles around her. The other girls join in dancing with Mary and the angel Gabriel. And a light shines down on Mary from above. Then all the little angels from the bambinas class will come out and dance around Mary in a circle opposite the older dancers. Soon they cover Mary with a large veil. When they open the circle, and pull the veil away, Mary is revealed holding a baby. All the mothers are watching on the sidelines.
Watching your child in dance class is a rite of passage for motherhood.

Ceci: Fantastico… fabuloso… genial.. I love it. You make me proud.

141. Preschool Drop off – The Judge visits

Ceci pulls up to the Pre-School in her funky black pick up truck. The three girls are playing in the school yard. Each has spent the day in Nursery (Jazmin), Pre-K (Angie), and Kinder (Roxana). This is a much different ambiance from the orphanage. All of these kids have parents and individual attention. They tell Ceci that Angie cried a bit when she left in the morning, but Roxana calmed her down. They all pile into the car with their art work and lunch boxes.

Arriving at the house there is a strange car. When they get out of the car, Ceci is greeted by the Judge, Irasema Guillien. She wants to know where Karla is. Ceci invites her into the house.

Judge Irasema: Dona Cecilia,,,, Vino el Director del SOS, y me dijo que las ninas estan viviendo aqui sin su madre, que fue la promesa cuando salieron del SOS. Yo conozco su reputacion aqui en la Ceiba, y aunque de yo se que sus intenciones serian buenos, hay que trabajar con la ley Senora. Dona Cecilia… The Director of the SOS came by and told me that the girls are living without their mother, which was the promise when they left the SOS. I know your reputation in la Ceiba, and even though I know that you have good intentions, you must work with the law.

Ceci: No hubo una ley, ni un camino legal abierto para buscar custodia y segurar el salud y las vidas de estas ninas. Con sus problemas medicas, yo creo que fue la sola manera Senora. Y cuando yo consegui la madre de nacimiento, ella me dio permiso para tener custodia. Tengo los papeles. Aqui estan…

Ceci goes to the desk to hand her a file… The judge holds her hands up. There wasn't any way… no open legal roads to get custody and secure the health and lives of these girls. With their medical problems I believe it was the only way Senora. And when I found the mother, she gave me permission to take custody. I have the papers. Here they are.

Judge: Ella no mas tiene la custodia permanente de estas ninas. Yo le di permiso condicional vivir con ellas con vigilancia de mi oficina…. A pesar de su neglegencia increible!! Ademas,

ellas todavía son la propriedad del estado. Dios mio! Senora Cecilia, sabes que… lo que ud. ha hecho es un crimen – una mentira – un abduction! Y donde esta Karla ahora? She doesn't have permanent custody of these girls any more. I gave her the conditional permission to live with them with vigilance from my office…. despite her terrible negligence. Besides the girls are still the property of the state. My God! Senora Cecilia you know that what you have done is a crime, a lie, and abduction? And where is Karla now?

Ceci: Lo hice para salvar las vidas de tres ninas bien enfermas que necesitaban tratamiento mas rapido que el SOS, la IHNFA, o cualquier hospital podrian darles… Y la systema no me dio ningun camino hacerlo… Aqui estoy yo con ellas…donde ellas tienen seguridad por la primera vez en sus vidas, con todos sus disabilidades … Ellas tienen atencion medico, agua limpia, comida… vitaminas… y pre-school bilingual …. conmigo… Que puede ser mejor?… I did it to save the lives of three really sick girls who needed treatment faster than the SOS, the IHNFA or whatever hospital could give them. And the system did not give me a path to do that. Here I am with them… where they are safe for the first time in their lives, with all their disabilities. They have immediate medical attention, clean water, food, vitamins, pre-school privada… all with me. What could be better?

The moment is tense as Ceci, the judge, and the three girls look at each other. The girls run to hug Ceci. Clearly, Karla is not living there as a worker, as promised upon the release of the kids from the SOS. Ceci has told the judge the truth about the charade, as there was no other provision under the law to get them out of the orphanage and into her custody. Karla has written them over to Ceci's custody and wants them to have the best possible future. Not Karla or the orphanage can come close to the care and opportunity that Ceci can offer them as a real Mom. The judge is visibly torn, angry, and confused.

Judge: Pues… Dona Cecilia… hay que venir a mi oficina a ver lo que podemos hacer para legalizar esta situacion, que nunca he visto en mi vida. Solamente una Gringa puede inventar algo asi. Ok

Dona Cecilia. You must come to my office to see what we can do to legalize this situation, that I have never seen in my life. Only a Gringa could come up with this.

Ceci: Disculpa Senora. Yo *tuve* que hacerlo. Y con mi perseverencia ellas van a ver una vida marvellosa, con los talentos que tienen. Necesito su apoyo….por favor… I am sorry Senora. I had to do it. And with my perseverance, they are going to see a marvelous life with all the talents that they have. I need your support… please.

The girls have been watching the ping pong between the judge and Ceci as they gaze upwards, back and forth in confusion.

Judge: Pues…. Venga manana a las 10am con la madre, Karla, que conozco bien… con las ninas, y hablaremos mas. OK, come tomorrow at 10am with the mother Karla, who I know well, and the girls… and we will speak again.

Ceci: Gracias Sra. Juez… gracias… Ninas… dele un beso a la juez…. Gracias Sra Juez.. thank you. Girls give the judge a kiss.

They comply.

La Juez: Son preciosas… y que pasa con su ojo? *Regarding Angie's eye and how she looks at things close to her face.* They are precious. And what happened with her eye?

Ceci: Ciega con abuso, llorando con fievre y hambre, Karla le pego para silenciarle. Y por eso vinieron los soldados para sacarles a las tres hermanas con el aviso de una vecina … Su ojo derecho sirve un pocito, Gracias a Dios… Se llama atrophia del nervio optico. Fuimos a ver un opthamalogo en el Progresso que dijo que no se puede curarla. Pero yo creo en milagros. Blind with abuse. Crying with fever and hunger, Karla hit Angie to silence her. For this the soldiers came to take the three sisters away with the advice of a neighbor. Her right eye works a little Thank God. It's called optic nerve atrophy. We went to see an ophthalmologist in El Progresso who said that there is no cure. But I believe in miracles.

La Juez: Ok Sra. Cecilia … vamos a ver lo que podemos hacer manana. Pero con Karla tambien por favor. Si Dios quiere, vamos a conseguir una manera. Ok Sra. Cecilia. Let's see what we can do tomorrow God willing. But with Karla please.

Ceci: Si Senora, Un grand gracias… a las diez manana… en el Corte. *Ceci and the girls watch the judge get back into her car.* Y el Viernes en canal 10 se puede ver el concurso de Ms. Honduras…. Las ninas van a participar en el espectaculo con la Reina del ano pasado. Yes Sra. A big thank you… at 10am tomorrow at the courthouse. And on Friday on Channel 10 you can see the Miss Honduras Contest.. The girls are going to participate with last year's Queen.

Angie: Si porque somos bellas como Miss Honduras!! Yes, because we are beautiful like Miss Honduras.!

Judge: Si, son bellas…. Hasta manana entonces…. Yes you are beautiful. Until tomorrow then.

When the car disappears, Ceci collapses holding her head in her hands. Roxana starts to cry.

Ceci: No,,,, nobody will ever ever take you away again. Uds. viven aqui conmigo… Soy su mama, and yes God wants that.

Jazmin: La mejor Mami del mundo. The best mom in the world.

142. <u>**Judge Irasema's Office - 2006**</u>

Next day Ceci arrives at the Municipal court house with three sleepy girls and Karla. The girls are wearing their traditional Honduran Folk dresses. Ceci carries Jazmin who is very tired. It is a strange dynamic with Karla, as she clearly feels very little for these girls, but knows that she is doing the right thing. Karla has given birth to so many children, she just doesn't have the ability to love or care for all of them. They sit outside the office of the judge and wait.

Karla: Ceci... tu sabes que no tenemos luz. Ceci. You know that we don't have electricity.

Ceci: Que paso... no hay luz en la calle? What happened? There's no light in the street?

Karla: No ... no pudimos pagar la cuenta... Necesito pistos. No.. we couldn't pay the bill.. We need money.

Ceci: *(sighing)* **Otra vez? Ya te di dinero para la luz. Karla, si la Juez sabe que yo te doy dinero, ella va rechezarme la custodia.** Karla if the Judge knows that I give you money, she is going to reject the custody.

Karla: Y porque? And why?

Ceci: Tu sabes... Hemos hablado de eso bastante veces.... Entonces... mas tarde OK? You know this.. We have talked about this many time. Later OK?

The door opens, and the judge invites them in. The girls stay near Ceci... Jazmin is still asleep in her arms.

Judge: Vengan sentar todos... Como estan ninas? Come sit down everybody. How are you girls?

Angie: Bien....

Judge: Voy a mirarles en el tele esta noche. *With a big mama smile.* I am going to watch you on the television tonight.

Roxana y Angie: *smiling shyly* Si gracias. Somos bellas.

Roxana: Somos princessas. We are princesses.

Judge: Empezamos. Karla, primero …la ley dice que ud. no tiene ningun derechos con las ninas a causa del abuso. Pero yo le di un chance cambiar. Todavia ellas son la propriedad de Honduras. Sin embargo, con este situacion con la Senora Cecilia …..quiero saber…. que es su interes en las vidas, el bienestar y la custodia de las ninas abajo la respondabilidad de ella. Let's begin. Karla, first the law says that you have no rights with the girls because of the abuse. But I gave you a chance to change. They are still the property of Honduras. Nevertheless, with this situation with Sra. Cecilia… I want to know. What is your interest in their lives, the wellbeing and the custodia of these girls under her care?

Karla: Quiero que ellas viven afuera del SOS con seguridad y medicina para sus disabilidades…. Y con una buena educacion. Eso no puedo darles… Y Si .. la señora Cecilia puede. Entonces ella debe de tener custodia de las tres ninas. I want the girls to live away from the SOS with the security and medicine for their disabilities. With a good education… This I can't give them.. and yes Ms. Cecilia can. So she should have custody of the three girls.

Judge: Si.. y recuerda ud. porque les sacaron de su custodia al principio Karla? And, remember why we took away your custody in the beginning Karla?

Karla: Soy pobre. No habia comida, ni medicina. Todas eran enfermas… una pesadilia. I am poor.. There was no food nor medicine and everybody was sick.. a nightmare.

Judge: Y quien es responsable por el dano de este ojo aquí? *Pointing to Angie's left eye.* Y Cuenta me también de esta mentira que tu tiene trabajo en Naranjal con una gringa. Estoy enojada Karla. And who is responsible for the damage to this eye here? And tell me also about this lie that you have work in Naranjal for a gringa. This all makes me mad Karla.

Karla: *Avoiding the eye incident…* Fue la unica manera quitarles del SOS, y ud. lo sabe!! Y todavia hay Cynthia Y Carlos en San Judas para cuidar. It was the only way to get them out of the SOS and you know it. And I still have Cynthia and Carlos to take care of.

Judge: Hay leyes Senoras. *Looking at Ceci also.* **Y quien esta cuidando ellos ahora? .... como tiene su nueva residencia.** There are laws ladies. And who is taking care of them now that you are in a different residence?

Karla: Cynthia y Carlitos estan con la Abuela, Celestina Alvarez, madre de su papa Carlos. They are with their grandmother Celestina Alvarez, mother of their father Carlos.

Judge: Y como puede la abuela cuidarles bien... con la meningitis en el barrio? And how can the grandmother take good care of them with meningitis in the neighborhood?

Karla: Si...Ella es una enfermera y tambien una partera. Yes, she is a nurse and also a midwife.

Judge: Entonces porque uds. no podian curarles de la meningitis antes? Then why couldn't you take care of the meningitis before? *The judge stands up and walks around.*

Karla: Porque no habian pistos. Because there was no money.

Judge: Hay el Hospital Atlantida? *She notices Karlas pregnant belly.* **Ooy Karla...Y de nuevo voy a preguntarle... que tienes en su bariga? Otra?** What about the Hospital Atlantida? Ooy Karla.... And I am going to ask you again... What is in your uterus? Another?

Karla: No senora. No tengo nada. No Sra. I am not pregnant.

Karla actually pounds on her belly again, to prove she is not pregnant, when she actually is pregnant again with Lilliana, daughter of Yarel, (the new BF). Many women try to abort through pounding on their abdomens to cause miscarriage. We believe this happened to Roxana, or she was the victim of physical fighting between Karla and the Dad while she was in the belly because of her later frontal lobe diagnosis of intellectual disability.

Judge: Y que pronto aparecio un nuevo novio despues del muerto de su papa, verdad? And how fast appeared a new boyfriend after the death of their father, right?

Karla: Si, y el trabaja. Yes, and he works.

Judge: Ooy senora... no mas ninos! En el nombre de Dios!!! *Pause* **Y Dona Cecilia, que son sus planes?** Oh Sra... no more kids! In the name of God!. Y Sra. Cecilia, what are your plans?

Ceci: Con su permiso, quiero criar estas ninas como su madre. With your permission, I want to raise these children as their mother.

Karla: Como co-madre. As CO-madre. *Correcting Ceci.*

Judge: Puede ser una sola madre Karla. There can only be one mother Karla.

Ceci: Pues, quiero adoptarles, con su permiso. Tengo 53 anos, y no se que son las posibilidades. I want to adopt them, with your permission. I am 53 and I don't know what the possibilities are.

Judge: Momento....

She gets on the phone to call the IHNFA headquarters in Tegucigalpa. She speaks to somebody there while filing her nails. Then gets off the phone after an intense and rapid conversation in Spanish..

Judge: I am sorry Senora Cecilia... el limite de edad para adoptar en Honduras es 50. Y no hay nada que puedo hacer para cambiar la ley. Lo que podemos areglar es algo como "foster care", pero yo no se como se puede salir del pais asi con ellas. Honduras esta conectada con el convencion de Hague donde hay reglas international de adopcion. I am sorry Sra. Cecilia. The limit in age to adopt in Honduras is 50. And there is nothing I can do to change the law. What we can do is arrange for foster care, but I don't know how you can leave the country with that. Honduras is connected with the Hague Convention where there are strict adoption laws.

Ceci's eye's water as she rocks Jazmin in her arms. Later Ceci discovers that Honduras is NOT affiliated with the Hague convention.

Ceci: OK, lo que se sea. Aqui vivo yo ahora. Ayudame con cualquier custodia de estas ninas.... Ellas me necesitan ahora ....tienen enfermidades que no van a cuidar en el SOS. Necesitan apoyo para acomodaciones académicas, médicos especiales, atención psychologica para su abandono y negligencia. Lo que quiero es que ellas son seguro conmmigo. Y si eventualmente podria darme permiso buscar visas para visitar los Estados con ellas. Au menos puedo conseguir ayuda medico y especial alla. OK.. whatever. I live here now. Help me with the custody of these girls. They need me… they have illnesses that can't be cured in the SOS. They need support for academic accommodations, special doctors, psychological attention for their abandonment and negligence. What I want is for them to be safe with me. And eventually if you can give me permission to apply for visas to visit the USA. At least I can find special medical help there.

Karla: Ir y vuelta Ceci. To go and come back Ceci.

Judge: Tengo dudas fuertes que la embajada Americana va a aceptar esta custodia. Usualmente permite salidas con ninos adoptados solamente. I have my doubts if the American embassy will accept this custody. Usually they permit exits with only adopted children.

Karla: No, mis ninas se queden en Honduras. No, my girls stay in Honduras.

Judge: Porque Karla? Para venderles a Cecilia cada vez que necesitas pistos? Ella no puede pagarte, ademas pagar para la vida de ellas.... No Karla.... Y ....Si oigo cuento de un solo transaction entre uds.... donde tu pides dinero de la Senora para tu mismo, cuando ella ya esta cuidando sus ninas.... ellas volveran al SOS. No vendemos ninos en Honduras. Entienden? Why Karla? To sell them to Cecilia every time you need money? She can't pay you and take care of the girls. No Karla. And if I hear about one financial transaction between you, where you ask for money from the Sra for your welfare, when she is taking care of the girls… they will go back to the SOS. We don't sell kids in Honduras. Do you understand?

Karla: *rolling her eyes.* Si Senora.

Ceci: Pues…Mi responsibilidad ahora es el bienestar de las ninas…. yo voy a buscar mi residencia para vivir aqui. Todavia, quiero visas medicas para ellas. Tengo mi madre alla en Virginia que tambien quiere ayudar. My responsibility now is the wellbeing of the girls. I am going to apply for residency to live here. Still, I want medical visas for them. I have my mother in Virginia who also wants to help.

Judge: Bueno… empezamos con un papel para la custodia, pero quiero ver las ninas cada mes, con sus notas de escuela, y cualquier cosa medica que pasa con ellas… Estamos todos claros? OK.. we will begin with a document for the custody, but I want to see the girls every month, with their grades from school, and whatever medical situation that takes place with them. Are we all clear?

Ceci: Si Senora… Gracias… Finally legal… I can't believe it… Gracias con todo mi corazon… Uds. han cambiado el futuro de ellas sin duda. *Ceci's mascara is running. She rises to hug the judge and then Karla as she maintains the sleeping Jazmin on her hip.* Yes Sra. Thank you. Finally legal. Can't believe it. Thank you with all of my heart. You both have changed their future without a doubt.

Judge: Entonces…. Karla… Hemos decidido que Cecilia tiene la responsibilidad y custodia completo de estas ninas… Y creo yo, que ud. debe de sentir agradecida de la Senora por salvar la vida de estas tres preciosas que criaste tu sin pensar de su bienestar…. ademas piensas en las posibilidades que tienen ellas con Sra. Cecilia. Es un liberacion para ti tambien Karla. Y mi palabra final contigo, es NO MAS NINOS…. Oye? Ahora estoy preocupada por Carlitos y Cynthia que me parece son menos importante que su nuevo hombre. *She shakes her head.* Si Dios quiere ellas puedan conseguir seguridad y amor sincero un dia. Tenga ud. acuerdo con estas condiciones Karla? So Karla, we have decided that Dona Cecilia has the responsibility and the complete custody of these girls. And I believe that you should feel thankful for the Senora for saving the lives of these three precious girls whom you have raised without thinking of their wellbeing. Besides, think of the miracle that the gringa is going to give them a future. It is a blessing for you also. And Karla, my final word with you.. is NO MORE CHILDREN. Do you hear? Now I am worried for Carlitos and Cynthia who seem to be less important than your new boyfriend while you leave them with the grandmother. God willing they will find some security and sincere love one day. So, do you agree with these conditions Karla?

Karla: Si senora.

The Judge Irasema, calls in Daisy the secretary to whom she dictates the document which gives Ceci her first legal foster care of the three girls. Overwhelmed with emotion, Ceci smiles and extends her hand to the judge.

Ceci: Gracias Senora. Ninas… digan gracias a la Juez Irasema…. Y también a Karla.

Ninas: Gracias Juez. Gracias Karla.

Judge: Bueno… Es lo mejor que puedo hacer. Se puede esperar afuera por el documento y firmarlo con Daisy. Vaya con dios… todos… Estas ninas son preciosas, y quiero un embrazo. Disfruten con el espectaculo de Ms. Honduras. Ciao ninas bellas!! Good… It's the best I can do.. You can wait outside for the document and sign it with Daisy. Go with God everybody. These girls are precious and I want a hug. Have a great time with the Miss Honduras show. Goodbye beautiful girls.

Jazmin has woken up and is drying Ceci's tears. The judge hugs the girls and opens the door.

Ceci: Let's go girls. We have school and then the show tonight. Got to get beautiful... Gracias senora…. Con muchisimas gracias….

They wait outside as other families with lawyers enter her office. Eventually Daisy brings out a paper that Ceci and Karla sign. Ceci cheers with delight.

As they leave the courthouse, and get into the car, Karla reminds Ceci that she needs money. Against Ceci's better judgement, the exchange is made once again, and Karla goes her way to the barrio across the street from the Court House…. pocketing the cash. Ceci is constantly amazed at how little she seems to care for these three sisters… her own flesh and blood. Some women just make babies. Ceci and the girls take off in the car, and pass some Garifunas playing drums. Ceci turns up the salsa on the car radio and wiggles in the seat with glee. She has official custody of the girls.

143. <u>**The Miss Honduras Beauty Pageant – The Beach Hotel Quinta**</u>

Eduardo Zablah introduces his event of the year, talking about Honduran nationalism, and how he has chosen local music to portray the cultural beauty of our country in times of hardship.

The opening number is a medley of authentic Honduran musical styles and culture, using all 30 of the contestants representing the different provinces, who sing and dance to the various pieces. There is bachata, merengue, salsa, punta, folkorico, and Mayan sounds, also using the music of famous contemporary Honduran singers. The sisters will carry the flags, wearing folklorico dresses. All of this is televised. Ceci coordinates back stage as the ladies open the show with a production number…. Then change into swimwear… and then evening gowns. All this is presented in video collage/from both the back stage and audience point of view.

Jazmin, Angie, and Roxana wait backstage with Vilma, as Ceci works the entrances and exits of performers. At the very end when the Queen is announced, the girls will enter in fluffy princess dresses, carrying the train of the former Ms. Honduras who will take her final walk down the runway and then present the new winner. They look beautiful, smiling in their look a-like gowns. When the new Ms. Honduras is announced and crowned, she bends down to get kisses from the girls. After receiving her flowers and her banner, a royal cape is placed on the new Ms. Honduras's shoulders, and the girls carry her cape train as she takes her victory walk down the runway. Ceci peeks from backstage with tears of pride…. Thinking about how proud they must feel.

Ceci: My God thank you, they are so precious!!

144. Tucking the Angels in bed

It is late when they get home. The girls have been experimenting with makeup. They are washing their faces, brushing their teeth, and singing the Ms. Honduras theme song. They are walking around in Ceci's high heels like models.

Roxana: Ceci yo soy Ms. Honduras. Ceci, I am Miss Honduras.
Jazmin: A mi tambien porque soy bonita. Me too because I am very pretty.

Angie: Soy yo bonita también, verdad Ceci? And I am beautiful too, right Ceci?

Ceci: Si son bellas todas… En mi libro?… Uds. son las mas bellas del mundo. And you were fabulous out there tonight. I was so proud of my little estrelllitas in Eduardo Zablah mini ball gowns. Pero ahora hay que dormir… You need your

beauty sleep. We have the show on the beach on Sunday for the President. *She sings CARRY YOU (Amy Grant) until they pass out.* **I love you my babies…Buenas Noches.** Yes you are all beautiful. In my book? You are the most beautiful in the world. But now you must sleep. She sings.

Carry You
Song by Amy Grant

Lay down your burden
I will carry you
I will carry you my child, my child
Lay down your burden
I will carry you
I will carry you my child, my child

I would walk on water
Calm a restless sea
I've done a thousand things you've never done
And I'm really watching
While you struggle on your own
Call my name, I'll come

Lay down your burden
I will carry you
I will carry you my child, my child
Lay down your burden
I will carry you
I will carry you my child, my child

I'd give vision to the blind
I would raise the dead
I've seen the darker side of
hell and I've returned.
I've seen those sleepless nights
And count every tear you cry

Some lessons hurt to learn
CHORUS

The girls have fallen asleep.

145. <u>Saturday at home - 2007</u>

Ceci is cooking breakfast and the girls are strutting around in high heels wearing Ceci's dresses, pretending they are modeling. Angie is narrating. It is comical to see them strutting around in Ceci's dresses as if they are models. Ceci is delighted, laughing and applauding.

Cut to the porch where Ceci delivers breakfast baleadas and fresh papaya from the tree. As they eat Ceci prepares art supplies to paint fabric banners.

Ceci: Sus baleadas estan listas... *They watch, eating their baleadas while Ceci shows them how to cut the fabric with scissors. After eating, Ceci turns on music and throws T shirts over their dresses, always talking.* **Y recuerden que manana es el desfile y espectaculo para el Presidente Maduro en la playa... con todos mis bailarinas... y uds. van estar con Vilma.** Your baleadas are ready. And remember that tomorrow is the parade and show for President Maduro on the beach... with all my dancers... and you will be with Vilma.

Roxana: Somos famosas ahora right mom? We are famous now right mom?

Ceci: Claro!

Jazmin: Yo quiero bailar en el desfile... I want to dance in the parade.

Ceci: Too young....

Angie: A mi tambien, porque no? Me too... who not?

Ceci: In a few years you can. It's a long walk. I have rehearsal in the morning and later you will come with Vilma. So let's see some fabulous art work now OK?

Angie is having a difficult time cutting fabric so she stops and goes to Ceci who is folding laundry while they work. Jazmin and Roxana begin to paint. Angie is still eating her baleada. She wants to fold socks with Ceci, but she can't and it is frustrating for her.

Ceci: **Venga Angie... no importa los calcetines... vamos a pintar.** Come on Angie... the socks don't matter... Let's paint.

Angie: **No puedo Ceci... no puedo ver... y no puedo usar las tijeras tampoco por nada! And I also wet the bed. What's wrong with me????** *She starts to cry, and Angie holds her close.* I can't Ceci.. I can't see... And I can't use the scissors either for nothing!

Ceci: **Oh baby I understand. Si poderas... You will do all these things one day. These things are like riding a bike. Once you get it you got it. You just need more practice. Tu pintas bien... con tiempo vas a cortar tela bien tambien. And you will definitely stop wetting the bed someday. It happens to lots of kids and they outgrow it.**

They all continue painting. They are interesting abstract designs. Suddenly we hear thunder and a tropical rain storm begins. The girls love this drama and take off their clothes and run into the yard wearing underpants and shirts. They run around like wild animals splashing in the rain puddles. In the street young boys start to play soccer barefoot. Ceci watches smiling.

Ceci: **Only in Honduras... La lluvia es como las lagrimas benditas de Dios... ... Ellas quieren sentirla.** The rain is like the blessed tears of God... They want to feel it.

146. <u>**Rehearsing for President Maduro Tribute – Dance Class**</u>

In the dance studio the next day, Vilma is sewing colorful sarongs and head pieces for the older Mazapan girls. Ceci enters... greets Vilma, and goes straight to the mirror to review the steps for the choreography she is preparing for the Zona Viva tribute to President Ricardo Maduro. The event will feature singers, Moises Canelo, Guilliermo Anderson, Aurelio Martinez and other famous

Honduran performing artists. Ceci is coordinating the musical mix of these three artists.

Female students enter and take their places at the bar. Ceci puts on the music… they do the jazz bar routine which has been memorized as part of the class warm up. Ceci walks around checking each of the 10 girls for technique and energy.

As they review the first part of the choreography, we see them enter as indigenous farmers, planting seeds ceremoniously to Moises Canelo's profound and dramatic tribute to Honduras after the famous flood caused by Hurricane Mitch in 1998. More farm women emerge in big work skirts, praying to the heavens for survival as they plant. This eventually turns into pieces of, "Vaya Pues" and an exhilarating, folk dance celebration of Honduras, dancing/ praying for the fertility of the land and the culture.

Vaya Pues – Honduras - Moises Canelo and Ricardo Cerato

Gracias a Dios dijo Colon, Por librarnos de estas Honduras Despues de una tormenta en el mar profundo Luego asi llamo a mi tierra. Lamas hermosa del mundo

Honduras para sonar, para el amor, para encontrar calor humano

Honduras para el estres, para gozar, Y porque es un pueblo sano

Honduras para cantar, para sentir, para llevar la frente alta

San Pedro Sula es pasion,La Ceiba ideal, Y un corazon Tegucigalpa

Vaya pues, te invito a mi tierra
Vaya pues, hey brother conoce a mi gente.

Vaya pues, te invito a mi tierra
Vaya pues, atrapa su cálido ambiente

Te vas a enamorar ya vas a ver nadie se escapa

Te puedo asegurar que a ti Tambien te va a guiar nuestra Suyapa

Orquideas bellas se dan bajo este sol, si ves Copan cuanta hermosura

Te hara decir como yo po resto y mas vaya pues vos, Que viva Honduras

Vaya pues, te invito a mi tierra
Vaya pues, hey brother conoce a mi gente.

Vaya pues, te invito a mi tierra
Vaya pues, atrapa su cálido ambiente

We watch the rehearsal of Vaya Pues, and then Ceci introduces another dance.

Cuando Llega El Carnaval -Guillermo Anderson

Ella se alegra cuando llega el carnaval Y le florece
un poco de felicidad

Ella se alegra porque baila en la carroza
Y le comentan que en ella se ve preciosa

Por un momento olvida el tedio y la tristeza

Y sale a relucir el sol de su belleza

Por un momento esa dulzura en confite sale
La Rutina gris de su escondite

Ella se alegra porque descansan sus penas y el
papelillo cae sobre su piel morena

Ella se alegra porque bailando se olvida De las
tristezas de las vueltas de la vida.

The song ends and Ceci applauds, gives feedback.

Ceci: Well that felt pretty good. Verdad? I am proud of you beautiful young ladies. You are concentrating well, which will help you fly when you dance on stage. See you next week and we will continue this choreography in the name of Viva Honduras. And also this will serve Mother's Day and Carnaval celebrations. This is a good number. Please memorize it and be proud girls.

147. Transition to Actual Performance – Ceiba beach

The sun is blazing on the beach stage, a sound system is being set up…. Chairs are being unloaded and Ceci is trying to work with her boom box. She is working the places of the dancers on stage, without the guest artists. Random nervous dialogue between the dancers flows during the rehearsal. The sisters are watching the preparations with Vilma in the audience. This show is a tribute to the President of Honduras, Ricardo Maduro. The musical medley versions will be headlined by guest artists of the songs, and the dance styles will change with the music. Guillermo Anderson,

Aurelio Martinez (punta king), Moises Canelo are just arriving. Ceci takes a moment looking out into the ocean to pray that all goes well.

Aurelio Martinez and Ceci

Ceci with Guillermo Anderson

......We shift over magically to the real performance. There is a fashion show, popular Latino folk dance and Ballet and a stunning performance by the Ballet Garifuna National of Honduras. The dancers perform what they rehearsed in class..... an indigenous Modern Ballet to Moises Canelo's ballad about Hurricane Mitch and Honduras – Starting with sowing corn.... Native flute   whistles... a land fertility ritual....Then the transformation into folklorico with "Vaya Pues".   Following this song, Guillermo Anderson takes over with his song "Carnaval". Ceci and the dancers come out in colorful Caribbean sarongs and dance merengue behind him. Other artists perform, and finally

Aurelio Martinez takes the stage with his punta hit "Canto a Mi Tierra".

Even the girls get to participate in the finale with their ropa típica, in which all the performers on stage receive thundering applause from the audience on the beach as President Maduro takes the stage. His "Evita" like wife Aguas Canas is there, who remembers meeting Ceci at a party for Doctors without Borders. Back stage they discuss their progress with custody and adoption. Ceci asks her what she will do, and Aguas tells her discreetly that she may be returning to Spain, hopefully with the children. Aguas thanks her for mounting the show, and they hug.

Ceci has held the show together, despite some backstage disorganization, cueing all the acts. Hondurans don't usually have rehearsals for these events. Her high school dancing girls are happy. The finale takes the various groups of dancers into a parade format as they dance off the stage down the isle and into the streets of the zona viva. Ceci and the girls follow the finale/parade in their tropical dance costumes. Hondurans love a musical parade to celebrate life and wash away all their troubles.

148. Carnaval Parade in the Zona Viva

The girls are following the Garifuna dancers with their drummers and are absolutely fascinated with the ladies' charismatic hip movements and all their African regalia, parading down the ocean road to live drumming. The famous Garifuna choreographer, Christoph is there again, with his National Garifuna Ballet of Honduras traveling with their hypnotic drumming and dancing. Jazmin is mesmerized by these Garifuna dancers and jumps right into the parade, swinging her hips, dancing punta. Everybody stops and circles around Jazmin and the lead female dancer doing the punta. Another enters and replaces Jazmin.... The parade carries on and there is a sizzling excitement in the air. A student of Ceci's stops by her to say hello. Ceci is smiling and chatting with her, not realizing that Jazmin was caught up with the Garifuna dancers and is travelling with the parade way ahead with them. What horror when she turns around and Jazmin is not there. She runs ahead with Angie and Roxana, calling out Jazmin's name frantically. Finally, they arrive ahead where the Garifuna girls are dancing in a circle stationary, and Jazmin is again dancing with them in the middle.... smiling and having the time of her life. What a relief.... Ceci dives into the circle, dancing, and lifting her high... She hugs Jazmin tightly and can barely let go of her.

As she walks back up the street, holding Jazmin's hand, she waves to the retiring Ms. Honduras who is the next float in the parade... There is once again a synchronistic memory of the last parade when they both saw the girls in a box. They touch hearts and wave.... She throws necklaces to the girls...

149. Unwinding on the Cangrejal River with the girls

As they are walking home from Carnaval in the hot sun, Ceci reminds the girls always to stay close to her.

Ceci: Jazmin, I almost lost you in that huge crowd. I almost had a heart attack.

Angie: Jazmin, now Ceci is our mother and you have to stay close to her.

Jazmin: Well I like the drums so much.

Angie: Ceci can we go swim? It is too much hot.

Ceci: Good idea Angie. I would like to get out of town, away from all these people and the noise. Let's go up the river and swim there OK?

Girls: Yes... Vamos!

They drive up the jungle road that borders the Cangrejal river to find a spot to go swimming. It is the place where Ceci originally saw the spirit of their father. Ceci watches the girls play in the water and on the rocks, and vows never to let them out of her sight. The River Song begins again and hovers over the images of the Ceci and the girls playing in the river.

Rio Cangrejal

150. <u>Next Day - Municipal Building for permission to travel for visa application #1</u>

As part of her custodial arrangement, Ceci and the girls go, well dressed and combed, on a monthly basis to the office of the Juez de la Ninez. They visit secretary Daisy, who is the hub of the municipal office wheel. This time Lawyer, Lucia Urbizo meets them there to submit the official request for visa permission. Daisy and the other ladies in the office have seen the multiple visits and lessons that Ceci has learned to be able to have custody of the girls. They all rush to see the girls in their school uniforms.

Daisy: Hola bellas. Como estan? Que bonita son sus trenzas, sus trajes. Siempre limpias y saludables. Estan estudiando? Hello bellas. How are you? Your braids and your outfits are so pretty. Always clean and healthy. Are you studying?

The Girls: Si Daisy...*Big smiles, which get lollypops.*

Daisy: Como esta Sra. Cecilia?

Ceci: Bien gracias... Pues, primero vengamos para reportar el bienestar de mis princessas con sus notas, y cosas medicales. *She hands over copies of their report cards and medical visits.* **Y Tambien somos con Abogado Lucia Urbizo....** I am well thank

323

you. So first we come to report the wellbeing of my princess's, their grades, and their medical issue. And also we are with Lawyer Lucia Urbizo....

Daisy: Si le conozco... Como estas Lucia? Yes I know her. How are you Lucia?

Lucia: Bien, Gracias Daisy.

Everybody knows everybody in La Ceiba.

Ceci: Tambien estamos aquí para pedir permiso para aplicar por una visa medica para viajar con las ninas y... pues quiero ver mi mama. We are also here to ask permission to apply for a medical visa for the girls to travel... and of course I want to see my mother.

Daisy: Aaaay Ceci....

**Ceci: Por favor Daisy... Yo se que ud. cree que soy loca.......
Puedo dejar el asunto con uds?** Please Daisy? I know you think I am crazy... Can I leave this with you both?

Daisy: Claro Ceci. *Daisy wants to help, but knows what Ceci's chances are.*

Lucia: Bueno, yo lo hago..... espereme a fuera. Ok.. I'll take care of it. Wait for me outside.

Lucia takes over with the paper work while Ceci and the girls wait out in the hallway, watching the local criminals and gang members pass handcuffed and defeated. An hour goes by, and the kids are antsy and missing school. Finaly Lucia emerges from the office with the paper.

Lucia: I am sorry this takes so long.

Ceci: Gracias Lucia.... Las ninas estan tarde para escuela. Tengo que ir.

Lucia: I will tell you Ceci... that your chances are very slim for a visa without legal adoption.

Ceci: I have to try. It's like a plant looking for sunlight... I bend in the direction of my family and my homeland. That's where I know the soil will have the best nutrients for these wildflowers to grow.

Lucia: Yo entiendo… Vaya con Dios. *She hugs Ceci*

Ceci: Thank you Lucia. *Handing her a check…* for your support. I truly appreciate all you are doing for me.

151. <u>Shopping with the girls in La Ceiba – El mercado</u>

It is Sunday morning and the downtown market is open with all of its colorful kiosks of fruits and vegetables. There are the Sunday radio sounds of religious sermons mixed with merengue and cumbia pop hits. There are also llaneras and bachatas romanticas (love ballads), interspersed with religious music. People have just come from church and are shopping for the noon meal. There are stalls with shoes, watch and cell phone repair, clothing, purses, backpacks, etc. Ceci takes the girls into the indoor market, which is noisy and teaming with life. There is fresh fish, a butcher, hot tortillas, juice, fruits and vegetables, herbs and cures, and every farm tool you might need. They stop for horchata and a baleada. Roxana sees and likes a pinata that they buy for her birthday.

Poor people on the street always beg with Ceci. They keep moving. She meets a Garifuna lady named Dona Magley in front of a spiritual Botanica selling herbs, crosses, magical tonics and candles. Ceci buys tableta de coco from the lady, who dotes over the girls for a while… inviting them all to come dance in Sambo Creek.

Dona Magley: Yes mam, I have all kinds of magical herbs and tonics for you. I want to invite you and your precious girls to any of our Saturday Garifuna ceremonies with drummin and dancin in Sambo Creek, just up the coast from Corozal. Any time Gringa... the girls will luv it.

Ceci: As a matter of fact, I know Dona Eva, and I went to a velurio session that she had a while back on the beach in Corozal for her late husband. She is a dear lady, and quite the medium.

Dona Magley: Yes, of course, I remember you, with a gringo man. Your children are beautiful. Come visit any weekend in Sambo Creek. Just ask for Dona Magley near the soccer field.

Ceci: Thank you for the tableta de coco. We all love it.

Ceci pays the lady and they move out onto the street with all the outdoor vendors and look at school shoes. As they walk, they pass young boys who live on the streets. Ceci purchases bananas and gives them to the girls to hand out to the sleeping boys. There is much color and demographic diversity in the street. The Ceibenos are Triguenos (3 mixed races) the African Garifunas; the rural indigenous indios, and the light skinned Spanish descendants. They are all working their trades, and add to the colorful life on the street. Roxana proudly carries her pinata.

Ceci brings them to the central Catholic Church Downtown to pay their respects. She prays to St. Joseph, for her father, Joseph. The girls say the Padre Nuestro in Spanish. Ceci prays for the visas. They walk out of the church past all the beggars and invalids.

Ceci: We must be thankful for what we have girls.

Roxana: Mama Ceci... Nunca quiero dormir en la calle. Mami, I never want to sleep on the street.

Ceci: I will never let you sleep on the street Roxana. I will take care of you.

Angie: Don't be sad Roxana... Remember what day tomorrow is?

Roxana: Mi cumpleanos!!! Yeah!!!!

152. Roxana's Halloween Birthday party

It's a beautiful October morning and Ceci is making arroz con pollo for Roxana's 9th birthday party. The theme is Halloween and guests are instructed to wear costumes. Vilma is working on tamales, pico de gallo, and guacamole. Sayda is fixing Roxana's hair, who is proudly admiring herself in the mirror in her beautiful gold princess dress. Jazmin and Angie are hiding orange eggs in the backyard. The piñata is strung, and balloons are everywhere. Angie and Jazmin are in costume. Ceci starts the merengue music and guests begin to arrive. Deni May, Ale, and a few kids from Roxana's school, Bright Beginnings come dressed in costumes, and the party officially begins. Sayda and Vilma bring out the food.

Roxana is upset that so few of the kids she invited have shown up. And Ceci sees the tears.

Roxana: Mom what happened to all the friends I invited from school? They told me they were coming.

Ceci: I don't know honey, and I do believe that it is bad manners not to RSVP yes or no. Sometimes people don't have the money to buy a gift so they have pena (shame) to come.

Roxana: Mommy, is it because I'm not very smart?

Ceci: Why do you say that?

Roxana: I don't think they like me because I'm slow. That's why they didn't come. I don't care about presents. I want friends.

Ceci: You know Roxie, the trick is to be around people who appreciate you, who understand you, and who care about you. That's not easy for sure, but that's the idea.

Roxana: You are the only person I know like that Mommy. I don't know how to find those people.

Ceci: Look Roxana...... Ale, some dance students, the neighborhood kids, and a few school buddies are here and they all seem to be having a good time, so I suggest you get out there and be a good hostess. This is your birthday party and I want you to enjoy it.

Roxana: OK Mom.. I love you.

Ceci: I love you too… and I want you to be happy….so let's get this party started.

There are definitely enough people to participate in a few races… the burlap bag race; the ball in the spoon in the mouth race; the three legged race; the egg hunt, and the race to wrap your partner in toilet paper. They bang the piñata, eat cake, and dance the freeze dance, until the sun falls. Roxana is happy at the end of the day. All the parents enjoyed socializing, along with Vilma and Sayda, who are always indispensable. Another birthday….

153. <u>Leaving dance class – driving home routine</u>

The scene begins with the end of dance class as Ceci leads a long, dramatic ballet bow and reverence. They pack up from dance class and close the studio. It is dark and she asks Vilma to help Angie get into the car as she has trouble navigating in the dark because of her vision problem. Ceci asks about homework, etc. Roxana has homework but says that she does not understand it at all. Jazmin, finished her homework, and wants to manipulate the car radio. Ceci drops Vilma off at the bus stop, and says:

Ceci: Mils gracias Vilma… Sin ud. nada pasa.

Vilma: Suerte en Tegucigalpa manana! Vaya con Dios!

Ceci: Ciao Vilma. Hasta el lunes… Dele besos ninas.

The girls kiss Vilma… Ceci returns to the road and driving.

Ceci: Girls… listen up, tomorrow we are going to Tegucigalpa to apply for visas.

Angie: What about school?

Ceci: You will miss school and fly on an airplane.

Jazmin: Now I like that! And I want to go to the US to become a rock star!

Angie: Tegucigallo is in Honduras Jazmin.

Ceci: Te-guci-galpa se dice. So we will get up early, dress up real pretty, drive to the airport, and fly to the capitol to visit the American Embassy.

As they pull into the driveway, there are boys playing soccer, barefoot on the street in front.

Roxana: Quiero jugar futbol en la calle Mami.

Ceci: Only if I am watching, and I have to print Doctor emails and collect many papers for the trip, AND cook dinner before you all stuff yourself with churros (Honduran chips). Go pick out Grandma's look alike dresses for tomorrow and make sure you wear your rain sneakers.

154. At home -Prepping for Medical Visas application interview #1

They all empty the car and pile into the house. Roxana goes to the street to play soccer with the local boys, Angie practices riding her bike, and Jazmin plays the guitar. Cows walk by with a humble old farmer. Ceci organizes her papers on the porch talking to herself.

Ceci: Ok Here is the American Neurological Ophthalmologist letter, who would see Angie about her eyes. And my brother in law's orthopedic practice for her spinal meningitis. Then there is the neurologist for Roxana, and the allergist for Jazmin's Asthma and the endocrinologist for her as well.. Then I have the translated recommendations from the psychologist for their aptitude scores. ... Their grades.... Their physicals...The foster child custody papers...their birth certificates... my passport... my legal United States police records clearance ... my work visa and the letter from the Mazapan School. They better give me those visas. My country tis of the.

She watches the girls play knowing how important it is for her to see the bigger picture of the future.

155. Plane Ride – La Ceiba to Tegucigalpa

The girls are all decked out in look alike dresses. Ceci is nervously walking them up the staircase to the plane. It is a small plane, and Ceci has nausea issues with flying ... so her mood is queasy.

Jazmin: Wow Mom... We are really going up there in the clouds!

Ceci: *Muttering to herself.* Please God, let my stomach make it to Tegucigalpa, and work your magic to get my babies into the USA, and to know that we can go to visit my Mom. Make this a great adventure for all of us, and give us a safe trip. I know you are out there. Please hear my prayers.

Angie: Amen...

Roxana: Todo bien Mami?

Ceci: Si baby... todo bien.

MID AIR TUMULT – Ceci is not really happy with this, as she has never had a strong stomach for tumult. The girls are clutching their seats, and Jazmin is screaming about being in the clouds with a running commentary on the views below. And then there is all the drama of landing with people crossing themselves as they bump onto the tarmac.

156. A taxi ride in Tegucigalpa

Tegucigalpa seems like an endless up and down urban sprawl... an opportunity to see what this third world Central American capitol city looks like...Bustling traffic, heat, smog, dirty streets, all kinds of people selling things, dated buildings in disrepair. Ceci is dizzy, and the girls are tired.

157. American Embassy – First Visa Attempt

They arrive at the huge American embassy, where there is a long line that twists around the block. This becomes another musical montage of waiting and witnessing everybody's immigration struggle. All cell phones must be stored outside the embassy with strange people in little tents along the way, who will hold your phone for a price. The girls are tired and growing impatient. But there are many Honduran people on line trying to get visas. Their stories are equally complicated. The montage of long line waiting shots eventually brings Ceci and the girls to the door.... More people are waiting inside after being screened. Finally, they get through security, into the long rows of musical chairs, and then work their way up to a window. They call out the girls' names: Iraheta Rojas por favor.

Ceci fumbles her way up to the window with the papers and the girls.... And pulls it together to present herself to the young American agent.

Ceci: Hello, I am an American living in Honduras with custody of three Honduran sisters who have disabilities…This is Angela Jazmin, Angie Nicolle, and Roxana Yadira. I am applying for medical tourist visas for the three of them.

Agent: Can I see your application and papers? *The agent takes the papers and disappears. Ceci and the girls wait anxiously by the window, standing…. It costs 3 X $400 each ($1200) … for Hondurans to apply for a visa. The agent returns with receipts.* Please take a seat over there and we will call you back.

Ceci: How long will this take? We have a return flight to La Ceiba today…

Agent: I'm sorry mam. My boss has to make a more intensive review of your case. Be patient. There is a line.

Ceci and the girls go sit down amongst rows of other Hondurans waiting for "a more intensive review" of their visa requests. There is money to be made in this business, as there are many more applications than granted visas. The girls fall asleep on Ceci's lap. Ceci makes character studies of all the people in front of her as they depart from the windows in either misery or ecstasy, depending on their visa awards or denials. Many life changing moments have taken place in this hall. This is Ceci's first time, and she does not realize how difficult the process is. Finally, last person has left.

*After what seems like hours we hear the girls' names being called on the loud speaker ...*Roxana, Angie, and Angela Iraheta Rojas

Ceci jumps to attention and they all wake up. The hall is empty. It is closing time. They run up to the window, and see the agent who had taken their papers hours ago. She hands back the papers.

Agent: Ms. Diaz.... We cannot grant medical visas to these children because their health issues are not life threatening. Nor is their foster custodial relationship with you solid enough for us to grant you passage with these children, as you fit the profile of American women who arrive in the USA with foreign children on a tourist visa, and never return to the child's country.

Ceci: I have no immediate plans of remaining in the USA with these girls... I have a job here in La Ceiba!!... and these letters I have presented to you are Doctors who will see the children gratis to do a state of the art analysis on their medical disabilities. This is something I feel very strongly about as their custodial mother. My brother in law is a Doctor and has offered his assistance in engineering these examinations. Why do you doubt my plans?

Agent: These girls look OK to me...

Ceci: Have you read the medical information in this application? They have disabilities that need sophisticated analysis that I can't get here. I am working in La Ceiba at the Escuela Mazapan, with a Dance Studio on the Standard Fruit Company Grounds. I couldn't be a more stable resident at this point.

Agent: Do you have your residency?

Ceci: I am working on that as we speak. At the moment, I have a work visa.

Agent: You will need to provide much more stability in Honduras for tourist visas, as well as more official custodial authority over these children, before you can cross any borders with them. And that means official adoption. I am sorry. We have had a lot of illegal child trafficking, and this will not be an easy path for you.

The girls are looking up at Ceci's face as she gets the bad news from the agent. They see that she is about to break into tears, as she crunches to the floor with her head in her hands.

They embrace Ceci and a nearby police lady helps her up and ushers her out the door of the embassy to the street.

Police lady: I am sorry Sra. You must try again.

Roxana: It's Ok Mom.

Ceci: No it's not... It's my country, my citizenship, my right to do this, and they are suspecting me of something wrong. I am insulted and humiliated.

Angie: They don't like Honduran people very much do they?

Ceci: Its' because you are not officially adopted. They want more papers.

Jazmin: Well then adopt us Mom!!

Ceci: Yes baby, I am working on it. Let's get a cab to the airport, I have a headache... and I love you so much, and at least, thank you God, that you are coming home with me, and not going to the orphanage. We must be grateful for the fortune we have. Don't worry, I won't give up. Let's go home. *They get in a cab.*

158. <u>Airplane return to La Ceiba – Phone call to Mom</u>

Ceci straps in the three girls as the plane takes off and they jerk around, up and down, until everybody gets sick all over their pretty dresses. Ceci herself is delirious from nausea... but cleans it up.... Sits back as the plane gains altitude... looks at the kids' big brown eyes looking up at her like WHY ARE WE DOING THIS? And she says ... as they are landing....

Ceci: Strike One... Volveremos, hasta ganamos!!... Entienden chicas? We will return until we win. Understand chicas?

<u>**Phone call from Mom**</u> - *As they are deplaning and collecting bags.*

Ceci: I am sorry I didn't call you. We just landed from this exhausting plane ride from Tegucigalpa.

Mom: I know you would have called with good news... So how did it go at the embassy?

Ceci: Not well Mom... They think I don't plan to return to Honduras... even with the medical request.... This is not going to be easy... but I won't give up.

Mom: I tried calling the office of our Virginia congressman, Tim Kaine. They said that Honduras is high on the list of discouraged visas.

Ceci: Mom, turns out that "no government office can override the visa decisions of a foreign embassy" anyway... So there is no political favor that will get the girls across the border, no matter how much tax you pay in Virginia.

Mom: Well I want to come see you at Xmas, is that OK?

Ceci: Of course Mom, we have room, and the kids would love it, and I would love it... *She fights back tears.* Absolutely... how exciting... OK... well just book the trip however you want... We will meet you at the airport in La Ceiba... or San Pedro... Just let me know. Wish you could come for the show. Bye.

Mom: I love you and my beautiful nietas... Bye.

Ceci hangs up and chokes back the tears.

Jazmin: Don't cry Mama.

Ceci: You are absolutely right... the show must go on... And the Christmas show is this week. That is our next challenge.... So lift that chin and be proud to be the daughter of an American.... No matter where you are. OK? I love you.

159. <u>Christmas Show at Mazapan</u>

Ceci is backstage with dancers in different classrooms, where parents are helping them get into costume and makeup. Vilma is dressing Jazmin, Angie, and Roxana while Ceci runs around checking the stage and the house, and the technical crew. The theater fills up rapidly and house lights blink and go down ... the curtains open.

**NOTE – Another reminder that there were 9 years of performances at Christmas and in the Spring at the Mazapan School. Different programs are included to show the scope of the work.

"ALAS" (WINGS)– 13 Diciembre - 2010

1. Tree Dance – Intermedios – "el Soldadito Cojo" – Cri Cri

2. Gift Babies in a box - Bambinas

3. "Root n Tottin Santa Claus "(tap) – Intermedios II – Tex Beneke & his Orchestra

4. Merengue/Feliz Navidad – Principios – "Potpouri Navideno" by Hitsong /Feliz Navidad –

5. Angel Party – Avancadas – "I'm your Angel"– Celine Dion/ It's a Party

6. Love Birds – Intermedios – SIDESHOW – The Broadway Musical – Henry Krieger/Bill Russell

7. Barney– Bambinas a. Tarraraboom b.The More We Play Together c.Baby Bop Hop d.Let's Play Together

8. "Santa Claus is Comin to Town" – Principios – Hilary Duff

9. Together – Intermedios II – "We're All in This Together" – HS Musical M. Gerrard & Robbie Nevil

10. Baile del Serpiente – Intermedios – "Miserlous" – Carlos Esquivel

11. "Salsa" – Avancadas – Marc Anthony

12. Nanita – Bambinas & Principios – "A la Nanita Nana" – Tradicional – Cheetah Girls

13. "Angel de la Guardia" – Bambinas & Principios – by Noelia

14. Statues to Flesh – Pygmalion

Six full bodied live statues on pedestals fill the stage covered with sheets, as the curtain opens. A sculptor enters the stage to begin his daily routine to complete his work in progress. Each frozen statue represents different aspects of a woman's personality and development: a young girl, a mother, a Doctor, an athlete, a Hollywood star, and a scholar/teacher. The sculptor removes the sheets to reveal these characters and begins to interact with each one as he brings them to life with his chisel. He is ecstatic as he watches them begin to dance. The clock strikes midnight and they all return to their pedestals taking their original frozen positions. He covers them with the sheets for the evening, puts on his coat and leaves. In the middle of the night the statue party resumes with an energetic liberation choreography that raises the energy so high that the dancers literally disappear in a cloud of smoke at the climax of the music. In the morning the sculptor arrives to find the empty pedestals which throws him into dismay and a crazy dance which ends with him mounting the central pedestal and assuming a frozen position. As night falls the statues return to dance around him and activate his lifeless state. Then they return to their positions on the pedastles and the lights fade as he takes a bow to the statues.

15. Ballet of the Nativity - "Breath of Heaven" – FINALE

These cultural events are family affairs in La Ceiba, attended by all the extended family. After the show, Ceci takes pictures and compliments... Has a few words with Margie Dip, the governor of La Ceiba, whose grandchildren, Cecilia and Rebeca Dip, were dancing in the show. Margie is an animated, redhead mountain mover who makes things happen in La Ceiba for people of all classes and colors.

A future Christmas production

"BUSCANDO LA LUZ" (Looking for the Light) – 12 Diciembre – 2011

1. **"Orguesta de Animales" - Bambinas y Principios - Cri Cri**
2. **"I'll Take you There" – Avancadas I – The Staple Singers**

THE NUTCRACKER SUITE – CASCA NUECES – Tchaikovsky

3. Overture

4. Danza de Las Madres – Bambinas Y Madres

5. Chinese Dance - Intermedios II

6. Russian Dance – Principios y Intermedios I

7. Arabic Dance – Alexandra, Ivana, Y Nelsiree

8. Spanish Dance – Intermedios II

9. Dance of the Reeds Intermedios I

10. Waltz of the Flowers – Principios y Madres Intermission

11. "Tell Me a Story"- Student choreography – Hilary Duff

12. "The Tide is High" Choreography – Nelsiree – The Atomic Kitten

13. "Noche de Paz" – Bambinas Y Principios – Jose Feliciano

14. "American Life " – Avancadas II – Madona

15. "The Frug" – Intermedios I & II – FOSSE – Broadway Show

16. "Prayer" Ballet – Avancadas I – Celine Dion

17. Salsa "Juliana" – Avancadas II

18. Feliz Navidad Medley – Avancadas II – Student choreography

19. Lament – La Reina Madre de Triana – Chita Urbizo – Malaguena -101 Strings

20. Flamenco – "Jaleo" – Avancadas I – Ricky Martin

    21. FINALE – TODOS

160. <u>**SATURDAY MORNING** – Post performance excitement</u>

Ceci wakes up to the three girls dressed in big girl clothes and heels ready for another fashion show. They ask Ceci to take the role of commentator. She sits up in bed and agrees to participate.

Ceci: Damas y Caballeros… Tengo el placer introducirles a la nueva linea de moda que se llama GITANA TROPICAL con las nuevas dibujantes hermanas – "Las Triguenas". Como se puede ver en nuestra primera modela, Angie, los colores son vivos y la ropa floja…. Para que se puede respirar en las noches del calor tropical…. Siempre andando con el espiritu de la musica Latina viene mas estilos exoticas. Les gustan estas rapsodias en tela, mi gente?? Ladies and gentlemen. I have the pleasure of introducing a new line of fashion called "Tropical Gypsy" with the latest designer sisters –"Las Triguenas". As you can see in our first model, Angie, the vibrant colors and the loose fit so that one can breathe in the tropical hot nights….. Always going with the spirit of Latin music come more exotic styles. How do you like our rhapsodies in fabric my people?

Jazmin: Soy fabulosa! I am fabulous!

Roxana enters in Mom's clothing, and then Jazmin herself in another Ceci dress and high heels.

Ceci: **Bravo bravo…** *Applauding, as she rises up from the bed.* **Show me more. Don't keep the audience waiting. Quick changes remember? Or I might go back to sleep.**

Roxana: Ay Mami!

Clearly there is chaos taking place... but it is comical. The modeling cycle goes around three times as we see more hilarious color combinations of clothes coming out of Ceci's closet, circus style... that don't fit but are highly amusing.

161. <u>Tropical Rain dance</u>

Suddenly it begins to thunder and rain, which is common in La Ceiba. The girls are thrilled. They go dashing for the plastic pool in the back yard in their clothes. This becomes a hysterical splashing party, until the pool literally deflates. Roxana sees guys out on the street playing soccer barefoot. She cannot resist, and wants to return to the pouring rain to join the soccer game. (This is common practice in Honduras... even barefoot on the street!) Once back in the house, they help Ceci set up pails where water is dripping from the ceiling. Then, without fail, the electricity goes out and flooding starts up in the streets.

Angie: *(Standing on a chair and talking into an artificial hair brush microphone)* As you can see ladies and gentlemen, La Ceiba is having a huge rain and thunder storm which has cut off our electricity and now is making our street into a river. In our barrio there are a group of boys who insist on playing soccer on the flooding street in the rain, WITHOUT their shoes. Even my sister, Roxana Iraheta Rojas wants to play water soccer the local boys. Will Roxana's mother give her permission to go back out on the street in this crazy rain? Only with shoes says the mother. OK, so Roxana gets her shoes and there she goes ladies and gentleman... out on our street to splash around with a soccer ball and the neighbors. We are on TV from La Ceiba, Honduras!

Ceci, Jazmin and Angie watch for a while, but the situation indoors is not ideal. They continue to empty the pails of water dripping from many places. What was such an exciting weather adventure, turns into a real uncomfortable, but familiar third world condition with candles. Ceci makes a fire on the back porch in a car wheel frame. They make "elotes", (grilled corn on the cob) as the thunder rolls and the lightning cracks. Night falls and there is still no electricity. Ceci sings MOTHER MOON (their lullaby) to her children by candlelight to get them to sleep, as the rain subsides.

162. **Sunday AM and Karla arrives**

Sunday morning everybody wakes up to an orchestra of tropical birds. The sun is shining. Roxana enters the bedroom. The street flood has drained but the pails are full.

Roxana: Ceci, Karla esta en el porton. Pistos... *She rubs her fingers together.* Ceci, Karla is at the gate. She wants money.

Ceci: Bueno..... *She gets out of bed and grabs a robe and goes to the front door.*

Ceci: Hola Karla como estas?

Karla: Embarasada y con hambre. Pregnant and hungry.

Ceci: Como puede ser? That's not what you told the judge.

Karla: Tengo hambre Ceci.

Ceci: OK come on in.

Clearly Karla sees Ceci as a banking mother figure. Ceci feels a mixture of compassion and annoyance, but knows that she must make room for Karla in her life... that the girls need to know where they came from, despite the lack of any demonstratable love. Karla enters and sits on the sofa. The girls come into the living room and stare at her. Ceci begins filling a bag with food.

Ceci: What do you think about taking the girls to the cemetery today to visit their Dad.

Karla: Como?

Ceci: Quiero llevar las ninas al cementerio para ver su papa. Yo fui alla para el papel de defuncion, pero nunca vi la tumba *(grave)*. Pienso que es importante para las ninas. I would like to take the girls to the cemetary to see their papa. I went there for the death certificate but never saw the tomb. I think it is important for the girls.

Karla: Si podemos ir. No he ido desde el morio. Y despues podriamos visitar la familia en San Judas si quieres. Pero, Ceci necesito pistos. No hay comida. Yes, we can go. I haven't gone since he died. And after we could visit the family in San Judas if you want. But Ceci, I need money… There is no food.

Ceci: Oye… Te doy la comida que tengo, pero… no mas dinero…. Karla, tu sabes que es peligroso para la custodia. This is starting to feel like blackmail. Deme 15 minutos para vestir las ninas. Listen, I will give you food that I have, but no more money. Karla, you know this is dangerous for the custody. This is starting to feel like blackmail. Give me 15 minutes to dress the girls.

Ceci puts together food for Karla and then dresses and combs the girls. Karla just watches.

Roxana: Donde vamos Ceci? Where are we going Ceci?

Ceci: A ver la tumba de su papa en el cementerio. To see the grave of your papa in the cemetary.

Roxana: Si?

Karla: El esta muerto Roxana. He's dead Roxana.

Ceci: Your father is in the sky… but he is buried in the tierra…. In what is called a cemetery… Y vamos alla para honorar su papa Carlos. OK? Buscame algunas flores del jardin para llevar. And we will go to honor your father Carlos OK? Get me some flowers from the garden to bring.

This confuses Roxana and she becomes very silent. She remembers and misses her father. Losing her father has a significant effect on Roxana as she grows up.

163. **Cemetery – Carlos's grave**

They arrive at the city cemetery. Ceci greets the proprietor of the public cemetery. The girls are following, timidly, with flowers.

Ceci: **Buenos dias senor.**

Proprietor: **Hola Senora. Te recuerdo. Vino ud. para confirmar el muerto de Carlos Alvarez.** Hello Sra… I remember you. You came to confirm the death of Carlos Alvarez.

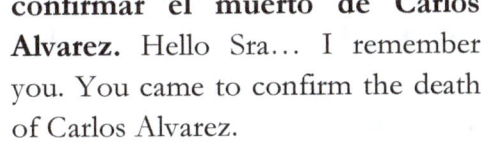

Ceci: **Si Senor. Estamos aquí para mostrar las ninas la tumba de su papa.**

Proprietor: **Hola Karla, como estas?** Hello Karla, how are you?

Karla: **Mas o menos. Venimos con las ninas para ensenarlas la tumba de su papa.** More or less OK. We come with the girls to show them their father's tomb.

Proprietor: **Bueno vamos. No tiene piedra… pero yo se donde esta.** Let's go. It doesn't have a tombstone, but I know where it is.

Angie: **Vamos a ver nuestro papa Ceci?** Are we going to see our father Ceci?

Karla: **Su papa esta muerto Angie… yo les dije.** Your father is dead Angie. I told you.

Ceci: **El esta enterrado aqui en el cementario, pero su alma esta en el cielo.** He is buried in the cemetery, but his soul is in heaven.

Roxana: Pero el puede ver nosotros verdad Ceci? But he can see us right Ceci?

Ceci: Claro – y el les quieria mucho…. Right Karla? Right… and he loved you very much.. Right Karla?

Karla: Si el les quieria.

Karla is clearly depressed. The proprietor is searching around, as there is no tombstone. But he finds the grave and tries to clean it up a bit. There are some plastic flowers sitting next to a rock.

Proprietor: Aqui esta Carlos. Yo le recuerdo…. triste como el morio…. Es una lastima como las drogas matan nuestra gente.
Here is Carlos. I remember him. Sad how he died. It's a pity how the drugs kill our people.

Jazmin: Eso es mi papa? That's my dad?

Proprietor: Si nina…. Fue un buen hombre… un amigo… Yes, nina… He was a good man, a friend.

Jazmin: Pero donde esta el? Yo nunca vi mi papa … nunca!!! Quiero verle! But where is he. I never saw my Dad.. never! I want to see him!

Angie: A mi tambien!! Me too!

Roxana: No entiendo… donde esta mi papi? I don't understand. Where is my dad? *She is visibly upset.*

Ceci: Recuerdan cuando un dia conseguimos un pajaro en la yarda… que no pudo mover? El pajaro morio, y perdió la vida en su cuerpo, pero su alma todavia vive en el cielo. Posiblemente volvera un dia en otro cuerpo. Vamos a regalar estas flores para el espiritu de su papa. Remember when one day we found a bird in the yard that couldn't move? The bird was dead, and lost life in his body, but his soul still lives in heaven. Possibly he will return one day in another body. Let's leave these flowers for the spirit of your father..

Angie: Como morio mi papa? How did he die?

Ceci: He was sick Angie.

Karla: Y en esos dias, el no estaba trabajando, y cuando sacaron las ninas, el fue loco. Tambien el me golpio muchas veces. No era facil. And in those days he wasn't working and when they took the girls away, he went crazy. He also beat me many times. It wasn't easy.

Ceci: I'm sorry Karla. Era importante que las ninas entienden donde esta su papa. Vamos. Gracias senor. It was important that the girls understand where their father is. Let's go.

Proprietor: De nada… Vaya con Dios.

Roxana finally lets go of her tears. She remembers her father. There is silence as they get into the car.

164. Visiting the Iraheta/Alvarez house in San Judas

Karla directs Ceci and the girls to drive to San Judas, their original birthplace. Grandma Celestina Alvarez lives on a mountain ledge with her family and all their children, her birthing hut, their farming tools, her animals, and acres of mountain crops. This was the family home of the father, Carlos. It is a series of mud brick houses sitting on a carved out cliff of a mountain rising up next to the Cangregal river.

After parking, and passing a poor family with a young child stricken with meningitis at the foot of the mountain, they climb a rocky, garbage ridden ravine to a chiseled out section of the mountain where a few houses sit alongside steep mountains covered in corn, frijoles, and cacao plants. Ceci carries Jazmin on her back and somehow, the girls climb up the wet slippery cliff. When reaching the top, they are greeted by the "pila", a large cement pool of running water. Animals like pigs, dogs, cats, and chickens run loose in small paths around the three adobe homes.

The main house belongs to Grandma Celestina, midwife, herbalist, and nurse. There is a kitchen with a fogata, a round clay Honduran oven, and 2 bedrooms. There is an older palapa hut where Celestina gives birth to all the grandchildren running around the narrow cliff. This is where Angie, Jazmin, and Roxana were born.

Their aunt Carmen, Celestina's daughter is also there, as is Cynthia, the girls' older sister, and Carlos, their younger brother, exactly one year younger than Jazmin. Grandma Celestina is thrilled to see her lost grandchildren. She makes an herbal, Honduran coffee drink for Ceci, and sends Cynthia to the local panaderia for sweet bread for the girls, carefully counting out her coins. Cynthia misses Roxana, and drags her along, telling her that she should put some clothes in a bag and move back in with them. Celestina shows the girls a picture of her son, their father Carlos, who was killed in February. Angie tells her that they just came from the cemetery but did not see Carlos. Celestina tells her that he is in heaven. Jazmin says "Everybody keeps saying that, but he never comes to see us." Jazmin never met her father.

Ceci tries to keep the subject on questions about the girls' medical history. Celestina says that Roxana and Angie had meningitis back in November, 2003 when they were taken away, because there was an epidemic in the barrio. This, evidently upset him very much. Ceci wants to understand what happened to them.

Clearly the poverty and circumstances with meningitis added to the mix have all contributed to lack of stability. The exit of her grandchildren, after losing her son, Carlos has been painful for her as the matriarch of the family.

Celestina also tells Ceci discreetly that Karla was impatient with the girls because of their fever, hunger, and crying. She whispers to Ceci that Karla struck Angie across the face when she was crying, and that's when a neighbor called the police. Soldiers came and took them away in a box as the police don't come to San Judas.

Karla walks back in at this time, and there is tension in the room, as both Ceci and Angie have heard the story of how she became blind. Karla has since moved out and has a new boyfriend.... Yarel, with whom she lives with his family near the courthouse. Celestina, shows them around the small complex of homes, to the parteras (midwife) hut where she gave birth to the girls. She tells Ceci that they should all come and live with them on the mountain. Ceci knows this is a kind remark, with undertones, but graciously declines the invitation. The girls are confused and somewhat uncomfortable walking around the primitive squalor of dirt floors that the family shares with chickens, dogs, and goats. Ceci thanks Celestina sincerely and tells her that she will invite the family to visit sometime soon. and they bid farewell. They all descend the slippery ravine very carefully.

165. Grandma Diaz comes to La Ceiba – Driving to the Airport

In the car on the way to the airport, the girls are excited, wearing costumes from the Xmas dance concert, and carrying balloons. They are very excited about Grandma's arrival from the USA.

Roxana: Abuela esta en un avion en el cielo, right Ceci? Grandma is in an airplane in the sky…

Ceci: Yes mam, and we are going to see her very soon.

Angie: I can't wait… now we have two grandmas.

Jazmin: And is she bringing gifts from Santa?

Ceci: Grandma will bring her gifts and Santa will bring his.

Angie: Can Santa bring me good eyes?

Jazmin: Yo quiero un papa. I want a father.

Ceci: You know I want all that too. Just don't know how to make those wishes happen.

Roxana: *Mumbling* . Yo quiero ser inteligente como ti Mami. I want to be smart like you Mom.

Ceci: You know that you have a special kind of smarts Roxana. Hey…this is beginning to sound like the Wizard of Oz…. I want eyes, I want a Dad, I want a brain.

Angie: Santa is supposed to be like the Wizard of Oz isn't he? He makes your dreams come true.

Ceci: Look….You are all perfect the way you are. I love you, and Grandma loves you, and so does my Dad, who is watching from heaven above just like your Dad. And here we are.

166. **La Ceiba Airport**

They park and rush to the arrival gate at the very small airport in La Ceiba. Grandma is the last to come through the gate in a wheelchair. The girls race over to hug her.

Grandma: Such beautiful girls… Mira que bonita son mis nietas!!

Roxana: *The girls give Grandma balloons.* These are for you Grandma.

Grandma: Thank you so much. This is so exciting. *Grandma has a chronic cough.*

Jazmin: And we are taking you to the beach today, so you can swim in our ocean.

Ceci: *joking…* So Mom, did you bring your bathing suit?

Grandma: I don't have a bathing suit anymore… but I love the ocean air.

Ceci: Soon as we get you settled, we are going to the beach. Or are you too tired?

Grandma: No no… let's go.

167. **The Zona Viva Beach in La Ceiba**

Cut to the beach in La Ceiba. The girls are dragging Grandma towards the ocean. She starts making sand castles at the water's edge with the girls and Ceci joins them. Everybody is laughing and enjoying the afternoon sun. But Grandma continues to cough.

Ceci: What's the story with that cough Mom?

Grandma: Evidently, it's a chronic infection called pseudomonas that is hiding in the scar tissue of my lungs. Can't seem to get rid of it... I've been to all the doctors.

Ceci: I'm sorry Mom, I don't like to see you suffer.

Grandma: You've got your hands full Ceil, don't worry about me.

Ceci: I worry about everybody Mom... that's my job.

Grandma: What I don't understand is why you took three. Why not one or two?

Ceci: Mom, how in the world could I break up sisters? All they have is each other.

Grandma: *Sigh of resignation.* And now they have you Ceil... and I'm proud of you... and I will do everything I can to help. I just worry about you. Just remember – when Roxana is 30, you will be 80.

Ceci: I know Mom, I do the math every day. I don't even know how many more years of dance I have in me... and even with all my experience, all I know is theater and dance.

Grandma: Well.... Don't give up on the visas. I will wait for you... the house is yours if and when you ever make it.

Ceci: Thanks Mom. I want to take care of you in that house. I really mean that and don't forget it. I will take care of you Mom.

Dark clouds and thunder begin to fill the sky. The girls bring shells to Grandma.

Jazmin: We love you Grandma. Feliz Navidad.

Grandma: And how I love you too.

Ceci: We better get home before the street floods... Let's go.

Grandma: What?

Ceci: The street fills up and we can't get the car in, although I have driven through it many times.

Grandma: Your kidding me!!!

Roxana: Mommy carries us on her back.

Grandma: What? Oh my God. I think you better take me to a hotel.

Ceci: It's not so bad Mom.

Jazmin: I don't think you can carry Grandma.

Ceci: Hey I can do anything. They told me I would never get you out of the SOS, and here you are... and they tell me that you will never get out of Honduras... but guess what... I will not give up until we are all in Grandma's house together. Getting into this house tonight is nothing compared to all that.

Angie: And Santa is coming tonight, so we have to get in bed and be good girls.

Ceci: But first we have to dress up and go to midnight misa.
Mass

Grandma: I want to go to a hotel, this is crazy. What about don't drown, turn around?

Ceci: Relax Ma... this is nothing.

168. Home with the flooded street

They have arrived at the gate, and the street is flooded. Ceci gets out and wades through the water in the pouring rain to unlock and open the gate. Grandma is freaking out.

Ceci: Hold on everybody, we're launching.

Ceci charges through the water, and the girls are laughing as Grandma covers her eyes.

Jazmin: Yeah we made it again!

Grandma: I don't know how you live like this.

Ceci: Don't worry. Hopefully it will drain before the mass begins

169. **Christmas Eve Mass**

Grandma, Ceci and the girls are all dressed up in Grandma's home made Christmas dresses, ready for the mass as they all emerge from the black truck and enter the downtown Catholic Church. Out front there are beggars, invalids, bums, and street kids of every level of poverty and hunger. This disarms Grandma, but they move on into the church. The girls imitate others who are crossing and blessing themselves with holy water.

People are dressed in their Sunday best and there are various saints to which people can light candles. Grandma goes to St. Joseph to light a candle in the name of her husband, Joseph, who died of cancer in 1998. After that they go to Santa Maria, to whom Ceci lights a candle with a whispered prayer for the welfare of her mother and her children, the miracle of getting visas to the USA and of course the healing of Angie's blindness and Roxana's neurological problems. They take a seat in a pew near the back. The mass begins.

A humble chorus of local parishioners belts out "Hark the Herlald Angels Sing" in Spanish. The girls are uncomfortable and can't sit still. When the priest begins to talk, Roxana whispers to Grandma pointing to the altar.

Roxana: **Grandma, eso es Dios.** Grandma, that is God.

Grandma: Donde?

Roxana points to the priest at the pulpit. Grandma looks at Ceci.

Ceci: They think that all priests are God. This happened with the priest at their baptism. They thought he was God.

Grandma: OK... *talking to Roxana* The padre is a priest, and he is the director of the church and talks to God for us. God is in everything. He is everywhere... even in you. Because you are so beautiful.

Roxana nods. People around them are dressed in their humble best. They all cross themselves, stand, kneel, sit, sing and pray with furrowed eyebrows. Angie knows the Spanish Our Father, or Padre Nuestro from her time in the SOS. Grandma is a Unitarian. She goes along with the Catholic routine, as she was raised in a Spanish Catholic family and went to a Catholic High School in New Jersey. Jazmin is fidgeting and starts crawling around... Roxana joins her. Angie has fallen asleep. Grandma is tired. They decide to leave. Ceci drops money in the plate by the door, while the girls splash themselves with holy water on the way out. They find the car and get on board.

Ceci: We'll have to try that next Sunday. It's hard for them to sit still.

Grandma: Maybe after I go back to Virginia.

Jazmin: But Grandma, we don't want you to go back to Virginia.

Grandma: I have a house there to take care of that will be yours someday.

Ceci: Let's talk about something else.

Angie: I know, let's go to the zona viva!

Ceci: Not tonight girls... I am sure Grandma is exhausted from such a big day. So...back to the house to leave cookies for Santa, and right to bed.

Jazmin: And don't forget the carrots and apples for the deer.

Chorus of "yeahs"

170. Christmas morning – Fashion Show

It is Christmas morning. The house is fully decorated. The Christmas tree stands out in the corner, and there are many gifts under it. Since there are no natural fir or pine trees in Honduras, Ceci has chosen an arty substitute. We can hear church bells and gun shots. The girls go to wake up Grandma, who is already looking out the window and freaking out because of the gun shots. Santa has come and eaten the cookies and carrots that the girls have left for him and his reindeer. Grandma thinks she is in a crime scene. Ceci enters in her pajamas.

Grandma: What's going on? Should we call the police?

Ceci: Mom, don't worry. People shoot into the sky to celebrate holidays, soccer games, and particularly Christmas in Honduras. Besides…. There are only a few police cars in La Ceiba, and they are used to it.

Grandma: Interesting tribute to the birth of Christ. I hope they don't kill any birds. *Grandma continues to cough.*

Jazmin: Can we please open the presents now?

Angie: But first we have to put baby Jesus in his cradle right Mom?

Ceci: Oh yeah I forgot… Here he is. Let's do it together.

Grandma: Are you sure it is safe to go outside?

The house is decorated for Christmas with a makeshift tree, decorated with ornaments. On the porch is a huge table with the layout of a typical Honduran village, with houses and trees, a church, fields of corn, beans, and coffee, and a small nativity, where Hondurans wait until Xmas day to lay the baby in the manger. They bring Grandma out to look at the village. They put baby Jesus in his bed, and then close their eyes and say the PADRE NUESTRO in Spanish together.

Roxana: Y los regalos Mami? *They go back inside.*

Ceci: Yes of course… I'll put on the Christmas music… Let me get the camera.

Angie: Look, Santa ate the cookies!

Jazmin: … And the reindeers ate the carrots and apples!! Mom, he really came!!

Ceci puts on the Christmas music, passes out all the gifts and then grabs her camera. There are bicycles, board games, more dolls and doll clothes that Granma made, funny wigs, and beautiful homemade white kindergarten graduation dresses also made by Grandma. The girls have handmade paintings for Grandma. Roxana gets a DVD and the book of Disney's SNOW WHITE. Jazmin gets a guitar, and starts singing immediately. Angie gets a microphone and stands up on the coffee table to begin narrating the news.

Angie: **Damas y Caballeros… Hoy es Navidad, pero no hay nieve en La Ceiba, Honduras. El sol brilla y Santa todavia vino.** Ladies and gentlemen… Today is Xmas but there is no snow in La Ceiba, Honduras. The sun is shining and Santa still came. *(pause, covering the microphone)* **Mommy, how does Santa fly in the air like that with a big sleigh and deer without wings? And why does he need a sleigh if there isn't any snow here?**

Jazmin: And how does he get to every single kid in the world in one night?

Roxana: **Porque Santa es magico!** Because Santa is magic!

Ceci: Right!

Jazmin: And I am only going to believe in Santa Claus for real if he brings me exactly what I asked for.

Angie: Never mind, I am doing the news now... **Presta atencion!** **Damas y Caballeros...** Grandma Diaz has come to La Ceiba to visit her **nietas,** and right now it is hot and sweaty. Probably it will rain later, because it rains every day and at our house it floods, so we will be stuck here all day playing with our Xmas presents!! Yay!

Girls: Yay!!

Grandma: Oh no... What if we can't get out?

Ceci: Don't worry mom, the water will drain eventually.

Roxana and Jazmin have been trying on their new homemade dresses that Grandma made. They go out to make a grand entrance, and come back wearing Ceci's high heels. Jazmin takes the microphone.

Jazz: **Damas y Caballeros,** now we will have a **desfile de moda.** How do we say that mom?

Ceci: *Behind the camera.* Fashion Show.

Jazmin: Yes and we are the models, and Grandma, you can sit over there.

Grandma: Thank you... I have the best seat in the house. *Ceci is still videotaping.*

Angie: Grandma, help me with my dress. *Grandma zips up Angie.* OK, Ladies and Grandma!! Welcome to our Fashion Show from La Ceiba, Honduras. You will see the most beautiful models and clothes in all of Honduras. First we have Roxana Yadira! *Roxana enters.*

Jazmin: Roxana is wearing a beautiful poofy dress with a blue bow for her Kinder Graduation made by Grandma Diaz from the Nited Stays of America.

Angie: *Making her entrance in high heels and grabbing the fake microphone from Jazmin.* And my beautiful dress is also from Grandma Jo, with a pink ribbon, cause my color is red, Roxana is blue..

Jazmin: And mine is poofy too with a purple ribbon. And I am Jazmin from Alladin.

Roxana: OK, Yo soy Cinicienta. *Posing....*

Angie: Y yo soy Blanca Nieves. *Posing....*

Grandma: Oh how beautiful you look... I just love it. *Applauding*

Angie: OK now put on the music Mom. Let's do our ballet dance to the Alladin song for Grandma.

This is a Disney song from the movie Aladin that they performed for the Xmas show, "A whole new world". They all begin to fly, jump and dance around the room waving scarves. Grandma and Ceci are laughing and crying and applauding, still videotaping. Suddenly Angie's arm starts shaking.

Angie: Mom everything is black... and I can't see, and my arm... Mom!!!

Ceci holds her close... the music stops.

Ceci: Oh Mom... this is what happened when I found her the first day... She was shaking all over. I don't know what it is.

Grandma: It's some kind of seizure. You have to take her to a neurologist.

Ceci: What's happening now Angie? Can you see?

Angie: Si Mommy... but my arm is like a rock.... Una calambre. A muscle spasm.

Ceci: Some kind of muscle spasm. It's going to be OK Angie... I'm here... Grandma's here. You know I can fix anything. I love you baby and we will go to the Doctor this week.

Ceci rocks Angie... massaging her arm. This will be the beginning of a condition that continues to the present day in which Angie, Jazmin, and Roxana, but mostly Angie, gets rock-hard muscle spasms that don't go away for 3 or 4 days. Jazmin and Roxana are staring at Angie, wondering what to do. Angie's seizures will continue in the form of panic attacks until she turns 22. She finally slows down her breathing and comes out of the seizure.

Ceci: Oh Thank God Angie. I won't let go of you baby.

Grandma: Is anybody hungry? I'm going to make my mother's Spanish arroz con pollo for my beautiful nietas. OK? So go change out of your princess dresses, and come help me in the kitchen. We must keep the ball rolling.

Roxana: *Holding up the Snow White video* - Y Blanca Nieves?

Ceci: Mas tarde, after Christmas dinner OK? Go change now.

Roxana and Jazmin change and go help Grandma in the kitchen. Angie remains in Ceci's arms.

Angie: Mom, what do I have now? I'm blind, I shake. What's wrong with me? *She cries.*

Ceci: Look at me. You are beautiful in every way, and you have been rescued from everything that made you sick, because, Angie Nicolle, you were meant to live and shine your beautiful light on the world. And I am your mother and I am going to give you every chance in heaven to have a beautiful, safe, and love filled life. And..... it's OK to cry. Because I cry about it all the time too, but Angie, you are alive and we can fix this. I will make sure we fix this shaking problem OK? I can't fix your eyes... right now... but we can fix this shaking thing.... *Holding her tight, muttering and looking up*. I promise. One thing at a time. I love you Angie.

171. <u>Walt Disney's Blanca Nieves and the Wicked Step Mother – At home</u>

Christmas Dinner is finished and the girls are seated on the sofa in their Christmas pajamas with their Christmas dolls, watching the Disney movie, Snow White. Angie sits in her own chair right in front of the TV. Ceci and Grandma are cleaning up and speaking privately.

Grandma: So I see what's wrong with Angie. What's going on with Roxana?

Ceci: I'm not sure yet Mom. It's pretty amazing that she can even speak Spanish. She used to grunt all the time in the orphanage. Then we looked under her tongue to see if she was mute, and it wasn't that. But I think that after the meningitis and the malnutrition, and possibly prenatal madness, her brain isn't operating on all 6 cylinders.

Grandma: Well, it's got to be neurological like Angie. Does she have seizures?

Ceci: No, I haven't seen it with Roxana, but I do know there are some learning disorders there. But this is the first time I've seen a full blown seizure with Angie, since the first day in the hospital. Although she did say something about it after school one day.... That when she pressed down hard on the pencil to write so she could see it, that her arm started shaking. I remember that, and now I realize that it's serious.

Grandma: Sounds like the mother didn't take folic acid and any prenatal vitamins.

Ceci: Mom, there's also a chance that Roxana got beat up while in the belly, because Vilma told me that's what women do to abort unwanted children. And it could be recreational drugs that the mother did. Not to mention the bad water and all the worms and amoebas they lived with in their distended bellies, all the way through the SOS. And of course there was no milk, only sugar water, and Angie and Roxana's teeth were all black when I met them.

Grandma: Or all of the above... Holy God, what have you gotten yourself into?

Ceci: Then somebody pulled all their black teeth out at the SOS. One day I arrived and they were gone... pierced ears and no front teeth... And, you're not supposed to pull them out so young, because then the adult teeth come in every which way after eating with your gums for a few years. So you can see the mess going on in Roxana's mouth. The kids at school call her "witchy".

Suddenly Jazmin comes running into the kitchen, screaming and crying. In the background you can see on the TV the part with the witch - Malevolent Step Mother, dressed as the old lady delivering the apple to Snow White (Disney version). Jazmin is truly terrified and angry. This is the first time they have heard this story.

Jazmin: Mama, mama..... Why is she so mean and ugly? Why does she want to hurt Snow White? *She begins to cry and hold Ceci close.*

Angie: It's only a movie Jazmin.

Ceci: But she thinks it's real. Look what she did to the book.

On the floor behind the sofa are strips of paper ripped from the page with the Malevolent witch from the Disney Snow White book.

Angie: I can't believe you ripped up this new book! We are not supposed to destroy books Jazmin. *Jazz bursts into tears again.*

Ceci: It's OK Jazmin. *She picks her up like a baby.* It's a fairy tale and you are not in it. I hope you don't think I'm the evil stepmother do you? I'm sorry. My poor baby.

Jazmin: No Mommy, but this bad lady really scared me, because adults aren't supposed to act like that.

Grandma: You know Jazmin… Even though we don't live in that make believe world of Snow White, there are some adults that are not good people, and they don't know how to protect and take care of kids. I'm sorry that we can't all live in a fantasy world…. But you are with your forever mama and grandma now, and we are going to take care of you, and nobody is going to hurt you, or make you eat a bad apple. Remember Jazmin, I am not your step mother, I am your forever and ever Abuela. And Ceci is your forever mother.

Roxana: **Ella nunca comera manzanas. Te digo.** She will never eat apples. I tell you.

Ceci: Look, I am going to tape the page back together, and hope that you don't freak out about this anymore. We must respect books. They live longer than we do. I still love you… I love all of you. And nobody will ever harm you like the wicked stepmother, for any reason. Understand? Group hug. OK Jazz?

Ceci: OK chicas, the sun is going down on a very big Jesus birthday… and it is time to go to bed.

Grandma: How about pancakes for Christmas breakfast?

We hear affirmative responses from the girls even though they are unfamiliar with pancakes.

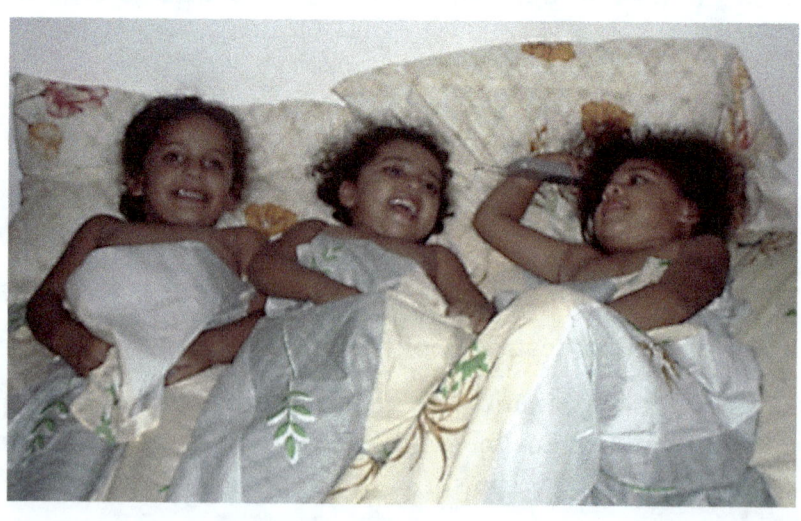

Ceci: But now it's bedtime. Say good night to Grandma... Kisses everyone... I will come tuck you in shortly, and then tomorrow morning we will have pancakes and bike riding.

Jazmin: Can we sleep in your bed tonight?

Ceci: I guess it's OK... I'll sleep in the guest room.

We fade out with Ceci singing Mother Moon, and fade back into the girls waking Ceil up at the crack of dawn.

Christmas Morning

Roxana: Mom can we ride the new bikes outside now?

Ceci: Let me get dressed OK?

Angie: Mom, there's just one problem, I don't know how to ride a bike.

Ceci: Well I'm going to teach you. Training wheels help a lot.

Roxana: Yo puedo.

Grandma wanders into Ceci's bedroom.

Grandma: This is when having a man in the house has its advantages. I don't ride bikes. So, I will make the pancakes.

Roxana: Que son pancakes? What are pancakes?

Ceci: They don't have pancakes in Honduras, but you are going to love Grandma's pancakes.

Grandma: Ellas van estar encantadas con mis pancakes!! They are going to love my pancakes. *She goes to kitchen*

Jazmin: Enough about pancakes. Mom I don't want to ride bikes; I'm too small for a two wheeler.

Ceci: Why don't you get your guitar and sing while we ride bikes in the street? And when you are ready I am going to teach you how to ride.

Jazmin: Do you think people will give me money?

Ceci: At Christmas we are supposed to sing Christmas carols for free. So go get dressed so you enjoy grandma's pancake because you won't find them too many places in Honduras.

Ceci's cell phone rings, and the girls look for Christmas dresses.

172. <u>Phone call – Dr. Harris- Merry Christmas</u>

It is Dr. Harris calling from Virginia to wish everyone a Merry Christmas. Ceci is happy to hear from him and she tells him about the bicycles and Grandma and the dolls, and how they will go to the beach later. She asks about the rest of his tour in Central America. He tells her that he is buying a villa in Italy and wants her to come with the kids in the summer. Ceci's jaw drops.

Ceci: Good morning Doctor. How are you?

Dr. Harris: I am fine and in Virginia visiting family. I wanted to wish you a Merry Christmas down there in the tropical sun…. How are you there?

Ceci: Well Grandma is here and we have spoiled the girls with loads of presents. We just had a wonderful Christmas dinner, and they are about to go to the street to ride their new bikes.

Dr. Harris: Ceci, I am about to move to Italy where I just bought a villa.

Ceci: Wow, the Doctor business must be booming.

Dr. Harris: I want to set up a practice there of international Doctors. But never mind all that… I am hoping you can bring the girls for a visit in the summer.

Ceci: Wow… I was about to thank you for making the monthly transfer and now this. I am overwhelmed. Can you afford this? As a missionary Doctor?

Dr. Harris: Don't worry about that. You will have to get Honduran passports for them.

Ceci: And permission to leave the country. Yes it is quite the choreography on many levels, but clearly worth it. I can do all this… And probably an invitation note from you could clear us at your end into Italy. I just can't believe this. I have always wanted to see Italy… and the girls will love it.

Dr. Harris: We can talk more about it later. I wanted to ask you about your twilight zone episodes. Are they still taking place?

Ceci: Interesting question Dr. Harris. You know, I haven't had any Ciudad Blanca visits in quite a while. I think I am just too grounded with the girls to go on supernatural excursions anymore. But I am very excited about a trip to Italy.

Dr. Harris: Yes… absolutely… well… wait for me before you have any more of that guiffity.

Ceci: Uh huh…..

Dr.Harris: So, yes….. Please begin this immigration paper work now so you can come in the summer.

Ceci: Yes, passports and all that. I will get right on it. Thank you Louis for your kind invitation and gracious philanthropy.

Dr. Harris: Of course, and most of all, I wanted to wish you a Merry Christmas and send my regards to the girls. I'm sorry about the visas… I know that they will eventually give it to you. Don't give up… Meanwhile you must come to Italy.

Ceci: Ok dear Louis. Yes… Thanks so much for calling… I will tell the girls…And thanks again for all your support… We could not do this without you. Bye…

Ceci gets off the phone, relieved, confused, and yet thankful. Grandma brings a stack of steaming pancakes to the porch and the kids follow.

Ceci: *Talking to herself.* I guess we do have angels. Venice, Italy… Oh my God. Life is good.

Grandma: A comer! Time to eat!

Ceci: What are we having?

Girls: PANCAKES!!!!

173. **Riding Bicycles on Avenida Roatan**

As the girls slide into their picnic table places on the porch, Grandma serves the pancakes with heaping spoonfuls of honey and strawberries.

Grandma: Pancakes deliciosos! Listos para todas las muchachas! Get them while they're hot.

Ceci: Yes… Eat, drink and be merry, for tomorrow you'll want more!

Their gastral glee is profound and that segues into the three new shiny Christmas bikes that Ceci is wheeling into the driveway. There are two 2 wheeler medium size girl bikes and a smaller bike for Jazmin. They are all still wrapped with big red bows. After a few pancakes, Ceci begins a silent modeling dance around the new bikes until Roxana notices.

Ceci: So are we ready to ride?

Roxana: Yo se que puedo. I know I can do it.

Ceci: I think Santa brought the big girl bikes for you and Angie. And Jazz gets the smaller one.

Angie – Wow Mom… I love it! But I need help so I don't crash.

Ceci: I am going to teach all of you one at a time.

Ceci patiently takes Roxana and Angie on their two wheelers with training wheels back and forth a few times. Grandma lifts Jazmin on to her little bike.

Jazz: Look Ma, I can almost touch the pedals!

The neighborhood kids have gathered at the gate with their scrawny old bikes. As this is unfolding, an indigenous woman with three kids approaches her and asks for food and clothing. The girls continue to ride as Grandma watches for their safety.

Ceci: Si pudieran volver en una hora, puedo ayudarle. Yo se que es Navidad y creo que tengo cosas para sus ninos que necesito recoger. Pero ahora quiero pasar tiempo con mis hijas. **OK?** If you could come back in an hour I can help you. I know that it is Christmas and I believe I have some things for your children that I need to collect. But now I want to spend time with my daughters.

Once again, Ceci addresses the woman with a secret guilt.

Ceci: Disculpa senora, si viene mas tarde puedo ayudarle, **OK?** I'm sorry Sra. If you come back later I can help you.

Without responding the lady walks away. It is almost a robotic action as if she knows what to do when she feels rejected. The girls are trying to ride their bikes. Angie has difficulty getting started, so Ceci helps her. Roxana gets the hang of it, and Jazmin offers her bike to one of the local kids. Ceci walks back to the house while the kids continue riding and joins Grandma who has taken a seat in front of the house. A neighborhood kid wants to ride Roxana's bike. Grandma addresses the poverty issue.

Grandma: There it is – the constant struggle between the haves and the have nots.

Ceci: Yes, I see it all the time, and I can't fix it.

Grandma: Your father and I never understood why you are so attracted to the dregs of the population.

Ceci: Are you saying that my kids are the dregs of the population?

Grandma: No, I am saying that if you keep this up, you will always be the provider providing for everybody. **Ceci:** That's the way they all see the gringos here.

Grandma: I just worry that you will be single for the rest of your life supporting these kids alone, and worse... taking on some crazy, unemployed boyfriend.

Ceci: Don't worry about that Mom. The only guys I meet here are 25 years old and want me to buy them a cell phone so they can call me, and then maybe marry them and get them a visa.

Grandma: Never mind all that. Just get the girls visas and come home Ceil.

Ceci: I'm doing my best Mom.

Angie, Jazmin, and Roxana are all proudly riding toward them. Jazmin is still struggling on her little bike. Ceci and Grandma applaud. Deni May calls.

Ceci: *on phone* Deni May... how are you? Oh... great idea... Yes it's a hot and tropical Christmas, and my Mom is here. She loves the beach. OK... Meet you there at 1.

Ceci: Wow, check this out. My babies can ride!

Angie: Mama tengo calor? Mom, I am hot.

Jazmin: Me too.

Ceci: Great, let's get your bathing suits and go to Helens on the beach. Deni May will meet us there. Jazmin: Come on Grandma, get your bathing suit.

Grandma: I think I'll just watch and be the life guard that yells for help OK?

174. Helen's beach restaurant and hotel – Grandma/ Deni

We are still celebrating Christmas vacation with Grandma. All are piled into the black pickup truck, singing their way down the beach highway with great Christmas spirit. When they get to the turn off, dirt road to the beach, Ceci begins the ritual of allowing each girl to sit on her lap and drive the car.

Grandma: I thought it was strange that they were allowed to ride in the back of a pick up truck, and now they are driving??

Ceci: *With Jazmin driving on her lap.* Mom, you know I wouldn't do anything to jeopardize your safety.

Jazmin is having the time of her life steering the car down the single dirt lane to Helen's resort. They switch.

Angie: My turn!!! *And Angie with her disabled vision, takes over Ceci's lap and the wheel. She does very well, with a little help from Mom. Angie really wants to drive someday.*

Roxana: Y Yo?? *And Roxana, who barely fits on Ceci's lap, squeezes in and takes us all the way into the parking lot at the beach. Grandma is clearly holding her breath the whole way.*

Ceci: I am so proud of my bambinas... They will all be driving me around someday you know.

"Helen's" is a resort on the beach run by French Canadians. Helen and her husband are tri-lingual, and employ members of the nearby Garifuna community called Sambo Creek, directly up the coast from Corozal. There is a small, but quaint hotel, an outdoor restaurant with tables and hammocks, a small but artistic pool, and direct access to a pretty secluded beach. The entire shore area is shaded by beautiful tropical palms.

Deni May is there when they enter. Ceci introduces Deni to her mom as her American Ex-patriot friend who teaches in the same school with her young custodial son named Ale, who hugs the girls when they enter. Grandma takes her time but manages her way to the corner where Deni has claimed a table and hammock. The girls dump their bags and jump into the pool with Ale.

Ceci: Hola Deni, Merry Christmas.

Deni: Feliz Navidad tambien... y tu mama!!

Ceci: Si, Deni, this is my mom Josephine.

Deni: You are the famous Ceci Mom , who sends all the tutus and dance shoes from the states. And the story books, and handmade dresses for the girls, and cool toys..

Grandma: I do my best for my beautiful grandchildren.

Ceci: That's Mom... and she taught me everything I know about costumes.

Deni: Too bad you can't see any of the shows. They are always really beautiful.

Grandma: I'm sure they are. Ceil has been doing this for a long time.

Ceci: Vilma does the measuring and the sewing... I design, buy the fabric, cut, and fit the outfits for each kid. But I learned the whole routine from you and my Spanish Abuela, and a few years doing costumes in theater and television.

Grandma: Plus you did the costumes for all of your *own* crazy movies and shows.

Ceci: Well, now, I am just trying to make a meager living in the third world, and maybe bring a little musical joy into my studio.

Grandma: Well, I'm going to watch the girls in the pool...

Ceci: I've got an extra bathing suit if you want to swim Ma.

Grandma: I won't be needing that. Thank you.

They watch her as she wanders off to the pool where the kids are having a ball jumping off the diving board onto floats. Ceci and Deni chat.

Ceci: My mom expresses her love through sewing for people. It is a very silent, lonely art. You should see the girls' dresses and the doll clothes she has made. They are so magical.

Deni: You are lucky she can still travel. My mom can't get out of her wheel chair.

Ceil: Do you plan to visit her?

Deni: I still can't get a visa for Ale. Now they want DNA to prove he's mine. Since they are hip to the fact that I am too old to have given birth to him.

Ceci: How old was Ale when you got him?

Deni: Maybe two months? Remember that gay Honduran guy, Omar, whom I married for citizenship... his and mine? He knew this lady in Sambo Creek, who is gay and did not want a baby she had just given birth to.... So Omar brought him to me... without papers... etc. He was a baby... and his mom never told me that there was something wrong with him.

Deni May and Ale

Roxana, Jazmin, Ale, Angie

Ceci: Then what's really going on

Deni: Besides the fact that he has delayed speech, I just don't know. Something else is not right in his brain.

Ceci: Maybe somebody dropped him, maybe he had meningitis... who knows? It could be so many things.

Deni: Most of what disables these kids is bad pregnancies. No prenatal care and all the poverty and confusion that comes with a surprise pregnancy.

Ceci: I wish they offered health and birth control education in the schools.

Deni: Nevertheless... he's mine, I love him, and I have to stay here until there are a new set of young American officers at the Embassy in Tegucigalpa. I just have to honker down. I've been here longer than you. This is a tough embassy.

Ceci: I guess we are in similar visa boats with the kids. **Como una pesadilla donde nunca se despierta.** Like a nightmare you never wake up from.

Helen approaches the table. The kids and Grandma work their way out to the beach. There are Garifuna children there waiting for customers to buy their shells, tableta de coco, coral jewelry, hair braids, coconut oil, etc.

Deni: Bon jour Helen!

Helen: **Bon jour mes ami! Comment allons nous ajourdui? C'est tu Mama, Ceci?** Hello my friends. How are we today? Is this your mother, Ceci?

Ceci: **Yes, and I am so happy to be able to bring her here to this little piece of tri lingual paradise. She loves the beach... and what a beautiful day.**

Helen: **Bienvenido Senora Deni... How are you?**

Deni: **Fabulous, and hungry. And we all want fried fish right?**

Ceci: **OK... Bring us 6 fried fish dinners with the platanos, frijoles and rice, 8 plates and lots of horchatas, and we will be fine. This is on me. Merci Helen.**

Helen: **Avec Plaisir, mais... un peu de temps si vous plait... parsque il ya beaucoup de gens aujordui avec les fetes.** With pleasure, but please give me some time as there are many people today with the holidays.

Ceci: **Pas de problem madame... Je suis enchante etre ici avec ma mere et mes enfants.** No problem madame. I am enchanted to be here with my mother and my children.

Helen: **Cervezas senoras entonces?** Beers Ladies... yes?

Deni: **OK... dos. Y cuatro horchatas para los muchachos,** And four horchatas (rice drinks) for the kids.

Ceci: **Merci beaucoup! Let me hear that distinct Montreal accent. I lived in Montreal for 7 years... had a dance studio on Blvd. St. Laurent, and choreographed the musicals Starmania and Pied de Poule, along with all the New Years Eve.. Bon Anee CBC TV specials... I also was Celine Dion's first choreographer... I love Montreal.**

Helen: **Vraiment! What are you doing here?**

Ceci: Montreal est trop froid… Vous savez… Montreal is too cold. You know that.

Helen: Oui ,,, Oui. That's why we're here dans cette paradis tropical! A pleasure to meet you Madame. I will be back with the bebidas. (Drinks)

Helen moves on to the next table as the restaurant fills up with local Honduran families. Deni and Ceci both sink into their hammocks. The girls have gone out to the beach and are building sand castles with the local Garifuna kids. Grandma is watching. Ceci eventually joins them with her camera.

Ceci: Wow, looks like a whole village of sand castles. Really beautiful.

Jazmin: I wish it could stay like this Mom

Grandma: Nothing is forever. You have to enjoy it now.

Ale: *Forms sounds and motions that indicate that Ceci should take a picture of the sand castle.*

Ceci: OK ,,, Great idea Ale… Everybody get behind the castle quick!

The entire gang, including Grandma and the Garifuna kids are hanging out on the beach. They set up for a group photo. Ceci snaps off one picture just in time as a wave suddenly slaps the beach and washes away the entire sand castle village in a flash. Roxana is upset by this and comes to sit by Mom. One of the Garifuna boys offers Roxana the shell he has been trying to sell to Ceci telling her it is a gift.

Garifuna boy: Vengan con nosotros caminando por la playa. Come walk with us along the beach.

Ale: Vamos a caminar por alla! *Ale can form some words in both Spanish and English. It is difficult to understand him.*

Roxana: Yeah – Take a walk he says.

Ceci: OK, but not too long. Helen is making us fried fish.

She gives the Garifuna boy 20 lempiras for the shell.

Garifuna boy: Y podemos tocar tambores... And we can play the drums.

Jazmin: Me gusta eso... I like that.

The Garifuna kids agree to accompany all of them down the beach and they leave. Ceci watches them walking in the waves down the desolate beach and returns to Deni and her Mom at the restaurant.

Grandma: Are you sure you want them to go alone?

Ceci: This is probably the safest place for them to be independent. *They sit around the table.* They went down the beach to play drums with the Garifuna kids.

Deni: What about the fish?

Ceci: The fish can wait. This is good for them.

Grandma: How is it good for them? This is the third world.

Ceci: Ma... You used to let me go on the bus to NY by myself, which was a lot more dangerous.

Grandma: When you were in high school... and even then I waited at the bus stop trembling.... Your kids are still in grammar school …. With disabilities… And you don't know these kids.

Ceci: OK Ma … yo me voy.

Ceci takes off jogging on the shore, skipping through the waves. It is a beautiful empty beach with few homes. In the distance she can see the kids playing drums and dancing in the sand with the Garifuna kids.

Cutting to the drum circle… Jazmin and Ale are playing drums with an older Garifuna girl while Roxana, Angie and several other kids are dancing punta. It is a beautiful sight to see, and Jazmin can really play. Ceci arrives and joins in with the punta dancers. More mature Garifuna drummers and female singer/dancers gather, emerging from the palapa shacks on the Sambo Creek shore. As the music intensifies and the back and forth singing increases in fervor, Ceci gets lost dancing to the rhythm, and there is a sudden dissolve into fantasy.

175. Mirage of Carlos

Ceci turns to look towards the ocean and sees a mirage of a man, fully dressed, walking out of the water at low tide… towards the shore. It is Carlos, the girls' deceased father. He starts to run towards them, crying out "Mis Ninas!". Ceci looks back at the circle, where the energy is intense. Ale and the girls are really having a great time. There is a spinning image of seeing Carlos and the drummers in a clockwise circle…. Until……

176. **Back to the beach**

Ceci's cell phone rings and brings Ceci back. She answers the phone and then turns back to the ocean, and the mirage of Carlos is gone. She removes her sunglasses and looks again. It was a mirage, and there is no one there.

Deni: Where are you? The fish is on the table.

Ceci: We are in a drum circle and it's crazy, but we will be there in 10 minutes.

Ceci gathers Ale and the three girls, and gives 200 Lempiras to the head drummer... They depart after goodbyes and go galloping back down the beach while intense drumming in the punta circle continues and other local vacationers gather around to watch the young Garifuna magic.

177. **Huevos rancheros and Doll Clothes – at home with Grandma**

Ceci is making huevos rancheros for breakfast. Grandma wanders into the kitchen coughing.

Grandma: Good morning.

Ceci: Buenos dias Mama.... Are you ok? I heard you couging all night. I wish I could fix it.

Grandma: Scar tissue in my lungs. Doctor says I won't die of it, but I will die with it. So I have learned to live with it.

Ceci: Mom, I just hate to see you suffer.

Grandma: You definitely have more important things to worry about.

The girls wander into the kitchen in their pajamas with the baby dolls that Grandma gave them for xmas, also in the same matching pajamas as the girls. They sit at the table and begin to devour their huevos rancheros, as Ceci gives out the vitamins.

Roxana: Look at my babydoll Abuela.

Grandma: She is pretty like you. What's her name?

Roxana: Ummm..... **Cinicienta...** (Cinderella)

Jazmin: Mine is Jazmin..

Angie: And mine is Aurora.

Ceci gets out her camera.

Grandma: OK, so now your baby dolls are in their morning pajamas which match your own. Where are they going after that? To school?, to play?, to church?, to a party? *Grandma has literally made three outfits for each doll. All the outfits match clothing she has already made for the three girls. But, confusion takes over as they have different dress up wishes.*

Ceci: Now wait Tengo un idea fabuloso. Come closer..... Let's do a fashion photo shoot with the dolls and you guys and Grandma.... First with the pajamas and then you can change OK?

They all seem to like that idea and Ceci ushers them into a family portrait pose at the kitchen table.

Jazmin: OK , now play clothes. Grandma, we have these same sun dresses right?

Grandma: That's right, why don't you put those on, and then you'll get the whole magic idea.

They take off looking for their dresses and box of doll clothes. Ceci is right there with their matching beach dresses.

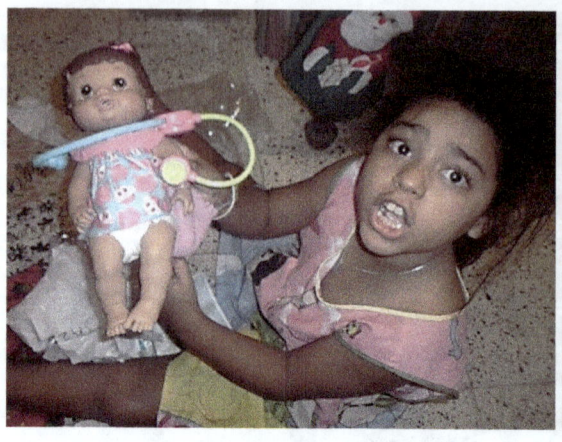

Jazmin: OK , now play clothes. Grandma, we have these same sun dresses right?

Grandma: That's right, why don't you put those on, and then you'll get the whole magic idea.

They take off looking for their dresses and box of doll clothes. Ceci is right there with their matching beach dresses.

Angie: Can I put the bathing suit under the play clothes?

Roxana: Para la playa!

Grandma: That's it, claro que si..... they are going to the beach.

As they dress, they sing together "Vamos a la playa" to a tropical beat. Grandma is loving this.

Roxana: OK... ahora... escuela...

Grandma: Who knows which is the school uniform? *They all dive into their doll clothes boxes.*

Roxana: Esta... falda beige y camisa azul oscuro.... Como las ninas en Santa Teresa. This beige skirt and dark blue shirt.. Like the girls at Santa Teresa.

Jazmin: I got it... *She holds up the skirt and blouse.*

Ceci: Somebody help Angie.

Grandma: Here they are. Don't forget the black Maryjane shoes girls.

Angie: Wow Grandma… This is fantastic.. Thank you.

Ceci tosses them all their school uniforms and they put them on. And another group photo is taken with Grandma, the dolls, and the school girls.

Roxana: I'm tire mom.

Ceci: Tired.. I know you're tired Roxie… OK,,, How about Grandma's blue, red, and green dresses?

Grandma: They can also be worn for church or a party. *Grandma poses too.*

Jazmin: Just like my doll's dress! *She holds up the matching dress.*

They all cheer waving their dresses around as Ceci puts on more Christmas music and they entertain Ceci and Grandma.

178. **Bedtime Stories with Grandma**

The frozen photo with the dolls fades into, the Spanish Silent Night, "Noche de Paz", a photo of Grandma reading to the 3 girls in their pajamas with their baby dolls in bed. She is reading "Are you My Mother", by PD Eastman

Roxana: Abuela, why you going manana?

Grandma: Because I have a house to take care of, bills to pay, bridge club, church, and my work for Homes for Habitat..... Some day you will come live with me.

Angie: We love you Grandma, and we want you to come back.

Grandma: And I love all of you too... more than you know. You are all very brave little girls.

Ceci: Let's get tucked in and I'll sing "Mother Moon" ... OK?

They get ready for bed. Jazmin pulls out her notebook. She likes to list the people she knows and trusts.

Jazmin: First I want to show you my list of everybody in our world. Mom, Grandma, Vilma, Sayda, my teacher, Deni and Ale, Who else Mommy?

Ceci: Well there's your God father David Ashby, my sister Tina, and her husband Fred... And there is Dr. Harris, who is like another God father who sends us money, and has invited us to Italy. And, I have friends, but they are all over the United States, and it seems like a lifetime since I had a coffee with an old friend.

Jazmin and the girls have been making their own lists of who is in their lives. This will be a recurring routine as the girls seek security and stability in their lives.

Angie: I want a big family someday.

Ceci: Well you may have to marry someone with lots of brothers and sisters. But for the moment we have to be thankful for what we have as a family... that we have Grandma in the United States, with a house where we can live someday. And that you always have each other.

Roxana: I am thankful for you Mom, and my Abuela.

Grandma kisses each one, tucking them in. Ceci sings Mother Moon."

179. <u>Airport – Grandma leaves</u>

Once again… the preceding shot of Grandma kissing Jazmin goodnight, the night before… fades into the boarding gate at the La Ceiba Airport with Grandma in a wheel chair being kissed by the girls. Everybody is crying. Roxana is particularly upset. They wave goodbye as the attendant takes her down the ramp.

Ceci: Grandma will be back girls. My mom is tough. *They all grab hands and leave the airport with sad faces.*

Ceci thinks about all the times Mom said good bye to her as she got on planes to see the world. Grandma Jo will make the trip 3 more times at Christmas, with people accompanying her. These visits became increasingly more difficult for her with the intensity of her cough and age, but she loved to travel… and have a purpose. She always brought homemade dresses and gifts for the girls and the love any grandma would have for her grandchildren. Watching her plane take off was never easy for Ceci… alone in Honduras. All the struggles Ceci made for her independence, and out of the box, artist lifestyle were possible because of Dad and Mom's support. The biggest struggle of all will be getting visas for the girls… And Grandma will be there for them,,, until her last breath at 93.

379

**(2018) 13,000 Latino refugee children are in prison like custody on the border in the USA now waiting to enter. They have escaped the danger in their countries. Without a parent or friend to fight for them, and support them, they await their fate... with only the dream of a safe place to land... safe from hunger, violence, gangs, maybe an education or a job. Meanwhile, they sit in cages, like animals, sleeping on cement floors with aluminum blankets.

180. **Dance Studio – Vilma misses her old home**

Ceci is working on a new choreography in the Mazapan dance studio for the next Mother's Day show, as Mazapan high school students enter and get dressed for class. Vilma is there organizing the office. Ceci asks Vilma about her abandoned house in las Mercedes.

Ceci: Hola Vilma, como esta la nueva casa? Hello Vilma, how is the new house?

Vilma: Estamos bien, por la voluntad de Dios. Mi madre todavia falta la otra casa. We are OK, for the mercy of God. My mother still misses the other house.

Ceci: Y que pasa con esa casa en las Mercedes? And what finally happened to the house in las Mercedes?

Vilma: No hemos ido por alla... y mi madre no quiere hablar mas de esa casa. Los mareros dominan las Mercedes ahora. We haven't gone by there, nor does my mother want to talk about the house anymore. The gang members have taken over Las Mercedes now.

Ceci: Y ellos no pagan renta, y no tienen miedo de nadie? ... y nunca se puede volver? And they don't pay rent, nor have fear of anybody? And you never can return?

Vilma: No Ceci.

Ceci: Yo no entiendo la mentalidad de los mareros. I just don't understand the mentality of these gang guys.

Vilma: La Policia no anda por alla Ceci. Estamos mas seguro en la casa en las Lomas. No hay tantos mareros alla. The police don't go there Ceci. We are safer in the las Lomas house. There aren't many gangs there.

Ceci: Cuesta mas yo se. No hay justicia, soluciones, ni razones aqui. *She mutters to herself.* **Poverty makes people crazy. Pero Vilma… siempre tengas trabajo conmigo OK?** It costs more I know. There is not justice, solutions, nor reasons here. *Muttering* Poverty makes people crazy.. But Vilma, you will always have work with me, OK?

Vilma: Gracias Ceci.

181. **DANCE CLASS – Mother's Day Show prep – Karla arrives in studio**

Ceci finishes her rehearsal with the Mazapan high school dancers for the next Mother's Day show. When the bell rings, very young students (3-6) and their parents enter for the after school dance class. Vilma and Ceci have set up the room with the pre-school obstacle course – hopping through the hoola hoops on the floor, leaping over benches, crawling under fences, somersaulting across mats, skipping, walking backwards to the best of one's pre-school ability. All of this is executed with ecstatic joy and laughter to Spanish kiddie songs. Jazmin and Angie are there after school and join the fun. Roxana comes in later for her class with other students. The place is bustling. They transfer into yoga meditation and sitting poses…. To baby ballet plies… and then into gleeful little choreographies for children… Hokey Pokey, Penguin Dance, Sesame St. favorites…

The next class with the girls and pre-adolescent older students, moves onto the dance floor. The dance sequences should be portrayed as montage shots of class with Ceci, Vilma and the students. This will give visibility to various traditional dance styles blending with the sensations of childhood fun and fantasy as all the different age groups of dancers express themselves in class. Angie, Jazmin, and Roxana always fade to the back of the class, and despite their childish distractions, they learn the routine.

At some point, Karla enters the studio... and waits until the class is over to speak with Ceci. Normally she waits by the guard at the entrance gate of Standard Fruit, but sometimes she sneaks through. Karla feels uncomfortable, and ignores the girls. They ignore her. She is now, clearly pregnant (with Lilliana, first daughter with Yarel). Class ends and Ceci approaches her.

Ceci: Hola Karla, como estas?

Karla: Necesito pistos Ceci – No hay comida, no hay trabajo. I need money Ceci. There is no food nor work.

Ceci: Esperes un minuto Karla por favor. *She walks into the office, annoyed, and Karla shouts after her.* Just wait a minute.

Karla: Y tambien, Celestina quiere ver las ninas. And also, Celestina, (the girls' grandmother) wants to see them.

Ceci: Primero... dejame terminar con mis estudiantes por favor Karla? First, Let me finish with my students.... Please Karla.

Ceci finishes chatting with parents and students, while Vilma closes up the office. Vilma is aware of the situation as she knows that Karla is exploiting Ceci as much as possible. She sees Ceci taking money from the daily earnings at the dance studio to give to Karla, and clearly disapproves. Before leaving, Ceci takes Karla into her office alone.

Ceci: Karla, manana me voy a buscar permiso de la Juez para dos cosas.... Primero a buscar permiso para viajar a Italia en el verano para visitar un amigo mio con las ninas. Segundo, creo que si nosotros dos pudieramos ir a la embajada con las ninas, con su permiso para viajar a los Estados, tenemos un mejor chance para conseguir visas medicas para las ninas. Que piensas de eso? Karla.. tomorrow I go to seek permission from the Judge for two things. First to ask permission to go to Italy in the summer to visit a friend with the girls. And second, I believe that if both of us go to the American embassy in Tegucigalpa with the girls, with your permission to travel to the States, we have a better chance to get medical visas for the girls. What do you think of that?

Karla: En avion? Nunca fui en avion Ceci. In a plane? I never went in a plane Ceci.

Ceci: Yo pagare por todo…like always… I will pay for everything.

Karla: Cuando? When?

Ceci: La semana que viene. Next week.

Karla: Esta bien… pero necesito pistos Ceci. That's OK. But I need money Ceci.

Ceci: *Ignoring her.* **Y tambien, tengo otra idea. Me gustaria invitar la abuela Celestina y su familia a la casa el Sabado para almorzar… medio dia. Se puede organizar eso, y llamar me?** And also, I have another idea. I would like to invite Grandma Celestina and your family to the house Saturday to have lunch around noon. Can you organize that and call me?

Karla: Si como no… Y Yarel tambien? Yes, why not. And Yarel too?

Ceci: Claro que si… Of course.

Karla: Y los pistos Ceci? Ud. quisiera que me voy contigo para Tegucigalpa verdad? And the money Ceci? You want me to go with you to Tegucigalpa right?

Ceci: This is what we call blackmail. *Talking to herself.* **Ok Karla… toma…** *She gives Karla another 500 Lempiras.*

182. **Karla – More money**

Ceci closes her office and Karla, Vilma, and the girls get into her car. Again there is an awkward silence… since the girls don't know how to relate to Karla, and it becomes more and more clear that the only reason she comes around is to ask for money. Ceci pulls over to the bus stop to leave Vilma and Karla. Vilma walks off rolling her eyes.

Karla: Por favor Ceci, es tarde *(counting the money)* **necessito mas pistos… quiero ir en taxi.** Please Ceci it's late I need more money. I want to go home in a taxi.

Ceci: Karla Do you ever think about the welfare of the girls? Karla.. Nunca piensas tu del bienestar de las ninas? Nunca? Siempre preocupada para ti misma y pistos pistos pistos! Yo no me gusta ser tu banco. *Pause* Hoy no hay mas pistos Karla... No olvides llamarme confirmar la fiesta el Sabado, y el viaje a Teguc. Ciao!! You are always worried about yourself and pistos, pistos pistos!. I don't like being your bank. Today there are no more pistos Karla. Don't forget to call me about the party on Saturday and the trip to Teguc. Goodbye!

Karla: Si tuviste mi hambre entenderias!! If you had my hunger you would understand.

Karla gets out and slams the door. Ceci pulls away from the bus stop.

Ceci: Oh.. this woman is impossible. I am not her mother.

Angie: She always wants money Mom! You have to say no.

Ceci: You look just like her Angie... It's like telling you no.

Jazmin: Come on Mom... this is no good. She can't come to school and bother you.

Ceci: *Resigned to the problem...*For some reason, I feel it is important for you to know who your real blood family is. And Karla is the connection. And how else can I get to the truth about what happened to you guys before I met you? And Celestina is your grandmother, and I know she wants to see you now and then.

Jazmin: But please don't leave us alone with them Mom. I don't want to go back there. It's dirty and no bathroom with the animals everywhere.

Ceci: OK... we're home and just in time cause it's gonna rain, and I can get the car in before it floods. Let's get into pajamas... I'll make dinner... and you can watch some TV... OK?

They all cheer and run into the house as the thunder begins.

183. Checking in with the Judge – 2ⁿᵈ visa permission request

Ceci walks into the La Ceiba Municipal court building with her three girls in school uniforms. Walking down the hall they pass lawyers, defendants, families and mareros with tattoos in hand cuffs.

Angie: Why are we here Mom? Tenemos escuela hoy no? Don't we have school today?

Ceci: First we have to show the judge that you are happy, clean, healthy and passing in school, so you can stay with me.

Jazmin: And if we don't go see the judge will we have to go back to the SOS?

Ceci: Of course not. We will always follow all the rules. That doesn't mean the world is a fair place. Just stick with mama Ceci...

They enter the office. The secretaries all know her and the girls. Daisy knows the whole story.

Ceci: Hola Daisy, como estas?

Daisy: Bien Sra. Ceci y las ninas son preciosas! Como estan uds.? Que bonita andan hoy. I am well Sra. Ceci, and the girls are precious. How are you guys? How pretty you look today.

Roxana: Si somos bonitas. *Smiling* Yes, we are pretty.

Ceci: Daisy... Me voy de nuevo por Tegucigalpa a la embajada... Daisy, I am going again to Tegucigalpa to the embassy.

Daisy: Tan pronto? Fue hace poco no? So quick? You just went.

Ceci: Si, pero me rechazaron. Esta vez me voy con la madre. Yes, but they rejected me. This time I am going with the mother.

Daisy: Ceci, tu sabes que hasta que tengas custodia fija, no veras visas. Ceci, you know that until you have a solid custody you will not see any visas.

Ceci: Que voy hacer Daisy? Son mis hijas ahora. Yo se que tengo 52 anos, y para adoptar hay que tener menos de 50... pero

estoy esperando por un excepción. What am I going to do Daisy? They are my daughters now. I know that I am 52 years old and to adopt you have to be under 50, but I am hoping for an exception.

Daisy: Tu tienes una fuerza increíble mujer. Vaya con Dios! Ademas recuerdas que necesitas preparar un papel legal antes que la Juez puede firmar. You have an incredible strength lady. Go with God! Also remember that you must prepare a legal paper before the judge can sign.

Ceci: Oh no!!! Olvide. OK.. otro abogado. Oh no, I forgot about that. OK another lawyer.

Daisy: Bien dificil Ceci. Yo se lo que estas haciendo. Yo conozco Karla, y yo se que las ninas estan mas seguro contigo... pero la ley es la ley. Really difficult Ceci. I know what you are doing. I know Karla, and I know that the girls are much safer with you. But the law is the law.

Ceci: Yo se Daisy.... Y ahora, otra cosa.... Que tengo un amigo que me ha invitado con las ninas a viajar a Italia... un sueno mio. Que hago yo para tener permiso para salir y ir por Italia con ellas este verano? I know Daisy. And now, another thing. I have a friend who has invited me and the girls to go to Italy... a dream of mine. What must I do to have permission to leave and travel with them to Italy this summer?

Daisy: Un otro papel legal escrito por un abogado, que la Juez puede firmar... Another legal paper written by a lawyer, that the judge can sign.

Ceci: *deep breath*....OK.

Daisy: No conozco nadie que dura como ti. Traigame el papel oficial y te llamo cuando los documentos estan listos. I don't know anybody who endures like you. Bring me the documents and I will call you when they are ready.

Ceci: Gracias Daisy... I do it becaue I love these little bambinas!!! . Vamos ninas... Hay que ir a escuela. Thank you Daisy. I do it for love. Let's go girls. Time for school.

Daisy: Ciao ninas bellas. Buena suerte Ceci.

Ceci is clearly overwhelmed, and even though the girls don't understand, they know Mom is upset. They leave the office, and get in the car. Ceci cannot bypass this system... She must buy legal paper and have the request submitted by a lawyer.

184. **In the car on the way to school with the girls**

Roxana: Vamos a ver Grandma en Nited States.... Verdad Mommy?

Ceci: No not yet baby.

Angie: And are we going to Italy?

Ceci: I am working on all of it... It is very complicated. Now I must get you all to school.

Jazmin: La vida no es fácil... right mom?

Ceci: Where did you get that?

Jazmin: From you.

Ceci: OK... You know I love you. So just to lighten it up, I have invited your family from San Judas to the house for a dinner party this weekend so they can see how you are. I feel like I have to prove this to everybody.

Angie: I'm healthy.

Roxana: I'm healthy.

Jazmin: Me too.

Ceci: Good then you can help me entertain them Saturday. Right now I want to move on all this paperwork to see if we can go to Italy.

Angie: So if we came out of your belly, then you wouldn't need all these papers right?

Ceci: Right. But it doesn't matter. I am still your Mom.

185. Montage – Legal paper, lawyer, signature for 2nd permit request to leave country

This is another step in a long red tape road for Ceci and the girls. The following montage flashes us through scenes that involve these documents. First she must go to a papeleria to buy legal paper at $30 a page. Then she goes back to Lucia Urbizo, one of the many Honduran lawyers who will write up the legal permits for minors to leave the country, and then back to the municipality to submit the papers to Daisy for the Judge's signature. And then to the American Embassy. if you are trying to immigrate to the USA you must pay everyone along the way.

All this information is included in the application for medical, tourist and residential visas for the American Embassy in Tegucigalpa, along with an application fee of $400 for each applicant, every time. Ceci will eventually meet Peter Thompson, the American Expat Immigration lawyer who constructs the argument for the fourth and fifth applications. The American Embassy earned (3 X $400) X 5 =$6000 in total revenue from all the applications made over a period of 10 years. Peter Thompson became the key to unlocking the stalemate because of his brilliant legal prose. That is years later on the 4th and 5th attempts.

186. Arrival of the family from San Judas

Roxana runs into the house from the porch to announce that Karla and Celestina have arrived. Ceci goes out to the porch to greet everybody, and it is EVERYBODY: Karla, her new boyfriend, Yarel, Celestina, Cynthia, Carlitos, Aunt Carmen, and several young cousins. The girls stand in the doorway shyly. This is confusing for them. Grandma Celestina (mother of Carlos) is overjoyed to see them and hugs and kisses them profusely. Karla is clearly pregnant again.

Celestina: Que lindas!!!…. Cuando veo sus caras pienso en Carlos. How beautiful!. When I see your faces I think of Carlos.

Jazmin: Ud. conoce mi papa? You know my father?

Celestina: Nina soy tu abuela... su papa fue mi hijo... *She sheds a few tears.* I am your grandmother. Your father was my son.

Ceci: Hola Karla... Y Yarel... como estan?

Karla: Bien Ceci... Mira, te presento Carmen, que es la hermana de Carlos, y la tia de las ninas. Look... this is Carmen, who is Carlo's sister and the aunt of the girls.

Ceci: Bienvenido Carmen. Welcome Carmen.

Carmen: Sabes que fue yo que ayudo con el nacimiento de Angie... Yo le di a la luz a ella...en la casa en San Judas. Le hale con su abuela! *She gestures the act of pulling a baby out of a woman's belly.* Do you know that it was me who helped with Angie's birth in the San Judas house. I pulled her out with her grandma.

Celestina: Las tres nacieron alla.. Yo soy una partera que es como una enfermera que ayuda mujeres embarasadas sacar sus bebes en la casa. . All three were born there. I am a midwife which is like a nurse who helps pregnant women give birth to their babies in their home.

Ceci: Yes .. En Englais se llama "midwife". Yes, in English we call it a midwife.

Carmen: Uh huh.. eso... Y mira como Angie parece como Karla!! La misma cara... increible. And look how much Angie looks like Karla. The same face... incredible.

Ceci: Y Cynthia.. como estas tu?

Cynthia doesn't answer. She is older than Roxana, and seems to have some kind of comprehension disability.... She is riding Roxana's bike around the house.

Ceci: Porque no habla ella? Why doesn't she speak?

Karla: Ella es asi. She's like that.

Celestina: Mira, yo tengo vestidos para las ninas. Look, I have dresses for the girls.

She removes three poofy, used dresses from a brown bag and gives one to each girl, holding them up to their little bodies to see if they will fit.

Ceci: Oh how pretty!!!

Celestina: Creo que van a caber bien. I think they will fit well.

Ceci: Digale gracias a Celestina ninas. Girls, thank Celestina.

The girls go to hug Celestina shyly with confusion, as they don't remember her.

Ceci: Celestina, quiere ayudar las muchachas poner los vestidos en su dormitorio? Ellas van a encantarlos... Y Karla, porque no vayas con todos los primos afuera para jugar en los columpios? Yo voy a preparer el almuerzo. Espero que todos les gustan arroz con pollo, estilo Espanol de mi Abuela Espanola, Cecilia. Celestina, do you want to help the girls put on the dresses?. They are going to love them. Karla... why don't you go outside to play with the cousins on the swings. I am going to prepare lunch. I hope that everybody likes chicken and rice... Spanish style from my Spanish Abuela Cecilia.

Celestina goes to the bedroom with the girls, and everybody else goes outside to play except Carmen, while Ceci makes lemonade in the kitchen.

Celestina: Gracias Sra. Cecilia por cuidar las ninas. Me alegre que no estan en el SOS mas. Thank you so much for taking care of the girls. I am glad they are no longer in the SOS.

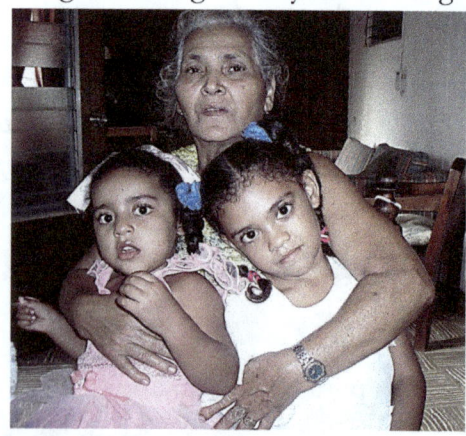

Jazmin, Celestina, Roxana   Yarel, Angie, Karla, Jazmin

Ceci joins Carmen at the kitchen table.

Ceci: Carmen, por favor.... Me gustaria clarificar de nuevo que paso exactamente con las ninas. Porque vinieron los soldados para recogerles? Carmen, please...I would like to clarify again what exactly happened to the girls. Why did the soldiers come to take them?

Carmen: *(whispering)* Primero, la policia no vienen a San Judas por miedo... Fue el vecino que llamo la policía cuando Karla pego a Angie en la cabeza, y la policia llamo el ejercito. First of all, the police don't come to San Judas out of fear. And it was the neighbor who called when Karla hit Angie in the head, and the police called the army.

Ceci: El vecino lo vio? The neighbor saw it?

Carmen: Si Ceci. Solo Karla estuvo en casa. Yes Ceci... only Karla was home.

Ceci: Saben uds... que ahora Angie es permanente ciega? You know that Angie is now permanently blind.

Carmen: *Also whispering with anger* Porque ella es mala!! No saben cuidar ninos... Ademas mire tan pronto que ella tiene otro novio. Because she is bad. She doesn't know how to take care of children. And look how fast she has another boyfriend.

Ceci: Pero todavia... no entiendo porque Karla le golpio. Como puede una mama pegar su bebe tan fuerte? But still, I don't understand why Karla hit her. How can a mother hit her baby that hard?

Carmen: Porque Angie tuvo hambre y fiebre de meningitis y lloraba y lloraba con dolor... y por fin para silenciarle... Karla le pego! Aay pobrecita!! Because Angie was hungry with meningitis fever and always cried and cried and finally to shut her up, Karla hit her. Aay poor thing!

Celestina returns with Angie, zipping her up. She has overheard Carmen's remarks. Ceci is stunned at the confirmation of the rumor about Angie's vision.

Ceci: Que bonita tu eres en rojo Angie! Ayuda sus hermanas vestir. Quiero ver todas juntas. How beautiful you are in red Angie. Go help your sisters. I want to see everybody together.

Angie returns to bedroom. Celestina whispers.

Celestina: El vecino nos dijo… Y yo lo creo. Hoy yo le dije que ella no puede dormir en la misma cama de mi hijo con otro hombre y hacer mas ninos. The neighbor told us. And I believe her.. and today I told her that she cannot sleep in my son's bed with another man and make more babies.

Ceci: Y porque no fueron al hospital con Roxana y Angie au principio del fiebre? And why didn't you go to the hospital with Roxana and Angie with the fever in the beginning?

Celestina: Porque yo tuve hierbas para esta enfermidad…. Because I had herbs for this illness.

Ceci: Para meningitis? For meningitis?

Celestina: Tengo hierbas por todas las problemas.

Angie, Roxana, and Jazmin come in all dressed up in their fluffy second hand dresses. They are smiling and pretending to model. Roxana is holding her soccer ball and wants to play with her cousins.

Ceci: Estas ninas podrian ser modelos con su belleza. These girls could be models with such beauty.

Celestina: Como yo veo el papa en sus caras. How I see the father in their faces.

Ceci: Digale gracias a Celestina. Thank Celestina girls.

Girls: Gracias por los vestidos, Celestina. Thank you or the dresses, Celestina.

Celestina: De nada, es lo menos que puedo hacer. It's nothing… and the least I can do.

Angie: Vengan uds. afuera. Come outside and play.

Roxana: Yo quiero jugar futbol, pero con este vestido? I want to play soccer, but with a dress?

Ceci: Mejor cambiar Roxana… No queremos ensuciar este vestido especial. Better to change Roxana.. You don't want to get this special dress dirty.

Roxana: Gracias Celestina. *She kisses Celestina and goes to change.*

Ceci: Si vayan afuera. Voy a servir limonada. Mas tarde me gustaria sacar photos de la familia. Yes, go outside. I will serve lemonade. Later I would like to take photos of the family.

Celestina and Carmen go outside where the kids are having a wonderful time with their cousins. Inside Ceci is preparing a tray, and there is a moment when she looks in the living room mirror and expresses a moment of private remorse to herself.

Ceci: Oh my God... I hope I am doing the right thing here. I will never be able to give them a big family like this.

Once outside, she distributes glasses of lemonade. Celestina takes Angie and Jazmin on her lap. Ceci begins to take pictures.

Celestina: Y Sra. Ceci... porque no vienen a vivir con nosotros en la montana en San Judas? And Sra. Ceci.. Why don't you come to live with us on the mountain in San Judas?

Ceci: Su invitación es muy generosa Sra... pero vivimos aqui y yo trabajo cerca en la Escuela Mazapan. Uds. pueden visitar cuando quieren. Lo que no entiendo es porque nadie iba a visitor las ninas cuando estaban en el SOS. Very nice of you to invite us Sra. But we live here and I work nearby in the Mazapan School. You can visit when you want. What I don't understand is why nobody went to visit the girls when they were in the SOS.

Karla: Porque no habian pistos. Because we didn't have the money.

Ceci: Karla... Cuesta 25 lempiras viajar en autobus al SOS. With the money I have given you there could have been many visits. Karla, it costs 25 lempiras to travel by bus to the SOS.

Big silence follows, while Ceci gets over her temporary annoyance and continues shooting photos. Ceci goes to little Carlitos and speaks. He looks just like Jazmin and is only a year younger.

Ceci: Carlitos… te gusta arroz con pollo? Carlitos, do you like chicken and rice?

Carlitos: Si tia… tengo hambre. Yes Aunt, I am hungry.

Ceci: Ok… voy a servir tu comida. I am going to serve your lunch.

She goes inside and Karla follows her with Yarel.

Karla: Ceci, hay un oportunidad para comprar un parcel de tierra en Peru, sur la playa. Yarel puede construir una casita alla para nosotros, con Cynthia y Carlitos. Ceci, there is an opportunity to buy a piece of land in Peru, by the beach. Yarel can build a house there for us with Cynthia and Carlitos.

Ceci: Que Bueno… That's fabulous. Here it comes again… Just what I need - to provide for more of your babies.

Karla: Cuesta solamente seis mils lempiras. It only costs six thousand lempiras ($500.)

Ceci stops working and looks directly at Karla.

Ceci: Y quieres que yo lo compro. *She sits… disgusted.* And you want me to buy it.

Karla: Por favor Ceci, para Cynthia y Carlitos. Please Ceci… for Cynthia and Carlitos.

Ceci: *muttering…* **Shit… when does this end? OK OK Karla… Primero almuerzo.** *Ceci takes a deep breath knowing once again she is being blackmailed.* OK, but first we eat lunch.

Yarel: Cuando puedes ir a ver la tierra? Manana? Domingo… a que hora? When can we go see the land? Tomorrow? Sunday..what time?

Ceci: Esperen uds. por favor…. Vamos a comer ahora… Ayudame. Wait Karla, please. We are going to eat now. Help me.

They go outside with the paella and everybody sits around the big picnic table for lunch. Everyone seems to be having a good time, despite the strangeness of the situation.

At one point Karla disappears during the meal. Roxana goes to use the bathroom and sees Karla come out of the bedroom with a brown bag which she brings to the garbage zone on the street. We later find out that she has gone into the girls' bedroom to take their clothing, which she disguises as garbage. Then she returns in the evening to collect the bag, and she sells the clothes. But, the party continues. Ceci discovers this technique later with Vilma's help.

187. Checking out the property in PERU on the beach

Ceci is driving Karla and Yarel down the dirt road to the beach in Peru, just up the coast from La Ceiba. They come to the railroad before the beach, and Yarel directs Ceci to park. This railroad was originally used to transport bananas, sugar cane, and pineapples to the downtown seaport in days past. There are several rundown shacks along the tracks where workers and their families who loaded the produce on the trains, originally lived. Yarel leads the way down the row of shacks until they come to a small empty lot not far from the beach. Pop music is blaring from a radio. There, a young man, named Manuel, is waiting for them, chopping away the weeds with a machete. Yarel and Manuel shake hands and greet each other.

Yarel: Sra. Ceci, te presento Manuel. El es el dueno de esta tierra. Ceci, this is Manuel. He owns this land.

Ceci: Buenos dias Sr. Yo soy Cecilia Diaz… mucho gusto…. Y entonces… digame… exactamente cuanto tierra vende y para cuanto? Hello Sr. I am Cecilia Diaz. Pleasure to meet you. So tell me, exactly how much land and for how much?

Manuel: Mira Senora…te muestro. *Manuel walks off about 400 square feet in a rectangle.* **Seis mils lempiras.** *($500)* Look Sra. I will show you… Six thousand lempiras.

Karla: Por favor Ceci…

Ceci: Y donde esta la agua, la luz, basura? Escuela para los ninos? And where is the water, the electricity, the garbage… School for the kids?

Yarel: Hay tubleria y conexiones cerca por agua y luz. There are connections for water and electricity nearby.

Manuel: Basura, cada semana. Garbage every week.

Karla: Y hay escuela y autobus para La Ceiba. There is a school bus for school in La Ceiba.

Long silence, as Ceci wrestles in her heart and mind what to do. If this will get Karla off her back, and more independent, then maybe it is worth it…. for the sake of security for Cynthia and Carlitos also.

Ceci: Y los papeles… para el vento… recibos? And the papers for the sale and receipts?

Manuel: No se preocupas… Yo trabajo con Yarel…. Verdad amigo? Los tendra manana. Don't worry about that. I work with Yarel, right my friend. You will have them tomorrow.

Yarel: Si Ceci, El es buena gente…. Mi padre conoce su padre por muchos anos. Y yo puedo construir la casa. Yes Ceci, he is good people. My father knows his father for many years. And I can build the house.

Ceci: *Reluctantly Ceci agrees.***OK… pero, no puedo pagar para las materiales.** Allright, but I cannot pay for materials.

Yarel: No hay problema. Donde yo trabajo hay mucha madera en la basura… que van a regalarme. No problem. Where I work there is a lot of garbage wood, that they will give me.

Ceci: Me parece una buena oportunidad para uds. Y particularmente para Cynthia y Carlitos si tu promesas que les guardarian… verdad Karla? It seems like a good opportunity for you. And particularly for Cynthia and Carlitos, if you promise to take care of them. Right Karla?

Karla: Como no co-madre.

With great hesitation Ceci pulls out six thousand lempiras in cash, holding it as she speaks.

Ceci: Manuel y Yarel... Quiero un recibo manana. Estamos claro todos? Yarel I want a receipt tomorrow. Is that clear?

Manuel: Si Sra... le lo dare a Yarel manana en el trabajo. Yes Sra. I will give it to Yarel at work tomorrow.

Ceci: Entonces... Lo quiero manana en la tarde en mi mano. Then I want it tomorrow in my hand in the afternoon.

Yarel: Si Senora ... Gracias.

Ceci: Y cuando pueden empezar a construir una casa? And when can you begin to build a house?

Manuel: Empiezo manana si Dios quiere. I start tomorrow Godwilling.

Ceci: Toma Manuel...*She gives him the cash. They all shake hands.* Vamos, tengo que recoger las ninas de escuela y trabajar despues. Let's go. I have to pick up the girls from school and then go work.

They march back towards the truck past other shacks with shoeless children running around. There are young mothers with babies strapped to their backs while they hang clothing up to dry, fill water buckets at a nearby faucet, or tend their fogatas (fires). This would be the lifestyle on the old railroad line... Panning into the background we see the deserted Peru ocean beach covered with weather worn palm palapas. Peru is a hot, deserted, tropical, 3ʳᵈ world coastline.

188. The pool at the Quinta Real with Deni

From Peru to the La Ceiba beach, we cut to the Quinta Real hotel in the Zona Viva. Ceci enters the pool area with the girls in their school uniforms. It is a hot tropical day ... there is no power.... And Ceci is meeting Deni and her son, Ale, for lunch by the pool. The Quinta is the closest thing to a "first class" hotel in La Ceiba. And if you can buy lunch, you can swim in the pool and use the private beach. Deni is there already... reading her book, and Ale rushes over to hug the girls. Almost all the service people are Afro-Caribe, or Garifuna, which reflects the colonial working classifications still designed by the wealthy.

Deni: Buenas tardes Gringa!

Ceci: Hi Deni … *fanning herself*….Dios mio it must be 100 degrees in the shade. I'm sweating more than I sweat when I dance!! *She hands bathing suits to the girls.* Can you change by yourselves?

Angie: Yes Mom… *They leave to change in the ladies room.*

Ceci: So how are you? Do you have power at your house?

Deni: No… and no fan, no light, no internet, etc. I think this is the only place in town with a generator.

Ceci: Well, we can't sleep without the fan, and I guess all the food in the refrigerator will go bad, because I feel like this power outage will take a long time.

Deni: Evidently the tower by the airport fell down because somebody welded off copper for personal use, and the whole thing collapsed!

Ceci: For sure it will be days. I think I'll have a drink.

Deni: So how's the visa hunt going?

Ceci: I'm going again on Friday and I'm taking Karla. And I went through all the backbends with the Judge to get permission for the embassy petition and for Italy.

Deni: But why are you taking Karla?

Ceci: I figure if it's another medical visa application, and they know that the mom agrees and trusts me to return… then I think I stand a better chance.

Deni: I think you are wasting your money.

Ceci: Well, it's better than pretending that I gave birth to them Deni.

Deni: Ale is whiter than your girls… and he could be my kid.

Ceci: Yes, but the embassy still didn't go for it, and now they want DNA proof… What's wrong with this picture?

Deni: Come on Ceil, every case is different, and I just have to wait until those embassy agents finish out their twoyear employment in Honduras... and then try again.

Ale starts talking in a way that only Deni can understand.

Deni: The girls are changing.

Ceci: Here they come now.

They all come running and jump directly into the pool. Ale joins them and he is happy.

Ceci: How's Ale doing?

Deni: Well, I have a speech therapist for him now, and I am going to enroll him in a private kindergarten.

Ceci: Do you have any idea what his clinical diagnosis is?

Deni: I think maybe he's autistic.

Ceci: You think? And how does that affect his speech?

Deni: I don't know exactly, and I don't really trust any of these doctors or therapists. And none of them speak English. I will raise him and maybe someday he will become an engineer or something like that.

Ceci: He's lucky to have you, Deni. Which reminds me. I need to call Karla about Friday... Can you order a pina colada for me, horchatas and the tortillas and fajitas for the kids? Thanks Deni...... Excuse me.

Deni orders while Ceci calls Karla... on a split screen... Ceci is facing the ocean, and Karla answers her phone in her shack with Yarel ... She is counting Ceci's money.

189. <u>Split screen phone call between Ceci and Karla</u>

Ceci: Hola Karla. Como esta? Llamo para dos cosas. Tengo su boleto para Tegucigalpa con nosotros el viernes que viene. Hello Karla... How are you? I call for two things. I have your ticket for Tegucigalpa with us for next Friday.

Karla: Si Ceci, para la embajada. A que hora quiere recogerme? Yes Ceci… for the embassy. What time do you want to pick me up?

Karla gets out of bed and leaves the shack to sit on a milk crate by the front door to talk on the phone. She is still pregnant with Yarel's first child…. Lilliana. There are neighbors nearby walking back and forth along the small alley next to the tracks… lined with more shacks, outhouses, animals, the occasional rigged shower, marching vendors, women carrying their laundry. It's afternoon.

Ceci: Temprano a las 7 para un vuelo a las 8:30am… OK? Early at 7am for an 8:30 flight.

Karla: Bueno.

Ceci: Y Digame… Donde esta mi recibo? Que pasa con la tierra en Peru? Ya empezaron a construir su casita? AND, tell me. Where is my receipt? What happened with the land in Peru? Have you already started to build your house?

Karla: Ceci……. Como te digo? Manuel nos enganaron. Ceci… how do I say this? Manuel tricked us.

Ceci: What?

Karla: Manuel no fue el dueno de la tierra. Nos robo! Manuel wasn't the land owner. He robbed us.

Ceci: Como puede ser? Me dijo Yarel que eran amigos. How can that be? You told me that he and Yarel were friends.

Karla: Lo siento Ceci. I'm sorry Ceci.

Ceci: *stunned* **OK Karla, I'll bet you're sorry. So sorry that you tricked me again. My mistake for falling for it**

again... Te veo el Viernes. Ciao! I will see you Friday.

Ceci hangs up irritated.

Karla walks back into the shack with Yarel, as they chuckle at Ceci's naivete. Ceci returns to the pool with Deni, more than rattled.

(Photo is of Karla's home with future kids Lilliana and Isaac in their shack by the railroad.)

190. Back to the Pool Lunch with Deni

Deni: What happened?

Ceci: I bought a piece of land in Peru for Karla and Yarel, and the guy who took the money was a fake.

Deni: How much this time?

Ceci: Six thousand lempiras

Deni: That's $500!!!!

Ceci: I know...

Deni: Wake up girl! She got you again Ceil. Haven't you heard the expression? No tengas confianza en NADIE!!! Don't trust anybody.

Ceci: Yes I have heard it, and have not yet learned the lesson. I am beginning to see why the gap is so great between the rich and the poor. The only problem is... I'm not rich.

Deni: I think your interest in 3rd world culture has taken you down some dark streets Ceil.

Ceci: Nevertheless, I am taking Karla to the embassy with us on Friday, so wish us good luck.

Deni: Por fin te digo... She's blackmailing you and keeping the cash... but!! Good luck girl... Let's eat.

Ceci: I don't know what is worse... that she gets the money, or that she thinks she outsmarted me in a new and creative way.

Deni: They are both bad, and you better hope that her selfish desperation doesn't run in the girls' blood.

Lunch has been served and Ceci calls the kids to eat. And for the moment, regular life resumes despite a typical power outage.

191. 2nd **Trip to Embassy in Tegucigalpa – with Karla and the girls**

Cut to the long line that wraps around the block at the American Embassy in Tegucigalpa, Honduras. Ceci, Karla and the girls have arrived after the rickety plane to Teguc, and then a roundabout taxi ride. As precious as the girls look in Grandma's homemade dresses, they are already confused and tired. Karla is holding it together, dressed in her best jeans, a new T shirt and looking very pregnant. Ceci runs to buy baleadas from a local vendor. There are Honduran visa applicants lined up for blocks, of all classes and colors. After a good 90 minute crawl on the line, they approach the door, and are approached by a vendor whose service is to hold and protect your cell phone while you are in the embassy. Ceci and Karla give up their phones. At this point Ceci is worried they will miss their appointment. Karla is clearly a fish out of water. The girls are really confused when they have to remove their shoes and go through security… and be body searched. Ceci takes her 3 vouchers to the cashier window and again shelves out over a thousand dollars for the three application fees. Karlas eyes bulge when she sees all that cash.

> **Cashier:** I'm sorry lady, we don't make change. It has to be exactly $1550.

> **Ceci:** Oh… So it went up? Where can I get change in dollars?

> **Agent:** I don't know lady, we don't do it here. Next!

> **Ceci:** *Muttering to herself as she walks away.* If this is the way they treat Americans here at my American Embassy, I can't imagine how they treat Hondurans.

Ceci goes into the main hall to seat Karla and the girls. There are rows and rows of applicants, shifting their way from chair to chair up to the front. Ceci stands in front of the crowd and yells.

> **Ceci:** **Disculpa! Hay alguien aqui que tiene cambio por cien dolares?** Excuse me… Is there someone here who has change for a hundred dollars?

A middle aged Honduran gentleman raises his hand and pulls out his wallet. They make the exchange and Ceci thanks him. The girls stand on their chairs trying to keep an eye on Ceci while she runs back to the cashier with the right change. They don't feel safe alone with Karla.

When she returns, the girls fight over Ceci's lap as they continue inching their way up the line to the interview. Ceci reviews her papers over and over again: the three applications with photos, the father's death certificate; the permission from the judge to travel, the foster paper custody paper, the statement from Karla, the birth certificates, the employment letter from the school, her birth certificate and passport, Karla's cedula number...

They watch people leave the interview booths either ecstatically happy, or miserably traumatized – It is very black and white... either you get the visa or you don't. So much time, energy, money and hope will go into every application for an American visa... and the privilege to cross the border into the United States. Thousands of Hondurans pray for this as their only hope for survival.

Finally, their number is called and they are ushered up to a glass window with the girls barely able to touch the ledge. Ceci will plead their case for another medical visa for the girls, with the consent of their blood mother to vouch for their illnesses and disabilities. Ironically it is the same 30-something American agent she spoke with 3 weeks ago.

Ceci: Good morning. *Handing him papers.*

Agent: Yes Ms. Diaz. Weren't you here recently for medical visas for three little sisters?

Ceci:: Yes I was, and I'm back, because I have brought along their blood mother, Karla Rojas, who understands the nature of their illnesses. I am going to visit my Mom and look into the girls' medical issues while there. Hence, once again, I am appealing the former rejection with another application.

Agent: OK OK Ms. Diaz... *addressing Karla*....Sra. Rojas, ud. es la madre de estas ninas?

Karla. Si.

Agent: *Looking down through the glass at the girls.* Roxana, Angie, and Angela? *They raise their hands when he calls their names.* That Angie looks just like you.

Karla: Si Senor.

Agent: **Y tiene acuerdo con la custodia de la Sra. Diaz, y sus intenciones?** And you agree with the custody that Sra Diaz has and her intentions?

Karla: **Si Senor... Yo tengo confianza que ella vuelva.** Yes Sr. I have confidence that she will return.

Agent: **Bueno... momento.**

The agent goes to a back office behind the glass. Ceci and Karla stand there motionless... The girls cling to Ceci. In what seems like forever, the agent returns asking them to sit.

Agent: **Please wait over there in the back. We have to review your case further.**

Ceci: **We have a 2:30pm flight back to La Ceiba. How long will this be?**

Agent: **As long as it takes.**

Angie: **Americans aren't very friendly Mommy.**

Ceci, Karla and the girls retire towards the back of the hall and wait, and wait. Ceci watches the clock tick way past the hour of the flight to Ceiba. Karla is asleep. Ceci and the girls continue to watch applicants laugh, cry, or kick chairs as they leave the interview booths. Ceci stares into the great hall where the last person has been waited on. They finally call the names of the girls, and once again they all enter the cubicle.

Agent: **Hello Ms. Diaz. I'm very sorry, again, to tell you that we can't grant visas to these kids with or without the permission of the mother. And with all due respect, the IHNFA still has jurisdiction over these children. The mother has no power.**

Ceci: **But I have permission from the Children's Judge in Ceiba to travel with them.**

Agent: I am sorry Mam, but your custody is not formal enough, and you still fit the profile of American women who come to Honduras as missionaries, fall in love with the orphans, and then take them away and never come back.

Ceci: I have a job and a home here.

Agent: You don't have your residency I see.

Ceci: I'll get it!! *She is becoming very agitated.*

Agent: Frankly mam, the only way to get these children visas is to adopt them. And here is their living Mom, which makes the whole thing impossible as they must be declared abandoned. *He looks at her like she is crazy for not understanding.* I am sorry. We have to close now mam.

He shuts the blinds. Ceci turns around, her face red, the tears gushing out… making it impossible for her to walk. The girls support her to the chair. They are the only ones left in the hall. The same police lady comes to escort Ceci out to the street again.

Police Lady: Don't give up. Eventually they will give it to you, si Dios quiere.

Angie: Mom it's OK, we'll try again.

Roxana: No lloras Mama. Don't cry Mama.

Jazmin hugs her and the girls will not let go as the guard ushers them out. It is raining outside, After collecting their phones, Ceci flags a cab, and they all go to the airport.

192. **Inside the Cab to the Airport with rejection**

Taxista: A donde van…? Where are you going?

Ceci: Al aeropuerto… To the airport.

Taxista: Y donde viajan con estas princessas? And where are you going with these princesses?

Ceci: La Ceiba.

Taxista: Pero no hay vuelos para Ceiba hasta las 10pm…. Y en la noche hay que ir a San Pedro primero. But there are no flights to Ceiba until 10 pm. And in the night you must go to San Pedro first.

Ceci: Shit... I must be cursed!

Karla: A que hora llegaremos Ceci? What time will we arrive?

Ceci: Llegaremos despues media noche... Disculpa. We will arrive in Ceiba after midnight. I am sorry.

Karla: Mas pistos Ceci. More money Ceci.

Ceci: Karla.... You just ripped me off for 6000 lempiras. Give me a break!!! *She turns her back on Karla.* **Ninas... Podemos comer MacDonalds en el aeropuerto OK?** Yes Karla. Girls we can eat at the MacDonalds in the airport OK?

The girls: YEAH!!!!!!!!!!!!!! *Thank God for kids and their resiliency.*

193. <u>**Dawn arrival at home – phone call to Mom**</u>

Due to travel circumstances beyond all control, Ceci and the girls arrive at their front door at dawn and stumble to their beds. Ceci's Mom has been calling... She answers the house phone.

Ceci: Hi Mom....

Grandma: Oh thank God... I've been worried sick about you, and haven't heard a word.

Ceci: We're OK... Just walked in the door... and I am sorry about the phone... there was no service for some reason.

Grandma: So what happened?

Ceci: Oh Mom... *Beginning to cry, she goes out to the porch.* **This is going to be so hard. Every road I take has a dead end.**

Grandma: I'm so sorry Ceil, I know how hard this is. My parents, your abuelos, went through hell to immigrate from Spain and become American citizens.

Ceci: Well I just don't feel like I fit in anywhere Mom. Everything I do is not normal. Don't make enough money, don't have a husband, and I am too old to bring my three kids back to my own country. I just don't want to die in Honduras.

Grandma: OK OK calm down... So what happened?

Ceci: Same old song… Adoption is the only way… and wouldn't you know that the government adoption agency is presently shut down because of corruption. Plus, I'm also too old to adopt. They don't want to take the chance that I would stay in the US without adopting them. I am going to see a lawyer who can maybe help me with Legal guardianship…. And maybe the embassy will go for that.

Grandma: Don't give up. Don't ever give up. I want to see you again, and I want you to come back. You know, I am going to contact Mark Warner, the governor of Virginia, and maybe Tim Kaine.. who is a senator. I'll write to him today. And I have talked to some people at the Dept. of the Blind in Richmond.

Ceci: I wanna come back too Mom… I want to take care of you. You've been really good to me, and I need you too.

Grandma: It may take many tries… but don't give up. I think you should go for the Guardianship and a residential visa. Just work towards that. That's the best direction right now.

Ceci: OK Ma…Thanks…. I will never give up because I want my girls to have *you* as their grandma. I am so exhausted, and I love you. I'll call you over the weekend.

Grandma: Yes I understand. Give my love to the girls… Will Roxana wear her Kinder Graduation dress?

Ceci: Oh yes I forgot. She is thrilled about it. It is beautiful and Roxana loves it. I'll send you photos. I love you Mom… Bye.

Ceci goes into the bedroom and finds the girls asleep on the bed in their clothing and shoes. She goes to kiss each one goodnight, taking off their shoes and tucking them in.

Ceci: I swear…. We will move to Virginia one day. All of us… together. You guys give me the strength to keep trying. There are no other options. Grandma is waiting for us. We don't give up in my family. I love you all. Goodnight.

194. **Preparing for Roxana's Graduation – at home**

The girls are in the living room finding Grandma's box with Roxana's graduation dress and accessories. Vilma arrives.

Vilma: Hola muchachas! *They rush to hug her.*

Ceci: Hola Vilma… me alegre que estas aqui. Hi Vilma… I am so happy that you are here.

Vilma: Es la graduacion de Roxana… nunca faltaria un evento tan importante. It's Roxana's graduation. I would never miss such an important event.

Roxana: Mira Tia, tengo el vestido, la diadema, calcetines, zapatitos, guantes, collar, aretes… TODO!! Look Tia. I have the fluffy dress, the headband, the socks, the shoes, the gloves, the necklace, the earrings… everything!!

Vilma: El vestido es bien bonito… tu abuelita es una buena costurera. The dress is beautiful. Your grandmother is a good seamstress.

Jazmin: Si, y vamos a llevar los vestidos de Angie y yo cuando temenos nuestra graduacion. Yes, and we will wear our dresses for me and Angie when we have our graduations.

Ceci: Si… el ano que viene uds. van a graduar con sus vestidos. Yes next year you both will graduate with your dresses.

Vilma: Entonces, vamos a peinarte Roxana para que tu eres bella. So, let's fix Roxana's hair so you are beautiful.

Ceci: Vamos a vestirnos ninas porque la graduacion es a la una and I want us to look gooood. Ok let's all get dressed because graduation is at 1pm, and I want us to look gooood.

195. **Phone call from Karla – Birth of Lilliana**

Amidst all of this chaos the phone rings and it is Karla announcing to Ceci that Lilliana was just born in the Hospital Atlantida.

Ceci: Karla… no puedo venir ahora. Como se fue? Baron o embra esta vez? Liliana?… que nombre bonito, como la madre de Yarel. Mira… Vamos ahora a la graduacion de Roxana. No puedo hoy. Please get some birth control woman. Vengo otro dia… Buena suerte, Ciao. Karla… I can't come now. How did it go? Boy or girl this time? Lilliana… what a pretty name, after Yarel's mother. Look.. we are going now to Roxana's graduation. I can't now. Please get some birth control woman. I will come another day. Good luck, Ciao.

New baby Lilliana

Vilma: Que paso Ceci? What happened Ceci?

Ceci: Otra nina… Lilliana… con el nuevo novio Yarel. She's a baby maker. Another baby girl, Lilliana. With her new boyfriend, Yarel. She's a baby maker.

We will eventually go to see her new baby.

196. Roxana's Kinder Graduation at the Quinta Motel

Graduation from Kindergarten in Honduras is a big family affair… almost like a **wedding or a baptism. Most people in the lower classes don't make it past 5th grade in the public school system. So Kinder graduation is highly celebrated amongst all Hondurans who can afford the private school tuition, with the fluffy white dresses and the shirts and ties to encourage future education and graduations.**

The ceremony is being held in a ballroom of a motel in El Sauce. Vilma has fixed Roxana's hair, and she looks like a princess in her white eyelet dress with blue accents and accessories. Ceci, Vilma, Angie and Jazmin sit in the audience watching the ritual with fascination and respect. All the children are formally dressed, as they march with great pomp and circumstance down the isle to their places on the teeny motel stage. They sing three English songs and then their teacher calls them individually to receive their diplomas. Roxana follows all her cues with her precious smile, except for her inability to learn lyrics and sing along with her classmates. We later discover that she can sing in Spanish but not English, and this issue goes well into her teens.
There is a psychologist parent sitting next to Ceci in the audience. Ceci chats with her about Roxana.

Jazmin: Mommy why doesn't Roxana sing?

411

Ceci: Honey, you know she has problems talking and understanding both Spanish and English... It will take time.

Lady (Psychologist): You know, I have patients with the same problem. Some children have great difficulty with two languages, switching over. Sometimes it is dyslexia, and other times it is just neurological panic. Take my card if you wish... I am a psychologist and I can do an evaluation for you.

Ceci: Thank you so much... I am really concerned about Roxana. She had some pretty rough prenatal damage, as well as early malnutrition and meningitis as a baby.

Lady: She will probably need a small bi-lingual elementary school...

Ceci: Her teacher has suggested the Episcopal.

Lady: That's because they are affiliated there. You can try it, but I suggest Bright Beginnings, where my older son goes. It is also bi-lingual.

Ceci: Thank you so much... I will be in touch with you.

All the children regroup for a final song after receiving their diplomas. And the photos begin. Ceci's phone rings. It is Doctor Harris. Vilma takes the camera.

197. **Phone call with Dr. Harris**

Ceci: Hello Doctor!! How nice to hear from you... where are you?

Doctor Harris: Here in Italy thinking about you guys... How is it going?

Ceci: As a matter of fact we are just finishing Roxana's Kindergarten Graduation ceremony, and she is all dressed in a fluffy white dress with all the accoutrement.

Doctor: Please tell her that I am very proud of her, and wish I could be there.

Ceci: I will, and she will love knowing that you care.

Dr. So what happened with the last visa attempt.

Ceci: Another rejection... not formal enough custody to qualify.

Dr: Why don't you look into legal guardianship?

Ceci: I have the name of a lawyer, who may be able to arrange all that who is highly recommended. I have been to so many already, I am dizzy with legal promises that never pan out.

Dr: And what about coming to visit in Italy? Do you think that would be possible?

Ceci: I am definitely working on it. So why are you in Italy?

Dr.: I bought a villa near Venice and I want to see the girls.

Ceci: You're really serious about this. Well that would indeed be exciting Doctor Louis...except for the fact that we would probably have to make connections in several different countries because we can't go through Miami without American visas.

Dr. So?

Ceci: You are right... it will be inconvenient, but absolutely thrilling for sure.

Dr: Go ahead and book it for June when they get out of school, and I'll pay for it.

Ceci: Wow... Louis... my jaw is dropping again... It's always been my dream to see Italy.

The girls come rushing over to her...

Roxana: Mommy vamos a sacar photos con mi profesora.
Mommy.. let's take pictures with my teacher.

Ceci: I have to go, the girls want to take pictures... Can we talk later?

Dr: Yes of course... give them my love... and make the reservations.

Ceci: Ok Louis... thanks for calling... Bye. *She hangs up confused but excited.* He's doing this for the girls. What a prince.

198. Conversation with Kinder teacher and Roxana

Roxana drags her teacher over to Ceci. They shake hands.

Ceci: Senora, I want to thank you for all your patience with Roxana. I know you are aware of her learning disabilities.

Teacher: Roxana is a lovely girl.

Ceci: Where do you think I should send her for first grade?

Teacher: With her disability I am not sure how good a bi-lingual school will accept her. She definitely struggles in both languages, and I believe she will think in Spanish for a long time.

Ceci: Part of it is that she has been traumatized from being removed from her family at an early age, then the SOS.... And along with malnutrition and meningitis, I believe all this change has created her comprehension and speech delay. She really didn't start talking until she was five. However ... She dances with me and does a fabulous job... other than her occasional left and right issues with dyslexia.

Teacher: I see that Roxana really needed nursery and pre-kinder.

Ceci: She did have some kind of Kinder in the SOS, but all they did was write Xs and Os on lined paper all day.

Teacher: We suggest the Episcopal, as it does not require entrance exams, and is still a private, bi-lingual school.

Ceci: I had hoped for CBS (La Ceiba Bi-lingual School), as I know she would never qualify for the Mazapan School where I work.

Teacher: She will have to pass an entrance exam at CBS too. You can try that and if they say no, I can help you get her into the Episcopal in September.

Ceci: I can see this will be a difficult educational journey for her anywhere in Honduras, because there is no Special Education program which addresses her delayed processing disability. I don't know why. So many of kids really need it.

Teacher: I know... I wish I could do more. But, I can tell you that Jazmin is quite exceptional. And Angie will be OK... even with her vision problem.

Ceci: Thank you so much for everything you are doing for my precious babies.

After much patience, Roxana proudly interrupts and takes her teacher's arm with a big smile.

Roxana: Mommy... un photo por favor.

Ceci: Con gusto!

She takes pictures of Roxana and her teacher. Angie and Jazmin want pictures too.

Angie/Jazmin: Me too Mommy.

Ceci: OK... of course. You are making me proud girls. *They have a short photo session with the teachers. Ceci thanks everybody* Now we have to go home and get ready for the Mother's Day show tomorrow night. I don't know how people work and have kids. But we do appreciate everything you are doing for my beautiful bambinas.

Teacher: The pleasure is mine. They make a big effort to do the right thing and I will try to help them as much as possible.

Ceci takes hands and walks away thinking out loud.

Ceci: Despite their disabilities, we will survive and thrive!

199. **Mother's Day Show – Mazapan**

The buzz at the outdoor theater on the Mazapan School cancha (outdoor court) is huge as parents, grandparents, and extended families arrive in their Sunday best for a Mother's Day tribute on the 2nd biggest holiday of the year in Honduras.... Dia de la Madre. Ceci has convinced the school to buy lights and a roof for the outdoor stage, and the entire arena is decorated with flowers and drapes. There is a huge, hand painted backdrop on the stage of a huge daffodil with "Feliz Dia de la Madre" script. Beginning with the Pre-Kinder and working the numbers all the way up through the senior class, interspersed with band, choral, and special choreographies... the show grips the spirit of the audience with tears, laughter, and admiration for their children's Mother's day gift performances.

"Alma" – Mayo, 2010

1.   Labyrinth of Acrobatics – Bambinas

2.   Primavera Ballet – Intermedios II

3.   The Big Bang Theory – Intermedios

4.   Munecas – Principios

5.   Immigrant Salsa – Avancadas - Mothers and daughters have arrived from some European country with suitcases and shawls over their heads. The music has an epic, Godfather quality. They move in a painful style waiting on the immigration line. As each family is processed, they leave the group and perform a repetitive dance of question and answer with the immigration officer. The agent rings a bell with each immigrant who crosses the line. When the last family crosses the line, the music changes to a Santana Salsa classic, "Candelito", and the immigrants return in gypsy skirts with American T shirts and flags to dance in celebration.

6.   Fresita Rosita/Polka – Bambinas

7.   Where is Love? – Intermedios II

8.   Jumpin – (Jump rope) Intermedios

9. **Blame it on the Boogie – Principios**

10. **Mariposas – Bambinas**

11. **Let's Dance – Intermedios II**

12. **Yolele – Avancadas**

13. **Suenos – Principios**

14. **Ballet de la Bella Dormiente – Intermedios II**

Roxana

** Sound track is a collage of different pieces of music which takes us through the various movements of the Sleeping Beauty ballet.

The ballet begins with a dirge like hymn that provides the processional journey beat as the pregnant Queen and King go to their summer home in the wilderness to pray for the safe birth of a special child. The north star guides them to a grotto where animals gather around a small cottage. There they perform a royal ceremonial duet.

As they retire for the evening, the wind picks up as does the music. A flurry of white angels circles the stage in front of the cottage and dances a fertility ritual. Comes the early morning and the Queen and King emerge proudly with their new born daughter, whom they hold up to the eastern sun and the fading north star. They place her in a golden cradle in front of the grotto. Suddenly there is a great transformation in atmosphere marked by music and lights and scenery change.

There is a grand ball at the castle of the King and Queen. They are celebrating the birth of their first born, Princess Aurora. The first dance is a minuet in which couples dance and create an isle down which the King and Queen march with their newborn daughter, and place her in a royal cradle. The guests pay their respects including a young boy, who is a royal prince. Then six fairies arrive and one by one present their symbolic gifts to Princess Aurora: Beauty – rose; Intelligence – book; Artistic talent – paint brush; love – a heart necklace; health – a golden apple; leadership – a crown.

Suddenly a cold wind blows through the ballroom and a witch-like fairy arrives. She is angry because she wasn't invited to the ball and she casts a sleep spell upon everyone at the party, including Aurora. Darkness falls as she recites/dances her curse. They see their beautiful daughter Aurora, grown to womanhood, motionless on a sacred altar. They are alarmed.

Then... out of nowhere comes Comizahual, the flying tiger, as the 7th fairy who has yet to bestow her gift of protection on the child. Comizahual has a dance off-duet with the bad fairy in which she banishes her from the kingdom. Then she makes the final blessing using a magical crystal on the baby Aurora's forehead. Magically, Aurora turns into a beautiful mature young lady. As everybody wakes up we see that they have aged, including the King and Queen. But then Comizahual and the fairies do a special circle dance which calls for the Prince who was the young boy who attended her baptism years ago.

The prince arrives, now a young man, sees Aurora.... bestows the magical kiss, she awakens, they dance, and the company dances. All celebrate, happily ever after....

As Ceci watches this performance on stage, her consciousness shifts to a dream state in the Ciudad Blanca where she re-imagines the Sleeping Beauty Ballet with a Mayan filter.

200. Flash Transition from dance concert to Ciudad Blanca – Sleeping Beauty/Comizahual

The scene is suddenly re created in Ceci's imagination at the grand plaza in the Cuidad Blanca in which the infant Mayan princess (played by Jazmin) is being baptized by the great Ancestors of Central America. The same fairies are transferred to this mystical flashback, surrounded by ancient ruins and all the great Caciques and Mayan priests.

Comizuhual, as the one remaining golden fairy, steps up and banishes the evil fairy from the floor with her dance and then ritualistically attempts to reverse the choreographed movements of the dark fairy to cancel the curse. This is a dramatic, non-verbal moment, which evaporates the dark fairy with the same choreography that was danced upon the arrival of Comizahual on the Mazapan stage. Comizahual bestows her gift of protection in the form of a star wand with 7 points. There is an air of caring and remorse in her performance, because she knows she cannot completely destroy the curse.

Nevertheless, the rejoicing of the elders for the safety and protection of the Mayan princess is great, and the spirit is heightened by new music. A great celebration of fertility that presents all the fairies dancing together is followed by a company of angels who begin to dance on the ancient steps of the white shining pyramids of the courtyard in the Ciudad Blanca.

Ceci then returns to Mazapan school stage as they all take bows at the end of the show... This has been a surreal moment for Ceci, as her visionary contact with the Ciudad Blanca had subsided, and remained an artistic memory, since having custody of the children.

She regains composure and graciously takes pictures with students and their parents, etc. Angie, Jazmin and Roxana are nearby always.

Jazmin & Angie – Proud curtain call

Madre Luna – Concierto de Danza – 13 Mayo 2011

**Note… the following program was a different Spring concert.

In this concert we integrated Father's and Mother's Day along with spring.

1. Daddy's Little Girls – Avancadas

2. Las Vaqueras (Cowgirls) – Bambinas

3. Tea Party – Beginners

4. Father's Wings – Intermedios

5. Body Rock – Avancadas

6. The Mommy Dance – Bambinas and Mothers

Mothers dance with their children in this dance, using a chair and many lifts. The music shifts several times to signal changes in mood and choreography. This is a favorite which the audience loves.

7. River Lullaby – Beginners

8. Single Ladies Hoola hooping – Intermedios & Avancadas

9. Rapunzel – Bambinas

10. Mambo – Beginners

11. Malaguena – Intermedios

12. Forest Fairy Ballet – Avancadas + Todos *A family goes camping in the woods near a stream. The number opens with the sounds of nature, water running, birds singing, wind blowing through trees. A Mom and Dad with two daughters arrive to camp. They set up a tent and the kids are sent out to look for firewood. As they wander through the forest picking up wood, the kids encounter the spirits of the forest who are only visible to children.*

First, they meet the GNOMES, the earth fairies, who appear to the girls as they collect wood. They are little dancers (Bambinas) who are dressed in shorts, big boots, and funny hats. They ring around the rosie with the 2 sisters to an earthy march with a heavy brass melody. This parade brings them to the stream where the girls decide to drink. The music shifts to a smooth, undulating melody which draws out the UNDINES (Beginners) who are the water fairies. *They lure the sisters into the stream with a modern, fluid swimming dance.*

As the wind picks up in the soundtrack, the air fairies, SYLPHIDES (Intermedios), arrive and blow the girls out of the water. They dance together. Eventually the girls get tired and remember to return to camp with the wood. The fairies lead them back to the campsite where the parents are trying to start a fire.

The Sylphides disappear and fly away. The sisters wave goodbye to them, but the parents are unable to see who they are waving to. The girls help their Dad to build the fires and the music changes to a rousing rapid beat with violins. This brings out the SALAMANDERS (Avancadas), or the Fire fairies who madly dance around fanning the fire with their turns and jumps. The sisters join the circle and become ecstatic as the rest of the fairy kingdom returns for a dramatic forest fiesta finale.

The parents feel the energy generated by the company of fairies, but can only see their daughters dancing wildly around the fire. They sit on their lawn chairs and enjoy the performance with their campfire drinks, while the audience sees the entire company of fairy dancers perform a rousing FINALE to the Forest Fairy Ballet.

Here is one of many photos of Ceci and the girls after a show.

201. Merlyn Vasquez – Lawyer's office – Tutora Custody

Ceci arrives with the girls at a small, second floor office not far from the center of La Ceiba. The girls are dressed up in lookalike clothes with their hair neatly combed in braids. When they get in the office the secretary tells them to wait for Merlyn. Ceci begins to organize her papers on the table in the lobby... stacks of files on each girl. The girls color pictures with crayons. Merlyn walks in... tall, young, thin and handsome... He is charming, yet very business-like. He shows her into the office after meeting the girls and asking that they wait in the lobby.

Ceci: Well, Mr. Merlyn... you come highly recommended by several people.

Merlyn: So I hear... I've been waiting for you to appear. Even my mother knows about your case. This is a small town. And your girls are beautiful...

Ceci: This is the first time in my life that I have ever seen so many lawyers, so I hope that you are the last lawyer I will need.

Merlyn: Ok Gringa. Plead your case. *Ceci goes into her speeded up paper presentation with birth certificates, pictures, medical documents, etc.*

Merlyn: You are too old to adopt I take it?

Ceci: Yes I am 52, but I was 50 when I met them. I also have the consent from their mother to care for them, although she wants me to stay in the country so she can continue extorting me for cash.

Merlyn: There is something we call "Tutora" in Honduras, which is like legal guardianship. This usually pertains to a family member, when the parents cannot care for the kids. They will also have to be declared abandoned to do this.

Ceci: Do you want to meet their Mom? I have all the papers of her consent.

Merlyn: She really has no power if the IHNFA took them away from her and placed them in the orphanage. But those consent papers will definitely help.

Ceci: And here is the death certificate of the father.

Merlyn: This is all good... You have really done some work... We will also require the back up of a Honduran custodian called a "Pro-tutora."

Ceci: And you know that the judge gave me the foster parent custody because I baptized them as their God mother at the SOS. Here is the photo and document.

Merlyn: Well that definitely gives you the family connection. But we still will need a Pro-tutora.

Ceci: OK... my trabajadora, Vilma might do it.

Merlyn: OK. The process is basically the same as adoption: background criminal checks here and in the USA; records of your financial status; recommendations from witnesses; a home visit; medical information, their school report cards, etc.

Ceci: OK. I can do all that. How long do you think it will take?

Merlyn: We are in Honduras Cecilia. Things go slowly here. Maybe two years?

Ceci: OK... I am overwhelmed with delays most of the time, but I will go with your plan.

Merlyn: You will have to be patient. The good news is that my mother is the Juez de la Ninez.

Ceci: What does that mean?

Merlyn: The children's judge.... It means I can make this happen, with her help.

Ceci: Do you think that Tutora status will get them visas?

Merlyn: As far as I know, it hasn't been done with all the present limitations of the IHNFA. Usually, formal adoption is required for residency visas. And with the corruption and closing of the IHNFA at the moment, it will not be easy. But my Mother will understand your situation and will definitely help.

Ceci: Merlyn... nobody on the planet will ever be able to advance the health, education, safety and welfare of these girls more than I can.

Merlyn: I can see that, and I will do everything in my power to make it happen. Your girls are beautiful and they deserve a mom like you. Leave me all these papers and I will get started on this right away and call you.

She gets up to leave and they go into the lobby where the girls are.

Ceci: Thank you Merlyn ... I hope your name precedes and follows you as the magician we really need.

Merlyn: Si Dios quiere Senora. Adios muchachas... preciosas.

They hug him... because they hug everybody.

Angie: Mommy is this the man who makes the visas?

Ceci: No, but he is the man who will make me your mother by the law, so help me God.

202. Roxana – First Grade Testing at La Ceiba Bi-Lingual School

It is June and Bi-lingual schools are out in La Ceiba. Ceci brings Roxana for first grade testing at CBS, La Ceiba Bi-lingual School. Bi-lingual schools are businesses in La Ceiba where educated, but unlicensed teachers, who speak English, are working. They use dated American textbooks, with basic teaching techniques, and do eventually teach many children to speak English. CBS is a private indoor/outdoor cement brick complex of buildings. It is a private school, but there is no special ed training there, and many kids drop out from educational frustration and family financial limitations.

Roxana is taken to a first grade classroom where she will be tested with other kindergarten graduates. Ceci waits outside nervously pacing, knowing that Roxana has no idea what is happening to her. Inside the classroom, Roxana is looking around, unable to focus on the test. She goes up to the teacher and asks for help.

Teacher: Sit down Roxana.

Rox: **Pero no entiendo nada!** But I don't understand anything!

Teacher: **I said sit down Roxana.**

Roxana goes back to her seat and starts to cry. The other kids laugh at her.

Roxana: **Quiero mi madre Ceci.** I want my mother Ceci.

Teacher: *Realizing that the situation is hopeless.* **Ok, venga aqui Roxana.**

She gives Roxana crayons and paper to color with. Roxana is so glad to have some show of compassion that she goes to sit on the teacher's lap.

Ceci looks in the door window and sees this, closing her eyes to blink back the tears. The teacher comes out with Roxana.

Teacher: **I am sorry Sra. But Roxana is not able to do this work and definitely will not qualify for first grade at CBS. I suggest the Episcopal School.**

Ceci: **Thank you Gracias.** *Ceci takes Roxana's hand.*

Roxana: **A donde me voy a escuela Mommy?** Where will I go to school Mommy?

Ceci: **Vamos a la Escuela Episcopal en Septiembre OK?** We will go to the Escuela Episcopal in September. **I love you baby.** *She kisses her and they leave.* **And guess where we are going right now?**

Roxana: **Donde?**

Ceci: **A comer pescado con Vilma y sus hermana en la playa...a Guity's!!** To eat fish with Vilma and her sister on the beach at Guity's!

Roxana: **Yeah!!!!**

203. <u>**Guity's Seaside Seafood Restaurant – Conversations with Vilma**</u>

Cut to Ceci, the girls, and Vilma walking the La Ceiba beach towards Guity's Seafood Restaurant... a favorite hangout for the family with Chef Guity. He greets them as they enter. Guity is a

Garifuna cook trained on the cruise ships, who has perfected Caribbean cuisine, with locally caught seafood, rice and beans, yucca, corn and homemade guiffity. It is an open air palapa, right on the water's edge, with typical music and all the atmosphere of a Friday night paradise at dusk, with the sun setting over the ocean to the west. Families, couples and Honduran tourists all migrate down to Guity's Palapa. A group of musicians serenade a couple in the corner. The girls like to run around with Guity's kids, while his sister and wife cook in the kitchen. Roxana goes from table to table, checking out everybody's dinner, and making friends with her beautiful smile. She still thinks she is in the orphanage and that the world is one big happy family. Ceci orders fried fish for everybody and enjoys her beer with Vilma, as they watch the beautiful, tropical sunset.

Ceci: Que bonita la noche Vilma. Me alegre que no hay escuela ni trabajo manana. What a beautiful night Vilma. I am happy that there is no school tomorrow.

Vilma: Yo tambien estoy cansada. Pero manana hay que lavar ropa en el rio. I am also tired. But tomorrow I have to wash clothes in the river.

Ceci: Yo le dije que se puede usar mi lavadora Vilma. Digame como esta la nueva casa? I told you that you can use my washing machine. Tell me how the new house is.

Vilma: Poco a poco la areglamos. Little by little we are arranging it.

Ceci: Y tu mama? And your mother?

Vilma: Ella todavia falta la otra casa... pero dormimos tranquila en la noche, porque no hay mareros alla. She still misses the other house, but we sleep at night because there are no gangs there.

Ceci: Siempre se puede dormir en mi casa Vilma.... siempre mi casa esta disponible si hay una emergencia. Actualmente, me gustaria saber si se puede cuidar la casa este verano cuando vamos en vacacion. You can always sleep in my house Vilma. My house is always available if there is an emergency. Actually, I would like to know if you can take care of the house this summer when we go on vacation.

Vilma: Y donde van Ceci? And where are you going?

Ceci: Recuerdas el Doctor Gringo que me ayudo con las ninas au principio? Remember the Doctor Gringo who helped me with the girls in the beginning?

Vilma: Si – el missionario en el Hospital Atlantida.... que tambien coquetio contigo? Yes, the missionary in the Hospital Atlantida… who also flirted with you?

Ceci: Si... pues... El nos invito a Italia este verano, y quiero saber si tu puedes cuidar la casa para dos semanas. Yes.. He invited us to Italy this summer, and I want to know if you can take care of the house for two weeks.

Vilma: Sola? Alone?

Ceci: Con Sayda si quieres... con tu mama... como tu quieres.... No hay otra persona en Honduras con quien tengo confianza. Nos vamos la semana que viene. With Sayda if she wants… with your mother… however you want. There is no other person in Honduras whom I trust. And we leave next week.

Vilma: Ok Ceci....

Guity's wife comes to the table to take the order with big smiles despite the sweat pouring off her face from working in the kitchen. Guity's kids are running around with the girls.

Ceci: Hola Sra Guity... como estas?

Guity's wife: Me alegre que tenemos negocios... estoy cansada cocinar, pero feliz a verte y sus bellas ninas. Como podemos servirles hoy? I am happy that we have a business, tired of cooking, but happy to see you and your pretty girls. How can we serve you today?

Ceci: Bueno, quereriamos 4 platos de pescado frito con limonadas. Great... we would like 4 plates of fried fish with lemonades.

Guity's wife: A tu orden Sra., con cerveza si tu quiere?. At your service Sra. , with beer if you want it?

Ceci: Si, por favor, y sus hijos son guapos. Yes please, and your boys are beautiful.

Guity's wife: Gracias Senora!

She returns to the kitchen with a big smile, and Ceci takes a moment to stare at the sunset.

Ceci: Bueno.... y tambien hay otra cosa, mas importante... y solamente tu puedes ayudarme con eso. And also there is something else, more important, and only you can help me with this.

Vilma: Digame Ceci.

Ceci: Fui a consultar otro abogado sobre la custodia de las ninas, y el me hablo de un opción que se llama "Tutora" que es como guardia legal. I went to consult another lawyer about the custody of the kids, and he told me about an option called "Tutora" which is like a legal guardian.

Vilma: Si, mi madre lo hizo para dos muchachos. Yes, my mother did it for two boys.

Ceci: Y como yo soy gringa, la ley dice que necesito una "Protutora" Hondurena para legalizar la transaction de custodia. Y tu sabes, otra vez, que no hay otra persona que conoce las ninas como tu. And as I am a gringa, the law says that I need a Honduran "pro-tutora" backup to legalize the custodial transaction. And you know, again… that there is no other person who knows the girls like you do.

Vilma: Como co-madre?

Ceci: Pues ... Como todo lo que ya estas – hermana, tia, co-madre!! Like everything that you already are to them – sister, aunt, co mother…

The girls continue to bounce around the restaurant, checking in with Ceci and Vilma periodically as they laugh and play. Roxana continues to visit every table of customers in the place.

Vilma: Para siempre? Forever?

Ceci: Si Dios quiere!

Vilma: OK Ceci... *They clink glasses.*

Ceci: Great!! **Hay que firmar con el abogado y un monton de otras cosas, estoy seguro.** We must sign with the lawyer and a lot of other things… I am sure.

Vilma: **Si Ceci... Tu sabes que amo estas ninas, y hare lo que puedo para ellas.** Yes Ceci, you know that I love the girls, and I will do anything I can to help them.

Ceci: **Bueno, gracias Vilma... el camino legal es largo, y no es seguro.** Thanks Vilma, the legal road is long and insecure.

Vilma: **Ok Ceci. Hecho…**

Ceci: **Gracias Vilma.** *Ceci slips her 500 lempiras. There are no transactions regarding labor or favors without cash in Honduras.* **Bueno… comemos.** OK … let's eat.

They fish arrives... the kids jump into their seats, and they eat. The Mariachi musicians come close around the table to serenade the blended family. Guity fills Ceci's cup with his private bottle of guiffity. Ceci stands up and bows graciously and dances with Guity for a moment, and then tips the musicians.

Ceci: **Saben que vamos manana a buscar pasaportes para nuestro viaje sorpresa este verano, y creo que necesito su firma como protutora por eso. Y en la noche te invito venir al circo con nosotros.** You know that tomorrow we go for passports for our surprise journey this summer… and I believe I need your signature as protutora for that. And tomorrow night I invite you to come to the circus with us.

Vilma: **Con gusto Ceci.** With pleasure Ceci.

Angie: But Mom why do we need passports for the circus?

Ceci: Honey, passports are like tickets for crossing borders. The circus is for fun and excitement. And what do we want?

Jazmin/Roxana/ Angie: Fun, fun, fun!!

Ceci: That's right and you deserve it! **Hay animales que bailan, payasos, bailarinas que vuelan, y magico!!!** – There are animals that dance, clowns, dancers that fly, and magic!! **The circus… the greatest show on Earth!!! But first things first…. Passports.**

The girls are excited, bouncing in their seats as they pull fish off the bones. Ceci helps Angie so she doesn't swallow any bones. Everybody is happy as the sun sets on the Ceiba harbor.

204. Honduran Passport Office – La Ceiba

The following afternoon scene includes passport photos of the girls at the local photo shop with Vilma. Then they dash off to the passport office where Ceci shuffles lots of papers for an agent who files an application for the three girls. She also looks at Ceci with typical gringa disapproval.

Passport agent: Disculpa senora pero que relacion tiene ud con estas ninas? Excuse me Sra. but what relationship do you have with these girls?

Ceci: Soy su madre. I am their mother.

Agent: Ud. no es su madre senora. You are not their mother Sra.

Ceci: Yo soy la madre adoptada y mis ninas necessitan pasaportes. Nos vamos a Italia con permiso de la Juez de la Ninez. Mire los papeles. I AM the mother and my girls need passports. We are going to Italy with permission from the Judge of Children. Look at the papers.

Agent: Entonces… Quien es la persona Hondurena que es responsable? Then who is the Honduran person responsible.?

Vilma: Aqui soy yo. Vilma Reyes. Here I am.

Ceci: Ella es la Tia de las ninas, y sera la pro-tutora con un transmite de Tutora Custodia que estamos esperando ahora con la Juez de la Ninez. She is the girls' Aunt, and will be the Protutora with a Tutora custody case that we are waiting for with the Judge of the Family.

Agent: No se senora. Esta situacion es extrano, sin papeles de adopcion. I don't know Mam. This situation is strange, without adoption papers.

Ceci: Si ,,,, pero... Yo soy la madre y ellas viven conmigo. Yes but I am the mother and they live with me.

Agent: OK Senora... Sabemos lo que esta haciendo. Ok Sra. We know what you are doing.

Ceci: Que estoy haciendo? Yo soy la Madrina y la madre. What am I doing? I am the Madrina and the Mother. *Showing more papers.*

Agent: Me parece que esta llevando las ninas por los estados. Que mas? No tenemos mucho confianza en los missionarios que cayen en amor con nuestros ninos. It appears that you are taking the girls to the states. And what else? We don't have much faith in missionaries who fall in love with our children.

Ceci: De nuevo.... Ellas viven conmigo Senorita, y yo vivo aqui en la Ceiba. Nosotros vamos a Italia a visitar el padrino de las ninas. Aqui es la carta de invitacion? Louis Harris... Entiende? They live with me Senorita, and I live here in Ceiba. We are going to Italy to visit the godfather of the girls. Here is the letter of invitation... Louis Harris. Do you understand?

Agent: Si entiendo bien. Vemos muchas gringas que quieren comprar nuestros ninos Senora. Yes I understand very well. We see many gringas who want to buy our kids Sra.

Ceci: Nosotros vamos a Italia y volvemos. No vamos a los Estados. Entonces, cuando podemos recoger los pasaportes? We are going to Italy and returning. We are not going to the US. So when can we get the passports.

Agent: Quien es tu mama ninas? Who is your mother girls?

They all point and run to Ceci with hugs

Agent: OK.... *Long pause...***Vamos a ver. Lo que no queremos es a ver las ninas en el orphanato de nuevo...... si la custodia no pasa Sra. Firmen aqui y aqui Senorita Vilma.... Y Senora Cecilia. Son bien bellas estas ninas..** We will see. What we don't want to see is the girls in the orphanage again…. IF your custody doesn't work out Sra. Sign here and here Srta. Vilma… And Sra. Cecilia aqui. They are beautiful these girls.

She gives them lollypops.

Ceci: Gracias. Pero no se preocupe Srta. Esta custodia va a pasar. Thank you. But don't worry Srita. This custody is going to happen.

Agent: Se puede pagar en la caja… y venga la semana que viene por sus pasaportes. You can pay at the register… and come next week for the passports.

Ceci: *Addressing Vilma.* **Rezo por el dia cuando no hay mas obstaculos.** I dream of the day when there are no more obstacles.

Vilma: No se Ceci. I don't know Ceci.

Roxana: Vamos al circo verdad Mama? Are we going to the circus now Mama?

Ceci: Yes honey… right now. Let's change the channel.

Ceci and Vilma look at each other as they grab the girls' hands and leave. Clearly this is another tedious milestone in the journey towards legal custody.

205. **The Travelling Circus in La Ceiba**

Cut to the inside of the big tent of a very humble, funky, third world Latino circus. Ceci, Vilma and the girls are seated in front because of Angie's vision. It is dark and the show has begun with an obese, jolly ring master and an opening number of oddly shaped and strangely dressed performers. The girls are fascinated despite the shabby tent and sets, the funky clowns and the smelly, rundown animals. The scratchy sound track includes dated American and Latino pop music which directs the continuity of the single ringed show. The dancers and trapeze artists are also dressed in well worn costumes, but the ring master presents all the dated acts with great pride.

Jazmin is clearly freaked out about the clowns and climbs into Ceci's lap with confusion and horror. (Clowns become a recurring nightmare for her over the years.) Angie cannot see things at a distance but there is so much going on... that she is riveted by the flashing energy around her. And Roxana is ready to jump into the ring. This is Vilma's first trip to the travelling circus, as she has never been able to afford the price of the ticket, and she is all smiles.

There is a funny dog and pony act that pulls ooohs and aaahs out of the girls. Then an old muscular man appears with a snake that scares them to death as he comes close to the audience. The various clown acts are humble, but amusing, and when they come close to Jazmin, she buries her head in Ceci's lap for some reason we will never quite understand. The trapeze act takes place without a net, and simple as it is, we are aware of its ambition and danger. A magician performs a few amateur acts with things going in and coming out of his mouth. When the elephant waddles through the ragged curtain, Roxana is the first to volunteer to sit in his saddle, which surprises and almost alarms Ceci. There is one old tiger who reluctantly jumps through a ring of fire. All of the performers double up with their roles, and it appears that they are one big family.

Despite the humility of the production, the girls are awestruck. There is nothing like this in La Ceiba, as there are no performing arts arenas in town other than the school auditoriums. The circus comes once a year and everybody goes. For Ceci this is like a Fellini movie, and she marvels at the ambition of the company, observing how dated and minimal the production is compared to Barnum and Bailey. Fortunately, it is affordable for the local, working "middle class", and the audience is clearly thrilled, laughing and cheering with great gusto for all the traditional circus elements. After a while nobody minds the smells and strange persona of the circus company. It is like a freak show filled with comic innocence.

The show ends with a company dance number to a Michael Jackson song, and the girls are dancing on their seats with excitement. As they leave, and walk through the muddy circus grounds, Roxana declares that she wants to join the circus.

Roxana: Mama, yo quiero trabajar en el circo cuando soy grande. Mama, I want to work in the circus when I am big.

Ceci: Well that's interesting.... porque?

Jazmin: Because she wants to ride an elephant standing up.

Angie: No... its' because she likes the attention.

Ceci: Well then, keep dancing with me in the concerts, and maybe you will have a future in show business.... although I can tell you that there is no financial security in it.

Roxana: Que quiere decir eso Mami? What does that mean?

Ceci: No importa mi amor. I am impressed that you had the guts to get on top of that elephant. *She addresses Vilma as they leave the big top.* **Te gusto el espectaculo Vilma?** Did you like the show Vilma?

Vilma: Si Ceci, gracias. Entonces cuando se van a Italia? So when are you going to Italy?

Ceci: Ah si, hay que hablar..... Vamos el viernes, y te doy la llave y dinero ahora para venir con Sayda a cuidar la casa. Toma dinero para el taxi tambien. Oh yes, we have to talk about that. We go on Friday, and I will give you the key and money now to come with Sayda to take care of the house. And here is money for your taxi. *Ceci gives Vilma a house key and cash for her salary and a taxi ride home. Vilma kisses the girls and wishes them a bon voyage.*

Vilma: Bueno... Espero que tengan un viaje marveloso... posiblemente con romance? I hope you have a marvelous trip.... Possibly with romance?

Ceci: Oooy Vilma!... Gracias... pero el es un Tio/Padrino para las ninas. Thank you Vilma, but he is an uncle/godfather for the girls.

Jazmin: Vilma, te llevo una pizza de Italia OK? Vilma, I will bring you a pizza from Italy.

Vilma laughs and Ceci waits until she gets into a cab. Taxis in La Ceiba are notoriously funky, driven by men of questionable character. Some drivers have cultivated two or three families in different homes by seducing multiple women passengers. Ceci waits for a suitable driver.

206. **Going to Italy**

Intro info

Why are we going to Italy? To have a relationship with a "Godfather", Dr. Louis Harris, who will arrange everything for the visit. Hondurans are permitted to go to Italy without visas, but not Canada, Mexico, or the USA, which Ceci doesn't fully understand. That is the eternal backbend.

This is an auspicious event, as Ceci has always had the fantasy of going to Italy. Her Spanish Grandfather, Florentino Diaz, always said that next to the Spanish are the Italians. This is because an Italian gave him 5 apples which sustained him for the five days he spent on Ellis Island in the New York harbor at the turn of the century, to immigrate to the United States.

Dr. Harris is an American, who would rather spend most of his time in Italy... but has a family in Richmond, Va. We will find out why he prefers Italy during the course of the visit.

Ceci's circumstance, to have the financial support of a man, without having a daily husband or father family presence is strange. The awareness that she will never have this in her life, or for the life of her kids, despite this kind man's distant financial support, is both comforting and painful. It haunts her constantly. The kids want a Dad. Their dad has been murdered. Ceci is the most dependable adult in their lives.

Dr. Harris has an Italian partner, Veronica, and her grown son, Daniel who recently moved in with him in a village north of Venice in the Dolomite Mountains. Ceci and the girls will learn about this relationship when they arrive. He has committed to Veronica and they are pregnant with a child. Veronica sees Ceci and the girls as a threat to her relationship with the American Doctor who comes and goes.

Ceci and the girls will make this trip to Italy twice, despite the immigration hassles and the antagonism it causes Veronica, whose pregnancy during this first trip is difficult. Louis also has grown children from a previous Italian wife. Yet despite all this responsibility, every month for many years, the financial transfer to Ceci for the girls will take place without fail, much to Veronica's disapproval. Dr. Harris's concern for the three Honduran girls is sincere.

Italy is beautiful, and as much as Ceci wanted to share its beauty with Louis and the girls, she is thankful for the gift of this luxurious trip. Hence, she maintains a platonic, respectful distance from Louis, and thinks of him as the brother she never had. He will show them Italy and they will have a first class experience.

We see that the girls can feel Louis's paternal love. They hug him like a father, and it is heartwarming. He is the only man in their lives who truly cares with a sincerity they have never known before. It is all Ceci can do to keep herself from throwing her arms around him with the deepest respect, admiration, appreciation and love. She always believed that God granted her this single status to live the strict, demanding life of a dancer and choreographer, free to travel the world and work for whatever wages, just to give people the joy of the dance. In the case of these three girls, her mission is the gift of a better life for these three sisters. Now that she is a mom, all her priorities will change.

207. **The Airport and Immigration**

Cut to Ceci and the girls at the San Pedro airport ticket window, where they are redirected to an immigration officer. Ceci has already anticipated all the roadblocks with the unadopted status of the girls. She nervously prepares her papers: the Judge's permission for their temporary journey; the custody papers; birth certificates; a letter from Dr. Harris inviting them to stay with him in Italy; and of course, all the passports and her work permit. The officer suspiciously interrogates Ceci and the girls.

Officer: Perdoname Sra, pero puede explicar su relacion con estas ninas? Excuse me Sra. but can you explain your relationship to these girls?

Ceci: Buenos dias Senor... Tengo custodia, y aqui estan todos los papeles. Good morning sir. I have custody and here are all the papers.

Officer: Donde van en Italia y porque? Where are you going in Italy and why?

Ceci: Vamos a un pueblo se llama Pieve d'Alpago cerca Venizia a visitar un amigo, y también vamos a ver doctores alla para las ninas. We are going to a village called Pieve d'Alpago near Venice to visit a friend where we will also see doctors for the girls. *The officer takes the papers, and directly addresses Roxana.*

Officer: Digame muchacha, quien es esta mujer? Tell me little girl, who is this woman?

Roxana: Ella es mi mama. She is my mother.

Officer: Y cuantos madres tienen uds.? And how many mothers do you have?

Jazmin: Tenemos Karla, Tia Conchita, Tia Dunia, y Mami Ceci. *Ceci rolls her eyes knowing this is a problem.* We have Karla, Aunt Conchita, Aunt Dunia, and Mami Ceci.

Angie: *She climbs into Ceci's lap and kisses her.* **Pero Ceci es la mejor de todas.** But Ceci is the best of all.

Ceci: Ellas viven conmigo Senor. Se puede ver la custodia en los documentos. They live with me Sr. You can see the custody in the documents.

Officer: OK... momento.

He takes the papers into an office and they all wait. Ceci is nervous.

Ceci: I hope we don't miss the plane. I can just see me going through this in every airport.

The officer returns after 15 very long minutes, hands Ceci the papers and wishes them a buen viaje. At this point, Ceci is sweating and biting her nails. With his rubber stamp, Ceci thanks him and they run to catch the plane to Panama, then Madrid, and finally Venice.

208. <u>Travel montage</u>

The following montage illustrates the 44 hour trip including several airports. Ceci does not travel well, and spends the layover time dealing with her nausea in the airports. The girls, however, are resilient and love the adventure, talking to everybody who will engage with them, in every airport. They are proud to use their English with anybody who will talk to them.

Finally, they land in Venice, where Dr. Louis is waiting for them, despite the delayed midnight arrival. Ceci tries to fluff everybody up to look presentable. As they are coming down the escalator in the Venice airport, the girls ask questions.

Angie: Mami who is Dr. Louis? I don't remember him.

Ceci: Dr. Louis actually saved your life when you were sick with meningitis in the Hospital Atlantida. And he is sending me money to take care of you in La Ceiba. You met him when you were very young.

Jazmin: But is he our new father?

Roxana: No, nuestra papa fue Carlos.... pero el morio. No, our father was Carlos. But he died.

Ceci: Dr. Harris is like a Godfather, como un padrino... But you can call him Tio Louis OK?

Angie: But David Ashby is our Godfather.

Ceci: You have two Godfathers… You will see how much Dr. Louis really cares about you girls. We are very lucky to know him, so I want you to treat him with respect. There he is!!!

When they see him, they all rush into his arms, even though they were very young when he first knew them. It is very obvious how much he cares about the girls as he lifts each one and gives them big hugs.

209. Dr. Louis's big car

They all get into Louis's big car with all its bells and whistles, and the girls fall asleep in the back seat. Louis explains what the arrangement is to Ceci.

Louis: The girls look great. You are doing a wonderful job.

Ceci: Thank you Louis… I'm sorry it's so late and the flight was delayed.

Louis: Don't worry about that. I'm glad you're here. So, I am taking you to a ski lodge on the mountain across from my villa. There is a kitchen there, and tomorrow I will arrange for you to have a car.

Ceci: At the moment all of this seems like a dream. I can't thank you enough for inviting us. This means a lot to the girls, and I never believed that I would actually visit Italy. Here I am. Lucky us… But Louis….. I thought you lived in Virginia.

Louis: Well…. there are some things I need to explain to you. I am originally from Richmond, which is where my practice is, but I have recently purchased a villa here……… because I have an Italian girlfriend who will be having my baby soon.

This news hits Ceci like a ton of bricks, and she is silent, and looks out the window…. masking her shock as they drive up long winding mountain roads with spectacular views.

Louis: I know I should have told you when I was in La Ceiba, but I didn't know she was pregnant at the time.

Ceci: It's OK, you don't have to explain anything. I am really grateful for everything you are doing for the girls. *Pause….* So… what have you told your lady friend about us?

Louis: Veronica knows that I treated them in the hospital while I was in Honduras, and I have told her that I wanted to support your ability to get them out of the orphanage. I have bought this villa, and she lives there with her older son in the house while I travel.

Ceci: Ok, I appreciate the clarification. Thanks for the heads up. *Ceci knows she must wrap her heart around that.*

210. The Ski Lodge Residence in the Italian Alps

It is late when they arrive at the ski lodge at the top of the mountain.

Louis: So here is the lodge and a cell phone. Tomorrow I will rent you a car, and this will give you some independence while you are here. I am setting up a practice here, so I will be working. I am hoping that you can see the sights.

Ceci: You know I don't speak Italian Louis.

Louis: Yes, but you are a world traveler. You will be OK I am sure. And here is a cell phone... I have made appointments with my best medical staff to examine the girls this week. I will pick you up tomorrow to get the car. There are many sights to see near the lodge, so I hope you enjoy it here.

They pull up to the lodge office and Louis speaks Italian to an all-night manager who takes us to a small apartment. The girls wake up, and in their stupor find their way into bunk beds and crash.

Ceci: Thank you Louis. This is way over the top.

Louis: It is the least I could do for them.

Ceci: Louis, you already saved their lives. I am overwhelmed with gratitude.

Louis: No *you* saved their lives... you called me and I came.

He tries to hug her, but Ceci carefully shakes his hand.

Ceci: Better this way. *She watches him as he drives away.*

Ceci: *Talking to herself.* **Well Dad.... That's as close as I'll ever get to a man like you.... But this guy is taken... and I'm too old for any hanky panky. Uncle Louis it is then.**

She locks the door and tucks the girls in for the evening.

211. <u>**First Full Day in Italy**</u>

Ceci has fallen asleep in the bottom bunk with Angie. Her new cell phone rings and she bangs her head on the top bunk looking for it. Early morning sun streams in the window.

Ceci: *(phone)* Hello?

Louis: *(phone)* It's me, I am outside. Open the door.

Ceci: OK. ...... Girls wake up!! It's Tio Louis!!!

Jazmin: Donde estamos?

Roxana: I have lag jet, and Angie will not wake up.

Ceci: It's called jet LAG, honey.

Ceci opens the door, and there is Louis with a winter hat, gloves, and groceries.

Louis: Good morning Honduras!! You are about to have breakfast with a breathtaking mountain view.

Ceci: I wish you could have warned me that July in the Italian Alps is like February in New York. I did not bring the correct royal wardrobe.

Louis: It's only cold at night. But don't worry, we'll buy clothes. Can you cook?

Ceci: Absolutely...*Looking at the contents of a foreign bag of groceries.* Did you bring coffee? Yes. And fabulous cheeses and prosciutto and salamis!!, and divine baguettes!! Oh yes I'm in Europe!!

Louis: And grapes for the princesses, with real orange juice and Italian strudel. *He has already tiptoed into the girls' bunk bedrooms and offered them grapes.... And Italian strudel. He cannot wake up Angie.*

Roxana: Mom... Angie doesn't wake up.

Ceci comes running in with a panic, as she knows that the altitude could be affecting her nervous system. She sits her up supporting her wobbly head... her eyes are open... but she does not respond.

Ceci: Get me that bottle of water,,, Quick!!

Jazmin hands her a bottle on the floor, and Ceci quickly douses Angie with it and forces her to drink like a baby from a bottle. Soon she is coughing and awake... her eyes popping.

Ceci talks to her constantly....

Ceci: Wake up baby... it's Mommy... Hello Angie? ... It's Mommy... I'm here... I love you.. Wake up honey... Angie? Talk to me baby!!...*She squeezes her tight, rocking her.* Louis... I think it's the altitude!!... What do I do? *She douses her with more water... Angie's eyes blink.*

Louis: Can she stand? Let's try getting her circulation going.

He gets on his knees and supports her from behind, while Ceci is right in Angie's face. The girls are standing there in pajamas, dumb founded. Angie comes to, sees Mo m and throws her arms around her.

Ceci: Que paso? What happened baby?

Angie: I wanted to wake up Mom, but I couldn't move and then everything went black when Roxana tried to shake me. I just couldn't wake up... until now.

Louis: Come here Angie.... I'm a Doctor and I want to check you out. *He looks at her eyes, in her mouth, listens to her chest... Does some reaction tests on her arms and legs.... Asks her to walk forward and backward.* How do you feel now?

Angie: A little dizzy... I remember that I couldn't get enough air. But now I am hungry.

Louis: It is the altitude... less oxygen, and more pressure. I think they all have suffered neurologically in one way or another from that meningitis epidemic in their home. And with Angie's trauma to the head...she is even more sensitive. I'll have her checked out in town with our pediatrician.

Ceci: Meanwhile, we are just going to have to hike around here and get all of our hearts, minds, and bodies tuned into this mountain air OK? So can you all get warmly dressed? And I will set up this lovely breakfast.

There are lots of YES MOMs!!... and Ceci gets to work in the kitchen, setting out the tempting array of cheeses, hams, pates, bread and fruit. The girls sit on Tio Lou's lap. She offers Louis some hot, black, Italian coffee.

Louis: Yes... so today we will get you a car, and then we can go for some authentic Italian pizza. And I also plan to set up some doctor appointments for the girls today.

Ceci: Feels just like Christmas... Thank you Louis. I mean... I never thought we would have this kind of red carpet, so excuse me if I constantly trip over my open mouth.

Roxana, Angie, Tio Lou, Jazmin

Louis: And also, this is a wonderful ski resort here, with rides in the summer, and hiking, restaurants, and a lovely church in the valley, called Aparicion de Maria.

Ceci: Well, I definitely want to go to there.

Louis; It's in a grotto, and run by nuns.

Ceci: OK, we'll do that later…. For sure. You know I'm a big Mary fan and I believe in miracles, right?

Louis: Yes, I know that.

212. <u>Car Rental Place</u>

Then we cut to a car rental parking lot, where Ceci is climbing into a little Fiat. It's a big thrill when Tio Lou hands Ceci the key.

Ceci: You must be kidding!

Jazmin: Mommy this is much nicer than our bumpy black pick up truck.

Roxana: It's so cute!

Angie: Come on Mom, start the car! *Ceci is flustered.*

Ceci: This is also too fabulous - but Louis.. I do not know my way around here, or anywhere in Italy, and I don't speak Italian.

Louis: You will follow me to lunch and then back to the ski lodge, and from there you can use the GPS, OK? Do you like your little princess chariot? Huh girls? I will lead you and we will see how you drive OK? Who's coming with me? We will go for lunch and you can have your first real Italian pizza OK?

The girls scream and yell and jump into Louis's big car. Louis clearly likes having three beautiful little girls on board.

Girls: Pizza Italiano!! Pizza Italiano!!

Ceci: Drive slow. OK? So glad you have so much confidence in my driving.

Tio Louis watches with a smile on his face as she chugs and stutters for a moment with the clutch.

Louis: If you can drive a funky old clutch pick up truck, I think you can drive a Fiat.

Ceci: Thank you for encouraging all this independence bro…

213.<u>Authentic Italian Pizza</u>

Louis leads her to a beautiful villa restaurant. He knows everybody, and the owner takes them to a special table on the terrace overlooking the lake on the road back to Pieve d'Alpago. Louis orders (in Italian) pizza for the girls and a bottle of wine. The waiter asks what kind of pizza….

Louis: What do you want on your pizza girls?

Jazmin: Pepperoni

Angie: Pepperoni

Roxana: Pepperoni

Louis: And I am ordering something special for you Ceci, if you don't mind… And a large antipasto salad for everybody. Andiamos manger.

Jazmin: How many languages do you speak Tio Lou?

Louis: Is that my new name? Tio Lou?

Roxana: Si, Tio Lou…

Louis: OK... I speak seven languages: English, Dutch, Italian, Slovenian, French, German, Russian and not much Spanish.

Ceci: So you can't tell secrets in front of Tio Lou in Spanish... Is that clear?

Angie: Well, we want to learn Italian while we are here.

Louis: Well let's start with Pizza 101. Here everybody gets their own individual pizza and in the north the crust is very thin. But the sauce is divino, and every restaurant has their own family recipe. Meanwhile repeat after me for your first Italian lesson: spaghetti (repeat), linguini, manicotti, penne, fusilli, fettucine, rigatoni, capellini, macaroni, calamarata, lasagna, etcetera... That was an excellent first Italian lesson. You guys are naturals!

The girls have cooperated and repeated after Tio Lou impeccably. They all laugh. The waiter brings two wine glasses, a bottle, and three cokes for the girls. He pours the wine.

Jazmin: I like Italy, they just bring kids coca cola, without even asking.

Louis: Wait until you have the gelato mis reinas…. The best ice cream in the world. But now, Let me make a toast to you in my bad Spanish… Las tres hijas bellas mias!!! To my three beautiful daughters!

The girls stand at attention with their coke glasses in their hands.

Louis: Jazmin, Angie, and Roxana….I want you to know that I believe in you so much, that I will make sure you are always safe and have what you need to live a good life….. a life that you deserve. I am your Godfather, Tio Lou who travels the world, with you always in my heart…. I give you my blessings. *(clink!)*

And the individual pizzas arrive. A very special pasta dish is served between Ceci and Louis, along with some calamari. There is a breeze from the lake, and it is a moment never to be forgotten.

For Ceci it is the dreamy, 5 minute, unrealistic illusion of a family, in a beautiful place, loving the food… and the surroundings. A short, portly waiter begins to bellow out an Italian aria, and everybody raises their glasses.

Even the people on the boat passing by wave. Ceci only dreamed of moments like this. The sun sets as the dancing begins on the terrace… The kids get up and dance with other kids, and Ceci and Louis take a friendly dance spin in the corner. The owner comes to fill their wine glasses.

With the darkness, Angie gets sleepy and falls asleep with her head on the table. Ceci quickly comes back to her mother senses, and insists that we all leave… The music continues over a sloppy exit that involves carrying Angie into the car. Tio Lou pays and hurries along to end the evening driving along the coast of the lake towards the ski lodge. It has been an evening Ceci will never forget.

214. Tio Lou's Villa

Next day, Ceci is fumbling her way up the mountain with the GPS and the three girls in the back seat of their rented fiat. Finally they pull into Tio Lou's walled estate with beautiful landscaping, tennis courts, rolling hills, and a tall, luxurious, over grown villa, with many levels and terraces.

Both Tio Lou and his pregnant Veronica come out of the house to greet them.

Tio Lou: Welcome to Villa Bella my bambinas bellas!!!

Ceci: Hello Veronica… nice to meet you.

Veronica: Welcome to you all… Now who is who?

Ceci: Jazmin, Angie, and Roxana. *Tapping them individually.*

Veronica: Mucho gusto… and you are very bellas.

Tio Lou: Let me show the girls the swings.

Veronica: I will show Ceci the house then. *She takes Ceci to the kitchen and makes coffee.*

Ceci: When do you expect your baby?

Veronica: In the next few weeks. She is a girl and we will name her Goia, and she is heavy and very active.

Ceci: Well that's a beautiful name, and I am sure she will be a beautiful baby. I want you to know that you don't have to go out of your way for us. I realize this is a difficult time for you. Please let me know how I can help you. I'm sorry about the timing of this visit.

Veronica: Louis knows that he is on "Goia priority call" and will not be travelling for work until she is born. *Her son, Daniel, enters the kitchen.* Ceci, this is my son Daniel, who is visiting for the weekend, and lives in Milan.

Ceci: How do you do Daniel? How nice to meet an Italian from Milan. What are you doing there?

Daniel: I am studying photography and living there with my girlfriend.

Ceci: Ah yes, how romantic... you are doing just what a young artist should be doing. I wish you well.

Daniel: And welcome to Italy; we have heard so much about you and the girls.

Ceci: Thank you, and please introduce yourself to the girls. I believe they are on the swings with Louis. Oh here they come now.

The house is a beautifully remodeled old villa with open beamed ceilings, fireplaces everywhere, tile floors, wooden archways, with ancient and modern art on all the walls. The kitchen is modern with all the updated Italian plumbing and appliances and lighting, along with a grand living room filled with magnificent antiques, anticipated female baby toys, classical music CDs, and art books. The veranda looks out upon the rolling mountain view of the property, and is the most spectacular seat in the house.

Tio Lou: I can barely keep up with these little puppies. Veronica ... I have to make a few calls; Can you and Daniel take Ceci and the girls on a tour of the property? Then I will take the girls to the clinic we are opening.

Veronica: Yes dear... Maybe we should get a golf cart for these tours. And on second thought I think I will leave Daniel as the tour guide and see you later. I have to go lie down. You know I am 43 and have to be very careful exerting myself in this pregnancy. I also forgot to take my prenatal vitamins this morning. Will you excuse me? Thank you, Daniel.

Daniel: Of course. I would be honored to show off my father's estate, as we are still in the process of remodeling a few things.

Tio Lou goes up to his office, Veronica to the bedroom, and Ceci and the girls follow Daniel. He takes them down to the tennis courts and around the orchard, and back around to the pine forest and across the mountain stream to a picnic table where they stop to rest.

Ceci: This is such beautiful property.

Daniel: Yes, I am glad he bought it, and I am doing a huge photo essay on the development of the land.

Ceci: Louis is very talented and very ambitious... I know this will become more and more beautiful. There he is now.

Louis is waving from the veranda of the house. The girls run to meet him.

Daniel: You have to see the clinic he has started in town. It is a coop of Doctors and technicians from all over the world... and will be an office for Italy's "Doctors Without Borders". I am doing a lot of photography for him for this business, as it exists mostly by donations. *They greet Tio Lou.*

Ceci: I believe we are going there this afternoon.

Tio Lou: Yes and we should get moving. Daniel, tell your mom not to worry about anything... just to rest. I will shop and get the barbecue going for later. We will be at the clinic and back for dinner.

Ceci: Yes.. And I will help in any way I can.

215. **In the yard outside the villa**

They all follow Tio Lou outside and wait for his next command.

Tio Lou: So Ceci, we continue the caravan as I must shop for dinner later.

Roxana: And can we go with Tio Lou?

Ceci: It's OK with me. And I will be the caboose! I am starting to like this little fiat.

Tio Lou: Good, and we will have an American barbecue with steak, corn, and potatoes.!!!

Angie: And marshmallows?

Tio Lou: But of course my bellas bambinas!! And I think I know right where to find marshmallows.... But first, we go to the doctor.

Roxana: But this is vacation,,,,, why the doctor?

Angie: I thought you were a doctor.

Tio Lou: Yes, and I want you to see the best doctors I know who can help you with your particular problems.

Jazmin: What kind of problems do we have?

Ceci: We have all different kinds of things to check out with special doctors.

Tio Lou: Put it this way... I am having all aspects of your physical health thoroughly analyzed, OK? We think that maybe your real mom didn't take baby vitamins when she was pregnant with you, and that she did not take care of herself during that time. Angie should have her eyes checked, and she and Roxana had meningitis, and all of you had bad water and malnutrition when you were babies. So we want to see how you are.

Jazmin and Angie: Ooooh! *Wrinkling their noses.*

Angie: That doesn't sound good.

Tio Lou: And wow, are we lucky that you don't have to live like that now. This is one of the reasons you have come to Italy. So I can check you out with the best doctors I know.

Ceci: Entienden todas? These are good doctors, and they will not hurt you. Don't be desgraciadas.

Jazmin: Mom, maybe you could meet a handsome Italian doctor.

Ceci: OK that's enough.

Roxana: **Si, porque Tio Lou ya tiene una novia.** Yes because Uncle De already has a girlfriend.

Ceci: **I said that's enough.**

Tio Lou: **What did she say?**

Jazmin: **You said you speak seven languages but no Spanish. Porque?**

Tio Lou: **I'm learning, if you will give me a break... and help me out OK? What's a novia?**

Ceci: *Quickly changing the subject.* **What about that Italian Gelato ice cream? Can we get some before they go to the doctor?**

Angie: **Mom says it is the best ice cream en todo el mundo.**

Tio Lou: **She's absolutely right, and that's one of the reasons that I live in Italy. So who is coming with me?** *They all chime in and climb into Tio Lou's big car.* **Do you think you can follow me to the clinic Ceci? It will be good practice for you.**

Ceci: **Just go slowly Doctor and I'll do the best I can.**

216. <u>Italian Gelato</u>

They take off down the mountain and Tio Lou pulls into the parking lot of a gelati shop across the street from a beautiful old Catholic church. Ceci follows. The girls love driving in Tio Lou's big car, and they are ecstatic when they see the choices in flavors.

Ceci: **Well now you have captured their hearts.**

Tio Lou: **I think it's a good idea to distract them with gelati before meeting all the doctors. And it doesn't take much to make them happy.**

Ceci: **They are happy to be here on an adventure with you. It's all a dream for them. Thank you so much for doing this. I am especially glad they can see some doctors before I take them to a Latina psychologist.**

Tio Lou: I have a great team here, and I know we can give them a complete physical with lab tests in the facility. I'm happy to help you with this. So what is your passion for gelato?

Ceci: I like raspberry and coffee. But if you surprised me, I'm sure I would be happy.

Tio Lou: OK … So girls, how did you order?

Roxana: **Hablemos Espanol!** We spoke in Spanish.

Gelato girl: **Il gelato e un linguagio universale**. Ice cream is a universal language!

The girls come up to Ceci with their cones and want to share the different flavors. Tio Lou brings ice cream to Ceci and they sit outside, while the girls climb on the swings with their cones.

Ceci: This is delicious… nectar of the gods… What's the name of that church?

Tio Lou: Santa Ana I believe. It's beautiful inside.

Ceci: I will bring the girls there for communion on Sunday. I want them to learn to pray, and to believe in miracles.

Tio Lou: If what you say about Angie's optic nerve is true, then you are really going to have to pray hard.

Ceci: I pray hard… because I believe she will see one day with two eyes. Because she deserves it. I will never let go of that wish, that belief, that possibility.

Tio Lou: Well I won't either. And I promise you this. If a procedure exists that will bring back her optic nerve, I will pay for it. You have my word. So Let's go… we have appointments.

He goes to round up the girls and they jump all over him. Ceci watches with her mouth open, dumbfounded as to how to react to what she just heard from Tio Lou … another miracle moment. They have never had this kind of paternal attention….

Except Roxana, who does remember her father and misses him. And when she thinks of him, she tends to revert to baby language. This personality switch lasted for several years in Honduras.

217. Tio Louis's Italian Medical Clinic

As soon as they walk into the clinic, it is clear that Dr. Louis is a well-respected man. A secretary comes up to hand him his messages, and greets the girls. A nurse comes to take them away, and Ceci follows. Louis tells the Secretary in Italian that they will get the full physical and lab workup. Roxana starts to cry, as she associates all office buildings with painful, backroom shots in the behind. Ceci faces her and tells her.

Ceci: Roxana... we are going to check out your health, and they may want to take some blood... so you will have to be a big girl OK? I will not let them hurt you.

Nurse Alma: *Starts to babble in part Italian / part English about not being afraid as she gets ready to draw blood.* Me name Alma... no hurt nobody....Jest a leetle peench.... *But Roxana freaks out and starts to cry. Ceci holds her close.*

Ceci: It's because where she was in the orphanage in Honduras, they would wait until the last minute to take kids to the doctor, and usually it meant going in the back room at the pharmacy in town. So Roxana associates office buildings with shots. You should see her at the dentist!

Angie: Mom, let me go first, I am not afraid. *She bravely holds out her arm.*

Alma: These good girls here.

Ceci: Ok good. Jazmin you go next, and Roxana you will see how your sisters survived and how you will be fine OK?

218. The Medical Interview – Ceci and the Italian Doctors

Eventually all three get blood taken, and then 3 nurses come to take them in 3 different directions for testing, while three young doctors come in to get the information from Ceci. One is a Pediatrician, an Ophthalmologist, another a Neurologist, and Louis as the directing doctor. He introduces Ceci, explains the nature of the examination, and he leaves. The questions and answers begin.

Ceci tries to give the background of the various deficits there were in the girls' very early years: the malnutrition, the meningitis, domestic and farm animal proximity, no electricity, the bad water, the parent's drug use, and probable physical abuse. They ask her about Angie's optic nerve blindness caused by trauma, and her meningitis, epilepsy and unusual muscular cramp attacks that last for days. Angie suffered a blow to the head while she had a meningitis fever of 104 degrees at the age of one. She sees mostly with her right eye, and we are hoping to have an operation to straighten out the pupil in her left eye, with which she does not see much.

Then she describes Roxana's speech, memory, and maturity delays which develop into clinical dyslexia, dyscalculia, disruptive mood disorder and depression, when combined don't provide for easy reading, writing, and arithmetic. She definitely needs special education. Ceci explains that she also suspects that Roxana was possibly beaten while she was in the mother's womb. Honduran women try to abort that way by punching their abdomens. We suspect that either that was the case, or the father may have beaten the mother while pregnant and injured Roxana's brain in the process. Either way, she has multiple personalities and she even reverts to baby talk when she thinks she is around a father figure. She is the most traumatized by the family separation and has learning disorders caused by malnutrition, meningitis, and abuse.

Jazmin has asthma and ankle cramps...and all the neurological anxiety that goes with being removed from a family with substandard living conditions at the age of three months. In college Jazmin is diagnosed with ADHD, although she is clearly very intelligent and learns fast. But she has trust issues, as they all do from being abandoned by adults. Jazmin is the 4th in line of Karla's immediate consecutive pregnancies, and definitely was malnourished and plagued by asthma. (We will later find out that this causes her stunted growth.)

The doctors all talk to each other in Italian, thank Ceci, and leave. Dr. Louis arrives and tells her:

Dr. Louis: The girls are in very good hands… I will take you to the lounge where you can have coffee, and I will see to their welfare. These are young, ambitious, curious doctors… who are the best in their fields… I will coordinate all of them. Don't worry about anything OK?

Ceci: And what if Roxana freaks out?

Dr. Louis: I will call you. This will take some time. Actually, I suggest you take a walk to the shopping mall down the hill.

Ceci: What? You must be kidding?

Dr. No… it's better this way.

Ceci: OK… Fine… Bye. *She hesitantly leaves.*

219. <u>The Medical Exam Montage – All three girls</u>

After giving blood we dive into a montage of medical examinations for all three girls. Roxana does not like any of this and is stubborn, but Lou does not allow her to call Ceci. They look into Angie's seizures and Roxana's neurological issues with EKGs… Roxana also is given an MRI of her brain. Angie goes through an intensive eye exam at Tio Lou's side, that involves special drops for dilation and lots of machines. They all get blood and urine tests. Tio Lou is vigilant for all of this.

Finally the girls emerge from the lab, smiling with Tio Lou and lollypops. They run to Ceci. Roxana has wet eyes behind her lollypop smile.

Tio Lou: They were really good patients.

Angie: But I can't see Mama.

Tio Lou: The ophthalmologist had to dilate her eyes, and says that her vision will be blurry for a few days.

Ceci: OK Angie… you just stay by me so you don't fall.

Jazmin: Roxana cried when they took her blood.

Roxana: **Callete Jazmin!** Quiet Jazmin!

Angie: She always cries.

Ceci: It's OK Roxie... come here.... Does it hurt in your arms? *She embraces Roxana.*

Angie: Just a little. Mom ... they gave us lollypops.

Ceci: That's because you were big girls. I am so proud of all of you. And I want you to thank Tio Lou for giving you such professional care. *They all rush to hug Tio Lou.*

Tio Lou: It's OK... I want my babies to be healthy.... *Embracing them.* It's all over now and we will get the results soon.

Ceci: Thank you so much for doing this Louis. I'm really impressed with this place and I know you will be very successful and happy here. I can see that you get to organize things your way, with the criteria of your experience.

Louis: You nailed it right there... And I hope to keep up the quality control with the best people I can find... in one location.... Along with superior lab testing, our missionary work, and global notoriety for Doctors Without Borders.

Ceci: Only the best for Tio Lou!!

Tio Lou: That's right...And we will get all the results in a week, with all the lab work. Meanwhile, I am surrounded by the most beautiful girls in the world at the moment. The sky is blue, and let's see you work that little fiat. Come on...

220. Parking Lot outside Clinic

Ceci and the girls get back in the little fiat.

Tio Lou: You look great in an Italian fiat. OK you are on your own. I am going to shop for dinner and will meet you back at the house later on around 6pm OK?

Jazmin: Don't forget the marshmallows papa.

Tio Lou: No problem.

Ceci: You know I am still nervous about general navigation Doctor.

Tio Lou: There is a GPS on the dashboard, and here are all the addresses and numbers you need to know.... And you have a phone. *The girls take the phone.*

Ceci: But...

Tio Lou: Don't but me... You are the crazy American who had the guts to move to Honduras, murder capital of the world... I think you can handle the suburbs of Venice.

Girls: Yeah Mom... Turn on the radio.

Ceci: Well then... you do think of everything now don't you...

Ceci smiles... changes her tone, takes the key and slithers into the car. She takes off smiling nervously as she faces independence in Italy. She jerks a bit in the little fiat and leaves Tio Lou laughing. Smiling as she pulls away she says:

Ceci: Now the question is... What if I don't understand GPS? Add what about my inability to speak Italian, and oh well... Si Dios Quiere!

Angie: Come on Ma... you can do this. No problema!

Ceci: OK, no problem!

The next few hours find Ceci and the girls lost, driving along a highway built on huge stilts, over the Dolomite Mountains, with no exit for miles. While the vistas are breathtaking, the vertigo and confusion rattles Ceci. Eventually they get off the highway and with sign language and Spanish, Ceci gets directions from an Italian road worker and finds her way back to the chalet. After spiraling through the mountain roads for hours, they arrive at the chalet just in time to spruce up.

221. **Dinner at the Villa**

Ceci and the girls arrive around dusk at Tio Lou's Mountain Villa. Ceci has dressed up. The girls see Tio Lou and Daniel firing up the grill and rush to greet them. Tio Lou directs them to go play on the jungle gym.

Ceci: What can I do to help?

Tio Lou: There's wine in the kitchen.

Ceci: Yes I think I need that after getting stuck on that suspended highway to Venice...

Tio Lou: You live and learn right?

Ceci: Yes Doctor... *She opens a bottle of red wine.* And how is Veronica?

Tio Lou: She's still not feeling well.

Ceci: Let me make a salad perhaps.

Tio Lou: Fine... Mi casa es tu casa.

Ceci: Pretty good Spanish Louis.

Ceci goes to the magnificent kitchen to explore the magnificent refrigerator. And begins to OOOh and AAAh over salad ingredients, as her creation begins. She festively drinks her wine and turns on the radio. The girls come inside and run around the house, eventually finding toys and dolls in the living room, for the future daughter. You would think they were in Disneyland with the excitement and laughter coming out of all three of them as they play with toys they have never seen before. Suddenly Veronica enters the room.

Veronica: Girls, what are you doing?! These aren't your toys. They are for my baby. Now please don't touch anything in this room.

This reprimand puts them into silent shock and they leave the room with their tails between their legs. In the other room, Ceci is kitchen dancing to Italian radio music as she drinks her wine, chops potatoes, and makes a salad in Veronica's kitchen. Ceci looks out the kitchen window and sees Vernoica arguing with Louis in Italian. The girls come into the kitchen looking depressed.

Ceci: What's wrong girls?

Jazmin: Veronica doesn't want us to play with her new baby's toys.

Ceci: Oh dear, I'm sorry, I should have checked that out.

Jazmin: Are we not like normal kids?

Ceci: What do you mean about that?

Angie: Well is their kid going to be more normal than we are because she's taking baby vitamins and resting?

Jazmin: Yes, maybe we are not normal, because Karla didn't take baby vitamins.

Roxana: **Pero no importa porque Tio Lou es como nuestro Padrino, si? Y Veronica es nuestra Madrina… No?** But it doesn't matter because Uncle Lou is like our Godfather right? And Veronica is our Godmother no?

Ceci: No I don't think so honey. She has a baby on the way, and she's just not feeling good today. And Vilma is more like a madrina than Veronica.

Roxana: Mommy did we do bad?

Ceci: No baby. You did absolutely nothing wrong. Veronica just isn't feeling well.

Dinner

Cut to an awkward sit-down dinner illustrating Veronica's clear discomfort with the social situation. She and Louis talk in Italian. Even her son, Daniel is uneasy. The table is topped with steak, hamburgers, buns, cheeses of all kinds, Ceci's salad, grilled potatoes, and wine bottles and juices. Yet despite the abundance, dinner is still uncomfortable. The girls are loving the food and ramble on in Spanish, English, and pretend Italian. As the meal ends, Ceci starts to clean up and loads the dishwasher. Louis and Veronica continue to argue in Italian.

Ceci: *As she clears the table* …You know, I think we better go… the girls have had a huge day and, I think we should get out of your way. Thank you for making such a wonderful barbecue.

Veronica gets up from the table in disgust and leaves the room.

Ceci: It's the hormonal state! You know… plus the full moon.

461

Jazmin: What about the marshmallows?

Ceci: Not tonight honey.

Tio Lou: We will save them for another night I promise. I am really sorry about this. She is not well. And this is a difficult pregnancy for her in her forties. You know I love you girls.

He hugs the girls as they help to clear the table.

Roxana: We love you too Tio Lou, and I wish that you are my real Dad.

Tio Lou: Well then tomorrow I can do Daddy things with you. I have to work in the morning, and in the after noon we can go shopping in Beluno *He hugs her.*

Angie: Shop for what?

Tio Lou: For Italian clothes for my beautiful bambinas of course.... And eat gelati and go to an Italian Carnival in the plaza with dancing and Comedia del Arte.

Girls: Wow!!

Ceci: Dios mio!!! Louis, this sounds fabulous...but... I just don't want to upset Veronica.

Tio Lou: I will deal with that. Maybe she will come.

Ceci: OK so, isn't there a church near the ski lodge... like a grotto or something?

Tio Lou: Yes it's called *"Santuario Maria Immaculata Nostra Signora de Lourdes".*

Ceci: Fabulous.... tomorrow morning we will go there and say some Padre Nuestros para agradecer a Dios por ud. y SUS regalos... say some Our Fathers to thank God for you and your gifts. And to pray for Angie's sight, Roxana's brain, and the American visas of course... etc. But most of all I really want to thank you Louis. It gives me faith in God that the girls have an angel like you.

Tio Lou: I don't know about the God part, but you are so welcome, and yes, I do care about the girls very much. Their welfare is my project... So I will pick you all up tomorrow around noon. For now, just give me big hugs and check out the full moon tonight on the mountain.

The girls give him big magnetic hugs. The stone villa is exquisite in the moonlight – the gardens and the paths around the property. The smell of roses and honey suckle and the warm summer night air create a beautiful ambiance. The girls drive away down the long driveway as Louis watches them again… disappear into the night.

222. <u>The Grotto Sanctuary – Next morning</u>
"Santuario Maria Immaculata Nostra Signora de Lourdes".

Cut to the image from behind of Ceci and the girls holding hands and walking towards the Church Grotto where high up, carved into the mountain rock, is a statue of Fatima de Lourdes… or the Virgin Mary. It is breathtaking.

Roxana: Porque vengamos aqui Mami? Why do we come here?

Ceci: Because I want to pray to the Virgin, high up on this beautiful mountain, in this beautiful country… with gratitude to be here, courtesy of Tio Lou and God, and the Virgin, and everybody who gave us this opportunity to be here as guests. So make some prayers to the Virgin…. and take her a candle, each of you.

She drops some Euros into a box and lights four candles, giving them each one.

Ceci: And I want to pray to the Virgin to ask for all the gifts you were meant to have in this life and to help you use them to achieve your dreams.

Angie: And what about my eyes mom?

Ceci: Yes, and to please take us wherever we must go in the world to regain Angie's vision… whatever it takes, if you can lead us to the right cure, you will be in our hearts forever.

Jazmin, Angie, and Roxana

Angie, Roxana, Jazmin

Angie: Amen que se sea… Because we believe in miracles right Mom?

Ceci: Absolutely 100% And if God and his team of Mary, Lourdes, Fatima, Guadelupe, and Maria Lionza… whomever can hear our Padre Nuestros, and beat science, and believe in my Angie and her sisters …   I am all for it.

The girls kneel at the Grotto altar and begin to pray their Padre Nuestros in Spanish. A nun approaches Ceci.

Nun: Ud. es una Americana, pero sus hijas son Latinas no?
You are an American, but your daughters are Latinas, no?

Ceci: Si, como sabia? Y porque habla Espanol en Italia? Yes, how did you know? And why do you speak Spanish in Italy?

Nun: *extending her hand.* **Me llamo Carmen y soy de Mexico, and I can hear a Padre Nuestro for miles. Your daughters are beautiful.**

Ceci: Yes, they are Hondurans, and we are here looking for the Virgin to help me with their disabilities. Angie is partially blind, and we really want her vision back. There are probably various levels of neurological damage from meningitis in all of them.

Carmen walks directly toward the praying girls.

Carmen: Que tenemos aqui? Tres Hondurenas que conocen el Padre Nuestro? What do we have here? Three Hondurans who know the Our Father?

Jazmin: Si.

Carmen: Como te llamas bella?

Jazmin: Jazmin

Angie: Y yo soy Angie, y ella es Roxana

Roxana: Yo soy Roxana.

Carmen: Well let me say this first. Sus Padre Nuestros son excelentes, y que la Virgin escucha todos que creen…. Y que uds. son tan bellas, y que me alegre conocerles. Your Our Fathers are excellent , and the Virgin hears all who believe.

Ceci: Can you tell us something about this place?

Carmen: Of course. The Sanctuary of Mary Immaculate "Our Lady of Lourdes" is located at 1000 meters above sea level, on the Nevegàl hill, a splendid terrace overlooking the Belluno pre-Alps. It is an oasis of the spirit immersed in the silence of nature, under the maternal gaze of Mary Immaculate.

There are two full-time diocesan priests, assisted by myself and two other Mexican nuns from the Congregation "Servants of the Heart of Jesus and the Poor". We are all dedicated to welcoming pilgrims who are devoted to our Lady of Lourdes,

and celebrating the Sacraments, especially the Sacrament of Reconciliation.

Jazmin: So does the Lourdes lady make miracles?

Carmen: To believers? Yes. Such beautiful spirits you are … And so I understand that Ms. Angie is looking for a miracle?

Angie: Yes I am. Do you know Mary? *Approaching her very seriously*

Carmen: Of course I know Maria, and this is Our Lady of Lourdes, who is connected to Maria.

Angie: Do you think she can make my vision to come back in both eyes?

Carmen: I believe she can.

Jazmin: How does she do that?

Ceci: Sometimes science and God and miracles all come together and we find cures to things.

Carmen: That is the best explanation I have heard … and I will gladly bless you and introduce you to the holy spring above at the altar mayor. This is where the Virgin does her best work…

Roxana: Can we all go?

Carmen: Of course. Come with me.

Carmen leads the way up the side of the grotto mountain on a small, stone carved staircase. At the top of the mountain is another small pond that is fed from still a higher mountain water fall… This is also a grotto with a statue of the Virgin. She takes Angie and her sisters and blesses them, with water from the waterfall, splashing the water on Angie's eyes, and over their heads … praying constantly. Carmen prays to Lourdes in Spanish, for the help of Santa Lucia (patron saint of vision), and all who can promise Angie a miracle to return her sight one day.

Roxana, who is slightly frightened, knows that Carmen is sincere. Carmen prays in Italian for her mind and damaged soul and slowly dowses her with the magical pool waters. Jazmin is the most willing and she decides to jump into the pool... They all laugh... but Carmen is serious and enters the pool with her to pray.

Carmen: This is holy, blessed, sacred water, and you will feel the cleansing when you reach out to the Virgin. I know this water is cold, but it will clear the darkness for light to come in.

It is a moving experience. Ceci bows her head, and closes her eyes to join the prayers. Then she looks up to the fading full moon in the morning sky and begins to pray silently, as a voiceover.

Ceci: Dear Maria, or Lady of Lourdes, or Guadalupe, or however you want me to call you. I know that you are the Queen of Mothers, the Mother of Queens, and that you grant miracles to the humble. I am here to ask you for help with my children... That my middle child will have her sight retained one day, so that she does not struggle so with her daily life... That my oldest child could have the missing part of her brain returned, and that they no longer suffer from anxiety. That they will get help with all their disabilities..... That we will have visas to go back to my Mother so I can take care of her in her home while we also begin a life in the USA. These are my biggest dreams, when before all I could ever imagine was a Broadway hit, and a husband to go with it. I was never able to make that happen, even though I could take them both in a heartbeat. Shine your light this way dear Mary, while we are lucky enough to be here as the guests of a very fine man. Please bless his generous soul, Dr. Louis Harris. My children need your guidance. Thank you for giving us Carmen as a bridge to your kind heart. Please hear these requests to heal my precious children, and give them the best possible future. Amen.

Carmen: Bueno... The blessing is made. *She takes Angie by the shoulders.* It's in God's hands, and the Virgin knows how to deliver my messages. I pray that you will see someday. Just keep your eyes open. When God is ready he will help you. You are all lucky to have your Mama Cecilia... Keep praying the Padre Nuestros... Besos Ninas...

Ceci: Sister Carmen, we better go now... Tio Louis will be looking for us.

Suddenly Tio Lou appears at the top step. He has been listening to Ceci's prayer.

Tio Lou: Tio Lou has found you!

Carmen: What a pleasure, are you the father?

Jazmin: We wish!

Tio Lou: I am their Godfather slash Uncle slash Papa.

Carmen: Well they are lucky to have you too. I can see that.

Roxana: I love Papa Louis!! *She goes to hug him.*

Ceci: Sister Carmen, Thank you for your blessings and messages to the Virgin. Girls, thank Sister Carmen.

The girls all give her wonderful hugs, and then descend with Tio Lou. Ceci remains for a final moment of thanks, and gives Carmen a donation for the Church and the Virgin. She leaves Carmen soaking her feet in the pool in silent prayer.

Once they are all on the ground the kids take hands with Tio Lou and Ceci as they leave the grotto and take the long winding path to the parking lot. They are all soaking wet. Tio Lou speaks to Ceci during the kids fun and excitement.

Tio Lou: Sister Carmen seems like a very nice lady. Unfortunately, I am an atheist, so I don't know much about religious miracles, but if there is any possibility whatsoever that science can correct Angie's vision.... *He stops everyone and picks up Angie high in the air....* Then I will pay for it, and we will make you see again. *Everybody applauds and laughs.*

Ceci: Well that in itself is a miracle – Just to HEAR that... But, I am sorry that you don't believe in God, because I truly believe that he sent you to us. *Long pause.* And I believe the Holy Virgin Mother, is the messenger.

Jazmin: So what do you think about that Tio Lou?

Tio Lou: I don't know… I have to think about it. I have seen so many God loving people suffer in my missionary work. And when I have done every thing I could to save children's lives… including pray… and they die under my care, I somehow found it easier to believe that no God would do this. Hence, I stopped believing in God. I take it day by day and try to fix what I can.

Ceci: I'm sorry to hear that you don't believe in God. Don't you think that medical missionary healing is spiritual?

Tio Lou: I am a fixer and I just want to fix whatever I can.

Angie: Well Tio Lou, I know that God likes you because you care about us and lots of other kids!

Jazmin: Hey guys….. there's the big Daddy car!

The long walk from the Grotto to the parking lot has ended and they arrive at Tio Lou's big car where Veronica is waiting. They divide up and Roxana and Jazmin go with Tio Lou and Veronica, while Ceci follows in the Fiat with Angie… It is a long ride to Belluno, and Angie must lie down as the altitude and mountain curves make her dizzy, despite the beautiful landscapes.

223. **Belluno, Italy - Shopping**

Belluno is a small urban city with ancient architecture and streets. The old stone buildings have very modern, state of the art, interior renovations, and only the most exclusive shops have a spot on the old cobble stone streets. In the plaza there are cosmetic and fashion boutiques, gelati shops, and luxurious side walk cafes. The Plaza is teeming with the European energy of a summer weekend renaissance festival. There are clowns, musicians, craftsmen, circus performers, with the artistic ambiance of Comedia del Arte. There are farm animals and pony rides. Tio Lou leads them through all of this, carefully leaving the pregnant Veronica in a café to bask in the sun. They walk down the picturesque stone alleys to the back entrance of a hip international clothing store. Across the alley from this is an Italian boutique. He gives Ceci a credit card.

Tio Lou: I am leaving you here with my credit card between these two cultural enterprises to shop. They will have interesting clothes for the girls, and there is a sale now. This Italian place will be fun for you. You have two hours. Then we can have dinner and enjoy the festival. What do you think of that?

Ceci: Louis, I don't know what to say.

Louis: Don't say anything... Just go for whatever you want... Fill the basket.

Ceci: I don't think anybody has ever said that to me before. *In semi trance.*

Jazmin: Mom ... It's because we are special.

Ceci: It's like Queen for a Day.

Angie: I feel like Cinderella and he is our fairy Godfather!

Tio Lou: It pleases me to see them so happy and to be part of your fairy tale. You know what they need. Work fast, and have fun. The day is young. I'll see you at 4pm. *With that, he kisses the girls, and disappears into the crowd, down the alley.*

Ceci: OK Cha chas! We are in Italy! Vamos hacer compras Let's go shopping, and you will learn about capitalism and desiarrhea!

They enter the first boutique and musical shopping madness takes over in accelerated motion as Ceci and the girls throw things into the cart. Everything catches their eyes: Pink shoes with red ribbons, matching purses, crazy socks, fancy dresses, ruffly skirts, sassy T shirts, cute bathing suits, hats and jewelry, wacky sunglasses.... on and on...Things they have never seen before... all on sale... A total delight! Once again, Ceci takes her initial ecstasy on a first gear run around the sale racks, thinking of getting three of everything in different sizes, but finally just grabbing necessities like jackets, shoes, underwear, shirts, skirts, dresses, etc. She is in shopping heaven. The girls have NEVER been in a store like this... so modern, so western. They are stunned, and chatter about things that perk their interest along the way. They are entranced with all the exotic merchandise.

After that they move over to the Italian boutique and go crazy on outfits for Ceci. Ceci models and the girls say yes or no. All these fabulous designs elevate Ceci's mood to the high fashion style she never quite achieved.

Even with knock off designer brands, Ceci is in heaven, after years of no fashion exposure in Honduras, except for the beauty pageants. At 4pm Tio Lou shows up in the alley with his big car… pops the trunk, and the girls load up bags of clothing. They have already changed into their brand new Italian party dresses and are flirting wildly. As they pack the trunk with bags and climb into the car, Ceci thanks him endlessly. Then she hands him the credit card and a stack of receipts, with a big kiss on the cheek. The shopping madness rhythm de-escalates into normal time.

They return to the Plaza where dusk has fallen and the mysterious fire lights of Italian festivalia take over, creating a romantic European atmosphere. Veronica waits for them in a beautiful outdoor café with grand chairs and artistic umbrellas. Tio Lou has already ordered for everybody. The girls are wide eyed and happy. Ceci is in awe…. Overwhelmed with the festivity, she drinks the wine and blisses out.

Musicians approach their table with performers all dressed in comedia del arte attire… Masks, wigs, big skirts, grand gestures and divine magical theater unfolds before them. There are masked clowns and court jesters, Scaramouches and Pierrots, young flirtatious maidens, merchants and aristocrats, dancing maids, seductive courtesans, and elegant rich women characters. The pomp and circumstance is everywhere. The kids are thrilled. Ceci is delighted and inspired theatrically by the café and festival magic. Carnaval and its true meaning (cars covered in flowers hauled along the venice waterway canals "car -naval"), along with the theatrical characters of Comedia del Arte, have always been one of her most passionate theatrical interests.

Veronica is uncomfortable in her pregnancy, but has dressed superbly in Italian designer silk for the Carnaval occasion, and "seems" to be happy with the venue. Tio Lou is really enjoying himself as the cuisine and service is impeccable, which fits right

471

into his demanding, Virgo character. The owner and waiters all know and treat him with extreme professional respect, as he frequents this café often. Three of the dancers cajole the girls to get out on the plaza and dance with them. Ceci and Tio Lou go to join the girls…. And probably could have danced all night as the entire plaza turns into a musical production number. The sun fades on Tio Lou 'ringing around the rosie' with the girls in front of an Italian fountain. This has been a night to remember.

Then Louis arranges for café for Veronica and Ceci as they watch the girls dance.

Tio Lou: Soon we must go back home. It's been a long day.

Ceci: They are having the time of their lives. Tell me where can I buy those masks? I want to make a ballet around all this Comedia del arte.

Tio Lou: Ah… In Venice are the most beautiful masks in the world. Every other shop has a world class artist who paints them all day. As a matter of fact, tomorrow I will take you to the train station to go to Venice for the day so you can see Carnaval there. You will love it … the girls will love it. There you can buy your masks.

Veronica: You will love Venice. All Americans love Venice.

Ceci: Yes I am ready to love Venice.

Tio Lou: Come on everybody…. Andiamos!!

They all dance their way to the car. The girls have balloons and painted faces and hold hands with Veronica and Louis and Ceci dancing. Veronica grips her stomach with her free hand, but seems to be enjoying herself. Clearly, she is struggling with this pregnancy.

With the music, the fantasy ambiance, the confetti, the theater and music, the fabulous pasta and anti pasto plates, along with the festive alcoholic beverages, and of course the gelati in all the glorious flavors…the evening was as close to an Italian version of a

Renoir painting depicting romantic café life as Ceci and the girls would ever see again.

224. **At the Chalet – Bedtime**

The girls are in their pajamas looking at their new Ipads, courtesy of Tio Lou. Ceci is on the balcony drinking tea and looking at the mountains. The girls come out to see her.

Ceci: Well girls, it's time to go to bed don't you think? Big day.

Jazmin: Really big day. Tomorrow we can have a fashion show for Tio Lou.

Ceci: That's a good idea.

Roxana: And why can't Tio Lou be our Dad?

Angie: Because he already is with Veronica, entiendes Roxana?

Jazmin: Sure would be fun... I like being a princess.

Ceci: What? I don't treat you like princesses?

Angie: Yes Mami... Roxana just wants a Dad. And lots of cousins and Aunts and Uncles.

Jazmin: I want a Dad too, but Tio Lou just isn't vailable.

Ceci: Available *(correcting her)* No Tio Lou is not available. But he is like your Uncle... like my brother... OK?

Roxana: I don't care. I want him to be my Dad.

Ceci: Well, vamos a llamarle Padrino – Godfather and/or Tio Lou. Whatever....

Jazmin: He likes to call himself our Dad.

Angie: Isn't David Ashby our Godfather?

Ceci: Well, two Godfathers are better than one. AND tomorrow Tio Lou is sending us on the train to Venice. Big deal... big adventure OK? So... now it's time to go to bed, close your eyes, and give me the Ipads, *She tucks them in.* and I'll sing Mother Moon OK?

Ceci sings her acapella lullaby MOTHER MOON, which the girls love, and the haunting melody puts them to sleep.

225. <u>Train Station to Venice – Next Morning</u>

The girls are in their new little day outfits with their sunglasses and hats and backpacks. Tio Lou is walking them to the ticket office at the local train station, and then up to the tracks. He gives Ceci the tickets and some Euros.

Tio Lou: Once again I am depositing you on the edge of a great adventure on this train ride to Venice, with vistas that will fill you with the richness of the Italian country landscapes. Here are the tickets and some Euros…and big kisses…. Do you have your phone?

Angie, Tio Lou, Jazmin, Roxana

Ceci: Yes Louis.

Louis: Call me on your way home.

Ceci: Yes Louis.

Roxana: **Porque no viene con nosotros?** Why don't you come with us?

Tio Lou: **Because I know Venice, and dislike all those tourists and smelly back streets, and have lots of work to do at the clinic while you all explore on your own. I will see you later. Have a great time.**

226. <u>Train Ride</u>

The train arrives. The kids hug Tio Lou and mount the steps of the train waving constantly all the way to the window of their seats. Tio Lou smiles and waves., and they watch him until he disappears. Ceci settles them down and the musical journey starts to unfold a moving montage of beautiful, Italian countryside …. Mountains, chalets, little towns, farms, churches, cows grazing, lakes, and forest……with people living their lives… waving to the train. It is like a dream for Ceci…. Just to relax and watch this cinematic European landscape with her awestruck children. Angie can never look out windows because it makes her dizzy, so she nests in Ceci's lap. Eventually they pull into the station passing over the Venice waterways.

227. <u>Venice – a montage</u>

Ceci makes a photo essay out of the journey from the Station to Plaza St. Marcos. The following sequence in Venice is presented as montage with music and improvised dialogue. Everything about Venice is romantic. Despite all the tourists, the unique European ambiance is riveting. Ancient architecture seduces the dreaming tourist back to days gone by.

Painted masks of brilliant designs and colors, bejeweled and gilded, glamorous and frightening.... are in shops everywhere. There are exquisite ball gowns and costumes to go with whatever ancient character you might desire to become. Ceci makes a project of finding souvenir masks of the famous Commedia del Arte characters as they run into them on the street: Harlequin, Pantaloon, Pulcinella, Scaramouche.

Players and musicians are everywhere ready to engage you in their masked dramas with their assumed personas and different languages. It is easy to look beyond the tourists, and the girls are entranced. This is an Italian Disneyland.

As the yellow brick road takes them beyond the dramas, across bridges and canals, they embark upon crooked little streets with high fashion shops where the most haute couture is dangled before the tourist ...in small, expensive, intimate designer boutiques where only the wealthy dare cross their thresholds. The shoe salons draw Ceci... as the beautifully crafted shoes remind her of the most elegant of Broadway dancer shoes. Her mouth waters at every turn.

The streets lead into Plaza St. Marcos where the girls become

hypnotized with the hundreds of pigeons and their movement. It starts to rain, so they take a tour of the Doge Castle. Then they dine in an elegant bistro under the arcade at St. Marks. The cook is charmed by the girls and their outfits and funny raincoats. They love his pasta.por bambinos.

Jazmin convinces Ceci to take a Gondola boat on the canals back to the train station. They find a friendly Gondolier who sings opera at the top of his lungs as he rows the gondola with three giggling girls. This is like a dream for Ceci. Never in a million years did she think she would ever see Italy

Music has carried them through this entire collage of Venice, until the train pulls into the dark station at Pieve d'Alpago, where Tio Lou is waiting. Angie is asleep and Tio Lou must carry her to his car, and up the stairs to the chalet. All is well. It is a new moon. As he leaves he tells Ceci:

Tio Lou: Oh I almost forgot... Tomorrow morning I have arranged for a conference with the doctors who will give the medical report on the girls. I will arrange for new glasses for Angie too.

Ceci: Oh ... And what have they discovered?

Tio Lou: No more than you have already seen, but this will help you define the conditions so you can do more analysis when you return.

Ceci: OK then. Molto grazzi again and again.... Today was a dream come true.

Tio Lou: Bonne note Signora y bambinas. I will meet you in the clinic in the morning. OK?

Ceci: Good night bro. Big grazzis! We all love you.

The girls have crashed into their beds with their clothes on. Ceci somehow gets them under the covers. Then she pours herself a glass of red wine, lights a candle.... and puts on Italian cabaret music that she bought on the street in Venice. She dances around the chalet balcony with her new masks.

Ceci: I dance in fantastic bliss in my chalet in the Italian alps after an afternoon in Venice with my beautiful daughters. What more could I want?

She suddenly gets serious and removes her mask. Looking up at the Italian Alp night sky with her hands pressed together she prays. What more? I want every miracle possible to restore the eye sight of my beautiful Angie, and to eliminate the disturbances in Roxana's brain that stop her from connecting.... To take away Jazmin's anxiety and asthma... to make them all healthy, and feel like they belong...... Yes dear God...I want every miracle possible. And I will never stop praying for these things. *Fade*

228. <u>**The Medical Conference Report at the Clinic**</u>

Next day, Ceci and the girls arrive in the Fiat at the Medical Clinic. Upon entering Tio Lou greets them, with big besos and arranges for the receptionist, Benina, to look after them while Ceci meets up with the Doctors.

Tio Lou: How are my beautiful bambinas? Ready for a trip to my office?

Jazmin: Do we have to go back to the Doctors?

Ceci: Oh come on... we're having a great time no matter what we do. We are in Italy!

Tio Lou: I'm going to have a meeting with your Mom and the doctors and you can go play with nurse Alma for a little while, and then I will take you for gelato. OK?

Benina takes them to the play area, and Tio Lou ushers Ceci to the conference room.

Tio Lou: So Ceci, I've assembled a team of specialists in the conference room to give you their report on all the lab tests we took last week. They are an international team of young doctors I have met through my travels with Doctors Without Borders, and they are very interested in the health of your girls. Feel free to ask them anything at any time.

They enter a conference room where there is a Pediatrician, an Ophthalmologist, a Neurologist, and an Endocrinologist whom are introduced to Ceci.

Pediatrician: First let me say, Ms. Diaz, that we are so impressed with the generosity and compassion you have demonstrated in rescuing these sisters. Without a doubt, the fact that they were born one after another to a mom who did not have any pre-natal care, in a barrio with bad water and a meningitis epidemic indicates the basis of their issues. Along with their severe malnutrition, this did not set them up for a healthy infancy. And from everything you have told us, these girls have come a long way from death's doorstep in the last two years. And although we did not find any more trace of meningitis in Roxana or Angie, the effects are there. So we will take each child individually and look at their current health and disabilities to the best of our ability, and make suggestions as to any medical treatments that will help. And because of so much neurological damage, I strongly suggest you take them to a psychologist when you return to Honduras. Our neurologist will explain Roxana's MRI to you.

Ceci: Well, that takes care of the overture. I guess I'm ready for the rest of the show.

Neurologist: So we will start with Roxana. Needless to say, as the oldest, she has endured the most time and abuse with the family. As we look at the MRI of her brain there you can see the dark parts which indicate trauma. You can see this especially on the frontal lobe, which controls planning, reasoning, critical thinking, problem solving, recognizing and regulating emotions and social skills.

Ceci: Well that sounds about right. *This is clearly not good news.*

Neurologist: Then here on the Temporal lobe there is damage, and that controls understanding of language, processing auditory information, organizing information, memory, and learning.

Ceci: *Eyes filling....* I know it's not her fault that she just doesn't understand. I had thought it was the transition to English.

Neurologist: No… its' the damage. And in the back is the Occipital lobe, which is for integrating and processing visual information – color, shape, and distance. When you go to the psychologist they will test her ability to reconstruct images.

Ceci: I just don't know if this trauma took place in or outside of the mother's uterus. Or if the meningitis caused this.

Tio Lou: Probably both, if the mother was trying to abort by beating her belly, from what you told us before. That would explain her problem with learning, sound, and language.

The tears start to flow, and Ceci has trouble controlling them.

Ceci: Oh God, what am I going to do?

Pediatrician: Shall we continue with the endocrinologist?

Ceci: OK bring it on. Sooner or later I need to educate myself.

Endocrinologist: So, Roxana's blood work shows hyper-thyroid issues which explains her underweight condition and thinning hair. This increases the metabolic rate which creates anxiety, sweating, and difficulty concentrating. There are drugs for this.

Ceci: Yes, she has all of these symptoms, and I really hope there is a more natural approach to fixing this, rather than a drug that she will need all her life.

Endocrinologist: That's your decision. I suggest you continue monitoring her blood to check her thyroid levels regularly.

Ceci: OK , thanks… my poor baby.

Pediatrician: And then there is her dental condition with the rotted tooth, and distressed gums.

Ceci: I believe that's from sugar water instead of milk, bad hygiene, and eating rocks in the dirt where she was born. We have been to the dentist, and she does not like that at all.

Pediatrician: If she maintains a healthy diet, with proper care and hygiene, she will be ok.

Tio Lou: Ceci, fortunately there is nothing life threatening at the moment, so just digest this information and take it with you. Now what about Angie?

Neurologist: Angie also has suffered the effects of meningitis and trauma. Her EKG shows that she is slow to react under stress, which can cause confusion. And the MRI of her brain does indicate neurological damage, not only to her optic nerve, but also to her neuromuscular connections which explains the seizures and tremors of epilepsy, which can be brought on through mental and physical stress. I can suggest medicine for that called tegretol.

Ceci: Her mom slammed her on the left side of her head which may explain this as well as the vision loss. And what about the muscle spasms that don't go away for days?

Neurologist: Those are also neuromuscular, which are triggered by physical and mental stress, which can ultimately lead to tremors. This also stems from the fever of bacterial meningitis in the brain.

Ceci: So will the tegretol take care of that?

Neurologist: You would have to experiment with that, because sometimes it can actually bring on more spasms. There is also a drug called Lamactil which is more suave.

Ceci: Oh my God. This is too much. How do you trust all these medications?

Tio Lou: The good news is… you saved her life… She could have died without the anti-biotic we gave her in La Ceiba.

He puts his hand on her shoulder. Ceci looks down, and then regroups.

Ceci: Ok now what about her eyes?

Ophthalmologist: OK… I had to put the drops in her eyes to dilate them. And I can see that there was trauma there, as well as the meningitis inflammation, which could have cut off the oxygen to this part of her brain. This affects her central, peripheral and color vision. She won't be able to distinguish contrast, and in low light she will have more difficulty, as the optic nerve has to do with sensitivity to light. So there is little to no vision in her left eye… And what there is causes it to move around with the struggle to connect with her right eye's focus. That's why her left eye is off center. Glasses may help this. And the right eye sees about 40%. So her vision is about 20/80. Unfortunately, there is no cure for this condition. And you must prepare yourself and Angie for the possibility of gradual vision loss.

Later, in her teens, Angie will have an operation in the USA (Strabismus) to center and correct the left blind eye. Her vision will also decrease to 20/200 at the age of 20 as she waits for a seeing eye dog, which finally arrives when she is 21.

Ceci: No…. I still believe there is a miracle out there for this… somewhere. What about stem cell therapy or electrical stimulus? I've been researching all the possibilities.

Ophthalmologist: The optic nerve is thinner than a strand of hair, and the stem cell work has not yet reached a level of enough sophistication to target the remaining nerve that was severed, just by injecting cells into her brain. And I don't know about the effectiveness of electrical stimulus. I will say that there are a lot of people with optic nerve blindness, and if there were a surefire cure, it would be in the international mainstream.

Ceci: I'm hanging in there for a miracle Doctor. She wants to see so badly. So will it degenerate?

Ophthalmologist: That I cannot tell you. I believe that glasses may help her somewhat at school.

Tio Lou: We will get her glasses.

Pediatrician: And you can get accommodations for her visual impairment at school. I can tell you that meningitis was caused by contaminated water and filthy living conditions. She will not have that again if she is with you.

Ceci: We have to boil our water in Honduras. And the mom gave them sugar water which came straight out of the stream where all the animals poop. She was born in a barrio with several cases of meningitis. Some of the kids that live there are like vegetables.

Neurologist: I also suggest that you take her to a psychologist to determine her learning capacity, which may be hindered by other neurological and intellectual brain trauma besides the optic nerve.

Ceci: You know, Angie is intrinsically intelligent and I believe her determination will help her overcome these obstacles. I will continue to observe her educational progress. *She takes a breath and a long pause* OK... what about Jazmin?

Pediatrician: As far as we can tell from her lab reports, her main issue is asthma. Fortunately, she was removed from the family negligence at three months, which allowed her to escape meningitis and the malnutrition that her sisters received.

Ceci: She definitely wheezes when she feels anxiety or hunger of any kind, or when it is humid, which is constant in Honduras. She also shakes her left leg a lot.

Pediatrician: We can give her an albuterol inhaler to open up her breathing passages.

Ceci: OK... and there is something going on with her ankles. She complains about that all the time.

Pediatrician: I would say that is growing pains. Basically, her brain is intact, and she will probably be a good student.

Endocrinologist: I did see some possible issues with human growth hormone deficiency. But I would have to do further tests. I hope that you can look into this in Honduras. Obviously, since she was the 4th in line without breaks, the mother must have been really run down by then.

Ceci: I don't know if there are endocrinologists in La Ceiba... but I will try to look into this. I just have to thank all of you for doing this for us. I had no idea that there was so much irreversible damage.... But..... I needed to know, and I will have to stay on it.

Tio Lou: Well, I believe we can arrange for glasses for Angie and an inhaler for Jazmin.

Ophthalmologist: I will write a prescription for her glasses now. I'm sorry Ms. Diaz. I wish we could have done more healing here.

Tio Lou: Thank you gentlemen... I believe that wraps it up.

The doctors leave the conference room. Ceci collapses on the table in tears.

Ceci: I just can't stand to see them suffer.

Tio Lou: They will not suffer with you. And like I said... I will send you money so you will be able to get whatever they need. And again Ceci, if there really is a cure for Angie's eyes, I promise we will find it and I will pay for it. OK?

She throws herself into his arms.

Ceci: Thank you Louis. You are such a fixer. *And I am such a cry baby.*

Tio Lou: Now you have to stop Ceci. You don't want the girls to see you like this. I'll get them and then we'll go for gelato. OK? And then tomorrow we will go to the beach.

Ceci: *smiling as she dries her eyes.* That sounds great... they will love that. *He leaves the room and she looks up at the ceiling as she pulls it together.* Hey God...Yes I am upset, but thankful, and if this is the road to miracles I will keep on walking.

The girls peek in the door, and then rush to Ceci. She embraces all of them together.

Roxana: Why do you cry Mama?

Ceci: I am so happy to see you, and love you all so much.

Tio Lou: *enters* Time for some gelati girls ... Let's go! *He lifts up Jazmin, Roxana and Angie grab Ceci's hands and they dance to the car.*

Girls: Yeah... gelato!!!

229. **Planning the Adriatic Sea beach trip**

Next day.... The doorbell rings at the chalet and it is Tio Lou blowing the wake up horn to pack up and get ready for the beach. The girls are fast asleep.

Tio Lou: Wake up mis bambinas... because I am taking you to Italy's finest beach, Lignano, Sabbiadoro on the Northern shore of the Adriatic sea.

Ceci: Good morning Dr. Harris. Please come in and have some breakfast with us, while I wake up the girls and get ready for another exciting event on our Italian itinerary.

Ceci: Chicas hay que despertarse. Nos vamos!! Estamos en Italia!!
Girls you have to wake up. We are leaving! We are in Italy!!

She whips up a quick breakfast and coffee.

Tio Lou: I'm sorry about throwing all of that medical information at you at once yesterday.

Ceci: Louis, I signed up for this and have to face it. I have learned to take the good with the bad. But now, gotta get ready for the Italian Riviera. *She goes into the bedroom to pack.*

Tio Lou: OK....So how did the girls like Venice?

Jazmin: I liked the boat ride.

Roxana: Me gusta la pasta. And all the birds in the plaza.

Angie: I like the clown people in the streets with the masks.

Ceci: *Shouting from the bedroom.* Actually, I was amazed at their tenacity, considering the completely unfamiliar territory we covered. But it was beautiful, and I got all my masks.

Tio Lou: So today we are going to a hotel on a beautiful beach, where the girls must dress every night for a magnificent dinner. So pack the pretty stuff.

Needless to say, this sends Ceci into a whirlwind obsession of finding the "right clothes" for the three girls, as well as bathing suits etc. She maintains conversation with him as she zooms around their chalet bedrooms.

Ceci: So how is Veronica? And will she come with us?

Tio Lou: I believe she will have the baby in the next few weeks, and she loves the beach…. So she will come with me to relax by the ocean before it is time………And perhaps two of the girls can come with us, and you can ride behind me with one of them.

The three girls: Me voy con Tio LOU!!! I am going with Tio Lou!

Ceci: I am sorry Angie … you must come with me, because of the altitude issues. I want to be near you if something happens. You can play with the radio all you like. Or just sleep so you don't get dizzy.

Tio Lou: It is a long drive, with beautiful scenery, so I believe you will enjoy the ride… Just follow me.

Ceci: OK… have another coffee, Louis, and we'll be ready in 10 minutes. Girls! Bring ALL your bathing suits… we are going to swim in the Adriatic sea!

230. **The Italian Riviera -** Lignano Sabbiadoro – Ceci and Veronica

Cut to the three girls and Ceci all decked out in swimwear with colorful hats and sunglasses… marching down the shore looking for Tio Lou and Veronica. There is definitely a comic visual to this brigade, as they are clearly fish out of water amongst the Riviera royalty. They see Tio Lou and Veronica on beach chairs and go to join them. Tio Lou immediately begins to dig castles in the sand with the girls. Ceci sits with Veronica.

Ceci: Veronica Hi….. How are you feeling?

Veronica: Constantly nauseous, but glad that it's almost time to deliver.

Ceci: Are you eating?

Veronica: As much as possible?

Ceci: I am so sorry you are going through this.

Veronica: I guess you wouldn't know, never having given birth. Which reminds me... How long are you and your bambinas planning to stay in Italy?

Ceci: We have another week.

Veronica: Ceci, don't you think it is a little strange that you are here running around with my man and your kids? Don't you have any idea how it looks? Or how I feel about this?

Ceci: *Stunned and caught way off guard.* Well, I'm sorry you feel so threatened by us. Because I understand this to be Louis's way of showing his love and charity for the girls.

Veronica: But he has children, and one on the way .... who very much need all his attention now. And I think it is dangerous for your girls to think of him as "Dad".

Ceci: Are you asking us to leave?

Veronica: I believe it would be easier for all of us.

Ceci: Well then... *Ceci is at a loss for words.*

Veronica: I am so glad you understand.

Ceci: What I understand Veronica... is that you are selfish and spoiled, and have been rude to my children, who have gone through hell, and have nobody else in the world but me, my mom, and Louis who really care about them. I have made NO romantic expressions or designs around Louis, so I think you better back off with your territoriality when it comes to me and my kids OK? I respect your relationship. We will be out of your hair soon ... I think you should be thankful for your fancy car, and your closet full of jewels and designer clothes, thankful for the generosity and company of such a philanthropic man ... and most of all, the future that he has given you and your son and future daughter. I am sorry if his charity to my children threatens your security. You should try living in Honduras on a shoe string budget..... and Veronica..... I know that you are pregnant, and will probably go into labor soon. I am sorry our presence is such an inconvenience. All I ask is that you please respect my children in the next few days. All children are children, and they all deserve love and respect. My children barely know what it is.

Ceci stands up, takes off her sundress, throws her glasses on the chair, and turns to enter the ocean with her kids. Veronica is left with her mouth open, clutching her big belly. Veronica shouts after her...

Veronica: I will make sure that you will never pass through Italian immigration ever again. Mark my words... I have connections.

Ceci turns around and returns to have the last word.

Ceci: Because of Louis, let's pretend this conversation never took place, because I am gracious and I want my children to know what true sincerity feels like. So you can try to slap me around, but again, my only request is that you please don't mess with my kids.... They have had enough rejection in their lives already. And if you agree to be civilized throughout this once in a lifetime- queen for a day vacation for me and my children, I will continue to be civilized in your presence. As a woman, I sympathize with your physical discomfort at the moment... but as a sister, it is difficult for me to understand your selfishness, in the midst of all your abundance. So..... if you go into labor tomorrow, we will leave tomorrow. Otherwise, our flight is next week. I am very sorry if my beautiful girls upset you.

Veronica: *Getting out her fan and smiles falsely.* I'm so glad we agree upon your immediate departure.

Ceci bows.... And smiles falsely back.

Ceci: Once again your highness, I apologize for the imposition. Clearly we are at your mercy. *She turns to walk towards the ocean, leaving Veronica speechless.*

231. Lignano beach scene – Adriatic Ocean

The girls are building sand castles on the beach at the ocean edge. Clouds are forming in the sky. Some other Italian kids join them.

Tio Lou is talking to the father of these kids in Italian. Ceci joins the girls and admires their work.

Ceci: This is such a beautiful sand village. I love the tunnels and bridges and pointed turrets. What do you guys think? *Addressing Tio Lou and the Italian father.*

Italian father: I think that your girls are professional sand castle builders.

Ceci: They get a lot of practice on the beach in Honduras.

Italian father: It's very creative.

Tio Lou: Yes my babies are very creative.

Suddenly a wave comes and washes over the little sand city. Everybody moans and groans together.

Tio Lou: Never mind. Let's all go swimming.

He grabs Angie and Roxana's hands…Jazmin takes the boys hands, and along with the Italian father they make a long chain and confront the waves together. There is a lot of laughter, and Ceci sits at the water's edge enjoying the love and joy that Tio Lou is showing the girls…. the fun they are having, that they deserve so much. She talks to herself.

Ceci: How could anybody think this is wrong? Am I crazy? But dear God… please don't trigger the tiger in my tank… because I will defend my daughters under any circumstances.

Dark clouds turn into rolling thunder and rain begins to fall. The girls start screaming with delight and run out of the ocean… Ceci wraps them up in towels and they run back to the umbrella with Veronica who is packing up. Tio Lou runs to help Veronica.

Tio Lou: *shouting to Ceci and the girls.* We'll see you later in the hotel dining room for supper tonight!

232. <u>Exploring the San Marco Hotel room – living the princess life</u>

The hotel room has a salon, a kitchenette, and two bedrooms with three princess beds and one master queen bed. The décor is bright with flowered wallpaper and large pinkish rose sofas and curtains. There are mirrors everywhere, with a huge window in the salon looking out upon the boardwalk and the ocean. The bathroom has a bidet and a strange looking bathtub, with a shower with many shower heads. The girls oooh and aaah at all of this, peeking into closets and built in drawers, turning the shower on and off.... They play with the fancy tea cups and wine glasses in the kitchen.

Ceci: OK girls, let's sit down and talk about cutlery and table etiquette.

Roxana: **Que es eso?** What is that?

Ceci: Etiquette and good table manners are very important. Come sit down with me and we will practice.

They all take their places at the table while Ceci sets up several pieces of silverware at each place with napkins, water glasses, etc. They practice without food.

Jazmin: *Lifting the bread knife.* I know, that this little knife is special for kids.

Ceci: No, as a matter of fact that is for the bread. So that may be the second thing you touch at dinner. However... let me continue. Are you all paying attention? What would be the first?

Pause She grabs the napkin. We talk about it every meal girls.

Roxana: Servilletas! *They all whip their napkins onto their laps.*

Ceci: Right!... Very good. Then you have your big soup spoon, which is just for soup over here. And then the bread knife for the bread that you graciously offer your neighbor from the basket before you take one.... Which you put on your bread plate, and tear off just a piece that you butter individually and eat that before you tear off another. Got that?

Angie: Yes mommy. Are you going to test us?

Ceci: You bet. This is a high class place and I want you to know what you are doing. So then your outer most fork is for the salad. The next fork is for the main meal, with the bigger knife that you use to cut ONE piece of meat at a time and then lay it across the plate without leaning it on the table.

Jazmin: How are we doing Mom?

Ceci: Very good. Now you never push your plate away. The waiter should remove it before you do that. Then you have your desert fork which is the little one. And the spoon if you have pudding... or you can use it for coffee. I am hoping you remember discussing this with me before. Me gustaria si pudieron recordar estas reglas de la mesa, OK? I would really like it if you could memorize these rules of the table OK?

Girls: Si mami!

Ceci: Ok time for the princess act - in the dresses Grandma made for you.

233. Dinner at the San Marco Hotel Salon

There is a grand staircase and entrance to the hotel restaurant. Ceci and the girls enter in their matching dresses all smiles and chin up. Tio Lou and Veronica are waiting for them in a corner table near the window, covered with a lace table cloth and dressed with flowers, candles, and crystal. Ceci is aware of Vernoica's ongoing discomfort with their presence but greets her graciously. It is a beautiful setting with white antique furniture, renaissance paintings and sculptures, and an air of European elegance. There are a cello and violinist playing Italian chamber music in the corner. The girls take their seats and all the tuxedoed waiters rush up to wait on them as Louis chatters away in Italian ordering wine and drinks for the kids. Louis switches back and forth in English and Italian to ask the girls what they might want. Ceci treats Veronica with appropriate graciousness. They agree on fried fish, and Louis then makes delicious seafood suggestions to Veronica and Ceci, which is all perfectly fine. Louis begins to teach the girls to count in Italian as the waiter pours wine... and the abundance begins to flow in various courses of appetizers, drinks, bread, salad, soup, entrée, dessert, gelati, aperitifs, cheese, coffee, etc.

Veronica and Louis chat with the owner and his wife, an elegant, aging couple who speak many languages. They graciously address the girls in Spanish. Other people in the restaurant notice that there are three brown little girls sitting at a table with white people. The girls are fish out of water but... still have a sparkle in their eye as they sit a little taller in Grandma's pretty dresses, at this elegant table, looking at all these people in their fancy clothes, speaking so many languages and eating food fit for royalty.

The sun and the overwhelming dessert choices have put the kids in sleep mode, as their silence and bedroom eyes begin to trigger an exit. The room is full of the sights and sounds of international, well dressed, bourgeois people laughing and chatting energetically over the ongoing chamber music... and after two bottles of wine and their cognacs. It appears that Veronica is tired... and they all parade to the elevator, as people stare at the "blended" family.

In the elevator, the irony and tension of Louis, flanked by Veronica, Ceci, and the three girls, is clearly obvious to all. As Ceci and the girls (half asleep) get off the elevator at their floor. Ceci speaks.

Ceci: Thank you so much for a lovely dinner. The girls have had a really big day full of sun and giant extravagance. Thank you again and good night.

Tio Lou: It was our pleasure... right Veronica?

Veronica: Of course. *She smiles.*

Tio Lou: And tomorrow we will walk the boardwalk, check out the shops, have some Northern Italian Pizza... and go to a fun park in the evening. What do you say gang?

Jazmin: Fun park? You mean rides?

Tio Lou: Yes rides, cotton candy, and all

Ceci: Well now they are awake?

The elevator door closes.

Tio Lou: See you tomorrow....

Veronica: Bye bye!

The girls hug and thank Tio Lou and the elevator doors close.

Ceci: Come girls… Shall we retire to our private suite?

They strut with exaggeration down the hall.

234. <u>Walking along the coast – Next day</u>

It is a foggy coastal summer morning at the beachside café where Ceci and the girls join Tio Lou and Veronica in the morning. The girls are dressed again in cute summer outfits with their pink sneakers… and sun glasses. They run to hug and kiss him whenever they see him.

Tio Lou: You girls make me feel like I am in a Hollywood movie with all your high fashion.

Ceci: You *are* the big daddy Tio Lou.

Tio Lou: I love being surrounded by beautiful women.

Veronica: So I've noticed.

Tio Lou: So here's the perfect plan on a cloudy day… to walk the length of the entire boardwalk… all the way down past the shops along the canal where the boats sail off… and then to eat real Italian pizza down there at the point by the light house. What do you say?

Ceci: Sounds great to me.

Veronica: I will make it until my friend's house, where I will gladly sun myself on her porch and await your return.

They have quick coffees, hot chocolates and croissants, enjoying the direct proximity to the tumultuous Adriatic rocky sea coast, filling with tourists despite the gray sky. Tio Lou buys six umbrellas from a local vendor and they begin their hike down the boardwalk… past modern hotels with unusual architecture…. One after another. They pass family after family, couple after couple, grandparents, lovers, tourists. Despite the drizzle, they continue on towards the point and weave in and out of the local craft and fashion shops. Tio Lou buys the girls sensible dress shoes, and they take turns holding his hand and making jokes as they make their way into an arty beach apartment complex of small streets and teeny balconies. Here Veronica will visit with her friend, while the caravan continues. It has begun to rain, but the girls don't care.... They climb on the rocky walls. Ceci talks to Louis.

Ceci: Louis, I am sorry that we are imposing upon Veronica. Our timing is not good.

Tio Lou: It was my fault... I didn't do the math when we booked the tickets. I apologize for her behavior.

Ceci: Hey... hormones... they are powerful... and she feels threatened by our presence... so I think maybe we should shorten the visit don't you?

Tio Lou: I want to bring them to the fun park tonight. It's huge, like nothing they have ever seen before....

Ceci: OK... and Veronica? I doubt she will like that. She prefers the beach and the sun. And she definitely dislikes sharing you with the girls.

Tio Lou: And I am very vigilant of the pregnancy, so don't worry. Let's have dinner tonight. Then the girls can change and we'll go to the fun park. It's like kiddie Vegas... they will love it.

Ceci: OK then tomorrow, we will take the bicycle carriage around Lignano, and you can decide how you want to do this. I don't want to rock the boat with Veronica anymore. She definitely triggers my protective motherly instincts.

Tio Lou: Look .. I'm sorry Ceci. *It starts to rain. The girls have run ahead.*

Ceci: You don't have to be sorry. You're taken Louis, and she wants me to know that. However, I can still think of you as my brother. I never had a brother, and you are an only child. It's perfect. Then we can always be family OK? I am so thankful for your appreciation of the girls, and your support Louis. Nobody else on the planet, other than my Mom, cares about these precious sisters. And you really are making a big difference in their lives. So... I don't want to jeopardize your relationship, nor disgrace your hospitality... because Veronica just doesn't like them very much. OK?

Louis: Well that was a lot. I am glad you got it out.

She continues her rant.

Ceci: I mean how could you not love my kids? *Long silence* I didn't know that pregnancy makes you selfish. Excuse me... As you can see I have a temper when it comes to my kids' safety when they are treated like second class citizens.

Tio Lou: OK I'm really sorry Ceci. It's because I haven't married her officially, and she was brought up poor, so she feels insecure and threatened by everything... I am sorry... OK?

Ceci: Plus she's pregnant in her forties... and she's Italian.

Tio Lou: Yes she's Italian and Italians love to fight... and she is pregnant in her forties.... And I knew what I was getting myself into...

Ceci: And you love her.

Tio Lou: And I love her... Yes... And I love these little girls too. So let's enjoy the rest of this hike out to the light house and back, and the girls will really work up an appetite for the banquet tonight, with the Fun park after that. And then we'll talk about going home tomorrow.

Ceci: *She shifts back into grateful.* Yes, and it is all over the top perfect in every way Louis. I still have to protect my kids. *Putting her hand on his shoulder.* And I don't want the girls or me to be the cause for any pain or confusion in your life. You have been so good to us, and they love you so much.

Tio Lou: Don't you think I feel that love? It's worth a lot to me Ceci. Come on let's run.

Ceci: But look at me Louis... Rejecting and attacking my kids puts me on my hind legs. I hope you understand that.

Tio Lou: Yes I do and it won't happen again.

235. North Italian Coastal Pizza

Louis and Ceci attempt to keep running with the girls in the rain on the boardwalk doing Mary Poppins dances with the umbrellas. They find a Fellini like pizza shop where the cook throws the pizza dough up in the air, singing at the top of his lungs to the music blasting from the radio. He brags about his pizza sauce, that it comes from his great grandmother... that the cheese comes from his father's cows... They take shelter from the rain and eat pizza.

Angie: Dios mio ... this is the best pizza I have ever eaten!

Roxana: Me too.

Tio Lou: You notice how thin the crust is? The hook is the flavor in the sauce... the quality of the cheese, and the crispiness of that crust. In the north they do it this way... thin crust and the flavor of the sauce stands out.

Jazmin: Mom, learn how to make this OK?

Ceci: Yes mam.. I am analyzing as I eat. So don't eat too much, or you will not be hungry for the elegant dinner hour at the hotel remember? Princess dresses? Food for days? Desserts beyond your wildest dreams? All this is a far cry from the orphanage.

Angie: Pizza is my favorite food.

Jazmin: And I don't care if it gives me a big pancha!

Tio Lou: They're on vacation... Ceci.

Ceci: Yes, why not spoil them sick.. then bring them back to the third world. *Exaggerating*

Tio Lou: Oh come on.

Ceci: I'm sorry... I didn't mean it that way. They deserve all of this, and they will always treasure these memories.

Tio Lou: Good... OK ladies, show me the Mary Poppins umbrella dance back to the hotel.

Ceci: Si... Andiamos...!!!

It is still drizzling, but not enough to dampen the spirits of the parade. They pick up Veronica on the way back. Ceci dances in the drizzle with the girls, giving up the umbrellas. as Tio Lou accompanies Veronica slowly behind. They arrive at the hotel and part ways.

Tio Lou: See you at 7:00pm for dinner then? In the hotel dining room?

Ceci: Yes Louis... That is if we can get our princess thing on in time.

Tio Lou: I'm sure you will manage. They are adorable, whatever they wear.

Ceci: Thanks for such an exciting itinerary... Arivaderci!

236. Hotel Room – Dining Room

The girls are giggling it up in the hotel bathroom with the fancy bathtub, shower caps and shower. Ceci is deciding what to wear. It is their final evening, dining like royalty with Tio Lou. She decides to go all out for the three look alike, fluffy, baby blue flower girl dresses she bought on sale in Belluno... because it reminded them of Cinderella at the ball. She lines up their silver sandals and hair bows. The phone rings... it is Louis.. they are waiting. She dresses them as they talk.

Ceci: Come on girls... we are late. You know how Tio Lou dislikes that. We're going all out tonight.

Roxana: Y su traje Mama? And your outfit mom?

Ceci: You know... I haven't quite decided.

Jazmin: Come on Mom.. You have to wear something fabulosa, and knock them all out.

Angie: What about that white dress you bought at the dress shop?

Roxana and Jazmin: Yes!

Ceci: OK… You finish up and go downstairs… and I will join you as soon as I am ready. Do you think you can handle the elevator alone like big girls?

Jazmin: We just have to push the number 1 button… no problem.

Ceci: Then stand up straight…. Hearts on a skyhook. Chin up… mis cha chas lindas - and strut down that staircase like you are going to the ball! Make an entrance.

Cut to the downstairs stairway as the girls descend the staircase into the dining room where Tio Lou and Veronica wait at their special table. The girls do their best with exaggerated chins up. Louis is wearing a beautiful Italian designer gray shiny suit. Veronica is wearing a beautiful long flowered gown. The restaurant is full, and the pride with which the girls carry their beautiful fluffy blue look alike dresses, pulls spontaneous attention from the room. They all curtsy at the foot of the stairs and go to kiss Tio Lou and take their seats. He is beaming with pride, and orders from the waiter in his typical managerial way. Veronica smiles.

Tio Lou: Please bring my precious bambinas three Shirley Temples.

Roxana: Y quien es Shirley Temple? And who is Shirley temple?

Veronica: Ginger ale with a cherry.

Roxana: La bebida?

Tio Lou: That's what we call the cocktail for kids. And where is your mother?

Angie: She didn't know what to wear, so she'll be a little late.

Veronica: Well then let's order. You always know what to do.

Tio Lou: Of course, so girls, do you want spaghetti or hamburgers?

Angie: Spaghetti is good, if the sauce is red.

Jazmin: And spaghetti is Italian.

Roxana: Do you have meatballs?

Waiter: Of course . This is no problem mademoiselle.

Tio Lou: And a bottle of Proseco please.

Tio Lou gets lost in his menu, as Ceci appears descending the staircase in a long white dress, rhinestone earrings, and her hair piled on top of her head. This is a show stopper, and the girls run to accompany her to the table.

Restaurant Dance Number – Latin Jazz, Ceci and the girls

Tio Lou looks up from his menu... the pre-recorded music changes to Latin jazz, and the four of them dance their way down the isle to the table for a full, two minute production number. This brings on applause. The waiters pull out the chairs for Ceci and her girls... Tio Lou toasts the girls and Ceci with Shirley Temples and Proseco. The meal becomes even more lively, as a short, robust Italian opera singer takes over the small stage.

Conversation in the room becomes more and more lively. Needless to say, Tio Lou is enjoying all this attention from the ladies. The waiter brings out cokes for the girls, and all kinds of exotic hors d'oeuvres. They pass the plates around, even though the girls are unfamiliar and uninterested in most of it. Ceci is enjoying every morsel, from the coquille St. Jacques appetizer, to the Caesar salad prepared before them, the divine dishes of magically spiced vegetables, and then on to heaping plates of spaghetti, a lobster entrée and finally the eye popping assortment of desserts that follow the meal.

As the last drop falls from the second bottle of Proseco, Tio Lou rises and makes a toast to the three Honduran sisters.

Tio Lou: I wish to make a toast to my three beautiful Honduran daughters, who have my blessings and whom I will always love wherever they go and whatever they do on this earth. You are beautiful and don't ever forget it. To Roxana, Angie, and Jazmin.... *They all drink.*

Ceci: Thank you Tio Lou. *The girls go to hug him.*

Tio Lou: Ok who is ready for the Fun park?

Girls: Me!!!

Ceci: We have to change of course into the next fashion show.

Tio Lou: OK meet us down in front in ten minutes. I am going to have some coffee and pay the bill.

Veronica: No not me... Needless to say I am very uncomfortable at the moment. So, I am going to retire and watch TV.

Ceci: I am sorry you are in pain Veronica.

Jazmin: Shall we bring you some cotton candy?

Veronica: No don't do me any favors.

Tio Lou has gone to pay the bill and the girls are playing in the isle. Ceci takes this opportunity to speak to Veronica privately.

Ceci: I want you to know I am sorry that we are distracting Louis from you and this pregnancy. The schedule was badly considered. I know how uncomfortable you must be, and how running after somebody else's kids, is definitely not on your exercise list. So we are planning to leave very soon. Please don't let us upset you. I'm sure this will be an early evening. Just remember... I will always defend my children.

Ceci says this sweetly with hidden subtext. Tio Lou returns to the table.

Veronica: I am so glad you understand.

Tio Lou: So I will finish my coffee while everybody gets ready to move on to a magical tour of the Fun park?

Girls: Yes yes yes..!!

Tio Lou: Great... Veronica,,, I will see you upstairs in a moment. And ladies see you in the lobby in twenty minutes. *And they make their exit through the salon of visibly interested dining clients.*

237. Funpark evening

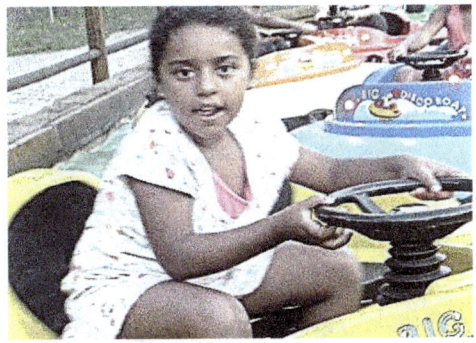

As the sun sets the five oddly blended family members (Ceci, Tio Lou and the three girls) take off for the neon beach Fun park. Carnaval music, penny arcades, gelati, and souvenir shops dazzle the girls along with rides of every imaginative shape and theme. For the first time the girls will drive their own bumper cars by themselves. This will be a featured experience for them in independence. Even Angie, who has been told she is too blind to drive, is having the time of her life in a little motor car that goes in circles. The super sound and visual stimulus has Ceci a little worried. She cues Louis.

Ceci: You know, it occurs to me that this kind of blasting, visual and audio stimuli could trigger reactions in Angie and Roxana. We may have to limit the intensity of the thrills.

Tio Lou: OK, I should have thought of that after our medical report. You're a good mama.

Ceci: When it comes to thrills, I have learned: That which gives the kids excitement, probably will give me anxiety.

Tio Lou: Well, let's keep an eye on them. The night is young.

The kids ride roller coasters, a swinging pirate ship that splashes in the water, a ferris wheel and spinning tea cups... They enter a scary dark house with loud noises and unstable floors. They can't laugh enough, and their joyous giggles and thrills are contagious for Louis. Ceci, however, notices that Roxana is unusually hyper, and is beginning to act like a baby with Tio Lou. Angie is looking dizzy and dazzled by the carnaval twilight. She becomes immediately concerned and bends down at eye level holding Angie and Roxana in front of her.

Ceci: Girls hello... This is mommy. I see that you are both a little crazy from all this noise and lights and action. Hello? *Angie is getting faint and starts to shake and hyperventilate.* Louis come take Roxana please.

Louis embraces Roxana while Ceci holds Angie close, talking to her the whole time.

Ceci: Angie baby, try to breathe honey.... breathe... we can fix this... Stay with me Angie... Mommy loves you. I'm right here baby. Can you try to slow down your breathing?

Ceci continues to rock Angie holding her very close to her own face. Louis has Roxana and Jazmin on his lap. Ceci takes Angie like a baby in her arms rocking her. Somehow this calms her down.

Ceci: Hi baby... It's Mama here. We're with Tio Lou and your sisters at the Fun park in Italy remember? You got dizzy from the roller coaster. Estas mariada? Como estas mi amor? How do you feel? Angie ...answer me!!

Angie: My stomach Mommy!...

Ceci: Uh oh.. Do you have to throw up? Oh OK? Over here ... come on... *Ceci instinctively leads her to a back alley.*

Roxana: A mi tambien Mommy!!!

Ceci: Oh OK.... Come on... Join the party. *Roxana runs to catch up with Ceci, and both she and Angie throw up at the same time.* Interesting purge timings..... I guess these are the affects of modernity on 3rd world kids. I'm glad that's over.

Tio Lou: Why don't you go clean them up in the lady's room of this café, and Jazmin and I will meet you on the terrace. Jazmin's having banana gelati and I'll be having vodka, how about yourself?

Ceci: At the moment I am out of tricks except plain water to clear their stomachs? And for me, perhaps a limoncello? Thank you Louis.

Tio Lou: I do what I can.

Ceci tries to send Louis a gracious smile, and then guides the stunned Roxana and Angie to a wash room in the back... and Jazmin takes advantage of having Tio Lou all to herself. She sits next to him proudly. They actually have the same birthday.

Ceci returns to the table with sleepy looking Angie and Roxana.

Jazmin: So you guys, how did you like the rides?

Angie: They were fantastic... I just can't think about them or I get dizzy.

Tio Lou: Ok ... enough Funpark, more gelato.

Girls: Yeah!

Ceci: I admire your ability to find a quick back pocket remedy for all ailments but after throwing up I think that's enough stimulus for one evening.

Tio Lou: Well I can't compete with your bag of tricks.

Ceci: I definitely don't have all the anti-dotes for their neurological problems. But the basic quick fixes come with the territory. You have to learn it from the person in pain. You know that as a Doctor.... And through everyday experience Moms have some of the best diagnostic tricks and cures. I'm just not sure about forever medications. That scares me.

Tio Lou: I understand that. And you should observe all of them carefully with that in mind.

Ceci: It's all a guessing game. I do my best.

Tio Lou: It's definitely time to go bambinas… Let's take a cab back to the hotel, and we'll see you at the pool in the morning.

Ceci: I can see that they all are wiped out. That sugar rush will only last for so long.

Jazmin: Mom.. Can I have gelato for breakfast?

238. <u>Dawn Wake up</u>

It is early and Ceci wakes up the girls to watch the dawn on the beach.

Ceci: Come on girls. This will be your last day on the Adriatic Sea and I want you to see the sun come up.

Jazmin: Mom I don't care about the sun and the moon. I want to sleep.

Ceci: Sorry, not today. We're going to take one of those family carriage bikes remember?

Angie: But I can't see anything out there Mom. It's still night time.

Ceci: Not for long. Vamos a ver la madrugada en Italia. Let's go watch the Italian dawn.

239. <u>Cruising the boardwalk- Buggy bikeride – Hotel Tamanaco</u>

The girls are riding in a family bicycle built for two to peddle in front and two in back, with a canopy. In the background the sun is coming up over the horizon. Not many people are on the beach. It is a beautiful and colorful dawn. They take turns peddling.

Jazmin: Wow Mom, that sky is beautiful.

Ceci: Angie can you see that?

Angie: Yes I can, I just don't know what color it is.

Roxana: It's pink and orange.

Ceci: I'm so glad to see all this with you guys. And this is a good time to see the rest of Lignano. Let's go inland here and drive around the streets.

This little tour gives us some insight into the local lifestyle. The streets are small and sunny with European balconies and crooked turns in the streets. Suddenly Ceci spots a sign that says "Hotel Tamanaco". She peddles faster in that direction.

Ceci: Oh my God… Tamanaco Hotel… This is surreal. What is my Indian Tamanaco doing here all the way from Venezuela?

Jazmin: Who is Tamanaco Mom?

Ceci: Oh you will never understand this…. But when I lived in Venezuela I studied with the brujos who go into trance and I met this Indian in spirit who was from the 16th century named Tamanaco, who actually became my protector and… It was a very special time for me.

Roxana: Mom that's a little crazy.

Angie: Isn't he the Indian doll that you have on your altar with the feathers?

Ceci: Yes... so we are going in, because this is indeed unbelievable.

Ceci makes a bee line for the desk and the concierge of this modest, back street hotel. When you walk in the lobby you can see two paintings of the great Indian chief Tamanaco. This is emotional for Ceci. There is a woman concierge there who speaks Spanish...

240. <u>Inside the Hotel Tamanaco in Lignano</u>

Ceci: **Disculpa senora, pero... me llamo atencion este Hotel porque yo vivia en Venezuela por algunos anos donde yo estudiaba con los brujos en Caracas y en la Montana de Maria Lionza... y pues... El Cacique Tamanaco fue mi protector... y aqui esta el en Italia!!** Excuse me Sra. but this hotel has caught my attention because I lived in Venezuela for several years where I studied with the brujos in Caracas and the Mountain of Sortes con Maria Lionza... and well Chief Tamanaco was my protector and here he is in Italy?

Concierge: **Si senora... Soy Venezolana, y mi esposo es Italiano... y pasamos los veranos alla en la Montana de Sortes, Venezuela donde trabajamos con Maria Lionza y Tamanaco... El tambien es mi protector.** Yes Mam. I am Venezuelan and my husband is Italian. And we spend summers there in the Mountain of Sortes, Venezuela where we work with Maria Lionza and Tamanaco. He is also my protector.

Ceci: **Y trabajan uds. con los espiritus aqui en Lignano?** And do you work with the spirits here in Lignano?

Concierge: **De vez en cuando. Mi hermana tambien conoce la practica de espiritismo en Venezuela, y ella es una materia.** Some times...My sister knows the practice of Spiritism in Venezuela and she is a medium.

Ceci: **Y esta ella aqui ahora?** And is she here now?

Concierge: **No.. esta en Caracas. Y veo que tienes hijas Latinas.** No she is in Caracas. And I see that you have Latina daughters.

Ceci: Ellas son Hondurenas. Y yo hiciera cualquier cosa para hablar con Tamanaco hoy... para ayudar a mis hijas. They are Hondurans. And I would do anything to speak to Tamanaco today to help my daughters. *Ceci suddenly jumps.* **You know I just got the chills!!!.**

Concierge: Si a mi tambien.. *She looks at the hair on her arms.* **Tamanco esta aqui. Pues, me llamo Benina. Mucho gusto.** Yes, me too. Tamanaco is here. Hello, my name is Mariana – a pleasure to meet you. *Extending her hand.*

The girls look a little confused. Ceci continues, speaking loudly to a painting of Tamanaco in the lobby as if spirit were listening.... even though there are other clients in the lobby.

Ceci: Si yo soy Cecilia... This is Jazmin, Angie and Roxana...... You know... **Estoy buscando milagros medicales para mis hijas....** Yes and I am Cecilia. And I am looking for medical miracles for my daughters.

Mariana: Ah hah... Me llamo Mariana.

Jazmin: Mom... what are you doing?

Ceci: Just having a little conversation with spirit. Would you please take my picture over here in front of his painting honey?

Jazmin snaps 2 photos. Mariana smiles and offers the girls "arepas."

Mariana: Quieres ver mi altar? Do you want to see my altar?

Ceci: Absolutamente!

Mariana: Ven conmigo. Come with me.

Mariana takes Ceci and the girls out back to her cluttered lean to porch where there is a huge altar with busts of Tamanaco and the Tres Poderosos (Maria Lionza, Negro Felipe, and el Cacique Guacipuro). She lights the candles on the altar.... And places some cocuy liquor in front of Tamanaco. She takes two cigars...conjures them and they smoke. The girls are dumbfounded. They all have wide eyes. Mariana examines the ashes of both cigars as they turn fluffy and white.

Benina: Si se puede hablar. Los caminos estan abierto para ti para rezar. Vaya pues. Yes you can speak. The paths are open for you to pray. Go for it.

Ceci composes herself to pray. The girls are wide eyed.

Ceci: En el nombre de Dios Poderoso, el hijo, y el Espiritu Santo… Con el permiso de la Reina Maria Lionza, el Libertador el Negro Felipe, y el Grand Cacique Guacaipuro… yo llamo mi protector … Tamanaco… que nos protéja con su ayuda milagrosa. Que pido… en el nombre de Dios por su sabiduria del corte medico… para remedios para las disabilidades de mis ninas adoptadas. Querida Tamanaco, tu ves lo que yo hago. Yo se que estas conmigo desde mi salida de Venezuela. And I thank you for that. Primero quiero pedir por la vista de Angie…. Que conseguimos una manera milagrosa para reconstruir su nervio optico. Para Jazmin, que ella puede sobrevivir sus problemas de crescimiento, su asthma y la angustia de estar abandonada con tres meses. Y para Roxana, que todos los huecos que tiene ella en su cerebro… todas las conexiones que ella falta, todos los deseos que ella tiene para ser saludable… que ella puede lograr.

Que ellas tendran amigas y una familia… una vida sin pobreza… Y ahora mismo, mas que todo las visas… que mi Madre me espera en mi pais… I'm asking for the future of my kids. Gracias… Tamanaco… por su protecion y interés en la seguridad de mis hijas. Deme el poder conseguir estes milagros para mis ninas. Deme direcion. Con su permiso… con su amor… Gracias.

In the name of God all powerful, the son, and the holy spirit. With the permission of the Queen Maria Lionza, the liberator Negro Felipe, and the great Chief Guacaipuro, I call my protector, the great chief Tamanaco… asking for his protection and for his miracle help. I ask in the name of your great power with the knowledge of the medical court… for remedies for the disabilities of my adopted children. Dear Tamanaco, you see what I am doing. I know that you are with me since I left Venezuela. And I thank you for that. So first I want to ask you for Angie… for her vision. That we can find a way to reconstruct her optic nerves. And for Jazmin, that she can survive her growth problems, her asthma and the anxiety of being abandoned at three months. And for Roxana, that all these holes that she has in her brain… all the connections that she seems to lack can be healed. And that all her desires to be healthy can be achieved. That they will have friends and a family… a life without poverty… And now, more than ever… the visas. My mother waits in my country for us. I am asking for the future of my children.

Thank you Tamanaco.. for your protection and interest in the safety of my daughters. Give me the power to find these miracles for my girls. Give me the direction… With your permission… with your love… Gracias.

Mariana: Amen que se sea. Eso fue mucho…. Si Dios quiere todo pasara. *Crossing herself.* Amen that it happens. That was a lot. God willing it will pass.

Jazmin: My mom believes in miracles.

Mariana: La vela verde de Tamanaco baila como loco. El te oyo. Tamanaco's green candle is dancing like crazy. He heard you.

Ceci: Me alegro. Gracias Mariana.

Phone rings… It is Tio Lou. Ceci answers it, despite her altered state of mind.

Ceci: Yes of course Louis… We are on the family buggy bicycle, and we watched the sun come up and now we are exploring Lignano. *Pause* **OK then, we'll meet you by the pool in half an hour.**

Roxana: Tio Lou?

Ceci: Yes... he is waiting for us... I think they are ready to leave. *Addressing Mariana*...Hay que ir Senora. Mils Gracias por su hospitalidad... y por el permiso usar su altar para hablar con Tamanaco...... un evento nunca creia yo que pudiera pasar de nuevo. We must leave Sra. Thank you so much for your hospitality, and for the permission to use your altar to speak to Tamanaco.... An event I never believed I could have again. *She hands her Italian Lira.*

Mariana: Su protector siempre esta contigo, Cecilia. Pero hay que trabajar con mi hermana para conversar directamente con Tamanaco. Sin embargo, yo se que el le escucho. Buenas tardes... Que Dios les bendiga. Ones' protector is always there Cecilia. But you would have to work with my sister to speak directly with Tamanaco. Nevertheless, I know that he heard you. Good afternoon... May God bless you.

They leave and get back on the bike.

Angie: Mom... that was weird.

Ceci: That all happened before you were born when I lived in Venezuela. And.... Who ever told you that your mother was normal?

241. Hotel Swimming Pool – check out

As they arrive in the pool area of the Hotel, we see Tio Lou and Veronica peacefully floating in the pool. When the girls see him, they start screaming, tearing off their sun dresses and jump into the pool. Tio Lou loves it. Veronica gets out of the pool immediately. Clearly, she is very pregnant and not comfortable. Ceci approaches her.

Ceci: Hi, how are you feeling?

Veronica: Like a ton of bricks. Can't wait to go home and have this child.

Ceci: Do you think it's time?

Veronica: Any minute... We're leaving shortly. I hope we make it home before I go into labor.

Ceci: Well my prayers are with you for a safe delivery, and for your little Goia. Veronica, I am very sorry about interfering with this pregnancy. I think of Louis as an American brother and that is all, and his generosity with these sisters has made a great impact on their lives. I wish so much that you could understand that. However, I am sorry again to upset you and cause you any discomfort. It was bad timing and I should have known more before accepting the invitation. Forgive me and good luck with your baby.

Veronica: Forgiven…. *She gathers her things and calls out to Louis.* Louis, I 'm going upstairs to pack. Goodbye girls.

This takes the girls by surprise.

Roxana: Are you going now? *You can see the separation anxiety kicking in as he leaves.*

Ceci: Yes honey… Veronica is very pregnant and needs peace and quiet… So you all will ride with me on the way home.

Jazmin: But we get to see you again right?

Tio Lou: Of course… I will take Veronica to the hospital when we get home, and will call you at the chalet. Are you OK with the Italian GPS?

Ceci: Sure. Louis… thank you so much for all of this. When all is said and done, the girls will remember this beach for the rest of their lives. Thank you.

The girls all hug Tio Lou. Roxana is crying.

Tio Lou: I will call you later this evening when we all get to Pieve D'Alpago OK? Don't cry Roxana. Now I must help Veronica. I will see you later.

The girls stand there in their wet bathing suits watching Tio Lou walk away. Ceci breaks the mood by tickling everybody into the pool. They spend the next few hours at the hotel pool surrounded by beautiful Italian women in beautiful Italian bathing suits.

242. <u>**Driving South in Italy – Return from the Beach**</u>

All four are in the Fiat with the music blaring. All three girls are stretched out and asleep. It's a 5 hour drive. Ceci is flying over the Dolomite Mountains again on the highway with huge stilt pillars and a long vertical drop to the valley below..

They stop and take pictures with the beautiful landscapes in the background, creating a little photo essay of the countryside, which is breathtaking. Ceci's cell phone rings, and it is Tio Lou:

Tio Lou: Ceci, this is Louis.

Ceci: Yes how are you?

Tio Lou: Well, Veronica just gave birth to baby Goia.

Ceci: Oh dear, where were you?

Tio Lou: Just as we pulled into town she went into labor. So we went straight to the hospital.

Ceci: Is she OK? Is the baby OK?

Tio Lou: Yes, everything is OK. Goia is beautiful and Veronica is glad to have her on the outside.

Ceci: Well, congratulations Louis. We are very happy for all of you.

Louis: Thank you, I will call you at the chalet later.

Ceci: You know Louis, I think we should cut our visit short and make plans to leave tomorrow. She's going to need you.

Louis: I know that. I'm glad you understand.

Ceci: So shall I call Iberia?

Louis: No, I'll take care of that and see what's available on short notice for four.

Ceci: OK Louis... thanks. We're having a wonderful time taking photos of the countryside along the way. Don't worry about us.

Louis: That's my Virginia girl... Ms. Independence.

Ceci: Ok so call us later?, and send our regards to Veronica. …. Good bye. *She sighs.*

The girls are spinning in a wheat field and falling down dizzy. Ceci calls them and they come running back to the car laughing.

Ceci: So I have news…. Veronica had a baby girl.

Roxana: Is she pretty?

Ceci: I'm sure she's pretty.

Angie: So what does that mean mom?

Jazmin: It means we gotta go soon and pack everything up.

Roxana: Pero porque?

Ceci: Porque Veronica is going to need Tio Lou to help her with the baby. And we'll just be in the way. So we will leave tomorrow.

Roxana starts to cry.

Jazmin: Oh come on Roxana. We have to go back to Honduras. We live there.

Ceci: It's OK Roxana. I am never going to leave you.

Angie: Mom you have to find a man who doesn't already have a girlfriend.

Ceci: It's all good… Tio Lou is the brother I never had. So guess what… tonight we can go for pizza when we get back to the chalet OK?

Angie: Our last real Italian pizza.

243. <u>Venice Airport - Departure</u>

Ceci, Louis, and the girls are at the departure gate at the Venice Airport. It is very early in the morning. Roxana is crying hysterically. Even Ceci is feeling it.
Angie and Jazmin are stunned.

Tio Lou: I am sorry about the hour … this is the only flight I could get. Hopefully you will make the connection in Madrid.

Ceci: We'll be going through Panama after that and then Honduras… so one way or another, we will be travelling all day. But don't worry about us. You have your hands full. Louis….Know that what you have done for me and the girls is almost unheard of in my world. I am aware of Veronica's disapproval… and yet from even a remote perspective, your generosity is truly compassionate and from the heart. Anybody can see that. So I thank you Louis. And I hope you can come and visit us in Honduras.

Tio Lou: Well I am hoping that I will visit you in the USA someday. *He bends down to face the girls.* Because I love these girls very much, and I want them to be successful and have a happy and safe life.

The PA system calls out the boarding for the flight to Madrid. Roxana won't let go of Louis.

Ceci: *Ceci goes to remove Roxana's grip on Louis.* Come on baby… We can't miss the flight. *With tears in her own eyes, she takes a last look at Louis and somehow drags all three girls towards the gate.*

Louis: I love all of you.

Louis watches as they disappear, and walks away… He has a tear in his eye.
They may never see Tio Lou again.

244. <u>Missing the connection in Madrid</u>

They land in Madrid. As the girls and Ceci run through the airport and arrive at the Iberia gate for Panama, it becomes clear that they have missed the plane, and must rebook the itinerary to Honduras.

Iberia travel agent: I am very sorry Ms. Diaz, but the only way we can do this is to put you through Mexico City and then on to San Pedro after that. And that plane leaves in three hours.

Ceci: Will you reroute our luggage as well?

Iberia Agent: Yes of course. Shall I book this for you Senora?

Ceci: Absolutely… without question. We want to go home.

245. <u>Immigration – Mexico City</u>

Ceci and the girls are exhausted from the travel run around, and stand in line at Immigration in Mexico City. When they get up to the window, Ceci gets the surprise of her life, after showing her American passport, and the girls' Honduran passports.

Immigration Agent: Excuse me Senora, but where are the girls' visas?

Ceci: What visas? We were rerouted here from Madrid after missing a connection to Panama.

Immigration Agent: I am sorry, but Hondurans must have visas in Mexico, just like the US and Canada. I will have to send you to Security.

He motions to a nearby policeman with dark glasses, carrying a rifle to escort us.

Ceci: What?

Agent: Please follow the officer Senora, with the girls. We will take care of your luggage.

Ceci: Come on girls.

Jazmin: Why does he have a gun mom?

Angie: Does he think we are bad?

Ceci: Because Hondurans are supposed to have special visas in Mexico, and I didn't know that, and damn it… that Iberian agent KNEW it and sent us anyway.

The officer escorts Ceci and the girls into a dark office where they wait for a Mexican Immigration officer to come and review Ceci's papers. When the girls have to go to the bathroom, the policeman with the rifle accompanies them. Finally, Ceci speaks to the officer, who assumes that she is trafficking Honduran orphans.

Immigration Officer: I will speak English with you Senora. I see that you are an American, and that you have, shall we say, interesting permits to travel with these kids. So why are you in Mexico?

Ceci: *Ceci repeats annoyed.* **Because we missed a connection in Madrid, and the Iberian travel agent put us through Mexico City instead of Panama on our way back to San Pedro, Honduras.**

Immigration Officer: OK, Senora Diaz... We have strict orders to arrest people on our soil who have no visas. And not having the proper adoption papers, makes your situation even more suspicious.

Ceci: You must be kidding!

Immigration Officer: Senora I will do my best to arrange to get you on the next plane to San Pedro as soon as everything has been reviewed. We reserve the right to go through your luggage.

Ceci: What? No lo creo. I don't believe it.

Immigrant Officer: Disculpa Senora... pero ud. es una gringa con tres morenitas. Y necessitamos averiguar lo que pasa aqui. Hay que hablar una por una con sus hijas. Espero que no hay problema. *He opens the door to let each girl in, one at a time.* Excuse me Sra, but you are a gringa with three little brown girls. And we need to look into what is happening here. I must speak one by one to the girls. I hope there is no problem.

Ceci: OK, pero permitame explicarles lo que pasa. Permit me to explain to them what is happening.

Immigrant Officer: Como no... Of course.

Ceci: Girls, listen to me. Because we don't have visas to be here, these guys think maybe I have you without permission.... And that maybe I am stealing you.....

Roxana: Pero tu eres mi madre. But you are my mother.

Ceci: Yes honey... so now he wants you to tell him that... each one of you alone... so they know you all will tell the truth. I will be right here in this other room. It will be OK... and then after that we will get on a plane to Honduras. So Jazmin... you go first.

Jazmin is angry. She goes in the room and tells the guy off.

Jazmin: Si, ella es mi madre. Vivimos con ella en una casa grande en La Ceiba. Y no me gusta como nos tratan. Yes she is my mother. We live with her in a big house in La Ceiba. And I don't like the way you treat us. **You make us feel like criminals. My mother is a good person. I don't like it here.**

Cut immediately to Roxana in the chair, who has her arms folded and is upset.

Immigration Officer: Y porque fueron a Italia? And why did you go to Italy?

Roxana: A visitar nuestro padrino. To visit our Godfather.

Immigration Officer: Y donde esta su madre? And where is your mother?

Roxana: Ceci es mi madre. Ceci is my mother.

Immigration Officer: Your REAL mother muchacha!!

Roxana: You scare me!!!!

Immigration Officer: Where is she?

Roxana: En La Ceiba. I want my Mom.

She goes for the door. The agent lets her out and calls in Angie.

Agent: And why don't you live with your real mother?

Angie: Because she hit me, and that's why I lost my sight, so the soldiers took us all away from her.

Agent: And does the Gringa know your mother?

Angie: Yes, she knows that Ceci is taking care of us.

Agent: And how long has the Gringa been taking care of you?

Angie: I don't know, but she is our real mother, and you are confusing me!

Agent: What if I don't believe you?

Angie: Then what are you saying? Are you going to take us away from Ceci? No... you can't do that? No puede senor!!! *She gets hysterical and starts to call Ceci.... Then she stars to* *convulse. She is having a seizure. Ceci comes bursting into the room. The guard tries to detain her but she manages to get to Angie and take her in her arms.*

Ceci: It's OK baby. I'm here. *She embraces her.*

Angie: No! *She begins to hyper ventilate. Ceci breathes slowly in and out.*

Ceci: Try to breath... with me in and out... in and out. You can do this honey. I'm not going anywhere.

The officer at this point is standing up in disbelief.... Other officers enter the room. A secretary gets water. Roxana and Jazmin are standing there hanging on to Angie. Finally, when she drinks the water she calms down. Ceci picks her up and rocks her. Then with rapid angry English she scolds the agent.

Ceci: Excuse me officer. I don't know what you said to my children, but I can tell you that you scared the hell out of all three of them. They have already been through separation anxiety a few times in their lives, and this experience has only added to the trauma they must carry with them every day. I am their mother, and I do everything I can to take them and their disabilities out of harm's way. This has been a negative experience, and I hope you understand that children do not lie about the people they truly love. You can see my papers are in order. Please let us go.

Officer: I am sorry Senora Diaz. We will arrange the travel plans for you.

Ceci: Gracias Senor. Please take us back to Iberia so we can go home, Por favor Senor... This has been a nightmare.... Una pesadilla!!

The officer tells his assistant with the rifle to take them to the plane. Clearly the girls are upset.

The secretary comes in with a wheel chair for Angie... and they all proceed to march through the airport accompanied by the armed guard with the sinister sun glasses.... as if they are criminals. They go to a side door near one of the gates and are picked up in a van, and driven to the airplane. For the entire van ride, Ceci is alarmed with wide eyes, not knowing where they were going. When they arrive at the plane on the tarmac the guard gives them their tickets. Ceci asks the guard.

Ceci: Y nuestras maletas? And our suitcases?

Guard: Ya estan Senora…. Buen Viaje. They are already there. *All without expression.*

They are weary as they climb the stairs to the plane. And Ceci asks the stewardess….

Ceci: Donde va este vuelo Senorita? Where is this flight going Srita?

Stewardess: *Confused as to why Ceci would not know, looking at her tickets.* **A San Pedro, Honduras… Are you OK?**

Ceci: Si, estoy muy bien!… Gracias…. Come on girls… we're going home.

Jazmin: Adios Mexico!! *She shouts to the guard with the rifle who is watching them from the tarmac go into the plane… still wearing his dark sunglasses even though it is 8pm.*

246. **First Morning back in La Ceiba**

Everybody has overslept when Vilma arrives banging on the door.

Vilma: Ceci… Buenos dias!!! Soy yo Vilma! Ceci, Good morning… It's me Vilma!

Ceci: Dios mio… Olvide… Lunes.. Escuela!!! Vilma… Voy! Oh my God, I forgot… Monday… School… Vilma…. I'm coming!

She wakes the girls up and tells them to get dressed… Vilma enters.

Vilma: Entonces? Como se fue? So, how did it go?

Ceci*: to Vilma* **Bello… Italia es bello… Pero tuvimos problemas con imigracion, y el vuelo y pues…lleguemos tarde. Gracias por cuidar la casa Vilma. Ahora hay que preperarles para escuela. Ayudame con desayuno y sus meriendas por favor?** Beautiful… Italy is beautiful. But we had problems with immigration, and the flight… we came in late. Thank you so much for taking care of the house. But now we must get them ready for school. Please help me with breakfast and their lunch snacks.

Vilma: Claro … voy. *Vilma moves towards the kitchen.*

Ceci: Bueno… yo les vesto si tu puedes ayudarme en la cocina. *Ceci goes to help the girls with their school uniforms.* Great… I can dress them if you cover the kitchen.

Vilma: Ya, Ceci.

Ceci: Gracias Vilma… por despertarnos… *shouting* - Thank you for waking us up.

Vilma: No se preocupes, Ceci. *Shouting back* Don't worry Ceci.

We see a musical runaround of dressing, breakfast, hair combing, and brushing teeth.

247. **Transporting Kids to Schools**

Ceci first drops Roxana at Bright Beginnings, and gives her money for a baleada.

Ceci: OK my Roxie… have a great day! Are you nervous?

Roxana: No… because I have some friends here.

Ceci: Don't forget… I'm picking you up early to go to the psychologist.

Roxana: What is that?

Ceci: She will help us to understand your brain, and how to help you in school. OK? I love you baby. Te amo mucho baby.

Next on to the Kinder to drop off Angie and Jazmin who are returning for the final Kinder level this year. When they arrive, they are happy to see their friends from last year.

Ceci: You both look sparkling fabulous…Give me besos.

Angie: Are we going to the bicycolagest today with Roxana?

Ceci: Yes, after school. I will pick you up... and I will take you to the PSY CHO LO GIST. OK? I love you.... Have a wonderful day.

Jazmin: Bye Mommie...

Angie: Bye Mommie... I love you.

Ceci: And me too, hasta la Luna!

Besos later... Ceci is pulling away from the kindergarten, seeing the girls in the rearview mirror and smiling and talking to herself, because...

Ceci: This is the way it's supposed to be... Because from now on you will always come home to <u>my</u> house.

248. **Dance Class – a new year – Dance Studio- Mazapan**

There is a new semester at the Mazapan school and Ceci is taking attendance with her class of teenagers, and running over the curriculum while Vilma takes their measurements for costumes.

Ceci: Buenas tardes ladies... Welcome to dance class. How many of you have ever studied dance before? *None respond.* That's OK... it is why I am here... and there is a first time for everything. So let's talk first.

Please know that I expect a strict dress code of a leotard and tights or black jazz pants in every class. When you have the right uniform, you are serious. I want you to decide if you are up to this.

We will begin with ballet technique at the bar. It is the foundation of Western classical dance. And I am interested in all kinds of dance like hip hop, flamenco, salsa and merengue, jazz, tap, modern dance, punta, African and ethnic dance too...., but the ultimate discipline in line and balance comes from ballet technique. Formal dance education demands that you get some of this first.

Yet... let me say this... What really interests me in the dance is what happens in all movement between the point of departure.... and the point of arrival. Someone who loves exploring the dynamics of what happens between these points in time and space…. is truly a dancer. *She demonstrates as she por des bras her arms.*

So we begin with plies, which means "to fold" in French… So please remember to apply this concept of your commitment to departure and arrival in exercise as well as when you are dancing. It will then become a habit… to take off with intention and fly artistically to a destination with every part of your body and soul.

So enough poetry… now we will sweat. It will be difficult at first but eventually you will understand the beauty and ritual of ballet. OK…. to the bar please.

The girls line up at the bar, and Ceci explains that there are five basic ballet positions with arms for plies… and slowly they begin with the piano music.

249. <u>Picking up the girls from psychologist – Hospital La Fe</u>

Ceci walks into the psychology office at the Hospital La Fe and the girls are playing in the nursery with the director. They see Ceci and run towards her. The Doctor follows with a big smile.

Doctor: **Buenas tardes Sra Diaz… Fue un placer trabajar con sus muchachas bonitas.** Good afternoon Ms. Diaz. It was a pleasure working with your pretty girls.

Ceci: **Gracias… Como se fue?** How did it go?

Doctor: **Well I worked with Roxana and my associates worked with Jazmin and Angie.**

Ceci: And what have you determined?

Doctor: With the medical and historical background you gave us, along with the tests and observations we have made, there will be a final report ready next week that includes a conference with each doctor about each child. And I will meet with you about Roxana.

Ceci: That sounds good.

Roxana: Mom – Yo hice juegos con la senora... y yo gane. I played games with the Sra. and I won.

Ceci: You won? That's terrific. And how did you guys do?

Angie: I was pretty good with the games.

Jazmin: They were really easy Mom.

Doctor: Everybody dances to a different beat, little Jazmin.

Ceci: How true...

Doctor: Can you come next Weds at noon?

Ceci: Yes that's perfect... Thank you so much. Now how much do I owe you for this?

Doctor: Seven thousand five hundred lempiras for the three girls... and a check is fine.

Ceci: OK.... Here you go... *She writes the check.*

Doctor: I will give you a receipt next week when I see you ... Ciao.

Ceci: Girls say bye to the Doctor,and I have a surprise for you

They comply with hugs, and Ceci rushes them out of the office into the truck which is already packed with suitcases.

Roxana: Tu sabes que no me gusta sorpresas... You know that I don't like surprises.

Ceci: Oh but you are going to like this. Now listen. Remember the man who always takes pictures at our dance concerts?

Angie: Si, Senor Nimer...

Ceci: Yes... well he thinks that you guys are SO beautiful, that he wants to take pictures of us in the botanical gardens near the dance studio. So I have maletas with costumes so we can make modelaje with different looks in the garden. OK?

Silence... She starts to drive.

Jazmin: But Mom, I want to go home and watch TV.

Ceci: Nimer wants to shoot the photos in the dusk light.. when the sun is going west. Oh come on, it will be fun, and we can do a few changes and that's it… OK? I also want to get some photos of you in the typical Honduran dresses for your school project. He is such a good photographer, and I want to have the pictures…

Angie: OK Mom… we'll do it for you.

Ceci: I know you are going to love it… and I have your favorite dresses.

250. <u>Botanical Gardens – Photo Shoot</u>

They drive through the Standard Fruit guard area near the dance studio, where Nimer is waiting for them, camera in hand. He is checking the light. The botanical gardens of the Standard Fruit company are on the same grounds as the dance studio, the Mazapan School, and the company offices.

Nimer: Hola munecas y mama.

Ceci: Hola Nimer. Vamos a cambiar rapido… Hello Nimer.. we will change fast.

Nimer: Si porque el sol baja… y me encanta esta luz tropical de la tarde. Yes, because the sun is going down and I love this tropical afternoon light.

Ceci: Si senor! Vengan cha chas.

This segment is a musical montage of the four posing in various natural settings in the park. Also including their native costume with Roxana showing the pottery. The number could be done to music as little dances, including freeze moments for the photos. All three girls are very photogenic.

Photos by Nimer Alvarado

251. Bedtime – Call from Grandma

Roxana and Angie are dancing around in pajamas while Jazmin has set up her desk/office in the bathroom in case she has to go. It is a school night. Uniforms are laid out. Ceci walks in as they are all belting out the lyrics to some Spanish pop tune. Telephone rings..Roxana answers… it's Grandma!

Roxana: Abuela!! Angie, Jazmin…. Grandma esta llamando!!!

Ceci: *Picking up on the other extension.* **Mom hi, how are you?**

Grandma: I am so glad to get you… I didn't get through on the skype last week, and nobody has been answering the phone.

Ceci: I am sorry Mom. We were without power last week again and of course the internet takes a while to kick in after power failures. How are you? We miss you. The girls miss you.

Girls: Hola Abuela…

Ceci: They are all on the other phone.

Grandma: Como estan mis nietas? Angie… Roxanna…. Jazmin???

Girls: Buenas!! Cuando vienes Abuela?

Grandma: No puedo ahora, pero tengo una sorpresa para su mama…

Ceci: What mom?

Grandma: I just shipped out your car yesterday from Delaware, and it should be there in a few weeks.

Ceci: A few weeks? Really!! Wow Mom… Good for you.

Grandma: They would absolutely not let me fill it with anything. So it is the key and the car. And it will cost you half the price of purchase with import taxes, as well as the shipping fee of $800… So we are into this transaction for a pretty penny.

Ceci: Yes mom… but it will be so much better for me and the kids. The old black truck has just about had it.

Grandma: Yes .. old age is not fun.

Ceci: How are you mom?

Grandma: I still have that cough… and did I tell you about the hurricane Isabel? That the three ash trees on the front lawn came crashing down on the roof.

Ceci: What? While you were in the house?

Grandma: Yes.. and without electricity.

Ceci: Oh my God Mom… so where are you?

Grandma: I am at your sister's house and they are repairing the roof this week.

Ceci: How did you have time to ship the car and deal with all of this?

Grandma: Because I am a mover and a shaker… Where do you think you get it?

Ceci: When are you going to move and shake yourself back down here?

Grandma: As soon as I take care of the house....

Ceci: Tell Grandma you love her...

Girls: *on the other phone listening*.....We love you Grandma!!!!

Grandma: And I love you too... Besos!!

Ceci: Take care of that cough... And say hi to my sister... Bye Mom, I love you.

Ceci hangs up with a tear in her eye.

Jazmin: Why are you crying Mom? Didn't I hear that we are getting a new car?

Angie: Yes and we should give her a name.

Jazmin: I know.. how about Karlota?

Ceci: I like that.

Roxana: Don't cry mom.

Ceci: I cry easily... Got it from my Dad. He used to cry at sad movies. It's OK... I just miss my mom. Time to dream girls – school tomorrow.

Roxana: **Mom – a veces tengo pesadillas.** Mom sometimes I have nightmares.

Ceci: **De que?** Of what?

Roxana: Like if I see a scary movie, I can't forget it, and I have bad dreams.

Ceci: Roxana, you have to know the difference between real and not real. And the movies are not real. They are stories that people make up. There are no monsters in your life.

Angie: So Mom why do they make scary movies?

Ceci: Excellent question, along with murder, violence and drug stories, wars, monsters, horror, crime and killing... and on and on all over TV and movies.... Because people need to feel something other than their daily routine, and for some reason that stuff wakes them up. Personally, I think it is bad information and is sick entertainment, which can inspire the worst crimes of humanity. And ....the United States generates most of the media violence in the world. Sorry girls... I should change the vibe at bedtime.

Jazmin: Sing mother moon mom.

Ceci: Ok my sweet bambinas... just so you know... you can do anything you want to do, and be anything you want to be, if you are realistic, you do the work, and find the people who can help you get there. And I am here to help you find that path. I want you to have dreams that come true.

You can hear the outdoor audio of the Evangelicals down the block, with their blood curling prayers for salvation from the pain of poverty, betrayal, sickness and hunger.

Roxana: Oye Momma... They are crying.

Ceci: Yes I hear... and I pity those people. I also know that crying and feeling sorry for yourself does not get you rescued. Only the strength and vision of a solution, a pathway, un camino abierto... that you can follow step by step until you reach your goal... that is the real path to miracles. You must believe in yourself.

Angie: But are people supposed to scream in church?

Ceci: Some people in Honduras have very hard lives. I will close the window and turn on the AC... and sing... OK? I will sing to you so you can sleep.

Jazmin: Mommy... Why are we the lucky ones? We don't have to scream and yell at God.

Ceci: That's because he picked me to lift you out of that world. This doesn't mean you will spend the rest of your life without pain. Everybody has pain.

Roxana: I have pain sometimes.

Ceci: I know you all do. But there is so much joy to share with people too. Just remember to bring your problems home, because I truly care, and will help you in any way I can. We have to share the good and the bad, because we care about each other.

Angie: I don't want to be a complainer.

Ceci: It's important to share the happiness. But I want you to come to me with any problems you have.

Roxana: **A cantar mami por favor.** Sing Mom, please.

Ceci: **Cha chas.. Les amo muchisimo.** *She dims the light and sings Mother Moon again.*

252. <u>Ceci wakes up – Sat morning – Angie talks about blindness</u>

Girls jump on Ceci for a late morning wakeup. Ceci has been lost in her dream.

Roxana: **Despiertete Mami!... Es tarde.** Wake up Mom, it's late.

Angie: **Tengo hambre y quiero pancakes!** I'm hungry and I want pancakes!

Ceci: **OK... todavia estoy en la luna.** Ok... I am still on the moon.

Jazmin: **OK Madre Luna... time to make breakfast.** Ok Mother Moon, it's time to make breakfast.

Ceci: **Si senorita ... Pancakes it is.**

Angie: **Mami... Tengo que decirte algo.** Mom, I have to tell you something.

Ceci: **Yes baby digame.**

Angie: **Sometimes everything goes black and I can't see anything. Then when it comes back I start to shake.**

Jazmin: **Yeah like when she pushes too hard on the pencil her arm starts to shake.**

Ceci: **Oh my God!**

Angie: But I have to push hard so it is dark enough to see it! Then that turns into a big calambre spasm and I can't control the shakes in my arm.

Ceci: This is something neurological, like when I found you. We will have to look into this more. I will take you to the Doctor soon.

Angie: Oh Mami... What's wrong with me... My eyes, my brain, my nerves... What else? I just want to be a normal girl.

Long, uncomfortable silence, as Ceci is at a loss for words. She embraces Angie.

Ceci: Right now, you are my pancake helper... So let's go make pancakes OK? I promise I will figure this out... Just always tell me about it OK? You are precious, remember that.

Roxana: Me too Mami... **Que paso conmigo?** What happened to me?

Jazmin: The "mengitis" ate your brain.

Ceci: Excuse me Jazmin. We all have disabilities and we help each other and learn how to do things right OK? And if you all have enough energy to eat pancakes ,,, well then you will have to help me make them.

Angie: Ok Mami...

Ceci: And Roxana you are very smart about a lot of things. So don't worry about it.

Ceci puts on the music, and they all begin to improvise pancake production in the kitchen. It is a mad laugh of learning how to use the spatula.

253. <u>**Bright Beginnings School - Roxana's teacher, Ms. Becerra**</u>

Ceci pulls up to Bright Beginnings, Roxana's private Bi-lingual school on the outskirts of La Ceiba. She parks the truck and goes to Ms. Becerra's, 2nd grade class, where Roxana is waiting. When she walks in, Roxana is fixing up her display of the Arbol de Mayo (May Tree). It is an indigenous fertility gift of flowers, corn, squash, and beans offered to the integrated Catholic form of a cross with the May tree to invoke abundance of the crops and food for winter. Ceci goes to admire the project, as she did most of it herself, but left enough of the flower work for Roxana to make her mark on the project. Ms. Becerra greets Ceci and they sit to talk. Ceci sends Roxana out for a baleada.

Ms. Becerra: I am so glad that you came to see me. I want you to know that Roxana is a beautiful little girl…. In so many ways… But clearly there has been emotional and mental malfunction. I am aware of her learning delays in certain areas. I can tell you for sure that she has all the characteristics of "dyslexia, dyscalculia" and some kind of language processing disorder, beyond bi-lingual difficulty.

Ceci: Yes *Big pause… as she breathes…* Well somehow she beat meningitis, without escaping its mental effects. I am aware of her learning delays, and now that you put a name on the disability it makes sense. She has trouble reading, adding and subtracting and more.

Ms. Becerra: And dyslexia is so much bigger than reversing the b and the d… or the 6 and the 9. It includes being unable to recognize groups of letters or numbers. Sometimes she says the words shake on the page when she is confused. Not only reading, writing and math become confused…. Also thoughts of sequential action, the steps to achieve a goal becomes shuffled as well. It is still a mystery for many educators and psychologists.

Ceci: And there are nervous reactions that concern me as well… around loud music, or loud crowd noise, she speeds up, and becomes irrational. I have also seen this when she is angry.

Ms. Becerra: Of course confusion gives her anxiety. I am sorry about this. I can only tell you about the dyslexia and dyscalculia, as an educator. As her teacher, I know how hard she tries, and what a beautiful little girl that she truly is. I love having her in class.

Ceci: Thank you... *Tears begin to fall, resulting from another reality check.* I am going to get the psychological analysis and learning aptitude results of all the girls today. It will be interesting if this also appears. And thank you for caring about Roxana.

Ms. Becerra: I see how disabled learners suffer socially, and Honduras has lots of them. That is why so many drop out at 5th grade, as they are becoming old enough to babysit, or work. I know how Roxana suffers with the rejections, and with God as my father, I try to protect children from bullying... but it comes from the parents of these children, who don't understand disabilities. Fortunately, Roxana is very pretty... but she is still lost and wants to be found. I commend you for your benevolent tenacity to get legal custody and keep the three sisters together. I am sure that they all need extra guidance.

Ceci: I don't want them to suffer socially, and I worry about that a lot, as it fits right in parallel lines to their academic disabilities.

Roxana walks in eating a baleada.

Ms. Becerra: You can only hope that you always put her in trustworthy hands throughout her care and education....

Ceci: Well I thank you for being one of those who care. I appreciate this information about her dyslexia and dyscalculia, which I will look into.

Ms. Becerra: You must research this yourself, as there are very few therapists who know how to treat dyslexia and dyscalculia. Maybe in the states... Good luck... Bye Roxana... Hasta manana.

Roxana: Adios Sra. Becerra. *With a hug, they take off in the truck.*

Ceci: I'm going to take you to the studio and then go see the psychologist about her report about you OK? Vilma is there waiting for you, and you can do your homework and get ready for class. OK baby? I love you.

Roxana: I love you too mom. Mom? Why do I have all these problems? A veces estoy tan confundida. Sometimes I am so confused.

She begins to cry. Ceci pulls her over and embraces her.

Ceci: Roxana, no matter what it is that is confusing you... I will always try to help you and understand you..... difficult as that may be sometimes. I love you... Look at me...You are growing a little slower in your brain than other kids. But you are healing and always getting better. I love you Roxana. Soy tu madre, cuando todo el mundo te rechaza... yo estoy aqui esperandote. Te amo... Tu eres mi hija... No te abondonare... nunca ... OK? I am your mother, when the whole world rejects you, I am here waiting for you. I love you. You are my daughter. I will never abandon you OK?

Roxana: Ok Mom... I have to pretend so much... that I understand what people are saying.... When I don't understand. Sometimes in Spanish too.... And the words on the page start to shake, and I shake, and everybody laughs at me. And then the noises around me get louder, and I can't concentrate...

Ceci: Ohhhh my beautiful Roxie ... It's because you are so frustrated. You just learn at a different speed. It's OK... I don't care how you learn, as long as you learn at your speed... we will get through this, and you will read and write and add and subtract, and do the times tables, which you already know from doing them in the car with me.... You get an A for that. And you are a very good dancer, and so beautiful... I love you Rox.

Roxana: Mom... Sometimes I am so lost - like I am going crazy.

Ceci: You are not lost. You belong to this family. Please come to me when that happens... Or Vilma... or Ms. Becerra... Whomever... Find help... calm down. OK.... So today I am going to see the psychologist to get her report so we can work on these things. So you stay here with Vilma, and the girls will be here soon. I love you baby.

Roxana: Te amo mucho Mami. I love you so much Mom.

254. **Psychological Report – Hospital La Fe office**

Ceci enters the hospital and walks down the modest, dated hallways to the Psychology department. She sits in a small waiting room and is soon greeted by the Director and is taken to a small office where two other young psychologists are waiting. After introductions the Director speaks:

Director: Ms. Diaz... I have thought it would be better to combine the session for the three sisters. We may have the possibility of illuminating parallel genetic and medical conditions which may have affected all of the girls.

Ceci: That sounds logical.

Director: So let's start with Roxana at 8 years old, who quite frankly, has suffered most from the length of time she sustained very substandard living conditions. We can only surmise that bad prenatal care, abuse, malnutrition, drug absorption and meningitis are the obvious causes of her learning disorders. Basically her skills reflect those of a child 3 years younger than her present age. You said she didn't actually start speaking until she was around 5 years old.

Ceci: She used to grunt when she wanted to say something. Even in pre-kinder at the SOS she could not copy from the board into her notebook without help. She has always had difficulty concentrating... so she is slow at writing and completely blocks math.

Director: I will tell you what I observed. First and foremost is her anxiety, impulsiveness, exhibitionist conduct and aggression. She has a low tolerance for frustration and difficulty organizing materials. Sometimes she was angry, other times she acted like a baby, and when she had drawn something, she wanted to show it to you.

Ceci is clearly uncomfortable with this information.

Director: There is a delay in all of her thought processes. Her range of information is deficient as is her memory. She is unable to think in concepts, and that leads to difficulty in critical thinking and establishing relationships.

Ceci: She was abandoned. Her communication skills are bad because she had a horrible relationship with her blood mother.

Director: And so it is difficult for her to select and verbalize appropriate connections to people and ideas.

Ceci: And then she just forgets where she belongs when she gets lost in the chaos. Oh God.

Director: With math she never really grasped the basic concepts of numbers and simple arithmetic. We call this "dyscalculia". In Pre kinder she was probably still in shock from being moved again. She has limited ability to calculate mentally and this affects her concentration. She says that you are trying to teach her simple math in the car.

Ceci: Yes... I am trying. I also see that her long term memory is better than her short term memory.

Director: Clearly Roxana is verbally deficient which goes beyond her bi-lingual confusion. She just can't retain enough linguistic information to access it and use it quickly.... and express herself. I see the delay in her responses. We have determined that some children were not meant to be bi-lingual, and for that reason of overload, she has problems speaking any language.

Ceci: She seems to understand my English.

Director: She may understand short sentences, but processing a series of directions or following a lecture in school is very difficult for her. And I also believe she is dyslexic.

Ceci: Her teacher just told me that.

Director: The dyslexia affects her sense of sequence... taking steps from A to Z... both as audio and visual explanations. Inverting bs and ds is just the tip of the iceberg. She may add or delete words or letters. I also noticed she has a speech and diction disorder pronouncing certain syllables or sounds.

Ceci: Yes, that too.

Director: When she has this difficulty expressing herself, her comprehension just shatters and she can't take personal responsibility for her actions or for making plans.... or for communicating with others. She does not have the space to store this information... Do you understand?

Ceci: You know what? This is all correct and I get it...but it is painful to hear any more of it without some hope of a cure.

Director: OK.. I know this is difficult for you to digest. Clearly Roxana has been through her most emotional trauma as a young child. You must always remember that she is three years below her normal age emotionally and intellectually. You will have to find the right schools.

Ceci: Where? Special ed does not exist in Honduras.

Director: I understand, and educators in La Ceiba are frustrated, because they have no technique to deal with special ed kids other than day care. Why do you think most adults don't go past the 5th grade in the public sector?

Ceci: I just need to get them to Special ed in the states as soon as possible. The public system at least recognizes the symptoms of a special needs kid in first grade, and begins the program there. My girls are not getting that kind of patience and connected education.

Director: Ms. Diaz, my heart goes out to you in every way. I can give you a list of important guidelines to help her teachers understand her disability, and plans to develop her memory, improve her concentration, deal with her dyslexia, and above all.... her self esteem. She will slowly mature and grow at her speed with a stable life style.

Ceci: Thank you.

Director: Now you may not appreciate or understand this now... But these guidelines are important methods to keep Roxana on track... and you will see that progress in 10 years. This will help her to grasp information and use it. She must feel connected to become part of the learning process.

Ceci: Ok thank you... At least now I understand her obstinacy. *She breathes deep and puts her head down for a moment.* Well now that I am completely exhausted, let's hear about Angie.

#2 Psychologist, Dr. Rosales: Yes Senora. I am pleased to meet you. My name is Marta Rosales, and I want you to know that I really enjoyed my time with Angie. Quite honestly I must preface my analysis by saying that her blindness, though partial, definitely affected her ability to take the visual perception and motor ability portion of our test fairly. Like Roxana, in an academic setting she has difficulty concentrating, with deficiency in memory and verbal information. The same in arithmetic... with hostility towards the exercises. Although in many ways she has a normal intelligence, her visual frustration and consequential impulsiveness make it difficult to test her.

Ceci: This sounds just like Roxana.

Director: I think Angie and Roxana were both affected by the meningitis, independent of Angie's visual impairment... Which requires brain scans and encephalograms. Although I agree that blindness would slow down anybody taking this test.

Dr. Rosales: I can see that there is a delay in her processing, which is why she is doubly frustrated. Both girls were late with speaking, which could be caused by neurological damage from the meningitis as well as the trauma of being removed from their family.

Ceci: OK... *She breathes in...* So where does that leave me with Angie?

Dr. Rosales: As for the seizures, I would suggest a change in the medication to Lamactil... which is more "suave" on the body. The Carbomecepina is harsh and can also cause muscle spasms.

Ceci: Yes, what are those calambres (muscle spasms) about? All my daughters get them for days on end.

Director: Nobody knows. We have met other children with this problem... and we can only surmise that it is bad circulation caused by physical or mental stress.

Ceci: OK, well I will get the Lamactil and see how that goes.

The doctor writes a prescription.

Dr. Rosales: I have made a list of medical suggestions for Angie... which include constant monitoring of her eyesight and of course, her neurological condition for her tremors and seizures. Both girls should have regular encephalograms.

Ceci: Frankly... I would like to take Angie off of all these meds.

Dr. Rosales: With time, I think that will be possible, with the guidance of a neurologist. For the moment, she really needs this drug, along with special visual accommodations in class, which I have prepared here for you to pass on to her teachers.

Director: Ms. Diaz, let's be clear. I believe Angie has intelligence. The three girls are experiencing the emotional trauma of change. Their lives have been ripped right out from underneath them several times, and you have presented them with many doctors, teachers, lawyers, and officials. They do not trust all these people, who are all here to judge them... to give them permission to live. They must recover from trauma, and learn to trust you and how to establish relationships.

Ceci: I do believe Angie is sensitive and intelligent. I just need to get her to the right people. The same with Roxana, and now what about my baby Jazmin?

Director: This is our resident psychologist, Dr. Cordoba who met with Jazmin.

Dr. Cordoba: Hello Ms. Diaz. The good news is that Angela Jazmin escaped much of the illness that her sisters endured. Despite her own anxiety at being evaluated, she did answer all my questions rapidly and followed directions very well. In almost all cases, her intelligence is superior to her age. I think she is hyperactive and distracted because she too was abandoned, and has her survival sensors always on alert. This may account for her asthma, which is sometimes caused by anxiety. I also see that she has eye allergies, which can stress her vision. Although she was, like the other girls, deficient with early childhood information, which usually comes with young abandoned children, I do believe that she is highly intelligent, and will need a lot of attention, after having been abandoned at three months. I can't imagine the insecurity that would come with that. You must foster her inquisitive mind... She is alert, and curious. You will see. This is so true for all of them. You must love them all as much as possible.

Ceci: Ahh yes I do. And Jazz.... Although I am relieved that she was spared intellectually, I believe there is still something else going on with her health, despite having escaped the meningitis. She looked very swollen to me when I first saw her, and I am almost positive that there was a lot of drug use by the mother. There are so many tests that I should be doing with all of them right now that I don't have access to, or just don't understand.

Director: And I hope these documents help you down the line, to get the visas. Their medical conditions will be better analyzed in the US. I also know that Special education is much more evolved in the states. So I wish you luck with the visa applications.

Ceci: Yes... as I continue to try to defy the impossible! And I must run to teach class now.

Director: Buena Suerte Cecilia. They are lucky to have you.

Ceci: And I am lucky to have them..... Angie and Jazmin will graduate Kinder tomorrow. Thank you... Gracias por todo.

All the doctors wish Ceci luck and encouragement with the girls. Ceci leaves, hiding her tears clutching the documents explaining all her daughters' deficiencies.

255. Preparations for Angie and Jazmin Kinder Graduation - Grandma calls

All the action is in Ceci's bedroom getting ready for Angie and Jazmin's Kinder Graduation ceremony at the downtown Quinta Motel. Vilma is doing their hair, placing the flowered diademas (headbands) that she has carefully made for them. They are wearing

Grandma's homemade white graduation dresses. Ceci is tuning in skype to speak to Grandma in Virginia.

Ceci: Hi Mom – Can you see me?

Grandma: Yes.. Oh hello... I am always so happy and surprised when this works.

Ceci: Me too.. So mom, we have a big surprise for you today...

Grandma: I am always ready for a surprise.

Ceci: Ok Girls, start the music.

And Angie and Jazmin begin an improvised ballet to a classical waltz in their fluffy white graduation dresses, complete with gloves, lace anklet socks and white shoes. They prance around while Grandma oohs and aaahs..

Ceci: So mom, the dresses fit perfectly and look so beautiful. Thank you so much. You are so good at this. When I think how many dresses you have made over the years... Girls your grandma is an artist!

Grandma: **Que bellas son mis nietas!!** How beautiful my grandchildren are!

Angie: **Yo amo mi vestido Grandma... Gracias...** I love my dress Grandma... Thank you.

Jazmin: **Hoy graduamos Grandma....Y cuando yo soy grande ... yo voy a ser una DOCTORA!** Today we are graduating Grandma... And when I am big I will be a doctor!

Grandma: You can be anyone you want to be. Follow your dreams.

Roxana: And we love you Grandma.

Grandma: And I absolutely loved the show.

Angie: When are you coming to see us again?

Grandma: Soon honey.

Ceci: The dresses are beautiful Mom. Thank you so much. You are truly an artist.

Jazmin: You are proud of us right Grandma?

Grandma: Of course I am. This is only the beginning. Maybe I will see you all graduate from high school and college. Congratulations… I love you.

Ceci: Bye Mom. I love you…

** Grandma made dozens if not hundreds of dresses for family and friends during her lifetime. They were works of art and love.

256. <u>Quinta Hotel Banquet Room – Graduation Ceremony</u>

Cut to the bi-lingual Graduation Ceremony with proud parents going photo crazy in the opening processional as kids walk down the isle. Vilma, Roxana and Ceci squeeze into a back row. Boys are dressed in formal shirts and ties, while some girls look like they are in a mini wedding, all in fluffy white. Angie and Jazmin look precious with their grand smiles, and Ceci prays internally that this graduation will one day take them to bigger, more important graduations. The children sing some songs in English as their teacher conducts them. One by one they receive their diplomas, and Ceci beams with pride in the audience as Angie and Jazmin get theirs.

257. **Bedtime – making lists**

The girls are in their beds. Ceci is reading them the story of

The Giving Tree, by Shel Silverstein.   She reads from the original text – final pages.

"And after a long time the boy (who is now an old man) *came back again.*

'I am sorry, Boy,' said the tree, 'but I have nothing left to give you. My apples are gone.'

'My teeth are too weak for apples' said the boy.

'My branches are gone,' said the tree. 'You cannot swing on them anymore.'

'I am too old to swing on branches,' said the boy.

'My trunk's gone,' said the tree. 'You cannot

climb' 'I am too tired to climb,' said the boy.

'I am sorry,' sighed the tree. 'I wish that I could give you something, but I have nothing left. I am just an old stump. I am sorry.'

'I don't need very much now,' said the boy, 'just a quiet place to sit and rest. I am very tired.'

'Well', said the tree straightening herself up as much as she could, 'well, an old stump is good for sitting and resting. Come, Boy, sit down. Sit down and rest.'

And the boy did.

And the tree was happy."   *The End*

She closes the book.

Ceci: Ok my bambinas…I want you to know how proud I am of all of you. Now it's time to go to sleep and dream after our grand graduation day.

Jazmin: Mommy I am not tired yet and there is no school tomorrow.

Angie: Mommy that "Giving Tree" is a sad story, and that little boy was very **desgraciada** (unthankful). He should care about the tree.

Jazmin: Yeah… The tree gave him everything he had.. the shade, the apples, the wood, the stump to sit on.

Angie: The tree picked the wrong guy to be his friend.

Ceci: Well we hope that the boy who became an old man learned his lesson.

Roxana: It's so hard to find friends.

Ceci: I know baby... that's why you and your sisters have to stick together... no matter what. OK?

Jazmin: OK so I am going to make a list in my special book of who is in my life.

Angie: Me too.

Ceci: OK, I see that we are really not tired.

They all grab their special diaries and a pen.

Jazmin: OK, so I have Angie and Roxana, and you and Grandma.

Roxana: Si... Grandma really loves us. We know that.

Angie: And Deni May, Ale, and David Ashby, and Tio Lou.

Jazmin: But what about Veronica? I'll put her in the other list.

Ceci: She doesn't hate you Jazz... she just wants Tio Lou all to herself.

Jazmin: Mom, I know when people don't really love us.

Ceci: Ok... so don't think about those people. Just make a love list.

Roxana: **Y quien mas?** And who else?

Ceci: You can write down all your friends who came to the party.

Roxana: They don't really like me Mom... **Casi nadie me quiere.** Almost nobody likes me.

Ceci: Roxana that is not true. You are a precious little girl. What about your teachers?

Jazmin: Yes but they don't treat us special.

Angie: What about Vilma and Sayda?

Ceci: Yes they love you....even though I do pay them. I know they will always love you.

Roxana: **Y tu hermana, Cristina?** And your sister, Cristina?

Jazmin: She is our Aunt Tina right?

Angie: And we are her sobrinas (nieces) right mommy?

Ceci: Well, she is far away.

Roxana: But she is supposed to care about us… doesn't she Mom?

Ceci does not answer. Her sister has told her to stay in Honduras to avoid the visa frustration, and that I should have checked out their DNA before taking custody.

Angie: And she is married to our Uncle Fred, and they have two daughters who are supposed to be our cousins. And what are their names?

Ceci: Katy and Megan.

Roxana: **Son nuestra familia y 549antasti verdad?** They are our family and they love us right?

Ceci: You can put their names on the list.

Jazmin: But Mommy, do they love us?

Ceci: Some day when they meet you I am sure they will love you because you are so adorable.

Jazmin: But they have to love us because they are our family.

Ceci: Yes of course.

Roxana: And what about Karla and our Abuela Celestina?

Ceci: I think that some people don't have time for love because they are struggling to survive. I do believe Celestina loves you. She just has so many people to take care of.

Angie: I really don't think Karla cares about us. I mean she did hit me and now I am blind.

Ceci: She just is unable to care for her kids. Angie, you are alive and healthy now. *She holds Angie close.* I am your mommy and I will take care of you guys. *Pause* And I know that your Abuela, Celestina, loves you very much.

Roxana: Then why did she let us get sick with mengitis?

Ceci: Se llama men in gi tis. It wasn't her fault Roxana. The water was bad in San Judas where you were born.

Jazmin: Then why did she let us drink it. We boil our water here.

Ceci: She is really a midwife honey. And they only have a fogata (open fire) to cook with... And also the medicine for meningitis was probably too expensive for them.

Angie: But you said you got medicine for me. Didn't you Mommy? Or I would have died from the "mengitis".

Ceci: I just showed up at the right time, and Tio Lou gave you the medicine. I know Karla would have helped you if she could.

Jazmin: But they were too poor. And it was lucky that you found us Mom.

Angie: Mom is our angel.

Ceci: No... you are MY angels... and I love you very much... hasta la luna. Until the moon.

They all have a group hug.

Ceci: And now it is time to dream my angels.

Roxana: Canta Madre Luna Mommy.

Ceci: Anything for my babies.... *Ceci sings Mother Moon and they all fall asleep with the short lists of who loves them in their hands. This question of who really cares about them will follow them forever, even when they get to the USA with Ceci's family.*

258. Dance Class – Mazapan – Marbella's Quinceanera

Ceci is working on a dance for the Xmas show coming. These are her advanced, adolescent students. As class is finishing one of the students, Marbella, approaches her.

Marbella: Ms. Ceci, you know I am turning fifteen this month and my Mom wanted to ask you if you would help us with choreography for my Quinceanera in Roatan?

Ceci: You know, this would be my first, but I would be delighted. I have heard that they are like Broadway productions. What does she want me to do?

Marbella: I know that there will be eight couples and we all do a waltz… and then we would like to change and do a special number with reggaeton, salsa, punta, and merengue for the party.

Ceci: So you have sixteen dancers including yourself who are willing to rehearse?

Marbella: Yes… and I want them to come after school as soon as possible so we can start. I have a sound mix for the choreography… but I need a waltz, and a processional… My Mom will call you this afternoon. Will you do it?

Ceci: Si señorita… A tu orden!! (at your service) Let's say 4:30 pm tomorrow here in the studio… 16 dancers. Have your Mom call me.. I will look for a waltz and make a copy of your music.

Marbella: I will. Oh thank you so much Ms. Ceci…

Ceci: Absolutely, I know how important this is for you.

259. **After School Dance Program, Prepping Xmas- Meeting Peter Thompson – expatriot, lawyer, musician, student dad**

At the dance studio students begin to arrive for the after school program. There are many groups today as they are getting ready for the next dance concert. Parents are there with their kids getting ready for class. Vilma is monitoring the studio and the office. Ceci enters and goes to her sound system to get ready for class. Students greet her with hellos and hugs. The bus driver has dropped off the three sisters, who enter in their school uniforms, all rushing over to kiss her. Vilma greets the girls and is patiently waiting to speak to Ceci. She will meet Peter, who is a retired immigration lawyer from San Diego, now living in La Ceiba with his wife Flor, a young beautiful Honduran woman. Jazzlyn is their daughter, six years old.

Vilma: Hola chachas… Vengan cambiar .. la clase va a empezar en poco. Hello girls, come in and change. Class will start soon.

Ceci: Gracias Vilma. *Vilma closes the office door and tells Ceci that Peter Thompson is here.*

Vilma: **Ceci... El papa de Jazzlyn esta aqui...alla...se llama Peter Thompson, esposo de Flor, la mama. El es abogado y me dijo que el puede ayudarte con sus visas para las ninas.** Ceci, Jazzlyn's father is here, Peter Thompson, Flor's husband. He is an immigration lawyer and told me that maybe he can help you with the visas for the girls.

Ceci: **No me digas! Verdad?**

Vilma: **Si Ceci** *She goes to change the girls in the office.*

Ceci rushes back to the sound system to put on some music, and approaches Peter and his wife, Flor, smiling.

Ceci: **Hola Flor ... como estas?**

Flor: **Bueno Ceci.. Mira.. Quiero presentarte a mi esposo, que es abogodo de imigracion.** I want to introduce you to my husband, who is an immigration lawyer.

Peter: **Hello Peter Thompson.**

Ceci: A pleasure to meet you... **Papa de Jazzlyn?**

Peter: Yes, and I understand you are wrestling with the visa applications for your girls.

Ceci: Yes,,, It is an overwhelming job. And you are American I take it.

Peter: Yes and I think I can help you present your case in a very legal and professional way on your next application. I practiced Immigration law in San Diego for years.

Ceci: **Dios Mio, Flor... me mandaste un angel!** You sent me an angel!

Flor: **I would not say that... Pero, para cosas legales.. 552antastic.** But for legal things – fantastic

Ceci: **Entonces Peter I hope we can talk soon. So Flor, vas a bailar con Jazzlyn para el numero de madres y hija? Ensallamos**

hoy. So Flor, are you going to dance with Jazzlyn for the mother daughter number? We rehearse today.

Flor: No Ceci, perdoname por favor... tengo pena. I am shy... BUT, Peter dice que el puede remplazarme. No Ceci, forgive me please. I am shy, but Peter says he will replace me.

Ceci: *Pause until she gets it* – Great I love it...but only if he is willing to wear an apron. **Come and join the rehearsal, Peter.**

They all laugh and Ceci goes to start dance class with the little girls, all sitting on their Xs in front of the mirror. Vilma is organizing the mothers to practice with their daughters today. Ceci explains that they are going to learn the dance for the Xmas show in honor of Mrs. Santa. She has spliced together a number of songs that have inspired many lifts and moves for ten Santa mother/daughter couples. Ceci dances with Jazmin. Peter also, is very comical.

260. Quinceanera Rehearsal – Next Day...Dance Studio

The sixteen Damas and Chambalanes for Marbella's Quinceanera begin to arrive. Ceci is chatting with Marbella and her Mom, Elena, who is a very classy lady. Marbella is adopted and her father owns a big hotel in Roatan. This will be a huge and elegant affair. Marbella's Mom has given Ceci a copy of the classic Quinceanera ritual and they are reviewing the needs for choreography. She also wants Ceci to MC the ceremony in English as many of the guests are international and do not speak Spanish. Jazmin, Angie and Roxana are hanging out in the background... very interested in the activity. Ceci welcomes the dancers and asks them to join her on the dance floor.

When the entire crew is present, and they have socialized sufficiently, Ceci lines them up by gender and height to establish partners. Marbella will dance with the Chambelan de honor (lead male). They first rehearse the military step which brings them into the hall with a processional. Then the mother explains to the group.

Mother Elena: Gracias por venir todos... Es un honor para nuestra familia tener su participacion en la Quinceanera de Marbella Edwards. Yo creo que el procession fue muy bien. Quiero explicar que va a pasar en este baile classico de la Vals... La Senora Cecilia va ayudarles con la coreografia. Yo voy explicar lo que pasa en el ceremonio. Primero Marbella baila con su papa... mientras uds estan en el fondo... Cuando cambia la musica, el papa entregara Marbella al Chambelan de Honor, Enrique, y ellos bailan, hasta que empieza la música de nuevo, y uds bailaran el valse en parejas. Y por el fin, uds invitaran a miembras de la familia a bailar como un baile de multiplicacion... hasta que todo el mundo esta bailando. Entiende? Es largo verdad? Pero es como lo veo. Thank you for coming everybody. It's an honor for our family to have your participation in Marbella's Quinceanera. I think the procession went very well. So I want to explain what will happen in this classical waltz dance. Sra. Cecilia will help you with the choreography. I will explain what happens in the ceremony. First Marbella dances with her father, while you are posed in the background. When the music changes the father will deliver Marbella to the Chamberlain of Honor, Enrique, and they will dance until the music begins again, when you all dance your choreographed waltz together. After two rounds of the pattern, you will invite members of the family and friends to dance like the multiplication routine, until everybody is dancing. Do you understand? It's long. But that's how I see it.

Ceci: Largo, pero magico, y bien interesante como un ritual elegante. Estan todos claro? Vamos empezar aprender la vals... y despues quiero ver sus talentos de reggaetón y hip hop Latino.. Long but very magical and very interesting like an elegant ritual. Does everyone understand the plan? Let's begin to learn the waltz... and later I want to see your reggaeton and Latino hip hop talents...

There seems to be a happy consensus amongst the dancers as they take their partners and begin the basic steps for sixteen bars of 6/8. There is laughing, clumsiness, talent, embarrassment, and finally determination in a montage of learning the valse. Angie, Jazz and Roxana attempt to keep up with the dances in the background. Marbella and her Mom are pleased. The Mom promises the girls a place in the procession following Marbella. They take a break, and Marbella plays Ceci a CD of the musical edit for the hip hop dance.

Ceci: This is a wonderful edit of tunes... Do you have any choreography for it?

Marbella: Si... Vas a ver... No tenemos todos los pasos, We don't have all the steps, but there is a little for each section with different choreographers. We will show you

Ceci: Can't wait..... Let me see what you have.

The boys start with a reggaeton choreography that is incomplete but really hot. Then the girls shuffle into an upbeat merengue, and do a few steps.... The boys take partners and improvise some merengue steps. Then when the music changes to salsa, they all face front and Marbella and her friends lead an independent salsa line... that then works into couples improvising... And the final dance is a punta in a group circle facing inward. The rehearsal is chopped into pieces with Ceci stopping the music and repeating or building on choreographies, and asking people to teach the steps that they know to the grou. All of this is a patch and glue job, until the performance piece is fully choreographed. And it will need polish.

Ceci: This is wonderful material, and with some organizing and cleaning up we can integrate everybody's ideas and have a great number. Pero hay que venir todos para los ensayos. Me entienden..? Poco a poco. But everybody must come to all the rehearsals... Understand? Little by little.

Mother Elena: Uds son fabulosos!!! Que rapido apriendieron... Bueno.... serian tres ensayos mas antes que vamos todos a Roatan en dos semanas. Y manana vamos a ver los vestidos con Eduardo Zablah... You guys are fabulous! How fast they learned. Great.. there will be three more rehearsals before we all go to Roatan in two weeks. And tomorrow we are going to see the dresses with Eduardo Zablah.

Jazmin: And big dresses for us too??

Mother: Claro.. Uds son las princesitas! Of course! You are the little princesses.

Ceci: Uds. todos son buenos bailarines, y vamos a ver una fiesta fantastica... Hasta el proximo ensayo el Sabado. Gracias... No olviden practicar... Ciao! You are all great dancers, and we are going to have a fantastic party. Until the next Saturday rehearsal. Thank you. Don't forget to practice. Ciao

Angie: Mama I want a Quinceanera when I am fifteen.

Ceci: Well we will have to have a big family and lots of friends for that. *Ceci turns to Marbella and her Mom.* **I want to thank you for this opportunity. This will mean a lot to my children.**

Marbella: And it will mean a lot to me, because I know how you can make things happen when they are supposed to happen, and I don't want me or my Mom to worry about the performance. And that's why I have to thank you for doing this. And you can be sure you and your daughters will be treated like family.

Ceci: Gracias Marbella...y Elena... Deles besos ninas... *The girls already know what to do...that this will be a great adventure for them... They hug Marbella and her Mama.*

261. Roatan – Arrival for the Quinceanera – Paradise Hotel

Ceci and the girls arrive at the Roatan Airport on the small tropical and tourist island off the coast of La Ceiba. They are picked up by a young guy with a sign that says "Quinceanera Marbella". The driver explains that he will take them to the Paradise hotel that is owned by Marbella's father and to meet at 5:30 pm for dinner in the dining room with Marbella and her parents. And there is a rehearsal tonight at 7pm in the hotel ballroom. They drive by palm trees and resorts, beautiful beach homes, restaurants. almost like Florida... Roatan has a very American feel. It is difficult to believe it is only a half hour plane ride from La Ceiba. Here is a reminder of how close modernity can move in on the third world for profit. The girls are amazed and thrilled with their apartment on the water... They unpack their bathing suits and run out to the beach...

We cut to the ballroom where all the couples practice entering to the processional music with a special military step. Each couple is introduced. The family enters and relatives are individually introduced... the Godparents, the Grandparents on both sides, the Mom, Sisters, Uncles and Aunts, etc.. and then Marbella with her Dad. Angie, Roxana, and Jazmin will follow with flower baskets.

262. <u>Church Ceremony – Quinceanera – Marbella Rodriguez</u>

This processional practice then cuts..... to the ceremony in the church with the same sixteen participants marching down the isle to the altar where a Catholic priest conducts a special mass for a young maiden. Marbella's parents stand behind her, ready to play their parts to launch her into society. Her Padrinos (Godparents) will keep Marbella on a path of spirituality and guide her into becoming a positive member of the community as well as a role model for younger female family members.

GOWN - Marbella is wearing a huge lavender gown with silver accents. The gown represents that this young girl is now a young woman, and is basically available for marriage. She will kneel on a special pillow, personalized with her name during the ceremony. Marbella receives Holy Communion, she makes an act of consecration to the Virgin Mary, offers her flowers, and receives gifts blessed by the priest:

TIARA – The priest first crowns her with a diadema or crown. The person wearing it is considered to be a benevolent princess in God's eyes.

BIBLE – Then the Priest gives her a bible. This cherished gift is the basis of Hispanic Catholic faith and will be something that one can turn to for companionship and advice throughout life

EARRINGS and a RING– The mother then puts diamond earrings on Marbella, which the priest explains are to remind Marbella that she must keep her ears in tune with the word of God as she becomes an adult. The ring signifies her unconditional and unending connection and love of God and family.

ROSARY – Her Abuela then gives her a beautiful Rosary which is to be with her always to practice her devotion to the Virgin.

The organ music begins and Marbella leaves her flowers below the statue of the Virgin Mary, and then turns to march out of the church followed by her entire eight couple entourage.

263. <u>Marbella's Quinceanera celebration at the Hotel Paradise</u>

We move to the Hotel ballroom where guests have been seated at tables enjoying drinks and boquitas (hors d'ouevres). The entourage of dancers and family takes the stage for a family portrait. She has asked Ceci to narrate in English. We can hear Ceci's amplified voice making introductions in English for the general comprehension of the guests.

Ceci: Welcome Ladies and Gentlemen to the Quinceanera of Marbella Edwards Rodriguez as she is accompanied by family and friends tonight. It is the pleasure of her family to host all of you and thank you for coming to celebrate this wonderful occasion with their beloved daughter Marbella. At this time we will continue with the traditional Quinceanera ceremony.

Marbella's father will change her <u>shoes</u> from flats to heels symbolizing her final shift from being a girl to becoming a woman.

The shoes are changed. A waltz begins.

Ceci: I ask the guests to rise to witness the famous Quinceanera waltz where Marbella will first dance with her father, who then hands her off to the Chamberlan and the full company.   After their performance guests are invited and requested to join the dance.

Marbella and her Dad begin the Waltz as everyone watches… and then Marbella is passed off to the Chamberlan…The Damas and Chambalanes are posed in the background in their full regalia of lavender gowns and classy black tuxedos. Then they all join in for a full company waltz choreography. After the waltz repeats three times, the dancers go into the crowd and find someone to join them to multiply the dance until all are dancing. When the waltz ends they all applaud and sit.

Marbella's Father: Welcome to the Paradise Hotel. We thank all of you for coming from so far to celebrate this day with our family and my beautiful daughter, Marbella. We invite all of you to enjoy the festivities you are about to witness in her name. At this time, I would like to make the presentations with my wife.

As these speeches are taking place, the girls join Ceci at her table and whisper in her ear how much they want to have their own Quinceaneras and a father who will dance with them.

Roxana: Mom when I am fifteen I want to have my own princess dress and a Quinceanera.

Jazmin: And I want a father who will dance with me like Marbella's Dad.

Angie: I just hope I can still see when I am fifteen. How could I walk in that dress?

Ceci: Well you have all asked me for some pretty miraculous things… so I will have to work on all of that… but the dress part is easy.

The party carries on in montage fashion with eating and drinking, until we see Ceci organizing the company of dancers back stage in their tropical dance wear.

The   music   starts   and   we   watch   a   hot reggaeton/merengue/salsa/punta mix of a choreography that is a raving success with a standing ovation. Everybody then joins the company on the dance floor, and the party goes on and on Latino style.

This will be a memory worth keeping for Ceci's girls, like going to Cinderella's ball.

264. <u>Regular Visit to Municipal Court with the girls – Margie Dip</u>

Ceci parks the black truck in front of the court house and enters with the girls in their school uniforms and clean braided hair. They are going for their regular visit to Daisy and to request permission for the next (3ʳᵈ) visa application.

As they enter, they see Margie Dip – Governor of Atlantida, and Grandmother of Rebecca and Cecilia Dip, dance students of Ceci.

Ceci: Well if it isn't Margie Dip, the Ceiba queen. Look girls, say hello to Cecilia and Rebecca's abuela.

They say hello in their obligatory way.

Margie: Hello hello... Mira que bellas son ellas. Bless your heart. How are you Ceci?

Ceci: Much better than the last time I saw you at your party when I lost myself dancing... I was so embarrassed.

Margie: First of all, you are a fabulous dancer, and I could tell you a few interesting stories about me and guiffity. It can take you away to una maravilla!! Why do you think I serve it cocktail style at my parties? So everybody will talk to each other, dance, have a good time!!

Ceci: Well the music was fabulous.

Margie: I can't get over how healthy and beautiful the girls are. So what are you doing here?

Ceci: Making my third request for permission to apply for visas for the girls. I am going to the American embassy in Tegucigalpa next week again trying for visas.

Margie: Do you have your residency?

Ceci: Not yet. I have to ask Standard Fruit for help with that.

Margie: Oh Ceci... I know how expensive, and frustrating this must be for you. But you are making a miracle for these girls. Listen... I know somebody in Tegucigalpa who handles residency for immigrants. His name is Jose Chinchilla. Take his number.... *She writes it from her book onto a papelito.* I will call him when I get back to the office. He can give you a ten year residency because of the girls' ages.

Ceci: Really??

Margie: Si Senora.

Ceci: How can I thank you for this Margie? Such fortune that I run into you now.

Margie: Just keep dancing... I love what you are doing culturally for La Ceiba... And the girls are just preciosa... Besos.. ninas... Good luck... I am running.

Ceci: Gracias Margie. Girls, I want you to thank Sra. Dip.

Girls: Gracias Sra. Dip.

Margie: De nada senoritas. I wish you luck in Tegucigalpa Cecilia... Give Senor Chinchilla my card, so he knows I referred you. Suerte.

Margie runs upstairs to the court rooms, and Ceci and the girls continue down the hall to enter the office where Daisy works. As they enter all the secretaries in the office turn and smile. The girls are neatly dressed and know the routine.

Daisy: Hola Sra Diaz como estas?

Ceci: Bien Daisy... Me alegre verle. I am happy to see you.

Daisy: Feliz a verte tambien con estas bellezas. Como estan ninas? Happy to see you too with these little beauties. How are you girls?

Ninas: Bien Daisy...

Daisy: Como puedo servirle hoy Dona Cecilia? How can I help you today Cecilia?

Ceci: Me voy de nuevo a Tegucigalpa para buscar mi residencia y otra visa para las ninas. Y de nuevo necesito permiso de la juez. I'm going again to Tegucigalpa to seek my residency and to apply again for visas for the girls. And again I need permission from the judge.

Daisy: Cuantas veces ahora? How many times now?

Ceci: La tercera. The third time.

Daisy has accepted Ceci's third request for the Judge's signature without a lawyer to save her the expense, in support of Ceci's custody.

Daisy: Te digo Cecilia.. hasta que tenga custodia… vas a perder su tiempo… Pero au menos se puede buscar su residencia. I'm telling you Ceci… until you have formal custody, you are wasting your time. But at least you can look for your residency.

Ceci: Yo se que ud. piensa que soy loca… pero Daisy que hago yo? Mi madre nos espera en los Estados. Ellas necessitan educacion y atencion medico especial. Tengo que seguir intentando. I know that you think I am crazy, but Daisy what can I do? My mother is waiting for us in the states. They need special education and medical attention. I have to keep trying.

Daisy: Oooy….. Si Dios quiere….*Taking the papers to give to the judge….***Y de donde viene su fuerza Ceci?** God Willing. And where do you get your strength Ceci?

Ceci: Mi amor para ellas… y mi madre…. Y mi pais. Ya… My love for the girls, my mother, and my country… there…

Daisy: Vuelvas manana… y te doy el documento firmada de la Juez. Olvide el abogado, y vaya con Dios… Aqui tengo dulces para sus dulce muchachas. *She gives the girls lollypops.* Come back tomorrow and I will give you the signed document from the judge. Forget the lawyer and go with God. Here you have some sweets for your sweet little girls.

Ceci: Oh Daisy, muchisimas gracias por sus favores.

Jazmin: Daisy…. Quiero decirle un secreto. Daisy I want to tell you a secret.

Daisy: Digame bella… Tell me beautiful. *Wagging her finger to come closer.*

Jazmin: Manana es mi cumpleanos, y si quiere venir a mi fiesta, te invito. Tomorrow is my birthday, and if you want to come to my party I am inviting you.

Daisy: No me digas… Cuantos anos? Don't tell me… How old are you?

Jazmin: Seis! *Holding up the fingers.*

Daisy: Pues tengo que cuidar mi sobrina manana… pero tengo un idea… sube…. *She helps Jazmin get up on a chair to take a bow……* **todo el mundo… cantamos para Jazmin…** *All the workers in the office stand and sing* **…Cumpleanos a ti… Cumpleanos a ti** *… all dancing around the chair singing and laughing.* Well tomorrow I have babysit, but I have an idea. Everybody, we will sing Happy Birthday to Jazmin. *Ceci and the girls leave feeling pretty important.*

Ceci: Adios todos!!! Gracias! *Jazmin is all smiles. They climb in to the black truck.*

Jazmin: Y mi piñata de Suzie Strawberry mommy? And my piñata Suzie Strawberry mommy?

Ceci: No te preocupas baby… Ya lo tengo. Don't worry baby, I already have it.

Angie: I just love parties…

Ceci: And then we go to Tegucigalpa again after that. **Don't worry, you know mommy thinks of everything. I have many hats. OK school bus is now in session. The times tables por favor… starting with the twos.**

Fade out on the recitation of the times tables in the car.

265. **Jazmin – Birthday Party in the garden – six years**

It is Sunday afternoon and Vilma and Sayda are helping Ceci prepare for Jazmin's 6th birthday party. Jazmin is wearing a pretty pink tutu outfit. It is a princess party theme. Sayda is doing

Jazmin's hair, the girls are blowing up balloons and placing them around the garden and on the gate, Vilma is helping Ceci in the kitchen, where Ceci has been cooking all morning. Ceci is icing the cake while Vilma steams the tamales. The piñata is strung up in the carport and food is collecting on the buffet for all to enjoy. The older housemate/siblings from Casa 9 in the SOS come early to help: Norma, Olvin, Juny y su hermano, Jimmy. The girls are happy to see them, and everybody chips in helping the decorations of papel cortados, comida, and bombas (balloons).

The clown, Reynaldo, arrives all dressed and in character. Jazmin has developed a fear of clowns, that Ceci doesn't fully understand, and she keeps her distance as he begins to make balloon animals and hangs them around the yard. This fear follows her for years.
Guests begin to arrive with their parents, and their siblings... dressed to the best of their ability as princesses. Angie and Roxana emerge from hair and makeup in their respective ballet/princess costumes. The local kids come without costume. The Mazapan dance students come dressed to the max in fluffy costumes with tiaras and magic wands. Others come in whatever long dresses with lipstick and flip flops.

Jazmin & Ceci

Norma and Olvin

Jimmy, Angie, Roxana, Juny, Olvin & Jazmin

The girls' SOS brothers and sisters come... Norma and Olvin, who are siblings... Jimmy and Juni... siblings also who were all very instrumental in the girls' protection at the SOS. Deni May comes with Ale, who is excited to be at the party. Peter and Flor come with Jazzlyn who is dressed in a pink gown. Ceci informs Peter that she is going for her third visa attempt in the coming week. Peter tells her that until she gets the Tutora custody it will be difficult, but that he will write a sterling request for her.

David Ashby, as the Godfather, shows up for a moment with his gift for Jazmin. And the music and the food buffet setup the party atmosphere. Later Ceci gets an after the party photo of the original family from the SOS orphanage. This is a production for Ceci, and multiply that times 3 daughters for several party years. And the games begin.

Puzzle piece egg hunt

Ceci gathers the young guests in a circle on the backyard lawn and introduces the first game as parents watch from the picnic table. In Spanish she explains that they are to find as many eggs as possible hidden in the garden, and gather them up in their baskets. When the music stops they must all come to the table with their eggs to play part two of the game. The music begins and with and without the help of mothers and older siblings, the kids scramble to collect eggs. The music is from Cri Cri, a popular Spanish children's song composer. Eventually they all bring their eggs to the table, open them and find some have candy and some have big puzzle pieces composing a big picture of Jazmin as a baby. They must assemble the puzzle pieces.

Races

After that they line up for a "carry the ping pong ball on a spoon in the mouth race (not an egg). With that also accompanied by music and the long princess dresses, the challenge is comical. Then comes the three legged race which is almost an impossibility in the long dresses, but also creates lots of laughter.

Guess the Princess

Finally, there is the GUESS the Princess game, where each guest pops a balloon which has a paper with a description of a famous Disney princess, that she must read... in the YO SOY (I am) first person, etc. The crowd must guess which Princess she is describing and then take their turn popping a balloon and impersonating the princess described on the paper.

1. Aurora – Sleeping Beauty – La Bella Dormiente - "The only way I can wake up is with a kiss. My name is _____."

2. Snow White – Blanca Nieves – "I live in the woods with seven little men. My name is _____."

3. Jasmine – Alladin – "I want to marry whomever I want and fly on a magic carpet. My name is _____."

4. Cinderella – Cenicienta – "I have two ugly sisters who can't fit into my shoes. My name is _____."

5. Ariel – The Littlest Mermaid – La Sirenita – "I had to give up my life in the ocean for love. My name is _____."

6. Beauty and the Beast – La Belle y La Bestia – "Belle – I fell in love with an ugly beast. My name is _____."

7. Rapunzel – Enredado – "An old witch locked me up in a tower and all I can do is grow my hair. My name is _____."

8. <u>Pocahontas</u> – "I fell in love with a man named John who invaded the native people of North America. My name is _____."

9. Tiana – <u>Princess and the Frog</u> – "All I ever wanted was my own restaurant, but I had to become a frog to get it. "My name is"

Cake

Ceci then enters with the birthday cake with six candles and everybody sings. Someone smudges cake on Jazmin's nose, which is a Honduran custom. Pictures are taken, and everybody gets a piece of Jazmin's cake.

Pinata

Ceci then passes out candy bags, and lowers the piñata of Suzie Strawberry, and the batting begins. Carefully each one is allowed to take five swings (not blindfolded because of their young age) starting with Jazmin and then the bat goes to the youngest in the crowd on up... They make a line and Ceci monitors the stick and the sequence until Angie gets her turn and whacks the pinata to pieces... so that everybody scrambles on the floor like frenzied ants for their candy.

The Princess Freeze Dance

The music carries on and they have the Princess FREEZE dance to some beautiful fairy music, as they laugh and dance as the music starts and stops. As the sugar starts to wear out and the sun sets, the guests leave, and Ceci cleans up the mess with the SOS kids and Sayda and Vilma.

266. Tegucigalpa – Residency – Justice building

Legal papers in brief case held tightly in hand, Ceci steps out of a Tegucigalpa taxi to a different government building. She is dressed in her most business like summer suit. She looks up at a modest government building and sign:

<u>Republica de Honduras – Secretaria de Gobernacion Justicia Direccion General de Migracion y Extranjeria – Relaciones Exteriores</u>

After paying the taxi, an armed policeman opens the door. They go through security.

Ceci: Me llamo Cecilia Diaz. Tengo una cita con un senor Jose Hernandez Chinchilla a la una.

Guard: Si senora… primero seguridad, y despues se puede ver Secretaria General Chinchilla.

Her body and baggage are cleared and she is ushered to a waiting room where she waits for not longer than a moment when Mr. Chinchilla enters with gracious and hospitable welcomes.

Sr. Chinchilla: Bienvenida Sra. Cecilia… Welcome to Tegucigalpa… Please come to my office.

Ceci: Muchas gracias Sr. Chinchilla por su hospitalidad tan simpatica…

He escorts Ceci into his office and closes the door. The desk is piled high with papers and legal documents, but he clears the way to look at all of her papers.

Sr. Chinchilla: Sra Cecilia, yo hable con Margie Dip, y ella me reconto todo lo que esta haciendo con las tres ninas, y tambien con su trabajo con la cultura en La Ceiba. Yo tengo una sobrina que es un estudiante tuya, y ella esta encantada bailar contigo.

Ceci: No me digas… Oh yes. Andrea Chinchilla – Of course!!

Sr. Chinchilla: You are the first person to make her dance and she loves your class.

Ceci: Pues Gracias… Me alegro oir eso. Andrea es una buena bailarina. Well thank you. I am happy to hear that. And Andrea is a beautiful dancer.

Sr. Chinchilla: We can speak English. I have arranged for my secretary to write up your residency papers which will allow you to carry an immigration residency for as long as you are employed by Standard Fruit. We have much respect for Margie Dip, and according to her testimony, she sees great value in the artistic work you are doing in La Ceiba, as well as for Eduardo Zablah and the Miss Honduras Contest, along with all the Festivals and Dance Concerts you mount for the Mazapan School. I know what you are doing for 3 young sisters from the SOS, and I also understand the struggle you are facing with transmites oficiales and visas for your young daughters. I hope to alleviate some of that inconvenience by arranging for your residency in our beloved Honduras.

Ceci: Dios mio you are quite the angel and detective.

Sr. Chinchilla: Margie Dip told me everything. You are the angel.

Ceci: Hombre!.... Thank you... I can't believe that all I had to do was get myself here and listen to you shower me with such beautiful and welcome words. If only you worked at the American Embassy!

Sr. Chinchilla: Senora, you must pursue full custody.

Ceci: I am working on this Tutora custody as we speak, but also requesting tourist visas for them this afternoon, after I leave you.

Sr. Chinchilla: Well I hope this residency helps you. This is as far as I can go with the Embassy. If you get permission on this end, it is up to them to grant the visa. *He hands her a formal paper in an envelope.* I will arrange to have your residency card sent to Standard Fruit. Goodluck with the visas.

Ceci: Yes, I know the embassy routine well... this is my third attempt.

Sr. Chinchilla: Don't give up... you will eventually win. I have faith in these things, and for this reason I help you... to give these girls a chance.

Ceci: Gracias Senor…. Por su ayuda, su bendicion y corazon… Thank you sir, for your help, your blessing and your heart. *She exits with the precious paper in her hand… Finds a cab.*

267. **American Embassy – Tegucigalpa – 3ʳᵈ visa attempt – no girls**

Not far from this office is the American Embassy. Ceci knows what to do as the taxi lets her off at the end of a long line. It is afternoon. She tries to read… Once again we overhear the applicants' stories around Ceci, as they all inch their way up the line, into the building. Like a robot, Ceci gives up her cell phone, removes her shoes, goes through security and joins other visa aspirants in the great hall. Ceci pays the $1500 fee for the three girls, and takes er seat on the musical chair line, waiting to be called up to a standing counter and window where their fate will be told… for the third time.

Once again, she watches people who were in line before her, exit the window area laughing, shouting, or crying or complaining in some form of pent up anticipation around scoring or not scoring a visa to the USA. The Iraheta Rojas names are called, and the same young American agent appears in the window.

Agent: Hello Ms. Diaz. How are you?

Ceci: Fine thank you. Interesting that you remember me?

Agent: This is your third time I recall.

Ceci: That's right.

Agent: And what is different about this time.

Ceci: Well, I just got my residency in Honduras based on my work at the Mazapan school at Standard Fruit in La Ceiba… and I also now have the custody of these children, with whom I would like to travel to visit my Mom in Virginia and seek medical help for them.

Agent: And where are they today? They are supposed to apply in person.

Ceci: In school in La Ceiba, under the care of my trabajadora.

Agent: And in the past you requested medical visas for them.

Ceci: And I would absolutely take them to as many doctors as possible during a visit.

Agent: And do you not eventually wish to immigrate these children back to the United States with your family?

Ceci: Yes I do, but not now. I am working in La Ceiba, and they are in school there.

Agent: And what else is happening with the custody of these children?

Ceci: I am waiting for Tutora custody of the girls, which is going through the courts as we speak. At the moment they have been under my care for three years.

Agent: Wait one minute. *He goes to a back room with her file in his hand. Five forever minutes go by, as Ceci shifts her weight back and forth in front of the window. The agent eventually returns.*

Agent: Ms Diaz, I am very sorry once again to decline this request for your children's visas.

Ceci: BUT WHY? I don't understand.

Agent: Because your custody is not yet formal enough to be considered a responsible parent.

Ceci: I saved their lives senor. They live with me. I pay for their doctor bills and their private schools. I have my residency. I am waiting for the Tutora custody. My car is being shipped over here... I plan to pick it up this week. *She speaks faster and faster as he shuts down.*

Agent: I am sorry Mam. You fit the profile of a gringa-get-the -papers-and-run mom. So I suggest you get those Tutora papers and come back when you have them in your hand. Even then they will want you to adopt... and you are too old to adopt. I don't know Mam. You can't change the rules. I'm sorry. *He closes the window shade.*

Ceci: *Speechless... Ceci turns and walks out of the great hall almost catatonic. She passes the armed guard who remembers her, and shakes her head. She grabs a cab to the airport, and as*

*soon as the taxi car door slams you can hear Ceci burst into
hysterical tears.*

268. <u>**Jazmin's Immigration officer act**</u>

*It is Saturday morning and Ceci is doing the dishes and staring out
the window sadly. She shouts out to the girls.*

    Ceci: Girls… get dressed, brush your teeth, clean your room.

    Angie: So what happened mom?

    Ceci: I don't want to talk about it right now, honey. Get
dressed.

*Jazmin approaches her in the kitchen wearing one of Ceci's blazer
jackets. She is also wearing Ceci's reading glasses.*

    Jazmin: Excuse me mam, I understand that you are
interested in visas, correct?

    Ceci: *Drying her hands, and realizing this is an act….*Why yes
I am. How did you know that?

    Jazmin: Never mind all that… please follow me, and let's see
what we can do.

*Jazmin has set up a desk with papers and a toy telephone in the
living room.*

    Jazmin: Please have a seat.

    Ceci: Thank you.

    Jazmin: So, now tell me how I can help you.

    Ceci: Well, I want to take my daughters back to the USA with
me, and the embassy will not give me even a medical visa.

    Jazmin: Well you have come to the right place. Are you an
American? *She starts to take notes.*

    Ceci: Yes I am, born in New York.

    Jazmin: And how many daughters do you have?

    Ceci: Three

Jazmin: Will you please write your name here, and their names right here. *Ceci writes.* And why do you want visas to the Nited States?

Ceci: Because my 83 year old mother is there and I want to bring my three Honduran daughters back with me so I can take care of her and the girls in the family home.

Jazmin: Wow, that's really nice. And are they YOUR daughters?

Ceci: No they are not, but I am their Godmother, and the judge has given me custody of them.

Jazmin: So they are adopted?

Ceci: No, not yet.

Jazmin: And why not?

Ceci: Because I am too old.

Jazmin: You don't look so old.

Ceci: Well thank you. I am actually 55.

Jazmin: Can you just wait a minute while I make a call. I have some good connections at the embassy in Gucigalpa.

Ceci: Really? In Tegucigalpa, the capitol? Looks like I have come to the right place. How much does it cost for your services?

Jazmin: Well I would say about $20 a person. So that is… just a minute… let me do the math… 20 plus 20 plus 20 is…… put down the 0 then 2 plus 2 plus 2 …. Sixty dollars… special for you… because I know you are a nice person and a good mother.

Ceci: Thank you Miss???

Jazmin: I am Officer Jazmin. How do you do? *Extending hand.*

Ceci: I am fine, except that I am afraid the embassy, MY American embassy, will reject me again.

Jazmin: But I know all the right people so you don't have to worry. Please excuse me while I make a quick call to the right people.

Ceci: By all means…. Take it away officer.

Jazmin dials a number, takes off her glasses, and puts her feet up on the desk. Ceci can barely keep from laughing.

Jazmin: Disculpa Senor, pero tengo aqui una Sra. Diaz Gringa. Ella tiene tres hijas Hondurenas y quiere visas para viajar con ellas a visitar su madre en Nited States. *Pause…..* Yo soy Officer Jazmin de la Ceiba, y yo conozco esta madre, y creo que ella es OK y no hay problema. *Pause* OK Bueno…. Uh huh…. Uh huh…... *E*xcuse me senor but I have here a Sra. Diaz Gringa. She has 3 Honduran daughters and wants visas to travel with them to visit her mother in the Nited States. I am Officer Jazmin in la Ceiba and I know this mother and I believe that she is OK and there are no problems. Ok good… uh huh… uh huh.

She covers the phone a moment to ask Ceci something.

Jazmin: When do you want to go for the visas?

Ceci: As soon as possible Officer.

Jazmin: *Back on the phone with the embassy….* El mas pronto posible Senor. *Long pause.* Muchas gracias Senor. La proxima vez que estoy en Tegucigalpa yo le invito para sushi OK? Bueno, ciao. *She hangs up the phone and puts her glasses back on and starts writing.* I have good news for you Sra Diaz. Just go to the embassy next week, give them these papers, and you will get your visas.

Ceci: Oh Officer Jazmin… thank you SO much for your help. Let me write you a check. And by the way… If you are ever in San Pedro, I know a great sushi place to invite you to.

Jazmin: You are very welcome, and I do love sushi. *She takes the fake check…* But please excuse me, because I think I have another customer who wants to see me now. Good afternoon and good luck. And one more thing… You don't have to cry anymore. *She shakes her hand.*

Ceci: That's good. *Ceci bends down to her level wiping a tear away.* Because we are having a huge Gringo Thanksgiving party tomorrow and I need your help because I will be cooking all night tonight and tomorrow.

Jazmin: OK mom.

Ceci: And Jazz. I love you so much for cheering me up. *Big hug.* Go get your sisters and let's get cooking and be thankful.

269. <u>An Expatriot Thanksgiving Dinner in Naranjal</u>

Ceci has been up most of the evening prepping and cooking. Vilma and Sayda arrive to help her complete a ten course buffet. Ceci has already finished the pastelitos de pavo (turkey), the pico de gallo, prepared the mix for the ham salad sandwiches, shucked the elotes (corn), sliced up the platanos, made the ensalada de habichuelas (string bean salad), and is stirring the sopa de caracoal.

Vilma and Sayda arrive with their tamales de pavo which they set up in a huge steamer. Ceci walks into the kitchen and hugs them, and thanks them for coming midday to help cooking. She reads off the Spanglish to-do list posted on the refrigerator.

Vilma and Sayda with the girls

Ceci: Hola bellas senoritas… Gracias por su ayuda en este Dia de Gringa Gracias!!! Tengo que preparar un monton de cosas. Dios mio…. los tamales de pavo son bellos. Tengo salsa de cranberry para acompanarlos. Hay que hacer *(reading her list)* the pureed yams con mantequilla americana; a cocinar los elotes en la fogata afuera; a cocinar los frijoles; friar los platanos; el arroz con pasas; la horchata, la ensalada de habichuelas, llenar pedazos de aguacate con pico de gallo. *she demonstrates*... y ya! Bueno, son hecho los pastelitos de pavo, los sandwiches de jamon, y sus marvellosas tamales. Los invitados traeran los dulces... Bastante complicada, verdad? Bueno vamos! Hello beautiful young ladies. Thank you for your help on this Gringo Thanksgiving Day. I have to prepare a million things. *She looks at the big basket of tamales that Vilma has.* My God the turkey tamales are beautiful! I have cranberry sauce to accompany them. We still have to do: the pureed yams with American butter; to cook the elotes over the outdoor fire; to cook the beans; fry the bananas; the rice with raisins, the horchata, the string bean salad; to fill the avocado halves with pico de gallo like this... and done! So the turkey pastelitos are made, as well as the mashed ham sandwiches, and your wonderful turkey tamales. The guests will bring the sweets for desert... *pause*... Pretty complicated right? OK let's go!

Ceci puts on classical music and the girls start claiming the food tasks they will take on. The bee hive buzzes!! There is a long table set up in the garden. Ceci covers it with white table cloths, sets up the chairs, and the table with bougainvillea flowers from the garden. She carefully arranges the buffet table inside to receive all food, and then returns to cooking. The girls help Vilma and Sayda cook.

Guests begin to arrive. Ceci greets them, offers them a glass of wine, beer, guiffity, soda, or juice. They wander into the garden after leaving their desserts on the table. There is arroz con leche; tableta de coco; dulce de miel; apple pie; pumpkin pie; flan, and bottles of wine. Deni May and her son, Ale... arrive. Some of the Mazapan American teachers, David Ashby, and Peter and Flor enter with Jazzlyn. Some of Peter's Gringo drinking friends from the Expatriados Bar, and their Honduran girlfriends arrive. The kids all play together while the adults enjoy a balmy, tropical cocktail hour Thanksgiving pouring wine and socializing. Ceci gathers everyone and invites them to raise their glasses before hearing the menu, and filling their plates. They all stand before the sumptuous buffet spread, which is a beautiful array of American and Honduran dishes... glasses raised. The kids all get pretty glasses with horchata.

Ceci: I just want to thank everybody for coming today. For me, I think that our American Thanksgiving is an excuse for everybody to have a global Thanksgiving around harvest time. It is so comforting to share it with others who understand why we celebrate abundance and grace together, and all the people we have to appreciate, along with the feast before us. I have to thank God for giving me these three beautiful daughters. Let us take a moment to be grateful and pray for others. Amen *A moment of silence.* A comer todos.. Please fill your plates and take a seat in the garden.

Peter: *Lifting glass.* A toast to friendship, and to Ceci for throwing such a great party...

Deni: And such a beautiful day.

They all clink again...Music fills the tropical festivity... Guests congregate around the buffet table, and move to the big table in the garden. Sayda and Vilma join the guests. The kids have their own table. The party takes on a life of its own after that. Peter tells Ceci over the meal.

Peter: Ceci, please come and see me. We will take a look at all your papers, and I will write up a case for your next visa application. I have been doing this for years, and I can construct a pretty good argument around your situation.

Ceci: Thank you Peter. I will take you up on that. I just got back from my third visa rejection yesterday. *She lifts her glass of wine and gets on a rant.*

Peter: Let me take a crack at it.

Ceci: Peter, I have tried everything. Even told them that my Mom was shipping my car over. Then we pull onto our street yesterday and the park is barricaded with limos and police. Turns out it is President Obama in our Botanical park, around the corner from here. So, I grab the girls and walk over there trying to get in and as close as I possible. Obama was there for some Biological dedication or something. There he was, maybe 25 feet away from me. But the secret service men were everywhere. I can't tell you how frustrating it was. I felt like screaming out "Barack... Hello... I'm American and I need to talk to you Mr. President. Can you call somebody over there at the embassy in Tegucigalpa for me? I need help!!!!"

Flor: Chica, estas loca con estas visas. *Laughter*

Ceci: Yes I am. *Peter fills her glass.*

Peter: Like I said... I will help you do it the right way... despite all your ineligibilities... Forget Obama... No outside agency can influence the decision of a foreign embassy with regards to visas anyway. Home Land Security goes by the local embassy rules. So we will play by the rules. *He holds up his glass of wine to toast with Ceci.* Come see me this week.

Ceci: I knew all that, but I just wanted to talk to Obama.... thanks Peter. I Know I have to do it the right way. I will be coming to see you soon.

She goes to the bar to get another bottle to fill up guest glasses. She takes the many comments about the food, as music and laughter fill the yard.

Deni May: So Peter, I see you guys have brought your guitars. Are you going to entertain us?

Peter: I thought you'd never ask. You ready to jamm guys?

American Guitarist *(Expatriot buddy)*: Sure nuf. Let's tune up.

270. Thanksgiving entertainment – Peter's Three Piece Combo

There is a table for the children, and they are all having a wonderful time, dressed up and laughing at each other. They take their fun to the swings and then to the street to play soccer and ride bikes. The music starts and everybody starts to dance and chat in between eating all the buffet food, draining every last bottle of wine. Some kids are playing hide and go seek in the garden. In between songs, Ceci reminds everybody about the dessert table, and to help themselves. These are the memories that are so meaningful, and so far between. The party goes into the evening as the sun sets on a hot, balmy night in November, to the sound of Peter and his three piece, California trio.

271. <u>**Duanes (customs) calls the house about Ceci's car**</u>

Next day, the phone rings, and wakes up Ceci who is still dressed in her long hostess dress from the Thanksgiving party the night before. It is Duanes (customs) and the customs broker at the dock north of La Ceiba. Ceci is half awake, until she gets the news.

Ceci: Hola... Si soy yo ... Como? No me digas!!! Cuando? Hoy? OK... Voy. *She hangs up ecstatic.* **Girls, wake up.. my car is here.. I have to go pick it up. Vilma? Where are you?**

Vilma is in the kitchen cleaning up. The girls wake up and come to the kitchen.

Ceci: Hola Vilma....Gracias a Dios que estas aqui... Tengo que irme a buscar el caro mio en Cortez, que llego en Duanes ayer... Entonces... Se puede cuidar las ninas hasta que vuelvo? Hello Vilma... Thank God you are here. OK.. I have to go pick up my car in Cortez.. that arrived at customs there yesterday. So can you take care of the girls until I return?

Vilma: Si Ceci...

Ceci: OK... Gracias ... Girls listen... We are getting a new car!!!!

Angie: And what about our black truck? What will we do with her?

Ceci: I don't know. Vilma, lo quieres? Do you want it back?

Vilma: Yo no manejo Ceci. I don't drive Ceci.

Angie: Debes de aprender Vilma. You should learn Vilma.

Ceci: Ella tiene razón.   Pero tengo un idea. Que transportacion tiene su hermano ahora? She's right. What transportation does your brother have now?

Vilma: Ninguno por el momento. None for the moment.

Ceci: Necesito alguien a manejarme. Llamale y preguntale si el puede manejarme en el camion negro hasta El Cortez para

que puedo recoger el mio.... Y...... digale.... Despues... el camion negro sera suyo de nuevo y tu puedes aprender a manejar. Call him and ask him if he can drive me and the black truck to Cortez so I can pick up my car from customs.... And tell him.... That the black truck will be his again and you can learn to drive it.

Vilma: Deveras.. Ceci? Really Ceci?

Ceci: Si ... llamale. Vamos a ver lo que dice el. Yes call him. Let's see what he says.

Ceci: Girls, when you see my 1999 Rav 4, you will love her. We will call her Carlota.

272. **Customs at the port in Cortez**

Vilma's brother drives Ceci to the port in El Cortez. Before entering the customs office she gives the car keys of the black truck to Vilma's brother. She signs back over the papers and asks him for 100 lempiras ($5) for the transfer. She smiles, and kisses the black truck goodbye.

Ceci: Vuelvo su burro porque ella te falta... I'm returning your donkey because she misses you!

Then Ceci meets up with a customs agent in the Import Office at the dock. She is giving the agent $2000 to negotiate the deal to get her car out of the yard. The customs fee is half the purchase value of the vehicle - A real rip off. Ceci has arranged for a cheaper sales receipt to lower the fee. She has become a well seasoned ex-patriot. The agent goes into the office, and she waits. Everything in Honduras has a middle man. He calls her in, and leads her to her car... She gets in and DRIVES AWAY... ecstatic to be reunited with her 1999 White Rav 4. She pops her salsa music into the dashboard, and turns up the volume, flying all the way back to Ceiba, thrilled to be back in her Carlota.

273. <u>Driving in Carlota to San Pedro with the Girls</u>

Ceci: OK, everybody get into our new car. We will call her Carlota... We are on our three hour trip to civilization in San Pedro girls.

Everybody has piled into Carlota, the 1999 Rav 4, for the long journey to San Pedro for costume fabric and a change of scenery. It is a beautiful drive on a two-lane highway past fields of sugar cane, corn, frijoles, coffee, pineapples, and palm oil crops. After leaving La Ceiba the route is rural into the center of the country.

At one point Ceci turns around and sees Jazmin and Roxana seated on the back door windows holding onto the sun roof hanging OUTSIDE the car. Ceci pulls over immediately.

Ceci: Oh my God do you want to give me a heart attack? How in the world did you ever come up with that idea? You could have fallen out. I was going 50 miles an hour!! Oh my God are you guys crazy?

They are all feeling very bad about this breach of behavior, as they had no idea it was dangerous. Once again, what gives kids a thrill, gives a parent anxiety. Ceci eventually gets over the tragedy and explains that they cannot do this again.

Ceci: OK ..promise me that you will never do this again, and that you understand how dangerous it is... OK?

Jazmin: Yes Mom... but it was so much fun... like a parade!

Ceci: Jazmin... please... I knew this was your idea.

Jazmin: OK Mom.. I will never do it again.

Ceci: Roxana... y tu? Entienden ninitas, que se puede caer y boom...adios!! Do you understand little girls, that you can fall and boom goodbye!!??

Roxana: Si mommy... no mas.

Ceci: OK... *She takes a deep breath, gets back in the car, and pulls back out on the dramatic highway to San Pedro. It is big sky country.*

People walk by the side of the road, carrying their machetes with wood on their heads. Sometimes you see horses, cows and sheep. Outside of the city, it is an agricultural life. They have passed the SOS orphanage where they originally lived. Next is Por Venir and la Union, where they were baptized. Then, through the lichee forest, where women and their children are parked every twenty feet, holding out their little bags of hairy red lichees for sale. As they approach El Progresso, where Angie had her first consultation with an eye Doctor, the sights become more urban and industrial. .... Ceci tells the story.

Ceci: So this is El Progresso, which is just on the outside of San Pedro. As you can see it is more urban, more city like. This is where I brought Angie for her first eye Doctor visit when you were just a toddler in the SOS.

Angie: And what did the doctor say mom?

Ceci: What they all say... That your optic nerve is shattered so that it does not connect with your brain so you can get a clear picture of what you are looking at.... that there is no cure but to keep monitoring your vision... which of course I will always do... but I, personally..... DO believe that one day there will be a cure for your optic nerve to grow or be replaced by some scientific miracle. We have to pray for that OK? I believe that with my heart and soul Angie.

They continue driving through zones that are urban residential outskirts of the city, with small businesses along the way. Traffic is chaotic... there are automatic rifled armed guards at the tolls and bridges. Young people jump onto public buses at the traffic stops to sell their food, candy, or novelties, and jump off as the bus accelerates. There is always somebody soliciting cash for their daily income of $5 a day.

274. Hotel Bolivar Lobby, San Pedro.

Eventually they pull into the Hotel Bolivar parking lot, where they always stay. It is an old, decaying hotel with Spanish overtones with a swimming pool in an overgrown courtyard at the center of the complex. There are shabby Christmas decorations everywhere. Ceci checks in and they go past the pool where several Honduran families are enjoying the sun.

275. Hotel Bolivar Pool

Cut to the girls in bathing suits entering the hotel pool area with Ceci. They jump in the water and Ceci strikes up a conversation with a Honduran woman. As they are talking…. Angie calls Jazmin to join her at the deeper end of the pool. Jazmin is young,

and still cannot swim. She creeps along the edge of the pool to meet up with Angie and gets on her back so they can swim piggy back to the island in the middle of the pool. At some point, Angie cannot support Jazmin so she lets her go to maintain her own flotation. Jazmin starts to sputter and sink. The lady with whom Ceci is speaking sees this and calls Ceci's attention to the pool. Ceci, who is fully dressed, immediately DIVES INTO THE POOL to rescue poor little Jazmin who cannot swim. It is a moment of truth and timing which makes Ceci realize never to take her eyes off of them while swimming. She carries Jazmin out of the pool who is coughing. She squeezes her close wrapping her in a towel.

Ceci: Oh my baby Jazz. You have not yet learned to swim, so you must stay in shallow waters.

Jazmin: There is no shallow water Mom… And Angie was supposed to carry me.

Angie: You were too heavy!

Ceci: Well then next time wait for me, and I will take you on MY back. I'm never taking my eyes off you again. I am so sorry. And I will sign you up for swimming lessons.

Jazmin: Angie dumped me Mom.

Angie: I couldn't breathe Jazz! No pude!

Ceci: It's my fault… I should have been in the pool with you… and I am sorry. I think it's time to turn in… I'll get some baleadas from the restaurant and bring them to the room. It's been a long day and I want you to be ready for shopping tomorrow.

Jazmin: Thanks Mom... Promise you will always be there ..

Ceci: I promise... Cross my heart. Hey, I jumped in with my clothes on. And next time you wait for Mom.

Cut to tucking girls in the hotel beds... after which Ceci takes a walk around the pool... It is dark and tranquil, even though you can hear the sounds of the city outside the wall. She dances a sentimental solo musical number in the tropical urban moonlight. This could be a musical number.

276. <u>AM Shopping in San Pedro</u>

It is morning in urban San Pedro, with all the musical and traffic sounds of a third world, tropical city at Christmas. Ceci and the girls are leaving the hotel, holding hands, and walking right past a group of young homeless boys who ask for money. Ceci grips the girls and walks faster.

Homeless boy: **Gringa quiere robar Honduras de sus muchachos!!!! Sin verguenza!** The gringa wants to rob Honduran kids without shame!

Ceci: **Don't look back. They are homeless, and don't have a mom to tell them right from wrong.**

Jazmin: **They look hungry and dirty Mom.**

Ceci: **They probably have no families..... I can't save everybody.**

They continue on down the busy boulevard covered with individual kiosks selling everything from underwear, to recorded music, to lottery tickets. The sidewalks are dirty and lopsided... This is the shopping mall of the poor. They pass old, pseudo fashion shops and restaurants until they find a vendor selling baleadas, pastelitos, and horchata, where they stop for a moment and watch people on the crowded sidewalk. It is a city freak show for Ceci and the girls.

277. Fabric store – San Pedro

Eventually they come to the big fabric store where Ceci gets lost in rows of different colored fabric and eventually finds her way up to the warehouse attic where bolts of stretchy fabric from Mexico lie disregarded. She pokes around measuring and checking her notes. Ceci racks up yards of fabric wrapped into six huge bags, while the girls run around playing in the store.

278. Sushi Restaurant – San Pedro

They take a taxi back to the hotel to drop the fabric, after which Ceci bathes them, dresses them up, and hauls them off to eat sushi in an upscale Japanese Restaurant with modern design and architecture. This is the other side of the tracks. The girls have put on Grandma's beautiful homemade dresses. This is a first - time experience for the girls, and we see the contrast between the upper and the lower class in the upscale metropolitan part of San Pedro... where one can see a Mercedes Benz with dark windows next to a donkey pulling a cart with platanos. These contrasts are everywhere, even in the higher class lomas (hills) of San Pedro. Ceci sips her sake and relaxes, surrounded by what appears to be educated upper class clients. Only Jazmin likes sushi, so Angie and Roxana have chicken teriyaki and rice. Ceci has taught them to put their napkins on their laps, and they behave like ladies.

The waitress wears a Japanese kimono, and this amuses the girls. She brings them blue drinks with pineapple and coconut juice.

Jazmin: Mami, I love this place.

Ceci: So what do you like?

Jazmin: I love the shushi, the blue drinkies, the waitress, everything... Can we come back tomorrow?

Ceci: Tomorrow we have to go back to La Ceiba and get ready for the Christmas show remember? That's why I bought all that fairy fabric.

Angie: Mom... I just want to see the whole world.

Roxana: But you can't see Angie.

Angie: I don't care, I still want to see what I can see.

Ceci: And I propose a double toast that not only will you all travel the world, but one day, Angie Nicolle, you will see everything in front of you.

Roxana: Because we believe in miracles right mama?

Ceci: **Absolutamente!!! Salud! Y Feliz Navidad!! Y vamos a montar el mejor espectaculo de Navidad que nunca!** To health and a merry Christmas... And let's mount the best Christmas show ever! *They clink their glasses twice, and laugh at the blue drinks.*

279. <u>After school rehearsals for Christmas Show #3</u>

Ceci and Vilma are in the dance studio office deciding what to do with all the new fabric from San Pedro. Ceci shows Vilma sketches of ideas for costumes for the various groups. The advanced dancers from the Mazapan school enter for class and Ceci gets ready to rehearse the Nativity ballet.

The following pieces will portray the process of working on choreographies for the 4 classes that will arrive. The sequential pieces of rehearsal will have a documentary style feeling. They are all works in progress.

1. *NATIVITY ballet – Ceci explains the idea of the ballet and the story line as she demonstrates choreography. Mary and her friends will enter the marketplace as belly dancers carrying produce to sell in baskets on top of their heads. They set up shop with their goods, and then stop to watch the arrival of the angel Gabriela. Ceci works with Gabriel and Mary on a duet in progress choreographing the gift of a lily to Mary, blessing Mary and circling her. This brings back the belly dancing girlfriends to join the circle and then snake around until the weaving and undulating puts Mary in labor. A light will appear from above and the baby will appear. Ceci explains that the Nativity will then be assembled and Gabriela will call on the Angels who will come in from the intermediate class... Then the three Queens will come, and etc. etc. The work commences.*

2. *TRINEOS – Bambinas – Ceci and Vilma show the girls their pretend cardboard box sleighs and how to get in them carrying them with straps around their necks. They work on skipping and a dance to the classic rendition of "Sleigh Ride" as galloping reindeer.*

3. *DOLL DANCE – Beginners -Ceci and Vilma show the girls their personal raggedy ann ballerina dolls (3 ft tall) who are dressed in identical tutus as the dancers. Ceci shows them how they will tiptoe into the living room on Christmas eve in their night gowns and open their gifts to find the dolls. Ceci shows them how they will remove their nightgowns to reveal the same outfit as the dolls and then perform a duet with the doll. She breaks down the moves with the doll.*

4. *SINGLE LADIES – Intermediates – Ceci explains that the hoola hoop is a symbolic prop for a wedding ring, and that works with the lyric from Single Ladies, "If you like it then you better put a ring on it", by Beyonce. The hoop is then used in every possible way in a rousing choreography. Ceci shows them different hoola hoop tricks that are challenging for the girls, but they all give it 100 percent - like using the hoop as a lasso, a jump rope, a boomerang, spinning it around all parts of the body, and tossing it in the air.*

280. <u>Hospital D'Antoni – with Angie , Neurology Dept.</u>

Ceci drags Angie by the hand as they search for the Neuro surgeon's office down long halls of the Hospital Vicente D'Antoni, the big hospital in La Ceiba. They go past fleets of nurses and patients waiting until they come to a waiting room that seems right and check in with the nurse at the desk.

Angie: So what do I say Mom?

Ceci: Just explain it to him the way you told me. That you were in class, and it was noisy and you were trying to write, and suddenly everything went black and when you woke up your arm was shaking….. Just like that OK? Dios Mio… It's a miracle you didn't fall and hit your head. I will explain the other episodes.

Angie: It's Ok Mom.

Ceci: *Fanning herself*…I am starting to flash on that time in the cafeteria when you tripped over the pipe and hit your head…. Come here baby… I love you so much… I am so sorry all this is happening to you. And you were so fabulous in the show last night.

A nurse appears and takes them to a room. She takes Angie's blood pressure and temperature. A doctor enters and puts Angie through a series of exercises to test her reflexes. He asks her lots of questions in Spanish.

Angie: Cuando vienen los ataques es como no puedo controlar mi cuerpo, ni mis palabras… y no puedo defenderme ni explicar nada, ni respirar. It's like I can't control my body or my words. And I can't defend or explain myself, nor breathe.

Doctor: Y que estaba pasando cuando empezo este ataque? And what was happening when this attack started?

Angie: Habia mucho ruido en la clase en Escuela Santa Teresa, y la profesora no podia controlar los estudiantes, y tambien el aire tuvo un sonido horible, y yo quieria exploder!!! There was a lot of noise in the class at Santa Teresa, and the teacher couldn't control the students, and the air conditioner was making a horrible sound, and I wanted to explode!

Ceci: Oh my baby… She gets overstimulated like Roxana. I'm taking you out of that school.

Doctor: OK.. Y como es con el tegretol? And how is it with the tegretol?

Angie: No se . Pero todavía tengo calambres de vez en cuando. Por dias y dias. I still have muscle cramps from time to time that last for days.

Doctor: OK, vamos a cambiar para Lamactil, que es mas suave, y va a calmarte mas. Chica, sabes que tu mama nunca va abandonarte… que siempre hay un luz al fin del tunel…. Entiende? OK Let's change for Lamactil, which is smoother, and will calm her down more. Little girl, you know that your mother will never abandon you… that there is always light at the end of the tunnel. Do you understand?

Angie: Si Doctor. Sabes que hay momentos cuando yo empiezo a temblar y me siento perdida, como hay peligro y yo respiro rápido y no puedo controlarlo. Yes doctor… You know that there are moments when I begin to shake and I feel lost, like there is danger and I breathe real fast and can't control it.

Ceci: These seizures always seem to happen when some emotional frustration or confrontation is happening… Oh baby I'm so sorry about this. *She embraces her.* **Is it epilepsy or panic attacks or what?**

Doctor: No se Sra. Vamos a empezar con el Lamactil. Aqui es la receta…. Uno diario… Y vuelve a verme en un mez. I don't know Sra. Let's begin with the Lamactil. Here is the prescription… One daily, and come back and see me in a month.

Ceci: Esta medicina es para bi-polar no? This medicince if for bipolar no?

Doctor: Si, pero tiene otra aplicacion para ella. Yes but it has another application for her.

Ceci: OK.. Y para cuanto tiempo la toma ella? And how long will she take it?

Doctor: Vamos a ver… senora… No se porque ella tiene esta condicion… sin conocer el salud de sus padres de sangre. Sin duda habian drogas, infection, malnutricion, abuso, etc au principio. Es algo neurologico seguramente. Hay muchos ninos de su edad con esta problema. Pero nadie lo entiende. Vuelve en un mez, y hablamos de los cambios. We will have to see Sra. I don't know why she has this condition without knowing the health of her blood parents… Without a doubt there were drugs, infection, malnutrition, abuse, etc. in the beginning. It is something neurological for sure. There are many children at your age with the same problem, but nobody really understands it. Come back in a month and we will talk about the changes.

Ceci: Si Doctor…. Gracias.

As they are leaving, Ceci is clearly upset. Angie is confused. Ceci is muttering to herself.

Ceci: Why didn't he order any tests? What's the deal here? Guess and prescribe? I don't know.

Angie: Mom, so now what is wrong with me…?? And why do I change pills? Is there really a cure for this shaking thing? Mom?

Ceci: *She stops in front of the truck and bends down at Angie's eye level, holding her tightly by the shoulders.* **Look Angie… I know one thing… that you are a sensitive, kind, and beautiful soul, and that I must do everything possible to keep**

you in a safe environment... but you know what honey? Not everybody is very nice, and sometimes when you can't see something, or don't understand what is happening, and maybe somebody is attacking you... You are not going to be ready for it, and that's when your nerves burn out and you start to shake. Eventually you will have to learn how to block this reaction. I know it's hard to explain how you feel when you are having this emotional meltdown. So for now we are going to try this new medicine Lamictal. And, I really think that you will be able to live without it one day. Also I am going to move you and Jazmin to Escuela Mazapan where you will be close to me, and that's all there is, and I will ask Tio De if he can help me pay for it. So come on.

Angie: Si Dios Quiere, Mommy.

281. Escuela Mazapan Director's Office–Registration Angie-Jazmin

Director: Ceci, you know we love the work you have done for our performing arts here at Mazapan. The Spring show was stunning and the parents are thrilled with the new outdoor stage and lighting you have created, and they can't wait until Christmas ... but the money is tight at Standard Fruit, and they are cutting back on us every day. So if you bring the girls in... assuming they pass the entry tests... then you will have to pay full tuition ... You are a part time teacher, and we are paying the electric bill for that AC in your dance studio.

Ceci: I know Martha, and I have to ask my friend in Italy if he can help with the tuition because I don't make enough to cover it. I just feel that they are not safe any place else, and if Roxana could come even close to passing the test I would have her here too... Special Education has not yet come to Honduras.

Martha: That's why we bring in the Special Ed teachers from the States... Let's get Angie and Jazmin over to Ms. Canahuati, the 2nd grade teacher for testing and we will go from there.

Ceci: Thank you for helping me with this.

Martha: Ceil, I know you think you are going to get visas for them one day, but I can tell you that you are dreaming an impossible dream.... I have seen many very disappointed American teachers come and go, leaving without the children they fell in love with in the streets, and in the orphanages.... It is very painful for the children too... But, I will accept them midyear if they pass the tests... You have taken them from the mud to the mountain and I will do what I can for them. But you must be realistic.

Ceci: Well I just will not leave until they come with me.

Martha: Well I hope you can dance forever!!

Ceci: We'll see about that. Thank you Martha...

282. **Phone Call with Louis about school change and tuition**

Ceci is walking out of the main office on her way back to the dance studio where she will have class soon. She calls Louis in Italy.

Ceci: Louis, how are you?....... Where are you? .... What are you up to?

Louis: *He appears as an aside or cutaway.* I am with Veronica in Milan visiting her son Daniel at his photography school. He has just moved into a new apartment with his girlfriend.

Ceci: Now that sounds exciting?

Louis: I got your message. And how are you and the girls?

Ceci: We are fine... But Louis I need to ask you a favor. Angie and Jazmin have been at Santa Teresa's, which is a local private bi-lingual school without any curriculum for special ed students. Also there is not enough discipline and control over the classes... and Angie has been having the shakes, like mini seizures because of the chaos in that class.

Louis: Is she taking her medication?

Ceci: Yes and we recently switched to a different drug called Lamictal on the advice of a neuro surgeon in La Ceiba. And I have decided to move them to the Mazapan school where I teach, which is a much better school which would reduce the stress and where they would clearly be closer to me. They are testing now, and if they pass I want to register them next week.

Louis: I think that is absolutely the right thing to do. Will they wave the tuition?

Ceci: That is the problem... I don't qualify for that status as a part time teacher, so I must pay $400 each for them a month. They would both go into 2nd grade together. I am waiting for them to pass the tests as we speak.... *She winces standing outside the dance studio, biting her nails.*

Louis: Then I will increase the transfer to 1000 Italian lire starting next month, and I will speak to the accountant in Belgium now. That should cover tuition plus some.

Ceci: Oh my God Louis, thank you so much. *She sits down on a park bench and her voice begins to shake.* I felt so guilty to ask you this, but I want to give them a better opportunity at this age, and I just don't know how to thank you.

Louis: Call me as soon as you know if they passed, and I will arrange an increase in the transfer. I think a good elementary education is crucial to their futures. I miss them... and what about Roxana?

Ceci: Roxana is still at Bright Beginnings, and thank God, because no other school will take her and deal with her disability. The classes are small, and I have to drive her every day, but she is OK there, and her English is improving every day. I believe she will always struggle with language.

Louis: Please send them my love... We are about to sit down to dinner.

Ceci: Ok, well Bon Apetit! And thank you again. Send my love to the family and baby Goia.

Louis: I will Ceci... and know that I am 100% behind what you are doing. Goodbye.

Ceci: Louis, thank you from the bottom of my heart.

Louis: I have been lucky in my life, and now I can give back.

283. <u>Angie and Jazz return from testing at Mazapan school</u>

She hangs up with composed relief. Again the Dr. Louis Harris has come through, and as she takes the tissue from her pocket, the girls come laughing down the path to her dance studio with Ms. Canahuati who is the 2nd grade teacher who tested them.

Ceci: Well hello, you finished so soon?

Ms. Canahuati: Yes they both did very well.

Jazmin: Mom I am really smart…. right Mrs. Teacher?

Angie: Stop it Jazmin, I am smart too.

Ceci: Yes you are both brilliant stars, now go get into your dance clothes.

Ms. Canahuati: *addressing Ceci privately…* Yes so they both passed, and I can tell you that Angie did struggle with the math, but I know I can help her. Angie is very sensitive and listens carefully. She is clearly a teacher pleaser. But she will need extra help because of her vision. And Jazmin…. Jazmin is very intelligent, and really has promise academically… a little distracted, but I think that is her social side.

Ceci: Oh this is great news. And now I am about to figure out how to pay for it.

Ms. C: I am sorry that it is the part time status that prevents the free tuition.

Ceci: I have been blessed by an angel in Italy who says he will help us.

Ms. Canahuati, Escuela Mazapan

Ms. C: Well hopefully you can bring them in on Monday, and we will do the best we can with Angie and her visual disability with accommodations, and I am sure they will adjust in no time.

Ceci: Thank you so much for doing this so fast... I have wanted to make the change for a while, but now that I have the money, I am ready and so are they. Thank you again, Ms. Canahuati.

Ms. C: I know what you have done here Ceci, and we all want to help however we can

Ceci: I needed to hear that today. Thanks...

284. <u>Karla's Black Eye Scam</u>

At the house, Ceci is on the porch combing the lice out of Jazmin's hair and Vilma is working on Angie's. Karla arrives at the gate, very pregnant again, on her bicycle. She has a black eye and is visibly upset. Ceci goes to the gate.

Ceci: **Hola Karla que paso con tu ojo?** Hello Karla, what happened to your eye?

Karla: **Yarel me pego Ceci. Peleamos porque no hay dinero, ni trabajo... y estoy embarasada.** Yarel hit me Ceci. We fought because there's no money, no work, and I am pregnant.

Ceci opens the gate and sees that she is pregnant again. This time it is with Isaac, Yarel's second child.

Ceci: **De nuevo? Karla! Donde esta Liliana?**

Karla: **En la casa con Yarel.**

Ceci: **Y que tienes en la bariga ahora?**

Karla: **Yarel quisiera un baron, y espero que aquí esta Isaac.**

Ceci: **Oh Karla!**

Karla: **Ceci, tu no sabes como es tener hambre y no hay pistos para comprar nada. Y Yarel no tiene trabajo. Entonces peleamos.** Ceci, you don't know how it is to be hungry and there's no money to buy anything. And Yarel doesn't have any work. Then we fight.

Ceci: Y Porque te pego? And why did he hit you?

Karla: Porque vivimos todos asi, con hambre, y no hay dinero Ceci... Con la rabia y frustracion, el me pego! Ya! Que mas quiere saber? Tu no sabes como es ... con su cuenta de banco que nunca se vacilla. Because we all live like that, with hunger, and no money Ceci. With the anger and frustration, he hit me. There… What more do you want to know. You have no idea how it is… with your bank account that never empties!

Ceci: OK Karla...basta... Dejame pensar... Chahcas... Go inside with Vilma... Roxana, traigame hielo por favor. Enough Karla.. Let me think… Girls, go inside with Vilma. Bring me some ice Roxana.

Ceci: Mira Karla... La violencia es mi primero preocupacion contigo y sus hijos. Gracias a Dios que estas ninas no vieron eso. *Roxana gives Ceci the ice for Karla's black eye.* **Entonces, creo yo que ahora debes de buscar su familia... su papa.. Donde esta el?** Look Karla. The violence is my first worry with you and your children. Thank God the kids didn't see that. So I believe that now you should look for your family. Your father… Where is he?

Karla: El morio hace poco, dijo mi hermana. He died not long ago… according to my sister.

Ceci: Y donde vivia el? And where did he live?

Karla: Estaba en Tegucigalpa... Yo no se que pasa con la casa. He was in Tegucigalpa.. I don't know what's happening with the house.

Ceci: Debes de ir ahora con sus hijos a ver que pasa con la casa de el. Puede ser un nuevo principio para ti Karla. You should go now with your children to see what happened with his house. It could be a new beginning for you Karla.

Karla: Como? Cuando no hay pistos para comer, como vamos a viajar? How? When there is no money to eat… how are we going to travel?

Ceci: Mas que todo tu necesitas un pedazo de seguridad que YO NO PUEDO DARTE Karla. Mire lo que paso con la tierra

en **Peru, donde me enganaste. Yo tengo sus hijas, pero no soy** *tu* **madre. Tu necesitas tu familia ahora Karla.** More than anything you need a piece of security that I cannot give you. Look what happened with the land in Peru, where you already fooled me. I have your children, but I am not *your* mother. You need your family now Karla.

Karla: Yo perdi mi familia hace anos Ceci. No hay familia cuando hay pobreza! Familia es la persona del momento que quiere o puede compartir su comida o su techo. O es el loco en la calle que te ofrece un trago de vino por la compania. Yo no se que es familia.... Yo se que morio hace poco mi papa Afro Cubano que nunca caso con mi madre, una india Maya de Belize, que nunca conoci. Y como yo siempre peleaba con mis hermanas desde llegue embarasada la primera vez, yo sali... Entonces no conozco mi familia. Ahora... como morio el papa de las ninas, ... pues... ahora mi familia es con Yarel. I lost my family years ago Ceci. There is no family when there is poverty Ceci. Family is the person in the moment who wants to or is able to share their food or their roof, or whoever crazy in the street offers you a sip of wine for company. I don't know what family is. I know that my Afro Cuban father died recently and never married my mother, who was a native Mayan… whom I never knew. And as I always fought with my sisters since I got pregnant the first time, I left. So I don't really know my family. And now … since the girl's father died… well now.. my family is with Yarel.

Ceci: Pero tuviste un Papa y debes de averiguar como el quiso dividir la casa. Mira Karla... la ultima vez... Yo voy a comprar boletos para ti y Lilliana para conseguir un hogar en Teguc que incluye Carlitos y Cynthia. Manana en la tarde te busco con Liliana para ir al estacion del autobus.... Eso es lo que puedo ofrecerte, OK? But he was your father and you should investigate how they are going to divide the house. Look Karla, for the last time. I am going to buy tickets for you and Lilliana to find a home in Tegucigalpa that includes Carlitos and Cynthia. Tomorrow in the afternoon I will look for you and Lilliana to go to the bus station. That's what I can offer you OK?

Karla: Y pistos?

Ceci: **Te dare dinero y comida manana ... Traiga una maleta ... y papeles de identificacion...** I will give you money and food tomorrow. Bring a suitcase and ID papers.

Karla: **Pistos, Ceci?** *Holding out her expectant hand.*

Ceci: **Karla... te dije. Te doy pistos manana cuando todo esta listo para tu viaje. Aqui es su chance para reclamar su vida. Hay que conseguir y preparar su propria casa, para sus hijos. No mas a buscar hombres para sobrevivir. Vaya con su familia Karla.** Karla... I told you.. I will give you pistos tomorrow when everything is ready for the trip. Here is the chance for you to reclaim your life. You must find and set up your own house for your children. Don't look for men for your survival. Go with your family Karla.

Ceci bags up some food and tries to usher Karla out towards the gate.

Ceci: **Vamos... Aqui hay frutas y arroz y frijoles. Te busco antes mi clase de danza manana a las once. Que sean listos OK?** Let's go.. Here is fruit... rice and beans. I will look for you before my dance class tomorrow at 11am... Be ready, OK?

Karla: **Bueno... OK Ceci...**

Ceci: **Y mantengas hielo en tu ojo!** And keep the ice on that eye!

The girls y Vilma join Ceci as she watches Karla drive away reluctantly on her bicycle. Ceci mutters to herself:

Ceci: I hope she finds a life.

Vilma: **Creo que ella te engano de nuevo Ceci.** I think she is tricking you again Ceci.

Ceci: **Que puedo hacer yo? Ella sabe donde estoy siempre.** It's definitely black mail... because I don't need any more daughters por favor Dios..!! What can I do? She knows where I am always.

285. <u>Following Day – Ceci takes Karla to Bus Station</u>

Ceci arrives at the shack where Karla lives with Yarel and his family and their daughter, Liliana. Ceci knows there must be a delicate situation in play since Karla is supposedly "leaving" while pregnant with Yarel's new baby. She quietly knocks on the shack door. Karla answers, half awake.. still with a black eye.

Ceci: Karla… vamos! We will miss the bus… Chica… Tengo clase en una hora… y el bus va a salir… Te espero en el caro.. Karla Let's go. I have class in an hour and the bus is going to leave. I will wait in the car.

Karla: OK cinco minutos Ceci.

Ceci goes to the car to wait and organizes her tickets with cash. Karla arrives with Liliana, smelly with a dirty face. She has a small back pack. They get in the car.

Ceci: Tienes sus papeles?, cedula, certificados de naicimientos? Do you have your papers? Your ID, birth certificates?

Karla: Si Ceci… los tengo aqui…

Ceci: Espero que tu entiendes lo que necesitas hacer Karla. Hay que estar fuerte. I hope that you understand what you need to do Karla… and you have to be strong.

Karla: Si Ceci… *She cleans Lilliana's face, and combs her hair.*

Ceci: Y que dijo Yarel? And what did Yarel say?

Karla: No dijo nada, no sabe nada… esta dormiendo.. He didn't say anything… he doesn't know anything… he is sleeping.

Ceci: Bueno…… Tienes el numero de su hermana? Good… Do you have your sister's number?

Karla: Tengo la direccion de la casa. I have the address of the house.

They arrive at the bus station. Kids and mothers are selling food to the passengers as they find their buses. They get out of the car in front of the bus going to Tegucigalpa. Ceci gives Karla tickets and 1000 lempiras.

Ceci: OK.. Aqui son los boletos. El bus sale en 15 minutos. Tomes el dinero, y mirame bien *(looking close to her face)* **Que seas fuerte.. Busques una vida sin hombres… una vida sincera…**

Trabajes para sus hijos… me oyes? Here are the tickets. The bus leaves in 15 minutes. Take the money and look at me … Stay strong… Look for a life without men… A sincere life… Work for your children. Do you hear me?

Karla: Si Ceci… *Liliana starts to cry.*

Ceci: No mires por atras. Aqui estan baleadas para el viaje. Karla… no mires por atras..oye? Don't look back. Here are baleadas for the trip. Karla.. don't look back.

Karla: Adios Ceci.

Karla gets on the bus with the kids… Ceci walks away after waving… and mutters.

Ceci: Adios… Si Dios Quiere….*She looks up* **Oyy! Por favor Dios…. ayude esta mujer!** Goodbye, Godwilling… Oyy Please God.. help this woman!

Ceci gets in the car and pulls out of the parking lot of this third world bus station…full of wanderers.

286. **Market Place – La Ceiba – Seeing Lillian, Yarel's Mom – Two days later**

Ceci is in the market downtown with the girls seeking a piñata. It is Saturday and she is shopping with the girls in the big crowded indoor mercado… teeming with sound, smells, life, and fresh products. There is music streaming from every vendor's shop, along with the repetitious shouts of barkers soliciting passer bys with their bargain prices. Inside the market place we see young girls making tortillas, farmers selling their fresh fruit and vegetables, butchers, botanicas and their magical herbs and elixirs… clothing, dishware, bookbags, and all of it jammed together. They pass a section selling pinatas and Roxana stops.

Roxana: Angie, mire esas pinatas lindas… para su cumpleanos!! Angie, look at the pinatas for your birthday!

Ceci: That's right… your birthday is coming in April.

Jazz: Look at the princesa!

Angie: Yes.. I want the princesa!

Ceci: OK.. We can get it now if you really want it.

Angie: Si la quiero Momi! Yes I want it!

At that moment a woman passes by them and stops to address Ceci.

Woman: Hola Ceci, como estas?

Ceci: Hola Sra. Liliana... Chachas... Saluden la senora Liliana *(senior)*... **Ella es la madre de Yarel.. el novio de Karla...** Hello Sra. Liliana,,, Chachas.. Say hello to Sra. Lilliana. She is Yarel's mother... Karla's boyfriend.

Liliana gives a hug to the girls. Ceci is walking on eggshells about Karla's exit from the family.

Ceci: Y como esta Yarel? And how is Yarel?

Sra. Liliana: Esta bien... trabajando... Gracias a Dios. He is good.... Working... Thank God.

Ceci: Y han oido algo de Karla? And have you heard anything from Karla?

Liliana: Karla esta bien... en casa. Karla is OK.. in the house.

Ceci: En la casa con Yarel? In the house with Yarel?

Liliana: Si, como siempre. Yes, like always.

Ceci: Entonces, ella no fue a Tegucigalpa con Lilliana. So, she didn't go to Tegucigalpa with Liliana?

Liliana: No. Ella me espera alla para cocinar tamales con mis compras. No she's waiting at home to cook tamales with my purchases.

Ceci: Y su ojo? And her eye?

Liliana: Esta mejor,,, Se golpio con la escoba por accidente... It's better... She hit herself with the broom by accident.

Ceci: Entonces... Ella y Yarel no estan peleando? So she and Yarel weren't fighting?

Liliana: No pues... Todo bien.. y ella esta embarasada de nuevo con otro nino. No, Everything's good.. and she is pregnant with another baby.

Ceci: Si yo se. Yes I know.

Liliana: Si... Yarel quiere un baron. Yes, and Yarel wants a boy.

Ceci: OK.

Angie: Mami, quiero comprar la piñata princesa Ok? Mom, I want to buy the princess piñata!

Ceci: Yes honey, we'll get this one. Pues, Sra. Liliana andiamos... Diga Karla que mando mis saludos... y saludos a la famiia.. Well... Lilliana, we have to go. Tell Karla that I send my regards and regards to the family.

Liliana: Si Ceci... Ciao!!

Ceci: Shit... tricked again. *Ceci rushes away stunned, as she realizes Karla has lied... Sra Liliana stands there confused.*

287. <u>Dance Studio – Mazapan –Christmas Kinder Rehearsal</u>

Ceci enters studio with coffee as kinder students line up outside who are eagerly ready to rehearse their Mazapan School Christmas show dance. She lets them in and they all rush to their small plastic chairs Vilma has set up on the dance floor facing the mirror. Vilma helps the kids settle down. The Kinder teacher speaks with Ceci.

Kinder Teacher: Yes they have practiced the song and are very excited to do this in the mirror again. It is a great choreography for them Miss Ceci, and a great achievement for them to memorize all of these movements.

Ceci: It is the perfect mix of English, classic, Christmas, kiddie songs, which they will never forget. Repetition really helps memorization... So let's get started.

Teacher: OK Ninos... silencio por favor.. Vamos a practicar la danza con Sra Cecilia ahora... Cuando hay silencio... OK.. OK Kids... quiet please. We are going to practice the dance with Sra. Cecilia now... when there is silence...

Without another word, Ceci starts the classic musical track mix... *(Frosty the Snowman, Rudolph the Red nosed Reindeer, and We Wish you a Merry Christmas) She faces the students with her back to the mirror and leads the 25 five year olds singing and dancing on, off, and around their little chairs. They know the choreography inside out and are ready to show off. Ceci, Vilma and the teacher laugh with delight watching them. Ceci maintains that little chairs keep young dancers in their spots.*

288. <u>After School Dance – same day – Nativity Ballet prep-</u> <u>Peter</u> <u>Thompson</u>

Dancing school begins when the school day ends. Ceci and Vilma are exhausted after hours of making costumes. But the dancing school routine begins full force. She continues to work on the Nativity ballet with the older girls. The rehearsal goes like this, and reviews a previous rehearsal.

Nativity Ballet

We hear a middle eastern gypsy like drone with Mary and her friends entering the stage carrying baskets on their heads with a belly dance as they go to the marketplace. At some point there is a freeze in the music and the angel Gabriel comes in with the lily for Mary, which she started earlier. We watch Ceci continue to work this choreography until the bell rings. (The birth of Jesus takes many forms for Hondurans at Christmas and is always popular).

In walk Angie, Roxana and Jazmin in between Ceci's classes. They salute their mom, and go with Vilma to get changed.

ANGEL Dancers - We cut to the next class with a fleet of angel dancers circling around another Mary to the chorus of Angels We Have Heard on High. This music takes Mary to a manger. Ceci starts and stops the music to work on the choreography.

Three Queens - Next we watch a rehearsal with the three sisters (Jazmin, Angie, and Roxana) portraying three queens in adult wedding dresses dancing to an instrumental version of "We Three

Kings". *They make a processional entrance which leads them to Mary where they bestow their gifts upon her and the holy child.*

Adestes Fideles – finale - The music changes to Adestes Fideles, which will be the finale eventually when the entire company dances.

There is one more class. Peter and Flor arrive with Jazzlyn... Peter will replace Flor in the Mrs. Santa Claus Mommy- Daughter Dance, and also play guitar in the show. Flor comes to say Hi.

Flor: **Ceci, tu sabes que tengo miedo del scenario y espero que tu entiendes porque no puedo bailar con Jazzlyn para su coreografia con las madres y hijas.** Ceci you know that I am afraid of the stage and I hope you understand why I can't dance with Jazzlyn for the mother and daughter choreography.

Ceci: *laughing*…Si esta bien Flor…. No te preocupes. He can wear his Santa outfit with an apron and everybody will love it. I am sorry you have stage fright, but I understand, and thank you for working this out so Jazzlyn can dance.

Peter: And I brought the guitar to practice the finale.

Ceci: Great, and I want to talk to you about your legal services and word smithing for my next trip to the embassy.

Peter: Yes I have a few more ideas about that.. When are you going?

Ceci: I am waiting to hear from the lawyer about my tutora custody within the next few days, which I am hoping will help… It has been two years in the processing.

Peter: Do you think you will get it?

Ceci: Well.. the Juez de la Familia is the mother of my lawyer, Merlyn Vasquez, which will also help. And my case is unique because no gringa has ever been awarded tutora status as a custodial arrangement.

Peter: This all sounds good. It will make a great argument to revisit the application. You know.. we will have to rethink this in terms of an "alternative adoption".

Ceci: Yes.. I am telling you, from everything I have researched... the tutora vetting and screening is exactly the same as the adoption process.

Peter: Only adoptions are on hold now because of the IHNFA corruption scandal, so your lawyer sounds pretty savvy to do it this way.

Ceci: Plus the girls have lived with me for almost five years.

Peter: This is worth rewriting just to keep your profile alive.

Ceci: OK... And Oh.. and listen to this this... I got an email from the embassy offering to return two of the three application fees from my third rejection.

Peter: So are you going to do it? That's $1000!!

Ceci: You know what? I am not. Because I want those guys to know who I am again and again .... To remember the gringa who was trapped in Honduras and kept doing it their way... the gringa who would not give up,,, paying every time to wait on long lines, paying into the pocket of the American Homeland Security... just to get rejected over and over again... For what reason? Because I don't fit in the right mother box. Why do I keep paying full price? Just so they won't forget that I'm the gringa who is dedicated to this. So next time.. Peter I definitely welcome your help with the application. They are going to know who I am.

Peter: And I will show you how we will fit you into the box.

Ceci: Deal!

Ceci refocuses as she sees little girls and moms gathering on the dance floor. She gives Peter an apron to wear for comic rehearsal relief and they begin.

Ceci: So now we have to work on the Mrs. Santa Claus Mommy dance... for which you need an apron so I can make it work with the other mothers. I see that as a great comedy opportunity!

Peter: Well I wouldn't go that far.

Ceci: Well if I am a mother/father all day every day, you can wear an apron for a Mrs. Santa Claus dance. Come and join the girls Peter. You will steal the show for sure. OK ladies let's get started! *Santa Claus Mommy- daughter Dance*

Just a beautiful mother daughter (ages 4-6) dance with lots of lifts and hugs and magic. Ceci dances with little Jazmin. The rehearsal is rough, but the music takes the students through it piece by piece. Vilma helps out checking on costumes in the background, and the scene fades with Ceci and Jazmin hugging.

289. Call from Merlyn – Tutora ready to go

Ceci is washing dishes when the lawyer, Merlyn calls.

Merlyn: Ceci... Everything is looking good to go for your custody transaction.

Ceci: Oh Dios mio! I thought you'd never call.

Merlyn: We have the testimony of three witnesses. You had the home inspection. We got the clearance from both Honduran and US law enforcement. Your financial papers have been reviewed. The children have been declared "abandoned". Now we need to register a Pro-tutora and then there is only the final assessment with the children and the judge. Fortunately, my mother has arranged to give your case priority examination, even though she will not skip over any formalities.

Ceci: Que maravilla! I think I have to sit down. It's been a long two year wait.

Merlyn: Yes, but all other adoptions have been put on hold with the closing of the IHNFA, and you are a gringa over the age for adoption.... I would say two years is not bad. And there has never been a gringa who has left the country with Honduran kids with Tutora status. That is your next mountain to climb.

Ceci: Well that remains to be seen of course... but I do appreciate this Merlyn... from the bottom of all four of our hearts.

Merlyn: OK ... now the Pro-tutora must be a Honduran citizen as a formal back up for this Tutora custody. This is absolutely part of the transaction. It should be someone who agrees to take over if something happens to you, etc, etc.

Ceci: OK.. Well Vilma Reyes, my assistant is ready to sign. She is the best possible choice. She knows the children and they love her.

Merlyn: Very good. Then she will have to sign some papers at the courthouse tomorrow when I have scheduled a meeting for all of you, in the morning with the judge, (my mother). She is fully aware of Karla and her inability to care for the girls. Basically this meeting is a formality to prove that the girls know Vilma and that she can sign as protutora... and mainly so the judge can testify that the girls think of you as their mother after individual meetings with her. Relax Ceci, you have nothing to hide... It is all a very clear case of what is best for these children, which you have already proven for the last five years. *Ceci smiles and touches her heart looking up.*

Ceci: Dios mio Merlyn... you are a magician after all. Wow, this means I can proceed with passports and my number four visa application.

Merlyn: This is truly unprecedented I admit... I hope you can celebrate this week.

Ceci: The next challenge is to get through US Immigration without a glitch someday. Si Dios quiere of course.

Merlyn: One step at a time Ceci... I will see you tomorrow with Vilma and the girls at 10am at the courthouse.

Ceci: Merlyn Vasquez, you are part of a significant historical shift in the future of these girls' lives. I could not do this without you. Thank you so much.

Merlyn: Hasta manana Ceci.

Ceci gets off the phone and starts jumping up and down. Vilma and the girls come running out to see what she is screaming about.

Ceci: Vilma... manana hay que ir a la municipalidad para firmar el documento de custodia para las ninas. Vilma... estas seguro que se puede hacerme este favor de ser la **Pro-tutora de mis ninas? No hay nadie mejor que ti...** Vilma tomorrow we must got to the courthouse to sign the Pro-tutora custody document for the girls. Are you sure you can dome this favor to be the Pro-tutora for my girls? There is nobody better than you.

Vilma: **Si Ceci.. tu sabes que les quiero mucho. Cuenta conmigo.** Yes Ceci, you know that I love them very much. Count on me.

The excitement starts to build.

Ceci: Thank you thank you thank you Vilma... OK.. Girls... we all have to go to see the judge tomorrow.... Manana vamos todas a ver la juez de la familia...

Angie: So she can make you our real mama!

Ceci: Exacto! We have to get all dressed up OK?

The girls hug and kiss her, and dance around with Vilma.

Ceci: *Looking up at the sky..* There is a God up there somewhere who loves us.

290. <u>The Courthouse – with the Juez de la Ninez (for children)</u>

Ceci and Vilma enter the courthouse with the girls dressed up in their Sunday best. Merlyn is waiting for them after they pass through security. He leads them to the Judge's chambers. Ceci is really nervous and keeps fixing the girls' hair. Merlyn coaches Ceci along the way.

Merlyn: So this is how the morning will go. You and Vilma will meet with the judge first to get the Pro-Tutora papers signed. Then the girls will be interviewed individually. You all look lovely by the way, and I want you to relax.

Ceci: After eight years of being told this would never happen, I am floating Merlyn.

Merlyn: She is my mother Ceci. And she knows por cierto that these girls stand a better chance to survive with you, more than any other possible situation with the family or the orphanages. You have passed all the tests so far. Just remain calm.

They arrive outside the chamber doors.

Ceci: OK girls, now listen to Abogado Merlyn. He will explain.

Merlyn: Entonces... todas son bien bellas con sus sonrisas...Hola Vilma... Gracias por venir. La juez va hablar primero contigo y Ceci para firmar los papeles de la Pro-Tutora. So... Everybody looks beautiful, with such happy smiles. Hello Vilma, thank you for coming. The judge will speak first with you and Ceci to sign the Pro-Tutora papers.

Vilma: Bueno soy lista. *Vilma pulls out her Cedula (ID).* Yes, I am ready.

Jazmin: Y yo puedo firmar tambien *She pulls a crayon out of her little purse.* And I can sign too.

Merlyn: Tu no tienes que firmar mi amor... solamente diga la Juez que Ceci es una buena madre y que quiere estar con ella para siempre, y que Vilma es tu tia. You don't have to sign my dear. Only tell the judge that Ceci is a good mother and that you want to be with her forever. And that Vilma is your aunt.

Angie: Si si...para siempre. Yes yes... forever.

Merlyn: Correcto... Y cada una va hablar con ella sola. Right, and each one will speak to her alone.

Roxana: Para que podemos ir a los Stados para vivir con nuestra abuela tambien. So that we can go with her to the states and live with our Grandmother also.

Merlyn: Bueno... eso es otro asunto. Well that's another situation.

Ceci: Au menos yo no necessitaria buscar permiso cada vez para viajar con ellas. At least I would not need to seek permission every time to travel with them.

Merlyn: Si claro.

The door opens and Judge Vasquez greets everybody with a big smile.

Judge: Buenos Dias todas.

Girls: Buenos Dias Senora.

Judge: Como se llaman estas ninas preciosas? What are the names of these precious girls. *She gives them lollypops.*

Angie: Yo soy Angie. I am Angie.

Roxana: Y yo soy Roxana y me gustan los chupetes. And I am Roxana and I like lolly pops.

Jazmin: Yo soy Jazmin y Ceci es nuestra madre. And I am Jazmin and Ceci is our mother.

Judge: OK... Quiero oir todo eso... Pero primero hablare con tu mama y Vilma. OK, I want to hear all of that. But first I will speak with your mother and Vilma.

Ceci y Vilma enter the office and Merlyn stays with the girls.

Angie: Senor Merlyn... que pasa con nosotros si la juez dice no? No quiero estar en el SOS, ni con Karla de nuevo. Sabes que no puedo ver bien, y solo Ceci puede ayudarme. Sr. Merlyn.. what happens with us if the judge says no? I don't want to be in the SOS, nor with Karla again. You know that I can't see very well and only Ceci can help me.

Merlyn: No te preocupas Angie... Todo va bien aqui... Yo conozco esta Juez bien.... y ella entiende todo lo que pasa contigas. Don't worry Angie. Everything will go well here. I know the judge very well and she understands what is happening with you.

Jazmin: Y yo quiero ir a Hollywood para conocer a Justin Bieber. And I want to go to Hollywood to meet Justin Bieber.

Angie: Abuela no vive en Hollywood Jazmin. Grandma doesn't live in Hollywood Jazmin.

Roxana: Ella vive en una casa grande en Virginia. She lives in a big house in Virginia.

Merlyn: Cuando llegas alla, se puede ir donde quieres, sin papeles. No hay fronteras entre los estados para viajar.. When you arrive there, you can go where you want without papers. There are no borders between the states for travelling.

As they suck on their lollypops. The scene switches inside the chambers with the Judge, Ceci and Vilma.

291. Inside the Judge's Chambers – Ceci, Vilma and girls

Judge: Dona Cecilia yo se que su viaje era bien largo y dificil para buscar una custodia legal para estas ninas. Y despues de averiguar todo, con la historia de las ninas... ud. ha pasado todas las inspecciones. Antes de hablar con ellas, quiero estar claro con su Pro-Tutora, Vilma Reyes, si? Puedo ver su identificacion? Dona Cecilia, I know that your journey has been long and difficult to get legal custody for the girls. And after investigating everything with the history of the girls, you have passed all the inspections. Before speaking with them, I want to be clear with your Pro-Tutora, Vilma Reyes yes? Can I see your identification?

Vilma: Si Senora... aqui esta. *She shows her identification card, called a "cedula".*

Judge: Ud. entiende que su posicion es como una co-madre para las ninas. Y si algo pasa con Dona Cecilia, que ud. deberia tomar la responsabilidad del bienestar de ellas... La ley dice que la Pro-tutora seria una Hondurena. You understand that your position is like a co-mother for the girls. And if something happens to Ms. Cecilia, that you would take responsibility of their wellbeing. The law states that the Pro-tutora is Honduran.

Vilma: Si, estoy claro... y creo que entiendo las disabilidades de ellas mas o menos.. Yes I understand, and I believe that I understand their disabilities more or less.

Ceci: Si, y Vilma y su hermana, Sayda, también, son como familia para ellas. Y Vilma es como mi mano derecho en mi escuela de danza por anos. Yes, and Vilma and her sister, Sayda, also, are like family for them. And Vilma is like my right hand in my business for years.

Judge: Uds. estan haciendo un grand servicio para estas muchachas, y me alegro conocerles. Entonces... Senora

Cecilia... por favor, firme aqui Y Senorita Vilma, firme por aqui. You are doing a great service for these girls, and I am happy to know you. So.. Senora Cecilia... please sign here, and Vilma... sign here.

Ceci y Vilma sign the papers.

Judge: Dona Cecilia, yo no se como su Homeland Security Americana va a mirar su caso... porque ningún Americano ha logrado visas para ninos Hondurenos sin adopcion...aunque de la sola differencia entra tutora y adopcion es el limito de su edad. El processo es casi el mismo. Dona Cecilia I don't know how the American Homeland Security is going to look at your case, because no American has ever gotten visas for Honduran kids without formal adoption, even though the only difference between tutora and adoption is the limit of your age. The application process is the same.

Ceci: Yo se.. y este papel seria un grand exito en el processo de casi ocho anos. Quiero agradedecerle mucho. I know and this paper would be a great success in this eight year process. I want to thank you very much.

Judge: Pues, ahora hablare con las ninas para confirmer sus sentimientos. Quiero ver Roxana primero sola – y se pueden esperar afuera. So.. now I will speak to the girls to confirm their feelings. I want to see Roxana first alone, and you can wait outside.

Ceci calls Roxana in who is very nervous, and waiting nervously.

Ceci: Roxana... La Juez quiere hablar contigo primero como tu eres la hermana mayor. Roxana, the judge wants to speak to you first, since you are the oldest.

The judge gives Roxana another lollypop. She follows her into her chambers. And Ceci and Vilma wait outside with the others.

One by one the girls enter and exit the judge's little chambers. It is a montage of innocent faces all expressing the awareness of a pivotal landmark in their lives. Finally, she calls them all back in... Jazmin sits on the lap of the judge. Angie sits on Ceci's lap, and Roxana on Vilma's.

Judge: Sra Cecilia, Felicidades... Este processo largo ha termindado y ud va a lograr lo que creemos aqui es la mejor decision para la vida de estas muchachas bellas... La custodia de Tutora. Felicidades Dona Cecilia..... *And the Ceci tears flow. The judge continues*.... Lo que quiero recordarte....... es que estas ninas tienen disabilidades que no van a desaparecer. Su trabajo va a crecer con los anos con doctores, educacion especial, y posiblemente dependencia por anos. Y tu no eres joven con 50 anos. Pero yo calculi la evidencia de su carera de bailarina, sus estudios, con su buena forma y salud en mi decision. Tiene mucho fuerza. Y veo tu amor para ellas... Entonces yo firmo este papel con la fe que su caracter y espiritu sigue apoyando el bienestar de estas preciosas muchachas como la madre que ellas necesitan. *She signs the final paper.*

Y me alegro que au menos estas tres huerphanes de Honduras han conseguido una familia buena. Vaya con Dios. Van a cambiar la vida de estas muchachas Dona Cecilia. Sra. Cecilia.. Congratulations. This long process has ended and you have achieved what we believe here is the best decision for the life of these beautiful girls – The custody of Tutora. Again Congratulations. What I want to remind you, is that these girls have disabilities that will not go away. Your work is going to grow with the years, with doctors, special education, and possible dependency for years. And you are not young with 50 years. But I calculated the evidence of your career as a dancer, your studies, and your good form and health in my decision. You are very strong. and I see the love you have for them. So I sign this paper with the faith that your character and spirit continues to support the wellbeing of these precious children as the mother that they need. And I am happy that at least these three Honduran orphans have found a good family. Go with God. You are going to change the life of these girls Dona Cecilia.

Ceci: *Blotting her tears with her blouse.* Es un milagro Senora.... Gracias por todo sus bendiciones. Y Merlyn también. Son buena gente. Dios me mando mas angeles. This is a miracle Sra. Thank you for your blessings. And Merlyn tambien. You are good people. God sent me more angels.

Roxana: No llores mami. Don't cry Mom.

Jazmin: Ella siempre llora. She always cries.

Ceci: But these are happy tears... Thank you so much... Girls go hug the judge. Where is Merlyn? Thank you Judge.

Ceci and the girls hug the judge. Merlyn enters the office. Ceci gives Merlyn a hug...

Merlyn: Now you can celebrate.

Ceci: Girls hug Merlyn. Oh Merlyn I can't thank you enough for doing this. How many lawyers did I talk to before finding you? I do believe in God.

Angie: Come on Mami... let's have a fiesta tonight.

Ceci: OK... Only if the magician Merlyn will come.... You can bring a friend Merlyn. I will make a 7pm reservation at Mango Tango in the Zona Viva. Y ud. tambien Judge... Please come if you can.

Judge: No puedo mezclar negocios con placer. Pero me alegre que podríamos hacer esta transacion para ud y sus preciosas hijas. Dios te bendigas. You have changed their lives.

Ceci: Thank you so much .. both of you.

Merlyn: OK Cecilia – Vaya con Dios.

*Ceci hugs them both again and they all leave dancing. Merlyn puts his arm around his Judge mother's shoulder as they watch the girls go dancing down the hall.*292. Custody Celebration Dinner at Mango Tango in the Zona Viva Impuestos de Guerra

Ceci, Vilma and the girls enter a popular outdoor restaurant in the Zona Viva called MANGO TANGO, which is owned by two lady gourmet cooks, Jane and Juanita. One of the owners, Juanita, approaches Ceci as she enters and gives her a big hug.

Juanita: Hola Ceci, ... I have a big table for your party on the beach deck... Follow me...

Ceci: Thank you so much... This is perfect.

Juanita: Ceci, let me congratulate you on this miracle. Yo se que tienes anos en esta lucha para custodia... Pero ganaste Ceci!!! Y Dios te bendices. Felicidades. I know how many years you have years you have come here telling me about this fight for the custody. But you won.. and God has blessed you. Congratulations.

Ceci: Thank you... Hay mas rios a cruzar... And this river was a wide and deep one...and we made it across,,, Thank you.. There are many more rivers to cross.

Juanita: I will bring you some cokes and your vino tinto... Disfruten! Enjoy!

Deni May and Ale arrive. He is happy to be there and hugs the girls. Peter enters with his wife and daughter, Flor and Jazzlyn. Then David Ashby shows up. Sayda has come to join her sister Vilma and the girls. Several Mazapan teachers come. Merlyn, his friend, and Dona Eva and her daughter arrive. All glasses are filled... Many hugs and congratulations are given to Ceci. Big platters of fried fish are brought out with sides of rice, beans, and platanos...
Peter stands with his glass and proposes a toast to Ceci...

Peter: Let us all take a moment before we dive into this beautiful presentation... to make a toast to Ceci for persevering through the system to finally win formal custody of these beautiful girls. She never stopped... followed one lead after the other for years... where others would have given up.

They raise their glasses.

Ceci: Thank you Peter... Well I want to make a toast to my three precious daughters whom have given me a passion for life that I never had before. They are beautiful and innocent and have great dreams before them that I hope to help them achieve. And I want to thank everybody who has supported us in this impossible challenge over the past eight years. Thank you Vilma for hanging in there with me and the girls... through dance concerts, and costumes... fevers and hair dos... birthday parties and graduations... Vilma has been there like an extra right arm. And I thank Deni May for being such a great friend and support who helped Vilma and I through the whole borderline coup that engineered the girls' original exit from the Orphanage. I also want to thank Conchita and Mami Dunia, their Tias at the SOS orphanage for rescuing their health and welfare. And of course I

must thank my Lawyer, Merlyn Vasquez, for engineering the whole Tutora custody after years of being lost. Also gracias to Dona Eva for giving me the faith in spirit to go on with visions of a positive outcome. David Ashby, their Godfather, who helped me baptize them, which enabled my initial foster custody. And I must thank our angel, Dr. Louis Harris, in Italy for giving me the support and confidence to continue the struggle until I found a way.

Thank you to Peter Thompson, American Immigration Lawyer, who will be the magician on my next visa application for the girls without whose brilliant word smithing, I could not face that embassy line in Tegucigalpa again.

And finally to my mother, Josephine Diaz Gruessing, for believing in me and my daughters. Amen! *Ceci raises her glass....* Ceci: Salud everybody! Buen Provecho!!! To your health! Enjoy!

Everybody raises their glasses, and begins to feast on the fabulous Caribbean dinner in front of them. Music pipes into the atmosphere and everybody is having a wonderful time. The girls and Jazzlyn are dancing until they begin to chase the restaurant kittens. The restaurant is packed.

Vilma and Sayda are sitting next to each other facing the entrance of the restaurant, when suddenly their jaws drop. Two gang men and a woman enter slowly with masks and guns. Ceci leans over to Vilma and whispers....

Ceci: **Que quieren ellos?** What do they want?

Vilma: **Oh Ceci... Les conozco... Viven en Las Mercedes... Quieren recoger Impuestos de Guerra..** Oh Ceci.. I know them. They live in Las Mercedes. They want to collect war tax.

Gang guy: **Nadie mueve!!** Nobody move!

The two gang guys stand at the doorway as the young lady goes to speak to the owner, Jane, who comes out of the kitchen. Everybody in the restaurant is frozen and clearly alarmed. Ceci is looking around frantically for the girls. The discussion between Jane and the lady marero who is demanding the money begins:

Gang girl: Ya hablemos de la cantidad senora!!! We already talked about how much.

Jane: Es demasiado! It's too much! *Juanita joins backs her up.*

Gang girl: Entonces Senora…. Podemos hablar directamente con todos sus clientes si quieres … Porque nadie sale hasta que recibimos nuestros impuestos. Entendiste mujer? Then we can speak directly to all your clients if you wish. Because nobody leaves until we get our war tax. Did you understand lady?

Juanita: Diez mils lempiras es demasiado! Ten thousand lempiras is too much!.

Gang guy: Es tu decision senora.. No podemos esperar mucho mas tiempo. Apurate! It's your decision Sra. We can't wait much more time. Hurry up! *He cocks his rifle.*

Jane: Esperes…. Lo Busco Wait, I will look for it.

She disappears in the kitchen with the armed gang lady.

Juanita: Deme permiso hablar con mis clients por favor. Give me permission to speak with my clients please.

The two guys with the rifles agree and she addresses the restaurant customers. **Disculpa todo el mundo… No hay problema… Les pagare a esta gente y se puede seguir con su comida.** Can I speak to my customers first? Excuse me everybody. There is no problem. I will pay these people and you can continue with your meals.

Jane returns with a handful of cash. The mareros count out lempiras in small bills, bag the cash, and then run into the street shooting their guns in the air. Juanita regains her composure, and turns back to the crowd, who is frozen in silence. The girls return to the table and Ceci embraces them.

Juanita: I am so sorry about this. Perdoname por esta inconveniencia. Por favor… Sigue comiendo *She begins to break down* **Porque seguramente esta noche es nuestra ultima noche de negocios en Mango Tango. No puedo seguir pagando estos**

impuestos de guerra, ademas amenezar las vidas de mis empleados y mis clientes. Vamos a cerrar. Estamos muy agradecidas a todos por anos de negocios… *Silence….* Forgive me for this inconvenience. Please finish your meals. Because for sure this is our last night of business in Mango Tango. I can't continue paying these war taxes and also threatening the lives of my employees and clients. We are going to close. We want to thank you all for years of business.

Her partner comforts her as they return to the kitchen to complete their last evening.

Deni: And where are the police when you need them?

Sayda: La Policia no hacen nada… tienen miedo. The Police don't do anything… they are afraid.

Vilma: Ni tampoco vayan a las Mercedes porque no quieren morir. Ceci … Sayda y yo nos vamos. Nor do they go to Las Mercedes, because they don't want to die. Ceci.. Sayda and I must go.

Ceci: Ahora? Con ellos en la calle? No… esperen un ratito Y yo les llevo. Now? With them in the street? No.. wait and I will take you.

People finish up and start to leave. The music comes back on, but the mood is bent. Ceci pays the bill. People pay their respects and leave in shock. Ceci thanks everybody for risking their lives to celebrate with her. Mango Tango has been a favorite restaurant in the Zona Viva for years. The celebrative excitement of the evening has faded.

Ceci: I am so sorry about this… Hoy debia de ser un dia de felicidad. This was supposed to be a happy day. We were so happy.

Deni May: Like everything else in Honduras… We take tropical paradise with a grain of sand.

Ceci: Well thank you for risking your life to celebrate my custody.

293. Peter Thompson preps 4ᵗʰ Visa application 2010 – his home

Ceci arrives at Peter's home to discuss her 4ᵗʰ visa application for the girls to US Homeland Security in Tegucigalpa. Peter lives the good life of a retired immigration lawyer from San Diego in a house he built in El Sauce, with Flor and Jazzlyn. They also live with Gabby, one of the few police officers in La Ceiba. Peter has strategically invited her to live there because of crime issues. Flor and Jazzlyn greet Ceci at the door.

Flor: Buenas tardes Ceci, como estas? Quieres una Salva Vida? *(Honduran beer)* Good afternoon Ceci, how are you? Do you want a Salva Vida?

Ceci: No gracias… quiero mantener mi cerebro izquierda el mas claro posible para trabajar en el asunto de imigracion con Peter. Pero gracias hermana… muy amable. And I am very sorry about what happened at Mango Tango. No thank you. I want to maintain the clarity of my left brain as much as possible to work in this immigration issue with Peter. But thanks sister, very kind. And I am very sorry about what happened at Mango Tango last weekend.

Flor: Ceci, eso no fue su culpa. Es parte de la vida aqui, desfortunatamente. Ceci this wasn't your fault.. It's part of life here unfortunately.

Ceci: And Jazzlyn? Are you excited about the next dance concert? *Addressing Jazzlyn.*

Jazzlyn: Yes I know all the steps to all the dances by heart..

Ceci: OK.. show me your favorite…

Jazzlyn starts to sing and dance one of the choreographies for the next show. Both Ceci and Flor are totally delighted with her confidence…. Flor whispers to Ceci..

Flor: She gets this from her father, as you know no me gusta estar en el scenario.

Ceci: Well she gets her beauty from you, that's for sure.

Flor. Gracias Ceci… Peter esta esperandote en su oficina… Vaya.. Peter is waiting for you in his office…Go ahead.

Ceci: Bueno.. I'll join you for a beer later.

Ceci goes to the office where Peter is strumming his guitar.

<u>Peter's Office</u>

Ceci: Peter, you are a really good musician. How does a lawyer come to be an artist too I ask?

Peter: Well what I always say is that Bruce Springstein and Julio Iglesias were lawyers.

Ceci: Well then it's never too late. The question is how do you do both simultaneously?

Peter: Can't answer that and will take it as a compliment. Retirement has definitely helped my music career.

Ceci: All I can say, on bended knee Peter, is that I thank the visa goddess that you are still practicing immigration law, and that she put you in my path at this fork in the road, because I was ready to give up quite honestly... thinking I would never see my Mom again.

Peter: Ok Ok... immigration stinks and is a tricky business. I understand how you feel because I have sat in front of hundreds of dejected immigrants looking for a better life, after countless rejections. *He takes a chair and sits right in front of Ceci...*

And.. listen to me... I have been around long enough to know what works and what doesn't work. Granted your situation is unique, but we have to present this as a legal opportunity for these three disadvantaged children to stand a better chance at survival with YOU than with anybody else in their world. OK?

Ceci: OK... *Ceci sits back with a sigh of relief, looking down, for once.. with nothing to say. Peter has captured her attention. She hands him the stack of papers that she has neatly identified with all her formal connections to the children including her residency, the recent Tutora custody document, report cards, doctor visits, etc. He takes the papers and puts on his reading glasses, and peers back and forth at her and the papers as he continues.*

Peter: So... I've been thinking about "the alternative approach" to this visa application and I want you to understand that having a lawyer prepare it from an outside point of view, will provide a much more formal and convincing presentation.... With the language of law, the paper format of classic protocol, and an argument which denies any other possible custody arrangement for the girls...as better than with you.... Ceci... you stand a much better chance with me than presenting handwritten forms.

Ceci: *Applauding* I can't believe I have been through eight other lawyers, and for once I am beginning to understand the concept of law and true legal services.

Peter: AND, now you also have a formal custody arrangement which puts you in a much better position... *along* with the five years you have had them under your roof.

Ceci: Thank you Peter.. The rejection makes me feel like a criminal sometimes, not to mention the fact that their mother wants me to stay in the country so she can continue bribing me for her financial survival.

Peter: Ceci.. these girls were taken away from her because of abuse. They have been declared abandoned. She has no more say in their welfare.

Ceci: What about all those papers she signed agreeing to let them live with me?

Peter: Those have been signed after she lost them, when they became wards of the state.

Ceci: You don't think I am robbing her children then... in any way?

Peter: Come on Ceci. You know she isn't able to take care of them, which is one of the reasons they were removed from her custody initially. She is living on the edge like most of these people. It's about survival for her. She doesn't care whether the girls make it to the dentist. She is not worried about them. She's worried about her guy, the new babies she has to feed, and your availability for cash. You don't have to do this... the custody is now in your favor. She lost any right to custody when they entered the SOS, and then she proved again that she can't handle all these kids, as she uncontrollably continues to make more.

Ceci: OK, I just don't want any trouble... She is always crazy desperate for lempiras. *(Honduran dollars)*

Peter: Agreed... all the more reason for you to be their only mother.

Ceci: And what about this other road block that keeps me up at night?

Peter: Which one Ceci?

Ceci: How do I get around the fact that I can't adopt them because of my age, and that they can't get visas unless they are adopted?

Peter: Once again... Here is the strategy... That you have always had formal custody arrangements with them for the last five years during which you have been and will always be prepared to deal with their disabilities and welfare better than the family and the orphanages from which they came. We will show them the girls' names in your mother's will. Voila!... You set new precedents, which change the laws... Nobody said this would be easy.

Ceci: OK that sounds pretty good Peter. Thank you..

Peter: Don't thank me .... it's not over yet. Look at me ... anything can happen... I am going to pull all my tricks for you. But anything can happen with Immigration law. As you know... There is no higher authorization over a local foreign embassy than the agent who takes your case. So you can write letters to Senator Warren from Virginia.. or even President Obama.. but they have no power over the Tegucigalpa Embassy. Each case is individually assessed by each embassy, and the laws within each embassy can be bent. That's all I can tell you... ...You can thank yourself for not giving up.

Ceci: It's just hard to see the forest through the trees.

Peter: I will put this in formal writing as a package worth thousands of dollars, which I give to you Pro-bono because you are letting my daughter live out her ballet dreams in your dance class, and of course I just want your girls to get the help they need in the USA. So... I can do this blindfolded and will have it ready to send in a week.

Ceci: Thank you so much Peter... I am speechless.

Peter: De nada bailarina... I got this.

Ceci: Ciao abogado Pedro... licensiado magico...

Peter: I will call you when I finish with my wordsmithing.

294. <u>Studio – Vilma and Costume construction</u>

When Ceci enters the studio, Vilma is laying fabric out on the studio floor to cut the final costumes for the Intermedios.

Ceci: **Buenos dias Vilma... pues, vestuario... casi me olvide.** Good morning Vilma... OK costumes.. I almost forgot.

Vilma: **Si Ceci, necessito una paterna antes de cortar. Se puede ayudarme?** Yes Ceci, I need a pattern before cutting. Can you help me?

Ceci: **Claro – tienes las medidas?** Of course... do you have the sizes?

Vilma: **Aqui estan... 4 grande, 6 mediano, y 5 pequenas.** Here they are: 4 large, 6 medium, and 5 small. *Ceci begins to draw out three different size patterns.*

Ceci: **Bueno, costures lo que puedes hoy. Yo sere ocupada trabajando por una coreografia para mis chachas. Creo que este concierto puede ser el ultimo, y tengo que hacer algo especial para ellas que esta en mi mente.** Good... Sew what you can today. I will be busy working on a choreography for my girls. I believe that this concert could be the last one and I have to do something special for them that I have in my mind.

Vilma: **Y porque el ultimo concierto?** And why the last concert?

Ceci: Porque la compania de Estandard Fruit esta cortando gastos y retirando gente que no son esencial... y sin duda los artes serian los primeros a cortar. Because the Standard Fruit company is cutting their costs and firing people that are not essential, and without a doubt the arts would be the first to cut.

Vilma: No me digas! Don't tell me!

Ceci: Si.. estoy esperando la llamada....pero Vilma... siempre te dare trabajo. Te necessito para ayudarme con las ninas. No te preocupas. Siempre tengas trabajo con migo Yes I am waiting for the call. But Vilma, I will always give you work. I need you to help me with the girls. Don't worry. You will always have work with me.

Vilma: Gracias Ceci.. Tu sabes que mi familia come con lo que yo gano contigo. Thank you Ceci. You know that my family eats with what I make with you.

Ceci: Entonces... trabajaremos... para hacer este concierto el mas bonito de todos... Allright.. Let's work to make this concert the most beautiful of all.

The next part is a fast action montage of cutting fabric spread across the dance floor for 15 dresses, after which Vilma gathers up the dresses to sew them in the office.

Ceci begins to warm up to prepare a choreography for herself and the girls with no idea where to go with it. She puts on some mystical music that feels modern, yet indigenous with the sounds of horns, flutes, drums and wind. She closes her eyes and begins to improvise to the music. Ceci is transported.

295. Choreography session about Comizahual and the girls

The scene then transforms into the mystical setting of the Ciudad Blanca ceremonial plaza again...which will include the girls. Ceci's voiceover recites the adapted legend of Comizahual to narrate the choreography over a musical track. There will be pauses in the narration as the dance/drama unfolds. Instead of Mary giving birth to Jesus, Comizahual becomes mother to three sisters whose destiny is to help others. It is an instrumental reprise of Amy Grant's "River Song" with voiceover in this dream sequence.

The story progresses with the choreography and this narration as the music dances them through the legend of Comizahual.

Several hundred years ago a princess came to the Lenca natives in ancient Honduras from far away. She was called Comizahual, or Flying Tiger, because she came from the sky and resembled the mighty tiger and jaguar who are highly respected and feared amongst the ancient Mayans. Her arrival from the heavens changed history for the Lencas.

Comizahual was a natural leader with great dignity and extraordinary beauty. Her people adored her despite the fact that she was different from the Lencas because of her white skin and blond hair. She had magical powers and attracted a great following as a sorceress and great, yet very strict ruler. She built a palace in Cealcoquin and had many servants and soldiers that grew as she developed her empire.

One day she rose into the sky and came back with a magical rock that was engraved with the faces of pumas. The special power of this rock kept enemies away.

Comizahual never married but had three beautiful daughters whom she raised after finding them in a basket near the river one day. These girls had been abandoned by their mother who was unable to feed them. She bestowed all her knowledge upon them, hoping that one day they might take her place on the throne of the palace in Cealquin. They loved dancing together by the river and cultivating the fertile fields of corn, beans and squash (*considered the "three sisters" in Latino food culture*).

Many years passed and the tiger princess became old and weak. Despite a sickness that made her dizzy, she continued to issue orders from her bed. But soon she felt her time had come...so she called her daughters and loyal chiefs around her bed and spoke.

"Soon I must leave you. My daughters will govern this land equally. Their rule shall be strict, but fair, and they should be obeyed as you obey me. My daughters… do not quarrel amongst yourselves… but divide up your responsibilities so that our people will prosper with your love and guidance. For you can preserve this kingdom and protect the people only if you live in harmony. Do not give unjust orders, nor tolerate injustice of any kind. Create the vessel in which your people are safe. Help the poor and make sure all have homes with enough to eat. I love you dearly and know that you will make our people strong, healthy and happy."

The girls wept at the thought of losing their mother who had saved them from drowning in the river. "Please do not leave us mother!" Comizahual replies: "My time on earth is over. Destiny calls me. So here …Get my crown and carry me into the streets so that I can bid farewell to my people." They followed her command as servants, lifted her bed, and brought her into the streets of Cealquin.

Suddenly a bolt of lightning appears in the sky and the air vibrates with thunder. Everyone throws themselves on the ground. And Comizahual vanishes skyward in a great spinning fog… as a rainbow colored bird flew up into the sky. The daughters shout with fear and amazement and reach towards the sky as she rises up to the heavens.

Ever since that day the Lenca natives have worshipped Comizahual as a goddess. They hold a yearly festival in honor of this mighty tiger princess.

There is an actual Lencan/Honduran myth about the flying jaguar with three sons instead of daughters.

Ceci is awakened by the sound of the school bell and realizes that she has gone back to her dream state in the Ciudad Blanca again and that she must have been "dance dreaming" for a while as she looks at her watch. She lays herself down on the dance floor and stares at the ceiling.

Ceci: *Talking to herself.* **Who is this Comizahual? And why does this Ciudad Blanca keep calling me?**

296. Christmas – "Palomas de Paz" Performance

These seasonal dance concert productions have become a routine and ritual for Ceci at the Mazapan School. The 4ʰ grade classroom has become the backstage, and the stage is part of the All Purpose room/gymnasium. Kids are running around in the audience in their costumes, when they should be backstage... Parents are arriving late, dressed to the nines, holding their daughters' hands whose makeup and hair are immaculate, despite their tardiness from being in the hair salon all afternoon. Classical Music is playing in the concert hall and Ceci continues to make the rounds checking backstage. Vilma has dressed the 3 girls, and then has taken her position backstage to check and prepare each group before they make their entrances. Ceci takes her final tour backstage and through the audience as the house lights dim. She has a little desk area in front of the stage where she runs the music and has enough space to dance backwards in front of the little dancers. Finally she takes the microphone:

Ceci: Buenas Noches todos. Feliz Navidad... y Bienvenido a nuestra decimo concierto de danza Navideno en La Ceiba para celebrar este dia especial... Y tambien para celebrar la libertad de reunir y celebrar con los artes. Quiero graciar todos los padres para la oportunidad de trabajar con sus hijos en el mundo de la danza. Arte, musica, teatro y la danza son regalos muy importantes en esta epoca cuando la vida familial esta bien distraída con technologia... con monitores y telefonos, televisions, computadores, y ipads para conquistar distancia. Yo entiendo la importancia de avancar nuestra evolucion electronica... pero no

quiero reemplazar la expression artistica y espiritual en vivo por machinas. **Muchachos quieren saber que sus padres estan cerca con sus ojos, abrazos, y aplauso. Testigos de la magica!** Good evening welcome to our 10th dance concert for Christmas in La Ceiba to celebrate this special day. And also to celebrate the freedom to congregate and celebrate the arts. I want to thank all the parents for the opportunity to work with your children in the world of dance. Art, music, theater and dance are important gifts at this age… when families are distracted with electronics - the monitors, telephones, televisions, computers and ipads which conquer distance yet create isolation. I understand the importance of advancing our technological evolution, but I don't want to replace live artistic and spiritual expression for machines. Kids want to know that their parents are near with their eyes, embraces, and applause. Witness the magic!!

She continues:

Yo soy coreografa porque quiero inspirar jovenes y comunidades con la importancia de celebrar las expresiones artisticas de la vida… con sus cuerpos y almas en vivo…. Con su gente… con musica, danza, y festividades collectivas y el magico de conciertos en vivo. Son rituales antiguas, que duran a causa del deseo humano a compartir con amigos y familia juntos. La madre tierra nos da tantas cosas como la fertilidad de humanos y la naturaleza para vivir bien. Que maravilla es participar en celebraciones de la vida con festivals, desfiles, fiestas, y conciertos con la mescla internacional de cultura Hondurena, Indio, Maya, Garifuna, Espanol, y Carribe y Americana. Tienen tantos costumbres y celebraciones que han sobrevivido por anos y anos. La Danza ha existida por siglos por el deseo humano conectar la alma y el cuerpo y la comunidad con felicidad y abundancia en dias importantes agriculturas, historicos, religiosos, civiles, y saisonal.

Hoy celebramos Navidad y familia, el invierno, el nacimiento de Cristo, las tradiciones Hondurenos, y la belleza de juventud. Bienvenido… a "Palomas de Paz!"

I am a choreographer because I want to inspire young people and communities with the importance of celebrating the artistic expressions of life with our bodies and souls in person. With your people.. with music, dance and collective festivities and the magic of live concerts. They are ancient rituals that last because of humanity's desire to be together with friends and family. Mother Earth gives us so many things, like human fertility and nature to live well. What a marvel it is to participate in celebrations of life with festivals, parades, parties and concerts with the mix of international Honduran culture, the indigenous, Mayan, Garifuna, Spanish and Caribbean and American. You have so many customs and celebrations that have survived for years and years. The dance has existed for centuries because of the human desire to connect the body and soul of the community with happiness and abundance on important agricultural, historical, religious, civil and seasonal holidays.

Today we celebrate Christmas and family, winter, the birth of Christ, Honduran traditions, and the beauty of youth. Welcome to " Doves of Peace".

Ceci: ON WITH THE SHOW!!!! Gracias por venir! And thank you for coming!

"Palomas de Paz" – Concierto de Danza – Diciembre

*All the ballets are designed around edited montages of music which set up the drama of the stories.

1. Mrs. Santa Claus Mommy/daughter dance - Bambinas

One by one little dancers enter in blue dream light dressed like Christmas girly elves carrying boxes that they deposit under the Christmas tree. They look beautiful in these different fluffy elf dresses. Suddenly there is a magical silence. They look at each other with fingers to their mouths and say SHHHHHH as they hide under the tree. There is a transforming twinkle in the lights The music begins.... And the Santa Mamas enter looking for their elf daughters who have been hiding behind the tree, (including Peter with Jazzlyn – Ceci with Jazmin). The girls pop out to surprise their Santa Mamas and perform passionate duets with lifts and poses and different moods of Christmas joy.

2. Honduran Christmas Montage – avancadas solos y duet –This is a medley of popular Honduran Christmas favorites including

merengues, bachatas, and reggaeton rhythms with dancers performing merengue with folklorico traditional steps in typical folk costumes. They are student choreographies.

3.Santa Baby – Principios – Tap - by Madonna

Beginners are facing the audience on their bellies writing a letter to Santa. They rise and begin a very simple tap dance. They are dressed in jewelry, sequins and gemstones… with a fur collar around their necks. Looking very expensive.

4. Modern Jaguar Dance – Avancadas y Ceci

Mystical, yet unusually modern music filters into a forest setting which embodies the slinky movement of jaguars, while emphasizing and portraying a deep yet haunting connection to spirit. This dance is more abstractly modern dance, and finds its character in depicting the movement of big cats. Ceci enters near the end characterizing a flying tiger…. The Mayan Goddess, Comizahual who dances with them. Jaguars are worshipped in the Mayan culture.

5. Doll Dance – Principios

The Doll dance opens with several life size (stuffed) Raggedy Anne ballerina dolls sitting under the Christmas tree. Young dancers tiptoe onto the stage in their nightgowns to wake up the dolls and take them into duets with their dolls as if they are teaching the dolls to dance. Little by little the beat escalates until the girls remove their nightgowns to reveal identical ballet costumes like the dolls. The energy increases until a circle forms where they all hold hands with the dolls in between the dancers. Then a mother's voice interrupts the dance asking: "Honey, are you OK?" A child's voice answers "I am dreaming about Santa Mom". The mother again is heard: "Go to sleep dear… goodnight". In the silence of the dark, the dancers return to their circle dance, giggling and jumping around joyously with the dolls, until they grow tired and they melt into sleep under the tree.

6.Honduran History – Int y Avancadas w/Garifuna guests

The haunting melody of a primitive flute and drum brings indigenous workers onto the stage who proceed to plant corn seeds. They then perform a native ritual dance to promote the fertility of their seeds.

The Spanish arrive with their folklore regalia, dance and music that evolves into romantic partner dancing. The girls have long flowing skirts with flowers in their hair... the boys are wearing white shirts and pants and have straw hats and a waving red bandana.

Then come the (African) Garifunas in a parade with drummers and dancers who perform an energetic punta dance with question and answer singing and dancing between the ladies. The young boys handle the homemade drums like magical weapons which dictate the accented and synchronized female hip movements.

The girls are dressed in lookalike kitchen dresses with their hair wrapped up in turbans. This evolves into a sentimental bachata that depicts the women of the mixed races in the market as they sell their produce and sing along with the recorded music. Then a few mariachi guitarists stroll through the market singing the same romantic lament that joins the bachata, which evolves into a lively Christmas merengue. The market ladies then find partners to dance together, which becomes a company production number ending a complete mix of the Trigueno musical culture of Christmas in Honduras.

7.Quartet – Ceci and daughters, Jazmin, Angie, and Roxana – Celine Dion – "Because you loved me". This dance is a tribute to Ceci and her daughters, and the journey of love they have been on to be able to be together as a family. The lyrics of Diane Warren, sung by Celine Dion to "Because You Loved Me", must be included because of their emotional relevance to Ceci and the girls. Ceci worked in Quebec, Canada as Celine Dion's first choreographer and takes pride in devoting this song to her children.

Ceci wanders onto the stage with a suitcase like a tourist and finds 3 girls asleep in a box like kittens on the street. She pulls each one of them out of the box and sets them on stage where she awakens them and begins to teach them a dance. They begin individual duets with Ceci and then all join hands to perform a family ballet. It is an emotional yet joyful expression of their love and devotion. (All 3 girls are at different technical levels, but still express sisterhood)

"Because You Loved Me" Diane Warren
Sung by Celine Dion

For all those times you stood by me
For all the truth that you made me see
For all the joy you brought to my life
For all the wrong that you made right
For every dream you made come true
For all the love I found in you
I'll be forever thankful baby
You're the one who held me up
Never let me fall
You're the one who saw me through it all

CHORUS

You were my strength when I was weak
You were my voice when I couldn't speak
You were my eyes when I couldn't see
You saw the best there was in me
Lifted me up when I couldn't reach
You gave me faith 'coz you believed
I'm everything I am
Because you loved me

You gave me wings and made me fly
You touched my hand, I touched the sky
I lost my faith, you gave it back to me
You said no star was out of reach
You stood by me and I stood tall
I had your love I had it all
I'm grateful for each day you gave me
Maybe I don't know that much
But I know this much is true
I was blessed because I was loved by you

CHORUS

You were always there for me
A tender wind that carried me
A light in the dark shining your love into my life

You've been my inspiration
Through the lies you were the truth

My world is a better place because of you
I'm everything I am, Because you loved me

8. <u>Nativity Ballet</u>

The entire sequence is a ballet montage with different types of dance and music which was foreshadowed in the previous rehearsal sequence. The ballet begins with the life of Mary and her friends selling goods in the market place in a belly dance sequence, whence comes the Angel Gabriel (Angie) to bring Mary a lily and bless her. Then the angels come and dance around Mary until she gives birth.

Then 3 Queens approach and make their offerings, and the female Jesus gets up and dances... It is the climax of the Christmas show, with all the magical amber light of holiday love and family. There is a finale to Pavorati's Adestes Fideles, and the house is ecstatic with applause.

297. <u>Ceci meets with the Mazapan school Director for the "Ax"</u>

Ceci is seated in the school office, waiting to speak to the Director. Teachers and students come in and out. She is gracious, but realizes that the ax is about to come down on her. The secretary expresses her kudos for the Christmas show, but also knows that good news is not around the corner. Ceci is part of a line-up of part time teachers who have been conveniently dismissed for budgetary reasons. As a teacher leaves the Director's office in tears, Ceci sighs and lifts her chin as she enters the office.

Director: Hello Ceci, come in… please sit down. *Uncomfortable pause* I want to tell you first of all what a wonderful show you put on last night… the dancing, the costumes, the music…. One of the best Christmas shows I have seen so far.

Ceci: Thank you.

Director: And also I want to thank you for teaching all of us how to mount a show professionally, so that there are lights and sound on cue, and that we don't have to wait 10 minutes between numbers, and that everybody knows in advance where they come in the line up. I realize that it is difficult to find someone who understands both the artistic and technical sides of theater.

Ceci: Thank you again. You can't present art without a frame. It has taken me years to absorb all of those professional details. I'm glad you appreciate the work.

Director: Which brings me unfortunately to my next item on the agenda.

Ceci: I think I already know.

Director: Yes… well as you know, Dole is having lots of financial problems now, and since we are under their umbrella on this campus, they are cutting costs right and left. And our budget has shrunk considerably… And despite the fact that we pay you the absolute minimum wage, we can't afford to keep it up anymore, along with the AC in the dance studio. So we will be able to offer you about 6000 lempiras in compensation at the end of the fiscal year, when we will have to let you go. You can use the studio for a final summer camp, but we can no longer keep you employed.

Ceci: I understand, although I believe parents are going to miss watching their kids dance.

Director: I am hoping we can continue mounting the annual Mother's, Father's Day and Christmas concerts through the music teacher, who I know has learned a lot from you. I am sorry that you have had to pay full tuition for your daughters, but we hope they continue studying here.

Ceci: I will have to think about that, as I probably won't be able to afford it unemployed. This dismissal will also affect my residency. At this point I am basically waiting for the embassy to give me visas for the girls.

Director: I don't know Ceci... It will be an absolute miracle if you get them. I have known so many American teachers who have tried to do this, and have had to leave orphans behind because of the IHNFA corruption and disorganization.

Ceci: Well I can't give up, because I now have formal custody and they would have to go back to the orphanage if I return to the states, which I could never do without them... They have disabilities which the orphanages and most schools don't accommodate.

Director: I think that you are kidding yourself, and you will probably have to stay here with them somehow.

Ceci: My mom is aging in the states and is holding on to the family home for us, and I want very much to go back and take care of her before she dies. Then the girls will have a home.

Director: You may have to choose between her and the girls. I am really sorry about this.

Ceci's eyes begin to water.

Ceci: I'm not giving up. I will get those visas on my next visit to Tegucigalpa.

Director: You have till the end of the year, with the spring shows, and if you want the studio for the summer camp, perhaps I can manage to convince management to allow it through July.

Ceci: Thank you very much... I would appreciate that, and thank you for the opportunity to work here and have a space to share my work.

Director: Buena suerte Ceci.

Ceci: I'll surely need lots of it. Thanks.

298. Visa Trip to Tegucigalpa #4

At home in the Naranjal house Ceci is preparing to go to Tegucigalpa for her 4ᵗʰ visa attempt and is leaving the girls with Vilma. She is nervous and has decided to make this trip alone to avoid the inconvenience of bringing the girls. Ceci is confident.

Ceci: OK girls, me voy. I'm leaving you with Vilma for the day so you don't have to ride in that bumpy old plane again.

Jazz: OK Mom – try not to throw up this time when you land.

Ceci: I'll do my best.

Angie: Don't we have to go with you?

Ceci: They already know who you are after three trips. And now I have the formal custody. I just don't want you to have to make that trip again to Tegucigalpa. So I will be OK this time.

Roxana: **Nada es facil con las visas Mommy.** Nothing is easy with the visas Mommy.

Angie; Bye Mom... who will catch you if they reject you again and you fall down?

Ceci: All that is over now sweetness... Don't worry about me. This time I am a winner.

Vilma: **Te mando suerte Ceci – Que se vaya con Dios.** I wish you luck. Go with God.

Ceci: Gracias, Si Dios Quiere.... *Ceci kisses everybody and leaves.*

299. On Line at the American Embassy in Tegucigalpa #4

Cut to the line at the American embassy in Tegucigalpa, which again, is around the block with hundreds of Hondurans inching their way up to the main entrance. When Ceci reaches the main steps, she again gives her phone to one of the many vendors and enters the sacred halls of the American Embassy Homeland Security building. Inside she goes through security, gets a number, then goes to the cashier to pay for the 3 visa applications, and then sits in the line up of chairs. Ceci knows all the routines. Slowly people slide from chair to chair inching up to the front of the line. Her head is spinning from the plane, the taxi ride, and the hot tropical urban sun beating down on the outside line. Slowly, after what seems like hours, she hears the names of her children called... Roxana, Angie and Angela Iraheta Rojas. *Ceci rushes forward to the #9 window.*

Officer: Hello, Ms. Diaz. What can I do for you?

Ceci: This is my fourth visit to apply for my children's US visas. I am an American.

Officer: Yes I remember you. And where are the children today?

Ceci: I left them home this time so they don't miss any school. I believe the papers speak for themselves. I now have Honduran custody of the girls called, TUTORA, through a Honduran lawyer with a Honduran Pro-tutora... and I also engaged an immigration lawyer this time to prepare my application.

Officer: Looking at the papers, Ms. Gruessing... It is always customary for the applicants to be present.

Ceci: I am sorry about that Officer. After three applications, and three trips to Tegucigalpa from La Ceiba, and three hotel bills, with taxis and food, the costs have gotten out of control and I was hoping my file would precede me with proof of my ongoing relationship with the children after years of care and previous applications.

Officer: I'll be right back Mam... Please give me a moment to check your file.

Ceci starts to sweat with anxiety. Tears come to her eyes. She takes out a picture of her and the girls from the Baptism. Fifteen minutes seems like an eternity until the officer returns.

Officer: Clearly this is a well prepared application. And I congratulate you on the Tutora custody you have earned which is without a doubt....

Ceci: Yes it took two years to get the Tutora...

Officer: Well I must explain to you Ms. Diaz, that even with a formal adoption, Homeland security requires that you live with the children for two years after the adoption paperwork is complete and official for observation purposes. And your custody is not even legitimate *adoption.*

Ceci: But these girls have been with me... under my protection for five years now!

Officer: I realize that, but you haven't adopted them, and even with this Tutora status, you must officially live with them for two more years after the documents are signed.

Ceci: Officer, please.... they don't know anybody but me as their only constant caretaker after several orphanage mothers. And my mother is waiting for us at my family home in Virginia. She is 86 and is losing her memory, and I must go take care of her... and she is offering my children the security of her home and estate.

Officer: I am so sorry Ms. Diaz. There is nothing more I can do but follow the rules. Please come back in two years and we will see if the rules have changed. Your case is highly unusual and since all adoptions in Honduras are on hold anyway since the IHNFA has closed... I cannot help you at all.

Ceci: You must be kidding. This is irrational. What if my Mom dies before we get these visas? I will never be able to go home again. And I won't let these girls go back to the orphanage. Oh my God!

Officer: I am sorry Ms. Diaz. *A security police woman moves in to calm Ceci down.* I repeat, come back in two years. I can not help you at this time.

Ceci starts to tremble, weep, and fall against the wall. The same police woman who has been standing by escorts her out of the building. The following shots are a litany of Ceci making her way back to La Ceiba in the midst of her despair. She flashes on her mother, on Obama, on the flag, on old boyfriends, even on her sister who does not approve of what she is doing. She calls Louis while sitting in the Tegucigalpa airport waiting for her late flight to La Ceiba.

300. Tegucigalpa Airport – Call to Louis

Ceci: Louis?.... Hi? ..... *starts to cry*...well .. not so fine.... I'm in the Tegucigalpa airport, waiting for a late night plane to Ceiba. No I didn't... They told me that I have to wait for two more years while living with them *after* being awarded the custody in Honduras, ... and then apply again .... This is the fourth time I have been here Louis. I am exhausted. *Pause*....Yes, I told them that. It doesn't matter. So I lost the job at the school.... Because Dole is losing money and laying off everybody they can. I had hoped I would be on my way by summer..... And I just put on a fabulous dance concert at the school... It was great, it was my swan song... I made a choreography for me and the girls.. it was beautiful...... I know, thank you Louis .. So .... How are you? How's baby Goia? And Veronica? I'm glad everything is good there. *Pause* No. There's nothing I can do or anybody can do. The Senator from Virginia, Mark Warner, told my mom that there is no federal agency, including the President, who can override an immigration decision of Homeland Security at a foreign embassy. This immigration thing is enough to put anybody in the funny farm...and you should see the lines of Honduran applicants around the block. I lose my patience...especially when I wait in line for 3 hours to talk to a 30 year old federal American agent, who is determining the fate of my children. *Pause* Yes I am blessed and they are blessed, and I love them.....You are right. OK...So I guess just have to wait it out. I may look for work at another Bi-lingual school here. Right now, I have to go home and face the girls.... *Pause* Yes Louis.... I'm sorry the news isn't better.... Of course I'll try again. I have no choice. I want to thank you for sending the money, and continuing to believe in us. I appreciate it... OK... Bye.

301. Return home to Ceiba rejected again

It is after midnight by the time Ceci gets home from Tegucigalpa. There was rain and all the flights were delayed. The street is flooded and Ceci has waded through the water in front of the house after returning from the airport by taxi. Vilma has been babysitting and the girls are asleep. She greets Ceci with an expectant look, and by Ceci's mood she knows not to inquire.

Ceci: Hola Vilma… debes de quedar aqui esta noche con la lluvia y inundación . Hello Vilma, you should stay here tonight with the rain and flooding.

Vilma: Bueno…

Ceci: Como acostaron las ninas? Did the girls go to bed easily?

Vilma: Bien… aunque de estaban preocupada para ti. Pero fuimos al parque botanica. They were OK except they were worried about you. But we did go to the botanical gardens across the street.

Ceci: Bueno.. Manana vamos a vender limonadas OK? Hay que organizar algo divertido para ellas… y tambien hay que hablar del campo de verano para emplear ud. Y su hermana Sayda…. como serian mis ultimos dias alla. Great, and tomorrow we will have a lemonade sale OK? It's important to organize something special for them. And also we have to talk about the summer camp to employ you and Sayda, since these will be my last days here at Mazapan.

Vilma: Oy… lo siento oir eso… pero, Ceci…. manana en la noche empieza las pequenas carnivales en Barrio La Isla… Todos podemos ir si quieres. Oh, I am sorry to hear that, but, Ceci, tomorrow night the little carnavals begin in Barrio La Isla. So we can all go if you want.

Ceci: Si, buena idea…manana hablaremos del carnaval… ahora necessito dormir… Buenas noches Vilma… Se puede dormir en el cuarto de Roxana. Gracias por todo. Yes, good idea. Tomorrow we will talk about Carnaval. Now I need to sleep. Good night Vilma.. you can sleep in Roxana's room. Thank you for everything.

Vilma: Buenas Noches Ceci…

Ceci goes to check on the girls who are fast asleep in their little beds. She then goes to her room and walks onto the balcony which looks onto a walled backyard orchard of fruit trees surrounding a swing set and a plastic swimming pool.

Balcony off bedroom

On her balcony there is an altar to the Virgin Mary, the Venezuelan Tres Potencias with Maria Lionza… and Tamanaco, her Venezuelan chief "protector", and some Mayan statues. Not tears nor rage can express Ceci's melancholy as she stares at the new moon.

Ceci: **What possibly is there left for me to prove Dear God? What have I missed? Why is my love for these girls so questioned, and doubted and unprecedented and unwarranted and illegal? I have to get back to Mom. There is no way Dear God that I will abandon her to a nursing home. She doesn't deserve that after all she has already sacrificed for me and the girls. And she has waited for us for so long. And now with her dementia, she just can't be alone. And I have to bring my girls home to their grandmother, to unite what is left of my family.** *Pause* **There is no delusion that Tio Louis is taken. I will not jeopardize his support for the girls by initiating any romantic suggestion whatsoever to our relationship. I will not participate in that kind of pain since I am already so familiar with unrequited love. Hence… I have no choice… and will wait two more years of this day by day existence in Honduras. I will work this life in La Ceiba until the American Embassy gets the divine logic of these visa requests. Give me strength Mother Mary… I rest my case. Venta de Limonada manana… La vida sigue!!** Lemonade sale tomorrow. Life goes on!

302. **Saturday AM at home planning**

In the morning Vilma is in the kitchen making tortillas con huevos. The kids are playing. Ceci enters in a bathrobe.

Ceci: **Buenos dias Vilma… Que sabrosa huele el desayuno. Cha chas… Vamos a comer y despues montaremos un** espectaculo de una **Venta de Limonada en frente de la casa.** Good morning Vilma. How good breakfast smells. Cha chas.. We are going to have breakfast and afterwards we will set up a big show with a lemonade sale in front of the house.

Jazmin: Y vamos a cantar con mi guitara para llamar clients OK?And we are going to sing with the guitar to call in the customers.

Angie: Yo puedo cantar tambien tu sabes. I can sing too you know.

Roxana: Si mas o menos Angie... Yo voy a jugar futbol. Yes, more or less Angie. I am going to play soccer.

Ceci: Claro... we can do all of that. I will make the limondada and we will also work on our bike riding.

Jazmin: And we will make lots of lempiras. Mom you know my legs are too short to ride a bike.

Angie: I can ride a bike.

Jazmin: But you're blind... You can't ride a bike or you will crash.

Angie: Si puedo! Yes I can!

Ceci: Now that wasn't necessary.

Vilma: Seran muchos clientes pasando hoy porque todo el mundo va al carnavalito en Barrio La Isla en la noche. There will be many customers passing by today because everybody is going to the Carnaval in La Isla tonight.

Angie: Oh Mom... can we go?

Ceci: Claro que si... Somos Ceibenas!

303. <u>**Lemonade Stand**</u>

There is a table with a pitcher of cold lemonade made with real limes. (There are no lemons in Honduras). Jazmin and Angie are singing a lemonade jingle and pretending to play the guitar. When there are no clients, Ceci helps Angie with her bike. Neighborhood kids are riding their bikes. Roxana is playing soccer.

There are musicians in the street walking towards Barrio La Isla in preparation for the Carnaval. Garifuna drummers and women in their look alike dresses are also making their way toward the beach to set up for the festivities. They will devote their entire day and night to Carnaval which always begins in Barrio Las Isla. Each night afterwards the Carnavalitos take place in different neighborhoods in La Ceiba. It is a beautiful day after the tropical flood rains have drained away from the street and the sun comes out. You can hear the sound of pumped merengue music coming from the stadium preparing for a big soccer game. Action starts to develop around the lemonade stand. Jazmin continues to sing and begins to play her guitar (that she fakes playing). Angie and Ceci join her. Business is good as thirsty kids drink up and are amused by Jazmin's jingle which does not rhyme.

Vengan vengan todos   Come come everybody

A comprar mi limonada   to buy my lemonade

Van a gustarla   Satisfaction guaranteed

por la limonada mia   for my lemonade.

Es la mejor limonada   It's the best lemonade

En el pueblo de La Ceiba.   In the town of La Ceiba

Fruta del sol tropical   Fruit from the tropical sun

Debes de beberla   You should drink it

Solo 10 lempiras   Only 10 lempiras

Para areglar tu sed.   To fix your thirst

25 por un grande   25 for a large

Van a sentir muy bien!   You will feel real good**Venga saborearlo** Come and check it out

Cuatro por cien!! Four for a hundred

After some applause and laughs, Ceci takes time to talk with Vilma

Ceci: Vilma… gracias por su ayuda esta semana. Solo contigo tengo confianza con las ninas… tu sabes. Vilma thank you so much for your help this week. Only with you do I have confidence with the girls, you know.

Vilma: Entonces… digame que paso en Teguz… Imagino que no fue bien. So tell me what happened in Teguz. I imagine that it did not go well.

Ceci: Tengo que esperar dos anos mas despues del primero dia de la custodia para aplicar de nuevo. Es la regla para adoptar tambien. No hay otra manera. I have to wait two more years after the first day of custody to apply again. It's the law for adoption also. There is no other way.

Vilma: Dos anos mas? Y el trabajo en la Escuela Mazapan? Two years more? And the work at the Mazapan School?

Ceci: Despues del campamiento en el verano hay que vaciar el estudio. Dole esta cortando sus fondos del presupuesto y no quieren pagar los gastos del estudio ni el salario mio. After the summer camp I have to empty the studio. Doles is cutting back funds for the budjet and they don't want to pay the costs of the studio nor my salary.

Vilma: No me digas. Wow… Don't tell me.

Ceci: Yes WOW… Sera un grand cambio por nosotros todos… y mi madre todavia nos espera en los Estados. It will be a big change for all of us. And my mother is still waiting for us in the United States.

Vilma: Que vas a hacer Ceci? What are you going to do Ceci?

Ceci: No se todavia. Pero quiero que tu sigues trabajando con el campamiento con Sayda en el verano y con las ninas en la casa. Sera mi ultimo trabajo en Mazapan… y las ninas no van a seguir estudiando mas alla…. I don't know yet. But I want you to continue working for the summer camp with Sayda and with the girls in the house. It will be my last job at Mazapan, and the girls will not continue studying there anymore.

Vilma: Y donde van estudiar ellas? So where will they study?

Ceci: No se todavia Vilma – Roxana seguira con Bright Beginnings … y posiblemente podemos hacer home school con Deni May para Angie y Jazmin. Pero hoy tengo que llevar Roxana a la dentista para frenos. Te dejo con las cha chas y la limonada OK? I don't know yet Vilma. Roxana will continue at Bright Beginnings, and possibly we can have home schooling with Deni May for Angie and Jazmin/ But today I have to take Roxana to the dentist for braces. Can I leave you with them and the lemonade sale?

Vilma: Si Ceci… Buena suerte con Roxana y la dentista. Recuerdas que paso cuando sacaron esa diente negro? Good luck with Roxana at the dentist. Remember what happened when they took out that black tooth?

Ceci: Si recuerdo eso… The dentist had to wrestle her into the seat. Dios mio.. Pero ella es demasiado bella para vivir con esos dientes torcidos. Yes I remember that…. Good God… But she is too beautiful to live with those crooked teeth.

Vilma: Ok… Yo le llamo a ella ahora… OK.. I will call her now.

Ceci: Gracias… Y cuando vuelvo vamos todos con Sayda a comer a Guity's en la Zona Viva antes de ir al carnavalito OK? Thank you, and when we return, let's all go with Sayda to eat at Guity's in the Zona Viva, before going to Carnaval.

Jazmin and Angie continue singing and selling lemonade as Ceci takes off in Carlota.

304. <u>The Dentist and Roxana</u>

Walking into the dentist office, Roxana starts to cry.

Roxana: No quiero ir Mommy. I don't want to go Mommy.

Ceci: Roxana… Don't be afraid. Remember how much you hate it when the kids call you "witchy" because of that tooth hole in your mouth? The braces are going to fix that beautiful smile of yours OK? It is so worth it to do this. And I will be there the whole time baby.

They enter the office and the nurse takes Roxana in to see the doctor. Ceci sits in the lobby with tears in her eyes pretending to read a magazine. This is another ongoing episode of many challenging adventures with Roxana going to doctors, dentists, and blood labs where she completely loses control and fear takes over. She trusts no one. The orthodontist tells Ceci to wait in the waiting room and to let her handle it. Ceci bites he lip as she hears Roxana scream and cry in the next room. There is silence and the assistant comes out to inform Ceci that Roxana has been sedated and they will install all the braces within an hour… not to worry. Although this is a momentary relief… Ceci is full of anxiety.

While waiting, Eduardo Zablah calls asking to see Ceci in his workshop to meet a girl he considers Miss Honduras material. Ceci promises to call him back.

Time passes, we can hear music in the streets as the Carnaval season begins. Finally, Roxana comes out waking up from her sedation, lightly groggy and somewhat happy. The nurse tells her to take the medication before she goes to bed.... She may or may not need it for pain. Ceci supports Roxana to the car. She slumps back in the seat.

Ceci: Roxie baby... como estas? *Trying to revive her. Roxie is sleepy but happy.*

Roxana: Agua... Quiero agua... I want water.

Ceci reaches for a bottle of water and gives it to her like a baby. This wakes her up a little. Ceci pours some into her hand and rubs it across her face.

Ceci: I am taking you home honey... I have to go to see Eduardo about some work... but I will take you home first so you can get it together for the carnavalito tonight in La Isla.

Roxana immediately wakes up. She talks funny with her new braces.

Roxana: Duele mama.... Pero todavía yo quiero ir al carnavalito! It hurts Mom. But I still want to go to carnival!

Ceci: You can go if the pain goes away by this evening. OK?

Roxana: I don't care... I want to go... *She starts to cry.*

Ceci: OK honey... Listen to me. We did this to bring out the beauty of your smile... the smile that God already gave you, which is tan linda ... mi hija... A veces la belleza duele... Te quiero... Sometimes beauty hurts. But I am taking you home where you will rest IF you want to go to Carnaval tonight. Entiende?

Roxana: Si Mami... *Clearly she is still woozy, which makes Ceci extra nervous as she tries to be a professional and a mother simultaneously. She drops Roxana off with Vilma.*

305. <u>Back Home</u>

Ceci returns to the house and all the lemonade is gone. The bikes are in the driveway and there is a group of kids in the back yard with Vilma on the swings singing the hit song, "Te amo".

Ceci: Vilma… me voy a trabajar con Eduardo en el studio. Roxana tiene frenos nuevos y su boca duele. Aquí esta hielo para darle… OK?… porque ella quiere ir con nosotros al carnavalito esta noche… pero primero la medicación… Vilma, I am going to work with Eduardo in the studio. Roxana has her new braces and her mouth hurts. Here is ice to give for the swelling OK? Because, she wants to come with us to carnaval tonight. But the medication first.

Vilma: Si Ceci…. Yo lo hago. Y como se fue con la dentista? Yes Ceci.. I will do it. And how did it go with the dentist?

Ceci: Pues…difícil. El le dio anasthesia para dormir… pero… ella no le gusta agujas y tampoco nadie en su boca. Fortunatamente ya estan los frenos. Gracias a Dios. Difficult. They gave her anesthesia to sleep, but she doesn't like needles nor anyone in her mouth. Fortunately the braces are on, thank God.

Roxana enters the kitchen feeling groggy still. Ceci gives Roxana ibuprofen. Vilma hugs her.

Ceci: Toma mi amor… this will reduce the pain. Inflammation is pain. This reduces the swelling. Remember that.

Vilma: Venga Roxana… te ayudo…. Come on Roxana. I will help you.

Roxana: Me duele Vilma… I hurt Vilma.

Vilma: Yo se… no se acuestas. Vamos a mirar tele. I know. Don't lie down. Let's watch TV.

Ceci grabs her dance gear, kisses Roxana, and leaves Vilma with a bag of ice and leaves Roxana in place on the sofa.

Ceci: Gracias again Vilma… Ciao… hasta luego.

306. **Eduardo Zablah's studio**

Ceci stops by Eduardo's taller(workshop) where he is dressing the new Carnaval queen and her princesses in huge fluffy gowns. He is also preparing his carosa (flower car - float) for the grand Carnaval parade the following week. Ceci is greeted by Eduardo who introduces her to the new Queen, Francesca, and all her runner up princesses. Eduardo takes her aside after the greetings.

Eduardo: What I want to ask you is if you feel this girl has what it takes musically to compete in this years' Miss Honduras contest.

Ceci: Can she sing or dance?

Eduardo: I don't know and I want you to find out.

Ceci: She is beautiful.

Eduardo: And very educated – bilingual, and very cooperative. She has all the qualities of a well bred Miss Honduras. I just don't know if she is musical enough to dance a solo in the opening number.

Ceci: OK I will check her out.

Eduardo: Ceci… I have been doing this for years… She has all the other ingredients, and I want a smart girl who can carry the role, looks good, talks good, and can dance… maybe go on to represent Honduras in the Miss World contest.

Ceci: Can you bring her to the studio for an hour at 3pm this afternoon before the Carnavalito starts?

Eduardo: She'll be there.

Ceci: OK… I will see you and your Feria Queen in the studio at 3pm… Ciao…

307. Dance Studio with the new Ms. Honduras Queen

We cut right into a salsa dance routine in the studio where Ceci is working with Francesca, the new Feria queen. She is a good dancer and the two of them are well synchronized in the mirror. It is a Christina Aguilera song that the girl knows well and can sing along to. They both sing the chorus together and she quickly achieves the ability to pick up both song and dance with great style and charisma. Eduardo enters on the phone having watched from a distance and is immensely pleased.

Ceci: As you can see, this young lady is an absolute natural and clearly undiscovered Honduran star material. I can vouch for that musically anyway. She seems very intelligent and cooperative. She can dance, sing on pitch, has great stage presence and picks up fast.

Eduardo: Exactly what I wanted to hear. I am hoping she will go from Queen of the Feria to Miss Honduras. Thank you so much for letting me see this. Franesca... Venga aqui... *He sits her down.*

Francesca: Si Eduardo...

Eduardo: Sin duda se puede ver su talento musico... De donde viene esta influencia? Without a doubt one can see your musical talent. Where does this influence come from?

Francesca: Well... my aunt lives in Miami, and I would spend my summers there studying dance, and singing in a salsa band. So that's where my English improved.

Ceci: And all that musical experience explains your quick pick up ability. I am definitely impressed. Good eye Eduardo....

Eduardo: Let us get through the parade next week and then we will talk about the next Ms. Honduras contest.

Ceci: I am available. Mostly working on visas for my girls....

Eduardo: Hay chica! You are crazy...

Ceci: Yes crazy!!! But I must run to get everybody ready for the carnival tonight in La Isla...

Eduardo: Yes of course, I almost forgot... Mils Gracias Ceci.

Francesca: Yes... Thank you so much, I really enjoyed this. I hope we work together again.

Ceci: Si Dios Quiere... as they say... Ciao... *As she is leaving, she mutters....* Aah show business... How it distracts us from life!!!

308. Guity's Seaside Restaurant - Carnavalito

Ceci, Vilma, her sister Sayda, and the girls are seated on the second floor of Guity's Palapa open air restaurant overlooking the ocean. Ceci knows Guity and his family well from having spent many solo hours dining alone upstairs watching the tide come in at sunset. This is a joyful meal and they all laugh as the girls get to feel as close as possible to what family feels like.

309. <u>Zona Viva – Carnavalito – Barrio La Isla – Musica from Guillermo Anderson. Chicas Roland, Salsa</u>

After watching the sunset and finishing dinner they all stroll down the zona viva beach boulevard to the Barrio La Isla. The canned music grows louder as they approach. The street fills with people of all ages who come from all over Honduras to escape their daily routine for a few days of carnaval magic... Many have their masks and friendship necklaces layered around their necks. Families have set up their home barbecue kiosks... artesans sell their homemade jewelry, there are arcades and games, toys, and souvenirs... and all kinds of food. Every corner has a stage where bands are preparing to perform.

Jazmin hears an acoustic guitar in the distance.

Jazmin: Mama, that's Marianella's father who sings "Arroz con Leche" Remember? Let's go.

Ceci: Yes... Guillermo Anderson... When you were very young I danced with him to his Carnaval song on the beach for the President.

Roxana: Vamos por alla!! Let's go over there!.

They approach the stage Left where Marianella is with her Mom and sisters. Guillermo and his band are setting up and he comes to greet the girls. Ceci greets Lastenia, Guillermo's wife, and his two other daughters Rocio and Mia.

Ceci: Hola amigos.... Happy Carnaval... The girls can't wait to hear you sing.

Guillermo: Si, ya voy... que guapas son las muchachas, Ceci. Y que grandes son.....The last time I saw them was in the SOS when I went there to sing years ago. You have really come a long way in this custody battle. I can't believe they are getting so big.... And that they are actually with you. Congratulations.

Angie: I remember when you came to sing at the SOS... and even you came into our little Casa Nueve.

Guillermo: Well you were so cute how could I forget you, and your English is so good. And I am so happy that you are here with your mama as a family to celebrate Carnaval right now.

Roxana: Vas a cantar Arroz con Leche? Will you sing "Arroz con Leche"?

Ceci: I taught all these kids a dance that goes with that song. I'll bet they can join the show.

Guillermo: OK. Con gusto... Let me tune up. *He finishes plugging in and tuning up with his musicians, and addresses the fast gathering audience of fans, friends and family. His wife, Lastenia and 3 daughters, Emilia, Rocio, and Marianella, sit on the side of the stage.*

Guillermo Anderson at the SOS orphanage

Guilermo speaks…**Damas y Caballeros, Bienvenida a Carnaval 2010. Es un placer tocar para mi gente de La Ceiba y Honduras… mi patria… Empezamos esta noche con un peticion de jovenes aqui para una cancion famosa para ninos, se llama "Arroz con Leche"…**. Ladies and gentlemen.. Welcome to Carnaval, 2010. It is a pleasure to play for my people from La Ceiba and Honduras… my fatherland. We begin tonight with a request from the young people here for a famous Latino children's song… "Rice with milk" *(rice pudding – a heterosexual metaphor)*

"Arroz con leche, me quiero casar, con una muchacha, que sepa bailar. Rice with milk I want to marry, a girl who knows how to dance.

Casa conmigo y yo te dare zapatos y medias color de café. Marry me and I will give you brown shoes and stockings.

Contigo si, contigo no, contigo mi negra me casare yo." With you yes, with you no, with me my negra I will marry you.

Guillermo begins and all the children in the audience who know the choreography to the song form couples and begin to sing and dance to it in the street in front of the stage. Lots of laughter ensues as

Guillermo's opening number is a production number with dancing couples in the street. Guillermo's family, friends and fans have gathered to sing along with all his original hit songs that have a modern influence mixed with his reverence for Honduran traditional poetry and folk music. He is truly a great Honduran poet. (We lost him to cancer in 2016. This was a great loss for Honduras).

Music from another corner takes over, and they move on to:

Las Chicas Rolands are 6-8 sexy female dancers of all racial colors, who perform in short shorts with high platform heels to quick Caribbean rhythms of sosa, merengue, punta and reggaeton. It is exhausting work and the crowd is mesmerized...especially the men, as they become riveted on the twerking pelvises of the sexy Chicas Rolands.

When Jazmin starts to imitate the pelvic moves, Ceci rolls her eyes and calls everybody to continue down the street to check out a pop merengue and salsa band with a huge horn section. The beat is a funky salsa that has couples firing up the dance floor in front of the

stage. Ceci dances with a musician friend and the girls love watching her show off. The Salsa ends and the band transitions to a romantic bachata.

310. Ceci consults Eva again - Garifuna sacerdota at Carnaval

The girls are thirsty and they stop for ice cream. Ceci suddenly spots a fortune teller tent across the street and asks Vilma and Sayda to stay with the girls while she goes to check it out. On automatic pilot Ceci bee lines for the tent *and is overjoyed when she sees it is Eva, the Garifuna lady from Corozal. Ceci points out the girls across the street before she goes into Eva's inner sanctum tent. They begin to talk as Eva shakes her shells... Soon she begins a Garifuna prayer and tosses the shells on her sacred table.*

Ceci: Eva! I am so happy to see you, and get a consulta.

Eva: Please sit. I am delighted to see your beautiful children. You have come a long way in this pueblo since your first Carnaval, yes sister?

She smiles with her big white teeth and peeks out of the slit in the tent door to look at the girls laughing with Vilma and Sayda.

Ceci: Thank you for seeing me Eva.

Eva: *Concentrating....* They are beautiful and you have rescued them from a shaky future. Give me a minute while I conjure this cigar. Spirit is calling you and I must open the road for my late husband, Melvin's spirit, to come down, and advise us since he is familiar with this matter?

Ceci: Yes, that was an incredible evening.

Eva: *She looks at the dancing candle on her altar.* Yes... Without a doubt the spirits are following you and want to help you with these little girls.

Eva takes out a cigar and bites off the end... then strokes it over the candle, saying a prayer, and repeating Ceci's name along with the three girls. As she lights the cigar and puffs away, she shortly falls into trance and speaks slowly with pauses.

Eva: Your tickets are almost within reach. You will see your mother before she dies, but her memory is leaving her. These three little girls need you so much. Oh mommy. They need this life changing opportunity... to SURVIVE... They deserve this chance. The Lords of Kharma commend you. As does Yemaya, African Mother Goddess of the Ocean. But Elegua is telling me that you will clearly have to sacrifice your creative contributions to the greater community to be able to keep up with the needs and paperwork for these girls. This will be a rewarding, yet lonely job, along with caring for your mother. You will not be around your artistic people. The children will also have many years of feeling like fish out of water, as you bring them out of poverty into a completely different world of possibilities. Again Cecilia... There will be many rewards for you as a single mother... despite the fact that you have always been alone without proper partnership. You must be thankful for the faith and love of your parents, who have believed in you. I am sorry that you have lived such a solo life, but spirit tells me that your rewards are yet to come.

Ceci: Eva...tengo 60 anos! I think the love songs ended years ago!

Eva: Look at you... You are not too old for love...There is an older man who cares for the girls very much. .... *Pause...* But yes I see that he is far away and has other loved ones he must attend to. Yes I see that he has a woman. Yet he will always care about you and the children.... You must maintain only a sisterly relationship with him.

Ceci: How do you know all this?

Eva: Because spirt is really watching you. You have accomplished a miracle to get custody of these girls and they need you to be strong and focused with your love.

Ceci: Eva, if I get the visas so I can go home and take care of the girls and my mother in the family home it will be a miracle. Because my Mom deserves this care and nobody else in the world but her and this man will ever love and care about the girls as much as I do.

Eva: There are complicated times ahead. More electronics... People looking at screens rather than being together. Children will become more isolated. I worry that they will not be able to communicate honestly and sincerely in a world full of false information. They must stay together.

Ceci: *With a sigh....* I always wanted a partner to help me...who is creative and crazy ambitious to make things happen like a real Dad… and to see the world… and to help me make a beautiful, forever home for me and the girls… to give them the perspective of an intelligent man of the world who understands survival… I don't know how to teach economics, nor make big money. You know, I dream on more as an artist for some reason. But God did not deal me the love card in this life, so I am the mom and the dad.

The girls come in the tent looking for Ceci. She puts her finger to her mouth for them to be quiet.

Eva: My child… in your last life you were a Tibetan monk and were killed by the Communists. You are not experienced in your soul for finding a mate… You are more inclined from your days as a monk, to do service in the world solo. The dancing is part of this… but the mothering is the lesson you have chosen to learn… and you must accept and bear this responsibility. Your father sees what you   are doing and truly wants to help.

Ceci's eyes are wide with wonder.

Angie: What is she talking about Mom?

Ceci: She is telling me what spirit wants me to know.

Angie: I don't know about this spirit stuff Mom.

Eva blesses and cleanses Ceci and the girls while uttering Garifuna prayers and shaking rue, blowing tobacco, and fanning incense around them. The girls are fascinated although they don't understand the importance of this ritual as they watch Eva with her eyes closed and the cigar hanging out of her mouth.

Eva: You will see green cards and airplane tickets for these girls, without a doubt. I don't know when. It will be a mountain to climb with many papers, but you will do this with another Gringo man who will help you with the documents.

Ceci: Yes the lawyer, Peter… He has promised to rework the application for us

Eva: Then you are in good hands. I do want you to know that you have the heart and instinct to be a good mother, despite doing it without a man in your life. This is very difficult, and you will have to give up your career I believe. These girls will need lots of time and attention. But your love is strong. *She is now waking up from her trance…..*I believe you have received what you were looking for?

Ceci: Oh yes Eva… thank you… so much for all of this. Please take this. *She hands her Lps 500*

Jazmin: So how does she know all this mom?

Ceci: Because she gets messages from spirit and I needed to hear it.

Roxana: I believe you mom.

Outside we can hear the sounds of a Garifuna band… the drums are warming up. The girls start to move to the beat.

Eva: Amen que se sea! Go and hear Aurelio… My Aurelio Martinez… the best punta artist in Honduras… You can shake up your spirit !!

Ceci: Thank you Eva. Once again you have soothed my soul.

Eva: You are being followed by God and his many angels my child. Learn how to ask for help and your call will always be answered….

311. <u>More Carnival with Aurelio Martinez – Garifuna Music</u>

Aurelio Martinez's punta band is down the street and Ceci and the

girls quickly join Vilma and Sayda who start dancing to the scintillating Garifuna rhythm. Aurelio is generating an intense African energy with his music. The women in the band have their kitchen dresses and turbans, and sing and dance in their powerful question and answer voices. There is a row of young drummers who follow Aurelio's command with the different rhythms as Aurelio directs the temperature of the performance with dance and magical energy. It is riveting, synchronous, spiritual, joyous, liberating, captivating, and pure Garifuna. It is getting late and everybody is happy... The old and the young, the races of many colors, the festive energy, and the friendship of the moment is a true Honduran memory for Ceci and the girls.

Ceci, Sayda, Vilma and the girls are having a wonderful time trying to keep up with the beat and the rapid hip circles characteristic of the punta. People of all ages are dancing. Ah, sweet Carnaval is truly a world, anybody can get lost in. Ceci is happy and for a moment realizes that this is why she came to Honduras... for this "old fashioned" native communityspirit of celebration.
We see the moon rise on the ocean horizon.

312. Visiting the tropical coastal Zoo – Rancho San Luis - Jutiapa

Ceci and the girls are in the car zooming southeast down the coastal road past Corozal and Sambo Creek, past Helen's Restaurant to a more remote part of the coast.

Ceci: So girls, we are on our way to a very special zoo called Rancho San Luis, where we will see all kinds of local animals...and we will be able to ride horses there...!! Isn't that fabuloso?

Roxana: Tu sabes Mami que amo tanto los caballos... You know Mommy that I love horses.

Jazmin: But you never ever even sat on a horse before Roxana.

Roxana: Si ... pero los amo. Amo todos los animales. Yes but I love them. I love all animals.

Ceci: OK ... so this zoo is owned by the Ponce Colindres family whose grandfather runs the place, and his grandson goes to the Mazapan School and he recommended to Angie that we should visit.

Angie: Yes and he told me that all of these animals have been rescued when their mothers leave them behind.

Ceci: That's right… when they are abandoned, or when they are injured. Y se dice aqui que *(reading in the tourist magazine)* "podrás encontrar una serie de animales como venados, faisanes, gavilan, mono araña, mico de noche, chachalacas, codorniz, pizotes, gato de monte"… I never even heard of some of these animals. This is going to be a magical mystery tour!!

Angie: So it's like an orphanage for animals…. It's just like us Mom. We were abandoned and injured.

Jazmin: I love you Mom.

Roxana: Me too Mom.

Ceci: OK so here we are.. You are going to love this place. Puro naturaleza!

She pulls into the long driveway approaching the farm. They are greeted by a stable boy who guides them into a parking spot not far from the main farmhouse. An elderly lady, Senora Ponce, comes out on the porch drying her hands, wearing an old apron, and smiling.

Mrs. Ponce: Bienvenida Sra Diaz… Te recuerdo del espectaculo en Mazapan para el Dia de la Madre. Siempre sus espectáculos me pongan a llorar. Bienvenida… Welcome Sra. Diaz. I remember you from the Mazapan School show for Mother's Day. Your shows always make me cry. Welcome.

Ceci: Gracias … es un placer llegar aqui en este paradiso suyo… Thank you. It is a pleasure to arrive here in this paradise of yours.

Roxana: Yo quiero montar un caballo Mommy. I want to ride a horse Mommy.

Sra. Ponce: Mi nieto, Esteban puede ayudarles mas tarde con los caballos. My grandchild isn't here today, but my other grandchild, Stephen, can help you later with the horse ride.

Ceci: Sra. Ponce… te presento mis hijas Roxana, Angie, y Jazmin. Sra. Ponce, these are my children, Roxana, Angie, and Jazmin.

Sra. Ponce: Bienvenidas y son bellas de la verdad!... Entonces… hay bastante animales que deben de conocer antes de montar caballos… Siguen los numeros… primero pajaros, conejos, venados, tortugas, serpientes.. mas tarde reptilios, crocadillos, bacas, patos, y por fin monos y jaguars por abajo. Welcome, and they are really beautiful. So.. there are enough animals that you should see before riding the horses… Follow the numbers… first the birds, rabbits, deer, turtles, snakes, later the reptiles, crocodiles, cows, ducks and finally the monkeys and the jaguars below.

Girls: Vamos Mommy!!

Ceci: Que trabajo de Dios estan hacienda aqui. What God work you are doing on here.

Sra. Ponce: No rechezamos nadie…qualquier animal con qualquier dano aceptamos. Y vivimos con las donaciones y venta de boletos de entrada aqui en el zoo. We never reject any animal who is harmed… we accept all. And we live on the donations and sale of entrance tickets here in the zoo.

Ceci: Le pagare por todo ahora, y quiero conocer su esposo para graciarle por su trabajo y donar un contribucion. I will pay you for everything now, and I want to meet up with your husband to thank him for his work and make a contribution.

Sra. Ponce: Claro, yo le digo. Gracias Sra Cecilia… For sure I will tell him. Thank you Sra.Ceci

Girls: Vamos Mommy!! Let's go Mommy!

Sra. Ponce: Vayan…Disfruten… Voy arreglar su reservacion para cuatro caballos!! Go, go! Enjoy yourselves. I will arrange your reservation for four horses.

The following montage takes Ceci and the girls through a magical mystery tour of exotic and rare birds on the mend. The cages are old, but neatly kept and suited for the injury of each animal

patient... The abundance of fruit and vegetables as their main diets, along with grain suggests an alternative wellness hospital for animals. They also see rabbits, snakes, deer, ducks, strange pigs, reptiles like lizards, turtles, crocodiles, and finally an island of monkeys and jaguars. At one point, they are watching an iguana struggle after surgery from having been cut open for her eggs (a delicacy) and abandoned on the road... Ceci speaks to the girls:

Ceci: You know girls, I really want you to have a respect for nature, not just for plants and mountains and rivers, and oceans, and all the beauty that goes with these places.... But also for the animals that God put on this earth with you. They are mystical creatures, struggling to stay alive, and in many places in the world... like where I am from, you don't see much more than dogs and cats, and the birds that fly around the suburbs. So Carpe Diem mis hijas... Angie: What's carpe diem Mom?

Ceci: Cease the Day!! Cease the day when you have the opportunity to be surrounded by this glorious nature to learn and understand. There is so much humility to learn from animals and plants.... Even when all we do is dominate them. It's times like this when I want to become completely vegetarian.

Here they just sit quietly and observe a jaguar staring at them, equally fascinated with the girls. The gazing becomes a spiritual experience. Ceci speaks her thoughts almost in a trance.

Ceci: I remember a time in Venezuela when I was practicing with a curandera who smeared fruit all over the body of a young woman who was unable to get pregnant. At one point, the shaman lady took on the spirit of a jaguar... who proceeded to crawl all over the young lady, covering her with watermelon, while flat on her back on the earth surrounded by candles. This cathartic growling and pawing went on for several moments until the curandera shook back into her rightful self and awakened. The young lady sat up with a huge smile as if a great weight had been lifted off her soul.... I remember the shaman lady prescribed a special tonic made with yams for the soman.

And then I later found out that she became pregnant, and her husband had to ask forgiveness for taking the life of a jaguar.

Jazmin: Mom, what are you talking about?

Ceci: Just one of my spiritual experiences with a jaguar in Venezuela. I don't think you would understand.

Sra. Ponce suddenly interrupts Ceci in her petit reve, calling her from the barn. The girls move on to watch the monkeys. Ceci awakens. Sra Ponce: Sus caballos estan listos con Esteban en el establo. Your horses are ready with Esteban in the stable.

Ceci: **Bueno... Gracias... Vamos chicas! V olveremos mas tarde a pasar mas tiempo con los monos OK?** Great! Let's go. We will return later to spend more time with the monkeys.

The girls are both thrilled and frightened to mount the horses that Sra. Ponce's grandson, Esteban, presents. Roxana immediately has an intuitive relationship with her horse, Midnight. He leads the group with Ceci in the rear, and they take off into the coastal jungle for an adventure they will never forget. The barn dogs follow along, the sun is shining, and the girls are on top of the world with an ocean breeze in their hair.

Ceci speaks to herself internally:

Ceci: *If only I could give them a nature based life like this, which would be so much like their roots, where they could learn about the medicinal value of plants.... like their partera (midwife) Abuela... and grow herbs, corn and beans and coffee... and know how to talk to animals. Just think how natural that would be...*

Alter ego Ceci: *OK... and then tell me how I am supposed to get them educated by American standards so they can go to American colleges and earn real degrees that are supposed to get them professional jobs, so they can make an incredible social class leap and become a consuming and bill paying member of white society like my parents and now me?*

Angie, Jazmin, Midnight, and Roxana

Ceci: OK Don't you think I have asked myself this a thousand times? I know how much they want a big family. I can only go towards the light, like a plant, I naturally lean in the direction of my family and my country where my survival and origins give me nourishment, and there is more hope of giving these girls a healthy life. There is special education in the USA which allows for accommodations. It would be selfish of me not to offer them this opportunity.

Alter ego Ceci: You are going to need a lot of accommodations Ceci. Lots of intervention at school... All the boat rocking that a Latino mother would never have the money or guts to do. And they may always struggle academically. But, nobody is going to care about their disabilities and how to work around them so they can keep up with a gringa lifestyle like yours ... So get ready sister... Your work is just beginning.

Esteban has stopped near a river which has been feeding the pineapple and banana fields they have been traversing while Ceci has her internal dialogue. The girls are happy. They dismount and Esteban helps the girls get a drink of fresh river water from the waterfall. Esteban talks about the view from the mountain top and they all remount and continue the journey up the mountain trail... There are birds and foxes and lizards of all kinds to behold. Once they reach the summit they dismount again, and tie up their horses to take some silent time to admire the view of the coast line and various off shore islands from this magnificent summit on the mountain.

Esteban: Miren... Por alla se puede ver Cayos Cochinos, y mas lejos...Roatan y tambien al norte esta La Isla Utila... y mas al sur esta La isla de Guanaja. Es bien claro hoy... Que bonito es nuestro pais.... Verdad muchachas? Look over there you can see Cayos Cochinos, and farther Roatan and also to the north is the Island Utila, and more to the south is the Island of Guanaja. It's really clear today. How beautiful our country is... right girls?

Angie: Yo no puedo verla... pero imagino que es bonito mi pais, y las islas en el mar. I can't see it, but I imagine that my country is beautiful, and the islands in the sea.

Jazmin: It's really beautiful Angie. I wish you could see it.

Ceci: Fuimos a Roatan cuando trabaje por la Quincineara de Marbella ... recuerdan? We went to Roatan when I worked on Marbella's Quincineara, remember?

Roxana: Si, fuimos en un barco grande por alla. Yes, we went there in a big boat.

Ceci: Entonces.. Aqui estamos hijas... en el mundo de Dios, con toda la vista natural.... Lo que me gusta es que podemos mirar una costa que todavia no tiene grand hoteles y conchas de golf, apartamentos, y centros comerciales... And so here we are, my daughters, in God country, with a completely natural view. What I like is that we can see this coast without big hotels, apartments, and shopping malls.

Esteban: Si .. entiendo... uno de los miedos de mi Abuelo... Y el nunca vendera.. Yes, I understand. One of my grandfather's big fears... and he will never sell.

Ceci: Girls.... I want you to remember this moment... as you look out upon all this untouched natural land that is so fertile... and is the home of so many people and creatures. They are all just trying to have a natural life for their families. May it not become like Miami. Amen.

Angie: We have a good life don't we mom…

Ceci: Yes you do… Let's have a group hug. I love you all so much. Can you believe how beautiful that big sky is? **Gracias por llevarnos aqui Esteban..** Thank you for bringing us here Esteban.

Esteban: **De nada…Sra Cecilia. Debemos de salir ahora antes que baja el sol…** It's nothing Sra. Cecilia. We should leave now before the sun sets.

Jazmin: Mom… I want to sleep here.

Ceci: Now that's the spirit!!! But not today… Come on, let me see you climb back up on that horse.

The hot afternoon sun begins to go down as the posse makes their way back to the ranch. As they pull in, we hear a huge scream from the monkey island.

Jazmin: Mom I want to go back to see the monkeys …

Ceci: OK…

Esteban: **Les traigo agua y se pueden sentar en la sombra alla cerca los monos.** I will bring you water and you can sit in the shade there by the monkeys.

Ceci: Perfecto … Gracias Esteban…

313. Sr. Ponce and the monkeys

The girls are hot and sweaty, but clearly inspired… They all take a seat across the moat from the island of monkeys. Suddenly they start cackling like crazy because here comes Don Miguel Ponce on horseback, the grand Patriarch of the Rancho San Luis.

Sr. Ponce: My wife tells me you want to see me.

Ceci: Yes we do and so do these monkeys want to see you. They ae going crazy.

Sr. Ponce: Yes… they are howler monkeys and they are very special… They bring me much inspiration.

Mr. Ponce dismounts, ties up his horse, and takes a seat on the bench with Jazmin on his knee, while the girls sit around him. He has brought them water and lichees. And he begins to tell Ceci about the monkeys as he tosses them old tortillas.

Ceci: We just love what you have done here with all these rescues Don Miguel... I am so impressed... Can you tell us more about your monkeys... as we are very drawn to this spot for some reason.

Sr. Ponce: Of course... Monkeys are a big part of the Mayan creation story as they were considered the result of an early failed attempt by the gods to produce humans. Let me introduce you to Hunahpu and Xbalanque.

Ceci: You mean from the Popol Vuh?

Sr. Ponce: Yes, and these howler monkeys are real twins... so you see we feel we have been blessed with their inherited magical powers.

Jazmin: Oh boy.. mom loves all that stuff.

Ceci: Yes I do, but the Hero twins were responsible for a lot of trickery, shape shifting, and crazy brujeria right?

Sr. Ponce: Yes Dona Cecilia, but they were also talented artisans, scribes, dancers, painters, sculptors and jewelers. When they call you... they are calling you to be creative and serve humanity. And I can see... Senora... that you are serving humanity by taking care of these three beautiful Honduran princesses. *He tickles them and they laugh...* And I have seen your work with the students at the Mazapan school, and I am very impressed with the way you get them to express themselves.

Ceci: Thank you... I am glad that you come to the shows and support the arts.

Sr. Ponce: You have been touched by the monkeys little Gringa... AND you know that our Ciudad Blanca is also known as the City of the Monkey King... which gives us the mythical power of the monkey in our Mayan culture.

Ceci: Yes.. I am very interested in the Ciudad Blanca. What a coincidence that you speak of the White City in the Mosquitia. I am trying to get my hands on more solid information about it.

Sr Ponce: Just let the monkeys bring you the information. Ask the spirits of Hunhupu and Xbalanque to accelerate your futures, overcome your obstacles, and evolve. They will pull all the spirit strings and grant your wishes... against all odds.

Ceci: Mystical monkeys... I love that. *Pausing almost in trance....* De verdad senor? You really think so?

Sr. Ponce: Si mujer...Within reason of course.... Pero tu tienes Dios en tu lado. But you have God on your side.

Ceci: Un Dios Maya? A Mayan God?

Ponce: Hay un solo Dios y los otros son sus ayudantes, sus angeles. Estos monos tienen la bendicion de Dios despues de sobrevivir mucho dolor y enfermedad.... Ellos volvieron de infierno... con el poder de curar, dar esperanza, y inspirar sabiduria. There is only one God and the others are his helpers and his angels. These monkeys have God's blessing after surviving much pain and illness. They came back from hell... with the power to cure, give hope and to inspire knowledge.

Ceci: Well I love all that.. thank you so much... Chicas-Digan adios y gracias a Sr. Ponce por todo lo que el esta haciendo aqui para los animales. Girls... Say goodbye and thank you to Don Ponce for rescuing all these animals.

The girls are having animated conversations across the moat with the two howler monkeys. Ceci and Mr. Ponce laugh. The girls give Mr. Ponce a big hug and thank him in Spanish... Ceci hands him a check. He smiles.

Sr. Ponce: This donation means a lot. Thank you. I will leave you with my monkeys. Gracias Sra. Cecilia y sus bellas hijas.

Ceci: Gracias a ud. senor... Lo qu e hiciste aquí es un trabajo de Dios. Ciao. Thank you to you Senor. What you have done here is God's work.

Mr. Ponce leaves and the girls continue to talk to the monkeys. Ceci says her private prayer to the monkeys…

Ceci: *in prayer* - "**If you can monkey the system for me spiritually, monkey away… Get my girls the visas we need to cross the border.**"

Roxana: **Que pediste mommy?** What did you ask for Mommy?

Ceci: **A visa prayer.** *sigh* **We have to go now. Say goodbye to the twins. We have camp tomorrow.**

Angie: **I love summer Mommy…**

Roxana: **Me too.**

Jazmin: **Te amo Mami.**

Angie and Rox: **Me too!**

314. <u>**Final Summer Camp at the Mazapan School**</u>

Ceci sets up for the first day of summer camp with young campers. Vilma and her sister Sayda are there to help. Ceci greets the parents as they drop kids off. Vilma and Sayda gather their lunches and sit the kids in a circle on the floor. Ceci has already run a multi arts camp for several summers, and this will be the last work she does at the Mazapan Dance studio before having to move out.

Young students between the ages of 4 and 10 are arriving, and as difficult as it may seem to work with such a varied mix of ages, Ceci and her team dive in for a full day of artistic group activity. The adolescent group arrives in the afternoons. Jazmin, Angie and Roxana are also there to participate and the action begins with the obstacle course set up which is already laid out when they enter. All of the activity is listed as lesson plans below, with descriptions of the activity. The schedule is similar for the older group with more mature activities.

SUMMER SCHOOL ARTS CURRICULUM

1. *The Obstacle Course is a Ceci invention mostly designed for preschoolers but is really loved by kids of all ages. The floor is*

set up like a game board with a starting point and end. This is always a great warm up for the day.

* First there is a chain of hoola hoops laid out on the floor. They must jump in and out of the hoops without touching them.

* Then they walk on a 5" width, 6" high narrow bench like a balance beam

* Next, they must jump over a series of foam blocks at different heights.

* Then they must crawl under a series of limbo sticks about a foot high

* Followed by a set of stairs that go up and down

* Then they are given a plastic spoon to hold in their mouths walking while balancing a golf ball in the spoon.

* And the final activity takes place on gymnastic mats where they do the wheelbarrow walking with their hands while a partner carries their legs; after that they learn how to do the crab walk and summersaults and cartwheels.

2. Chorus – Ceci then gathers everybody around the piano to sing scales using Do Re Mi Fa So La Ti Do in several keys. Some can sing and some can't, but the focus is on opening the mouth, hearing changes in tone, and expressing the voice. Then she teaches "Doe a Deer" from the Sound of Music. The kids love this and of course Ceci's kids have watched the movie so many times they know the lyrics inside out. Most of the kids are not quite bi-lingual but they catch on to the moves as Jazz, Angie and Roxana make up silly choreographies to go with the song.

The children remove their shoes and get ready to dance, and the floor is cleared.

3. Dance – Ceci teaches across the floor movement to music

* They walk across the floor with a "style"

* They walk backwards across the floor

* *They hop on two feet, and then on one foot*

* *They chasse side ways*

* *They learn to skip... step hop, step hop, step hop*

* *They walk on all fours like dogs*

Then they all stand on the X's facing the mirror and learn the Penguin dance, which is a fun song that talks about flipping flippers and sliding on the ice and falling. The kids love this dance and laugh like crazy.

The teenage group learns a hip hop dance to a reggaeton song.

4. *Outdoor Art Outside on the patio - Vilma and Sayda have set up painting stations with large pieces of fabric to paint big faces. There is a hem on one end that will eventually be stuffed with a tree branch attached to a rope, so they can hang them up. With much supervision and mess the kids paint for a half hour. The children must decide to paint themselves or their moms, or both together.*

5. *Running the Labyrinth on the field while the paintings dry... Ceci lays a huge canvas of a painted Hopi labyrinth on the tennis court outside the studio. She puts on music and they have a blast running in and out of the maze as they meet and greet each other in character along the way.*

6. *LUNCH – By now they are all hot, thirsty, and ready for lunch back in the air conditioned studio.*

   *Ceci so appreciates the help from Vilma and Sayda, as it is non stop bi-lingual prep, setup and clean up.

7. *Drama – After lunch Ceci provides costumes with matching puppets. Students can pick their characters and then they are paired off and must make conversations with their partners using the puppets. After they practice for a while, everybody sits with their backs to the mirror and couples perform for the group in Spanish or English by choice.*

8. *Finally, Ceci brings out a trunk of musical and percussion instruments and they all become part of an orchestra which Ceci leads, instructing them to play loudly, softly, at certain rhythms with silences and attacks. No particular musical notes are necessary. Just to follow the dynamics of the conductor.*

By now parents are arriving and are loving the show. The children are exhausted but happy and ready to show off their fabric art, which Vilma and Sayda have prepared to take home.

This will be the routine every day for 2 weeks and then another group will come in as the summer progresses. It is a bi-lingual event which introduces kids who speak absolutely no English to the language through music, drama, art and dance, with constant, healthy stimulus and creativity.

315. Expatriados Bar Goodbye Party

Ceci takes Vilma, Sayda, and the girls to the Expatriados Bar where there is a celebration for Ceci and all her dancers as a goodbye to her work at the Mazapan school, and for her contribution to the arts in the community. Many of the parents approach Ceci to thank her and express their regrets for her departure. Dancers come to hug her and have their pictures taken with her.

There are many retired gringos at the bar, mixed with young international back packers and some European folks. Peter's band is setting up for the happy hour entertainment. Jazzlyn and her mom, Flor, are helping Peter. The girls take off, circulating with Jazzlyn. Ceci approaches Flor and Peter.

Ceci: Quieo graciarles por esta celebracion. Thank you for organizing this.

Flor: Ceci, te digo…. Jazzlyn le gusto mucho bailar contigo. Ceci, I'm telling you… Jazzlyn really liked dancing with you.

Ceci: Me alegre, porque ella aprende bien rapido. Como estas tu? I am so glad to hear that, because she learns fast. And how are you? *Knowing that she has been diagnosed with cancer.*

Flor: Estoy bien. Vivo para Jazzlyn y Peter con el tiempo que tengo. *Changing the subject fast.* **Me alegre que hiciste este campamiento porque no habia ningun actividad de calidad en el pueblo para ninos este verano. Solamente las piscinas y la playa.** I am OK. I live for Jazzlyn and Peter with the time I have. I am so glad you did this summer camp because there was no quality activity for kids in town this summer. Only the pools and the beach.

Peter: Yeah… Jazzlyn is a big fan. We love how you tie in all the different arts…

Ceci: Well…She is an artist in so many ways. But, with me… it's all over. We are moving out of the studio tomorrow, and remember… I have my fifth appointment with the embassy in a few months. It's been a long two year wait.

Peter: I heard that they are letting people go right and left at Dole and the school for financial reasons. So many parents are

sorry to see you go.. Nobody knows how to mount a show like you do...

Ceci: I did what I had to do... and now I have to keep my eyes on the bigger picture. I have to go home to be with my Mom, and the girls have to come with me.

Peter: I know....and we are going to rework the package to perfection this time OK? They said two more years... you waited, and we are going to cover all the loop holes for your next and final application.

Ceci: Thank you Peter... I appreciate your optimism.

Peter: How about next weekend?

Ceci: Perfect... Go tune up. You've got a full house, ready to dance all night.

Peter returns to his sound check. Young dancers have taken over the floor as
Peter speaks

Peter: Damas y Caballeros, Ladies and Gentlemen, Boys and girls, Muchachos... Bienvenidos a el Expatriados... Your home away from home.. Su casa en La Ceiba. Estamos aqui celebrar la vida divina en Honduras and to thank Ms. Cecilia Diaz for her artistic services as dance teacher, choreographer, and show director for the last seven years here In La Ceiba...

Applause And so.. fittingly I would like to dedicate this opening number to Ceci and her students.

Everybody gets up and dances. Ceci struts to the middle of the floor with all her students and initiates a dance combination from a previous choreography to Peter's music. Even some parents are on their feet. When the song ends, Ceci takes a bow with everybody. There is applause, and Peter's band starts playing again. The girls keep dancing, and Deni May enters with Ale to join Ceci at her table. Ale goes to join the girls on the dance floor. Ceci and Deni talk.

Ceci: I'm so glad you made it. How are you?

Deni: Well, aside from the fact that the truck won't start again... We're fine.

Ceci: Do you want a drink?

Deni: Cranberry juice, Ale will have a coke.

Ceci orders drinks and anafres for everybody (Honduran hot bean dip with cheese and sausage in a clay pot with a candle beneath.)

Ceci: Deni... I want to hire you to homeschool the girls for a few months until I find out what's happening with the visas. I move everything out of the studio tomorrow... Angie and Jazmin aren't enrolled anywhere, and I just need to keep the academic ball rolling... and you are the perfect teacher for their level. And the Ceiba Bilingual school has offered me work and I might put Angie and Jazmin there until I go to the embassy.

Deni: You really think that you will get the visas this time?

Ceci: Yes... I really believe it's time. In May it will be two years with official custody, besides the five years of foster care before that, and all the other boxes have been ticked. They are running out of rejection excuses.

Deni: Except for the fact that they aren't officially "adopted." This is why I can't apply.

Ceci: You can't apply because you told them Ale was your kid and you can't prove it. Once you start a lie it is difficult to turn it around. But I think I am paving the way with this Tutora custody so that you can do the same with my lawyer, Merlyn. Deni it is possible. You can eventually apply and qualify for a visa for Ale to move back to the states.

Deni: I don't know Ceci.. I hope you are not kidding yourself.

Ceci: Well Deni... I am playing the game changer card, and praying every day. Peter will help me tweek the application again before I go. So will you help me out with homeschooling? I'll pay you 300 lempiras an hour.

Deni: How can I refuse? When do I start?

Ceci: Monday

Deni: Great, I need the work. *They toast*

316. Moving out of the Studio

Ceci and the girls drive through the guard at Standard Fruit to get to the studio for the final hours of moving out in one day. She walks into the studio with the girls and walks for the last time to the bar, and then to her position in the front center where she taught in front of the mirror for years. The girls are running around.

Sayda and Vilma arrive and there is a wordless, sympathetic exchange before the difficult task of moving everything out of the studio -- costumes, fabric, supplies, props, paint, backdrops, dance shoes, sewing machines, sound system, music CDs, photos and furniture.

There is no discussion for the first five minutes until music takes over as the sound track to an accelerated montage of the demolition, boxing, categorizing, and moving takes place. The girls help move boxes to the car. Ceci drives several loads to the house. Eventually the studio is stripped except for the bars and the mirrors.

Ceci takes her last look at the empty studio, bowing her head in prayer.

> **Ceci: Gracias por todo lo que me ha dado para realizar mis suenos artisticos.** Thank you for everything you have given me to realize my artistic dreams.

This is not the first studio Ceci has built and left (Montreal, Los Angeles, and Caracas, Venezuela) Hours of movement and creative spirit have taken place in this space. She wipes her tears, locks the door, and takes the last load with Vilma and Sayda.

317. On the home Driveway

Everybody finishes unloading at the house. Ceci, the girls, Vilma and Sayda are exhausted and are lounging around all the "stuff" which has been vacated from the studio.

Vilma: Ceci, que vas a hacer con todas estas cosas? Ceci, what are you going to do with all these things?

Ceci: Pues... Creo que debo de regalar el vestuario a David Ashby para los ninos en su orfanato, pero hay que organizarlos. Y posiblemente muebles para La Casa de Ninos. Y que toda la tela, machinas, y materiales de coser te los doy cuando estas lista Ok Vilma?... Y tambien hay cosas para vender... porque necesito dinero para vivir... como no trabajo mas. Well... I believe I should donate the costumes to David Ashby for the kids in his orphanage HOGAR... but we have to organize them. And possibly the furniture to the Casa de Ninos. And all the fabric, sewing machines and materials for sewing I give to you when you are ready to take them... OK Vilma? And also there are things to sell, because I need the money to live, since I am not working anymore.

Sayda: Poco a poco Ceci... tranquila. Hoy estamos desocupando el estudio... Hay tiempo. Little by little Ceci... relax.. Today we are emptying the studio. There is time.

Ceci: Si Gracias... tienes razon. Yes thank you... you are right.

This is visibly difficult for Ceci. It will be the last major dance studio of her career.

Vilma: Vengamos manana para organizar todo OK? We will come tomorrow to organize all this OK?

Ceci: Si Gracias para ayudarme hoy. Estoy cansada... Basta para hoy. Aqui estan pistos para el taxi. Yes thank you for helping me today. I think I'm tired.. enough for today. Here is money for the taxi.

Ceci goes out to the street with Vilma and Sayda as she always does to make sure they get in a cab with an "appropriate" driver who will honor the price they agree upon. Fortunately, it is a beautiful night with a full moon... and no danger of rain on the cluttered driveway.

Back inside the house Ceci puts on some Spanish guitar music and pours herself a glass of wine. The kids hang out on the swings.

Angie: So are you sad mom that you had to leave the studio?

Ceci: It won't be the first studio I've had to leave.

Jazmin: But will you keep dancing Mom?

Ceci: What else am I going to do? That's all I really know.

Roxana: What about all of these things?

Ceci: Just gotta let go eventually. Have a garage sale. But first I have to see if I get work at CBS, and then of course we are still waiting for the visas.

Angie: I just don't want you to be sad.

Ceci: How could I be sad when I have three beautiful daughters to keep me laughing huh? *They have a little tickle session.* Come on it's time to go to bed. We'll clean this up tomorrow. And after that we are going swimming up the river, so get your new bathing suits ready.

318. Oscar's Cangrejal River Resort – Crazy Gringo

Ceci and the girls are in Carlotta heading up the river to Oscar's River quarry resort, which is also a mecca for tourists and serious river rafters. Oscar is a Honduran who loves nature and is married to an American woman with two sons who go to the Mazapan school. Their resort on the river hovers on decking over a huge rock formation of little rolling rock pools of all depths, edged by boulder cliffs allowing flow from the Cangrejal river. It is one of the most beautiful parts of the river. Oscar's hideaway has a bar and restaurant and humble, tropical hotel accommodations literally built on top of the cliff dwelling deck. His crew offers river rafting trips and tours along the way with the help of a competent, Honduran crew of young men. Or you can casually sun bathe in the shallow rock pools with a beer in hand.

Ceci and the girls zig zag down the cliff from the edge of the road above and enter the restaurant/porch where various campers and international tourists and sports enthusiasts are eating and sitting at the bar. Ceci grabs a table for her kids and goes to the bar for a beer and kid drinks. The girls toss their gear and go running for the pools. There is an American man at the bar in his late 50s, who apparently is chaperoning several young American boys on a river rafting expedition. Ceci takes three horchatas to the table and returns for her beer.

Oscar: Como estas Senora Cecilia? How are you Sra. Cecilia?

Ceci: Bien Oscar. Me alegro que su negocio va bien. I'm well Oscar. I am happy that your business is going well.

Oscar: Si, bastante bien. Sabes que... la familia absolutamente fue loca con el ultimo espectaculo. No creo que podia interesar mis muchachos a bailar. Fue incredible. Gracias.. Yes, good enough. You know that the family loved the last show. I can't believe how you got those boys to dance.

Ceci: Fueron ellos que decidieron hacerlo seriosamente... Tienen la fuerza tuya y la gracia de su madre. It was really their decision to take it seriously. They have your strength and their mother's grace.

Ceci: Cuanto te debo ahora? How much do I owe you?

Albert: Let me pay for that Oscar. *The gringo man steps forward.*

Oscar: Yes of course... Ceci, this is Albert. Alberto - Ceci. She is the dance teacher in my son's school at Dole Fruit and makes wonderful shows.

Albert: How do you do?

Ceci: I'm fine and .... Thank you for the beer.

Albert: May I join you?

Ceci: *hesitant, as he seems a bit tipsy to her.* OK, have a seat. *Ceci fusses with the family gear.* And you are?

Albert: Albert Hilger, from Pittsburgh.

Ceci: MY name is Ceci Diaz, and my family is in Virginia, but I live here now.

Albert: Pleased to meet you. *They shake hands.*

Oscar comes with an anafre, the classical hot bean dip appetizer.

Oscar: What can I get for you and your girls Senora Cecilia? We have pescado frito, pollo asada, carne asada, chuletas de puerco, sopa de caracol, pupusas, platanos, arroz y frijoles. Fried fish, barbecued chicken and beef, pork cutlets, conch soup, pastries, bananas, rice and beans.

Ceci: Oscar can you make me a big plate for the family with a little of this and that?

Oscar: A tu orden.

Albert: Cheers madame.... *Toasting beers*

Ceci: To Honduras... and it's untouched natural resources.

Albert: *He interrupts.* Yes... that's all good. So tell me. What are you doing in this corner of the earth and who are these children?

Ceci: Hmm... That's very direct. Let's see.. Do you want the 25 words or less version or..

Albert: *He interrupts again.* Well I know you are a professional dancer and that you work at the Dole school, and that you must have a big heart by taking these girls away from the orphanage for the day. But I don't know where you are from?

Ceci: That's pretty good, but not quite.....OK...So my Mom lives in Virginia, and I have travelled a lot over the years.

Albert: I can see you are single.

Ceci: I can see you are married.

681

She looks at his ring and then walks over to watch the girls in the pool below. Albert tells Oscar to put everything on his tab. Ceci yells to the girls:

Ceci: Girls! We will eat in a little bit OK?

She returns to the table and sits.

Ceci: So what about you?

Albert: I am an almost retired CEO of a clothing manufacturing biz in Pittsburgh. I am with my two sons and their scout troop river rafting in Honduras. And yes I am married and interested in all people, and why the hell a lady like yourself would give up a career in show biz to move down here and work for peanuts to hang out with Honduran orphans, is beyond me.

Ceci: Ok so I am interested in Honduran culture. The music, the naturaleza, the food, the history, the Mayas, the ruins?? All of it is interesting.

Albert: And the kids?

Ceci: I actually have custody.

Albert: So they are adopted.

Ceci: I wish. Unfortunately, I'm too old... which is making it difficult to get visas. But I got them out of the orphanage by a miracle of God... and that's why I am here.

Albert: And I imagine there are disabilities?

Ceci: Yes there are too many to list or even predict. I take it day by day and love them all as much as I can to make up for the neglect they went through.

Albert: Well. I wish you luck with all of that because the disabilities don't go away, and will require more and more attention to launch them ... And your dance thing will just drop by the wayside. It must really be a sacrifice, and I hope you are doing the math.

Ceci: **What math?** *Ceci is beginning to suspect the integrity of this gringo.*

Albert: The math about the age difference my dear, as I suspect you are in your fifties by now?

Clearly he has had too much to drink. The food suddenly arrives when the girls return to the table all wet from swimming. They wrap themselves up in towels looking at the guy. Ceci is irate and stands up.

Ceci: I beg your pardon?

Albert: OK I'm sorry….. I just wanted to say that as much as I admire you madame, I hope you realize how many more kids you could be teaching and inspiring if you didn't have three disabled half breeds.

Ceci: You know Mr. Hilger, it might be time for you to take your American white boy attitude back to the bar. My children are hungry. And thank you for your charming company. *She is simultaneously cutting up the meat and fish furiously with a knife.* My children would like to eat. Will you excuse us? …. So how was the water girls?

Albert goes back to the bar with a bozo look on his face.

Roxana: Bien frio mama… Tengo hambre. Really cold Mom. I'm hungry.

Jazmin: So who is that man momma?

Angie: Is he American?

Jazmin: Esta casado? Is he married?

Ceci: Oh Please! Enjoy your food so we can take another dip before sundown. *Ceci grabs her Spanish albanico and starts to fan herself vigorously.* After all, we come to the river to cool off, not to get all hot and bothered…

Angie: Are you hot and bothered mom?

Albert: *Across the room from the bar …* You know I picked up your dinner tab too.

Ceci walks over the bar to whisper in his ear so as not to cause any more commotion.

Ceci: Well I hope it was worth the 10 minute toxic release of your critical white supremacist insight into my destiny as a caregiver. Because those 10 minutes are all you get, and I would have introduced you properly to my children, but I doubt they would appreciate the uncalled-for, condescending remarks you made about them. *She returns to her table as the restaurant watches.*

Albert: *Macho game on.* Well they clearly won't be going to Harvard.

Jazmin: What's Harvard Mom?

Ceci: It's a college honey, where you may go to study one day. *Redirecting her comments to the gringo.* And where did you go to school to be such a talented insulting gladiator?

Now there is an audience.

Albert: At least I would be smart enough to check out a kid's DNA before I take them for the rest of my life.

Ceci almost chokes on her beer... then stands up and announces:

Ceci: Excuse me, whose father is this? *The place goes silent and two teenage boys step forward.* Would you mind taking your Dad for a swim. I think he needs to cool off.

The boys take him away and tell Oscar they will take care of the bill on the way out. Ceci returns to the table.

Roxana: Que paso Mami? What happened Mom.

Ceci: No te preocupas. Learn one important rule... No one is better than you are. You are beautiful the way you are. Nobody can judge or manipulate you...even if they buy your dinner. Entienden?

Oscar: *approaches* I am so sorry Senora Cecilia. He had too much to drink.

Ceci: It's OK Oscar.. I am sorry for all the rumba. Gringos like him make me realize what we might be facing in the USA. Thanks Oscar, the food is delicious. We are going to take some doggy bags and leave. This is for you.

She gives him a tip and he goes for boxes. Ceci starts babbling to herself as she collects the food to go.

Ceci: *Mumbling* Now why would somebody like that come to Honduras where there are lots of brown people if he thinks they are all inferior?

Jazz: What are you talking about Mom?

Ceci tries to shake it off. One of the waiter/raft assistants come to clear the table and over hears Ceci and responds.

Waiter: **Porque este tipo puede visitar el mundo tercero y vivir mas barato aqui que en los estados, mientras se siente mas superior que los Hondurenos... Y la cerveza cuesta menos!** Because this type can visit the third world and live cheaper here than in the US... while he can feel superior to the Hondurans... and the beer is cheaper.

Ceci: **Tiene razon hombre... But even though *he* is American ...... we are not all like that.** *Oscar comes with boxes... She fills them with the leftovers...*

Oscar: Come during the week when it is more tranquila.

Ceci: Thank you Oscar... Come on girls lets go.

Ceci loads the girls in the car in her bad mood.

Ceci: You know girls I think we all need a change of scenery. Since we don't have much going on now I am going to take you to Copan to see the Mayan Ruins and I will make reservations at Thelma's hotel. So tomorrow we go to Copan.

319. Taking the girls to Copan

It is mid afternoon when Ceci and the girls arrive in Copan after a five hour drive. Ceci drives up and down the hilly, bumpy, cobble stone streets until she finds Thelma's Hotel. The girls have awakened and are curiously taking in the old world surroundings. Ceci gets out of the car and runs up the steps to Thelma's indoor/outdoor kitchen where she is making tamales.

Ceci: Thelma!

Thelma: Ceci!

Ceci: Yes I came back!

Thelma: **Y las ninas?** And the girls?

Ceci: **Estan conmigo abajo!** They are with me downstairs.

Thelma: **Dios Mio! Te dije mujer!** Oh my God… I told you lady.

Thelma's Rooftop Altar

The scene changes to dinner on Thelma's rooftop. The girls are playing with the exotic birds next to Thelma's altar until she serves a huge plate of Honduran arroz con pollo.

Ceci: Thank you so much for taking us at the last minute..

Thelma: I am proud to host you anytime because you are caring for these beautiful Triguena sisters.

Ceci: It's so beautiful here, your food is delicious and the girls just love the birds.

Thelma: They are Lionel's and he wants to see you. I called him last night. How long will you be here? He wants to take you to some special places and have a session with the girls.

Ceci: By all means…

Thelma: Leonel suggests that you accompany him tomorrow first up to the mountain to the Jaguar hot springs… to cleanse before you go to the ruins. It is a beautiful place.

Roxana: Do they have jaguars there?

Thelma: Not anymore. But they do have hot water pools.

Angie: So we can swim?

Ceci: You actually soak in hot springs.

Thelma: And it cleanses your body and soul.

Jazmin: Mom… isn't my soul clean?

Ceci: Yes your soul is clean, beautiful and innocent. The hot springs make you extra clean.

Thelma: We go to the hot spring to cleanse so spirit can hear us and talk to us. Spirit anchors in hot water. And after that Leonel will bring you to the Copan Aviary where all the macaws and colorful, sacred birds are. These birds are very special and will help you understand more about your Mayan heritage.

Roxana: I just love animals. They always want to talk to me.

Thelma: Ceci, why don't you take the girls for a walk around Copan before the sun sets?

Ceci: Great idea ... girls finish up and we'll put on our walking shoes.

320. Walking around *Copan*

The following sequence gives the reader an idea of the ancient style of Copan with its colorful small houses nd cobblestone streets. Three wheeled, open air mini taxis take you anywhere you want to go. There are charming hotels and restaurants and many artisan shops selling local jewelry, busts of Mayan Gods, clothing, and souvenirs.

321. Next day – Luna Jaguar Hot Springs

Ceci, Leonel, and girls arrive, after driving up the mountain to the Jaguar hot springs.

Leonel: Ok ladies, are you ready to enter the world of spirit?

Roxana: Mom, are we going swimming in hot water?

Ceci: These hot springs are for healing more than fun.

In the following montage Leonel leads Ceci and the girls through the elaborate chain of hot spring pools in the Luna Jaguar hot spring in the community of Agua Caliente. There is a mystical glow about this place with the steam floating over the string of pools situated up the mountain path. They climb up to the highest pool where there is an altar of cement Mayan statues to all the Mayan Gods and Goddesses. He takes out and feathers and prays over the girls in a Mayan tongue. The tourists are fascinated and the girls are completely hypnotized.

Jazmin: Mr. Leonel, Have I washed my soul enough now?

Leonel: Not quite. Now you are ready for the macaw birds.

Angie: OK… so my spirit can fly, right?

Ceci: Now you are getting the idea.

322. **Same day – the Copan Aviary**

We cut immediately to the Macaw Mountain in the Copan Aviary where the girls are giggling nervously over the exotic birds which are landing on their head and hands. Leonel blesses the birds with the same copal incense. The girls are delighted to interact with such magical creatures, and Leonel is pleased that they are attracted to the birds.

Jazz

Roxana

Angie

Roxana: These birds really like me.

Ceci: You know Leonel, I am getting the chills.

Leonel: Porque el espiritu esta aqui. Creo que las ninas estan listas para ir a las ruinas manana. Because the spirit is here. I think the girls are ready to go to the ruins tomorrow.

323. **Next day – the Copan Mayan Ruins**

In the following montage we see Ceci and the girls wandering through the Copan ruins with Leonel passing all the stellae sculptures, the ball court, the hieroglyphic staircase, the Great Plaza and the Acropolis.

Leonel: This is your heritage ninas. Be proud that the Mayans were so advanced. They watched the stars, the sun and the moon... they watched the animals and their ways... the land and what it could grow for their nutrition, with very sophisticated irrigation systems. They understood time and the calendar. This knowledge is in your blood. Be proud... because you can use this knowledge to walk between worlds and help others.

Jazmin: *Tilting her head upwards as she looks at a pyramid.* But Sr. Leonel, I don't understand how they lifted up these big blocks so high. They weigh a lot more than legos.

Leonel: Buena pregunta. The star people did that for them.

Angie: You mean like magic?

Leonel: It was a science and still is. Just way too advanced for people today.

Roxana: What are star people?

Ceci: They are people from another star system called the Pleiades, who came here to help the Mayans.

Leonel: And to teach them very advanced ways of living.

Angie: Mom is he making this up?

Ceci: No baby. You know there are millions of stars up in the sky. And each one of them is a sun with planets going around them. And don't you think that maybe some of those planets have people on them that are smarter than us, with rockets that could visit our planet Earth?

Angie: I don't know.

Jazmin: You mean like those ETS with big heads?

Leonel: You think that everybody in the universe should look like us?

690

Ceci: Think about it girls.

Leonel: So maybe they were smart enough to show the Mayan people how to make those pyramids and lift those big heavy blocks up high.

Jazmin: I thought we were the smartest people in the world.

Ceci: I don't think so honey.

They continue walking as they talk. They come to the court of the Jaguar.

Leonel: And so now we come to the court of the Jaguar.

Ceci: Dios mio Leonel. This is where I blanked out and went to the Ciudad Blanca!

Leonel: Yes, I remember, and you said that I was Quetzalcoatl!

Angie: Please don't pass out on us Mom. *Holding on to her.*

Ceci: I promise. I just get so inspired by these spaces. I see dozens of dancers and costumes, music and lights. It accelerates my heart and the art goddess just takes over.

Leonel: It was probably Comizahual, the flying tiger queen, who is following you and protecting the girls now that you are a real mother. She also came from the stars.

Ceci: Yes I know about Comizahual. She is haunting me.

Roxana: Mom I want to be the star of your show and dance in a feather costume.

Ceci: You are my shining stars, and my life revolves around your happiness. May all the gods and goddesses hear that.

Leonel: Amen que se sea, Ceci. And there is no doubt in my mind that your mother will have her grandchildren in her house in America one day soon.

Ceci: I hope so. Thank you Leonel for everything.

Leonel: What's good for my people is good for yours. Remember the Mayan saying: "I am another you and you are another me." Yes, they will walk between the worlds and learn to give back.

324. Home School – Deni May

It is Monday and Vilma has washed her final third head of hair and is braiding all of them. Ceci has set breakfast on the table outside on the car porch. She cleans up the schooling area where the white board is hung. The radio is broadcasting the news about what happened in Tegucigalpa last night with a military coup.

2009 Honduran *coup d'état* - *La Tribuna*

"The Honduran *coup d'état*, part of the 2009 Honduran constitutional crisis, occurred when the Honduran Army on 28 June 2009 followed orders from the Honduran Supreme Court to oust President Manuel Zelaya and send him into exile. Zelaya had attempted to schedule a non-binding poll on holding a referendum on convening a constituent assembly to rewrite the constitution. Zelaya refused to comply with court orders to cease, and the Honduran Supreme Court issued a secret warrant for his arrest dated 26 June. Two days later, Honduran soldiers stormed the president's house in the middle of the night and detained him, forestalling the poll.[8] Instead of bringing him to trial, the army put him on a military airplane and flew him to Costa Rica. Later that day, after the reading of a resignation letter of disputed authenticity, the Honduran Congress voted to remove Zelaya from office, and appointed Speaker of Congress Roberto Micheletti, his constitutional successor, to replace him.

International reaction to the 2009 Honduran coup d'état was widespread; the United Nations, the Organization of American States (OAS), and the European Union condemned the removal of Zelaya as a military coup. On 5 July 2009, all member states of the OAS voted by acclamation to suspend Honduras from the organization.

In July 2011, Honduras's Truth Commission concluded that Zelaya broke the law when he disregarded a Supreme Court ruling ordering him to cancel the referendum, but that his removal from office was also illegal and a coup. The Commission found Congress' designation of Roberto Micheletti as interim president had been unconstitutional, and the resulting administration a "de facto regime."

Deni May arrives amidst this activity and is listening to the same English station on her car radio. She enters with great drama.

Deni: So have you heard that the Honduran Supreme Court is bringing President Zelaya back to power after he engineered a coup de etat? Remember when the military took him out of bed in his pajamas and flew him to Costa Rica! It's going to be crazy in the streets now.

Ceci: Wasn't he trying to create a second presidential term by altering the Honduran Constitution instead of going through congress?

Deni: Yes, and this being a third world oligarchy who knows what these guys are really up to? It's taking years to get any truthful information about this.

Ceci: But the Honduran Supreme Court declared this illegal. Interesting how all these dictators think they can change history and convention.

Deni: Both Hilary and Obama called the kidnap unconstitutional. I don't think they realize that Zelaya is a friggin dictator. With all this hulabaloo the US could cut off aid, and stop all Honduran immigration.

Ceci: This is definitely bad timing for me. It may ruin my 5th visa attempt. Do you want some coffee? Here are the girls... ready to go. I am going to the Registro.

Deni: All I can say is this is your last chance, because if the Republicans get into power, you will never get visas, no matter how big the promises at the embassy or your backbends along the way.

Ceci: Ok Deni, I'm already a neurotic mess over this, with my Mom all alone at home. I don't sleep about it. I have to do some errands around this.

Deni: Ok well I am ready to teach.

Ceci: Vilma, se puede dar un café a Deni porfa? Gracias... Me voy al Registro OK? Bueno... Saluden a Deni May chicas.. Vilma, can you please give Deni a café. Thank you. I am going to the Registro OK? Say hello to Deni May girls.

Chicas: Hello Deni May...

Deni: Hola bellas

Ceci: I love you babies! – pay attention!

Ceci jumps into Carlota and takes off.

Deni: Hello muchachas... Are you ready for home school... We are going to start with a story that I will read, and then ask you questions about at the end to see who understands English.

Angie: I already speak English...

Jazmin: Me too. Roxana isn't so good.

Roxana: I am good.

Deni: OK girls. just get comfortable and listen to this story about.... Dora Exploradora.

Chicas: Yeah!!

325. The Registro

Ceci gets on the long line of people waiting for copies of their birth, marriage, or death certificates. Ceci has done this many times, but wants to get a recent copy that might indicate her name as custodian on the girls' birth certificates for the visa applications. She reaches the head of the long line composed of a cross section of Honduran society. The three birth certificates do not have her name on them. She is directed to a back office for help. She waits on another line to speak to a secretary.

Ceci: Disculpa Senora. Tengo aqui los certificados de nacimiento de tres hermanas que estan en mi custodia como Tutora, y quiero saber si es posible inscribir mi nombre en sus certificados de nacimiento? Excuse me Sra. I have here the birth certificates of three sisters who are in my custody as Tutora, and I want to know if it is possible to register my name on their birth certificates?

Secretary: *looking at Ceci with confusion and impatience....* **Que quiere senora Gringa?** *Looking at the three birth certificates and Ceci's custody papers.* What do you want gringa?

Ceci: Yo soy la madre de estas ninas y creo que mi nombre debe de estar en sus certificados de nacimiento. Tengo papeles de custodia aqui. I am the mother of these girls and I believe that my name should be on their birth certificates. I have custody papers here.

Secretary: *Smiling as if Ceci is eccentric.* **Gringa... vamos estar claro. Ud esta ayudando la madre... tu no eres la madre. Y no podemos entrar su nombre en este documento.** Gringa..........you are helping the mother... you are not the mother. And we can't enter your name on this document.

Ceci: *Composing herself with a low voice...* **Excuse me... por favor... no me hable asi. Yo pongo la comida en las bocas de estas ninas... Yo compro su ropa y las traigo a la dentista. Ellas viven conmigo por anos. Yo soy la mama. Puedo hablar con su jefe?** Please don't talk to me like that. I put the food in these girls' mouths, I buy their clothes and take them to the dentist..They live with me for years. I am the mother. Can I speak to your boss?

Secretary: Si Senora... Espere por alla.

She disguises a giggle and rises to go into the office behind her. She then attends to the next person in the line. Ceci waits in the corner until a man exits the office and invites her in.

Manager: Como puedo servirle senora? How can I help you Senora?

Ceci: Senor, gracias por su tiempo. Yo tengo custodia "Tutora" de tres hermanas que estaban en el SOS y ahora han estado conmigo por seis anos. Estoy pidiendo visas para ellas y creo que es importante tener mi nombre en sus certificados de nacimiento como la persona responsable por su bienestar. Aqui son los papeles. Senor, thank you for your time. I have Tutora custody of three sisters who were in the SOS and now have been with me for six years. I am applying for passports for them and I believe that it is important to have my name on their birth certificates as the person responsible for their wellbeing. Here are the custody papers.

Manager: Senora... Aunque de yo entiendo el razon por este requisito, es la primera vez que alguien en La Ceiba pide algo asi. Sra. Even though I understand the reason for this request, it is the first time that someone in La Ceiba has asked for something like this.

Ceci: *Earnestly repeating herself again.* **En realidad yo** *soy* **la sola madre responsable ahora. Here are the papers from the judge for custody. Aqui son los documentos de custodia.** But Sr. In reality, I am the only responsible mother now.

Manager: Claro ... OK, I see this. *He looks over the papers and sees her cedula identity.*

Ceci: Y me enojo su secretaria cuando me insulto, disputando mi custodia, con sus sonrisas y disrespecto. Sabes que el trabajo, tiempo, y frustracion que yo he pasado para obtener custodia y darles seguridad y salud? Hombre! ..... Disculpa... I feel better now. And your secretary made me angry when she insulted me, disputing my custody, with her smiles and disrespect. Do you know the work, time, and frustration I have been through to get this custody to give them security and health?

Manager: Please senora... accept my apologies. I know how difficult it is to adopt with the IHNFA situation. It was not like this before. But we must protect these Honduran children from being purchased like a bag of bananas.

Ceci: Yes, I see them everywhere on the street. There are many good people who want to adopt, and they are being discouraged. I have been in Ceiba for years seeking custody and immigration. How is Honduras caring for these kids? I have to do backbends to justify everything I do with these girls. And now I am trying to get visas for them with papers that link our names.

Manager: OK, look… This is what I will do. My assistant will go in the back room with you and will hand write the following information on these three birth certificates with your name on them as Tutora, and I will personally sign it. That is the best I can do for the moment. Will you accept this as the only solution I have?

Ceci: I assume this can't be written in type?

Manager: Not now… maybe sometime.

Ceci: This paper will help with the visas and I need this to accompany the custody papers. I have my doubts about a hand written document, but it is better than nothing.

Manager: Then it is done… follow me.

Ceci: Thank you sir. You are part of this long story.

Ceci follows the manager to a back room where he instructs a young woman to copy by hand and then photo copy information regarding Ceci's custody on the back of each birth certificate.

Ceci looks at her watch, and knows, with a sigh, that this is an important move. She waits in a wobbly chair next to the young lady's desk as she slowly copies the information.

326. In the car – Phone call to Lawyer Peter

Cut to Ceci bursting out of the Registro sweating and fanning herself with a precious file in her hands. She climbs into her Carlotta and drives home.

Ceci: Dear God, when is this going to be easy?

On the way home Ceci stops by the Ceiba beach to walk and think. Ceci sits and stares at the ocean and then calls Peter.

Ceci: Hola Peter! Como estas? I wonder if you are ready to work on tweeking this final visa application. I still have 6 months to go but I want it to be stellar with all your Socratic arguments OK?

Pause, listening to Peter.

Ceci: I don't know what I am going to do. I have applied for work at the Ceiba Bi-lingual school and I can put Jazz and Angie in school there with me. Roxana couldn't pass the entrance exam, so she will stay at Bright Beginnings.

Pause

Ceci: Deni May will home school them for a while... And I know leaving Mazapan is going to be as difficult for them as it is for me, but I want them to be near me... and they have to be around other kids, and as you well know, Mazapan is expensive. I am working it out.

Pause

Ceci: So right now Peter... the most important priority in my life are these visas. I think this is my last chance. My mom is waiting for me, and I will never forgive myself if I don't go take care of her. I think dementia might be kicking in and if I am going to inherit the house for the girls, I have to get there as soon as possible before my sister puts her in a home and sells the house. I want to take care of her in the family home, with the girls. It's the right thing to do.

Pause

Ceci: Thanks Peter. I am banking on your dicho (saying) that "I may have lost some battles, but I am going to win the war". That is for my next trip to Tegucigalpa. So I will see you tomorrow. Thanks...

She hangs up and flops down in the sand on her back. We see shots of the horizon and the empty beach.

327. <u>Returning to Deni and home school at the house</u>

Deni and girls are doing math on the porch white board.

Ceci: So how are my geniuses doing? How are those times tables going?

Deni: They are doing great. Let's show her the 4s ok?

In confused unison the girls recite the 4 times tables.

Ceci: I love it... Thank you Deni... *Ceci gives her lempiras*

Deni: Oh I almost forgot... CBS called and wants you to work in the fall and to bring the kids over for an assessment check. I guess they want a dance teacher.

Ceci: I guess they know that Mazapan let me go. This is a small town.

Deni: Maybe they want some of your really big shows.... Every proud mother wants to see their kids on stage.... Future Stars of La Ceiba!

Ceci: Whatever... I will call them later... and thanks so much... How are you doing?

Deni: OK... But Omar is in town and I told him the only way he could see Ale is if I dropped him with his family, because I trust his family. You don't think that was too harsh?

Ceci: You mean too harsh for the gay man you married for convenience so he could get a US visa cause he brought you a kid who is not even his kid – so Ale could have a Dad who asks you for money and you can't get out of Honduras with Ale anyway because of the DNA problem?

Deni: Right...

Ceci: No that is NOT a harsh condition. You should have never lied that he was your kid. But I understand how desperate custodial parents get.

Deni: OK OK... I am as desperate as you are to go back to the states. Desperation calls for drastic measures... as you already know...

Ceci: I'm sorry Deni. I don't know how anybody normal has kids and a husband anyway. I can barely keep up with these kids let alone the politics of immigration.

Deni: And keep up with a job.... You better call the Ceiba Bilingual School. They are looking for you ... I'll see you Wednesday.

Ceci: Ok bye Deni… you know I appreciate your sisterhood.

Deni: Us expats gotta stick together. Right?

Deni leaves… The girls are singing La Tortuga (A Honduran kid song about a turtle) with Vilma. Ceci joins them on the swings.

Ceci: So how do you like home school?

Angie: Well you know we love Dora Dora Exploradora.. but we miss other kids.

Ceci: Deni will come a few times every week until I figure out what to do with you. It's very important that you have some kind of regular schooling OK?

Jazmin: Yes mamaaaa

Roxana: So what will we do tomorrow mom?

Ceci: Well if Vilma will join us tomorrow I would like to take you to the Casa de Ninos where I used to teach when I first got here. Quieres ir con nosotros a la Casa de Ninos en Barrio Englais manana Vilma? Do you want to come with us to the Casa de Ninos in Barrio Englais tomorrow Vilma?

Vilma: Si Ceci

Angie: Isn't that for boys?

Ceci: Yes.. It's a very poor orphanage in Barrio Englais by the ocean. I want you to see this place OK?

Jazmin: Is it like the SOS?

Ceci: It's not as nice as the SOS… I am going to do some yoga and art with them and I need you all to help OK?

Jazmin: OK mom. You want us to know how lucky we are right?

Ceci: Hear me about this, girls. It just breaks my heart to see kids without moms and dads. Because they just don't know what to do about so many things. This is a complicated world even for me and I am old. So I know how much kids need a solid education, guidance and sincere love to point them in the right direction… or at least to give them good choices to go towards their dreams safely and in good health – protected from the bad stuff. Right?

Girls: Right mom…. *Hug session.*

328. <u>**Casa de Ninos – Yoga and Art - Adan reappears**</u>

Ceci, Vilma, and the girls enter the Casa de Ninos, in Barrio Inglais on the ghetto shore. They help Ceci to carry art supplies, music CDS and a boom box. The boys rush to hug Ceci as the Director shakes her hand in greeting.

Director: Bienvenidas Sra Diaz. Hace mucho tiempo desde veniste. Me alegro verte de nuevo con sus ninas. Welcome Sra. Diaz. It's been a while since you came. I am happy to see you again with your girls.

Ceci: Si, buenos días. Disculpame. He pasado mucho tiempo y energia buscando custodia de estas bellas hermanas… y tambien estaba trabajando. Yo llame ayer y deje un mensaje que yo pudiera venir hoy. Yes, Good morning and forgive me. Yes… I have spent a lot of time getting the custody of these beautiful girls, while also working. I did call yesterday and left a message that I was able to come today.

The boys surround Ceci, Vilma, and the girls like magnets. They are hungry for adult care, love, attention and supervision and they rush to any adult in the room who has a plan. They immediately refer to Ceci and Vilma as "Tias".

Director: Pues, nadie me aviso… entonces que suerte que esta aqui hoy. Podemos arreglar algo rapido. Well.. nobody told me. But what luck that you are here today. We can arrange something quickly. *He directs some of the boys to move tables in the cafeteria.*

Ceci: Si…Y he pensado de sus muchachos muchisimo con toda la situacion de huerphanes sin familias en este pais. Se rompe mi corazon. Pero aqui estoy hoy con mi gente para hacer lo que puedo… Vilma es mi ayudante. Y aqui estan mis hijas: Roxana, Angie, y Jazmin. Y el proyecto de hoy es a celebrar las siete CHAKRAS en yoga con meditacion, exercicio, y arte.

Tenemos todo lo que necesitamos aqui. Yes, I have thought a lot about your boys with the situation of orphans in this country. It breaks m heart. But here I am with my people to do what I can. Vilma is my helper. And here are my daughters, Roxana, Angie and Jazmin. And today's project is to celebrate the seven CHAKRAS in yoga with meditation, exercise, and art. We have all that we need right here.

Director: Fantastico! – Con mucho gusto Sra. Cecilia, la cafeteria esta lista para uds. Fantastic!... With much pleasure, Sra. Cecilia, the cafeteria is ready for you.

Ceci follows the boys into the cafeteria. They are clearly hungry for organized activity. Ceci shows the boys how to sit in the lotus position in a circle. Vilma walks around correcting posture and crossed legs. Angie, Jazmin and Roxana sit with straight backs making good examples.

Ceci: OK. Presten atencion caballeros. Lo que vamos hacer ahora es estudiar las siete chakras del cuerpo con meditacion, haciendo exercisios de yoga, y pintando las chakras con los colores del arco iris… Entienden? Que es meditacion? Cuando descargamos la mente de todo, concentrando en su respiracion y nada mas. All right. Now pay attention gentlemen. We are going to study the seven chakras with meditation, doing yoga exercises, and painting the chakras with the colors of the rainbow… Do you understand? And what is meditation? When we empty the mind of everything, concentrating on your breath and nothing more. *She shows off her straw yoga mat with an outline of her body and the seven chakra symbols in their respective colors located along the spine in the body form.* **OK… Que son las chakras? Estes siete puntos son centros de energia en su cuerpo… y cuando estan meditando, se puede concentrar fuerte con su respiración y mente en cada chakra empezando abajo con el rojo, y subiendo con la naranjada, el amarillo, el verde, el azul, morado, y blanco** *indicating each one,* **uno por uno, con su respiracion y concentracion… subiendo arriba hasta su corona… con sus ojos cerrados…. desllenando su mente, espiritu y cuerpo con la basura del dia…. Pensando en los colores.** OK and what are the chakras? These seven points are centers of energy in the body, and when you are meditating, you can think strongly with your breathing and mental attention to each chakra, beginning below with red, and rising with orange, yellow, green, blue, purple and white *(indicating each one)*, one by one, with your breathing and concentration, rising upwards until your crown, with your eyes closed... emptying your mind, spirit and body of the garbage of the day... thinking of the colors.

Some of the boys are already beginning to meditate with their eyes closed. Ceci puts on some beautiful Hindu music, and magic fills the air of the dark, cold, cement orphanage cafeteria. Jazmin has one eye open to see who is cheating. Ceci keeps reminding the boys to empty their minds and concentrate on their breathing. She repeats herself many times to reinforce the directions.

Ceci: Yoga es una practica ancien de India que es un país en el otro lado del mundo, y fue parte de la religion Hindu. Pero se la usa en esta epoca moderna para salud y ejercicio en todos partes del mundo...para estirar el cuerpo y la mente. Recuerden que su concentracion empieza con la primera chakra color roja, y poco a poco su mente puede subir a la segunda, color anaranjada, etc... abriendo su mente y imaginacion con su respiracion... se puede desorallar este control de cuerpo y mente con mucha practica. Despues, amarillo en el estomogo, verde – el corazon, azul – la garganta, y morado – el tercer ojo aqui. Hay que concentrar fuerte con respiriacion hasta que llegan encima de sus cabezas en su corona con la luz blanca... Con practica... poco a poco... Bueno... empezamos a estirar...
Yoga is an ancient practice from India which is a country on the other side of the world, and was part of the Hindu religion centuries ago. But it is used in modern times for health and exercise in all parts of the world.... to stretch the body and mind. Remember that your concentration begins with the first chakra, red in color, and little by little your mind can move up to the second, orange color, etc. By opening your mind and clearing your imagination with your breathing, you can develop your mind/body control with a lot of practice. Afterwards comes yellow at the stomach, green for the heart, blue is the throat, and purple, the third eye. You must concentrate strongly

703

with your breathing until you arrive above your head at your crown with the white light, number seven.

Ceci begins to demonstrate and leads the yoga floor postures, which goes on for the next 20 minutes. To see these boys so quickly entranced in meditation and yoga truly indicates a desperate need for education and spiritual guidance in the orphan population. These boys are big candidates for the gang world. Several of the boys are very thin, and are clearly suffering from malnutrition and drug damage (resistol – glue sniffing). Vilma and the girls help put boys in the proper yoga positions.

Suddenly another boy walks in the room on crutches and sits in the corner. As she changes the music and puts on her glasses, she realizes that this crippled boy in the corner is Adan, the boy she had accompanied to his family home in Tocoa. She approaches him.

Ceci: Adan?

Adan: Hello Senora Cecilia. No puedo bailar. Hello Sra Cecilia. I can't dance.

Ceci: *Pausing and giving him a hug…..***OK Adan mas tarde hablamos. Pero se puedes participar ahora con el arte. OK? Give Adan a mat Angie.** Ok Adan.. we will talk later. But you can participate now with the art OK?

Adan appears willing to draw.

Ceci: OK Todo el mundo… ahora Vilma y las muchahcas van a distrubuir sus proprios carpetas de yoga… con marcadoras para pintar. Van a trabajar en parejas como yo les demostrare con Roxana. OK everybody… Now Vilma and the girls will distribute your own yoga mats, with markers so you can draw on them. You are going to work in partners like I will demonstrate with Roxana. *Ceci demonstrates outlining Roxana's body shape with black marker as she lies on her yoga mat.* **Y uno por uno van a dibujar los simbolos de las siete chakras con sus colores adentro el dibujo de su cuerpo en su proprio lugar. Repeto… las chakras son los siete centros de energia y glandulos en su cuerpo.** And one by one you are going to draw the symbols of the seven chakras

with your colors inside the outline of your body in the right spots. I repeat... the chakras are the seven centers of energy and glands in your body.

Ceci hangs her mat on the wall as a guide, and continues explaining as she walks around. Vilma keeps the markers coming, the girls help with the symbols.

Ceci lectures in Spanish walking around looking at the boys' work:

1. Primera Chakra – Color Rojo –Se llama MULADHARA chakra – - el baso de su espina. Representa el simbolo de un raiz – fundacion – la vida physica – energia primal. con colores de tierra rojo. Tambien quiere decirles que es energia de fuego impulsivo.

2. Segunda Chakra – Color Anaranjada – SVADHISTHANA chakra – Agua - Socializacion – La zona de reproducion – fertilidad – conexiones – atracion – relaciones, emociones, polaridades, sexualidad, cambio, movimiento - Simbolo – Yin / Yang sign

3. Tercera Chakra – Color Amarillo – MANIPURA chakra – Del umbligo hasta el plexis solar... con imagen de un triangulo puntrado abajo a la tierra – Poder, voluntad, nutricion, salud, presencia, fuerza...

4. Chakra Cuatro – Color Verde – ANAHATA chakra – Simbolo triangolos dobles – Representa amor, curar, compasion, generosidad, relacion, unidad, carino, rezar

5. Chakra Cinco – VISUDDHA chakra – Color Azul - Zona del cuello y la garganta – Con este simbolo OHM... un canto Buddhista para rezar por el mundo... Entonces esta chakra representa expression, creatividad, communicacion, vibracion, purificacion.

6. Chakra Seis – Color Morado – AJNA chakra – ojo tercero – Intuicion, visualizacion, imaginacion, y espiritualidad,

7.Chakra Siete – Color Lavender/Blanco –SAHASRARA chakra – corona - conexion con el universo, sabiduria, liberacion, understanding, enlightenment, etc…

Ceci: Entonces… por favor sigue pintando… Que bueno trabajo… que bonito… Muchachos… para mi, yoga es una practica para estimular mi mente, mi cuerpo, mi sanidad, y mi espirito. Con un mente fuerte, se puede controlar su vida. Entonces…desllenando la mente de toda la basura del dia para concentrar en su cuerpo y alma es medicinal… y yo queria compartir esta pequena parte de mi sabiduria de yoga y las chakras con uds para que se usa cuando lo necesita. Gracias por su atencion, su energia bonita, su arte, y su participacion. So.. please continue painting. What good work… how beautiful. Boys, for me yoga is a practice to stimulate my mind, my body, my health, and my spirit. With a strong mind, you can control your life. So… emptying the mind of all the daily garbage to concentrate on your body and soul is medicinal… and I would like to share this little part of my knowledge of yoga and the chakras with you so that you use it when you need it. Thank you for your attention, your beautiful energy, your art, and your participation.

The boys all respond with big thank yous and hugs and want to show Ceci and Vilma and the Director their artwork.

Ceci goes towards Adan, who is painting in the corner of the room. The director follows.

Ceci: Adan … que bonito su trabajo! Adan how beautiful your work is.

Adan: Gracias, me gusta dibujar. Thank you, I like to draw.

Director: Conoce este muchacho? Do you know this boy?

Ceci: Si, nos encontremos hace anos? Como estas Adan? Que paso con su pierna? Yes, we met each other yeas ago.. How are you Adan? What happened to your leg?

Adan: *Without shame.* **Fue un tiro de un watchie cuando estaba robando una casa.** It was a bullet from a watchman when I was robbing a house.

Ceci: Oh Adan porque? y en la misma pierna... segunda vez? Oh Adan why? And in the same leg the second time?

Adan: Desfortunatamente, si. Unfortunately yes.

Ceci: Y como llegaste aqui? And how did you arrive here?

Director: Adan ha venido y salido mucho aqui en la Casa de Ninos. Esta vez el llego medianoche con una policía que no quiso ponerle en el cárcel de nuevo. Adan has come and gone a lot here at the Casa de Ninos. This time he arrived in the middle of the night with a policeman who didn't want to put him in jail again.

Ceci: Oh Adan........Lo siento muchísimo. Yo se que has sufrido mucho. Y todavia tu prefieres la calle en vez de la casa de su mama? Oh Adan.... I am really sorry. I know you have suffered a lot. And still you prefer the street instead of your mother's house?

Adan: Si Ceci. La calle es mi hogar donde estoy libre. Yes Ceci... the street is my home, where I am free.

Director: Si, libre para romper la ley. Yes, free to break the law.

Adan: *He continues drawing.* **Y finalmente estas son sus hijas?** And finally, these are your daughters?

Ceci: Si, Roxana, Angie, y Jazmin...

Adan: No puede imaginar la suerte que tienen muchachas... no la olvenden. You are luckier than you can possibly imagine chicas. Don't forget it.

Ceci puts her arms around Adan for a big sincere hug, and as she pulls away with a tear, the Director replaces her embrace with a strong arm around him.

Ceci: You are too smart for this kind of life. Adan.. escúcheme por favor...se puede cambiar su vida si buscas adultos buenos que pueden ayudarte. Rezaremos para ti.

Adan...please listen to me.. you can change your life if you look for good adults who can help you. We will pray for you.

Adan: Si.... Gracias.... Si Dios Quiere. Yes thank you. God willing.

Angie: Dios lo quiere Adan. God wants it Adan.

Ceci: *Addressing the other boys.* **Quiero haligarles todos, por su buen trabajo. Es excellente. Se puede guindar las pinturas en la pared y tambien uslarlas para yoga. Buenas tardes, fue un placer.** I want to compliment you all for your great work. It is excellent. You can hang these paintings on the wall and also use them for yoga. Good afternoon. It was a pleasure.

Director: Gracias de nuevo por su ayuda hoy... Vuelvan cuando quieren por favor. Thank you again for your help today. Come back when you want please.

Ceci: Gracias tambien... Ciao.. *Ceci holds back tears.* **Come on girls...**

The director unlocks the gate and Ceci, Vilma, and the girls are liberated into the street, as all the boys look through the fence as they leave. They are trapped, stuck there, as the only other option is the street. Ceci looks at Vilma and her eyes load up with tears as they drive off.

Roxana: Mami, porque lloras? Mom, why are you crying?

Ceci: I don't know baby. Because it breaks my heart how many kids don't have parents that care about them. *Pause* **Adan has a mother but prefers the street. I feel badly that I can't help him. I just have to take you guys home with me where it's safe. It's hard to forget about the others... Dear God, I can't save every lost kid in the world.**

Jazmin: Really mom... You belong to us, and that's it, OK? We are enough, aren't we?

Ceci: Definitely enough. And I love you more than you know.

Angie: But it IS really very sad that these boys don't have moms or dads.

Ceci: But on a lighter note.... we are on our way to Desiree's pizza pool to meet Deni and Ale. *She turns up the music on the radio in Carlotta so she won't cry.*

Ceci: With time you will really understand how lucky you are. Maybe this was your destiny.   So you could help others.

329. Desiree's Private Pizza Pool Estate/Restaurant

Ceci, Vilma and children are arriving at a favorite swim spot in la Ceiba run by Desiree, an Italian tourist stuck in Ceiba with the clever vision of renting an estate with patio and pool as an authentic pizza restaurant. This is a favorite spot for birthday parties and a general kid/pool/ family solution to a hot afternoon. She meets up with Deni and Ale there.

Ceci: Ok girls... You were so helpful at the Casa de Ninos today, I am going to get extra pepperoni on two pizza grandes OK?

Desiree is there at the table holding one of her little baby pitbulls that she breeds. The girls are admiring the puppy.

Desiree: **Les gustan a mis peritos? Hay mas nuevecitos por alla...** Do you like my little puppies? There are more new ones over there.

She directs the curious and enthusiastic girls to the yard where the puppies are.

Desiree: **Entonces, Senoras... Como puedo servirles hoy?** So ladies, what can I serve you today?

Ceci: **Bueno... Dos pizzas grandes... uno de queso y el otro con extra pepperoni.. Y limonadas para todos... Vino tinto para mi... Gracias... y con mucho gratitud estamos aqui en su paraiso para ninos... Solo los Italianos saben hacer ambiente familiar en restaurantes...** Ok... Two large pizzas, one with cheese and the other with extra pepperoni. And lemonades for everybody. Red wine for me. Thank you, and with much gratitude we are here in your paradise Desiree... Only Italians know how to create good family ambiance in a restaurant.

Desiree: Ahh Gracias, y a su orden. Bueno... Me voy a ensenarles los perritos primero.. Ahh thank you... and at your service. But first I will show them the puppies. *She hurries off to monitor the show and tell of her Pitbull mom and puppies.*

Deni: Con cuidado por favor. Carefull please. **The mother is a pitbull... and protects her babies for sure.**

Ceci: Wow what a beautiful day... Thanks so much for helping me with the home schooling. You are doing a great job with the times tables. It's all about repetition, just like dance.

Deni: So you got the dance job at CBS? Yes - no?

Ceci: Yes.. and there is no studio so I have to build it.

Deni: Will they pay for it?

Ceci: I think so. I have to engineer the construction.... again. You know I have built five studios already in my life? And it has been traumatic leaving all of them. I even dream about them.

Deni: Uh huh... and so what about the girls?

Ceci: Well Roxana is doing OK at Bright Beginnings. So she will stay there. Angie and Jazz passed the entrance exam at CBS and will go in to the 4th grade together there and wear the famous CBS pink skirts.

Deni: I hope it works... It will be an adjustment for sure.

Ceci: Yes and I am charging myself up for it slowly. So what about Ale?

Deni: I just enrolled him in a summer kindergarten class that he really likes and makes him feel like a big brother to his classmates... while he is learning.

Ceci: Well that's really good news Deni. Amen que se sea... So be it.

Deni: He is happier there than he was in the Ceiba Special School.

Ceci: I don't know why they don't teach *everything* in bilingual schools at special ed speeds. I mean step by step, from A to C, instead of A to P on steroids. If the primary level is

substandard and rushed there is no foundation for more advanced material.

Deni: I see this in most of the bilingual schools in town where the teachers are there mainly because they speak English, and the programs are not tailored to uneducated families. So they move so fast through the basic studies that most students never quite grasp the concepts. At the elementary level, if your parents don't speak English, your chances of comprehension go way down.

Drinks arrive. The girls are in the pool with Ale.

Ceci: When you think about the fact that most of the population doesn't get educated beyond the 5th grade level, the chance of reading and writing, or learning a trade or critical thinking skills to survive economically in a digital world... is just so out of reach.

Deni: It's the constant reminder of being in the third world, with that huge gap between the classes. Girl.. we were born white in America. We got educated early on and had the guts to travel.

Ceci: Well I am not that secure financially... but I do know that I feel guilty about Honduran poverty all the time. You know my maternal grandparents are Spanish from Spain.

Deni: Yes well... Your grandparents' generation were not the conquistadores.

Ceci: No. You are right. They were immigrants who struggled to give my Mom a life in the USA in the twenties, where she eventually got a graduate degree.

Deni: Just be careful with your guilt and generosity because people like Karla will suck your white shame to the bone...

Ceci: Ok .. I have no case ... plucked by another gringa.

Deni: Just learn the lesson Ceci.

Ceci: Si Dios quiere. I am working on it. Thanks Deni.

330. La Ceiba Bilingual School – CBS - New Job

The following sequence of events takes place at the La Ceiba Bilingual school, which is a more humble private school, heavily populated with Honduran students Pre-K – 11. Honduran schools consider 12th grade as "collegio" if one continues their education.

This is presented as a montage of Ceci's four month employment at this school. In a musical montage, Ceci coordinates the construction of the dance studio, converting two joined classrooms, installing ballet bars and mirrors, and a place for her sound system. She will teach 35 classes a week, and mount a school wide Christmas show.

Ceci takes on weekly classes for mostly the elementary age students. Creating order is a challenge for Ceci as she is training more students who have never been in a dance class before. The younger children get Ceci's traditional obstacle course to introduce basic body movement and balance skills to little kids. They travel through, up down and over various hoops, blocks, sticks and tubes to gymnastic mats where they learn to somersault (with assistance) to the finish and then start over... laughing to the music all the way.

Three Christmas Queens for CBS show

Then we move to the ballet bar with older students, and Ceci's typical Ballet/ Jazz class with isolations port a bras, stretches, across the floor steps, and pieces of different dance styles. We see pieces of choreography being prepared for a Christmas show in which Roxana, Angie, and Jazmin will play the three queens. It is strange to watch children in their school uniforms dancing, but Ceci goes with whatever works.

Meanwhile, Jazmin and Angie are struggling with the adjustment to yet another school... a new population, different curriculums, different teachers. Jazmin avoids her stress by going to the nurse a lot. She has trouble sitting still. Angie is confused academically as she struggles in the rows of chair- desks packed in the overcrowded, hot classroom. She keeps trying. They are presented with the scientific method formula in science, which is never clearly explained and goes way over their heads. Ceci tries to grow sweet potatoes at home to illustrate that good soil produces a much more nutritious sweet potato, but it is a guessing game with regards to the use and concept of the formula. Clearly the educational approach is over the heads of fourth graders.

Spanish classwork at the 4th grade level is also the same as all the advanced classes above it. Ceci can't figure it out. Where is the step by step? They are breaking down two dozen categories of adjectives in Classical Spanish linguistics ... which crossover with similar definitions of each so as it is impossible to distinguish one from the other... and it becomes increasingly obvious that Angie and Jazmin don't understand the work. There is also constant teacher absence for pregnancy. So... Angie and Jazmin are failing Spanish. The classes are crowded. Everybody is doing the best they can. Jazmin has discipline problems... and she gets suspended for a day for rolling her eyes when a teacher refused her 3rd trip to the nurse. (Ceci doesn't discover/acknowledge that Jazmin has ADHD, despite her intelligence until she is in college in the USA).

713

331. La Ceiba Bilingual School – one month later

Ceci continues to teach dance and drama classes in factory line style. During her free class she paints hopscotches on the sidewalks.

One day, after the lights went out... again. (Typical electricity outages take place every other day) Ceci frantically loads batteries into her boom box to continue giving class in the dark. Everybody is sweating because there is no AC. Along with the humidity, it is the end of the day with her teenage group and they are working on a tribute to La Ceiba's annual Carnaval, for which Ceci has cut a soundtrack medley. Poco a poco the kids crowd in front of the mirror to hear the boom box and recreate the choreography they have been working on.

Ceci looks on and jumps in as needed to remind them of steps forgotten, but the basic structure is there. As they repeat it the second time, Angie and Jazmin enter with their report cards. The girls sit and watch, as Ceci shakes her head in disappointment to see what bad grades they are earning. She mutters to herself that "they are lost and being set up to fail and it is my fault for moving them so much".

Ceci makes a few comments to the group as the medley ends for the third time, complimenting them. They are all fighting over the hoola hoops and new music brings on the frantic whirling dervishes of crowded hoola hooping. Clearly they are all having a great time while Ceci stares at her children's report cards.

The bell rings, they all run, and Ceci is left alone in the studio with Angie and Jazmin. She picks up the studio and sweeps. The girls know that Ceci is upset with their grades, but she does not complain or reprimand them. She tells them to meet her by the car.... Suddenly the electricity returns.

Alone in the studio she speaks to the mirror internally.

Ceci: Mother Mary, my children must come first. *Long pause* I think this is it. The last time I will teach dance... my last dance studio...

the end of hours creating steps and ballets, searching and finding music… dealing with parents…. I can't do this anymore, and never

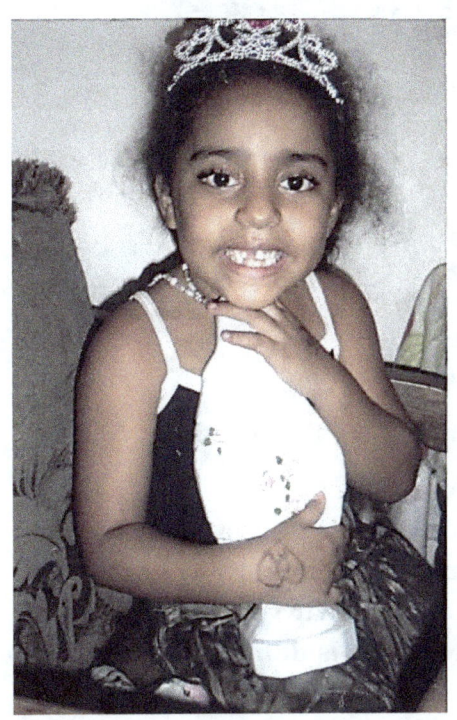

did I think this day would come… this moment when… just like in Chorus Line… when you realize… "What I did for love…" is over. It's now or never. I have to get those visas so I can get them the help they need academically and medically before it is too late. I don't know how to do it myself. And look at me…

I have lost weight, I am 63, nobody is going to hire a senior choreographer from nowhere again. It's time for me to go home and take care of my mom, right God? She and my Dad made all this artistic freedom possible in my life. It's time for me to give back. I have worked hard as an artist, a dancer, choreographer, director and producer… and teacher of many, many children and dancers in my day. But now it is time for my family. And these girls are my family. My art has lived well for a long time. I kiss it goodbye. Eso es todo.

Ceci puts on her lipstick and kisses the mirror thinking of her precious daughters. She packs up her music and boom box and says good bye to the studio…

332. Telephone Conversation with Louis

Ceci is seated on the beach at dusk watching the girls play at the shores edge. Her cell phone rings and she answers it. Tio Louis is calling from Italy. She is happy to hear from him.

Ceci: So tell me how is baby Goia?

Louis: She is fat and healthy and fine. Tell me about you and the girls.

Ceci: Well... the appointment at the embassy is next week and I am fine tuning the application again tomorrow. I now have an expatriate, American immigration lawyer preparing the application. He seems to know what he is doing. It will have to happen this time because I am unemployed and the girls are no longer enrolled in any school.

Louis: What happened with the last job?

Ceci: Mazapan ran out of money, and I took a job at another bilingual school with no special education. Then the girls started to fail there because the material was spinning around their heads too fast... And I was working too hard for too little money and getting burned out. So now I am just running on the hope that this number five visa attempt will be the one to change our lives. There it all is Louis.

Louis: I believe it's in your favor this time. Keep showing them what you are doing for the girls. You mustn't give up.

Ceci: I hope so Louis. Again, I want to thank you so much for helping us.

Louis: I wish I could do more.

Ceci: You have done plenty.

Louis: No, I mislead you romantically, when I had a previous relationship.

Ceci: I think that happens to a lot of people who travel in the tropics.

Louis: Ceci, I clearly care about you and the girls, and forgive me please for not being able to be the father they really want and need.

Ceci: It's OK, because I *can do* both mom and dad. Here come the girls… Talk to Tio Louis…

On speaker phone the girls all babble at once about everything, including their sand castle in Italy and how much they want to come back and see him one day. This causes Ceci to drop a tear or two, which she quickly wipes away as an unrealistic emotion, while telling the girls to thank Tio Lou for supporting us in La Ceiba. They do so, and Ceci takes the phone as they run back to the shoreline sunset.

Ceci: The sunset is glorious, and we wish you could come.

Louis: I do too Ceci. Again I want to apologize.

Ceci: Remember Louis that we can be siblings forever… maybe longer than we could have been mates. And you have made the rescue of these children possible, and for that I will never forget you, nor will the girls. You are their fairy God father, and always will be.

Louis: Thank you Ceci… I will be thinking of you next week when you go to the embassy. Let me know right away will you?

Ceci: Yes Louis.. I will. Thanks for calling…

Ceci hangs up the phone and falls back into the sand now being lit up by a full moon. She can hear the waves and the sound of the girls laughing as they dance in and out of the moving shoreline. Life is not perfect, but it's pretty good for now.

333. <u>One week before #5 Visa attempt – Homeschooling</u>

There is one week before the next embassy appointment in Tegucigalpa. The girls are again with Deni May in homeschool reciting times tables. Ceci returns from picking up Roxana from Bright Beginnings.

Th phone rings. It is Ceci's mom in Virginia calling to wish her luck on the next visa attempt. Mom tells Ceci to be strong and realize that this request is the legitimate culmination of all the preceding ones. Ceci pretends to be confident in her visa acceptance chances this time... She tells her mom that she will be there soon to take care of her... that the girls love her and to hang on. She gets off the phone depressed. Vilma goes to tell Deni... They come to comfort

her. Clearly the built-up stress of so many visa rejections, the squeezing of their lives in La Ceiba, the medical, and educational needs... and the critical nature of Ceci's Mom's mental and physical health .... constantly hovers in her immediate concern.

Vilma suggests they go to the beach to see Dona Eva in Corozal. Her daughters can braid the girls' hair. Then they can all hang out and eat at Stella's Restaurant.

Vilma: Vamos a Corozal a visitar Dona Eva... Ceci... se puede pedir la bendicion de ella antes de ir... Y las muchachas pueden nadar, y disfrutar en la playa. Let's go to Corozal to visit Dona Eva. Ceci.. you could ask for her blessing before going to Teguz, and the girls can swim and play on the beach.

Deni: Vilma's right... You need a nature break before throwing yourself into the embassy routine again. Go to the beach. Go see your bruja. Eat fish and have a great day.

Ceci: You and Ale can come with us then...

Deni: No, it's late in the day and he has school tomorrow and he really likes being a big brother with his kinder classmates. It makes

him feel useful you know. He needs to get as much of those kudos as possible. You go.

Ceci: Yes, I do get it.

Vilma: Entonces – nos vamos? Preparo? So are we going? Should I prepare?

Ceci: OK.. Porque no? Tienen razon. Vamos a la playa chicas! Why not? You are right.. Let's go to the beach ladies!

The girls cheer jumping up and down. This will be the last time they see the Honduran Garifuna village. So much of this culture is in their blood.

334. Driving through Corozal

Driving the coast road, Ceci, Vilma and the girls arrive at the dirt road that cuts off to Corozal. All three take turns sitting on Ceci's lap to steer the car. Ceci takes over when they get to the Garifuna streets of Corozal. They pass palapa huts interlaced with colorful, cement, sun baked homes, children playing soccer in the streets, old black women sweeping their front walks, hanging laundry, women carrying banana and coco bread, tabla de coco, and aceite de coco in baskets on their heads. Upon arriving at Stella's restaurant, they go to the beach where Ceci sees Eva's daughters and arranges for them to braid the girls' hair. Eva passes by with goods on her head. Ceci runs down to the water's edge to greet and hug her. Ceci truly loves Eva. They talk, sitting with their feet in the water and then return to the shade of the hair salon tree. Eva says something to her daughters in Garifuna and she hugs the girls.

335. Stella's Restaurant – Arrangements with Eva

Eva: You get bigger and bigger every time I see you. I see your mother is feeding you right. Que bonitas son ellas…! *Addressing Ceci and Vilma* Mira.. Vengan a verme con ellas cuando terminan y se puede pedir a Stella para mandar la comida por mi casa, porque es tarde ahora. Yo voy a preparar mi altar y trabajamos a las 7pm cuando baja el sol… OK? How beautiful they are! Look… come to see me with the girls when you finish with their hair and you can ask Stella to send the food to my house… because it is late now. I will prepare my altar and we work at 7pm when the sun goes down. OK?

Ceci: **Perfecto.. Gracias Eva.** *She discreetly tucks 500lps into Eva's hand.* **Hasta luego.**

Ceci goes to the bar to have a beer and chat with Stella and order food for everybody to be sent over to Eva's. The girls are having their hair braided by several girls. Garifuna fishermen come in from the ocean after spending the day on their wooden boats. Boys play soccer barefoot in the sand. There are local Honduran tourists

sunning on the beach. Young girls sell sea shells, mothers nurse their babies and sell food… Old ladies sit together. There is radio music all round with the background of live Garifuna drums.

A boy with a drum appears on the beach in front of the hair salon tree. Angie and Jazmin get excited and join the drummers after finishing their braids. Ceci pays the hairdressers who will also bring the food to their momma Eva's house, and they finish up with Roxana. We see that both Angie and Jazmin have rhythm in their blood as they dance to the young Garifuna drummers. The sun begins to set. They all parade down the beach towards a bon fire in front of Eva's beach house. The drumming continues as Eva prepares the indoor altar with candles, tobaccos, and offerings of fruit and drink. Eva's daughters arrive with three huge, banana leaf platters of food on their heads… Fried fish, platanos, rice, beans, salad… all presented on the buffet altar. It is an abundant and friendly atmosphere. Everybody eats as the official ceremonial drumming begins.

336. Eva's Ceremony and Trance – Final session - Maria Lionza

Ceci has ordered a bottle of guiffity for Dona Eva, who pours shots for Ceci and herself. The drum circle outside grows with the fire and the darkness of sunset. Eva begins to chant. The girls dance with Eva's daughters to the vibrant drum beats. Ceci and Vilma watch.

Suddenly Eva begins to shake and vibrate ever so dramatically... like an electric current was streaming through her body. She withstands the intensity of this force. The drums stop. There is silence. Eva begins to speak in Garifuna and it is her late husband, Melvin, the drum maker, coming through. Eva's daughters translate as Eva's voice has changed.

Eva and the spirit of Eva's late husband, Melvin: Welcome to our home again gringa! Our people appreciate your open heart which can see beyond colors of the skin. You are blessed ... And your beautiful daughters are blessed... by the spirits of our Garifuna community, and those of the girls' Afro Cuban maternal blood line from I believe the Grandfather.

Ceci: Yes that's right... Afro Cuban on the Grandfather's side.

Spirit of Melvin: Elegba will open their roads. Yemaya will nurture their health.. and there are Mayan ancestors on the maternal Grandmother's side which give them an ancient, strong, and mystical tenacity for survival... Then there are the native warriors from Honduras on their fathers side... natives from Guerero where his blood originates... I am getting many spirits who wish to speak... and who is this white woman from Sud America?

Ceci: Oh Dios Mio.. Maybe it's Maria Lionza from Venezuela!!

Spirit of Melvin: Yes!! Hola mi hija she says... And also there is an Indian with many feathers...

Ceci: Tamanaco!!

Spirit of Melvin: Yes! Tamanaco dice que el siempre esta contigo para protegerse... con un ojo en las ninas. Pero esa Reina quiere hablar contigo primero. Tamanaco says that he is always with you to protect you... with an eye on the girls. But this queen wants to speak to you first.

Ceci: I can't believe this is happening!!

Eva begins to tremble and "the channel" changes.

Spirit of Maria Lionza: Soy yo Cecilia – tu madrina Maria Lionza. Recuerdas cuando te corone? Quiero decirte que fue yo que arrelgo su primero encuentro con las ninas en la calle en frente del hospital. Recuerdas las mariposas eso dia en la calle? Fue yo Cecilia. Recordabas que tu me dijiste que en cualquier momento que yo quisiera re-encarnarme ... que yo podria usar su cuerpo... It's me Cecilia. Your Godmother, Maria Lionza. Remember when I crowned you? I want to tell you that it was me who arranged your first encounter with the girls in the street in front of the hospital. Remember the butterflies that day in the street? That was me Cecilia. Do you remember that you told me that in whatever moment that I wanted to reincarnate that I could use your body?

Ceci: Oh my God! Si yo recuerdo. Yes I remember!!

Spirit of Maria: Y en vez de sembrar mi alma en su vientre para reencarnarme... decidi en eso momento el dia de Carnaval con Dios a cambiar la opcion de su promesa cuando viste las ninas casi muerto en esa caja. Fue un momento sagrado para poner la vida de estas tres ninas en sus manos. Recuerden todas esas mariposas? And instead of seeding my soul in your womb, I decided with God in that moment on that Carnaval day, when you saw the girls almost dead there in the box... that I decided to change the option of your promise. It was a sacred moment to put the lives of these three girls in your hands. Remember all those butterflies?

Ceci: Oh mi madrina Maria... ud. toca mi corazon. Oh Godmother Maria... you touch my heart. *Ceci pauses for a moment to collect herself.* **This is unbelievable. Spirit is every where all the time... You see that girls? Even in butterflies. Si, yo recuerdo cuando me dijo que ud. me prometio aparecer como una**

mariposa. Yes, I remember when you promised me that you would appear to me in the form of a butterfly.

Spirit of Maria: Y por fin... aqui y ahora te digo que tienes el apoyo de todo lo que necesitas para sus visas. And finally... here and now I tell you that you have the support and all that you need to get your visas.

Ceci: Seria un milagro. It would be a miracle.

Spirit of Maria: A causa de su tenacidad has conseguido la oportunidad llegar en los manos de una mujer Americana alla en las oficinas de la embajada que esta pendiente de su caso. Creo que ella es buena - una rubia creo yo. No estoy seguro.. puede ser... Because of your tenacity you have found the opportunity to arrive in the hands of an American woman there in the embassy office who is aware of your situation. I believe that she is good.. A blond I believe. Not sure... maybe...

Eva, still embodying the spirit of Maria Lionza, takes another puff of her cigar.

Ceci: Oh Maria, reina sagrada. Un monton de gracias. Es increible, que despues anos ud. todavia me recuerda. Siempre esta en mi corazon y mi altar. *Ceci is overwhelmed.* **She could be talking about Catherine Ventura maybe. Did you hear that girls? I hope she's right.** Oh Maria, sacred queen .... I thank you. It is incredible that after all these years you still remember me. You are always in my heart and my altar.

Maria blesses Ceci and the girls with water, making the sign of the cross on their foreheads. And then she leaves, as the spirit of Eva's husband returns.

Spirit of Maria: Si, hija... siempre te recuerdo. Nuestras corazones son similares. Y su protector Tamanaco también todavía te guarda. En el nombre de Dios Poderoso, el hijo, y el espirtu santo te bendigo con toda la fuerza del espiritu sagrado. Adios mi hija. Soy siempre tu madrina. Siempre pendiente. Si, daughter... I always remember you. Our hearts are similar. And your protector Tamanco also still watches over you. In the name of God the powerful, his son, and the holy spirit, I bless you with all of the strength of the sacred spirit. Goodbye my hija. I am forever your madrina. Always vigilant.

With a puff of her cigar, Eva then shifts back into the body of her late husband, Melvin.

Spirit of Melvin : Bueno – aqui estoy de nuevo. Y otra cosa gringa Cecilia. Yo veo un gringo maduro, musico, abogado? Ok … here I am again. And another thing gringa Cecilia. I see a mature gringo, musician, lawyer?

Ceci: You mean Peter?

Melvin: Si Sra. *Pause* **Algo con los papeles legales para ti y las ninas.** Something with legal papers for you and the girls.

Ceci: Oh yes… That's Peter. He is writing the application. El escribe con palabras lógicos y elegantes. He writes with logical and elegant words.

Melvin: Si.. El va a abrir sus caminos, y también hay otro hombre, blanco, medico, que vive lejos que te ayudara. Yes . He will open your roads. And also there is another white man, doctor, who lives far who will help you.

Ceci: Tio Lou of course. He is helping me.

Melvin: El ama mucho a las ninas y quiere ayudar mas, pero vive lejos. Yes he loves the girls very much and wants to help more, but he lives far.

Ceci: Yes that's Tio Lou, and he sends money for them. El manda dinero.

Melvin: Gringa tu eres bien bendecida con todos estes ángeles que están contigo. Vaya con Dios y los futuros de estas ninas preciosas. Gringa you are well blessed with all these angels who are with you. Go with God and the futures of these precious girls.

Ceci: Oh thank you so much for this opportunity to hear all this and speak with my madrina from Venezuela. I had no idea I would speak to her. I don't think the girls understand.

Spirit of Eva's husband: It's OK mi hija… They do not understand, but some day they will. You and these girls are

blessed. Now let me speak to my own beautiful children whom I love and miss oh so dearly. Toquen los tambores por favor! Play the drums please!!!

The drums start again as people begin to line up for their healings with Eva. Ceci thanks Eva's daughter, and they make their way out to the beach with the full moon. Ceci washes the faces of her daughters with the ocean water, thanking God and all the spirits and ancestors for making this experience possible.

337. Peter helps with final Visa Application #5

Ceci is in Peter's office. The girls are playing with Jazzlyn and Flor in the garden. Ceci is nervous. Peter comes in with a bottle of rum and two glasses. It is the day before the fifth appointment at the embassy.

Peter: Ok Ceci... sit down.. relax... I got this OK? I did the tweeking. You are going to love it. Here, drink this first.

Ceci: I can't relax about this Peter.

Peter: OK. Let me talk... It was exactly two years ago this week since you last filed... since then you have added another two full years to the five preceding years during which you cared for them under your roof. That makes a total of seven years that you have had some kind of formal live in custody.   So listen....

He reads. "Cecilia has proven, beyond a shadow of a doubt that she has saved and improved the lives of these three sisters. Their special educational needs are not being met here in La Ceiba without exorbitant private school tuition costs that she can't afford. Hence... in the USA there is a free public school system within walking distance of Ceci's mother's home in Richmond, Virginia, where the girls would get special ed support and accommodations to proceed with their educational needs.

Because of the medical and psychological issues presented by both Angie and her blindness, and Roxana with her intellectual disability, they need medical and therapeutic resources, which are all available in her home town. Ceci is meant to inherit this home some day which will eventually be inherited by the children to insure their constant security."

Ceci: Wow... Sounds so real and undeniable... And what a package Peter... all these chapters. It is a manuscript... And one for each child. How could they say no again?

Peter: A declaration of freedom Ceil... because, if you think that Honduran immigration into the US is difficult now in 2012 with the imminent conservative majority about to take over... just wait until it is totally illegal and the embassies are really closed. There will be hundreds of thousands of Latinos walking to the border with the hopes they can just run across. This is the right time for you guys. So have another drink of this fine Honduran rum, and let's celebrate your inevitable visa #5 success. OK? *Ceci takes the manuscript, hugs it, kisses it... and toasts Peter.*

Ceci: Thank you Peter. You have truly given me hope.

338. The day before the 5th Visa Attempt – AM at the house

Ceci wakes up early after a sleepless night, makes her coffee, and wanders into the girls' room to watch them sleep for a while. Then she goes out into the garden and sits on the swings looking at the fruit trees around her. She goes back in to check her email. There is an urgent email from Peter. She is shocked.

Ceci: What? *She mutters out loud as she reads.*

USCIS will close its field office in Tegucigalpa, Honduras, on Thursday, June 20, 2013. The USCIS Field Office in San Salvador, El Salvador, will assume Tegucigalpa's former jurisdiction (Costa Rica, Honduras, and Nicaragua), and the U.S Department of State (DOS) Embassy in Tegucigalpa will assume responsibility for certain requests. Please visit for more information.

Ceci *scrambles to write....and reads out loud as she goes...*

From: Cecilia Gruessing [mailto:sanghita5@yahoo.com]
Sent: Friday, May 31, 2013 4:20 PM
To: USCIS, Honduras
Subject: For Ms. Ventura

Ms. Ventura I got word from my lawyer today about the US embassy in Tegucigalpa closing. I am planning to come for my 5th appointment for visas for my three Honduran daughters tomorrow. Exactly 2 years ago today, after getting the Tutora custody status for myself with the girls, I have waited until applying again. This is my 5th visa attempt.

I am hoping you will be open tomorrow and again willing to hear our continued and revised plea for visas to bring these three sisters, with their disabilities to the home of my aging mother in Richmond, Va. There they can get medical attention and go to good schools. We will be there tomorrow. I am praying you will be open, because we are on our way and it is now or never.

Thank you,
Ceil Gruessing, La Ceiba.

Ceci: Send!!!

Ceci spins around on her desk chair in time to catch all three of the girls in a big hug.

Roxana: Mom who are you talking to?

Ceci: I am talking to the computer and those people in the embassy who are controlling our lives... And they better be ready for me this time because you all know how many times we have done this... and we are ready for the right answer this time.

Jazmin: But Mom you can't fall down in the embassy this time.

Ceci: Well Peter says that our chances are way better now. So we are going to look fabulous tomorrow in Grandma's best dresses and get up early and go to the airport.

Angie: And Mom you better take your belly medicine so you don't get sick on the plane.

Ceci: Good idea Angie… Oh I love you all so much, and we are so ready for a miracle.

Jazmin: So let's go by your altar and pray mom.

Ceci: Now that's a good idea… *They go out to the porch balcony where Ceci has a garden and an altar and a hammock. They kneel down.*

Angie: Mom I'll go first OK…. Dear God… Please give us the visas so we can go take care of Grandma in her house and she can live with us, instead of being alone in some old people's home. Right mom?

Ceci: Right baby.

Jazmin: And I really want to go to Disneyland.

Roxana: And I pray that I can find an easy school.

Ceci: I want a school that understands you.

Angie: And helps me with my bad eyes.

All: Si Mama!!!

Ceci: OK … repeat after me..

Ceci: *Ceci starts a beat where she calls out a phrase and the girls repeat*

Deme la fuerza…….Deme la suerte… Give me the strength, give me the luck

Deme courage…. para separar fuerte. Give me the courage to stand up strong.

Saber lo que soy….. Saber lo que quiero. To know who I am.. To know what I want

a vivir libre…….. Seguro, yo vengo!!. To live freely… For sure I am coming.

Es la hora dear God ….. por una otra vida. It's the hour dear God, for another life.

Estamos muy lista…volar enseguida! We are so ready to fly right away!

They all applaud and laugh at their little song and dance. They all join Ceci on her bed.

Jazmin: But mom, what if all those white people at the embassy really don't like us.

Angie: Do you think they don't want us because I can't see?

Roxana: What if they make me take a test?

Ceci: No no, that has nothing to do with visas. Girls girls … escuchame! I want you to remember. You are good girls. You have good hearts… You will help other people some day. People help you and you help others. You try to learn as much as you can, to be curious and go after something you think you can do well…But all because you are giving – that is an important reason for living. *She continues holding them close.*

And you all have contributions to make in the USA. Everybody you know, see, and have ever met… are all trying as hard as possible to survive and do the right thing. They all were innocent babies once, with Moms… They grew up with and without disabilities, money, education, or moral direction… and they all are trying to make a life for themselves and a family somewhere in the world. This is the big family of man that we are part of. And my family is in Virginia… my precious Mom. I keep saying…. Just like a plant leans towards the sun, I keep wanting to go home. And you are my daughters and you will come home with me to Grandma's house. So tomorrow we go to Tegucigalpa… to get our visas. And te digo… DIOS QUIERE que logramos estas visas… para cuidar mi madre, y para sembrar sus futuros… Entienden mis vidas? And I tell you GOD WANTS us to get these visas. To take care of my mother and to begin your futures. Do you understand?

Roxana: Si mami…

Ceci: Entonces, vamos a esperar que la embajada estuviera abierta manana… Now we are going to hope that the embassy is open tomorrow.

Girls: Si Dios Quiere…

Ceci: Repeto.…Si, senoritas… I know that DIOS QUIERE!!!
I think I need a nap! Give me a moment in the hammock please.
*Ceci takes the opportunity to escape in her porch hammock
while the girls play in the back yard.*

339. <u>Tegucigalpa American Embassy – Visa Attempt # 5</u>

*Skipping all the unpleasantries of the airplane ride from La Ceiba
to Tegucigalpa, we pick up as Ceci and the girls get out of a taxi at
the end of the line of hundreds of applicants waiting to get into the
American Embassy. The four of them are wearing Grandma's look
a like dresses, all made of the same fabric. Ceci carries a brief case
with which she fumbles over and over with Peter's latest rendition
of her petition for the girls' visas. They inch forward in the hot sun.
Ceci fans herself and the children, watering them constantly as she
eavesdrops on everybody's stories in front and in back of them on
the line. They work their way up to the "phone hotel" where you
leave your cell phone until you get out of the building. Then into
security, off with the shoes, everything on the conveyer belt. Check
the papers, the appointment, and then into the lobby, when.…. Ceci
sees:*

*Mellissa Calix, who was the IHNFA administrator who came to
investigate Ceci's involvement with the girls when they were with
Adila years ago. With her pejorative gaze Melissa recognizes Ceci
and the girls and approaches her.*

Melissa: **Dios Mio… Que grandes estan las ninas. Mucho ha
pasado desde nuestra ultima reunion.** My God.. How big the girls
are. A lot has happened since our last meeting.

Ceci: **Si, ellas han crecido mucho. Como esta Sra Calix?** Yes,
they have grown a lot. How are you Sra. Calix?

Melissa: **Estoy bien. Trabajo aqui ahora… Y que estan
hacienda en la embajada?** I am well. I work here now. And what
are you doing in the embassy?

Ceci: **Buscando visas para volver a mi pais con mis hijas.
Ahora tengo papeles de Tutora para ellas.** Applying for visas to

return to my country with the girls. Now I have Tutora papers for them.

Melissa: Interesante... Puedo verlos? Interesting. Can I see them?

Ceci pulls out her custody papers which are laminated.

Meissa: Sra Diaz no se permite laminar papeles formales como estos! Sra. Diaz laminating formal papers is forbidden like this....!

Silence. Ceci panics.

Ceci: No sabia eso... Pero son validos Sra. I did not know that. But they are valid Sra.

Melissa: Senora Cecilia , ud. sabe que necesita adoptar las ninas para lograr visas. Mira... Busquen su lugar en la cola y yo entrigo estes papeles. Senora Cecilia, you know you must adopt the girls to get visas. Look. Find yourself a place in the line and I will deliver these papers.

Ceci: Disculpa Sra... estos son mis papeles que son para mi cita con Catherine Ventura. Demelos por favor? Excuse me Sra. These are my papers and they are for my appointment with Catherine Ventura. Give them to me please.

In shock, Ms. Calix returns the Tutora Custody laminated original copies to Ceci. She truly has no jurisdiction over these papers. Ceci continues in English.

Ceci: Thank you. If you don't mind we'll just wait our turn.

Ceci turns abruptly and leaves Ms. Calix with her mouth open.

Ceci then goes to the cashier to pay more fee money for three applications, as it goes up every year. Then they get in the musical chair line. The girls are fidgety and nervous and can't sit still. Ceci watches people entering and exiting the small alcove booths to learn their fate. Some leave ecstatic, others joyous, some in tears, stunned, crying, violently mad, defeated, proud, indignant, paralyzed, thrilled etc. It wrenches one's soul to see the power of the American embassy changing the course of human lives every day.

Finally, their names are called…… Iraheta Rojas!

Ceci fumbles with her brief case and awkwardly shuffles all the girls up to window number 9 which has a small shelf and is way too high for the girls. The blinds open suddenly and there is the same young male agent Ceci always has.

Agent: Hello Ms. Diaz… What can we do for you today?

Ceci: Here is my latest application within the two year time frame to try again.

Agent: Yes, as a matter of fact we have been expecting you.

Ceci: Well that's a relief. I'm glad because I thought you might be closed before I got here.

Agent: No, we are honoring previously made appointments, and not making any more…. So you are OK… Meanwhile whom do we have here today? Roxana? Angie? And Angela?

Jazmin: Yes sir, But I'm Jazmin.. Angela Jazmin.

Agent: Oh, OK.

Ceci: We don't want people to mix up Angie and Angela…

The girls have all curtsied and are looking up at the guy behind the glass … smiling as hard as they can… Ceci is standing there like a stage mother with a nervous smile.

Agent: Yes so you all wait right here and I'll be right back.

Ceci: And excuse me… is Ms. Ventura here?

Agent: Just wait right here OK?

The blinds close. They all four start buzzing like over-zapped bees. Ceci whispers loudly….

Ceci: So let's just pray real hard and squeeze everything for the moment to HOPE THAT MS. CATHERINE VENTURA is in IN THE HOUSE TODAY!!!

ALL: Yes.. **CATHERINE VENTURA** – in the house!
Whispering loudly….

The agent reappears.

Agent: Ms. Diaz, If you will take the girls to the far corner of the room where there is a hallway with seats, someone will call their names again and help you there.

Ceci: OK? Thank you? Someone will help me?

He smiles and slams the blinds closed. The policewoman guides them to the corner dispatch for the next ride in immigration. She is the same policewoman that Ceci sees every time she was escorted out of the building in the past.

Ceci: Hola… Wish me luck this time, so I won't be needing your exit services.

Police lady: I have a feeling this is your lucky day… How many times have you applied?

Ceci: Number five.

Police lady: You got this lady.

They sit and wait, heads against the wall. The girls are restless. Ceci continues to remain positive despite the dramatic parade of the rejections and the acceptances. After what seems like hours, the police lady calls out their names:

Police Lady: Iraheta Rojas!

340. <u>The moment of truth – with Catherine Ventura</u>

And they all jump up to follow her down the hallway to a door leading into a small cave like seating area bordered by a big window covered by more blinds. Everybody finds a seat and stares at the window. Suddenly the blinds go up and there, in the flesh is a blond woman in her thirties, smiling and greeting Ceci and the girls.

Ms. Ventura: Ms. Diaz and girls… My name is Catherine Ventura… I am so happy to meet you.

Ceci: *Dropping her hands and head on the counter in front of the glass window...* Hallelujah! Prayers answered... Did you get my email last night? I was so worried you would be closed.

Ms. Ventura: Yes I did, and did you get mine this morning?

Ceci; No, we have been travelling since early this morning.

Ms. Ventura: Well, here is a copy of the email I sent you... just to calm you down a little.

Ms. Ventura hands Ceci a copy of the following email through the crack in the window:

From: "USCIS, Honduras" Honduras.USCIS@uscis.dhs.gov
To: Cecilia Gruessing sanghita5@yahoo.com
Sent: Friday, May 31, 2013 5:35 PM
Subject: RE: Ms. Ventura
Dear Ms. Gruessing,

Please do not worry. I approved all three applications today. You and the girls are fine. Our office will send you the approval notices on Monday and refer the cases directly to the U.S. Consulate, requesting expedited handling. The Consulate will retain all your original documents until the girls come for their immigrant visa interviews. Then they will return all originals to you. Please contact us if you have any other questions or concerns. Enjoy your weekend and again, thank you for your patience throughout this difficult process. <u>You have forever changed the lives of your daughters and this is the true meaning of being a mother.</u> All the best to you and your family.

Regards,

Catherine Ventura

Ceci: *In astonishment after reading the letter, Ceci's eyes start to water, her mouth open, with the girls reading over her shoulder. She is speechless.*

Angie: What mommy?

Ceci: Does that mean?

Ms. Ventura: Yes it does…

Ceci: Girls… Yes ,… This is it! We have the visas! *The girls start jumping up and down…*

Angie: We're going to see Grandma, and maybe Disneyland, and American pizza and hamburgers.

Ceci: Ok tranquila! We will party later. Ms. Ventura, thank you so much. This is the day the future has shifted for these three little girls and my mother too. We all thank you and I will prove that you made the right decision. God bless you for doing this.

Ms. Ventura: Ms. Diaz… You deserve this… so much so that what we have done here today for you is unprecedented based on your custodial status. But this last application was written with even more heart, soul, and solid proof that only you are the key to a better life for these three girls. Ms. Diaz, your tenacity and noted professional contributions to the La Ceiba Cultural community over the past ten years strongly demonstrate the stability you will be able to give them in the USA as your mother country. I salute you for your bravery in the face of constant adversity, and your compassion for these children. Not many blood mothers can do for their children what you have done for these three sisters.

Please sign here.

Ceci: *With trembling hand, signs the documents…The girls are silent with big eyes.* Oh thank you so much. Thank you for understanding. So I sign here and that's it… Then what?

Ms. Ventura licks the seal on a big envelope full of documents and slides it to Ceci.

Ms. Ventura: You will guard this with your life and take this sealed and unopened package of papers to the immigration officer when you land in the USA.

She then stamps papers that go in their Honduran Passports…

Ms. Ventura: These are their visas and they stay in their passports... Now you must pass the TB test and medical review, and the interview at immigration, and you are good. This will get you across the border, but this envelope will get you through immigration.

Ceci: And I am still mystified about the process of getting their citizenship.

Ms. Ventura: After you get there you will get them Social Security numbers, and hopefully you can adopt them in the USA since you will have had them under your custody for so long. I don't think you will have an age problem there. With the adoption you can get them foreign born US birth certificates, and THEN, with that paper you apply for an American Passport, which gives them citizenship. Your journey is not finished Ms. Diaz.... But the biggest river, you have crossed today. You are free to go... and cross any border now.

Ceci: Whenever we want?

Ms. Ventura: Yes, God Bless You!

The girls kiss the window. Ceci stands up and dances around the little room... arms wide open .. she bows to the window.

Ceci: Thank you, Ms. Ventura. You have answered a ten year prayer.

Ms. Ventura: You worked for it. Good luck girls. You have no idea how much your life will change.

Ceci: Say God bless you babies!

Girls: God blesses you!

Ceci: Say Gracias!

Girls: Gracias! *Angie kisses the window.*

The blinds go down with Ms. Ventura's angelic smile. Ceci's mouth drops open, and the tears of joy flow. She looks at the girls who are confused.

Angie: So is this really real mom? Did we win?

Jazmin: Yes we won! We got the visas! We are going to America

Roxana: We will see Grandma again!

Ceci: Come let's go girls... I can't believe this day has come.

The same police lady who always ushered Ceci out of the building when she was devastated with previous rejections, has overheard the meeting. She now ushers her out with a smile. She helps Ceci, who can't stop crying in disbelief, to reclaim her phone and get a cab. As she helps the girls into the car she says....

Police lady: I always knew that one day you would win. I can see all the love, and what you have done for these children over the years. We all need to be with family and now, God wants you to go home. Good luck to you and your beautiful girls... God Bless you and your mother for helping these girls.

Ceci: Thank you officer. *She shouts to the sky.* Thank you God. Thank you Mom and Dad... Thank you my beautiful bambinas. I have seen the light!!! *She laughs through her tears.*

When she gets out on the street and retrieves her phone she calls Peter immediately.

Ceci: *On the phone juggling the girls as she hails a taxi.* Peter... We did it! Yes. Catherine Ventura kept her word. And it was your brilliant formal proposal that made it work. Yes! Thank you Peter. You are an angel in disguise. Bravo... OK.. Bye!!

341. <u>Musical montage – garage sale, give aways, donations</u>

At Ceci's house, limbo has shifted to movement in this musical montage of unloading possessions. She boxes and ships lots of personal items along with books and CDs. The garage sale did not produce much cash, so Ceci moves furniture and clothing and costumes to the Casa de Ninos, the SOS, and David Ashby's new "Hogar" orphanage, Helping Honduras Kids. We give all our children's books to Deni May. Ceci's mother's beautiful hand made dresses go to Jazzlyn. A shady looking guy comes to buy Carlotta and pay for her and drive her away. All this is emotionally difficult *for the girls. Then a car comes to carry Vilma and her donation of yards of fabric, the sewing machine, and lots of clothing. This is difficult as Vilma believed that she would move to the USA and be part of the family as a caretaker. Ceci gives her $1000 in Lempiras. The goodbye is heartbreaking for Ceci too... as Vilma was her co-madre and co-worker.*

The neighborhood goodbyes are short and sad. Roxana cries as the house gets more and more empty. The memories run deep. Change is difficult for those who have no control over their future. Deni May and Ale show up for final goodbyes.

342. Final goodbye ride around La Ceiba

Deni takes Ceci and the girls for a final ride in her pick up truck past all the memorable places: The zona viva, the beach, the schools, the downtown area, the mall, the river. It is difficult for everyone, but necessary.... As Ceci has no idea if or when they will ever return to La Ceiba. The taxi van comes. They load up lots of suitcases, say their goodbyes to Ale and Deni... and kiss La Ceiba goodbye. This is difficult, as Deni was Ceci's closest ally in the struggle.

343. Tegucigalpa Hotel – waiting for TB shots

The scene shifts to Tegucigalpa where they are getting TB shots for which they must wait three days for results. The girls are watching Spanish cartoons on TV in a Tegucigalpa hotel. Their luggage is stacked in a corner. Ceci then goes to the window and gazes down into the city street with all its urban chaos.

Ceci: *Thinking out loud as a voiceover.* Honduras is a beautiful country. What happened to the Maya and the indigenous who lived off this fertile land and cultivated its beauty? Why did they disappear? My children are leaving their homeland because there is no opportunity for them here... insufficient special education... no services for their specific medical needs, no work, no income, no future .... and yet history begs to understand the mystery of why the Maya left this country suddenly, as Latinos are leaving their patrias. Historical theory blames drought and depleted soil conditions with over population….an inability to provide for the masses. This generation is stuck in time, between the ideologies of nature and technology…. To be on or off the grid. So this Latino exodus is exactly the same… drought, no work, poverty, no social or medical services, gang violence, bad water, and substandard education. It all boils down to economic, educational, and managerial deterioration… when the administrators see the end coming and selfishly get out with the goods, before the whole thing collapses, and then leaves the lower class in shambles. Please… Just get my babies out of here before President Obama steps down to some Republican. There won't be much dancing then.

Angie: Remember Mommy how you always say "We have to be thankful for what we have"? This is our happy time right?

Ceci: Yes baby, you are absolutely right. Thank you for reminding me. Let me see that TB vaccination on your arms. Looks good to me. I think I need a nap.

Ceci checks the TB test on all three girls' arms again and then lies down to take a nap and dreams while they watch TV.

344. Final Blessing Ceremony – Comizahual and the ancestors -

Ceci begins to dreamwalk through a wormhole with the girls. They emerge into a plaza in the Ciudad Blanca with pyramids and statues of white stone. She leads them into a fertile garden with pools and flowing water. They sit, and Ceci transforms into Comizahual. The other ancestors are also there. And please note that these ancestor characters should also be played by characters in the lives of Ceci and these sisters, such as David Ashby, Deni May, Conchita, Dunia, Tio Lou, Vilma, Doctors and Teachers. This will give a deep dimension to the power of the ancient flashbacks. The girls are dressed in Mayan ceremonial clothing and sit on a rock together. They are there to participate in a ritual ceremony, to make an offering dance, and to receive a blessing for their protection and wellbeing, with great hopes for their ability to help other children like themselves one day.

Ceci as Comizahual: I am here to bless you and prepare you for a great journey. You have just come through a time tunnel into a world that you were not originally intended for. Your karma has changed. As your godmother, I will not be with you forever, but I will show you the ways of medicine that will keep you healthy on your journey. And you will have the academic opportunity to study for a respectable profession of your choice. You must seize the day and rise to the occasion for these opportunities. So you can make something of yourselves as proud Honduran Americans. Make progress daily... Move forward. Use your youthful time and energy wisely. Remember to improve the life of those around you. America has these opportunities and you must recognize truth and sincerity to get connected to these people. You will also be surrounded by fast moving, robotic, electronic minds. You will see competition, disinformation, false advertising, corruption and racism. So always... remember where your values are, and establish truth and trust within this family. Know who is sincere. Look at each other and promise to take care of each other always. You are bound by blood and by faith in love, and as my children – to put family first. *Comizahual continues:*

Remember this great Mayan proverb: In lak' ech, Hala ken" which, in a literal translation, means "I am you, as you are me" or "I am another you, as you are another me".

They take hands in a circle repeating this phrase over and over, with drums and flutes and a haunting melody enveloped by a rhapsody of primitive sounds. This sound accompanies a ritual of initiation for the girls. This all takes place as a dream choreography where the girls dance in parade fashion as if they are on a moving train. They pass each of the characters that have participated in their lives up until now, dancing in and out of them until they return to Comizuahual who speaks again as she anoints them.

Comizahual: All human beings are trying to survive, be happy, and coexist. You girls have been blessed by this Gringa to live in another world. It is a fast world and you were not designed to run at this pace, so you will have to catch up, develop the unused parts of your brains, learn to make friends with good people. This will be difficult, but above all… Respect your mother. She will show you a love you have never known. Bring your Latina spirit of love, family and kindness with you. Take care of each other. Respect the higher powers that have given you this opportunity to be survivors and good citizens. Go with love and strength in your heart. I am your spiritual Madrina. I will be watching you. I am another you as you are another me.

Please repeat again 3 times girls: I am another you, you are another me.

Girls repeat: I am another you, you are another me. 3X

Fade out….. as Ceci visualizes a huge American flag that flies dramatically, billowing over a car dealership in Richmond, Va at Parham and Broad Sts. This is a reoccurring dream that will finally come true in the near future.

345. <u>**Interior of Airplane – Ceci wakes up**</u>

The girls are trying to wake Ceci up as she is talking in her sleep, repeating "I am another you, you are another me." The plane is about to land in Atlanta and we hear the stewardess command to prepare for landing. Ceci is disoriented for a minute and then tries to get the girls organized. Again, she is overcome with emotion.

Ceci: Oh thank God, we are here, finally. *The reality of the moment is overwhelming her.*

Angie: No llores Mommy. Don't cry Mommy.

Jazmin: Why does she always do this?

Ceci: I am really happy. I just can't believe that after all these years this moment has finally arrived.

There is a Latina woman seated across the isle who over hears Ceci.

Latina: First you must pass through immigration. THEN you can celebrate.

Ceci: I forgot about that. I just thought the visas were enough.

Latina: It all depends on the officer who screens you. I can see these are not your children, so don't be surprised if you have to jump through some hoops before you get to pick up your luggage. I have been there before, but now I have my American passport which changes the filter. Just hang in there, and good luck.

Ceci: Thanks for the heads up.

346. <u>Immigration line - Atlanta, Georgia USA</u>

They disembark the plane and proceed to immigration and take the line for non-residents. It has been a long flight, and the girls are groggy and Ceci is seasick, with tear- stained eyes. They finally reach an officer and Ceci presents the unopened package of papers with her American passport and their three Honduran passports.

Officer: Good afternoon, what have we here?

Ceci: Good afternoon sir. I am an American and these are my three custodial daughters from Honduras, for which we have visas, and look forward to citizenship some day.

Officer: OK let's have a look.

Ceci: Here are all the documents.

He opens the envelope and spends a good 15 minutes looking through each girl's portfolio as he compares photos to the faces of the girls. The girls are staring at him like he might be God.

Officer: And you say you adopted these girls?

Ceci: I have legal guardianship, called "Tutora" under Honduran law. But they have lived with me for seven years now in Honduras.

Officer: Normally, you need a formal adoption to get a residential visa for children.

Ceci: Yes I realize that, but the agent at homeland security in Tegucigalpa gave us the visas, after several previous applications.

Officer: OK, just wait while I talk to some people.

He goes to the other side of the wall and through the window we can see him on the phone. Ceci is rolling her eyes, and catches the eye of the Latina woman who is in the next line, who looks at Ceci sympathetically and crosses herself. After what seems like twenty minutes, the officer comes back accompanied by a more senior looking officer who checks out Ceci and the girls while holding a private, muttered conversation.

Officer: I'm sorry mam, you'll just have to wait.

Ceci: Wait for what?

Officer: These aren't your kids mam. It's complicated. Can you wait over here for a minute?

Jazmin runs after the senior officer who had walked away, Roxana follows. Jazmin tugs on his jacket.

Jazmin: But we are her kids. She's our mom.

Roxana: Senor... That lady is my mother and she loves me.

Angie: *(holding on to Ceci)* What's happening Mom? I'm hungry. How long is this gonna take? *Ceci reaches into her pockets for some crackers as she tries to corral the girls all to her side. At that moment, with the chorus of three sincere daughter comments... the two officers actually freeze, looking at the three girls and Ceci. The entire hall freezes watching the scene unfold. The senior boss officer looks down at the girls, takes them by the hand and returns to where Angie and Ceci are waiting. He looks at the attending officer and speaks.*

Officer Boss: Officer, you can process this family please, and I will sign off on it.

The pen the attending officer gripped, which had been stuck to the sign off paper on his desk, finally starts to move with his signature.

The Officer Boss then bends down to speak with the girls.

Officer Boss: So you all speak pretty good English. Am I right?

Girls: Yes sir.

Officer: And I hear that you are hungry - am I right about that?

Girls: Yes sir.

Officer: Well let me tell you something girls… We're not the bad guys. Welcome to the USA And… when you get upstairs you will see more fast food than you have ever dreamed of. Welcome to America muchachas. It may not be healthy, but it's fast.

Girls: *With besos…* Gracias Senor!

Ceci: So now we're OK?

The attending officer hands her the four stamped passports. The Officer Boss walks away waving goodbye.

Officer: OK that's it. You can go.

Ceci: Excuse me officer, but can you just tell me why the hesitation?

Officer: We needed to see the proof that you were their legal mom. Their behavior clearly demonstrates that. And we checked you out electronically. So now there's no doubt in my mind. Welcome to America.

Ceci: Well you got it right officer. It has taken me ten years to prove it. Thank you very much. Say thank you to the officer. Say it loud girls… SI SI -DIOS QUIERE!!!!!

Girls: SI SI - DIOS QUIERE!!! Gracias Senor!

Officer: Buena suerte muchachas!

The entire crowd of lines waiting behind them, who have been riveted to the drama, begins to cheer and in unison echos:

Crowd: Buena suerte muchachas!!!

And Ceci, Jazmin, Angie, and Roxana go skipping off to baggage holding hands. There is the following voiceover.

En lak' ech, Hala ken" - "I am you, as you are me" or "I am another you, as you are another me".

THE END

The day before leaving June, 2013

347. Where the Heart Is – Style Magazine

In Henrico, three sisters from Honduras go back to school — for the first time.

BY **TINA GRIEGO @TINAGRIEGO**

- Scott Elmquist
- A decade after Ceil Gruessing spotted the three sisters Angie, Jazmin and Roxana, from left, in a cardboard box in Honduras, the new family has moved to Henrico County where the girls start school this week.

Ceil Gruessing had been in La Ceiba, Honduras, for 11 months when she first saw the three sisters. The choreographer from Richmond was used to seeing orphaned children by then. Her walk to the school where she taught dance brought her regular encounters with street boys, begging and hustling and sleeping amid passersby who casually stepped over them. The poverty of Honduras is notorious. So, too, is the abandonment of children to orphanages or gangs or worse.

Still, the sight of the girls stopped Gruessing. In part, because they were girls. In part, because they were naked and nestled in a cardboard box. Like kittens.

The box sat next to a police truck, which was parked outside a hospital. The officer, a woman, told Gruessing she was taking them into the emergency room.

"What's going to happen to them?" Gruessing recalls asking.

They'll go to the IHNFA, the offer replied, referring to the state-run orphanage. Two were suffering from meningitis, which left them with lasting disabilities.

"They were half-dead, malnourished, sick. The youngest was three months old," Gruessing says. "I followed them inside the hospital. It was like a message from God saying, 'You know, nobody is going to care about these kids.'"

That was in November 2003. Nearly 10 years later, Gruessing sits in the living room of her mother's house in Henrico County. Dancing about her, buoyant and chattering away, are the three sisters: Jazmin, 9, Angie, 11, and Roxana, 12.

They are now Gruessing's daughters. She brought them home a month ago.

"This is grandma's house!" Angie shouts, throwing her arms in the air. She is pig-tailed and chubby-cheeked and given to dramatic gestures. She and her sisters attended a bilingual school and speak fluent English. "I want to live here forever!"

They have their green cards and their Social Security cards, and this week — dressed in their new shoes, carrying backpacks and notebooks and pencils — they join the thousands of local students going back to school. They will be in the fourth, fifth and sixth grades.

"I'm nervous ..." Jazmin says.   "... and excited," her sisters interrupt.

"That maybe they won't know me and maybe they won't like me," Jazmin continues.

"Maybe they won't play with me and sit with me at lunch," Angie says. On the other hand, she continues, "I'm excited about meeting the new teacher and new friends and a new school and the bus driver and the seats of the bus."

It took years of legal wrangling, of denials and petitions and more petitions, mostly of the U.S. embassy in Honduras, which four times refused visas for the girls, Gruessing says. It took tracking down the girls' birth mother and finding the death certificate of their father.

It took Gruessing taking residency in Honduras, following every step of protocols designed to protect children in international adoptions.

"It's tremendously difficult," says Richmond immigration lawyer Emily Sumner, who didn't represent Gruessing, but spoke generally of international adoption. Sumner says she no longer handles such cases because of their complexity. "You make one mistake and that can be the end of the process," she says. "It can't be undone."

It was all the more complex because Gruessing couldn't adopt the children. She surpassed the age limit of 50. Instead she has custody as their legal guardian.

"I remember when you used to come to the [orphanage] and you would stay with us for hours and then you would go and we would cry for you," Roxana says. "I would drive away and watch them in the rearview mirror, watch the gate closing," Gruessing says, choking up. Angie rushes to comfort her. "Now, we are here and we are yours."

Gruessing, 63, is aware she persisted where others would not. It wasn't something she planned, she says. She went to Honduras to teach dance and work as a choreographer because she couldn't find a job in Richmond. She took care of the girls because she saw how unrelenting poverty destroyed dreams, and she couldn't bear that for these three talkative, bright-eyed children.

"It wasn't that I was looking for daughters," she says. "It was just like falling in love. It was not clear-minded at all. It was just instinctive." "Mommy, it was un caso cerrado," Roxana says, a closed case. Yes, her mother says, it was a done deal.

THE ATTORNEY FOR THE STARS

Peter Thompson, Attorney
PART 3: MORE MEMOIRS (OTHER INTERESTING OR
FAMOUS PEOPLE I MET)

Chapter 23: CECILIA GRUESSING and the Miracle of the 3 orphaned Honduran sisters Roxana, Angie, and Jazmin

I first met Cecilia "Ms. Ceil" Gruessing shortly after we moved to Honduras in 2009. Ms. Ceil had been a professional choreographer for 40 years in the U.S., teaching hundreds of people to dance, when she went to La Ceiba, Honduras after 9/11 to teach dance at Mazapan School, a bilingual school where my daughter Jazlynn was enrolled. Ms. Ceil (as everybody called her) also gave private ballet and dance lessons, which Jazlynn also attended.

I soon met Ms. Ceil's 3 daughters, Roxana, Angie, and Jazmin whom she had followed through the orphanage system since 2003 when she found the little sisters abandoned in a box on a street. Alone, for ten years, Ms. Ceil dealt with the girls' disabilities, their health, education, their orphanages, and all the red tape involved with adoption in a third world country. Despite intense poverty, gang violence and political upheaval, Ms. Ceil carved out a family life in La Ceiba with a proper home, a bilingual education and vigilant medical care for Roxana, Angie, and Jazmin.

Although she went to the official Honduran adoption agency and also to the local family court, they refused to let Ms. Ceil formally adopt them, on the grounds that at 50 she was "too old", even though the birth mother gave her written consent. Finally, after years and fees to local lawyers, she convinced a judge to grant her custody and legal guardianship (called "Tutora") of the girls.

Jazmin, my wife Flor, myself, daughter Jazlynn, Angie   2011

Ms. Ceil had tried 4 times before over the 10 year period to get visas for the girls, and was denied every time.

It had always been Ms. Ceil's goal to obtain U.S. "green cards" (legal permanent residency) for her girls, so she could bring the girls home to her own mother in Richmond, Virginia, who had been waiting for 10 years to give the girls refuge and a life with her blessing in the USA. But, U.S. immigration law states that a foreign minor child must be "adopted" in order to qualify as a "son or daughter" of a U.S. citizen in order to qualify for a green card.

Nevertheless, I took the immigration case on a *pro bono* basis, because the cause was righteous and my family had grown close to Ms. Ceil and the girls. I looked for a way to convince USCIS and the U.S. Consulate in Tegucigalpa, Honduras to approve the girls for green cards.

There is a saying in the legal community that if you don't have the facts on your side, argue based on the law, and if you don't have the law on your side, argue the facts.

Since it appeared at first glance that I did NOT have the law on my side, I based the case on the persuasive facts, namely, the honorable work Ms. Ceil had done in taking in these orphaned, disabled girls and supporting them for many years, as well as the fact that sufficient help for their disabilities was not available in a poor, third world country such as Honduras. And then we prayed for a Miracle. AND GOT IT. AN ANGEL HELPED US.

The entire case got referred to the Visa section of the U.S. Consulate, and (after a waiting period of some months to complete the requirement of 2 years of formal guardianship) our lady angel in the Consulate, Catherine Ventura, approved green cards for all 3 girls. Her reasoning was that the guardianship that Ms, Ceil obtained in a Honduran court was the <u>functional equivalent</u> of adoption. Soon the girls had their green cards. Soon after that, they all moved to Richmond to live with Ms. Ceil's mother. They were all formally adopted there, got their citizenship and earned their high school diplomas.

Ms. Ceil recently told me: *As of 2023, two of the girls are in college and one is working in the USA. Roxana earned a certificate in Early Childhood Development and works with young children. She understands the emotions of young toddlers separating from their parents every day because of her own issues with abandonment. Both Jazmin and Angie are studying at Universities and want to go into criminal law. NOT because I suggested it... but because they hate injustice. They have experienced racial and disability discrimination as Latin American immigrants several times. But have all transcended these obstacles and more to follow distinguished paths, rising to all occasions. This is an impossible story of a successful adoption that clearly was "God Willing".*

Photos from Richmond, Va. USA

2020

2021

2022

2025